D0184615

DOUGLAS REEMAN

THE IRON PIRATE
IN DANGER'S HOUR
KILLING GROUND

CHANCELLOR
PRESS

The Iron Pirate first published 1986 by William Heinemann Ltd
In Danger's Hour first published 1988 by William Heinemann Ltd
Killing Ground first published 1991 by William Heinemann Ltd

This collected volume published 1994 by
Chancellor Press an imprint of
Reed Consumer Books Ltd
Michelin House
81 Fulham Road
London SW3 6RB
and Auckland, Melbourne, Singapore and Toronto

A CIP catalogue record for this title is available from the British Library

ISBN 1 85152 714 1

The Iron Pirate © Highseas Authors Ltd 1986
In Danger's Hour © Highseas Authors Ltd 1991
Killing Ground © Highseas Authors Ltd 1991

Phototypeset by Intype, London
Printed in Great Britain by Bath Press

Contents

THE IRON PIRATE

To Dorothy, Frank and Stan

from us, with love

1

Charmed Lives

The sea's face that morning rose and dipped in an endless formidable swell. There were no crests, and the deep troughs gleamed in the early light like molten glass. A heavy mist drifted above the water, broken here and there into clearings while close by it barely skimmed the surface.

In a few days it would be August, but in the Baltic the dawn air was already like a knife, a threat of the winter which would soon grope down from the Gulf of Finland to torment ships and sailors alike.

Occasionally scattered groups of gulls and other sea-birds lifted on the successive swells like broken wreaths, pale in the dull light, unimpressed by the steepness of the troughs which in happier times could hide one fishing boat from another even when they lay less than half a cable apart. From end to end the Baltic had been one of the busiest waterways in the world where fishermen and coasters, timber ships and colliers created their own patterns and trails. Now, apart from a few wary neutral Swedish vessels, the waters were the hunting ground, and a burial place for friend and foe alike.

It was 1944 and for many, the fifth year of war. The sea noises were muted or dampened by the mist; it was like a wilderness, an abandoned place for a while longer on this particular morning. The gulls which floated silently and waited to begin their search for food were as usual the first to sense they were no longer alone. To begin with it was more of a sensation than a sound, not close enough to be a beat or throb, just a tremor through the water which soon made the birds rise flapping and mewing, disturbed, anxious yet unwilling to quit their territory.

Had there been an onlooker he would have been startled by the suddenness of the ship's appearance. First a great shadow, and then with a contemptuous thrust of her high, raked bows she swept through the mist, parting it, and cleaving the steep swell with impressive ease. Although her three screws were throttled down to reduced speed she threw a sharp white moustache from her stem which spattered against her faded camouflage paintwork to give a hint of her true power. As she thrust across the grey water she grew in size and strength, but her four twin turrets and towering bridge structure did nothing to spoil the perfection of her lines. She was a heavy cruiser, one of the most powerful afloat, yet she retained all the dash and grace of a destroyer.

No figures explored her wet decks, and only occasional movements at gun mountings and on her bridge gave any sign of life. For a few moments she lay fully exposed in a clearing, like a graceful animal crossing a glade in a forest, and the reluctant dawn made her upperworks shine like glass and touched the flag, a solitary patch of scarlet with its black cross and swastika.

Before the mist closed in again the cruiser's secondary armament seemed to come to life, the slender muzzles in their separate mountings around the superstructure training and lifting as if to sniff out a possible enemy. Each gun crew was fully aware of the cost of carelessness, the lack of constant vigilance. In these contested waters there was rarely a second chance.

Closed up at their various action stations, as they had been for most of the night, there were some 950 officers and men scattered throughout her armoured hull. Separated by the needs of safety, and yet welded into a solitary team to fit the demands of their ship, the wishes of their commanding officer.

At the rear of the open bridge, alone for a few more precious minutes in his spartan sea-cabin, Kapitän zur See Dieter Hechler sat at his desk, outwardly relaxed from long practice, but with his mind recording each movement and untoward sound beyond his small refuge. He rarely visited his spacious quarters below except in harbour, for time taken in running to the bridge in any emergency was time lost. He rarely thought about it. This was his world, and had been for the eighteen turbulent months since he had been given the honour of this command, one of the remaining crack cruisers in the German navy.

In a moment or so, Viktor Theil, his second-in-command, would call him on the red handset above the sea-cabin's crumpled bunk. Then Hechler would get to his feet, take a quick look round to ensure he had forgotten nothing, and walk to the bridge.

They would greet him with varied feeelings. Relief, doubt, dislike even, but all would accept him as their captain.

He sat back in the chair and stared unseeingly at the chart on his desk, the personal one he kept for his own guidance. When he joined the others of his team he would need to know everything, be ready to answer any question, even the stupidest one. He knew from hard experience that any man rebuked for asking something which in all truth he should have known, would never dare to ask another question, perhaps when it was vital.

His jacket hung from a rail beside the bunk, the four gold stripes glinting dully in the light from the desk lamp. His cap, like the medal ribbons on the jacket, showed his authority and skill at a glance, but any casual visitor would see him now as the man, not the commander. The cap and jacket were necessary trappings, just as banners and flags identified the old sailing men-of-war in the height of battle in another century. But for now, in his favourite roll-necked fisherman's jersey in thick grey wool, and the extra pair of flannel trousers beneath his uniform ones, he looked at ease. Hechler was thirty-six, the youngest captain to command such a ship as the *Prinz Luitpold*, and the responsibility was clear to see in the deep creases on either side of his firm mouth. His hair was dark and had remained unruly despite all the caustic comments of his superiors over the years. His strength, his qualities, the depth of the man himself showed mostly in his eyes. They were blue with the shadow of grey, like the sea itself.

In his youth he had discovered that his eyes had made him vulnerable. If they had showed his confidence, so too they had betrayed his doubts. He had taught himself to contain his inner emotions, and had seen the effectiveness of his control when he was dealing with his day-to-day life. A seaman to be punished, or to be promoted with a word of congratulation. A man to be told that his family had perished in an air raid. It was all part of his world, as was watching people die, sometimes horribly, knowing as he did that others would be looking at him to see his reactions if only to gauge their own fates.

Like last month when he had cleared the lower deck and had every officer and man assemble aft beneath the twin muzzles of Turret Dora, to tell them about the Allied invasion of Normandy. To most of *Prinz Luitpold*'s ship's company the other theatres of war had seemed remote and with little meaning. The Pacific, Italy, even the Atlantic, the bloodiest sea war of all, meant little. Their war had been here, or in the Arctic against the Russians. Normandy had changed all that. The official news was optimistic, adamant that the British and their allies would soon be driven back into the sea and in turn leave England ripe for invasion. And anyway Normandy was a long, long way from the Fatherland.

But to many of the listening faces it seemed like a stab in the back, an enemy gnawing away at another front, which would make even greater demands on their own resolution and resources.

The deck gave an unexpected shudder and Hechler had to make himself relax again, muscle by muscle. Perhaps he was too tired. Maybe the war had pared away his resistance without his realising it. He smiled and ruffled his hair with his strong fingers. Then with a sigh he leaned forward and stared at the chart for the last time.

The coastline was familiar enough. It was useless to consider what might have been, to despair over the loss of ground in the past few months. Safe anchorages had come under constant air attack; now they lay in enemy hands. All the time, the Russian armies kept up their pressure along thousands of miles of savagely contested land. Up here in the North, the Finns, Germany's allies, were under terrible pressure, and an entire German army was in danger of being cut off from retreat. Hechler's mouth moved in a wry smile. *Strategic withdrawal*, as the news reports termed it. The heavy cruiser always seemed to be at an hour's notice to get under way even after the briefest respite in harbour. Now, with her escort of two destroyers divided on either beam, she was back in the same fiercely contested waters where she had once been able to rest; where she had been like a symbol to the army shore.

As he ran his eye along the chart, or checked a measurement with his dividers, Hechler could see the coast in his mind's eye, like a painting, a watercolour. Abeam was the northern coast of Lithuania, the gateway to the Gulf of Riga. During the night they had slipped past the low, sandy point, Kolkasrags, with its wooded darkness beyond, and would soon begin to turn in a wide sweep towards the land once more.

South-east and deep into the Gulf of Riga, where they had been ordered to supply artillery support to the beleaguered German army. Riga was the only point from which the army could retreat if the worst happened, and there had been nothing in the regular signals to suggest that the Russians were losing steam in spite of their horrendous losses in men and tanks.

It was always a risk, a ship against sited shore batteries. Those who gave such orders saw only the overall strategy, the latest necessity, and rarely considered the danger.

It was a task which *Prinz Luitpold* had carried out many times. Originally she had provided covering fire for their own landings, had supported a victorious army through one advance to the next. If winter closed in early there might be some respite on this front at least. Hechler pitied the poor devils who endured the bitter cold and privation, who would face it yet again with the added knowledge that the Allies were nearer their homeland than they were. *Unless.*

Hechler glanced up at the framed picture of his ship. The glass shivered in the frame to the gentle vibration from several decks below his feet. It made it look as if the photograph was alive. *Prinz Luitpold* was a lucky ship, and had become something of a legend in the tight world of the navy. Bombardments, hurling aside air attacks, or matching gun-for-gun with British cruisers of the North Cape, she had sustained only negligible damage, and had lost but two men killed. One of the latter had fallen overboard after slipping on an icy deck. Not a very proud death for his family to remember.

Hechler thought of other ships similar to his own. *Prinz Eugen*, another legend even in the enemy's navy, *Admiral Hipper* which had been rammed in a hopeless attack by a British destroyer early in the war – they were both fine ships. Another of the class, the *Blücher*, had gone to the bottom back in 1940, torpedoed by the Norwegians of all people. One more was still building.

But *Prinz Luitpold* seemed to lead a charmed life. Her launch, shortly after *Blücher*'s end, had been delayed by several fierce air raids. They had played havoc with the Blohm & Voss yard in Hamburg where her keel had been laid. And yet despite the devastation all around her, she had survived, waiting patiently for the smoke to clear and the work to continue.

Hechler had been serving in a small, elderly cruiser when she had been launched by the Führer himself, her name chosen to cement Austrian friendship. He had seen her several times, and as his own advancement had progressed he had set his heart on her, this cherished command.

He stood up, his body balanced automatically to feel the strength of the ship beneath him. Fourteen thousand tons with the machinery to drive and sustain her every need, the weapons to fight anything faster or of equal size, she even carried three Ardo float-planes, Hechler's eyes when he needed them.

Hechler was a tall man, with broad shoulders, yet despite this he moved in the confined cabin with the ease of a cat as he slipped into his jacket and patted each pocket without really noticing this regular precaution.

He opened the drawer of his desk and placed the dividers and parallel rulers inside. As he did so he saw her face looking up at him from the worn leather case which he had always carried at sea. He sighed, his eyes distant. *Next to my heart*.

He heard a steel door slam shut somewhere below the cabin. A last bolt-hole for anyone whose nerve might waver?

The ship, this ship, had helped him to get over even that, he thought. He could look at her face now, even study it without the old surge of bitterness and despair. Inger was not smiling in the photograph. When he thought about it now he realised that she had never smiled very much.

The red handset buzzed above the bunk, like a trapped insect. Hechler smiled and lifted it. Relieved at the interruption, to be freed from the sudden shadow, the depression. He closed the drawer as he spoke. Shutting her away, until the next time.

It was Theil, as he had known it would be. A man so dependable that Hechler had once found himself searching for flaws and mistakes. He had been in the ship since she had first commissioned at Hamburg and had served under the one other captain before Hechler. A competent officer in every way, one that commanded most people's respect and liking, qualities which rarely went hand-in-hand in a warship.

Theil should have had a command of his own; they were desperate for experienced captains in larger vessels. Each promising junior was snatched up and sent into submarines to combat the mounting toll in the Atlantic. Like cutting down a forest before the trees had had time to mature, as one elderly staff officer had complained.

Theil reported, 'Five minutes to the final change of course, sir.'

It would be. *Exactly.* Hechler replied, 'Very well, Viktor. I shall come up now.'

He put down the handset and reached for his cap and binoculars. A glance in the bulkhead mirror made him grimace as he tugged the cap tightly across his thick hair. He looked calm enough. He examined his feelings as he would a subordinate.

Nothing. It was as if all pointless doubts had been worked out of him. He studied his image in the glass and saw the strain fall away. He was young again, like the day he had stood in church with Inger, had walked beneath an archway of drawn swords of his fellow officers.

The thought made a shutter fall across his blue eyes. Hechler snapped off the light and left the cabin. He never thought that each time might be the last. That too was a waste, an unnecessary burden on his mind.

He waited a few moments more in the deep shadows, his shoulder touching the damp steel plating, his eyes adjusting, preparing for the open bridge, and the sea. For the enemy.

Fregattenkapitän Viktor Theil, the heavy cruiser's second-in-command, stood on a scrubbed grating in the forepart of the bridge. His booted feet were wide apart so that he could feel the ship rising and slithering down beneath him, tasting pellets of salt spray as they lifted occasionally over the glass screen. A new hand aboard ship took days, longer if he was allowed, to grow accustomed to objects and fittings even in pitch darkness. Theil knew them all, just as he could picture the faces of the intent bridge party on either hand and behind his back. Signalmen and petty officers, the massive, oilskinned bulk of Josef Gudegast, the navigating officer. Theil had some reservations about officers who were not regulars, but like the rest of the team he had cause to be grateful that Gudegast was the navigator. In peacetime he had earned his living in the merchant service and had been for much of the time the chief petty officer of a Baltic timber ship. Gudegast knew all the niceties and the perils of these waters like his own considerable appetite.

Theil analysed the captain's voice on the telephone. Calm. Nothing to worry about. Not like the previous captain who had cracked up when the ship had been under constant air attack for three whole days. Theil felt the old hurt like a physical pain. He had taken command, had got the ship back to Kiel when others had been less fortunate. He had dared to hope he would be promoted, and be given *Prinz Luitpold*. He had deserved it. He knew it. Instead, Hechler had stepped aboard to the trill of calls and the proud salutes. A man of excellent reputation who had since proved his worth a dozen times. But he was several years Theil's junior nonetheless.

Theil thought of the other faces, some of which were new to the ship. In the armoured superstructure above the bridge, the conning tower and fire-control stations, the officers he saw each day were waiting for the calm to shatter. Tired faces at the meal table, or flushed with drink after a trip ashore in some port or other. Faces which hid things or revealed too much. Like the youngest officer here on the bridge, Leutnant zur See Konrad Jaeger. A fresh-faced, green young-ster of nineteen. He would be perfect on a recruiting poster. Apart from training, *Prinz Luitpold* was his first ship. He had a pleasant manner, and the confidence of one used to authority. His father was a much-decorated captain who had been put ashore after losing an arm and one eye in the North African campaign. Jaeger's father still had influence, Theil decided. Otherwise the youngster would have been a junior watch-keeper aboard a U-boat instead of serving a thorough-bred like this ship. It was rumoured that a junior officer's life expectancy in a combat U-boat was about that of a lieutenant on the Russian Front.

Theil shivered. It was best to leave it as a rumour these days.

He heard the steel gate at the rear of the bridge open, noted the way the dark figures around him seemed to come to life as the captain entered and touched his cap casually to the bridge party at large. Theil faced him, and recalled suddenly how he had resented, hated this man.

From beside the compass platform Jaeger watched the two senior officers, the men who between them controlled the ship and his destiny. They made a com-plete contrast, he thought. The captain, tall, powerful, yet with a calm unruffled tone. Theil, stocky, with short fair hair, given to angry outbursts if anything slipped below his very high standards.

Hechler could feel the youngster's scrutiny just as he could sense the navigat-ing officer's indifference. The latter knew his charts with an uncanny accuracy; he was often known to scoff at the ship's new navigational aids, the first things to break down when you needed them, he proclaimed.

Beyond his long hours of duty as the ship hurried from one sea area to another, Gudegast rarely mixed with his fellow officers. Another surprise about him was his skill as an artist. Despite his bluff seaman's appearance and colourful lan-guage he could paint and sketch everyday scenes with accuracy and compassion. Now he was rising on his toes to watch some circling gulls, one of his favourite subjects, like patches of spindrift against the mist. Another sketch maybe?

Hechler ducked his head beneath the canvas hood which hid the light of the chart-table and peered searchingly at Gudegast's neat calculations, bearings and fixes. Like his artwork, each pencilled note or figure was clear and delicate. Perhaps a frustrated artist from another age lurked inside his rugged frame. In his shining oilskin he looked like a sea-creature which had unexpectedly come aboard.

Theil joined him by the chart. 'The shore batteries are there sir. Our main armament is alerted and will be kept informed of any change of intelligence.'

From far beyond the hood's shelter Hechler heard the scrape of steel as the aircraft catapult was manoeuvred around ready to fire off the first float-plane. Each had a crew of two, and apart from cannon and machine-guns would today be armed with two heavy bombs.

Thinking aloud Hechler said, 'That is the railway station. We are ordered to destroy it. Ivan will bring up reinforcements by that route. We'll give him a headache.'

He withdrew from the hood and climbed on to the forward gratings to let the salt air sting away any lurking weariness. He thought of his men, sitting and crouching through his command. Some able to see the heaving water like himself, others confined to their armoured turrets, waiting to feed the big eight-inch guns, or down in the bowels of the engine- and boiler-rooms, deafened by the din of machinery and fans, watching dials or each other. Trying not to think of a shell or torpedo changing their roaring world into a merciless inferno.

In the streets of Kiel or some occupied seaport you would not notice many of them as individuals, Hechler thought. It was a pity the people at home could not see them here, in their environment. It might give them heart and perhaps some hope.

Theil said quietly, 'Time, sir.'

Hechler nodded. Glad they were committed. 'Alter course. Full ahead, all engines.' For a second his guise fell away and he added softly, 'Another time, Viktor, but the same enemy, eh?'

Fifteen minutes later the ship surged away from the mist to greet the first weak sunlight like an enraged tiger.

As the four main turrets swivelled soundlessly on to the prescribed bearing, all eight guns opened fire.

'Alter course, steer two-three-zero!' Hechler lifted his eyes from the gyro-compass repeater and tensed as the sea lifted and boiled into a solid cone of white froth some cable's length beyond the port bow.

He felt the deck tilt as the order was passed to the wheelhouse, the instant response as the raked stem bit into the glittering water. The forward turrets swung slightly to compensate for the sudden change of direction and then each pair of guns recoiled in turn, the shock-wave whipping back over the bridge, hot and acrid as the shells tore towards the land.

Hechler waited for the hull to steady and then raised his glasses once more. The land was blurred with smoke, the colour drained out of it by the hard, silver sunlight. Shell-bursts pockmarked the sky where the ship's three Arado float-planes ducked and dived over their targets, and the fall of the cruiser's shells was marked by great smokestains, solid and unmoving. They made the landscape look dirty, fouled, he thought vaguely.

Tracer lifted from the rubble of some dwellings near the water-front, and he guessed that the army were using their fire to retake their old positions, the bitter house-to-house fighting which was an infantryman's lot.

Hechler thought briefly of his father, and the unexpected distraction disturbed him. He was unused to having his mind shifted off-course when he needed it most.

His father had been a soldier in the Great War, and had been wounded several times on the Western Front until he had been badly gassed and sent home, a coughing, broken wreck of a man. In clear moments he had described war at close quarters, and had chilled his family with tales of wiring parties in no-man's land, raids on enemy trenches armed with sharpened spades, nailed clubs and long knives. No time to load a rifle, and a bayonet was next to useless in a hand-to-hand encounter, he had said. You could smell your enemy, feel his strength, his fear as you tried to kill him with the same methods they had used centuries earlier.

At sea you rarely saw the enemy. Gun flashes, the fall of shot, a shadow against the moonlight or fixed in a range-finder. It was better that way. Cleaner.

A great gout of fire, bright orange and tinged with red, erupted from the shore and Theil, who had a handset jammed beneath his cap, shouted, 'Railway station, sir!'

A seaman nudged his friend and they grinned at one another. The young officer, Leutnant Jaeger, shaded his eyes to look up at the control station with its narrow observation slits, like the visor of a massive helmet. He did not even duck as something whistled above the bridge and Hechler saw a seasoned petty officer glare at him behind his desk. He probably wanted him to get down; any fool could die a hero.

'Aircraft, sir! Bearing red-one-one-oh! Angle of sight three-zero!'

The secondary armament were already swivelling round on their sponsons and in their small turrets, tracking the tiny, metallic dots which had suddenly appeared out of the smoky haze.

Hechler thought of Kröll, the gunnery officer, and was glad of his efficiency. Kröll, lean, tight-mouthed and devoid of any sense of humour, was a hard man to serve. Constant drills in every kind of exercise, switching crews around with loading numbers from the magazine and cursing any officer or seaman who failed to respond to his immediate satisfaction, had nevertheless made the ship a living example to many others.

The anti-aircraft guns and then the lighter automatic weapons clattered into life, the bright tracer streaking across the sea and knitting together in a vivid mesh of fire through which the approaching planes would have to fly.

One of the escorting destroyers was turning in a steep welter of foam, an oily screen of smoke trailing astern of her as she headed closer to her big consort, her own guns hammering sharply to join the din.

Prinz Luitpold's main armament recoiled again. Hechler had lost count of the number of rounds they had fired, and he heard the abbreviated whistle of the shells as they ripped towards the target.

'Alter course. Steer due west.' Hechler let his glasses drop to his chest as Gudegast passed his orders through the brass-mouthed voice-pipe by the compass.

'Two-seven-zero, sir.' The rest of his words were drowned by the throaty roar of engines, and the increasing bang and clatter of gunfire as the enemy planes flashed over the water.

Hechler did not see which one straddled the destroyer, but the explosion just abaft her squat funnel made a searing flash and flung fragments high into the air even while the ship staggered round in another turn, her deck laid bare as she tilted over. Another great explosion blasted her from between decks and fire spread along one side like lava, masking her hull in steam and surrounding her struggle with bright feathers of spray from falling debris. Distance hid the sound of her destruction but it was clear enough for anyone to see.

Two of the Russian aircraft were weaving away, their own wounds revealed by smoking trails as tracer darted after them, and the sky around them was filled with drifting shell-bursts.

Gudegast said thickly, 'She's going! God, look at her!'

Hechler watched the destroyer as she began to settle down. One boat was in the water, but was carried away from her side by the swell with just a handful of men aboard. Floats were dotted about, but the first two explosions had obviously taken a heavy toll of life. Hechler had met the destroyer's captain at several conferences. It was a moment dreaded by every commander. *Abandon ship*. Even thinking the words was like a surrender.

Two more Russian planes roared over the listing vessel, and the sea around the solitary boat was torn apart by machine-gun fire. Hechler felt his stomach muscles contract, but made himself watch as the tiny, unreal figures clawed at the air or floundered in the swell before they were cut down.

Theil hurried to his side. 'One of the Arados is finished, sir!'

They looked at each other. Theil's voice was harsh; his words were not just a report. They sounded disbelieving, like an accusation.

Hechler strode across the bridge, his boots scraping on empty cartridge cases from a machine-gun, and watched the pall of smoke beyond the waterfront. The float-plane must have been hit just as she had released her two bombs and had exploded directly above them.

'Signal from escort, sir! Request permission to pick up survivors.'

Hechler glanced at Jaeger's handsome face. He had not yet learned to conceal his emotions, Hechler thought; his eyes looked wild, full of pain for the men who were dying out there.

It was an additional, unwanted drama. The remaining destroyer's captain knew better, even if the other one was his best friend.

It could have been his ship. The two after-turrets roared out again and sent a violent shock-wave through the bridge as if they had hit a sandbar. *Or it could have been us*. It would be no different. You must not even think about it.

He heard himself reply flatly, 'Denied. Discontinue action.'

He glanced quickly at his watch, aware of the tension around him, the shock at what had happened so swiftly.

His voice seemed to move them again, voices called into telephones and pipes, and Gudegast passed his prearranged course to the wheelhouse. Parts of a pattern. There were things to be checked, not least preparations for another air attack before their own covering fighters flew out to shepherd them to safety.

Hechler raised his glasses and stared at the mounting curtain of smoke where the railway station and surrounding streets had been under fire. It was already falling away as the cruiser swung on her new course and threw spray over the forecastle like heavy rain. The signal would be sent, the army would be left to use whatever advantage and breathing space the bombardment had offered. Hechler moved his glasses and saw the stricken destroyer hard on her side, the swell around her smooth and stained with oil. A few heads bobbed in the water, but as the distance increased they seemed without meaning or purpose. Two aircraft shot down or severely damaged. A small price to pay for a destroyer and her company, he thought bitterly.

He lowered his glasses and moved to the opposite side to watch the other destroyer increasing speed to take station again. Nearby he could hear the watch-keepers whispering together while the voice-pipes kept up their constant chatter. Routine and discipline kept men from fretting too much. Later they would remember, but their pain would be mellowed by pride. The legend lived on. They had lost one Arado. Two absent faces at the mess table, telegrams to their homes, and later Hechler would write a letter to each family. Now, as he watched the drifting smoke he was dismayed to realise he could barely remember the faces of the dead airmen.

A messenger scrambled on to the bridge, wide-eyed and anxious, the first time he had left his armour-plated shell since the guns had opened fire.

Theil took the signal pad from him and after a quick glance said, 'Priority Two, sir. To await new orders.' Their eyes met.

Hechler nodded and removed his cap. The air felt clammy against his forehead. He thought suddenly of a bath, hot water and soap, an unbelievable luxury. He wanted to smile, but knew he would be unable to stop. It was madness. A helplessness which always followed a risk. He glanced up at his ship, the smoke trickling past her funnel-cap and the shivering signal halliards. She was not built to act as a clumsy executioner, a tool for some general who had failed to outwit the enemy's tactics. He thought of the destroyer which would soon come to rest on the bottom, how her survivors would still be floundering about and dying, but still able to see *Prinz Luitpold*'s shadow fading into the mist. Abandoned. In the twinkling of an eye they had become mere statistics.

He realised that Theil was watching him. Waiting, his features controlled and impassive.

The signal was brief, but said all that was needed. Fresh orders probably meant they would be ordered away from this battleground. The news would flash through the ship like lightning. It always did. Where to? What mission had been dreamed up this time?

Hechler gripped the nearest handrail and felt the ship respond to his touch. Like a great beast whose respect had to be constantly earned and won.

So many shells fired, and each selected target bombarded without damage and without cost to any man aboard. One aircraft was lost, and the others would be retrieved as soon as it was safe to stop the ship and hoist them inboard.

He felt suddenly angry, contemptuous of the fools who had risked the very survival of this ship for a gesture, one which would and could make no difference.

'Perhaps we shall be given bigger game to hunt, Viktor.' He looked at him searchingly and saw him flinch. 'Unless some politician has already thought up some wild escapade for us.'

Theil dropped his voice. 'I am a sailor, not a man of politics, sir.'

Hechler touched his arm and saw Jaeger relax as he watched them. 'Sometimes we must be both!' Then he smiled, and felt a kind of recklessness move through him. 'This ship is a legend. She cannot remain one while she sniffs after fragments left by the army.'

The two Arados flew over the mastheads and rolled their wings. They had already forgotten. Survival was a great tonic.

Theil said, 'Normandy, do you think, sir?'

Hechler walked to the gratings again and rested his hands on the rail below the glass screen. The destroyer was already zig-zagging ahead of them, ready to seek out and depth-charge an enemy submarine, although it was unlikely there would be one in this area, he thought.

He considered Theil's question and pictured his ship charging through the invasion fleets and their supply vessels like an avenger. A proud but short-lived gesture it would be too.

No, it was something else. He felt a shiver run through him. A war on the defensive could not be won. He looked down at the forecastle, at the two pairs of smoke-grimed guns as they were trained forward again.

It was what he was chosen for, and why the ship had been built. To fight and to win, out in the open like *Scharnhorst* or the cruisers of his father's forgotten war.

Hechler nodded to himself. Nobody would forget his *Prinz Luitpold*.

2

Faces of War

Kapitän zur See Dieter Hechler emptied another cup of strong black coffee and glanced around his spacious day cabin. Sunlight shone brightly through the polished scuttles, and he could hear some of his seamen chattering and laughing as they went about their work on deck.

The ship felt at peace as she swung to her cable, and it was hard to believe that they had been in action less than two days back, and had seen the destroyer go down.

Hechler stood up and walked to one of the scuttles. From a corner of his eye he could see Mergel watching his every move, his pen poised over a bulging pad as it had been for an hour or so since they had anchored. Mergel was a petty officer writer and would have made someone a fine secretary had he been a woman, Hechler often thought.

Even the weather was different. He shaded his eyes and looked towards the shore, the high shelving slope of green headland, the clusters of toy houses which ran all the way down to the water's edge. Untroubled – from a distance anyway.

Hechler was moved by what he saw. It was the east coast of Denmark, and the port which was set in a great fjord was named Vejle. He smiled sadly. He had visited here several times during the war, and earlier in a training ship, or to holiday with his parents and brother. Happy, carefree days. It gave him a strange feeling to be here again in *Prinz Luitpold*. Many eyes would be watching the ship, but how would they see her? Would anyone admire her lines, or would they see her only as an extension of the occupation forced on their peaceful country?

He saw a fuel lighter move away slowly from the side, men staring up at the ship, some soldiers with their weapons slung carelessly on their shoulders, a world apart from the Russian Front, he thought. With the taste of good coffee in his mouth he felt vaguely uneasy, as if he should be doing something useful. Another fuel lighter cast off and followed the first one towards the fjord. Stück, the chief engineer, would run him to earth eventually to report on his department. Even in harbour there was no obvious rest from routine. Visitors came and went. Requests, demands, questions – it was like being responsible for a small town.

The thought of going ashore touched something in Hechler and made him eager to leave, if only to smell the land, feel the lush grass beneath his feet.

He sighed. It was not to be. Not yet anyway.

He looked at Mergel. 'Have the letters done first, and I'll sign them.' He tried to picture the faces of the two dead airmen. Did such letters ever help, he wondered?

Mergel gathered up his papers and moved to the door. 'May I ask, sir, will there be leave?'

Hechler shrugged. 'You will probably know that before I do.' He waited for the door to close. In the ship's crowded world he treasured the moments he could be alone. Alone with his ship perhaps?

He poured a last cup of coffee and ran his eyes over the pad of signals and news reports again.

There was some sort of security blanket on Normandy, he decided. Only one thing was certain. The Allies had not been flung back into the sea, but were pushing deeper into France. There was a mention of some possible secret weapon which would soon change all that, and enemy losses were still heavy in the Atlantic due to the aggressive tactics of the U-boats. Hechler bit his lip. Many words, but they said little.

The sentry opened the door and Theil stepped into the cabin, his cap beneath his arm.

Hechler gestured to a chair. 'It will be quite a while before the admiral arrives, Viktor.' He had seen the surprise in Theil's eyes, as if he had expected to find his captain unshaven and still in his seagoing gear.

Theil said, 'The upper deck is washed down, sir, and the boats are being repainted. The admiral will find no fault in the ship's appearance.'

Hechler looked away. There it was again. The defensive, bitter note in Theil's tone. As if the ship was his sole responsibility. Hechler pushed the pad of signals towards him. 'Read these, Viktor. They may amuse you.'

He put on his best jacket and buttoned it carefully. In his mind he could see the admiral very clearly. One of those round, ageless faces with wide confident eyes. He smiled. Unless you knew him. He was only a year or two older than himself and already a rear-admiral. One of Dönitz's shining lights, everyone said, highly thought of even by the Führer himself. Or so it was claimed. Looking back it was not so surprising, Hechler thought. He had first met him when they had both been cadets, and then later they had served together in an old training cruiser which had unexpectedly been called to speed to the assistance of a burning cargo-liner in the Mediterranean. The event had captured the headlines, and in Germany had been blown up enormously to cover other less savoury news of attacks on Jews which had been giving the country a bad name abroad.

While others who had once been cadets in those far-off days had progressed or fallen by the wayside, he had always managed to seize the limelight. Now he was a rear-admiral. It would be interesting to see how that had changed him.

Theil said, 'Will there be leave, sir?'

Hechler looked at him and smiled. *You too?* 'I expect so. Our people can do with it. This kind of landfall makes the war seem far away.'

'It's not for myself, sir, you understand – '

Hechler nodded. 'We *all* need a break.'

Theil shifted in his chair. 'I hate not knowing. What is expected of us? I am not afraid of fighting, even dying, but not to know is like a weight on your back.'

Hechler thought again of his father. *Like waiting to go over the top.* Theil was right, but it was not like the man to express it so openly. Perhaps he should have looked for some additional strain earlier?

Hechler said, 'We both know that we cannot go on like this. The *Prinz* was not built to nurse an army. She was designed to fight.' He waved his hand towards the sunlit scuttles. 'In open water, like she did off North Cape.' The picture rarely left his thoughts. It had been the first battle he had fought in this ship. Up there off the Norwegian coast which had been shrouded in day-long darkness. Two British cruisers and some destroyers in a blizzard like the one last year which had covered the end of *Scharnhorst* in those same terrible seas. At the end of the day *Prinz Luitpold* had won the battle, even though her escorts had been sunk, and another cruiser set ablaze. The British had hauled away, their losses unknown, and had left this ship almost unmarked.

Both sides had claimed a triumph, but Hechler knew in his heart that *Prinz Luitpold* was the only victor.

There was a tap at the door and after a small hesitation the executive officer, Korvettenkapitän Werner Froebe, stepped inside. Froebe was tall and ungainly, with huge hands which seemed forever in his way. Next to Theil he was responsible for the running of the ship and the supervision of the various watches and working parties.

Theil glared at him. 'Well?'

Froebe looked instead at his captain. 'I apologise for the intrusion, sir, but there is an officer come aboard from the town.' He dropped his eyes. 'A major of the SS, sir.'

Hechler studied him gravely. 'What does he want?'

'He wishes to load some stores on board, sir.' He held out a piece of paper. 'He has the admiral's authority.'

Hechler took it and frowned. 'It seems in order. Have the boatswain select a party of hands to assist him.'

Froebe said glumly, 'The major has some people, er, workers – '

Theil was looking from one of the scuttles. He said shortly, 'Civilian prisoners, more trouble!'

Hechler saw their exchange of glances. Civilian prisoners could mean anything in wartime, but with an SS major in charge it probably meant they were from a labour camp.

'Deal with it.' When Froebe had left he added, 'The admiral will be here soon, Viktor. I don't want the ship cluttered up with working parties when he steps aboard.'

Theil picked up his cap. 'I agree.' He seemed suddenly pleased to go, all thoughts of the next mission, even home leave forgotten.

Hechler examined his feelings. Like most of his colleagues he had heard stories of overcrowded labour camps, and the rough handling by the SS guards. But it was not his province; his place was here in the ship, or another if so ordered. It was what he was trained for, what he had always wanted.

He could almost hear himself saying much the same words when he had asked Inger to marry him.

He walked to a scuttle again, but the day was spoilt. It was like having a bad taste in the mouth. Something you could not explain, and certainly something you could do nothing to change.

Somewhere overhead a speaker came to life, followed by the trill of a boatswain's call. The boatswain was already mustering a working party for the unexpected and as yet unidentified cargo. The deck gave a sudden tremble as one of the powerful generators was switched on, while down in the shining galley the chief cook would be ranting and cursing about having to delay the midday meal until the admiral had been piped aboard.

Hechler left the cabin and walked along the starboard side, his eyes on the choppy water, but missing nothing of his men who worked above or around him. They moved aside to let him pass, while petty officers saluted and called their men to attention if he caught their glance.

They respected him, he had brought them back to a safe anchorage, and that was enough.

He saw some seamen by the float-plane catapult, and Brezinka, the massive boatswain, wagging his finger as he explained what he needed done.

Froebe stood slightly apart with the SS major, a man who would have been utterly insignificant but for his uniform and the death's-head badge on his cap.

Something made Hechler pause. He asked, 'Is anything wrong?'

Froebe jerked to attention. 'N-no, sir. These hands will go ashore to man a lighter and bring it alongside – '

The major interrupted. 'They must be under my orders, Captain.'

Hechler glanced at him coolly. 'They are also under mine, Major. I will be pleased if you remember that.' He saw the man's flush of anger, but felt no pity for his embarrassment. He glanced at Froebe. 'Make it quick.' He saw a young acting petty officer who had been placed in charge of the party and thanked God for his gift of remembering names.

'You will be taking your final exam soon, Stoecker?'

The sailor had an open, pleasant face. One you could rely on.

Stoecker smiled. 'Yes, sir. Three weeks' time if – '

Hechler touched his arm. '*If*, a word that carries much weight for all of us, eh?' He walked on, knowing that Stoecker would remember how the captain had spoken to him after snubbing the major. Cheap? Possibly. But it *made* a ship's company.

With the warm sunlight across his shoulders Hechler walked alone right around his ship's upper decks. Past the towering bridge structure and capped funnel, beneath the long guns and over the white-painted anchor cables, his eyes missed nothing.

Germany had broken the treaty made by her old enemies to build the *Prinz* and her sister ships. Ten thousand tons had been the maximum which had been allowed, but secretly they were over 15,000 tons when they had been launched. From her raked stem to her handsome quarterdeck the heavy cruiser would make any shipbuilder proud.

The armament and gunnery controls in each of the class were unmatched anywhere. The ill-fated *Bismarck* had been given the credit for sinking the British battle-cruiser *Hood* early in the war, but it was believed throughout the fleet that *Prinz Eugen*'s guns had fired the fatal salvo.

Hechler looked at the two after turrets and forgot about his irritation over the SS officer.

Just given the chance. That word *if* again.

He smiled at the thought, and two seamen who were polishing the deck plate which bore the ship's name, where the admiral would step aboard, nodded to each other and grinned. There could be nothing to worry about.

Later as the gleaming launch, with a rear-admiral's pendant streaming from it, curved in a frothing wake towards the accommodation ladder, Hechler, with the unaccustomed weight of a sword at his side, felt the same sense of pride.

For a moment at least the war itself had become a backcloth, and only the manned anti-aircraft guns, both here and ashore, gave any hint of possible danger.

The ship's company were dressed in their best blue uniforms, unlike their drab seagoing rig, and all but the duty officers were in ranks, with Theil, unsmiling and grim-faced, at their head.

The launch vanished beneath the rail and Hechler saw the top of the accommodation ladder give a tremble as the boat nudged alongside. He controlled the desire to laugh. All it needed was a band. But as they were always being reminded, there *was* a war on.

Konteradmiral Andreas Leitner lay back in one of the cabin's deep chairs and regarded the glass in his hand.

'Good, eh?' He chuckled. 'I find it hard to admit that only the Frogs can make champagne!'

Hechler tried to relax. Leitner was exactly as he had remembered him, youthful, confident, and so buoyant that it was impossible to imagine him ever being ruffled.

He had come aboard with a bounce in his step and after saluting the quarter-deck and side-party had faced the assembled company and thrown up a stiff Nazi salute which had seemed theatrical in spite of his gravity. An act? It was still difficult to judge. Hechler watched him while Pirk, his steward, refilled the glasses. Leitner must have brought a dozen cases of champagne aboard which his flag-lieutenant was now having stowed for future use.

Leitner had not mentioned their mission or his sealed orders; he was taking his time. In that respect too, he had not changed.

His hair was fair and well-groomed, and his skin had a kind of even tan, although Hechler had not heard of his being out of Germany for a year or more.

The admiral nodded to the steward. 'Well trained, eh? Pours it like a head waiter at the Ritz.' He grinned broadly. 'You have a fine ship, Dieter. I am quite jealous the way you are spoken of in the high command.'

He waited for Pirk to withdraw and said, 'I shall hoist my flag aboard very shortly.' He watched him evenly. 'A private ship no longer, how does that strike you, my friend?'

'I am honoured, sir.'

'You are not. I know you too well to accept that!' He laughed and showed his even teeth. 'No matter. You are the right captain. We shall do well together.'

'Shall we return to the Gulf, sir?'

Leitner became serious. 'I cannot discuss it yet. You and your ship have performed wonders, have given pride where it was lacking, a sense of destiny when some were only thinking of comfort and a quick end to the war.'

He wagged the empty glass at him and added, 'I have often thought of you, and the old days, believe me. Your parents are they well?'

Hechler replied, 'They are managing.'

'I felt it personally when your brother was lost in *Scharnhorst*. A good ship too. He lies with a brave company, an honour to our country.'

Hechler tried to compose his features and his reactions. It seemed strangely wrong to hear Leitner, or anyone else, speak of his brother like a part of history. He could see him without difficulty, so full of life, excited at being appointed to so famous a ship.

Leitner was saying, 'Young men like Lothar are an example, part of our heritage –'

Hechler refilled their glasses, surprised that his hand was so steady. His young brother's name had come off the admiral's tongue so easily, as if they too had been close, and yet he knew they had never met.

He tried again. 'My people have had no leave, sir, and they deserve it. Whatever we are called to do –'

Leitner gave a mock frown. 'You will be told, but now is not the moment. I can only say that I am here for the same reason. You have earned a rest, albeit a short one, but the needs of Germany rise far above our own petty desires, eh?' He laughed lightly. 'When I watched your ship anchor, my heart was filled, I can tell you.'

Hechler realised he had drained another glass, but Leitner's mood was unnerving. For just a few seconds his pale eyes had filled with misty emotion, then they hardened as he continued, 'We shall have vengeance, Dieter, for Lothar and all the other fine young men who have died for our cause.'

The admiral stood up suddenly and paced about the cabin, touching things as he moved. He said, 'I have arranged some leave, but it will be short, I am afraid. I have my temporary headquarters in Copenhagen. It is not like Berlin, but it must suffice.' He shrugged. 'We do what we can.'

Hechler said, 'You were in America too.'

Leitner swung round, his eyes pleased. 'So you followed my career as I watched over yours, eh? That is good. Friendship is too strong to be parted by events. Yes, I was in Washington as a naval attaché. I learned a lot, mostly about American women. If their men fall on their backs as willingly this war will soon be brought to a successful conclusion!' He laughed and wiped his eyes. 'God, what a country. I was worn out!'

Hechler watched him as he moved about the cabin. Leitner had always excelled in sporting events, but he never recalled any great attachments with girls as a junior lieutenant. He had not married either.

Leitner paused by a bookcase and said without turning, 'I was sorry to hear about your marriage, Dieter.'

16

It was as if he had been reading his thoughts. Like a single bullet. 'It was a mistake.'

'I can tell by your tone that you blame yourself. I doubt that you have any cause, Dieter. An idealist, yes. A bad husband, I think not.' He sighed. 'Women are admirable. But never treat them as equals.'

Hechler relaxed slightly. Another problem solved. Was that how Leitner had gained flag rank, he wondered?

Leitner said, 'My gear will be sent aboard this afternoon. You have quarters for flag officers, that I do know.'

Hechler nodded. 'Had I known you were coming sir, I would have had the quarters properly prepared. As it is – '

Leitner shrugged indifferently. 'Castle or charcoal burner's hut, it is the same to me. All I ask is a little luxury here and there.' He did not elaborate. Instead he said, 'Your last mission failed, I believe?'

It was so blunt after his affable chatter that Hechler sensed his own resentment rise to meet it.

'We carried out the bombardment, the objectives were all destroyed. We lost one escort because – '

'I know the hows and whys, thank you.' The smile broke through again like winter sunlight. 'But it was a failure nonetheless. I heard from OKM Operations Division an hour ago that we have at least a whole infantry brigade cut off, surrounded.' He closed his fingers like a claw. 'They will fight to the death of course, but we lost a good destroyer for nothing.'

Leitner looked directly at Hechler but his pale eyes were faraway. 'No matter, my friend. The Führer has ordered the beginning of an aerial bombardment by rocket, the like of which will make Rotterdam, London, Coventry and the rest, seem like mere skirmishes. The first rocket was launched yesterday. I can say no more than that, but you will soon hear of it. There is no defence. The RAF had some success against our flying bombs over London, but against the V–2 there is *nothing!*'

Like most serving officers Hechler had heard about the much-vaunted secret weapons. They never seemed to appear. The fanatical confidence in the admiral's voice made him believe that this one was real, terribly so.

Leitner said, 'I know what you are thinking. War on civilians is foul. Perhaps it is. But to shield Germany from invasion any means are acceptable. God will always congratulate the winner!' It seemed to amuse him and he glanced at his gold wrist-watch before adding, 'We shall dine together tonight. In the meantime my flag-lieutenant will present a brief summary of immediate requirements.' His eyebrows lifted as the sentry's booted feet clicked together beyond the door. 'My aide is not blessed with all the arts, but he is ever punctual.'

There was a tap at the door and Hechler called, 'Enter!'

Kapitänleutnant Helmut Theissen strode into the cabin very smartly, a heavy file under one arm. Like his superior he had fair hair, and the same even tan. Maybe they had both been on a secret mission, Hechler thought, to Spain for instance, whose one-sided neutrality had often proved a great asset.

Theissen was young for his rank, with anxious eyes and a willowy figure which even his immaculate uniform could not disguise. At the sight of the admiral his confidence seemed to melt.

He said, 'I have brought the file, Admiral.'

Leitner glanced at him coldly. 'Don't stand there like a Paris whore, man, prepare it for the Captain.'

He looked at Hechler and winked. 'A mother's gift to a war-starved nation, yes?'

Hechler heard the harsh echo of commands and the clatter of the main winch. The mysterious lighter was about to leave. Froebe's men had done well. They had hardly made a sound.

He would escort the admiral to his quarters or wait until he was ready to go ashore again. He glanced briefly in the bulkhead mirror then looked away quickly. It was like uncovering a secret – worse, sharing it.

In those brief seconds he had seen Leitner and his anxious-eyed aide looking at each other behind his back.

There had been no animosity. Affection was the nearest description he could think of. He was surprised and troubled to discover how the possibility left its mark.

Later at the gangway before they exchanged formal salutes, Leitner said, 'I shall send my car to the pier tonight, Captain.' He glanced at the side-party and rigid guard of helmeted seamen. 'We shall speak of *old times*.'

Then he was gone, and Hechler saw his aide staring up from the launch, something like relief on his face.

Hechler nodded to the duty officer. 'March off the guard, Lieutenant.'

He watched them clump away, doubtless thinking of their delayed meal. It was a pity that life could not be that simple for us all, he thought.

When he looked again, the launch had vanished around an anchored freighter with the Swedish flag painted on her side. Her only frail protection against bomb or torpedo.

Life would not be quite the same again, he decided grimly.

A muffled explosion echoed against the superstructure and made several seamen come running, their faces taut with alarm.

Froebe panted along the deck and saluted. 'Captain, the lighter is on fire, an explosion in her engine, I think!'

Hechler thought suddenly of the young acting-petty officer's face. 'Call away the accident boat at once. Send help.'

It had been on the way back to the shore after unloading the mysterious cases.

Froebe watched men running for the main boom beneath which the duty boat was already coughing into life.

Then Hechler glanced at the placid shoreline. 'I want to know immediately what happened. Everything.' He strode away and wondered if the admiral's launch had seen the explosion, which must have been near the fjord's entrance.

In war you never accepted even the smallest disaster as an accident.

Hans Stoecker walked abreast of the lighter's long hatch-covers and turned to watch the cruiser, his home for about a year, as she drew astern, and her details and personality merged like a misty photograph.

Astern, *Prinz Luitpold*'s motorcutter kept a regular distance, her crew relaxed and unconcerned about the brief break in routine.

Stoecker was twenty-five and very conscious of his small authority. Even this rusty lighter represented *his* ship until he could gather the small working party together and return in the motorboat. He watched the SS major, hands in pockets as he chatted quietly with two of his men, machine-pistols crooked under their arm and not slung on their shoulders.

Stoecker glanced at the wheel, aft by the low guardrail. Künz was the helmsman. They had had a few rows since his acting rank had been awarded by the captain. Now he seemed to accept him. And he was a reliable seaman despite his foul mouth.

Stoecker walked along the side and kept the hatch covers between himself and the SS men. Locked down below there were ten prisoners who had carried the heavy steel boxes to the cradles to be hoisted up the cruiser's side. They had needed careful watching, for Stoecker knew that if just one tackle had been allowed to scrape the paintwork he would have felt Froebe's wrath.

He smiled and thought of his father who had been recalled to the navy after a few years' retirement. Too old for active duty, he was in charge of some naval stores in Cuxhaven. How pleased his mother would be after he qualified and they both went home in the same uniform!

Something touched his ankle. He glanced down, and saw a wiry hand reaching for him.

He looked quickly around the deck. The SS men were in deep conversation and peering at their watches, the few seamen who had not transferred to the motorboat were sitting on the hatchcovers, looking up at the sun, their eyes slitted with pleasure. Stoecker crouched down and peered through a narrow air vent at an upturned face.

He had mixed feelings about the prisoners. He did not after all know what they had done – they must have done something. They were dressed in clean, green, smocklike overalls, unnumbered, unlike some he had seen. They had been very docile, even cowed, and any sort of contact with the sailors had brought a scream of anger from the little major. There was one naval officer aboard, a pale, listless, one-striper who was said to be on light duties after his E-boat had been blown up in the North Sea. Stoecker and his companions had watched the young officer until his indifference and his sloppiness had made them bored.

He was up in the bows, his back to all of them, shutting them out.

Stoecker lowered his face. 'Yes, what is it?' He tried to be clipped and formal.

The man gazed at him, his eyes almost glowing in the gloom of the hold.

'I have a letter.' His German was perfect. 'Could you give it to my family?' He paused and licked his lips. '*Please!*' The word was torn from his mouth.

'I can't – I don't see why – '

A dirty, folded letter was thrust through the hole, and Stoecker saw the man's thin wrist and arm beneath the green smock. It was raw, and covered with sores. Like something diseased.

The man whispered, 'I am going to die. We all are. In a way I am glad.'

Stoecker felt the sweat break out on his neck like ice. The address on the letter was Danish.

The weak voice said, 'I am, *was* a teacher.'

'Ah, *there* you are!' The major's boot glinted in the sunlight as he came round a hold-coaming.

Stoecker snapped to attention, his eyes on the sea alongside as the boots clicked towards him.

He knew that the prisoner's hand had vanished, just as he was sure that nobody had seen him in conversation. But he felt something like panic, the prickle of sweat beneath his cap.

He was a good sailor, and was secretly proud of the way he had behaved in the actions and bombardments which had been the cruiser's lot since he had joined her. His action station was high up above the bridge in the Fire Control Station, one of the gunnery officer's elite team. Kröll was a hard and demanding officer to serve, but Stoecker had noticed that he was rougher on his officers than the rest of them. Perhaps because he had once served on the lower deck and had had to build his own standards.

Stoecker knew what he should do, what he should already have done. But he could feel the grubby letter bunched in one hand, and anyway he disliked the major with his snappy arrogance. He doubted if he had ever been near the front line in his life.

The major snarled, 'The motorboat is falling too far behind. Tell it to draw closer!'

Stoecker climbed on to the hold cover and raised his arm until the boat's coxswain had seen his signal. What was the matter with the man? The boat was at exactly the right distance. The coxswain would not hold the job otherwise, Froebe would have made certain of that.

The major watched as the motorboat's bow-wave increased and said sharply, 'See that it keeps up!'

Stoecker saw the two SS men watching, the way they were gripping their machine-pistols. Afterwards he recalled that they had looked on edge, jumpy.

The explosion when it came was violent and sharp, so that the side-deck seemed to bound under Stoecker's feet, as if it was about to splinter to fragments.

The dozing sailors leapt to their feet, and even as the motorboat increased speed and tore towards them, the lighter's engine coughed, shook violently and died.

Künz shouted, 'No steerage way!' He stood back from the wheel, his eyes fixed on a billowing cloud of smoke which was spouting up through the ventilator.

The major shouted, 'Get that boat here!' He glared at Stoecker. 'What are you gaping at, you dolt?'

Stoecker stared at the hatch coaming. Smoke was darting out as if under great pressure, and he could hear muffled screams, and the thuds of fists beating on metal.

The major flipped open his pistol holster and added, 'Sabotage! There may be another bomb on board.'

The motorcutter surged alongside, but when some seamen tried to climb aboard the major screamed, 'Get back, damn you! It's going down!'

Stoecker looked at the pale-faced naval officer and pleaded, 'We could get them out, sir!'

Over the officer's shoulder he saw one of the SS men swinging the clamp on the ventilator to shut off the dense smoke.

The officer stared at him glassily. 'Do as you are told. Abandon *now*!'

Stoecker felt his eyes sting as the smoke seared over him, and he peered at the little slit where the prisoner's arm had been. Only smoke, and even the cries had stopped. Like a door being slammed. He felt Künz grip his arm and hiss, 'Come on, Hans! Leave it!' Then all at once they were clambering into the motorcutter, and when he looked again Stoecker saw that the lighter was already awash and sinking fast in the current.

The major said, 'Take me ashore.'

The boat turned towards the land again and Stoecker saw a naval patrol launch and some other craft heading towards the smoke at full speed.

He looked down at his fingers, which were clasped together so tightly that the pain steadied him. Some of the seamen sighed as the lighter dived beneath the surface, and one said, 'Lucky it didn't happen when we was alongside the old Prinz, eh, lads?'

No one answered him, and when Stoecker again lifted his eyes he saw the major was watching him. He appeared to be smiling.

They barely paused at the pier before turning and heading back at speed for the ship. It seemed important to all of them that they should be there, with faces they knew, and trusted.

There had been a black car waiting for the major and his men. He apparently offered a lift to the young naval officer, but the latter merely saluted and walked away.

Stoecker put his hand inside his jacket and touched the letter. The man had known he was going to die. He remembered the SS men looking at their watches. Most of all, he remembered the major's smile.

He looked up as the heavy cruiser's great shadow swept over them. He had expected to find comfort in it, but there was none.

3

And So Goodbye

One day after the admiral's visit to the ship the news of leave was announced. It was little enough of an offering and brought a chorus of groans from most of the mess-decks and wardroom alike. Only seven days' leave would be allowed, and first preference for married men only. The rest of the ship's company, by far the greater proportion, was confined to local leave on Danish soil, with no sleeping-out passes below the rank of petty officer.

For the lucky ones seven days would be precious but pared away by the time taken to reach their destinations and return to the ship. It was rumoured that rail transport was always being delayed or cancelled due to day and night air raids.

As the men were lined up and inspected in the pale sunshine before rushing ashore to the waiting buses and trucks, Fregattenkapitän Theil reminded them of the seriousness of careless talk and the damage it could do to morale. Anyone who witnessed bomb damage or the like would keep it to himself, nobody would gossip about the ship, the war, anything.

Viktor Theil left the ship himself as soon as the others had departed. His home was in Neumunster on the Schleswig-Holstein peninsula, so he had less distance to travel than most.

As he sat in a corner of a crowded compartment in a train packed to the seams with servicemen and a few civilians, Theil reflected on the choice of a home. Not too far from Denmark. Now it seemed ironic, something to mock him.

The train crossed the frontier and clattered at a leisurely pace through the Hans Anderson villages, and the green countryside with its scattered lakes and farms. It was a beautiful part of the country, especially to Theil who had been born and brought up in Minden. At least, it should have been.

He thought of his wife Britta, their nice house on the town's outskirts, the perfect retreat for a naval officer on leave. He was known there, and certainly respected, especially when he was appointed to the *Prinz Luitpold*.

But he sensed people watched him, wondered what he really thought, if he cared. For Britta was Danish, and marriages from across the border were common enough before the war. It was often said that the Germans on the peninsula were more like Danes than they were. That too had a bitter ring for Theil.

When the German army had invaded her country Britta had tried to discover what had happened to her parents. Her father was a printer in Esbjerg, but he also managed a local newspaper. It had begun with letters and telephone calls, none of which had been answered. In despair she asked Theil to make enquiries but he had met with a stone wall of silence from the security offices. Eventually, when he was on a brief home leave, a plain-clothes police officer had called to see him. He was fairly senior and eager to be friendly and understanding.

'Your wife probably does not understand the need for security in these matters – '

Theil had tried to delve deeper and the policeman had said, 'You are a well-respected officer, a fine career ahead of you. Why spoil things, eh?'

When he had departed Theil had explained as well as he could to his wife. Perhaps her father had been in some political trouble, and was being kept out of circulation until things settled down. It had been the first time which he could recall when she had turned on him.

She had shouted, '*Settle down!* Is that what you would call it if the Tommies came here and started locking people in jails for wanting their country, their freedom!'

That leave had ended badly, and Theil had returned to his ship, which unbeknown to him was about to be called to action when the captain finally cracked under the strain and he himself by rights should have been promoted and given command. If not of the *Prinz Luitpold* then another of similar status. Instead, Hechler came.

Then Theil had received a message from a friend in Neumunster. He had not said much, but had sounded frightened, and it had been enough to make Theil hurry home after giving a vague explanation to his new captain. The ship was to be in the dockyard for a week, and anyway he knew that Hechler wanted to come to terms with his command on his own, and at his own speed.

22

The news had been worse than he had imagined. Britta had gone to her parents' home alone. In spite of the strict travel restrictions, the impossibility of moving about in an occupied country without permission, she had managed to reach the port of Esbjerg.

When Theil had confronted her he had been stunned by her appearance. She had been close to a breakdown, angry and weeping in turns. That night when she had finally allowed him to put her to bed she had shown him the great bruises on her arms. The military police had done that to her when they had dragged her from the house where she had been born.

When he had tried to reason with her, to calm her, she had pushed him away, her eyes blazing, and cried, 'Don't you see? They've killed my mum and dad! Don't you care what those butchers have done!'

The doctor, another old friend, had arrived and had given her something.

When she had finally dropped into a drugged and exhausted sleep he had joined Theil over a glass of brandy.

Theil had asked desperately, 'What should I do? There must be some mistake, surely? The authorities would never permit – '

The doctor had fastened his bag and had said crisply, 'Keep it to yourself, Viktor. These are difficult times. Perhaps it is best not to know all the truth.' He had fixed him with a grim stare. 'You are a sailor. Be glad. At sea you *know* your enemies.' He had gone, leaving Theil with his despair.

As time wore on Britta withdrew more and more into herself. The local people tried to be friendly but she avoided them for the most part. She had been a pretty girl when he had married her; now she seemed to let herself go. Theil always regretted that they had no children, preferably boys to grow up in his footsteps and serve Germany. Once it had distressed her that she could not give him a child. The last time it had been mentioned Theil had found himself almost wanting to strike her.

'A *baby*! What would you give it? A black uniform and a rubber truncheon to play with!'

Theil walked the last part of the journey from the railway station. It had always been a pleasant little town but he noticed that the queues of people outside the provision shops seemed longer, and the patient women looked tired and shabby.

And yet the town had escaped the war apart from a few stray bombs from homebound aircraft. The sky was empty of cloud as it was of the tell-tale vapour trails of marauding aircraft. It was almost like peacetime.

Theil was too deep in thought to glance at the bulletin boards outside the little church, and the people who were studying the latest casualty lists which like the queues were longer than before.

He thought of the case which he shifted from one hand to the other to return the salutes of some soldiers from a local flak battery. It was heavy and contained among other things, cheese and butter, Danish bacon and eggs which might bring a smile to her lips. She had enough to worry about without the damned shortages.

He had written to her several times since that last, unnerving leave. She had only replied once, a loose, rambling letter which had told him very little. Britta was never a great writer of letters. Their leaves spent together had always made up for that. He quickened his pace. This time it would be all right again. Just like all those other times. It *must* be.

Whatever his personal worries might be, Theil was a professional to his finger-tips. He had noted all the recent happenings, not least the arrival of the rear-admiral, an officer whose face and reputation were rarely absent from the newspapers.

It might be his chance. The *Prinz Luitpold* was obviously earmarked for something important. That meant dangerous, but you took that for granted.

Perhaps he had been hard on Britta, or had written something in a letter which had upset her without intending it.

She had to understand, and be seen to be with him, no matter what. It was bad about her parents, but then he had never really got to know them. They should have considered her before they became involved with some political or subvers-ive activity.

It was so unfair that because of it, his future might be endangered and her health also.

He thought of the ship lying up there in Danish waters. He knew the *Prinz* better than any of them. They would all need him when they were really up against it.

He turned on to the quiet road which led to his house; it was the last one in a line of five. Nothing had changed, and the flowers and shrubs in every garden made a beautiful picture after grey steel and the Gulf of Riga.

They would have three, maybe four days together. Then he would go back to the ship. As second-in-command he must be on time even at the expense of losing a day or so. But the leave would be just right. Like a reminder and a memory. A hope too for the future.

He thought he saw a woman in the neighbour's house, bending perhaps to pick up some flowers. When he looked again she had gone. He was glad. He did not want to loiter and discuss the war, rationing, and all the other complaints.

Theil reached the gates to his own garden and shifted his grasp on the heavy case. He squared his shoulders and wondered if anyone was watching. 'He's back.' He could almost see himself in his best uniform with the decorations and the eagle across his right breast.

He looked at the garden and hesitated. It was not like Britta to allow it to become so neglected. It was dry, and dead flowers drooped over the neat drive-way, running to seed. It was unheard of. He held back a sudden irritation and strode to the main door. He fumbled with his key, expecting at any moment for the door to open and for her to stand there staring up at him. Her flaxen hair might be untidy but he would see it as before. Her dress would be for doing jobs about the house, but to him it would be like the silk one he had once brought her from France.

The house was so quiet that he stood stock-still within feet of the open door. Without looking further he knew it was empty. The sunlight which streamed through the back windows was dusty, and there were dead flowers in a vase near the framed picture taken on their wedding day. He paused by it, off-balance, uncertain what to do. He stared at the photo, her arm through his, the faces in the background. That one was Willi, who was lost in the Atlantic two years back.

Theil put down his case and flexed his fingers. What did he feel? Angry, cheated, worried? All and none of them.

Perhaps she had gone away? He stared at the dead flowers. Where? He turned away, a sick feeling running through him. She had left him.

He walked about the house, opening doors, shutting them again, then went upstairs and looked out at the neighbours' house. So quiet and deathly still.

He opened a wardrobe and touched her clothes, remembering her looking up at him as he had undressed her.

What was she thinking of? He tried to contain it, as he would aboard ship when some stupid seaman had made a mistake. Did she think it could do anything but harm to behave like this? He touched a curtain which was pulled aside. Untidy. Again, out of character, or was it deliberate?

Theil went slowly downstairs and then saw some letters neatly piled on a hall-table where she kept her gloves.

He recognised the official stamps, his own writing. Unopened. She had not even read them.

He looked fixedly at his case by the front door. Abandoned, as if someone else had just arrived, or was about to leave.

What the hell had she done? There was no point in calling the police or the hospital. He would have been told long ago. An army truck rolled past, some soldiers singing and swaying about on the rutted road. How sad their song sounded.

He thrust the letters into his pocket and after a momentary hesitation picked up the heavy case once more.

He would ask the neighbours; they were decent people and had always liked Britta.

But he hesitated in the doorway and looked back at the silence. He thought of the future, the ship lying there waiting for him, for all of them, and was both apprehensive and bitter.

He *needed* her, just as she had once needed him, and she was gone.

Theil slammed the door and locked it and walked down the drive and then round to the next house.

Once he glanced over at his own home and pictured her in a window, laughing and waving. It had all been a joke, and now she wanted him.

The doorbell echoed into the far distance and he waited, knowing somehow that nobody would answer. But as he walked down the road again he felt someone was watching him.

What should he do? He thought of his friend the doctor and walked all the way to his house, ignoring the weight of his case, his mind snapping at explanations like an angry dog.

The doctor was pleased to see him, although he had to leave for an urgent visit almost immediately.

He listened to Theil's story impassively and then said, 'I think you must face up to it, Viktor. She has left you.' He raised one hand as Theil made to protest. 'She will be in touch, be certain of that, but she has to sort things out in her own way, d'you see? Women are like that. All these years, and they still surprise me!'

Theil made to leave. Britta had some other relatives somewhere. He would check through his address book. He looked at the heavy case. 'You take it, Doctor. For old time's sake, eh?'

The doctor opened it and gazed at the array of food.

'Thank you, Viktor. Some of my patients – '

Theil nodded and tried to grin. 'Of course.'

Outside, the shadows of evening were already making purple patterns on the road. Theil did not look towards his house. If he went back now he knew he would go crazy.

She had left him, had not given him a chance to make things right. He compensated by telling himself that she had no warning of his coming.

But all this time? Another man? He hastened towards the main road and did not even see two saluting soldiers as they went past. Never, not Britta. No matter what. Then back to Denmark? He looked at his watch. What should he do?

He felt his fingers touch the black cross on his jacket; like his other decorations it had always given him pride and confidence. For a few moments longer he stared unseeingly around him, hurt and then angry when he thought of what might have been, *could* have been. Because of Britta's anguish over her parents his own advancement and career had been scarred for all time. He had lost the *Prinz* because of it, because of her.

When she did come back, pleading for understanding, what would he do?

Theil turned towards the railway station. There was nowhere else he wanted to go now.

To some members of *Prinz Luitpold*'s ship's company the seven days' leave were as varied as the men themselves. To many of the lucky ones it was as lifeline, something precious and yet unreal against the harsh background of war. For others it might have been better if they had stayed with the ship, men who eventually returned from leave with the feeling they had lost everything.

Amongst those who remained aboard there was one who, after a quick visit to a dockside telephone, made the most of each day and night in Vejle.

Korvettenkapitän Josef Gudegast, the cruiser's navigating officer, not only knew the ways of the sea and the landmarks which he had used in peace and wartime, he also hoarded a comfortable knowledge of harbours and what they could offer. When he had earned his living in timber ships he had often visited Danish ports, and Vejle was one of his favourite places for a run ashore.

On the last day but one of his leave he sat in a big chair, his reddened face tight with concentration as he completed a charcoal sketch of the woman who lounged opposite him, on a couch, her naked body pale in the lamplight.

The small house was quiet, more so because of the shutters and dark curtains across the windows. The place had always been his haven, stocked with food and drink, some of which he had carried with him from the ship to which he returned every morning, keeping an eye on his department and the work done by his assistants.

The room was very hot, and he sat in his shirtsleeves, his jacket with its three tarnished gold stripes hanging carelessly from the door, a reminder, if he needed it, that his time of freedom was almost over.

'There.' He sat back and eyed his work critically. 'Not bad.'

She got up and stood beside him, one arm around his massive shoulder. He could feel her body against him, her warmth and the affection which they had shared with passion and quiet desperation in turn. Soon they would lie together again and later they would sleep, wrapped around one another like young lovers.

Gudegast was forty, and felt every year of it. He tugged at his ragged beard and murmured, 'You're still a bloody fine woman, Gerda.' He gave her a squeeze. 'I've never forgotten you.'

She touched his hair. It was getting very thin, and without his uniform cap he looked his age, she thought. She could remember him as the bright-eyed mate of a visiting ship, the way that they had hit it off from the start.

She said, 'Get away with you. I'm sagging everywhere.' She peered at the picture. 'You've made me look nice.'

He covered it with some paper and said abruptly, 'It's yours.'

She stared at him. 'But you've never given – '

Gudegast stood up and glanced towards the bedroom door. 'I'll be off soon. Something to remind you of old Josef, eh?'

She gripped his arm, disturbed by his mood. 'It'll be all right, won't it?'

'*All right?*' He took his pipe from the mantelpiece and filled it with slow deliberation. It gave him time.

He was surprised that he cared that much. At the same time he did not want to alarm her.

He said slowly, 'No, I don't think it will, as a matter of fact.'

She sat on the couch and dragged a shawl over her naked shoulders.

Gudegast added, 'Did you see the way they buggered us about in the café this afternoon?'

She replied uneasily, 'They said they were full up.'

He frowned. '*Said.*' He lit his pipe and took several deep puffs. 'Little bastards. I had to put my foot down.'

She watched him and smiled. 'You got us a lovely table.'

'Not the point.' Puff, puff. 'They're more scared of the bloody Resistance now than they are of us, don't you see?' He studied her full mouth and barely covered breasts. She had been such a pretty girl. He should have married her, instead – he turned his mind away from his wife in Hamburg. It was all a mess. Like the bloody war.

He tried again. 'What will you do, Gerda, when it's all over?'

'I – I shall be here – '

He moved to her side and ruffled her hair. 'We're losing. Can't *you* face it either?'

'You mustn't say things like that, Jo! If anyone heard you – '

He grinned, his whole face crinkling. 'Christ, you care, don't you?'

'You know I do.'

'All these years.' He stroked her hair with one big hand while he gripped his pipe with the other. 'I know you're Danish, but there'll be plenty who'll remember you had German friends when it's all over.' He felt her stiffen and almost regretted saying it.

A few more days and he'd be off again. Probably for good, if the mad bastards at headquarters had anything to do with it. What sort of a war was it becoming?

27

He was not even allowed to see his new charts. He felt angry just thinking about it so that when he spoke again his voice was unexpectedly hard.

'You must get out, girl. You've relatives in Sweden, go there if you can.'

She clung to his arm. 'Surely it won't come to that, Jo?'

He grinned, the rumble running through his massive frame. 'I expect our high command have it all worked out, some sort of treaty, a compromise. We've only wiped out half the bloody world, so who cares?'

She stood and looked up at him, her eyes misty. 'I never thought – '

He smiled at her gently. Too many German friends. No, they'd not forget. He had seen it in Spain after the Civil War. All the *heroes* who showed up after the fighting was finished. Brave lads who proved it by shearing the hair and raping girls who had backed the wrong side. It would be a damned sight worse here.

He held her against him and ran his big hands across her buttocks. Neither noticed that his fingers had left charcoal marks on her bare skin.

Their eyes met. He said, 'Bed.'

She picked up a bottle of schnapps which he had brought and two glasses. Gudegast stood back and watched her march into the other room with a kind of defiance. She would not leave. Perhaps she would find a nice officer to look after her when the Tommies marched in. He felt sweat on his back. God, you could get shot for even thinking such things.

He pushed through the door and stared at her, the abandoned way her legs were thrown on the crumpled sheets, unmade from that morning, and probably from all the rest.

He would do another sketch tomorrow. If he got time he might try and paint her in oils when he was at sea again. He shivered and then stepped out of his trousers.

She put out her arms and then knelt over him as he flopped down on the bed. He was huge, and when he lay on top of her it was like being crushed.

He watched her and said, 'I wish we'd wed, Gerda.'

She laughed but there was only sadness there. She took him in her hand and lowered herself on to him, gasping aloud as he entered her.

It was as if she knew they would never see each other again.

The cinema screen flickered and with a blare of trumpets yet another interminable newsreel began.

Hans Stoecker tried to concentrate but it was difficult to see anything clearly. The air was thick with tobacco smoke. The cinema had been commandeered from the town, and he guessed it had once been a church hall or something of the kind. Between him and the screen were rows and rows of square sailors' collars, broken only occasionally by the field-grey of the army.

The newsreel was concerned mainly with the Eastern Front and showed thousands of prisoners being marched to the rear of the lines by waving, grinning soldiers. The commentator touched only lightly on France, but there were several good aerial shots of fighter bombers strafing a convoy of lorries, and some of burning American tanks.

The major part of the reel was taken up with the *Bombardment of London*. The usual barracking and whistles from the audience faded as the camera panned across the great rocket, the V–2, as it spewed fire and dense smoke before rising from its launching gantry and streaking straight up into the sky.

The commentator said excitedly, 'All day, every day, our secret weapon is falling upon London. Nothing can withstand it, there is no defence. Already casualties and damage are mounting. No people can be expected to suffer and not break.'

There were more fanfares, and etched against a towering pall of flame and smoke the German eagle and swastika brought the news to an end.

Stoecker got up and pushed his way out of the cinema. Several voices called after him. There must be half the ship's non-duty watch here, he thought.

Outside it was dusk, with the lovely pink glow he had first seen in these waters. He thrust his hands into his jacket and walked steadily away from the harbour. There were plenty of German servicemen about, and they seemed carefree enough.

He thought again of the sinking lighter, the terrified screams of the prisoners trapped below. He had passed the place in one of the cruiser's motorboats when he had been sent on some mission ashore. It had been marked by a solitary wreck-buoy, but as one of the sentries on the jetty had told him, there had been no investigation, nor had any divers been put down. *Prinz Luitpold* carried her own divers but had not been asked to supply aid.

It was obvious, whichever way you looked at it. It was not sabotage. He thought of the SS major's face. It had been murder.

Stoecker crossed the street automatically and paused to peer into a shop window. He had done it merely to avoid three officers whom he would have had to salute. It was childish, but like most sailors he disliked the petty discipline which the land seemed to produce. He thought of the captain, how he had spoken to him, called him by name, from a company of nearly a thousand men. Hechler never laboured the point about discipline. He had his standards, and expected them to be met. Otherwise he was a man you always felt you could speak to. Trust.

A hand touched his sleeve. 'Hans! It *is* you!'

He turned and stared at the girl who was smiling at him. It all flashed through his mind in seconds, the brown curls and laughing eyes, school uniform, but now in that of a nursing auxiliary.

'What are you doing here, Sophie?' At home she lived just three doors from his mother. 'A nurse too, eh?'

She fell into step beside him, the pleasure at seeing him wiping away the tiredness from her eyes.

'There is a big hospital not far from here.' She glanced away. 'Mostly soldiers who were in Russia.'

Stoecker thought of the jubilant newsreel, and of the ship's superstructure shaking like a mad thing when they had fired on the enemy position.

Later he had heard the deputy gunnery officer, Kapitänleutnant Emmler, say angrily, 'Ivan still smashed through and decimated a whole brigade! When will we hold the bastards?'

He said quietly, 'They are lucky to be in your care, Sophie.'

She put her hand through his arm. It was so simply done that he was moved.

She said, 'They have been in hell, Hans. Some of them are – ' she shrugged and smiled, but there were tears on her cheeks. 'Now look what you've made me do!'

He guided her from the main stream of people and traffic and together they entered a narrow street, their footsteps their only company.

They talked about home, people they had known, and the last time they had seen some of them.

He said suddenly, 'I'd like to see you again.'

She looked at him gravely. 'I have every evening off unless – '

He nodded and gripped her hands. 'Tomorrow. Where we just met. I have to get back to the ship now.' His mind was unusually confused. If he had not gone to the cinema he would have missed her, would never have known.

'I'll be there.' She touched his face. 'You've not changed, Hans.'

She saw his expression and asked quickly, 'What is it?'

Stoecker stared past her, his hand on her arm as if to protect her. The street name was faded and rusty and yet stood out as if the letters were on fire. It was the same street as the one on the letter. Almost guiltily he touched his pocket as if to feel it there. He knew it was the house even though he had never been here in his life. There was a shop beneath the living quarters, but the windows, like the rest of the building, were burned out, blackened into an empty cave. But on one remaining door post he saw the crude daubs of paint, badly scorched but still visible. The Star of David, and the words, *Dirty Jew!*

The girl looked with him and whispered, 'Let's get away from here.'

They walked down the narrow street towards the main road again. Who was it, he wondered? Parent, wife, girlfriend? He tightened his hold on her arm and could almost hear the man whisper. *I am going to die. We all are.*

'Are you sick?'

He smiled, the effort cracking his lips. 'No. It is nothing.'

They looked at each other, sharing the lie as if it was something precious and known only to them.

'Tomorrow then.'

He watched her hurry towards a camouflaged van with red crosses painted on it.

Perhaps he had imagined it all. There was only one way he would find out and he knew that he was going to read that letter, no matter what it cost.

As darkness closed in over the anchorage, the boats which plied back and forth from the shore ferried the returning sailors to their ship. The duty officer with his gangway staff watched as each returning figure walked, limped or staggered away to the security of his mess.

Like a resting tiger the *Prinz Luitpold* was blacked-out, with only the moonlight glinting on her scuttles and bridge-screens.

Almost the last launch to head out from the shore made a broad white wash against the other darkness, her coxswain steering skilfully between anchored lighters and a pair of patrol boats. Hechler seemed to sense that his ship was drawing near. He climbed up from the cockpit and stood beside the coxswain, the collar of his leather greatcoat raised around his ears, his cap tugged firmly down. Spray lanced over the fast-moving hull, but he did not blink as he saw the great shadow harden against the pale stars, and he felt a strange sense of relief.

He saw the bowman emerge from forward, his boathook at the ready, heard the engine fade slightly as the helmsman eased the throttle.

The proud talk, the dinner parties, the uniforms and gaiety – he had had enough in the past few days to sicken his insides. Only here was reality. His ship.

A voice grated a challenge from the darkness and the coxswain shuttered a small hand-lamp.

The ship's raked bows made a black arrowhead against the sky and then they were turning towards the long accommodation ladder.

The captain is back on board. Maybe there will be news.

Hechler ran lightly up the ladder and folded back his leather collar so that the faint gangway light gleamed dully on the cross around his neck.

Prinz Luitpold's captain felt as if he had never left her.

4

Maximum Security

There was a tap at the door to Hechler's day-cabin and then Theil stepped over the coaming and closed the door.

Hechler was glad of the interruption. His table was covered with intelligence files, packs of photographs and even vague news reports. In a matter of days he had soaked up everything he could find about the war so that he felt his mind would explode. It was the first time he had seen Theil since he had returned from leave, other than for the brief requirements of reporting aboard.

Theil looked paler than usual, and tight-lipped. Hechler had felt a change of atmosphere throughout the ship when the married men had returned from their brief escape. They might make laws about spreading gloom and despondency, but they could never enforce them, Hechler thought.

Several men had requested extra leave on compassionate grounds. Relatives killed or missing in the constant bombing. Unfaithful wives and pregnant daughters. The list was endless.

He waited for Theil to be seated and for Pirk to produce some fresh coffee.

Theil said, 'Everyone is aboard, sir, except for two seamen. I have posted them as deserters.'

Hechler frowned. A tiny fragment set against the war, and yet in any ship it was distressing, a flaw in the pattern.

Pirk opened one of the scuttles and Hechler saw some trapped pipesmoke swirling out towards the land. Gudegust the navigating officer had been one of his visitors; in fact Hechler had seen all of his heads of departments.

Gudegust never actually complained, but his dissatisfaction over the charts was very apparent. It was useless to tell any of them that he did not know the ship's new role or mission either. Nobody would have believed him. *Would I in their place?*

'They may have their reasons, Viktor. They won't get far.'

He thought of the news from the Russian Front. The enemy were making a big push, perhaps to gain as many advances as possible before winter brought its ruthless stalemate again.

Theil said, 'We sail this evening, sir.' It was a statement. 'The escorts have already anchored as ordered.'

Hechler looked at him casually. Theil sounded almost disinterested. It was so unlike him and his constant search for efficiency.

'Is everything well with you, Viktor?'

Theil seemed to come out of his mood with a jerk. 'Why, yes, sir.'

'I just thought – how was your leave?'

Theil spread his hands. 'The usual. You know how it is. A house always needs things.'

Hechler glanced at the papers on the table. So that was it. An upset with his wife.

'Anything I can do?'

Theil met his gaze. It was like defiance. 'Nothing, sir.'

'Well, then.' Hechler looked up as the deck trembled into life. It was a good feeling. He never got tired of it. The beast stirring after her enforced rest.

He said, 'Norway. We shall weigh at dusk and pass through the Skagerrak before daylight.' He studied Theil's reactions if any. 'I want to be off Bergen in thirty hours.'

Theil grimaced. 'I doubt if the escorts will be able to keep up.'

'So be it.' He pictured the jagged Norwegian coast, the endless patterns of fjords and islands. It would give Gudegast something he *could* grumble about.

'After that we shall keep close inshore and enter our selected fjord to await further intelligence.'

Theil nodded. 'Another fjord.'

Hechler guessed he was thinking of the great battleship *Tirpitz* which had been hidden in her Norwegian lair many miles from the open sea. Safe from any kind of attack, and yet about a year ago they had reached her. Tiny, midget submarines with four-man crews had risked and braved everything to find *Tirpitz* and to knock her out of the war by laying huge charges beneath her as she lay behind her booms and nets.

Hechler thought of his young brother again. *Scharnhorst* had been sunk a month later, the day after Christmas. The seas had been so bitter off North Cape that only a handful of survivors had been found and saved by the victors. His brother had not been one of them.

Hechler tried to push it from his thoughts and concentrate on what his ship would be required to do. The North Russian convoys again? Any pressure on the Russians and the destruction of much-needed supplies from the Allies would be welcomed by the army. Or was it to be still further north, and round into the Barents Sea itself before the ice closed in? Attack the Russian navy in its home territory. Hechler tightened his jaw. It might be worth a try.

Theil said, 'I had expected to see an admiral's flag at the mast-head when I returned, sir.'

Hechler smiled. 'The admiral intends to keep us guessing, Viktor.'

He thought of the mysterious boxes which had been taken below. All the keys of the compartment where it was stowed had been removed from the ship's office. The admiral had one key, and Hechler had locked the other in his cabin safe. He was determined to get the truth about them out of Leitner.

He recalled Leitner's temporary headquarters in Copenhagen where he had been driven that first evening and almost every day since. Copenhagen was still beautiful. A war and occupation could not change that, he thought. The green roofs and spires, the cobbled squares, even the huge German flags which hung from many commandeered buildings could not spoil it.

Leitner seemed to have created another world of his own there. His HQ had once been an hotel, and the people, men and women, who came and went at his bidding seemed to treat it as one. There was always good food and plenty to drink, with a small orchestra to entertain his official guests with music either sentimental or patriotic to suit the occasion.

If Leitner was troubled by the news from the Russian Front he did not reveal it. He was ever-optimistic and confident and seemed to save his scorn for the army and certain generals whom he had often described as *mental pigmies*.

If any man was enjoying his war it had to be Leitner.

Theil watched him across the table, half his mind straying to the shipboard noises, the preparations for getting under way once more. But Hechler fascinated him far more. Was he really as composed as he made out? Untroubled by the weight of responsibility which was matched only by its uncertainty?

Theil thought of the rumours which had greeted his return. The arrival of piles of Arctic clothing on the dockside had added fuel to the fires of speculation even amongst the most sceptical.

He should feel closer to Hechler now. *His* wife had left him, although no one had ever discovered the whole truth. Did he fret about it and secretly want her back again? He watched Hechler's grave features, the way he pushed his hair back from his forehead whenever he made to emphasise something.

Theil tried not to dwell on Britta's behaviour. Perhaps she only wanted to punish him, as if it had all been his fault. He felt the stab of despair in his eyes. It was so unfair. Just when he needed her loyalty, her backing. If only –

Hechler said, 'I wonder how many eyes are out there watching us right at this minute, eh, Viktor?' He walked to a scuttle and rested his finger on the deadlight.

He looked more relaxed, more like a spectator than the main player, Theil thought desperately.

Hechler felt his glance, his uneasiness. It was not time for Theil to be troubled. Their first loyalty was to the ship, and next to the men who served her. After that – he turned, hanging from the deadlight like a passenger in a crowded train.

'We're going to fight, Viktor. I feel it. No more gestures, no more bloody bombardments with barely enough sea-room to avoid being straddled.' He looked at the nearest bulkhead as if he could see through it, to the length and depth of his command. 'Have you ever read about Nelson?'

He saw from Theil's expression that the change of tack had caught him off balance.

'No, sir.' He sounded as if he thought it was somehow disloyal.

Hechler smiled, the lines on either side of his mouth softening. 'You should. A fine officer.' He gave a wry grin. 'Misunderstood by his superiors, naturally. Nothing changes in that respect.'

Theil shifted in his chair. 'What about him?'

'The boldest measures are the safest, that's what the little admiral said. I believe it, never more so than now.' He eyed him calmly, weighing him up. 'We'll lose this war if we're not careful.'

Theil stared at him, stunned. '*Impossible*! I – I mean, sir, we can't be beaten now.'

'Beaten – I suppose not. But we can still lose.' He did not explain. Instead he considered Norway. The first part of their passage should not be too dangerous. Air attack was always possible, but the minefields should prevent any submarines from getting too close. He thought of the new detection gear which was being fitted. As good as anything Britain and her allies had. Kröll, the gunnery officer, had shown rare excitement, although he obviously disapproved of having civilian technicians on board telling him what to do. They would still be in the ship when they sailed; it was that sort of priority.

The unseen eye, one of the civilians had described it. The *Scharnhorst* had been tracked and destroyed with it even in a dense snowstorm. *Prinz Luitpold*'s was supposed to be twice as accurate, and they were the first to have it fitted.

Hastily trained men had been rushed to the ship, new faces to be absorbed, to become part of their world.

There was also a new senior surgeon, the original one having been released because of ill-health. It had been something of a cruel joke amongst the sailors.

Hechler considered discussing the surgeon with Theil but decided against it for the moment. The man's name was Stroheim; he was highly qualified and a cut above most naval doctors. The best were usually in the army for all too obvious reasons.

Hechler had skimmed through his confidential file, but only one part of it troubled him. There was a pink sheet attached to it. Hechler hated political interference. It was like being spied on. Nevertheless, Stroheim had come to him under a cloud. You could not ignore it. He held a mental picture of Oberleutnant Bauer, the signals and W/T officer. On the face of it a junior if important member of his team. Bauer too had a special form in his file. He was the ship's political officer, a role which even as captain Hechler could not investigate.

Hechler shook his sudden depression aside. 'I would like us to walk round the ship before the hands go to their stations for leaving harbour.' He forced a smile. 'To show a united front.'

Theil stood up and grasped his cap tightly to his side.

'It will be an honour. For the Fatherland.'

For a moment Hechler imagined he was going to add 'Heil Hitler' as Leitner would have done. He said, 'No one goes ashore from now on.' He thought suddenly about the explosion which had sunk the lighter. It was always unexpected when it happened. Vigilance was not always enough. *Sabotage.* They were out there watching the ship, the same people who had placed the bomb aboard the lighter. To damage the ship or to destroy Leitner's boxes, the reason made little difference. It could have been serious.

In London, quaking under the new and deadly rocket bombardment, a telephone would ring in some Admiralty bunker. *Prinz Luitpold is leaving Vejle.*

A brief radio message from some Danish traitor was all it took. He smiled again. Or patriot if you were on the other side.

Another more persistent tremor came through the deck plating from the depths of the engine-room.

He looked away from Theil's strained face. Like me, he thought. Eager to go.

The *Prinz Luitpold*'s swift passage from the Baltic into Norwegian waters was quieter than Hechler had anticipated. They logged a regular speed of twenty knots and passed Bergen within minutes of Gudegast's calculations.

For much of the time, and especially for the most dangerous period in the North Sea when the Orkney Islands and later the Shetlands lay a mere 200 miles abeam, the ship's company remained closed up at action stations. Every eye was on the sky, but unlike the Baltic the weather was heavily overcast, with low cloud and spasms of drizzle which reduced visibility to a few miles. They were able to test some of the new radar detection devices, and Hechler was impressed by its accuracy as they plotted the movements and tactics of their escorts even though they were quite invisible from the bridge.

Further north and then north-east, still following the wild coastline which Hechler knew from hard-won experience. Past the fortress-like fjord of Trondheim and crossing the Arctic Circle until both radar and lookouts reported the Lofoten Islands on the port bow. To starboard, cut into the mainland itself lay Bodø, and an hour later the cruiser's cable rattled out once more and she lay at anchor.

A grey oppressive coast, with sea mist rising around the ship like smoke, as if she had just fired a silent salute to the shore. They were not alone this time. Another cruiser, the *Lübeck*, was already anchored in the fjord, and apart from their escorts there were several other big destroyers and some supply ships.

Some if not all of the tension had drained away on the passage north. To be doing something again, to accept that a sailor's daily risks put more personal worries into their right perspective, made Hechler confident that his ship was ready for anything.

With the ship safely anchored behind protective nets and booms, and regular sweeps by patrol boats, Hechler found time to consider the wisdom of his orders. Bodø was a good choice, he thought, if only for the enlarged, military airfield there. Bombers and fighters could supply immediate cover, as well as mount an attack on enemy convoys or inquisitive submarines.

Routine took over once again, and after the fuel bunkers had been topped up from lighters, they settled down to wait.

Less than twenty-four hours after dropping anchor Hechler received a brief but impatient signal. He was to fly immediately to Kiel. After the uncertainty and the mystery of his orders it was something of an anti-climax. But as he was ferried ashore and then driven at reckless speed to the airfield in an army staff car, the choice of Bodø as a lair for his ship became all the more evident. Everything was planned to the last detail, as if he had no hand in anything. He did not even know what to tell Theil before he left. He might even be going to Germany only to be informed he was relieved, that perhaps Theil was taking command after all.

The aircraft, a veteran Junkers three-engined transport, arrived at Kiel in the late afternoon.

Hechler had been dozing in his seat, not because he was tired but mainly to avoid a shouted conversation with an army colonel who spent much of the four-hour flight fortifying himself from a silver flask.

As the plane tilted steeply to begin its final approach Hechler got his first glimpse of Kiel through a low cloud bank. He had not returned there for about a year and he was unable to drag his eyes from the devastation. Whole areas had been wiped out, so that only the streets gave any hint of what had once been there. There was smoke too, from a recent air raid or an uncontrollable fire, he could not tell. He had seen plenty of it in five years of war. Poland, Russia, even in the ship's last bombardment he had watched the few remaining houses blasted into fragments.

Smoky sunlight glinted momentarily on water and he saw the sweeping expanse of the naval dockyard before that too was blotted out by cloud.

It was hard to distinguish serviceable vessels from the wrecks in the harbour. He saw fallen derricks and gantrys, great slicks of oil on the surface, black craters instead of busy slipways and docks.

In such chaos it was astonishing to see the towering shape of the naval memorial at Laboe, somehow unscathed, as was the familiar, gothic-style water-tower, like a fortress amidst a battlefield.

The drunken colonel peered over his shoulder and said hoarsely, 'We'll make them pay for this!' He wiped his eyes with his sleeve. 'My whole family was killed. Gone. Nothing left.'

The plane glided through the clouds and moments later bumped along the runway. Here again was evidence of a city under siege. Sandbagged gun emplacements with grim-faced helmeted crews lined each runway. Parties of men were busy repairing buildings and filling in craters. It seemed a far cry from *Prinz Luitpold*'s ordered world and Leitner's luxurious headquarters.

It felt strange to be here, he thought. More so to be amongst his fellow countrymen, to hear his own language in every dialect around him.

A camouflaged staff car was waiting and a tired-looking lieutenant seemed eager to get him away from the airfield before another alert was sounded.

No wonder some of his returning ship's company had seemed so worried and anxious. If all major towns and cities were like this – he did not allow his mind to dwell on it.

Naval Operations had been moved to a new, underground headquarters, but before they reached it Hechler saw scenes of desolation he had not imagined possible. There were lines of men and women queuing at mobile soup-kitchens, their drawn and dusty faces no different from those he had seen on refugees in Poland.

They drove past a platoon of marching soldiers who carried spades and shovels instead of rifles. They were all in step and swinging their arms. Some looked very young and all were singing in the staccato manner of infantrymen everywhere. But their faces were quite empty, and even their NCO forgot to salute the staff car.

The lieutenant saw his expression and said dully, 'It's been like this for weeks.' He dropped his eyes under Hechler's blue-grey stare. 'I – I'm sorry, sir.'

Another small cameo came and went as the car picked its way around some weary-looking firemen.

A stretcher was being carried from a bombed house, the front of which had tumbled out on to the street. Hechler caught a glimpse of some torn wallpaper and a chair hanging from the upper floor by one leg. An old man was being led to safety by a nurse, but it was obvious even at a distance that he wanted to remain with the blanket-covered corpse on the stretcher.

Hechler said, 'Night raids?'

The lieutenant shrugged. 'The Yanks by day, the Tommies by night.'

Hechler wanted to ask about Kiel's air defences but said nothing. *I am a stranger here.*

The lieutenant gave a sigh and wound down a window as some armed sentries blocked the road. The new headquarters was like a slab of solid concrete, not much different from the outside to one of the great U-boat pens, he thought.

But once inside, with the huge steel doors shut behind them, it was more like a ship than anything else. Steel supports, shining lifts which vanished into the ground like ammunition hoists, and even the officers and seamen who bustled about with briefcases and signal folders looked different from the embattled people he had just seen on the streets outside.

The lieutenant guided him into a lift and they stood in silence as it purred down two or maybe three levels. More doors and brightly lit passageways where the air was as cool and as fresh as a country lane.

Hechler had the impression that the lieutenant was taking him on a longer route than necessary in spite of his haste, perhaps to show him the display of businesslike efficiency. Hechler had not been in the bunker before and he looked into each room and office as they hurried past. Teleprinters, clattering typewriters, and endless banks of switchboards and flashing lights. There were several soldiers about too, and in one map-covered room Hechler saw that the Luftwaffe was also represented.

He felt his confidence returning, the dismal pictures he had seen on the street put momentarily aside. It was just that when you were involved in the fighting you never thought of those at home who had to stand and accept whatever was hurled at them. He thought of his parents and was glad they lived well away from the city.

The lieutenant pressed a button and another steel door slid to one side.

Several uniformed women were busy typing, while an officer was speaking intently on a telephone.

All of them jumped to their feet as Hechler appeared in the bright electric glare, and stared at him as if he was from another planet.

The lieutenant was relieved. 'The Admiral is waiting, sir.'

Two more doors, and each new room became less warlike. There were rugs, and pleasant lamp-shades, and the desks were of polished wood and not metal.

Leitner was sitting in a comfortable chair, a glass in one hand, his uniform jacket unbuttoned. He looked fresh and untroubled, as if he had just had a swim or a shower.

'Right on time, Dieter.' He gestured to another officer, a captain who was vaguely familiar.

Leitner said, 'Perhaps you know Klaus Rau? He commands *Lübeck*.'

They shook hands, and Hechler recalled the other captain who had once commanded a destroyer during the attack on Narvik.

He was a stocky, dark-jowled man with deepset eyes which seemed very steady and unblinking. Hechler sat down and pictured the cruiser which lay near to his own ship. *Lübeck* had been in the thick of it from the outbreak of war. The Low Countries, France and then in the Baltic against the Russians, she too had a charmed life despite being heavily damaged by gunfire and bombs alike on several occasions. *Lübeck* was an old ship, built in the early thirties and about half the size of *Prinz Luitpold*.

Leitner put down his glass and looked at them blandly.

'We shall be working together, gentlemen, just as soon as I hoist my flag. It will be a small but crack squadron, and the enemy will have cause to remember us.'

Rau glanced at Hechler. 'My ship has already given them reason enough.'

Hechler kept his face impassive. There it was again. Like Theil. He wondered briefly if it was coincidence or an accident that Rau had arrived here ahead of him. He had not been aboard the old Junkers. He smiled inwardly. It was unlikely that Leitner would ever permit a coincidence.

The rear-admiral added, 'You will receive your final orders when you return to your commands. This is a maximum security operation.' He gave a quick grin, like an impish schoolboy. 'If it leaks out, I shall know where to come looking, eh?'

A telephone buzzed, and the flag-lieutenant appeared as if by magic through another door and snatched it up before his superior had time to frown.

Hechler could not hear what he said, but saw some dust float down from the ceiling; he would not have seen it but for the lights.

Leitner listened to his aide and said, 'Air raid. They are going for the harbour again.' He gestured for his glass to be refilled. 'Our fighters have brought down four already.'

Hechler looked at the ceiling. Was that all it meant down here? A tiny trickle of dust, and not even a shiver of vibration. He thought of the drunken colonel on the plane, his despair. How could a man like that lead his troops with conviction? He had been damaged as much as any man who loses a limb or his sight in battle. It was dangerous to cling to the past merely because he imagined he had no future.

Leitner glanced at his watch. 'We must see the head of Operations.'

Rau stood up. 'Until tomorrow then, sir.' He glanced at Hechler. 'A pleasure meeting you again.'

Hechler watched the door close. A man without warmth.

Leitner smiled. 'He is jealous of you. Nothing like envy to keep men on their toes.'

He walked to the other door. 'Come with me, Dieter. The time for cat-and-mouse with men like Rau can keep.'

Admiral Manfred von Hanke was an impressive figure by any standards. He was standing straight-backed in the centre of a well-lit map-room, his heavy-lidded eyes on the door as Leitner and Hechler were ushered in by another aide.

Hechler knew a lot about the admiral, although he had not found many people who actually met him.

Von Hanke had been a captain in the Great War with a distinguished career ahead of him. He had been in the United States attached to the German Embassy where he had been engaged for several years in organising a powerful intelligence and espionage ring. In the final months of the war when America had abandoned her umbrella of neutrality, he had found himself arrested as a spy. Even that, and the possibility of summary execution, had not broken him, and despite his aristocratic family background, something frowned on in Hitler's New Order, he had survived and prospered. Today he was second only to Donitz, while his grasp of strategy and naval operations took second place to no one.

He had iron-grey cropped hair, and because he had just come from an investiture was wearing his frock-coat uniform and winged collar. He could still be one of the Kaiser's old guard, Hechler thought.

Leitner began brightly, 'This is our man, sir – '

Von Hanke raised one hand in a tired gesture and Leitner fell instantly silent.

Von Hanke said, 'Be seated. This will not take too long, but of course if you have any questions?' He gave a dry smile. 'In that case – '

He pressed a button on his deck and several long wall panels slid away to reveal giant maps of each of the main battle areas.

Hechler stared at one of the Baltic and the Gulf of Finland where his ship had been mostly employed. It all seemed so long ago instead of weeks.

His eyes fastened on some red flags where one of von Hanke's staff had marked the various army units.

Von Hanke watched him steadily, his hooded eyes without expression. 'You have seen something, Captain?'

Hechler hesitated. 'The Twenty-First Division, sir. It is still shown south-west of Riga.'

'Well?' Not a flicker of emotion although Hechler could sense Leitner's irritation behind his back.

'It no longer exists. It was decimated weeks ago.' The admiral's silence was like an unspoken doubt and he added, 'I was there, sir.'

Leitner said, 'I expect it has been regrouped – '

The admiral clasped his hands behind him.

'I am glad you show interest as well as intelligence, Captain.'

Von Hanke gestured to the adjoining map which showed Norway and the convoy routes from Iceland to North Cape. It was pockmarked with pointers and flags, and Hechler felt a tightness in his throat when he saw his own ship's name on a metal pennant placed on Bodø. Pictures leapt through his mind. Theil's anxiety, the straddled destroyer heeling over in a welter of fire and steam. Men dying.

The straight-backed admiral said in his slow, thick tones, 'The Allies are throwing everything they have into France. Even now there are advance units within miles of Paris, others breaking out towards the Belgian frontier. Our forces will blunt their advances of course, and already the army's pincer movements have taken many prisoners and valuable supplies. But the advance goes on.'

Hechler glanced at the flags nearest to the Belgian frontier. It was said that the new rocket-launching sites were in the Low Countries. The Allies would use every means to reach them before they could do their maximum damage in England.

Von Hanke continued calmly, 'Intelligence reports are excellent. The British intend to do something they have not attempted before and have two convoys in

Northern waters at the same time. A loaded convoy routed for the Russians in Murmansk, and an empty but nonetheless valuable one on the reverse route to Iceland. The Normandy campaign has made the Royal Navy very short of escorts, that is their only reason.'

Hechler could see that too in his mind. The endless daylight, the convoys drawing further and further north towards Bear Island to avoid air and U-boat attack. It had always been a murderous battleground for both sides.

He examined his feelings. It was what he might have expected. An attack on two convoys when Allied warships were deployed in strength in the English Channel and Biscay. If they destroyed one or both of the convoys it might give a breathing space. Even as he considered it, he sensed a nagging doubt. Just to look at those probing red arrows, the British and American flags, made such an operation little more than a delay to the inevitable.

Much would depend on the army's counter-attacks in France. They had to hold the line no matter what if they hoped to gain time to break the enemy's determination with an increasing rocket bombardment.

Von Hanke said softly, 'You look troubled, Captain.'

Hechler faced him. 'I think it can be done, sir. My ship – '

'Your *ship*, Captain, is possibly the most powerful of her kind afloat, and she is one of half a dozen major units left in the fleet.' He glanced absently at the maps. 'Others are supporting our troops in the Baltic, as you will know better than most. Some are marooned in ports on the Biscay coast. And there are those which are damaged beyond repair by air attacks.' He turned again and fixed his eyes on Hechler. '*Prinz Luitpold* is the best we have. If she is not properly employed, she may end up like her less fortunate consorts.'

Hechler glanced at Leitner. He looked bright-eyed; inspired would be a better description, he thought.

'At the right moment you will leave Bodø and seek out one of the convoys as directed by OKM.' His eyes never left Hechler's. 'And then, Captain, you will take full advantage of the disruption caused and – ' He walked towards him and then gripped his hands in his. 'You will take your ship into the Atlantic.'

For an instant longer Hechler thought he had misheard or that the admiral was about to add something.

The Atlantic. A ship like *Prinz Luitpold* could create hell on the sea-lanes until she was run to ground.

Von Hanke said, 'You do not question it?' He nodded slowly. 'That is good. I would not like to give the ship another captain at this stage.'

Leitner exclaimed, 'It is a perfect plan, Dieter!' He could not contain his excitement. 'A tiger at large, with all the chain of supplies to make it possible!'

Von Hanke frowned. '*Later.*' He looked at Hechler. 'Surprise will be total. It will show the world what we can do.' He gripped his hands again. 'You will do it for Germany!'

A door opened and Hechler knew that the interview was at an end.

It was so swift, so impossibly vast he could barely think of it as a feasible plan. At the same time it was like a release, perhaps what he had always been looking and hoping for.

Von Hanke folded his arms. 'Nothing will be said beyond these walls. Only the Führer knows, and he will let nothing stand in your way.'

Hechler thought of the colonel on the plane, the frightened-looking people he had seen in the bombed streets.

Perhaps this *was* a way. Maybe it was all they had.

Outside the map-room Leitner said, 'Return to your ship. I will fly up in two days.' He shrugged. 'After that, who knows?'

Hechler found the tired lieutenant waiting for him and the car was ready to take him to the airfield.

He barely noticed the journey and was astonished that he could accept it so calmly.

The Atlantic. The vast Western Ocean. *The killing ground*, where every ship would be an enemy.

Leitner's words stuck in his mind. *A tiger at large*.

He touched the peak of his cap to a saluting sentry and walked out to the smoke-shrouded runway.

The waiting was over.

5

Rank Has its Privileges

Dieter Hechler opened his eyes with a start and realised that his face was pressed on to his forearm. Two other facts stood out, that he had been writing a letter to his parents, but had been awakened by the clamour of alarm bells.

He jumped to his feet, his mind still refusing to grasp what was happening. He was in his day cabin, his jacket hanging on a chair, an empty coffee cup nearby. Normally the sound of those alarm bells would have brought him to instant readiness and it was likely he would have been in his tiny sea-cabin, or dozing in the steel chair on the bridge.

The telephone buzzed through the din of bells and running feet with the attendant slamming of watertight doors.

It was Theil. 'Red Alert, sir. Air attack.'

Hechler slammed down the handset and snatched his jacket and cap even as Pirk scampered past him to screw the steel deadlights over the scuttles.

On deck the ship seemed deserted, and only abandoned brooms and paint brushes marked the sudden alarm.

He climbed swiftly to the upper bridge, aware that the anti-aircraft guns were already traversing towards the land, and men were putting on helmets and dragging belts of ammunition to the short-range weapons.

It was still a bright afternoon with just a few jagged clouds towards the open sea.

Hechler barely heard the quick reports from the officers around him but stared instead at the long stretches of camouflaged netting which hung between the masts and above the main armament. It was the same aboard the *Lübeck*. It did not hide a ship from an inquisitive aircraft, but it acted as a disguise and broke up a ship's outline.

Theil took a pair of binoculars from a messenger and then handed them back with a terse, 'Clean the lenses, damn you!'

Hechler looked across the starboard screen. The airfield was invisible from here, but there ought to be some fighters scrambled by now, he thought.

He hated being at anchor. Like lying in a trap. The bait. The ship had been at short notice for steam since his return from Kiel, but not that short. It would take an hour to slip and work out to some sea-room.

He turned his attention to the other cruiser. All her secondary armament was at full elevation, and in his mind's eye he saw Rau, watching the heavy cruiser and probably comparing the times it had taken for both ships to clear for action.

Theil muttered irritably, 'Come on, get those planes airborne!'

He must be thinking much the same. Too many warships had been caught in enclosed fjords and damaged beyond repair by daring hit-and-run raids.

An inland battery had opened fire and every pair of glasses scanned the clouds as the shells left their familiar dirty brown stains in the sky.

Theil exclaimed, 'I can't see a bloody thing!'

The young one-striper, Konrad Jaeger, called suddenly, 'I see it! One aircraft, sir, at red four-five!'

Hechler sensed Theil's annoyance but concentrated on the bearing until sunlight shone like a bright diamond on the plane's cockpit cover.

Another voice hissed, 'Nowhere near the thing!'

Hechler watched the shell-bursts gathering in an untidy cluster while some earlier ones broke up and drifted downwind.

Hechler had to agree with the unknown sailor. The shooting was very poor and the tiny sliver of metal in the sky did not even alter course.

It was not a bomber anyway, and seemed to be quite alone.

Bodø was described as a safe anchorage and better protected than most. It was likely that enemy agents would know of *Prinz Luitpold*'s presence here, just as her departure from Vejle would be known and plotted in London. However, there was no need to invite some reckless reconnaissance plane to confirm everything.

Theil said between his teeth, 'Our Arado replacement is expected, sir.' He sounded anxious. 'I hope to hell that headquarters have ordered it to stand away.'

Hechler looked over the screen and past the nearest gun-crews as they tried to track the aircraft, their anti-flash hoods making them look like members of some strange religious order.

The aircraft derrick was already swung out, the tackle prepared to hoist the new Arado inboard as soon as it landed in the fjord.

'Gunnery officer requests permission to use main armament, sir.'

'Negative.' Hechler knew that Kröll would shoot at anything just to exercise his men. But it was a waste of ammunition and with as much hope of hitting the reconnaissance plane as a bow and arrow. In fact the solitary aircraft was already heading away, flitting between the clouds, the shell-burst too far away to catch it.

Theil said, 'Here they are! *At last.* Late as bloody usual!'

Two fighters streaked from the land, the echo of their engines roaring around the fjord with a throaty vibration. The sun shone on their black crosses as they tilted over and then tore towards the sea.

42

Hechler lowered his binoculars and glanced at Theil and the others. Theil was furious, too angry perhaps to notice the coincidence. The anti-aircraft battery had been haphazard, just as the fighter cover had been far too late to do anything.

It was as if they had been ordered to hold back. If that was so, it meant just one thing. Headquarters wanted the enemy to know they were here. It was like being in the dark. Being told only a part of von Hanke's strategy. Hechler tried to shrug it off. It was not the first time that air defences had been caught napping. He pictured the admiral in his winged collar, the dry grip of his hands. Von Hanke of all people would know each step before it was made. Just as he had known about the army division which existed only on his map. How many more divisions or battalions were represented only by coloured markers and flags? A million men lay dead from the last campaign. How many more were there now? He tried to dispel the sudden apprehension, the sense of danger.

'Aircraft at green one-one-oh, angle of sight one-oh!'

The gunnery speaker snapped into life. 'Disregard! Aircraft friendly!'

Some of the seamen grinned with nervous relief, but Hechler crossed the bridge to watch the float-plane as it left the land's protection and followed its own reflection across the flat water.

He snapped, 'I want to see that pilot as soon as he comes aboard! We may be short of a plane and the man to fly it, but by God I'll send him back double-quick unless he can explain himself!'

All the smiles were gone now. Even young Jaeger had enough experience to realise the cause of the captain's cool anger. If there had been a proper air attack, especially by carrier-borne torpedo bombers, the Arado replacement would have been right in the middle of it, and Kröll's flak gunners would have had to hold their fire or shoot it down with the attackers.

'Fall out action stations.' Hechler controlled his anger.

Moments later the guardrails were thronged with men again as the new float-plane made a perfect landing and then taxied towards the anchored cruiser.

Theil dropped his glasses. 'Extra passenger, sir.' He bit his lip. 'It looks like the rear-admiral.'

Even as the plane glided towards the side Hechler saw Leitner grinning up at them, before removing his flying helmet to don his oak-leaved cap.

He said, 'I don't care if it's Christ Almighty. That was a damn stupid thing to do!'

Hechler was as much concerned at his own anger as he was about the admiral's unorthodox arrival. Was it because there were so many questions still unanswered? If they engaged one of the British convoys for instance. Would Rau's *Lübeck* be able to withdraw safely? That, almost more than the mission itself, had filled him with uncertainty.

Followed by Theil he hurried from the bridge and down to the catapult, where a side-party had been hastily assembled.

Leitner pulled himself up from the Arado without waiting for it to be hoisted aboard. He was flushed and excited, and could barely stop himself from laughing aloud at Hechler's grave features. Together they watched the plane being hoisted up the side, water spilling from the floats as the handling party used their guy-ropes to sway it round. The Arado was brand-new, and bore no camouflage paint. As it came to rest on the catapult before being manhandled inboard

Hechler saw the bright red stripe on the side. Like something from the Great War, he thought grimly.

Leitner stood with his arms folded, still dressed in a white flying suit, his cap at a rakish angle as he had appeared many times in the newspapers.

Hechler watched the pilot and observer climb down to the deck and then said, 'I'll see *you* later. You might have got your arse shot off!'

The pilot turned and stared at him and then pulled off the black helmet goggles.

Hechler stared as a mass of auburn hair tumbled over the other man's shoulders.

The admiral made a late effort to contain his amusement and said, 'Captain, may I introduce Erika Franke. One of the finest pilots in the Third Reich, I believe!'

She eyed him without curiosity, her lips slightly parted as she shook out her hair from her flying suit.

'Quite a welcome, Captain.' She did not offer her hand.

Hechler could feel the side-party's astonishment giving way to broad grins, and Theil's pink-faced disbelief that this had happened.

Hechler looked at the admiral. 'What I said still goes, sir.'

She was watching him, amused or merely bored he could not tell.

Erika Franke, of course. Her father had been an ace pilot who had died in attempting a lone flight across a desert in Africa. She had won several prizes within a year of obtaining her licence. And she had even made her name in the war when she had flown into an encircled army position in Italy to rescue one of the Führer's top advisers before the whole place had been overrun.

He said, 'I am not used to – ' It sounded defensive, foolish.

She turned away to watch as the two fighters came roaring back across the water.

'Evidently, Captain. We must try to change that, mustn't we?'

Leitner clapped him on the shoulder.

'It will be a different war, Dieter.' He became serious again. 'For all of us, yes?'

The girl turned and looked at them calmly. 'I'd like to change and have a shower, if I may.' She touched her upper lip with her tongue. 'Even at the risk of getting my, er, arse shot off, eh?'

Hans Stoecker in his best uniform with a holstered Luger at his belt stood nervously outside the wardroom. He felt on edge, unable to concentrate on anything, even the prospect of meeting Sophie again.

It was all so strange and unreal, he thought, after the patrols and bombardments, the wild elation of watching from his position high above the bridge when the main armament had fired on the enemy.

The wardroom throbbed with music, and was packed from side to side with officers and visitors alike. Like the peacetime navy must have been, he thought, without fear of a sudden air-attack or torpedo.

With the rear-admiral's flag hoisted over the ship everyone had expected things to move swiftly, that the *Prinz* would head out to sea again.

He recalled seeing the girl pilot as she had climbed down from the catapult.

Like most of the company he had read of her exploits, especially the last one when she had flown through enemy flak to lift off an important politician. Stoecker did not really like the idea of women in the firing line, but after meeting Sophie he was not certain of anything. She was not a schoolgirl any more. She was a woman, and had probably seen more results of war than he had.

Now he had two secrets to hold. One was the letter, still unopened. He had nearly destroyed it several times but something made him hold back. The other secret was what Sophie had told him.

She was ordered to a hospital in Norway. Suppose it was where they were based? They would meet again. Like that last time when they had kissed and clutched each other, hearts pounding while they had tasted a new and delicate love.

A curtain swirled back and Leutnant zur See Konrad Jaeger stepped over the coaming. He took a pistol from the rack and clipped it around his waist.

He grimaced as a great burst of laughter came from beyond him.

'Time for rounds, Stoecker. Others have all the luck.'

It would take all of an hour to go round the flats and messes, to check padlocks and magazine and to sign all the log-sheets. By the time they had finished some of the guests would have left.

Stoecker nodded to a boatswain's mate and messenger who were waiting to accompany the young officer on his rounds. There was a faint smell of schnapps in the damp air, and he hoped Jaeger had not noticed it. He was a good officer, for a one-striper that was. But he'd come down on Stoecker if he found someone had been drinking on watch.

Jaeger was not aware of the acting petty officer's wary glance. He was thinking of the wardroom party, the first one he had ever attended in a real combat warship. The *Prinz* was famous; you could see the excitement, even awe, on the faces of the guests, and especially the women. The admiral must have a lot of influence even in that direction, he decided. There were lots of women aboard, and most appeared to be German except for the wives of some local officials.

Preceded by the boatswain's mate, Jaeger and his little party climbed to the cooler air of the quarterdeck, where Korvettenkapitän Froebe was waiting by the accommodation ladder to welcome guests below the shaded police lights.

It was a rare sight, and Jaeger paused to watch as two women in long, colourful dresses with some officers from the airfield stood by the guardrails, their hair moving in the evening breeze, their eyes exploring the ship.

Jaeger thought of the young girl he had met in the wardroom. It was unlikely he would get a look-in there, he thought. Hampe, the torpedo officer and a well-known womaniser, had been watching them, waiting for rounds to be called. For him to leave.

A figure moved from the shadows and Jaeger called his men to attention.

The captain touched his cap and smiled. 'Hard luck, Jaeger, but rank has its privileges, you see.'

Jaeger grinned. He could recall standing like a ramrod at attention for minutes on end in his last ship, where he had completed his training. That captain had been a tyrant, a bully you would never want to speak to even if it had been allowed.

Hechler was so different. Did he never have any worries or doubts?

Hechler saw the youngster's glance in spite of the gloom. He had also noticed the faint tang of schnapps. That would be the boatswain's mate. His mother and sister had just been reported killed in an air raid. He would let it pass. Hechler strode on, half-dreading the party and Leitner's exuberance. *This* time, he would say nothing.

Theil was waiting to meet him outside the wardroom and Hechler asked, 'All going well?'

Theil nodded. 'Like old times.'

Hechler stepped into the wardroom and moved through the packed figures. It was hard to see this place as it usually was, or used as a sickbay for wounded troops brought offshore from the fighting.

He sensed the glances and the occasional bold stares from some of the women. Why should he feel so ill at ease? This might be the last time for a long while that they could relax and drink too much. It could just as easily be the last time ever.

He heard a woman laugh and saw the auburn hair shining beneath a deckhead light.

Erika Franke wore neither a gown nor a uniform, it was something in between, dove-grey which set off her hair and her skin. She was speaking with Zeckner, a quarters officer, so that Hechler made to step aside before she saw him.

He was still uncertain what to do. Leitner had explained that the orders came from von Hanke and even higher. Erika Franke was to stay aboard. Incredibly, there was also a camera team. That in itself was not unusual in major warships, but with the prospect of immediate action it could put their lives at risk. Leitner seemed to treat the whole matter like a personal publicity operation.

She called, 'Why, Captain, so you have come amongst us after all!'

He faced her, surprised and angry at the way she got under his skin and made him feel clumsy.

He said, 'I hope you are being looked after?' She had long lashes and eyes which seemed to change colour as he watched. Hazel and then tawny.

She smiled. 'You are staring, Captain.'

Hechler took a glass of champagne which someone thrust into his hand.

'Yes. I'm sorry.' He raised the glass and lowered it again. 'And I apologise for the way I greeted your arrival on board.'

She touched her lip with her tongue as she had when she had faced him at their first meeting.

'That must have cost you a lot, Captain.' She nodded, her eyes grave. 'I suspect you are not used to bending your knee.' The smile moved into her eyes again. 'Especially to a mere woman.'

Leitner joined them before Hechler could answer. He said, 'Good party. It will make everyone believe we are here as a part of a local squadron.' He beamed and showed his perfect teeth. 'Let them all relax and enjoy themselves, eh? Who cares about tomorrow?'

Theil was making signals from the door and Leitner remarked, 'A night full of surprises. As it should be.'

Hechler glanced past the noisy, laughing figures and saw her as she stepped over the coaming. He felt as if his breath had stopped, that even his heart was still.

Her hair was quite short so that her small, perfectly shaped ears were visible, as were the pendant earrings as she turned to look around.

Several officers stopped talking to stare, questions clear on their faces.

Hechler put down his glass. Inger had always commanded a lot of attention, like the first time he had seen her and lost his heart.

She had an escort, a much older man in an olive-green uniform, a political officer of some kind and obviously quite senior. That too was pretty typical, he thought bitterly.

Leitner was watching him, one eyebrow cocked. 'She asked to come.' He spread his hands with mock gravity. 'What must I do? How could anyone refuse her?'

'Your wife, Captain?'

Hechler looked at the girl with auburn hair. He felt suddenly lost. Trapped.

He said, 'Yes.'

'She is very beautiful.' But she was studying him, her eyes quiet with interest. 'You seem surprised?'

Leitner smiled. 'It is only right, Dieter.'

Hechler said, 'She has no place here.'

But she was coming across, men parting before her or trying to catch her glance.

She wore a red silk gown with thin shoulder straps. It was cut very low both front and back and Hechler guessed that she wore little if anything underneath it.

She presented her hand for him to take and kiss. Even that was perfectly done. The perfume on her skin, it too he could recall as if it were yesterday.

Leitner was shaking hands with her escort, but Hechler did not even catch his name. It was as if nothing had happened, that the fire still burned. The touch of her hand, the movement of her breasts which were barely concealed by the red silk, seemed to render him helpless.

He knew Theil and some of the others were watching. They were learning more about their captain every day. Why had she come?

She said softly, 'You look tired, Dieter. Doing too much.' She observed him calmly. 'As always.' Her eyes moved to the girl. 'And who is this?'

Erika Franke met her gaze, unruffled by the casual but faintly imperious tone.

She replied, 'I work here.' She gave a quick smile. 'I shall go and enjoy myself.'

Inger watched her leave and said, 'That's the flier. I thought I knew her.' She seemed to relax. 'She's been in some bother, I believe.'

Hechler did not want to discuss it. 'I was not expecting – '

'*That* is evident.' She smiled and touched his cheek but her eyes were quite cool. 'No matter. You are a man, a *hero*, some say.'

Leitner had moved away and was in deep conversation with her escort. The latter was staring across, unwilling to be shelved so soon.

Hechler felt the old anger again. Why should he have to put up with it?

Theil was watching too, although he was at some pains to cover it.

He heard himself ask, 'Why here and now, Inger? It's over.'

'You think so?' She rested one hand on his sleeve and touched the four gold stripes. 'You need me. You always will. Nothing's changed.' She seemed to become impatient and thrust her hand beneath his arm. 'Can we talk? In private?'

Hechler heard the lively dance strike up as another record was put on the gramophone and was grateful for the interruption. Voices grew louder and some of the guests began to revolve although there was barely room to move. Perspiring stewards and messmen pushed amongst the throng with laden trays of glasses. This evening was going to cost the wardroom a small fortune.

She said, 'Your cabin?' She looked up at him, her eyes steady, her lips shining, inviting.

They walked along the deck, the noise growing fainter as if the ship was reasserting herself, rising above them, grey steel and hooded guns.

Once she turned and looked across at the darkening water, the thin white line of a motor-launch's wake.

He asked, 'What about your friend?'

She shrugged. Even that motion stabbed him like a knife.

'Ludwig? He is head of a mission here, something to do with fisheries, I think. Don't worry about him.'

The cabin was quiet, with a tidiness which showed Pirk had been busy clearing up from the last official visitors. But there was some champagne and two glasses, as if it had all been planned. She saw his expression and said, 'Thank you, I should like some.'

He could feel her watching as he opened the bottle and wiped it free of ice. She never looked tired; he could not recall her ever refusing an invitation to a party or a reception. Like the time he had returned home with the knowledge he was being given *Prinz Luitpold*. He had been in bed reading when he had heard her come into the house, then the sound of men's voices.

When he had gone down he had found her in the arms of an artillery major, while another officer was on his knees beside a girl who had obviously passed out with drink. The man had been tearing the clothes off her, stripping her naked while Inger and her friend ignored what he was doing.

Somehow, he could barely recall how, they had made it up. She had even been excited when he had thrown the others out of the house, had pleaded for his forgiveness and then given herself to him with such wild abandon that he had surrendered.

Looking back he must have been mad. But he had loved her then. Hechler turned with the glasses. He still wanted her. Was that the same thing?

He sat beside her, feeling the longing and the pain of it as he studied her face and her mouth. When she took his hand and put it around her breast he could feel the drumming in his mind, could think of nothing but taking her, here and now. As Leitner had said, who cares about tomorrow?

She stretched out and put down her glass so that one shoulder strap slipped away and her breast was almost lying bare in his hand. She watched his face as if to test each emotion there and said, 'You are sailing soon. Why else would Andreas invite me?'

He should have guessed that Leitner was behind it. It was a game to him. He used people with little thought for what might happen.

'What do you want, Inger?'

She touched his mouth with her fingers. 'I need you to love me.'

It made no sense, but he wanted to hold her, tell her everything. Hopes, fears, all the things which were bottled up inside him . . . The telephone shattered the silence and she smiled as he reached out to take it.

It was Theil, his voice hushed and troubled. One of the guests had fallen down a ladder. It was someone important. He thought the captain should know.

Hechler watched her, the way she smiled as she slipped the other strap from her shoulder and allowed the red silk to fall about her waist. Her breasts were lovely, and she touched one, her lips parted, knowing it would provoke him.

He said quickly, 'Get the senior medical officer, Viktor.' He had not met the newcomer yet and as he watched the thrust of her breasts he could barely recall his name. 'Stroheim.'

He put down the phone and looked at her. She was staring at him, her eyes full of disbelief. 'What name?'

Hechler said, 'Karl-Heinz Stroheim. He's new on board. I – '

She struggled into her dress and knocked over her champagne without seeming to notice it.

Hechler stood up while she looked around the cabin like a trapped animal. 'You know him?'

She faced him, her eyes hot. 'Don't you *dare* question me! I'm not one of your snivelling sailors?' She recovered slightly and glanced at herself in the mirror. 'Take me back. I must go.'

He blocked her way. 'Tell me! For God's sake, you said you wanted me!'

She stared at him, and he could see her self-control returning, like a calm on the sea.

'What will you do, Dieter? Knock me down? Rape me?' She tossed her short curls. 'I think not – your precious Andreas would not care for *that*!'

Hechler could not recall walking back to the wardroom. More curious stares, her bright laugh as her escort lumbered over to claim her. He heard her say something about a headache, and then as she turned to look towards him she said, 'It will be a relief to be alone.'

Leitner watched as she followed Theil towards the door. He asked softly, 'Not going with her, Dieter? Tch, tch, I am surprised.'

Hechler turned his back on the others, his voice dangerously calm.

'You did it deliberately, sir. For one moment I thought – ' He shook himself angrily. 'I don't know what I thought.'

Leitner glanced towards his willowy aide who had just entered, his eyes everywhere until he had found his lord and master.

Hechler saw the brief nod. Nothing more.

Leitner picked up a fresh glass and watched the busy bubbles rising.

'I shall set an example and retire, Dieter.' He looked at him for several seconds as if making up his mind. 'First-degree readiness.' He shook his head as Hechler made to speak. 'Not *yet*. People are watching. We shall weigh tomorrow evening. As soon as the guests have departed, pass the word to the other commanding officers.' Some of his self-control slipped aside. 'You will brief your heads of departments as soon as we clear the anchorage.'

Hechler watched the crowd of guests thinning soon after Leitner had followed his flag-lieutenant outside. It was like an unspoken command, and he walked to the guardrails opposite Turret Caesar to watch the boats and launches queuing at the accommodation ladder to collect their passengers.

Perhaps he hoped to see the red silk gown. He did not know any more. But he could picture her sitting beside him, her lovely body naked to the waist. Then her anger – or was it fear?

Some of the departing guests were singing. The ship, deep in shadow, must look quite beautiful from the boats in the water, he thought.

First-degree readiness. Like the opening of sealed doors. Page one.

The squadron would slip away unseen in the darkness, but not a man in any of the other ships would know *Prinz Luitpold*'s true purpose. When they did there would be few who would wish to change places with them.

As one of the duty officers, Jaeger, with Stoecker standing close by, stood by the gangway and watched the visitors being guided and helped down the long ladder. The sailors were taking much greater care with the women than the men, he noticed.

He saw the girl pause and look up at him. She had waited until he returned from rounds, and he had spent the rest of the time speaking with her.

He raised his hand in salute and saw her blow him a kiss.

He did not see the pain on Stoecker's face as he spoke her name aloud. *Sophie*.

By midnight as the watchkeepers changed round for the next four hours Hechler still walked the decks alone.

When he eventually went to his cabin he saw that the glasses and ice-bucket had gone, the stain of her champagne all but mopped up from the carpet.

A light burned beside his bunk, some coffee in a thermos nearby.

He thought suddenly of the new medical officer, and her expression when he had spoken his name.

There was so much he wanted to know, so much more he dared not ask.

When Pirk entered silently to switch off the light he found the captain fast asleep, still fully dressed.

Pirk sighed and then swung Hechler's legs on to the bunk.

He thought of the newly installed admiral and what he had heard about him and his flag-lieutenant. If the other stewards knew, it would soon be all over the ship.

Pirk smiled with satisfaction and switched off the light.

The captain would see them all right. He always had.

Hechler slept on, and with his ship waited for the dawn.

6

The Unexpected

Hechler slid from his steel chair on the port side of the bridge and stamped his feet on the scrubbed gratings to restore the circulation. One of the watchkeepers jumped at the sound, and Hechler noted the tense backs of the bridge lookouts as they peered through their powerful glasses, each man to his own allotted sector.

Hechler glanced at the armoured conning-tower and past it to the fire control position. Beneath and around him the ship vibrated and quivered but the motion was steady, and even some pencils on the chart table remained motionless.

He tried to dampen down his own anxieties. It was always like this when a ship left the land. For him in any case. Now, with the additional knowledge of what might lie ahead, he had to be certain of everything. *Confident.*

There had been no flaws, nothing serious anyway. He looked past two signal-men and saw *Lübeck* following half a mile astern, her faint funnel vapour stream-ing out abeam like her flags. The destroyers too were exactly on station, as if they were all on rails. They dipped their bows occasionally and Hechler saw the sea creaming over their forecastles before cascading down through the guardrails again. A small but powerful force, he thought, with air cover to make it easier. Every few minutes, or so it seemed, they sighted one of the big Focke Wulf Condors which acted as their eyes and escorts.

Two bells chimed out from below the bridge and the men relieved from watch would be having their lunch, the main meal of the day. It had been sixteen hours since they had weighed and with little fuss had steamed out of Salt Fjord, soon to lose Bodø in the gathering dusk.

Hechler had been on the bridge throughout that time, watching the cable clanking inboard with the usual chipped paint scattering to each massive link.

Westward to skirt the Lofoten Islands and then north, the ships closing in protectively on either beam.

All the captains had come aboard just prior to sailing, but Leitner had kept his comments on a general level. They all knew about the enemy convoys, each captain had an intelligence pack as big as a bible. The British might have a change of heart, or perhaps one of the convoys would be re-routed at the last minute.

Sixteen hours at a relatively gentle fifteen knots, although the destroyers were finding station-keeping hard work.

It was a strange feeling to be heading out into an ocean instead of sighting land every so often as in the Baltic. Now as *Prinz Luitpold*'s raked bows ploughed across the seventieth parallel nothing lay ahead unless you counted Spitzbergen or Bear Island. Scenes of other sea-fights, Hechler thought, before every eye had turned to Normandy and the Eastern Front.

He walked to the chart-table to give himself time to glance at the men around him. Most of them were warmly dressed, for despite the fact it was August, the air had a bite to it. Soon there would be no escape from the ice.

Their faces looked normal enough, he thought. That morning he had sensed the silence throughout the ship when he had spoken on the intercom to the whole company.

Leitner had been ready to make a speech, but Hechler had bluntly asked permission to speak to his men, in his own way.

He had pictured them as his voice had echoed around each deck and compart-ment like a stranger's. Gun crews and engineers, the damage-control men and those who cooked and served the hundreds of meals it took to feed the *Prinz*'s people.

'We are going out into the Atlantic – ' There should have been rousing music, cheering; instead there was a silence which meant so much more to him, no matter what Leitner might believe.

Some had tried to tell him privately that they would not let him down. Others, like the huge Gudegast, had merely joked about it. *Good a place as any to lose a ship!*

He wondered what Rau would say if he knew.

Hechler shaded his eyes to look at the horizon. It was so eerie. A great, unbroken swell which roamed on and on for ever. And the sky, which was salmon-pink, painted the ragged clouds in a deeper hue, like copper. The ship's upperworks too were shining in the strange glow. Endless daylight, empty seas.

Another Focke Wulf droned overhead; a lamp winked briefly to the ships below.

The camera team has been on the bridge for much of the forenoon, but they seemed to have exhausted their ideas, and even the big four-engined Condor did not lure the cameras on deck again.

Oberleutnant Ahlmann, who was officer-of-the-watch, put down a handset and said, 'The lady flier wishes to come to the bridge, sir.'

Hechler thrust his hands deep into his pockets. He had not seen her since they had left Bodø, except once when she had been on the admiral's bridge with Leitner. Like the two girls who were in the camera team, her presence gave a sense of unreality. According to Leitner, they would be transferred before the ship headed deep into the Atlantic. Their films would be invaluable, he had said with all of his usual enthusiasm. A tonic to the people at home. It all depended on the first move. Von Hanke would decide after that.

Hechler had the feeling that the rear-admiral intended to use von Hanke as an excuse for almost everything.

He said, 'Very well.' He might get to the bottom of it by asking her what exactly she was doing aboard, in his ship.

Her voice came up the ladder and he pictured Inger, as he had a hundred times since the party. Her anger, her contempt, were so different from that earlier seduction. If it was to happen again . . .

He turned to face her as she was ushered into the bridge.

She wore a black leather jacket with a fur collar turned up over her hair. Her skin was very fresh from the wind and he guessed she had been exploring the upper deck.

'A wonderful view, Captain!' She climbed on to the gratings and peered through the salt-blotched screen. 'I should love to fly right now!'

Hechler watched her profile, her neat hands which gripped the rail as the deck tilted slightly to a change of course.

Ahlmann looked up from a voice-pipe and reported, 'Steady on Zero-Two-Two, sir. Revolutions one-one-zero.'

He turned and saw her watching him.

She shrugged. 'So different.' She gestured towards the upper bridge and radar, Leitner's flag leaping stiffly to the wind. 'So huge. You feel as if nothing would stop her, as if she could run away with you.'

Hechler nodded. 'When I was a young watchkeeper I often thought that.

Especially during the night, the captain asleep, nobody to ask. I used to look at the stars and – '

'Gunnery Officer requires permission to train A and B turrets, sir.'

Hechler replied, 'Yes. Ten minutes.'

'It never stops for you, does it?'

He looked at her. 'I hadn't thought about it.' Together they watched as the two forward turrets swung silently on to the same bearing.

Kröll never missed a chance, which was why he had given him a time limit for this, another drill. At any moment, any second, the alarms might scream out. Men had to be clear-minded and not confused by too many exercises.

He thought of what Inger had said about this quiet-eyed girl. In some sort of trouble.

She said, 'Seeing those great guns makes me realise what your kind of war is all about.'

'Are you afraid?'

She seemed to consider it. 'I don't think so. It's like flying. There are only certain things you can do if the plane gets out of control.' She shrugged again. 'I don't feel I have any hold on things here.'

Then she laughed and one of the lookouts tore his eyes from his binoculars to glance at her.

'I *know* you are going to ask me, Captain, but like you, I am under orders. I am on board your ship because I have been so ordered. I am a civilian but I fly for the Luftwaffe.'

'I heard what you did.' Hechler tried to adapt to her direct manner. 'It's more than I'd care to do.' He scraped the gratings with his boot. 'Give me something solid . . .'

Theil appeared at the rear of the bridge and saluted, although his eyes were on the girl.

'The admiral sends his compliments, sir, and would you see him.'

'Yes.' Hechler was annoyed at the interruption. Being captain usually gave him all he needed, but he craved a conversation with someone who was not committed or involved with the same things. Leitner had probably seen them chatting, and was merely calling him away although it could hardly be from jealousy.

The thought made him smile and she said quietly, 'You should do that more often, Captain.' She turned away as the two forward turrets purred back to point fore-and-aft again.

Theil stepped forward so that he seemed to loom between them.

Hechler said, 'If there is anything I can do while you are aboard . . .'

She watched him, her eyes tawny in the strange light. 'Attend your ship, Captain. Her needs are greater than mine, I feel.'

Hechler turned away. The brief contact was broken. And why not? His own self-pity was a poor enough bridge to begin with.

He found Leitner on his armoured bridge, leaning with his arms spread wide on the plot-table.

Leitner glanced up, his neat hair glossy beneath the lights. 'All intelligence reports confirm my own thinking, Dieter. Tomorrow, we shall meet with the eastbound convoy. The British will know we are on the move. No matter, they will expect us to strike at the westbound one, to protect their friend Ivan's supplies, eh?' He nodded, satisfied. 'All working out. There are six U-boats in this area, and round-the-clock air patrols.' He stood up and clasped his hands at his sides. 'I can't *wait* to begin. Into the Atlantic, all that planning and von Hanke's preparations. God, it makes one feel quite humble!'

Hechler watched his emotion. It came and went like the wind. He thought of the reams of orders, the methods of fuelling, rendezvous, and alternatives. This would be a million times different from previous raiding sorties.

Leitner said, 'I know it is important to you, Dieter, the close comradeship amongst your people. I heard it in your broadcast this morning. Saw it on their faces. Just boys, some of them, but the older ones who can be so hard and cynical – ' he gave an elaborate sigh ' – you had them eating out of your hand.'

Hechler replied, 'Comradeship is everything.'

'I *knew* it.' Leitner looked down at his plot-table again. 'Your second-in-command. I had a private signal about him.'

'Viktor Theil?'

'His wife has gone missing.' He sounded almost matter-of-fact. 'Of course I'm certain it will be all right. After all, ration books, identity cards, a civilian can't just vanish, eh?'

Hechler recalled Theil's face, the way he had parried questions about his leave.

Leitner said softly, 'I know what you're thinking, Dieter. *Don't*! He is a good officer, I'm sure, but he *is* the second-in-command. Should anything happen to you, well . . .' He shrugged.

'I trust him, sir.'

'Good. I shall remember it. But if he trips up on this mission, he goes, do I make myself clear?'

Hechler nodded. 'Very.'

Leitner yawned. 'Pretty girl, that Franke woman, eh? I wonder if she's as good in bed as in the cockpit.'

Fortunately a telephone rang and the flag-lieutenant appeared again like magic to answer it.

Hechler returned to the bridge. He felt strangely disappointed to find she was no longer there. Theil had gone too. For that at least he was glad.

He climbed into his steel seat and listened to the deep throb of engines, the occasional clatter of a morse lamp as signals were exchanged between the ships. Tomorrow that would all cease. He glanced over the screen at the same heavy guns. Moving targets, not rubble and houses, or a position on a range map.

He tried not to let Inger into his thoughts, to recall how she had looked, and shifted uneasily in the chair. He was getting rattled just when he needed every thought honed to a knife-edge. Tomorrow they would engage the enemy. Right now, at this very moment the convoy was being attacked by U-boats. Like sheepdogs gone mad who were driving the convoy on a converging course.

He thought of Theil, then of himself. Two deserted husbands. It was laughable when you considered it. Was that all it meant? Voices muttered in voice-pipes, while guns moved in their mountings as the faithful Condor droned past the formation yet again. No, it was anything but laughable. He gripped the arms of his seat. Men would die, cursing his name, ships would burn.

Wives and petty squabbles were as nothing.

The bows dipped and he saw his reflection in the smeared glass. No, that too was a lie.

Hans Stoecker slammed yet another watertight door behind him and wedged the clips into place. Below the ship's waterline where one compartment was sealed from another the air felt cool and damp, the motion more pronounced. He passed the massive circular trunk of B turret, Turret Bruno, and paused by a brightly lit door to the forward starshell room.

He had been carrying a message from the gunnery officer for one of the lieutenants but had purposely taken a roundabout route, and had parried not a few questions from sentries who guarded some of the vital bulkheads which in an emergency might prevent serious flooding. Stoecker glanced at the studded rivets and rough steel. It was best not to think of it, of those who might be trapped on the wrong side to face a terrible death by drowning.

He heard the familiar whistle and saw a grey-headed petty officer rummaging through a box of tools. Oskar Tripz was probably the oldest member of the ship's company. He had served in the Kaiser's navy, and when you got him going over a quiet glass of brandy or schnapps, would dwell with relish on the Battle of Jutland, and clashes with the Grand Fleet off the Dogger Bank. Even when he had quit the service he had been unable or unwilling to leave the sea and returned to it in the merchant marine and eventually in the famous Hamburg-Amerika Line. There again he could open the eyes of young sailors with his yarns of great liners, rich widows and randy passengers who chased the girls and sometimes the stewards with equal enthusiasm.

He was a rough, self-made seaman, and one of the gun-captains, despite his great age, great to younger men like Stoecker anyway. Stoecker was never bored by his stories of that other navy, another world, and was ever impressed by the man's knowledge of the sea. Tripz had even managed to teach himself at least three languages, with enough of some others to get him around in ports all over the world.

Tripz looked up and squinted at him questioningly. He had a round, crumpled face, as if that too had been carved from old ship's timber.

'You're a bit off-course, young Hans?'

Stoecker sat on a steel chest and eyed him awkwardly. Of all the people he knew he probably trusted the old petty officer the most. It had been due to his patience and private coaching that he had risen this far, with the hope of confirmation to petty officer in the near future.

With Tripz it was not learning. It was more like listening to well-told history.

'A job for the gunnery officer.'

Tripz wrinkled his nose. 'Oh, him.'

They both glanced up as the sea, muffled but ever-present, boomed along the outer hull. Thick steel and one of the great fuel bunkers separated them from it, but they both knew it was not enough to withstand a torpedo.

Tripz asked casually, 'Bit bothered, are you?'

Stoecker shrugged. Straight to the point. As always. This rough, outspoken man was respected by almost everyone, even if some of the young recruits made fun of him behind his back. God help them if his wintry eyes saw through them.

'It's the first time I've been in a battle with other warships.'

Huh. Maybe it won't come to that. The Tommies might have other ideas.'

'When I heard the captain explain what we're going to do, I – '

Tripz grinned slowly. 'The Old Man knows more than *we* do, Hans.'

Stoecker bit his lip. It was useless to go on like this. He could barely sleep even when he got the chance, and he had been off his food since that day at Vejle.

Suppose he was wrong? Tripz might go straight to his divisional officer. He had been known to pass the time of day even with the captain, the Old Man as he called him, though Stoecker guessed that Tripz was old enough to be his father.

But he couldn't go on. He would certainly fail his exams and let down his parents unless – he made up his mind.

'I found a letter.' He hesitated as the petty officer's faded eyes settled on his. 'Somebody told me that – '

'Show it to me.' He held out one calloused hand. He saw the lingering hesitation. 'I'll make it an order, if you'd prefer it?'

Stoecker passed it across and momentarily the prospect of action, even death, faded into the background.

Tripz prised open the much-folded envelope and scanned the letter with great care.

He said, 'It's in Danish. But then you'd know that, right?' He did not look up to see Stoecker nod. 'One of those prisoners.'

'Yes.' He was surprised the admission came out so easily. 'Just before he was killed.'

Tripz eyed him grimly. 'Before the explosion.'

'Yes.'

'Told anyone else?'

Stoecker shook his head and thought of the others he had almost confided in. Even the young one-striper Jaeger. Until he had discovered about him and Sophie. That moment still gnawed at his insides like teeth.

'Good.' He folded the letter with great care. 'This is hot stuff.'

Stoecker found himself blurting out about the SS officer, then the ravaged shop.

Tripz grunted. 'Jews, eh.' He added vaguely, 'Well, they started it all, you know.'

Stoecker waited; at any moment Tripz might put him under arrest, take him to Korvettenkapitän Kröll. He could face detention barracks or much worse.

Tripz said, 'Best leave it with me.' He looked at him strangely. 'Just between us.'

'But I don't even know . . .'

'Better that way, my son.' Tripz placed the letter inside an oilskin pouch and buttoned it in his tunic.

He added, 'It could get both of us shot. Do I make myself clear?'

Stoecker nodded, glad to have shared his secret, moved by Tripz's confidence in him.

'When I've fathomed it out, I'll tell you.' His battered face split into a grin. 'Feel better?'

Stoecker gave a shaky smile. 'Much. I – I'm just sorry I got you mixed up in it.'

Tripz looked up quickly at the deckhead as if he had heard something. It was like an inbuilt sixth sense for at that moment the air cringed to the strident clamour of alarm bells.

Tripz was thickset, even ungainly, but he was through the steel door and on the rungs of a ladder before Stoecker had grasped fully what was happening.

Tripz peered down at him. 'Move it, boy! No time to hang about! You'll get a wooden cross, not an iron one, if you do! Remember what I once told you, one hand for the Führer, but keep one for yourself!' Then he was gone and would doubtless be in his turret before the bells had fallen silent.

Stoecker ran after him; he had further to climb than anyone. And yet despite the crash of steel doors he felt as if a great weight had been lifted from him.

'Ship at action stations, sir!'

Hechler returned Korvettenkapitän Froebe's salute and glanced briefly around the bridge. In war what a short time it took to know their faces, to forget them after they had gone.

Everyone stiffened as Leitner entered the bridge and strode unhurriedly to the gratings.

Hechler watched him curiously. The whole scheme might go badly wrong from the outset. There had been plenty of examples like *Graf Spee* and *Bismarck*, he thought. But Leitner looked very much at ease, even theatrical with a pure white silk scarf tossed casually around his throat, his rear-admiral's cap set at a rakish angle.

Leitner remarked, 'The stage is set, eh?'

Hechler could picture his men throughout the ship, as he had when he had told them their missions. Theil as second-in-command was down in the damage-control section, as far from the bridge as possible. Not too many eggs in one basket, as his father would have said. Did he ever hope a shell might fall on the bridge and give him the command he craved so desperately?

'I assume the engine-room is warned for full revolutions?'

Hechler nodded. It was almost amusing if you knew Wolfgang Stück, the taciturn senior engineer. He had been like a midwife to the *Prinz*, had been with her within weeks of her keel being laid, had watched over every tube and wire, valve and pump until her birth, when she had slid confidently into salt water at Hamburg.

So many miles steamed, thousands of gallons of oil, and a million day-to-day details. Stück would need no reminding. They got along well, allowing for the unspannable gap between bridge and engine-room, he thought.

Leitner was saying, 'Looking back, it all seems worthwhile now. Remember breaking the ice on those buckets with your head aboard the training ship before you could wash in the morning, eh? It would make some of these mother's boys puke!' His eyes were almost dreamy. 'And the electric shock treatment to test your reaction under stress at Flensburg Naval Academy. I'll bet we know more than those old has-beens ever did!'

Hechler raised his glasses and studied the nearest destroyer.

'Signal the first subdivision to take station ahead.' He glanced at Leitner. '*Now.*'

A lamp clattered and Hechler saw a young signalman staring at the admiral with something like awe. He had probably never been so close to a god before.

Hechler asked sharply, 'What are those people doing here?'

Leitner smiled. '*My* orders, Captain.'

The camera team huddled by a flag-locker, the two women looking ill-at-ease in their steel helmets.

Leitner added smoothly, 'A record. We must all take risks in war.'

Hechler watched the camera being mounted, the way Leitner was adjusting his scarf. But he thought of the battered streets in Kiel, the faces of his men who had lost their relatives and their homes.

The flag-lieutenant hurried across the bridge and handed Leitner his signal pad.

He took his time while the camera purred into life and all eyes watched as the scene was recorded.

Hechler thought for an instant it was an act, but Leitner said briskly, 'The attack on the convoy was a success. The one escort carrier was hit by torpedoes. She is out of the fight.' He returned the pad to his aide. 'Two U-boats were destroyed, but they carried out their orders. Brave men, all of them.'

Hechler tried to shut him from his thoughts. Voice-pipes and telephones kept up their muted chatter and he saw the two forward turrets turn slightly, the four big guns lifting and lifting until they appeared to be trying to strain themselves from their mountings.

The first subdivision of destroyers were tearing ahead and heeling over in a great welter of spray as they formed into line abreast, well ahead of their big consorts. The others were on either beam, with one solitary vessel lifting and plunging across *Lübeck*'s wake as she followed like a spectator. To sniff out any submarine, to pick up survivors, to stay out of trouble.

Leitner had made his name in destroyers; he was probably remembering it right now.

Froebe, the executive officer, tall and ungainly, his huge hands gripped around his binoculars, stood in Gudegast's place by the gyro-repeater. The navigator and his small team were up there in the armoured conning-tower, waiting to plot every manoeuvre and change of course, to advise, to take command even, if the main bridge was demolished.

Hechler could feel the younger Jaeger standing as close as he dared to the steel chair. His action station was here too, and unlike the other junior officers he was privileged to hear and see everything. He was also more likely to be hit if the Tommies got too near.

Hechler thought suddenly of their sister-ship the *Admiral Hipper*. She too had carried out a raiding cruise in the Atlantic, and after a successful attack on a convoy and other ships had returned in triumph to her Norwegian lair.

But that had been in 1941. Things were different now.

Hechler examined his feelings again. What were their chances? His ship was the best there was anywhere. If skill and audacity counted they stood every chance of success.

It was strange to realise that *Hipper*, powerful though she was, had been rammed and severely damaged by the little destroyer HMS *Glow-worm*. A brave, hopeless gesture which had cost her captain his ship and most of his men. He smiled to himself as he thought of Theil's expression when he had mentioned Nelson. It was exactly what the little admiral would have done had he lived in this century.

The flag-lieutenant returned with his pad and Leitner said quietly, 'The British are concentrating on the eastbound convoy, Dieter. Von Hanke is a shrewd old devil. They have a battleship and two heavy cruisers as a covering force, but well to the north as expected.'

Hechler put one hand in his pocket and felt the familiar shape of his favourite pipe. It was somehow comforting, and he would have dearly liked to smoke it. It reminded him of Inger again. She had wanted him to give it up, change to cigars. Like Leitner who usually appeared in press photographs with a jaunty cheroot, although he had never seen him actually smoking one. Just for the record.

He walked to the rear of the bridge and peered aft past the funnel. The new Arado looked bright and incongruous beside one of the camouflaged ones. Was she really going to fly it as Leitner had vaguely outlined? He never gave the whole story about anything. Again, that was exactly how he had been as a junior lieutenant. A touch of mystery. He thought of the photographs Leitner had shown him prior to weighing anchor. The fjord at Bodø, shot from several thousand metres up. Even the camouflaged nets had looked the same. It could have been *Prinz Luitpold* lying there. But Leitner had explained, two old supply ships had been preparing for weeks. After this sortie they would be moored together in such a way that any reconnaissance aircraft would imagine the *Prinz* had returned to her anchorage. It was so simple, it was almost ridiculous. But if it worked it might give them the extra hours they needed.

Ahlmann, the lieutenant in charge of bridge communications, handed him a telephone.

'Gunnery officer, sir.'

Even the telephone could not disguise the satisfaction in Kröll's voice.

'Enemy in sight, sir. Bearing Green one-oh. Range two-one-five.'

Hechler wanted to turn and look up at the fire control station. The unseen eye reached beyond the empty horizon so that Kröll could already watch the enemy formation at a range of over 21,000 metres.

Leitner jabbed his sleeve. 'I am going to my bridge.' He grinned. 'This is a great day!' He brushed past the bridge party and Jaeger said, 'They are almost within range.'

Froebe watched him over the gyro-repeater and muttered, 'So will we be soon.'

Hechler raised his glasses and stared past the leading destroyers. Even their wakes were salmon-pink, their shining hulls like coloured glass.

Intelligence had reported a dozen merchantmen in the convoy. Probably twice that number had originally set out for Murmansk, he thought. Homeward bound, and with all the heavy support groups to the north of them waiting for an attack on the other precious array of supply ships. He listened to the regular ranges and bearings coming over the bridge gunnery intercom and pictured the two converging formations in his mind as he had studied it on the chart and had planned for such a moment. As Leitner had said, all that training was bearing fruit now. *Observation, method, conclusion, attack.*

The forward guns shifted slightly, the muzzles high-angled for the first salvo.

Astern, *Lübeck*'s gun crews would be ready too, but they would have to be patient a while longer.

He wanted to glance at his watch, but knew such a move might be mistaken for doubt, anxiety.

Above the whirr of fans and the surge of water against the hull he heard the dull thud of an explosion. Far away, like someone beating an old drum. Another torpedo hit, one more ship gone to the bottom. Leitner did not seem to care about the cost in U-boats. To him nothing mattered but this moment.

Ahlmann asked, 'Permission to open fire, sir?'

'Denied.' He pictured the convoy again. Liberty ships for the most part. It would be a fast one, probably about fifteen knots. They would scatter if they fired too soon. It would be harder, and there was always the covering force to consider. A battleship and two heavy cruisers.

'*Aircraft*, sir!' Several of the men gasped aloud. 'Red one-five! Angle of sight one-oh!'

Froebe said between his teeth, 'Torpedo bombers, for Christ's sake!'

Orders rattled out from every side and the short-range weapons swung instantly on to the bearing.

Hechler stood in the corner of the bridge and levelled his Zeiss glasses, surprised that he should feel so calm, almost detached.

Two aircraft, so they had to be from the crippled carrier. They must have been flown off just prior to their being torpedoed. He considered it, weighing it up. Each pilot would know he had no chance of returning to his ship.

Like the little *Glow-worm* all over again, the unexpected factor. It would be the worst kind of attack – bravery or cold-blooded suicide, you could take your pick.

One of the aircraft might even be radioing a sighting report. So much for radar. The British senior officer must have outguessed von Hanke, or was it just luck?

He tightened his jaw. 'Short-range weapons stand by. Secondary armament – ' his eyes watered in the powerful lens as he saw the two small dots heading towards the ships. They were so low now they appeared to be scudding across the water. He knew their outdated silhouettes well enough. Swordfish, twin-winged torpedo bombers, like relics from the Great War.

He cleared his mind and shouted, '*Open fire!*'

The line of destroyers were already firing and the sky soon became pockmarked with shell-bursts. It would be tracer and cannon-shell soon, and then –

Alhmann said thickly, 'The Admiral, sir.'

Leitner sounded faraway. 'The convoy may scatter. Increase speed. Signal the group to engage the enemy as ordered.'

Hechler saw the signalmen bending on their flags and said, 'Full ahead. Prepare to take avoiding action.' He saw Froebe nod. Then he forgot him and the others as the power surged up through the bridge like something unleashed until the whole structure quivered around them.

He had to shout above the sharp bang of the secondary armament, which poured acrid fumes over the bridge as the ship swept forward, faster and still faster.

'Main armament. *Open fire!*'

He barely had time to adjust his ear plugs before both forward turrets blasted the air apart to fire upon the target which was still invisible, below the horizon.

He looked for the two aircraft and saw them weaving amongst the shell-bursts while bright tracer lifted from the destroyers and crossed their path in a fiery mesh. One of the Swordfish was trailing smoke and it seemed impossible that either of them could survive the barrage.

One thing was obvious. *Prinz Luitpold* was their target.

7

Aftermath

Neither of the Swordfish torpedo bombers stood any chance of survival, and each pilot must have known it. As they pounded past the line of destroyers, the one trailing smoke seemed to stagger as tracer and cannon-fire tore into it.

Hechler jammed his elbows below the screen and stared at the weaving silhouettes as pieces of the damaged plane splashed into the glistening swell. Seconds later it exploded in a vivid orange flash. When the smoke drifted clear there was nothing to be seen. But the second aircraft was dodging the flak, and even as he watched Hechler saw the torpedo drop from the plane's belly and make a small feather of spray as it hit the water.

The plane continued towards them, shell-bursts, tracer, everything which would bear hammering into it. Perhaps the pilot and crew were already dead, but the Swordfish rolled over and then dived into the sea with a dull explosion.

'Torpedo running to port!'

'Hard a-port!'

At thirty knots the cruiser seemed to lean right on her beam, men falling and clutching anything for support as she thundered round.

'*Steady*. Hold her!' Hechler thought he saw the thin thread of white as the torpedo streaked towards the port bow.

The ship was steadying up, and Froebe croaked, 'Two-eight-zero!'

Leitner's voice broke through the din, distorted and wild on his intercom.

'Signal *Hans Arnim* to –' He got no further. The destroyer received the torpedo halfway down her port side even as she dashed protectively between it and the flagship.

At full speed the effect was instantaneous and terrible. Half of the forecastle collapsed and then rose in the air as the ship broke in two, the thrust of her screws driving her on and down as they watched.

Hechler said, 'Bring her back on course.' From one corner of his eye he saw the *Lübeck* surging past to take the lead into battle. He could picture Rau laughing as he watched the *Prinz* reeling from the line in confusion. His guns suddenly opened fire, and moments later he saw the tell-tale flash-flash on the horizon to mark the fall of *Lübeck*'s salvo.

Gudegast's voice intruded from his armoured conning tower.

'On course, sir. Zero-two-zero.' He sounded calm, even disinterested, even though the destroyer was turning turtle in a welter of smoke and foam.

The intercom reported dully, '*Hans Arnim* has sunk, sir.'

Hechler snatched up the gunnery handset. 'This is the Captain. I am turning to starboard. Bring the after turrets to bear on the enemy!' They had a better chance with four turrets in action.

He said, 'Alter course. Steer Zero-seven-zero.'

He raised his glasses again and winced as the fire-gong preceded the violent crash of the main armament. Kröll was using each turret in sequence, so that the bombardment seemed unbroken and deafening.

Jaeger wiped a smokestain from his cheek and gasped, 'The Admiral, sir!'

Leitner strode across the bridge, his silk scarf no longer so white.

He snapped, 'Can't see a damned thing up there. Too much bloody smoke.' He gritted his teeth as the two after turrets fired, gun by gun, the great shells shrieking past the ship and lifting towards the unseen enemy. They sounded like express trains.

Leitner shaded his eyes to look for the destroyer. If there were any survivors they were left far astern, forgotten.

Hechler waited for the guns to shift slightly and asked, 'Can I signal *Lübeck* to take station again?' He grimaced as the guns thundered out once more, their long orange tongues showing that Kröll was using semi-armour-piercing shells.

The intercom shouted, '*Straddling!* Two hits!'

Leitner scowled. 'Get up there, Theissen! I want to know what we're hitting today!' He seemed to realise what Hechler had said. 'No. Let Rau have his fun. He can take the lead.'

Flash-flash. Flash-flash. The blink of gunfire, partly masked by a mist along the horizon. It looked like copper-coloured smoke. The screeching hiss of a falling salvo and then the tall waterspouts which betrayed the fall of the enemy's shells made every glass turn towards the *Lübeck*.

Leitner said, 'Not even a straddle.'

The intercom shouted again. 'Another hit!' Somebody sealed behind thick steel was actually cheering. Or going mad.

'Gunnery officer, sir.' The lieutenant named Ahlmann looked pale, and was biting his lower lip as another salvo screamed out of the sky and burst into towering columns of spray. They seemed to take an age to fall, as if they were solid.

'Captain?'

Kröll said between explosions, 'We've sunk a wing escort and have hit two merchantmen. One ship is leaving the convoy, range closing. I would say it's a cruiser by her size and speed.'

More waterspouts shot from the sea, changing from white to copper in the weird light.

Hechler stared at the *Lübeck*, which was almost stern-on, her turrets trained hard round to bear on the enemy. Where his own ship should be. The bridge quivered again and yet again and Hechler could feel the din of gunfire probing into his ears like hot wires.

'Enemy in sight, sir! Bearing Red four-five!' Hechler lifted his glasses and scanned the distant mist. No longer empty. A dull, blunt silhouette suddenly wreathed in smoke as her guns fired at extreme range.

Hechler did not lower his glasses. 'Tell the Gunnery Officer to concentrate on the cruiser.' The forward turrets fired instantly, but it was too far away to see the results.

He heard the gunnery intercom mutter, 'Short.' Then Kröll's voice. 'Four hundred metre bracket!' A pause. '*Fire!*'

'Straddling!'

Leitner clasped his hands together. 'Signal *Lübeck* to go for the convoy. We'll take care of this upstart!'

'Two hits!' The rest was drowned by a violent explosion and as Hechler twisted towards *Lübeck* he saw smoke and flame burst from below her bridge and spread upwards and outwards in a fiery scarlet mushroom.

Lübeck was altering course again, her forward guns firing and recoiling as she concentrated on the convoy as ordered.

The British cruiser had been hit too, but there was no let-up in her gunnery or its accuracy.

The next salvo straddled the *Lübeck* as if she was smashing through columns of ice, and another fire had broken out aft, the smoke trailing astern in an oily screen.

Hechler saw a boatswain's mate start with shock, his eyes glow like twin coals as the *Lübeck* received another direct hit. She was slowing down, her bow-wave dwindling.

The speaker intoned, 'A hit!'

Hechler tried to keep his glasses steady. It was as if they were all struck by some terrible fever. Nothing would hold still, only the guns which fired again and again until thought became impossible. He saw the glow of fires amidst the smoke and knew that the enemy too had been badly hit.

Kröll announced, 'Convoy's scattering, sir. Cruiser's disengaging.'

Leitner snapped, 'What about the other escorts?'

'Some destroyers, I think, sir.' He sounded guarded, aware that he was speaking with his admiral.

The first merchantmen were now in view, ungainly and pathetic as they tried to head away from the oncoming warships.

The damaged cruiser was standing off with two of the destroyers closing around her to take her in tow if need be, or to make a last stand against *Prinz Luitpold*.

'Shift target! *Open fire!*'

The merchantmen had no hope of survival. One by one they were straddled and set ablaze until smoke stretched across the horizon like a dense curtain.

'Cease firing.' Hechler glanced at the conning-tower, knowing that Gudegast would be watching the helpless merchantmen burn and die. Would be recalling his own life in a peaceful timber ship. There were others in his command who would see beyond the destruction, who would feel disgust as their mindless companions cheered and slapped one another on the back.

The enemy cruiser had been outgunned from the start, but it only took a lucky shell. That was different. But merchant ships were vital to the enemy, who knew that each convoy route had to be kept open, no matter at what cost.

Hechler said quietly, 'In my opinion we should return to Norway, sir.' He stood his ground as Leitner stared at him. '*Lübeck* is down by the head. Even under tow – '

Froebe called, 'Signal from *Lübeck. Unable to make more than six knots. Request assistance.*'

Hechler watched his admiral. That must have cost Rau a lot, he thought.

Leitner shrugged. 'Signal the senior officer, destroyers, to escort *Lübeck* back to base.' He watched the lamp stammering, the young signalman's face white as he shuttered off the signal. The aftermath of battle. A convoy destroyed; God alone knew how many had died in the twinkling of an eye, or so it seemed.

Lübeck's signal lamp flashed again, almost hidden by the dense smoke which billowed from her lower bridge. Through his glasses Hechler could see the splinter holes in her funnels, the great crater left by a direct hit. But the fires were under control.

'From *Lübeck*, sir. *I require a tow.*'

Leitner said, 'Has the destroyer leader acknowledged?' He sounded more impatient than concerned.

'Acknowledged, sir.'

'Very well.' Leitner seemed to take a long breath. 'Discontinue the action, Captain. Phase Two, *if* you please.'

He turned as the smoke-grimed camera crew emerged from where they had been hiding.

Leitner went to the prettier of the two girls and pinched her chin.

'Warm work, eh, my child?'

She stared after him, still too dazed to understand any of it.

'Fall out action stations.' Hechler picked up the damage control telephone. 'Viktor? This is the Captain. Come up, will you. We have disengaged.'

Gudegast already had his orders. He spoke on his own intercom. 'On new course and speed, sir. Revolutions for twenty knots.' It was all he said, or had to say.

Even the men who had appeared on deck as they were stood down from first-degree readiness must have felt it, like a sickness as their ship turned away from the others, the strange light playing into shadows through upperworks and guns, leaving her wake in a wide, crisp arc.

Rau would be watching. Cursing them and their ship, Leitner most of all. But he was too good a sailor to speak out even with a bitter signal as the sea opened up between them.

Left to the wolves. The British would be out for blood, and every aircraft which could be flown from the nearest carrier would be after Rau's *Lübeck*. And he would know it. In the same way that the captain of the *Glow-worm* had known, or the pilots of the two elderly Swordfish. Death or glory. It was no choice.

Gudegast came to the bridge and waited for Hechler to see him.

Hechler said, 'In ten minutes I'll join you in the chart-room.'

Gudegast nodded, his beard on his chest. He knew what Hechler meant. In ten minutes *Lübeck* and the others would be too far astern to matter.

He watched Hechler's grave features and did not know whether to pity him or to thank God he was in command.

He had seen one of the merchantmen die. A big freighter, high out of the water, in ballast. That feeling. *Going home*.

Gudegast decided to make a sketch of the unknown victim.

For the first time in his life he was suddenly afraid.

That evening as *Prinz Luitpold* steamed south-west into the Norwegian Sea she was greeted by a thick mist which cut down the visibility to two miles.

All signs of the brief attack on the convoy were cleared away, and ammunition racks and magazines were refilled and ready for instant action.

Every turn of the great triple screws carried them further and further from land, paring away the safety margin should they have to turn and run for home again.

Hechler had to admit there was some value in Leitner's confidence. Every radio message and intercepted signal was checked and plotted by Gudegast and his team, while high above all of them their new, triumphant radar kept up a constant search for unwelcome visitors. A pack of U-boats had forced home an attack on the big eastbound Russian convoy, and every available British warship was apparently engaged. The flimsy plan might just work, he thought, and *Lübeck* would reach Norwegian waters where she could carry out her repairs. Hechler could not accept that part. It stuck in his throat like a bitter taste. To leave *Lübeck* to her fate had been part of the plan, but at no time had Leitner allowed for such a spirited defence of the convoy by the lone British cruiser.

When he had voiced his opinion to Leitner the admiral had given him a dry smile.

'*You*, Dieter, of all people? I thought you had the stomach for this mission!'

There was no point in pressing the argument. It was said that an open row between the captain of the *Bismarck* and his admiral had sealed her fate as much as enemy gunnery.

Hechler considered it. They had destroyed the convoy, just as the enemy had tried to finish them in return. It was war. He thought of the radar and was glad of it. Apart from its vast superiority over anything else they had used, its range meant that they had some warning of possible attack by sea or air forces. It meant that the company need not stand at action stations all day and night. They could sleep for four hours at a time off-watch. It was little enough, but they were used to it. To lie down, even for a few moments, made all the difference. Escape.

Despite the frantic manoeuvring to avoid the torpedo, there had been no damage in the ship, apart from some broken crockery in the main galley.

There had been plenty of minor injuries, two men scalded in the boiler-room when they had been hurled from their feet, another with a broken leg after pitching down a ladder to the deck, and several other casualties.

One of the latter was Erika Franke, who had suffered a severe sprain to her wrist.

The medical report had been handed to Hechler with all the other items from the various parts of the ship. It was customary for the doctor to report in person, but he had sent a brief message to say he had too many casualties. Nervousness at meeting him, or a kind of arrogance, Hechler did not know. Yet.

Theil joined him on the bridge, his coat glistening as if it had been raining. The mist was wet and made everything shine in the failing light.

Hechler said, 'We seem to be clear, Viktor.' He spoke quietly. The men on watch were obviously straining their ears. Perhaps this lull after the roar of gunfire seemed like an anti-climax, or intimated that they had the sea to themselves.

He looked up at the sky, at Leitner's flag curling damply above the ship. 'We shall stand-to tonight.'

Theil looked away. 'Do you still intend to run south of Iceland, sir?'

Hechler nodded. 'Unless we're challenged, yes. At this time of year there's no advantage in taking the northern route through the Denmark Strait. Too much daylight, too many air patrols. If we head between Iceland and the Faeroe Islands it will give us 150 miles on either beam to play with.'

Theil grunted. 'Do you think we'll get through, sir?'

Hechler watched two seamen carrying an empty stretcher into the shelter of the forward turret. It made him think of the girl. Theil was right to question him; he would be required to execute Leitner's wishes should anything happen to him. He looked strained, anxious. He was not worried about their mission, it would be out of character. He was a book man, and rarely trusted personal opinion. Maybe that was why he had never been recommended for a command. No, he was worried about his missing wife. That was bad. You could not afford that kind of diversion when you were at sea. It could be fatal. For all of them.

Hechler listened to the steady vibration, felt the confident power of the great engines. They had been doing thirty knots when they had made their turn. She could manage thirty-five if need be. Even a destroyer would find her a difficult one to outpace.

It seemed to get darker as they hurried to the south-west, the night an ally, their only friend in this hostile sea.

Hechler tried to contain the excitement. It was like heady wine. After the stark pictures of battle and burning ships, the prospect of actually getting into the Atlantic seemed suddenly real and clean.

Theil saw the lines at Hechler's mouth soften and wondered how he would have felt in his place.

Like all the senior officers in the ship Theil had studied their orders with great care. The plan was marked both by its audacity, and its very scale. The naval staff under von Hanke must have been working on it for many months just in case the chance presented itself. Perhaps too many people were already involved? Secrecy was vital; without it they might as well give up now.

Von Hanke's son was a U-boat commander, or had been until he had been lost in the Atlantic. Maybe he had first given the old admiral the idea. For two years at the beginning of the war, U-boats had been hampered by the length of time it took them to reach their patrol areas in the Western Ocean, with the same delay in returning to bases in France to refuel and rearm.

To counteract this a building programme had started to produce a flotilla of huge submarines which could stay at sea for months. Their sole duty was to carry fuel and stores for their smaller, operational consorts. In prearranged positions on a specially charted grid, a rendezvous could be made or rejected according to the needs of each U-boat commander. It more than trebled their time at sea, and the enemy's losses had mounted accordingly. Nobody ever mentioned what this extra time on active service did to the morale of the submarine crews.

Now, these same supply submarines, milch-cows, were to be employed as tankers for the *Prinz*. Daring it certainly was. Practical? Nobody knew, as it had never been done before.

None of the others had voiced any doubts, and after today they might be glad they had not shown any lack of confidence. Once again the ship had come through unscathed. It was a pity about the *Lübeck*, but if it had your number on it, there was not much you could do. *Lübeck* had got off lightly, Theil thought. While she was in port, licking her wounds and enjoying all the glory, the *Prinz* would be in the Atlantic, in the thick of it. It was some comfort to know that a pin's head laid on a chart of the Western Ocean represented as far as a man could see in any direction.

Hechler said suddenly, 'I was sorry to hear about your wife.'

Theil stared at him and then at the nearest of the watchkeepers. He lowered his voice. 'The admiral?'

'He had to tell me, Viktor. I would have been informed anyway if Leitner was not aboard. What's the matter, did you think I'd see you as a lesser man?'

Theil felt the colour draining from his face. 'It makes no difference to my ability. None whatever, and anyone – '

Hechler slid from his chair and moved his legs to get rid of the stiffness.

'I'm going to the sick-bay while it's quiet. Take over.' He eyed him calmly. 'Shake the load off your back, Viktor. I just wanted you to know that I am concerned for you, not your bloody ability!'

Theil was still staring after him as he clattered down the internal ladder.

It felt strange, wrong to be off the bridge while the ship was at sea. Hechler saw the surprise on the faces of his men when he passed them while he made his way down two decks to the sick-bay. As a boy he had always hated hospitals, mostly because he had had to visit his gassed father in one; that was when they had promised there was still a good chance of a cure.

His poor mother, he thought, facing up to those daily visits, passing all the other veterans. No legs, no arms, gassed, blinded, some would have been better off lying in the mud of Flanders.

And always the bright cheerfulness of the nurses. *Coming along nicely. As well as can be expected.* It had all been lies.

He wondered how his father was managing now. He would soon be reading about the *Prinz* and their exploits.

His father, so sick but quietly determined to stay alive, was beyond pride. Love would be a better word, he thought.

The sick-quarters were white and brightly lit. Two medical attendants were putting bottles into shelves, and there was a lot of broken glass in a bucket. The same violent turn had done damage here too.

Some of the injured men were dozing in their cots, and one tried to sit to attention when he saw his captain enter, his plastered arm sticking straight out like a white tusk.

Hechler removed his cap and forced a grin.

'Easy there. Rest while you can, eh?'

The new doctor was not at all as he had expected. He was forty years old but looked much older. He had a heavy, studious face with gold-rimmed glasses. A lawyer, or a school teacher, you might think if you saw him as a civilian.

He made to stand but Hechler closed the door of the sick-bay and sat down. Then he pulled out his pipe and said, 'Is this all right?'

Karl-Heinz Stroheim watched him warily, one hand plucking at the three gold stripes with the Rod of Aesculapius on his sleeve.

He said, 'I have dealt with all the casualties, Captain.'

Hechler lit his pipe. A good feeling, almost sensuous, after being deprived on the bridge.

'I thought we should meet, so – ' He blew out some smoke. 'So, Mohammet and the Mountain, you see?'

'I'm honoured.'

'You'll find this a different appointment from your last. The barracks at Wilhelmshaven, right?'

The man nodded. 'Before that, well, you know about it too.'

'You were in trouble.'

A flash of anger came and went in Stroheim's brown eyes. 'I was too valuable to be thrown out. They put me in uniform instead.'

'No disgrace in that.' Hechler tried not to listen to the engines' beat. So much closer here.

He asked casually, 'Abortions, wasn't it?'

Stroheim's jaw dropped. 'How did you know?'

'I didn't. I guessed.' He smiled gravely. 'And I shall put down your lack of respect to the suddenness of your appointment, right?'

Stroheim thrust his hands beneath the table. 'I – I am sorry, Captain. I went through a lot. One day they will accept my views. Too late for many, I fear. But I have always believed – ' he hesitated, as if he expected Hechler to stop or reprimand him – 'a woman must have the right to choose.' His voice was suddenly bitter, contemptuous. 'There should be a better reason for having a child than producing soldiers and more mothers for Germany.'

Hechler stood up, his eyes on a bulkhead telephone. 'We'll talk again.'

Stroheim got to his feet. 'I'd enjoy that.'

Hechler glanced round the little office. A pile of records and a portable gramophone, some books, and a box of chessmen.

Hechler said, 'Don't make this too much like home. Mix with the others. It's not good to be cut off.'

Stroheim took off his glasses and held them to the light.

'Like you, do you mean, Captain?'

Hechler turned away. 'I don't need a consultation just now, thank you!'

He paused by the door. 'Take good care of my men. *They* did not ask to be here, so you see, they are like you, eh?'

He made to leave and almost collided with Erika Franke, her left hand bandaged and in a sling.

She gave a wry smile. 'Next time you change direction, Captain, please let me know. I need both hands for flying, you know!'

He looked past her at the doctor. 'I was sorry to hear of your injury.'

She laughed. It was the first time he had seen her really laugh.

He said, 'Can I see you to your quarters?'

She became serious, and gave him a mock scowl.

'So correct, so proper, Captain.' She relented. 'I shall walk with you. I find the ladders a bit difficult at the moment.'

They reached the upper deck, the passageway in shadows, the steel doors clipped shut.

She said, 'I would like to visit the bridge again. I hate being shut away down here. I feel trapped.'

'Any time.' He watched her, the way she moved her head, the colour of her eyes. He had hoped to see her. The doctor had been an excuse.

A messenger skidded to a halt and saluted. 'There is a message from the bridge, Captain.'

Hechler strode to a handset which was clipped to the grey steel and cranked the handle.

He heard Theil's voice, the muted sound of the sea and wind.

Theil said in a hushed voice, 'The admiral had a signal, sir. *Lübeck* was sunk.'

Hechler replaced the handset very slowly.

She watched him, her eyes concerned. 'May I ask, Captain?'

He looked at her emptily. '*Lübeck*'s gone.'

He could see it as if he was there. As if it was now.

She said quietly, 'You didn't want to leave her, did you?' She saw the question in the brightness of his blue eyes.

She shrugged and winced; she had forgotten her injury. 'I was told. Everyone knew. They're very fond of their young captain, you know.'

He rested his hand on one of the door-clips. 'There are no secrets in a ship, no matter what they say.' He faced her again. 'Yes, I wanted to stay with her. Now she's gone.' He thought of the burning convoy.

They had had their revenge. He touched the girl's sound arm. 'Later, then.'

He opened the heavy door and stepped out into the damp air. *Lübeck* had been sacrificed. He quickened his pace to the first ladder, oblivious of the watchful gun crews.

It must not have been in vain.

8

—— —— —— —— ——

Flotsam

The South African naval base of Simonstown was packed to capacity with warships of every class and size. It was like a melting-pot, a division between two kinds of war made more apparent by the vessels themselves and their livery. The darker hues of grey and garish dazzle paint of the Atlantic, at odds with the paler hulls of ships from the Indian Ocean and beyond.

Powerful cruisers which had the capacity and range to cover the vast distances beyond the Cape of Good Hope seemed to make the greater contrast with a cluster of stubby Canadian corvettes which had fought their convoy all the way from Newfoundland.

Freighters and oilers, ammunition vessels and troopers. There was even a cleanly painted hospital ship.

The largest cruiser in Simonstown on this particular afternoon lay alongside the jetty, her White Ensign hanging limply in the harsh sunlight.

She was HMS *Wiltshire*, a big, 10,000-ton vessel, typical of a class which had been constructed in accordance with the Washington Treaty in the late twenties. She was heavily armed with eight, eight-inch guns in four turrets, with many smaller weapons to back up her authority. An elderly Walrus flying-boat perched sedately on the catapult amidships, and her three tall funnels gave the ship a deceptively outdated appearance. She stood very high from the oily water, and because of her comparatively light armour plating her living quarters were both airy and spacious when compared with other men-of-war.

It was Sunday, and apart from the duty watch and men under punishment *Wiltshire* was deserted. Officers and ratings alike took every opportunity to get ashore, to visit Cape Town and enjoy the colourful sights, untouched by war.

In his day cabin Captain James Cook Hemrose, Distinguished Service Order, Royal Navy, sat beneath a deckhead fan and regarded his pink gin while he wondered if it was prudent to take another. On one chair lay his best cap which he had worn for Divisions and prayers that morning. Beside another stood his golf clubs, a reminder of the match he had had to cancel.

He was a heavy man, and in his white shirt and Bermuda shorts looked ungainly. There were dark patches of sweat at each armpit despite the fans and he hated the oppressive heat.

He was in his late forties, but service life had been hard on him. He looked older, much older, and what was worse, he felt it.

The door opened and the ship's commander entered quietly.

Hemrose gestured heavily to the sideboard. 'Have a pink Plymouth, Toby. Do you good.'

The commander looked at the signals on the table and said, 'It's all true then, sir?'

'Pour me one while you're at it. Not too much bitters.'

The commander smiled. As if he did not know his ways. He had been with him over a year. The Atlantic, convoys round the Cape, Ceylon, India. It suited the commander. Routine, and often boring. But you could keep the Atlantic and Arctic runs. Let the glory boys do them if that was the war they wanted.

'Yes, it's true.' Hemrose's eyes were distant. 'The Jerries have put one of their big cruisers to sea. They think it might be *Prinz Luitpold*.' His eyes hardened into focus. 'I hope to God it is.'

The commander sipped his gin. Just right. 'She won't get down here. Not at this stage of the war.' When Hemrose remained silent he added, 'I mean, it's just not on, sir.'

Hemrose sighed. The commander, Toby Godson, was a well-meaning fool. He ran a smart ship, and that was enough. Until the signal had arrived anyway.

Hemrose recalled his excitement, although he would die rather than display it. The war might indeed end soon, maybe even next year. Being captain of a big cruiser, a ship well known as any of her class, was some compensation. But he had seen himself, still in command when the war ended. Then what? Passed over for promotion again, or merely chucked on the beach like his father before him.

They had some saying about it. 'God and the Navy we adore, when danger threatens, but not before!'

He looked at the lengthy signal from the far-off Admiralty. As from today he was promoted to acting commodore, to take upon himself the command of a small squadron. To take all necessary steps to seek out and engage the German raider should she manage to penetrate the defences and come to the South Atlantic.

It was unlikely, as Godson had said. But it had given him a well-needed boost. *Acting commodore*, a temporary appointment at the best of times. But it was his chance. The all-important step to flag-rank. It was not unknown in this war. Harwood, who had commanded the little squadron which had run the raider *Graf Spee* to earth, had made flag-rank immediately afterwards. It was something to think about.

One of his new squadron was already here in Simonstown. She was the small Leander class cruiser *Pallas* of the Royal New Zealand Navy. She looked like a destroyer compared with the *Wiltshire*, but her captain and her ship's company were well trained, and had been together since she had commissioned.

He heaved himself up and walked to one of the scuttles, one which faced away from the glare.

He thought vaguely of his home in Hampshire. His wife Beryl would be pleased when she heard. There were too many naval officers' wives who lived in the county whose husbands seemed to have been promoted ahead of him.

Acting commodore. He nodded. It sounded good. Old world; he liked that. He was distantly related to Captain James Cook and was proud of it, although it did not seem to have helped him over the years.

The commander asked carefully, 'I'd forgotten, sir. You crossed swords with *Prinz Luitpold* before. North Cape, wasn't it?'

'*I* don't forget.' He stared through the scuttle. Two sailors in a dinghy were calling up to some black girls on the jetty. A bit of black velvet, as his father would have said.

The commander ignored the warning signs. 'They say that Rear-Admiral Leitner's in command.'

Hemrose glowered. 'I don't give a bloody damn about *him*. Her captain's the man – Hechler. He was in command at North Cape, when – '

The commander said, 'She's a miniature battle-cruiser, sir. Makes our armour plate look like cardboard.'

Hemrose ignored him. 'Came out of the snow like a cliff. It was gun-for-gun.' He looked around the pleasant cabin, remembering it as it had been. 'This place was riddled, like a bloody pepper pot.'

The commander had lost his way. 'She made off anyway, sir.'

'Aye, she did that. Just as well. It was a right cock-up, I can tell you.' He saw the sailors paddling away. They had probably seen him looking at them. 'I hope it *is* Hechler in command. I'll get him this time.' He gave a rueful grin. 'Now he's like I was at North Cape.'

'How so, sir?'

71

Hemrose laughed out loud. 'He's got his fucking admiral breathing down his neck, that's why!'

The commander downed his gin. He was used to the captain's coarse speech and blunt manner. Perhaps his temporary promotion would mellow him. But it could not last. The fleet would catch the German raider before they got a look-in.

Hemrose rubbed his hands. 'Recall all the senior officers. I want 'em aboard by the dog watches.' He eyed his golf clubs. 'See how *they* like it.'

The commander nodded. 'I see – '

'You don't, Toby.' He became grave. 'I meant what I said. For the first time in my life their bloody lordships have given me a free hand, and by God I intend to use it.' He clapped him on the shoulder. 'Make a signal to *Pallas*. Captain repair on board.'

Godson said unhappily, 'He's playing cricket with the South Africans, sir.'

Hemrose beamed. 'Good. I want us out of harbour by this time tomorrow and I'll need you to form your own team to monitor all despatches and signals. Every damn thing.' He slammed his fist into his palm. 'So get that Kiwi aboard, *chop, chop!*' He bustled to the sideboard and groped for some ice, but it had all melted. He slopped another large gin into his glass.

'*Lübeck*'s gone to the bottom anyway. That's one less. Scuttled herself when our lot were almost up to her.' He frowned. 'I wonder if Hechler knows?' He turned. 'Somehow I doubt it.'

But he was alone.

Kapitän zur See Dieter Hechler closed the conning-tower's steel door and pushed through the fireproof curtain.

Outside it was dusk, but in here it was like night, with only the chart-table lights and automatic pilot casting any glow on the thick armour plate.

Hechler could sense the tension as well as the controlled excitement. Gudegast was leaning on the vibrating table, his face in shadow, only his beard holding the light. His team stood around him, boys most of them, in various attitudes of attention as Hechler joined them.

Hechler looked at the chart, the neat calculations and pencilled fixes. Then at the plot-table which told him all the rest. Course, and speed, time and distance, variations, fed in by a dozen repeaters from radar, gyro and log.

'We're through.'

Gudegast nodded. Then he pointed his dividers to the chart where the course had crossed the Iceland-Faeroe Rise, where the seabed rose inexplicably like a hump. To U-boats, and blockade-runners alike it was known as the *meat grinder*. Not a good place for a submarine to run deep to avoid a depth-charge attack, and no scope for a surface vessel to manoeuvre.

And yet they had made it. This great ship had passed through the 300-mile gap without opposition. Not a ship, not even a distant aircraft had been sighted.

Luck, a miracle, or a direct result of von Hanke's decoy, it was impossible to tell.

The curtain swirled aside again and Leitner strode in with his aide behind him. He stared unwinking at the chart and said, 'We did it. As planned.'

He looked at the darkened figures around him. 'Two days since the convoy, and now we are here!' He slapped the chart with unusual fervour. 'The Atlantic, gentlemen! They said it could not be done!'

Some of the men were shaking hands and grinning at each other; only Gudegast remained unmoved and grim-faced.

He said, 'I should like to alter course in fifteen minutes, sir.'

Hechler nodded. 'I shall come up.'

A seaman called, 'From the bridge, sir.' He held out the telephone.

Hechler shook himself. Fatigue or anxiety, which was it? He had not heard it ring.

It was Froebe, who was in charge of the watch.

'Radar has reported a faint echo at Red one-oh, sir. About five miles.'

That was close. Too close. Hechler calmed himself. 'What is it, man?'

He could picture Froebe shrugging his gaunt shoulders. 'Very small, sir, barely registers.' Someone shouted in the background. 'It will be dark very soon.'

Hechler said, 'Alter course to intercept.' He felt Gudegast brush past him to adjust the chart.

Leitner muttered, 'Something small, eh? God damn them, it might have been a submarine's conning-tower. At five miles anything might happen!' Another flaw. The unseen observer.

Froebe spoke again, relieved. 'We've identified it, sir. It's a boat.'

Hechler hurried from the conning-tower, not caring if Leitner was in agreement or not.

On the main bridge it was quite cold, and the clouds had thickened considerably.

He raised his glasses and felt the deck tilt very slightly as the helm went over.

Then he saw it and felt his taut muscles relax. There would be no attack from this lonely boat. It was a common enough sight on the Atlantic, but new to most of his company, he thought.

Theil had arrived on the bridge, panting hard as he snatched some binoculars from a messenger.

He said, 'A boat full of corpses.' He sounded angry, as if the drifting boat had wronged him in some way.

Hechler watched the boat. Would their journey ever end, he wondered?

'Slow ahead, all engines.'

Theil was peering at him with disbelief. 'You're not going to stop?'

Hechler said, 'Boatswain's mate, call away the accident boat.'

The boat would automatically have an experienced petty officer in charge. He glanced at young Jaeger. 'You go. Keep your wits about you.'

Theil said between his teeth, 'In the name of God, sir, we're a sitting target.'

Hechler said quietly, 'Keep your voice down, Viktor.' He gripped his glasses more tightly. A trick of the fading light, or had he seen a movement amongst the silent, patient figures in the listing boat?

'Stop engines?' He hurried to the side as the motorboat hit the water and veered away on the dying bow-wave. Jaeger had only just clawed his way aboard in time.

He remarked, 'Someone's alive out there.' When Theil said nothing he added coldly, 'Would you have me fire on the boat?' He raised his glasses once more, sensing the rift between them. He saw the motorboat speeding across the swell,

Jaeger looking astern at the cruiser and probably wondering what would happen if there was an attack.

He knew Leitner was beside him, could smell his cologne. But he kept his eyes on the little drama as the motorboat hooked on and Jaeger with a petty officer scrambled over the gunwale. The petty officer was Tripz. He was used to this kind of work. He saw Jaeger lean on the gunwale with a handkerchief to his mouth. Jaeger was not.

A signalman lowered his glasses. 'Two alive, sir.'

'Call the sick-bay.'

More feet on the ladder and he heard her thank a seaman for helping her through the gate. She was wearing her black leather jacket again, her hair ruffling in the breeze.

Theil moved aside so that she could stand between Hechler and the admiral.

How huge the ship looked as the long forecastle lifted and then fell again very slowly, the motion increasing as the last of the way went off the hull.

She asked, 'Just two?'

Hechler nodded. She was probably thinking of its futility.

Ships sunk and men killed, two aircraft shot down, and we stop because of these living dead. The unwritten law of the sea perhaps? Or to make up for those they had already left to die.

He saw her right hand grip the rail beneath the screen so tightly that her knuckles were white through the tanned skin.

When he glanced at her he saw moisture in her eyes, or were they tears?

Leitner remarked, 'Flotsam of war, my dear.'

She said huskily, 'My – ' She tried again. 'I knew somebody who died at sea.'

Hechler glanced down at her. She looked sick. The motion was getting worse as the *Prinz* rose and dipped like a huge juggernaut.

'Sit in the chair.' He took her elbow. 'Take some deep breaths.' Then, so that the others should not hear he added quietly, 'Stay in the air, little bird. The ocean can be a dirty place.'

He glanced across her head. 'Take over. I'm going to the sick-bay.'

Someone yelled, 'Boat's hooked on, sir!'

The motorboat rose swiftly on its falls, and Froebe asked, 'The lifeboat, Captain? Shall I have a shot put into it?'

'No.' He raised his glasses once more and knew she had turned in the chair to watch him. 'They have found their harbour. Leave them alone.'

A great tremor ran through the deck and he felt the men sighing with relief as the great screws began to beat out their track of white froth again.

Leitner called sharply, 'Find out what you can, eh?'

Hechler ran down the first ladder and paused, gripping it with both fists.

What is the matter with me? Is it that important?

He found Jaeger and Petty Officer Tripz already outside the sick-bay.

'All right?'

Jaeger made an effort, but he looked ghastly.

'All the rest were dead, sir.' He was reliving it. 'Bobbing about together as if they were really alive. The gulls had got to some of them – ' he retched and old Tripz said, 'Easy, sir. You'll get used to it.'

Jaeger shook himself. 'We brought two of them aboard.' He stared at the deck for a long moment until he could continue. 'One of them is an officer. The other – ' he shook violently. 'He wouldn't leave without the cat.'

'Cat?'

Tripz said, 'The animal was dead, sir. We left it in the boat.' He looked despairingly at the young officer. 'Must have been adrift for weeks.'

Hechler said, 'You did well.' He gave Tripz a meaning glance. 'Both of you, go to my steward. He'll give you something to warm you up.'

Tripz gave a sad grin. 'It was worth it then, sir.'

The doctor was wiping his hands on a towel, and Hechler saw that both blanket-wrapped survivors were lying in bunks inside the office and away from the injured sailors.

An armed seaman stood outside but it seemed unlikely their passengers would create any problems.

One, the young officer with two tarnished stripes on his sleeve, was conscious, but only just. Hollow-eyed and filthy, he was staring at the white deckhead with shock and disbelief.

The other man was much older with a white beard. Perhaps he had already seen and done too much when his ship had been blasted from under him. He had his arms wrapped into a cradle, as he had been when Jaeger had found him, clutching the ship's cat to his body to protect it.

The doctor said, 'I've given them something, Captain. They'll sleep. I shall get them some hot soup later on.' He nodded to the pathetic belongings on the glass table. 'They were aboard the *Radnor Star*, a freighter.'

The officer was probably the second mate. He was too young for much else, Hechler thought. In charge of a lifeboat, perhaps the only officer to get away when the torpedo struck. Watching them die, one by one, until he was alone but for the old man with his dead cat. Some last thread of discipline had made him hold on. He had been in charge. What else could he have done?

The doctor took off his glasses and polished them as he had done at their first meeting.

He said, 'So this is the Atlantic, the *killing ground* they warned me about?'

Hechler looked at him. 'Don't be clever with me, Doctor!' He jerked open the door as the sentry snapped to attention. 'Report when they recover enough to speak.'

He waited outside, breathing hard, angry with the doctor, more so with himself for dropping the guard he had built up so carefully. When he reached the bridge he was greeted in silence. He looked for the drifting lifeboat but it had already disappeared into the darkness astern.

He walked to the gratings, and with a start realised she was still sitting in the tall chair, wrapped about with somebody's heavy watchcoat.

She did not say anything and he was grateful. He saw Jaeger return to his place on the bridge, the way Gudegast moved across to pat his arm. That would mean more than anything to Jaeger just now. He was accepted. One of them.

And what of me? The captain without a heart? Do they imagine I have no feelings?

He stared down with surprise as she placed her hand on his wrist. She did not move it or grip with it. It lay there, separate, as if to listen.

She said quietly, 'I am here, Captain. I shared it with you. I saw it through your eyes.'

Hechler looked at her neat hand and wanted to seize it, press it against himself. She had understood, as if he had shouted aloud.

He said, 'I would like to talk –' He felt her hand move away very slightly. 'Later, afterwards –' He was lost for the right words.

She said, 'Afterwards may not be ours, Captain.' She slid from the chair and handed the coat to a seaman with a quick smile. Then she melted into the shadows and he heard one of his men assisting her on the ladder.

He touched the chair; it was still warm from her body. He climbed into it and wedged his feet against the voice-pipes.

She would probably laugh in his face if he even laid a hand on her. What about the man who had been lost at sea? She had nearly said something else. 'My lover' perhaps?

Afterwards may not be ours. Her words seemed to linger in his mind. His head lolled and he was instantly asleep.

The *Prinz Luitpold*'s petty officers' mess was in complete darkness apart from shaded blue lamps and one light above one of the tables. A different story from an hour before when the men off watch had been watching a film in the other part of the mess, one of the luxuries which went with their status. The film had been a noisy display of German armed strength, backed up between the excited commentary by rousing music from *Tannhäuser*.

The air had been electric, and had remained so since the intercom announcement from the bridge that they were forging deeper and deeper into the Atlantic, unchallenged as they were unbeaten.

Hans Stoecker sat in the pool of light, sipping a mug of bitter coffee, restless, unwilling to sleep although he had only just come off watch.

Opposite him, his grey head nodding in a doze, was old Oskar Tripz. His chin was covered in grey stubble so that he looked almost ancient.

His eyes opened and he stared at Stoecker, his gaze searching. Trying to discover something, to make up his mind.

'Why don't you turn in?' Tripz sniffed at the coffee and shuddered. 'What do they make this muck from – acorns?'

A dark shape shrouded in blankets called irritably, 'Hold your noise! Think of the watchkeepers!'

Tripz grinned. In harbour the mess housed a hundred petty officers, the backbone of the ship, as of any other. Now, with many of them on watch it seemed quiet, deserted by comparison.

Stoecker lowered his voice. 'I keep thinking about *Lübeck*.'

'You're always thinking about something. You should keep your mind on your exams. Do you more good. Let the bloody officers think. It's what they're paid for.'

Stoecker persisted, 'I mean, *Lübeck* should have been with us surely? Together we'd have made a stronger force.'

'Easier to find too.' Tripz rubbed his chin with a rasping motion. 'I reckon she was meant to return to base.'

Stoecker stared at him. 'We wouldn't just leave her!'

Tripz shrugged. 'Who knows anything any more? They'd sell their mothers for a bit of glory.'

'You don't mean that.'

Tripz became impatient. 'I've got more important things on my mind at present.' He leaned across the table until their faces were only a foot apart. 'Those boxes, for instance.'

They both glanced along the silent bunks like conspirators, then Stoecker asked, 'Do you know what's in them?'

'It's all in that letter. If half of it's true, and I see no reason why that prisoner should lie about it, our gallant admiral is carrying a bloody fortune with him, though I can't imagine why.'

Stoecker blinked. 'What kind of fortune, I – I mean, how much?'

The man watched him grimly. 'Do you know how much the *Prinz* cost to build?'

Stoecker smiled. 'You're joking – '

Tripz tapped his arm with a thick finger. 'You could build three ships like this one with what he's got tucked away.' He dropped his voice again to a hoarse whisper. '*If* that letter tells the truth.'

Stoecker thought of the man's face in the air vent, his despair. He often thought about it, also the man's quiet courage in the shadow of death. *Murder.* The word was fixed in his mind.

Tripz seemed satisfied with the young man's acceptance; he had never doubted his sincerity.

He said, 'It seems that the prisoner was writing to some friends. To warn them that the boxes were being moved.'

Stoecker recalled the burnt-out shop, the crude insults.

Tripz continued, 'His friends were Jewish, right enough. One of them was a jeweller. Probably why he was still at large.' He dropped his eyes. 'Or was.'

'I still don't understand.'

Tripz's gaze softened. 'You wouldn't, Hans.' He hurried on. 'All I do know is that we're probably carrying a bloody great fortune. If so, my guess is that Rear-Admiral Leitner's no more entitled to it than we are.' He changed tack before Stoecker could speak. 'What will you do when this lot's over, Hans? Always assuming you're still in one lump, of course?'

Stoecker hesitated. 'The navy. A career, I thought – '

The finger jabbed his arm again. 'Suppose we lose? D'you ever think about that?' He did not wait for an answer. 'Me? I'll be good for nothing, no matter who wins. I saw it after the last war. You couldn't even sell your bloody medals for a crust of bread. No, peace will be hard, even for the kids.' He shook his head. 'They'll toss me out like so much waste.'

Stoecker felt vaguely uneasy. 'Anyway, we'll probably never know. The boxes are locked away, under guard.'

'I know. The admiral's got one key, the captain's got the other.' He tapped the side of his nose. 'But there's a duplicate, my young friend.' He saw his astonishment and grinned, showing his uneven teeth. 'You've caught on. It's mine.'

A figure, naked but for a lifejacket, lurched past on the way to the heads.

Tripz stood up. 'Say nothing, or we'll both end up on the wrong side of a firing-squad. And that would be a pity, eh?' He leaned over and patted his shoulder. 'Thought you should know. In case I stop a bit of the Tommies' steel. After all, we're partners, right?'

He walked away, leaving Stoecker alone beneath the solitary light.

The *Prinz Luitpold*'s senior medical officer looked up from his book and saw the girl standing in the open door.

'Can't you sleep either?'

She walked to a chair and glanced at the two motionless survivors, swaying gently in their white cots.

'My wrist. It's bothering me. If I lie on it – '

He took her hand and reached out for some scissors. The girl was very attractive. It was hard to think of her as the professional flier, as good as any Luftwaffe ace, they said. It seemed wrong that she should be here, in this iron machine.

'You're new aboard the ship?' She had a direct way of asking. As if she was telling him.

He looked at her. She seemed strained, and there were shadows under her tawny eyes.

'I am. Lost amongst strangers.' It seemed to amuse him.

She said, 'Call me Erika. If you like.'

He cut the last of the bandage. 'I do like.'

Her skin felt hot, feverish. He remembered all those other women. The scandal which had almost got him into prison, a ruined man. But the women who came to him 'in trouble' were people of influence, or those who had powerful friends. Curious that such power could be smashed because of an unwanted baby, he thought.

Like the captain's wife, for instance. Well-bred from an old family, she was always in the centre of society, that jungle which was safe only for the privileged few. It was strange how the high party members, *men of the people* as they liked to be known, were so in awe of women like her.

He wondered if the captain really knew what she was like. One of his colleagues had once described her as a thoroughly delectable whore. That doctor had been indiscreet in other ways too. Then one day he had simply disappeared.

He said, 'It is a bit stiff, er, Erika.'

She watched him, unsmiling. 'I have to fly in a day or so.'

'It will be all right by then.' What were they thinking of? Flying? They would meet up with the enemy at any time now. The British would not give up until they had brought them to action.

She glanced at the gramophone and the pile of well-used records. She raised her eyebrows. 'Handel? You surprise me. Is it patriotic?'

She smiled then, at some private joke perhaps.

'I like it.'

'You always do what you like?'

'I try to.' He looked at her, and tried not to think of her on his examination couch, naked.

She said, 'I wanted to talk. I knew you would still be awake. It's not like a ship down here.'

He chuckled. 'I suppose not. I shall attempt to keep it that way.'

'I was with the Captain when these survivors were brought aboard.'

He said nothing and waited. So that was it. There was certainly nothing wrong with her wrist which could not wait until daylight.

She said, 'He is different from what I expected.'

'An enigma perhaps?'

She smiled at him. 'You are leading me.' She added, 'He seems to care so much about people. How can he do his work?'

Stroheim spread his hands. 'Perhaps it is tearing him apart. I do not know him that well. Yet.'

'But you know his wife, don't you?'

He started. 'How do you hear these things?'

'A friend told me.' She had been going to say *a little bird told me.* But at that instant she remembered his face, the concern in his voice as he had said so quietly to her, 'Stay in the air, little bird.' To use the expression loosely would seem like a betrayal, like sharing a secret.

Stroheim said vaguely, 'She is very beautiful.'

'I met her.' She thought of the other woman's searching stare, her arrogance giving way to caution when she realised who Erika was. Because she was a flier and had carried out a mission for the Führer, people often thought she too had influence. Yes, she recalled that stare, her perfect body, so carelessly displayed in the cutaway gown. Try as she might, she could not see her and the Captain together. Maybe they had both changed.

'Well, you know what she's like.'

'Are they still married, or anything?'

He warmed to her. '*Anything* would be closer, I believe.'

She opened and closed her left hand, her face expressionless as she tested the pain, the discomfort.

Stay in the air, little bird.

'I'll say goodnight then.' She looked at the two sleeping figures. Flotsam, Leitner had called them. 'Or, good morning now, I believe?'

He watched her leave and then reopened his book.

Every so often, even in the midst of danger and death there was one small light. Like a flower in a forest, a lone star.

He sighed and crossed his legs. She had made him feel human again.

9

Viewpoint

Apart from the regular swell the sea's face was like glass, blinding bright in the sunshine. There was a fine haze which never seemed to get any closer, so that there was no break between sea and sky. For the Atlantic it was unusual, even this far south.

The two ships stood close together as if for support, which was true, and at a greatly reduced speed appeared to be almost motionless above their quivering reflections.

The SS *Port St Clair*, a freighter of some 8,000 tons outward bound from Sierra Leone, had the second vessel in tow. It was a slow, painful passage, with the other ship yawing out clumsily until she seemed to be overtaking, before veering back again with all the maddening alterations of course and speed until they were under command once more.

The first mate of the leading ship watched his captain, who was standing out on the bridge wing, staring astern at their companion. It was almost funny, when you thought about it. Both the captains were rivals of many years, and yet that same rivalry seemed to join them more persistently than any tow-line.

The other ship, the SS *Dunedin Pioneer*, had joined the convoy with them at Freetown, but after a few days had broken down with engine trouble. It was hardly surprising, the mate thought, she was probably older than he was.

The convoy escorts had been unwilling to leave them astern of the main body of twelve ships on passage for Liverpool. At any other time the senior naval officer would have ordered the *Port St Clair*, with her precious cargo of rice, New Zealand butter and meat, to keep station and leave the other ship to fend for herself until a tug could be sent from somewhere, or a hungry U-boat had found her.

But the rivalry, which over the years had often been akin to hatred, had carried the day.

The mate considered the news. A German raider at large in the Atlantic again. The navy had probably got it all wrong. The enemy warship had either returned to base, or had already clashed with Allied patrols.

It was a strange feeling to be out here, alone, on such a fine day. Soon the Atlantic would show its other face, but by then they would have turned round, and be on their way back to the sunshine and New Zealand.

He walked out on to the bridge wing and waited for the master to notice him. The latter had his stained cap tilted over his eyes as he watched the tow lift from the water, hesitate and then dip into it again.

He remarked, 'Bloody old cow.'

The mate replied, 'What about the raider?'

The master rubbed his bristled chin. He would not shave until they crossed the Liverpool Bar. There was no point in shaving while there was a chance of being blown up.

They had passed the Cape Verde Islands to starboard in the night, and tomorrow, or maybe the next day, would meet with ships of the screening squadron. Cruisers from Simonstown, it was said.

Half to himself he said, 'Should have left the old bugger.' He turned and eyed the mate cheerfully. 'If there *is* a raider, and that I doubt, it's a comfort to know that the convoy will run smack into it before we do! Justice for leaving us behind!' He chuckled.

The mate agreed and rested his hands on the rail, but withdrew them instantly with a curse. The bridge was like an oven. But you could keep Liverpool. A sailor's town, they said. Blackouts, air raids, and tarts outside the clubs who looked as if every one of those sailors had had a go at them. You could keep it.

Steam spurted from the ship astern, wavered around her poop and then faded away.

The master said unfeelingly, 'If his Chief can't get her going, I'll tow the sod all the way. That'll give him something to bite on!'

A whistle shrilled and the mate walked into the wheelhouse and hauled a little brass cylinder up the tube from the radio-room.

He returned to the glare and said sharply, 'Intercepted a signal. Convoy's under attack. German raider.' They stared at each other and the master hurried to the chart-room abaft the wheel-house and snapped, 'Give it here. Where the bloody hell are they?'

He did not speak again until he had plotted the convoy's approximate course and bearing on the chart. 'Call up *Dunedin Pioneer*.' He held him with a grim stare. 'On the lamp. Tell him. He may not have picked it up on that relic he calls a receiver.'

Alone in the chart-room he stared at the chart. It was worn and stained. So many convoys, too many risks, and always a target for torpedoes and bombs.

It must be serious, he thought. He pictured the other ships as they had weighed anchor and had formed into two lines with the destroyer escorts bustling around them like sheep dogs.

The mate came back, breathing hard. They were all used to danger, and both the master and mate had already been torpedoed in other ships and knew the margin of survival. The U-boat, the most hated and most feared of any war machine. The unseen killer.

The master looked at his second-in-command. 'Rouse the lads, Bob. Have the gun manned, and set two more lookouts.'

The gun was mounted aft on the poop, an elderly four-inch weapon from another war.

This was something else, he thought. A raider, one of their bloody cruisers. How could she get through the patrols at this stage of the game, he wondered? The invasion was said to be going better than anyone had dared to hope – a newspaper in Freetown had proclaimed big advances all along the front. No longer beachheads, not just another wild hope; they were going all out for a grand slam.

He heard some of his men clambering up ladders and protesting at the call to arms. He gave a tight smile. They might soon have something to moan about.

He looked at the sky. A few clouds, but it was clear, washed-out blue. And it was another eight hours to dusk. He glared at the ship astern through the chart-room scuttle. Six knots. Without her dragging along like a sick elephant, they could increase speed, go it alone if need be. They would stand a better chance.

The mate and the second mate entered the chart-room and watched him without speaking. The second mate was just a kid, wet behind the ears, but he was learning.

'Look.' The master eyed them gravely. 'This bugger might come our way. But she's more likely to stand off before the screening squadron comes down on 'em like a ton of bricks. He stared hard at the chart. 'It's like being blind and deaf.'

The mate asked, 'Can't we make a run for it?'

'Is that what you'd do?'

The second mate said, 'We could turn back, sir.'

The master smiled. *Sir.* That showed how green he was.

He said, 'Can't leave the *Dunedin Pioneer.* He wouldn't cut and run if it was us.'

They looked at each other for support while the ship noises intruded. Usually they gave confidence. Now they seemed to represent their sudden vulnerability.

The master exclaimed angrily, 'No, sod 'em, we'll keep going as we are.'

There was a clang from aft and he strode out to the sunlight again to watch as the four-inch gun trained round on its mounting. Fat lot of use that would be against a bloody cruiser, he thought. But some of the seamen saw him and grinned up at the bridge. For some peculiar reason the old captain wished he had shaved, that his cap cover was crisp and white like those bloody RN characters.

The second mate clambered on to the bridge and said, 'Call from the tow, sir. Will be getting up steam in fifteen minutes.'

They all breathed out and the master said, 'Tell the silly bugger to get a move on.' He hid his relief from the others. 'And about bloody time!'

It was just minutes later that a seaman called, 'There's a plane, sir!'

'What? Where away?' The master strode through the wheel-house and out on to the other wing. 'Why can't you learn to report the thing properly?' He ignored the lookout's resentment and raised his massive binoculars.

An aircraft. Out here. Hundreds of miles from anywhere. It could not be hostile. Maybe they were looking for them? To tell them to alter course, or to rendezvous with a tug. They'd get a surprise when the other ship cast off the tow and began pouring out her usual foul smoke, the bane of every escort commander.

He saw the sunlight glint on the little aircraft and stared at it until it misted over.

He said flatly, 'It's a Jerry.'

The second mate said, 'But it's too far – '

The master turned away. 'From the raider. Call up *Dunedin Pioneer* right now. Then tell Sparks to prepare the emergency signal – '

But it was already too late even for that. As the little toylike aircraft cruised back and forth against the pale sky, the horizon's mist seemed to raise itself like a frail curtain.

They saw the blurred flashes, almost lost in the fierce sunlight. The master waited, counting the seconds, until with a terrifying screech the salvo fell close astern, the white columns bursting high above the ships before cascading down in a torrent of spray and smoke.

The old captain shouted, 'Send that signal! Plain language, tell the bloody world! *Am under attack by German raider!*'

The next salvo shrieked down from the sky and he felt the hull shake as if it had run aground. He staggered to the rail and peered aft. It was almost impossible to see anything through the smoke, but the other vessel was still there, standing away at right-angles. The tow must have been slipped, or had parted in the explosions.

Then he stared incredulously at a solid, black shape as it rolled over and began to sink. It was their own stern, the useless four-pounder pointing at the sky, its crew nowhere to be seen.

He seized the rail and yelled, 'Sway out the boats! Abandon ship! What the hell is Sparks doing?'

Glass shivered from the wheelhouse windows and men fell kicking and screaming under a fusillade of glass and wood splinters. The ship had stopped, her holds already flooding as bulkheads burst open and turned the engine-room into an inferno of scalding steam.

Another earsplitting screech, and the shells burst alongside and on the foredeck.

The master slid down the bridge wing, his eyes glazed with agony while he tried to call out. His mind recorded the crash of falling derricks, the savage roar of water through the hull below, and the fact he could not move for the pain. He was still staring at the top of the bridge canvas-dodgers when the sea boiled over the edge and swamped the wheelhouse as the ship plunged to the bottom.

Then there was silence, as if the whole world had been rendered speechless.

Aboard the other ship, the men on the bridge and along her rust-streaked decks, stared dumbly across the empty sea towards the horizon. Like beasts waiting for the inevitable slaughter, for their own execution.

But nothing happened. Even the tiny aircraft had disappeared.

The master crossed the bridge and peered at the carpet of oil, the rising litter of fragments which spread across the swell in a great obscene stain.

Around him his men stood like statues, shocked beyond words or movement.

Then the master said, 'Lower a boat, Mister. Fast as you can.' He made himself stare at the floating pieces, all that was left of his old enemy. His best friend. He added brokenly, 'Seems they've no time for us, the bastards!'

As if to mock him the engine began to pound again.

'Stop engines!' Acting-Commodore James Cook Hemrose sat stiff-backed in his bridge chair and surveyed what was left of the convoy. A battlefield. A junk yard.

The commander stood beside him as the way went off the ship, and the endless litter of wreckage, bodies and pieces of men parted across the *Wiltshire*'s high stem.

Half a mile astern, her signal lamp flashing like a diamond eye, the New Zealand light cruiser *Pallas* followed reluctantly amongst the remains.

The convoy had scattered at the last moment when the first salvoes must have come crashing down. Hammers of hell, Hemrose thought bitterly.

'Stand by to lower boats!'

Hemrose trained his binoculars across the sea, hating the stench of escaping fuel oil and burned paintwork. A few figures floated or splashed amongst the filth, their bodies shining and pitiful in the oil. There were more corpses than living, but it was worth a try.

'Signal *Pallas* to cover us, Toby.'

The lamp clattered again. Even it sounded subdued.

A distant voice called, 'Lower away!' That was one of the whalers. The motor-boat was all ready to slip from her falls, the surgeon in the cockpit with one of his SBA's.

He looked long and hard at a black line which lifted and dipped above the water like a crippled submarine. It was the keel of one of the escorting destroyers. Of a corvette there was no trace at all.

Another destroyer had escaped without a scratch and was now lashed alongside a listing tramp-steamer, hoses dousing some fires while men passed back and forth with stretchers and inert bundles. An oil tanker was awash, but still afloat, her engines and pumps working manfully to keep her going. Some wag had hoisted a Union Flag on the stump of her remaining mast.

The commander returned and watched the light cruiser increasing speed to circle around the scene of pain and death, her pale hull streaked with oil like an additional waterline.

Hemrose said savagely, 'Whole convoy wiped out except for these pathetic remnants!' He pounded the arm of his chair with his fist. 'All they needed was another day. The escort group was on the way from Gib, and three destroyers from Bermuda. And us.'

The commander stared at the drifting filth and spreadeagled corpses. Some of them wore naval uniforms, or bits of them. It was like being with them, part of them. He resisted the urge to shiver. Even Hemrose must know that they would have stood no chance either.

The Admiralty had confirmed that the raider was *Prinz Luitpold*, and fresh details came in every hour. He watched his superior, suddenly glad that he did not share his responsibility.

Hemrose watched the boat coxswains signalling to one another with their shortened, personal semaphore. He knew what the commander was thinking. It made it worse. If *Wiltshire* had been on the spot, she might have scored a lucky hit, enough to cripple the bastard, or at least slow him down.

Now the German could be anywhere. He thought of the signals, and the information from the lone freighter *Dunedin Pioneer* which had been left untouched. Somebody aboard that poor ship, a spectator to the total destruction of the one which had been towing her, had kept his head. Had reported seeing the enemy's faint silhouette as she headed away at full speed to the south-west.

The commander had asked, 'Give chase, sir?'

Hemrose had studied his charts with the navigating and cypher officers for an hour while they had steamed at full speed towards the convoy's last position.

The raider had steamed away without sinking the *Dunedin Pioneer*. There had to be a reason. Now as he watched the oil-streaked boats picking their way amongst the human remains, he went over it again for the hundredth time.

Give chase. To where? To the coastline of Brazil, or back along the same course?

It had certainly put the cat amongst the pigeons, he thought. Every available ship was under orders. A nightmare for the Admiralty and the Allied Command. There must be no let-up in the lines of supply to the armies in France. The Channel was filled with vessels of every kind, carrying fuel and ammunition, transport and the precious cargo of men to replace the convoys which passed them on the way back. The wounded and the dying.

According to the latest intelligence there were seventeen major convoys at sea. Well escorted for the most part, but to resist U-boat and bombing attacks, not a bloody great cruiser like *Prinz Luitpold*.

Hemrose still could not fathom how it had happened. The RAF recce boys had reported that after the battle near Bear Island, *Prinz Luitpold* had been seen and photographed back at her lair in Bodø. It did not make any sense. Somebody's head would be on the block over it, but it offered no satisfaction for all this horror. He pictured the pandemonium in Whitehall. It made a change for them to be under siege. First the flying-bombs, then the massive V–2 rockets. The Allied HQ which controlled the Normandy invasion would be worried too. You could not ignore a raider, any raider. Convoys had to be diverted, held up, cancelled altogether.

Hemrose glanced around the open bridge, the intent figures and anxious faces. A midshipman was retching into his handkerchief as he stared at the bobbing remains which surrounded the tall hull.

Hemrose rasped, 'Get off my bridge, damn you, until you can act like a man!'

It was cruel and unfair. Hemrose knew it but did not care.

There was a third cruiser coming at full speed to join his little group. They should meet up with her in two days, unless . . . He said to the commander, 'I want a full team on this, Toby. The paymaster-commander, even the bloody chaplain. See to it.'

The man's words came back to him and he heard himself say, 'Give chase – I don't think so, Toby. He had a reason for letting the *Dunedin Pioneer* stay afloat. He wanted her to see him steam away, to report his course.' It felt easier now that he had decided. 'No, I reckon he changed direction as soon as he was clear of all this. Get the convoy lists, and we'll study the chart. Outguess the bastard.' He eyed him grimly. 'It's up to us. As I see it, Toby, we'll get precious little advice from their lordships just now.' He wrinkled his nose. 'Signal a recall to the boats and we'll get under way. That destroyer can stand by the survivors until the escort group turns up.'

He heard one of the boats creaking up to the davits and felt the commander let out a sigh. No U-boats were reported in their vicinity. But if they could miss a big cruiser there was no point in adding to the risks.

The deck began to tremble and the *Pallas* headed round to take station astern again.

When the third cruiser joined them it would make all the difference. He looked down from the bridge and saw the first survivors being led away, wrapped in oil-sodden blankets. There did not seem to be many of them, he thought.

'Resume course, cruising speed, Toby.' He settled back in the chair. 'Send for a brandy. I need to *think* about this one.'

Astern, the listless ships, and the great span of oil and fragments seemed to fill the horizon.

For Hemrose the war had suddenly become a personal one.

It was like fighting free from a nightmare, only to discover that it was real. Even the overhead light, although it was partly screened by some kind of curtain, had a hard, unreal shape. Cold and still. Like death.

The man lay motionless, his hands balled into fists at his sides while he waited for his senses to return, or to fade again and leave him in peace.

In tiny fragments his mind recorded that he was suspended in some kind of cot, high-sided and white. He felt the surge of panic. A coffin.

He tried again and groped for clues, explanations, like piecing together parts of a puzzle.

He made his taut limbs relax but kept his hands pressed against his sides. His body was naked, but warm beneath a sheet and a soft blanket. Again, he felt the surge of hope. A nightmare after all. He could feel the pulsating tremor of engines through his spine, the gentle clatter of unseen objects. But he felt despair close over him once more. It was not his ship. He closed his eyes tightly as if to shut out the stark, leaping pictures, the great fountain of searing flames, exploding metal as the torpedo, maybe two, had exploded into them. He tried again, and in his reeling thoughts seemed to read the vessel's name, as he had once seen it at the dockside. The *Radnor Star*. An old ship, then part of an eastbound convoy from St John's to Liverpool, packed to the gills with engine spares, bridge-building equipment, armoured vehicles, all heavy stuff. The poor old girl must have gone down like a stone afterwards.

He opened his eyes wide and stared at the solitary light. *Afterwards*. What then?

It was almost painful to work it out. He had been in the open, something in his hand. Had to see the captain. Then the explosion, wild faces, mouths open in silent cries, smoke, dense choking smoke which he imagined he could still taste.

Then the boat, water swilling over his feet and thighs as someone had fought it away from the ship, the terrible suction as she had dived for the last time. Why had nobody seen them? It was coming back, sharp and hard, like heart-beats, the panic of a child who wants to hide under the blankets.

It had been at night. That was it.

He felt the sweat break over his chest and stomach. The lifeboat then. Why did his mind refuse to examine it?

He heard a distant bell, the clatter of feet somewhere. *Where the hell am I?*

He tried again. *My name is Peter Younger*. He wanted to laugh, but was closer to weeping. He had a name after all. He could not be dead.

It was difficult not to cry out as another picture loomed through the mist.

Men bailing and working at a handful of oars, a great sea which lifted and flung the boat about like a sodden log. Later still, the deathly quiet, the silent figures, some seared by fire, others who had died of exposure, a few eyeless, victims of seabirds. *They were all dying*. He vaguely recalled the hoarse voice of Colin Ames, *Radnor Star*'s second mate, close against his ear. He must have been dying too. The whole bridge had collapsed, and it was a miracle he had made it into a boat.

'Take the tiller, Sparks.' That was all he had said. Sparks? It was coming back. He had been the radio officer. Had been on his way to the bridge with a signal when the world had exploded. He recalled the other man wrapping his jacket around him. He must have lost his own. Younger examined his body limb by limb without moving a muscle. He ached all over, but he was whole. Then more distorted faces, alien voices, hands hauling him into another boat, a huge ship away in the distance. He tensed. This must be the one.

He remembered that he had been too weak to protest or struggle, but knew that in some strange way he had not wanted to leave his dead companions, and the boat he had steered until the last oar had drifted away.

All dead. Like the old ship, nothing left.

Another twist of terror as he pictured his mother reading the telegram. God, there had been plenty of those in their street. He could not remember its name, or that of the town. A seaport. Pictures of his father and uncles, all in uniform. Sailors.

Feet scraped on metal and he tested his strength, tried to raise his head above the side of the cot.

His eyes would not focus at first. All glaring white, bottles and jars on neat shelves, like a hospital, while nearby lay a pile of gramophone records.

Perhaps he had gone mad?

Bit by bit, section by section, like a complicated, coded message over the receiver.

He stared uncomprehending at two uniform jackets which hung from a brass rail. One with three stripes, the other with two, with some odd insignia above them, and – he caught his breath – the Nazi eagle on the right breast. He had seen enough of those. Again the urge to laugh. But only in films.

Then he saw the other cot, the untidy white beard, the ancient face creased with pain or some terrible memory.

He held on to what he saw. Like a life-raft. It was Old Shiner. A bit of a character in the *Radnor Star*, listed as boatswain but one who could do almost anything. He had been at sea since he was twelve. *A bit of a character*.

He caught a brief picture of him in the boat, his pale eyes wild while he had clutched the cat against his scrawny body.

Younger attempted to bridge the gap between the boat and here. All he could remember was warmth, the fact that he felt no urge to hold on, even to live.

He imagined he had heard a woman's voice too, but that was impossible. A part of something else maybe.

So he and Old Shiner were in a German ship. Prisoners. Survivors. But not a U-boat. He recalled the misty silhouette of the ship. He also remembered a needle going into his arm, oblivion, but not before the world had begun to shake and thunder to gunfire. He had wanted to scream, to escape; instead there had been nothing.

He winced as a shadow fell across the cot and he saw a man in gold-rimmed glasses looking down at him.

'Well, now, Herr Ames, are you feeling better?'

Even his voice made him shake with silent laughter. Shock.

The man must be a doctor, and he spoke like one of those Germans in the movies.

He prised his lips apart, or so it felt, and tried to explain that his name was Younger. Then he saw the crumpled, oilstained coat with the two tarnished stripes lying on a table. Ames's jacket, the one he had used to shield him from the wind and drenching spray. It flooded through him like fire. Anger, hatred, and an overwhelming sense of loss.

The doctor leaned closer and took his wrist. 'You had a narrow escape, young man.'

Younger moved his dry lips again. 'What ship?'

'*Prinz Luitpold.*' He lowered the wrist. '*Kriegsmarine.*'

Younger was not sure if the name meant anything or not.

'How is Old Shiner?'

'Is that his name?' The doctor gave a sad smile. 'He will live, but I fear his mind may be scarred.'

Younger heard himself shouting, but the words sounded wild, meaningless.

A door opened and he saw an armed sailor peer in at them, his eyes questioning. *Just like the movies*, a voice seemed to murmur. It must be his own, he thought despairingly.

The doctor waved the sailor away and said, 'You must try to eat something soon. You are young, it will pass.'

Younger could feel his strength draining away, and twisted his face to the pillow to hide the tears which spilled down his cheeks. They were all dead. He saw the needle glinting in the overhead light and tried to struggle, but the doctor's grip was like steel. 'You killed them!' He saw the needle hesitate. '*Bloody murderers!*'

Stroheim felt the fight go out of the young officer and stood back to watch his face lose its anguish, its hate.

He moved to the other cot where the old man still cradled his lost cat in his arms.

They had no part in their ship's destruction, but the fact gave no comfort.

He thought of the guns thundering and shaking the ship from deck to keel, the muffled shouts of the intercom as one by one the convoy had been decimated.

Karl-Heinz Stroheim examined his hands. They were surprisingly steady.

He had been sent to the *Prinz Luitpold* as a punishment or a reprieve. All things considered it seemed likely they would come to rely on his skill.

The twist of fate which had brought these two strangers to his care was like an additional challenge. The oldest and the youngest in the lifeboat had survived.

He put on his jacket and gestured to the sentry. If hate was a reason for survival, the young officer named Ames would outlive them all.

10

Beyond Duty

Hechler wriggled his shoulders deeper into his watchcoat and felt the damp air exploring his bones. By leaning forward in his tall chair he could see much of the *Prinz Luitpold*'s long forecastle, which glistened now as if from a rain squall. But there was no rain, and as the high bows sliced through the Atlantic swell he saw the spray drift over the anchor-cables and breakwater to make the angled gun turrets shine like glass.

It was afternoon, and the sky was almost hidden by dark-bellied clouds. He heard Gudegast's rumbling tones as he passed another helm order before checking his ready-use chart again. How many times had he done that, Hechler wondered?

He saw the rear-admiral appear around Turret Anton, head high despite the misty spray, his face flushed and youthful in the distance. He was walking in step with Oberleutnant Bauer, the signals and communications officer. They could be brothers, he thought. Bauer was also the political officer and had been having a lot of private conversations with Leitner. What did they discuss? The *Prinz*'s captain probably.

Gudegast called, 'New course, sir. Two-one-five.'

It was a strange relationship, Hechler thought. Leitner had been as good as his word for the most part, and had let him handle the ship in his own way.

As they had steered south-west away from the broken convoy and the additional freighter which the radar had plotted with unnerving accuracy, Leitner had only once questioned his judgement.

Hechler had answered, 'The British will look for clues. By heading south-west in view of that ship which was under tow, they will assume it was a ruse, and expect us to alter course immediately to throw them off the scent. I think I would.'

Leitner had considered it, his eyes opaque, giving nothing away.

'But if *not*, Dieter? Suppose the British admiral thinks as you do?' Then he had nodded and had given his broad grin. 'Of course, that other convoy – they will think we are after it.'

OKM Operations Division had signalled more information about a vast troop convoy which was scheduled to head around the Cape of Good Hope en route for England. Commonwealth soldiers with all their equipment and vehicles, life-blood for the armies in France. A prize which would draw every U-boat pack in the Atlantic, and which would have a massive escort to match it.

Heavy units of the Home Fleet would be hurrying at full speed to meet it and swell the defences. Suicide for any attacking surface raider, but with such high stakes, the end might justify the means. Because of that risk no admiral would dare leave the convoy underguarded.

It was one of the biggest of its kind, too large to turn back, too vital to stop.

So the *Prinz Luitpold* had carried on as before. Nothing further had been sighted. If anything showed itself now they would have to forego their first rendezvous with a milch-cow. They had plenty of fuel, and Leitner intended it would remain like that. A little and often, as he had termed it.

It was too early to expect enemy submarines in their path. The simplicity of von Hanke's strategy had worked perfectly, and there had been no time to deploy submarines from their normal inshore patrols in the Baltic and the North Sea.

Hechler watched the two windswept figures until they vanished beneath the bridge. He thought of Leitner's broadcast that morning to the ship's company. Rousing, passionate, compelling. It was all those things, if you did not know the man.

Hechler had watched him as he had stood with the handset close to his lips in the armoured admiral's bridge. The flag-lieutenant and Bauer had also been present while Leitner's clipped tones had penetrated the ship above and below decks.

He had spoken of *Lübeck*'s loss at some length. Her sacrifice. 'We must not fail her, can never forget they fought for us, to give us the freedom to break out into the Atlantic! For *us* and our beloved Fatherland!'

Hechler had watched as one hand had darted to his cheek as if to brush away a tear. An act? He was still not sure.

Of one thing he was certain, however. There were two faces to the youthful admiral. After the attack on the convoy Leitner had walked around the upper deck, chatting to the jubilant gun crews, lounging against the mountings or slapping a seaman on the shoulder to emphasise his satisfaction.

Then, on the bridge, almost in the next breath, he had snapped complaints about this man or that, and had ordered Theil to deal with their slackness. So the reprimands would come from the bridge, not from their popular and untiring rear-admiral.

Then there had been the flash of anger over Leitner's mysterious boxes.

Hechler had requested permission to move them deeper in the hull, so that their space could be used to store additional short-range ammunition.

Leitner had snapped, 'They belong to me! I will not be questioned! I am entrusted to this mission, to carry it out in *my* way!' He had been almost shouting, his voice trapped inside the armoured bridge. 'It is a mark of my trust in this ship's ability, surely? If we are crippled or sunk in battle, my boxes will go to the bottom too!'

So they were that valuable, Hechler thought.

He heard Theil's footsteps on the gratings and shifted round to look at him.

'All well, Viktor?' Things were still strained between them, although Theil had shown his old pride and excitement when the enemy convoy had been destroyed.

Hechler had thought about that often enough. It had been so easy, he had found no satisfaction from it. It had been slaughter, the careering merchantmen and their escorts falling to their massive bombardment like targets in a fairground.

He had told himself that they would have done the same to *Prinz Luitpold*, would have cheered like his own men, if they had been left to burn and drown.

It was their war. What they had trained for. What they must do.

Theil shrugged and stared moodily at the grey ocean, the lift and dip of the raked bows.

'Yes, sir. I have just questioned the prisoner, the officer named Ames.' He shrugged again as if to sum up his irritation. 'The other one is raving. I can't imagine how he ever got to sea.'

Hechler eyed him thoughtfully. The old sailor should have been ashore with his grandchildren, not fighting for his life in an open boat. They had been adrift for five weeks. How could the human body stand it? But it was pointless to say as much to Theil. It would sound like one more disagreement. Perhaps he was more worried about his missing wife than he would admit.

Hechler tried not to let his mind stray to Inger, but even in distance her will seemed too strong to resist. In that low-cut gown, when he had held her, had seen her perfect breasts. In another moment – he sighed. She could never be kept out of his thoughts for long. Her betrayal and her contempt were like deep scars.

He had felt clumsy by comparison, and she had scorned his reserve as being stuffy, and dull.

Maybe she had been right?

Theil said abruptly, 'The Englishman knows nothing. Just that the torpedoes hit his ship in the forward hold. She sank in minutes, apparently.'

Hechler glanced at his watch. The rendezvous was in twenty minutes' time. If it happened at all. It seemed impossible that two such diverse vessels could meet on a pinpoint in this ocean.

There was a coughing roar from amidships and Hechler stirred uneasily in his chair. He wanted to walk aft and watch the brightly painted Arado as it was tested on the catapult. Leitner had told him that it would be launched without further delay. The camera team would be down there too, waiting to record their audacity as they flew off their new aircraft, indifferent to the enemy and what they could do.

Hechler had seen the girl when he had left the bridge to visit the various action stations while the ship had steamed away from the last fall of shot. She had been in the hangar, where her new Arado had been housed throughout the bombardment, its wings detached and stowed separately rather than folded, like a toy in a crate. They had faced one another awkwardly like strangers; perhaps each was out of his or her depth.

Hechler had heard himself enquiring how she had accepted or endured the din of salvoes, the hull's shaking to each ear-shattering crash of gunfire.

She had watched him as if to see her own answers without asking the questions. How small she had seemed against the wet, camouflaged steel, and the smoke-blackened gun-muzzles.

Now she was down there with the aircraft-handling party. Ready to fly off, so that some lunatic's desire for patriotic realism could be filmed.

Theil said dourly, 'I think it is madness to put that plane in the air. Suppose – '

The word hung between them. There were no enemy carriers anywhere in this part of the ocean if the OKM's reports were to be believed. Submarines, then? Even the hint of a plane would be enough to make them increase speed and head away. The Arado might fly after them, like a fledgling abandoned by its parents, until it ran out of fuel.

Theil whispered, 'He's coming up, sir.'

Leitner strode on to the bridge, the familiar silk scarf flapping in the keen air, but otherwise unprotected by a heavier coat. He smiled at the bridge-party and then returned Hechler's salute.

'According to my watch – ' He frowned as Gudegast called, 'Permission to alter course for take-off, sir?'

Hechler nodded. 'Warn the engine-room.'

Leitner's good humour returned. 'See, the sky is brightening. It will do our people at home a lot of good to see these films.' He glared at his willowy aide as he clambered on to the bridge. 'Well?'

The flag-lieutenant eyed him worriedly, hurt by his master's tone. 'The camera team would like you to join them, sir.' He glanced shyly at Hechler. 'I have a list of the questions you will be asked.'

Leitner clapped one hand across his breast and gave an elaborate sigh. 'What we must do in the name of duty!'

Gudegast lifted his face from the voice-pipe as the helmsman acknowledged the change of course. He watched Leitner march to the after-ladder and then looked over at Jaeger, who shared the watch with Korvettenkapitän Froebe.

He said softly, 'Does he fill you with pride, young Konrad? Make you want to spill your guts for your country?' He grimaced. 'Sometimes I despair.'

He thought of the painting he had begun of Gerda. Just imagining the softness of her body, the heat of their passion, had helped him in some strange fashion to endure the massacre of those helpless merchantmen. Bomber pilots who nightly released their deadly cargoes over Germany did not care about the suffering they created; the U-boat commander did not see ships and sailors in his crosswires, merely targets. Any more than an escort captain spared a thought for that same hull being crushed by the force of his depth-charges as the sea thundered in to silence the submariners' screams.

Hechler heard him, but let it pass. Gudegast was releasing the tension in his usual way.

'Ready to fly off aircraft, sir!'

'Slow ahead all engines.'

Hechler walked from his chair and leaned over the screen, the damp wind pressing into his face.

He saw the camera team down aft, some sailors freshly changed into their best uniforms, outwardly chatting to their admiral. Hechler looked at the vibrating Arado on the catapult, trained outboard ready to be fired off.

He saw the girl's helmeted head lowered to speak with one of the deck crew before she closed the cockpit cover and waved a gloved hand.

He felt his stomach contract and was stunned by the sudden concern. There was nothing that they could do or share. What was the *matter* with him? Was it Inger's fury or his own loneliness?

He tensed as the shining Arado roared from the catapult and without hesitation climbed up and away from the slow-moving cruiser.

Leitner returned to the bridge, his eyes squinting as he watched the little plane weaving and circling over the water.

He said, 'I hope she flies nearer than that. It's a camera down aft, not a bloody gunsight!'

Hechler lifted his binoculars and watched the weak sunlight lance through the clouds to pick out the plane's thin silhouette.

'Five minutes, sir!'

Gudegast's voice made him pull his thoughts together.

Leitner remarked, 'Now we shall see, eh?'

It was more like a shoal of fish than a surfacing submarine. Long flurries of spray and frothing bubbles, so that when the hull eventually appeared some half-mile distant it rose with a kind of tired majesty.

Jaeger exclaimed, 'God, she's *big*!'

Leitner heard him and turned to look. 'Another idea with vision and inventive skill!'

The huge submarine surfaced and lay on the heaving water like a gigantic whale. Unlike an ordinary combat U-boat she lacked both menace and dignity. Even as they watched, men were swarming from her squat conning-tower, while from her casing, untidy-looking derricks and hoses were already rising from hidden compartments like disturbed sea-monsters.

The tannoy blared below the bridge, and men ran to the prepared tackles and winches, ready to haul the fuel lines to the bunkers. Hechler saw the men waving to each other across the water. It must be a heartening sight to see such a big warship at large in enemy waters, he thought.

There would be no news from home as yet, but his own men could send their letters across while the two vessels lay together. It might be many weeks before those letters were read by wives, mothers and girlfriends. He wished now he had a letter written for his own parents. But they would understand. Without effort he could see the photographs of himself and his dead brother in the neat, old-fashioned house where he had been born. His mother preparing the evening meal early, in case there was an air raid, although they had been mercifully spared most of those where they lived. His father, reading the newspaper and coughing quietly at painful intervals.

A telephone buzzed and Jaeger called, 'Chief engineer reports hoses connected, sir.'

'Very good. Warn the wheelhouse to hold her steady.' It was probably unnecessary to warn anybody. Severed hoses might take hours to replace, and every minute exposed like this was too much.

Hechler watched the oily hoses jerking busily as the fuel was pumped across the gap of heaving water. What a strange war it was becoming. He glanced down at the deck below as an armed seaman walked past beside the captured English officer. The latter was downcast, and did not appear to be looking in any direction as men scurried to tackles to release the strain or to take up the slack.

A victim and a survivor.

Theil said, 'I think it unwise to let him walk about like that.'

Hechler smiled. 'He is hardly a threat, Viktor.'

He looked up to seek out the Arado, but the sky seemed empty. She would be feeling free right now, he thought. Unlike the sad-faced prisoner who walked alone despite all the seamen around him.

But the young officer who wore another man's uniform jacket was anything but despairing. On his way to the upper deck, with his guard sauntering beside him, a machine-pistol dangling from one shoulder, he had heard the one sound which was so familiar that it pulled at his reserve like claws.

The urgent stammer of morse and waves of hissing static. The radio-room with at least three headphoned operators at their bench was like a laboratory compared with anything he had been used to. But the idea had formed in his mind even as they had passed the open door.

It was his one chance. His life would be forfeit, but he found it surprisingly easy to accept that. He had died back there in the open boat with his gaunt, eyeless companions.

When the time was right. It would take just one signal to bring the navy down on this bloody German like a force of avenging angels. He looked up and thought he saw the captain framed against the low clouds.

It would all be worth it then, even if he was dead when the first great salvoes came roaring down on the raider.

The armed guard saw him give a wild grin and sighed.

It could be no joke to be adrift in this ocean, he thought.

The girl named Erika Franke adjusted the clips of her safety harness and peered to starboard as she eased the Arado into a shallow dive. She had flown several of these float-planes when she had worked for a while as a delivery pilot, before she had been asked to serve with the special section of the Luftwaffe.

She watched the grey wastes of the Atlantic tilt to one side as if it was part of a vast sloping desert, the occasional white horses where the wind had broken the swell into crests.

The cruiser had already fallen far away, and it was hard to picture her as she had first seen the ship. Huge, invulnerable, and somehow frightening. But once aboard it had seemed so much smaller, the great hull broken up into small intimate worlds, faces which you sometimes saw only once before they were swallowed up again. She watched the ship in the distance, her outline strangely broken and unreal in its striped dazzle paint. Beyond her was the austere shape of the great supply submarine which Leitner had described to the ship's company.

She saw the perspex screen mist over very slightly and adjusted her compass accordingly. They were too high for spray. The looming clouds said *rain*.

She bit her lip. If the visibility fell away she must return to the ship immediately.

She touched the microphone across her mouth. 'Rain soon.' She heard the observer, Westphal, acknowledge her comment with a grunt. A thickset, bovine man, he obviously resented being in the hands of a woman. She ignored him. It was nothing new in her life.

She deliberately altered course away from the ship and the motionless submarine. If only she could fly and fly, leave it all behind, until – she checked herself as Hechler's grave features intruded into her thoughts.

A withdrawn man, who must have been badly hurt and not just by the war. She remembered his voice, his steady blue eyes when he had visited her after the encounter with the enemy convoy. His presence had calmed her, like that moment when you fly out of a storm into bright sunlight.

During the bombardment she had felt no fear. There had been no point in being afraid. Her father had taught her that, when he had first taken her flying, had given her a taste for it. If you could do nothing, fear had no meaning, he had often told her.

But the feeling of utter helplessness had been there. The ship, powerful though she was, had shaken like a mad thing, with every plate and rivet threatening to tear apart, or so it had felt. Then Hechler, his voice and his quiet confidence had covered her like a blanket.

The Arado swayed jerkily and she quickly increased throttle until the blurred propeller settled again into a misty circle. The plane was unarmed, or at least it carried no ammunition. Just as well, she thought. That was one kind of flying she had not tried.

She thought of the two survivors who had been brought to the ship by the young officer, Jaeger. He was a nice young man, she thought, and she had seen him looking at her when she had joined the others in the wardroom for meals. It made her smile within the privacy of her flying-helmet. She was twenty-eight, but far older in other ways than Jaeger would ever dream. Why did they have to be so predictable? Those who saw her only as an easy victory, a romp in bed. Others who saw her reserve as a coldness, like something masculine.

When she glanced down at the endless, heaving water, she recalled another face with sharper clarity. Claus had loved her, and she him. He had been married, but the war had brought them together in Italy.

Had they ever really decided to take a step beyond the endless anxiety of being lovers? He had promised; she could almost hear his voice in her hair as he had held her, had pressed down to that delicious torment when he had entered her.

She had learned of his death through a friend. After all, she had no *rights* to him.

His ship had been torpedoed, lost with all hands. It was over.

She came back with a start as Westphal's surly voice intruded into her memories.

'Time to turn. Visibility's down.'

They would fly back now, she thought, and the camera crew would film her landing near the ship, and again as she stepped aboard to be greeted by Andreas Leitner. Strange how people of his kind always professed to be such men of the world, with an eye for every pretty girl.

She had met plenty like Leitner. It was surprising that the war machine attracted so many who might have been happier as women. She considered Hechler again. Dominated by his wife? Hardly. What was it then with women like Inger Hechler? She had seen her occasionally at those staid parties in Berlin which so often had changed into something wild, repellent.

She moved the controls sharply so that the plane tilted over to port. She could feel the pull of her harness, the pain in her breast as the Arado went over even further until it appeared as if the wingtip was cutting the water like a fin.

The changing light, the endless procession of unbroken waves, or was it a shadow?

'Dead ahead!' She eased the throttle with great care. 'Do you see it?'

Westphal had been deep in thought, watching her hair beneath the leather helmet, imagining how she would fight him, claw at him, when he took her.

He exclaimed, startled, 'What? Where?'

She found that she could watch the submarine quite calmly, for that was what it was. It looked dark, blue-grey, like a shark, with a lot of froth streaming from aft, and a faint plume of vapour above the conning-tower.

Westphal had recovered himself, his voice harsh as he snapped, 'Enemy boat! Charging batteries and using her *schnorchel*!'

He reached forward to prod her shoulder. 'Back to the ship, *fast!*'

The girl eased the controls over to port. Westphal had seen what he had expected to see, but had missed something vital. The submarine was trimmed too high – most of them would be almost at full periscope depth to charge batteries, and in their own waters it was unlikely they would submerge at all.

The submarine must be damaged, unable to dive.

Thoughts raced through her mind and in her imagination she could hear Hechler's voice, then see the cruiser and the supply submarine lying somewhere back there, totally unaware of this unexpected threat.

Damaged she might be, but her commander would not hesitate when *Prinz Luitpold*'s silhouette swam into his crosswires.

Erika Franke had learned quite a lot about the navy, and one of the things which stood out in her mind was something which Kröll the gunnery officer had said about his new radar. That a submarine on the surface nearby could interfere with accuracy, and that was exactly what was happening right now.

She thrust the controls forward and tilted the Arado into a steep dive. She felt the plane quivering, the rush of wind rising above the roar of the BMW engine.

Westphal shouted wildly, 'What the hell are you doing? They'll see us!'

Sure enough there were tiny ant-like figures on the submarine's deck. They might have picked up the supply boat's engines on their sonar, or even the heavier revolutions of the *Prinz Luitpold*, but the sight of a brightly painted aircraft must have caught them on the hop.

She laughed. 'Scared, are you?' The Arado's shadow swooped over the water like an uneven crucifix, and then tumbled away as she brought the nose up towards the clouds.

It was responding well; she could even smell the newness in the fuselage and fittings.

She shouted, 'By the time we made contact with the ship it would all be over!'

Then she winced as several balls of livid green tracer floated past the port wing, and the plane danced wildly to shell-bursts. The clouds enfolded the aircraft and she peered at the compass, her brain working coolly but urgently as she pictured the other vessels, the enemy submarine's bearing and line of approach. She was probably American, one of their big ocean-going boats, which she had studied in the recognition books. She held her breath and pushed the stick forward, and felt the floats quiver as they burst out of the clouds into a great span of watery sunlight.

Just right for the camera team, she thought vaguely. Then more shell-bursts erupted on either side, and lazy balls of tracer fanned beneath her, so that she instinctively drew her legs together.

The plane jerked, and she heard metal rip past her body. But the engine was behaving well. It was time to turn back. They must have heard the shooting. There was still time.

She twisted round in her seat to yell at Westphal, but choked on a scream as she saw his bared teeth, his fists bunched in agony at the moment of impact. His goggles were completely filled with blood, like a creature from a nightmare.

The plane rocked again, and she almost lost control as more bursts exploded nearby. She felt as if all the breath had been punched from her body, and when she looked down she saw a tendril of blood seeping through the flying suit and over her belt.

Then the pain hit her like a hot iron, and she heard herself whimpering and calling while she tried to find the compass and bring the plane on to the right bearing.

She felt the pain searing her body, so that her eyes misted over. She dared not turn her head where her hideous companion peered at her, his teeth set in a terrible grin.

Nor could she call up the ship. Dared not. The submarine would know instantly what he probably only suspected.

'Oh, dear God!' The words were torn from her. 'Help me!'

But the engine's roar drowned her cries and every vibration made her swoon in agony.

There were no more explosions, and for a brief moment she imagined she had lost consciousness, was dying like the men in the lifeboat. Clouds leapt towards her and then writhed aside again to bathe the cockpit in bright sunlight.

She cried out, then thrust one hand against her side as blood ran over her thigh and down into her flying boot.

There was the ship, the supply submarine almost alongside, with tiny lines and pipes linking them like a delicate web.

She saw the ship begin to turn anti-clockwise across the windshield, revolving faster and faster, blotting out everything until it seemed she was plunging straight for the bridge.

Her mind recorded several things at the same time. The lines between the two vessels were being cast off, and a great frothing wash was surging from beneath *Prinz Luitpold*'s bows as she increased to maximum speed.

The girl fought to control the spin, to bring the aircraft's nose up and level off.

All she could think of was that she had warned him. She would never know if she was in time.

11

The Truth Can Wait

Hechler joined Gudegast at the compass platform. It was going well, but any sudden cross-wind might bring the unmatched vessels too close together.

'Alter course to two-two-zero degrees. Signal the submarine's commander yourself.' He touched the big man's arm. 'Don't want oil spilled all over the ocean.'

He walked back to the gratings and imagined he could feel the fuel coming through those long, pulsating hoses.

His ship was the best of her class for performance, and with the additional bunkers she had been given last year could cruise over 7,000 miles unless she was called to offer full speed for long periods.

He thought of the girl in her brightly painted plane. It worried him more than he cared to admit to have her aboard. At the same time he knew he would miss her when she was ordered to leave. Maybe she did not have a genuine mission? Perhaps after all she was only a piece of Leitner's public relations puzzle.

Theil lowered his glasses. 'The Arado's a long time, sir.' He eyed him worriedly. 'Completely lost sight of it.'

Hechler peered over the rear of the bridge wing. One of the regular float-planes in its dappled camouflage was already standing on the catapult, the handling party lounging around with nothing to do.

Hechler contained his sudden impatience. One thing at a time. It was the only way. The collection of charts with their plotted rendezvous marks were all in the future. Nobody could say how much future they still had.

Leitner strode on to the bridge, his mouth set in a tight line. 'Where the *bloody hell* is that woman?' He moved this way and that, almost blindly, so that men on watch had to jump out of his path.

Theil suggested, 'Perhaps we should send up another aircraft, sir?'

Leitner stared at him. 'Don't be such a bloody idiot!'

Hechler saw the seamen nearby exchange glances. Some worried, others pleased that a senior officer was getting a choking-off for a change.

Hechler said, 'I agree with him, sir.'

Their eyes met. Hechler felt very calm and relaxed even though he wanted to yell at Leitner. *Go on, tell me I'm a bloody idiot!*

Leitner recovered his composure somewhat. 'It's taking too long,' he said mildly.

Hechler looked at Theil and winked. The admiral had climbed down. For the moment anyway.

Then Hechler moved to the opposite side of the bridge to watch the fuelling operation. In the Great War, German raiders had been tied down to coaling stations, built up in readiness for such a dangerous form of sea piracy. He smiled in spite of his anxiety for the girl. *Piracy. Is that what we have come to?*

He glanced at his team, the watchful faces, the occasional padding of an order for helm and engines.

And yet, in spite of the quiet discipline, or perhaps because of it, there was something not quite right. Like a fault in a painting. He knew it was not Leitner's outburst, or Theil's embarrassed confusion at being reprimanded like a first-year midshipman in front of the watch. You got used to the petty whims of superior officers. *Maybe I am like that myself now?*

No, it was a feeling of uneasiness.

He made up his mind. 'Warn the milch-cow, then sound off action stations.'

Leitner heard him and glared from the other corner of the bridge.

'It'll make them jumpy!'

Hechler forced a grin. 'I *am* jumpy, sir.' He heard the clamour of bells, muffled and far away beyond the thick plating.

To Theil he said, 'You stay here.' He shrugged. 'It's just in case.'

Leitner climbed on to the bridge chair and tugged his cap down over his eyes. When one of the camera team requested permission to come to the bridge, Leitner snapped, 'When I'm ready, damn him!'

Hechler lowered his voice. 'Pass the word to the catapult, Viktor. Prepare to launch aircraft.'

A telephone buzzed and seconds later the Arado's engine spluttered, then bellowed into life.

Leitner swung round. 'Of all the bloody useless – '

He got no further as the gunnery control intercom filled the bridge.

'Gunfire to the north-west!'

Hechler moved like lightning to the compass platform. 'Discontinue fuelling!' He snatched up the red handset and waited, mentally counting seconds. Then he heard Stück's voice from the depths of the engine-room, machinery sighing in the background like some insane orchestra.

Stück began, 'I'm sorry about the delay, Captain, but we're almost topped-up. I – '

Hechler said, 'Stop immediately, Chief. Maximum revolutions when I give the word.' He slammed down the handset. There was nothing to add. Stück better than most knew the narrowness of their margin.

He waved his arm. '*Cast off!* Take in those wires!'

Leitner was beside him, peering at him wildly. 'What the hell's going on?'

'Gunfire means an enemy, sir.' He swung round as a lookout yelled, 'Aircraft, Red four-five, angle of sight four-oh!'

'Stand by, secondary armament!' Without looking Hechler pictured the twin turrets along the port side already lifting and training. But for what?

He levelled his glasses and found the Arado almost immediately. It was rolling from side to side, but apparently intact. He felt his heart throbbing as he followed every painful movement.

Theil called, 'Clear that breast-rope, damn you!'

Hechler lowered his glasses and saw the remaining wire dragging the heavy submarine dangerously close alongside.

'Cut that line! *Now!*'

He turned back again but the plane had plunged into some low clouds.

The gunnery intercom intoned, 'Submarine on the surface, bearing Red two-oh. Range four thousand!'

Leitner was almost beside himself. 'How can it be?' He peered over the stained screen. 'In the name of Christ!'

Hechler called, 'Full ahead all engines!' He felt the sharp tremble through the deck plates. Now or never. If that wire refused to part they would take the milch-cow with them.

The port lookout was leaning against his mounted binoculars, his legs braced behind him as if he was taking the whole weight of the ship.

'Aircraft in sight again, sir. Closing. Shift bearing to Red six-oh!'

Hechler gripped the rail as the deck seemed to rise and then surge forward beneath him.

'Line's parted, sir!'

'*Open fire!*'

The three twin turrets along the port side opened up instantly, their sharper explosions making men grope for ear-plugs, others crouch down away from their savage back-blast.

Theil called, 'Supply boat's diving, sir!' He sounded breathless.

Great fountains of spray shot from the milch-cow's saddle tanks as water thundered into them, and her wash indicated a frantic increase in speed.

Hechler tore his eyes from the Arado as it reeled over the ship and then appeared to level off on an invisible wire. Not before he had seen the bright, starlike holes in the paintwork, some of which appeared to cross the cockpit itself.

'Port twenty!' He wrapped his arms around the voice-pipes with such force that the pain seemed to steady his mind, the ache which that last sight had given him.

She had drawn enemy fire. There was no other possible reason but to warn the ship.

He felt the deck going over. Like a destroyer. '*Steady!* Hold her!'

Voices yelled on every side and then the secondary armament recoiled in their mountings yet again, their shells flinging up thin waterspouts against the horizon where the enemy lay hidden in the swell.

'*Shoot!*' Again the urgent cry, and again the sharp, ear-probing crashes.

'Torpedoes running to port!'

Theil jumped to the voice-pipe but Hechler snapped, 'As she goes!'

He looked quickly at the supply-boat. Her bows were already under water, her squat conning-tower deserted as she prepared to run deep and head away. She would not even be a spectator, let alone wait around to pick up survivors.

The explosion was like one great thunderclap which rendered men blind and deaf in a few seconds, as if shocked from every known sense.

Dense black smoke billowed across the water, so thick it seemed solid, then it rolled over the decks and through the super-structure and masts, and for a while longer it was like the dead of night. Through it all the intercom kept up its continual babble.

'Short!' Then, 'A straddle! Got the bastards!'

Hechler groped to the forepart of the bridge and almost fell over a young signalman. He could barely remember the boy's name as he was their newest addition. Logged as seventeen years old, Hechler guessed he was a good deal less.

He dragged him to his feet by the scruff of his tunic and shouted, 'Hold on, Heimrath!' He could hear his gasping and retching in the foul stench and dense smoke. 'It's not us this time!'

The torpedoes must have hit the big submarine just as she made to lift her tail and dive. There could be nothing left. Fuel, ammunition, spare torpedoes, they had all gone up together, scattering fragments for half a mile, while some had clattered across *Prinz Luitpold*'s forecastle and maindeck.

'Target is diving, sir.'

Diving or sinking, it made no difference now. That last salvo would put her out of the fight. It was far more likely that she was falling slowly into the depths, blacker than any death pall, until the weight of water crushed her and her crew into a steel pulp.

'Slow ahead.' Hechler dabbed his mouth with his sleeve. The smoke was streaming over and around them, and men were peering for one another, dazed and with eyes running while they sought out their friends.

Hechler gripped the rail with both hands. 'Tell the accident boat to stand by.' He saw Theil's disbelief, his eyes bulging in his smeared face. 'Lower to the waterline. Now!'

Reluctantly almost, training and discipline reasserted themselves. Like a great beast, rising and shaking itself before it had time to consider the fate which had taken one and spared another.

Leitner wiped his binoculars and glared through the fading smoke.

'Another minute and we'd have shared the same end, Dieter.'

Hechler steadied his glasses as the Arado's bright paintwork gleamed through the smoke. It was settled on the water, and rocking like a wild thing in the powerful rollers.

He said, 'Stop engines. Slip the boat!'

He raised his glasses once more, thought held at bay while he searched for the aircraft, made himself ready for what he might find.

A voice murmured on the intercom, 'Sounds of ship breaking up, sir.'

It must be the enemy submarine. There was not enough of the milch-cow to disturb their sonar.

He flinched as he saw the horrific face in the rear of the cockpit. Eyes of blood, hands in raised fists behind the slumped figure at the controls.

'Get the doctor on deck!' There was a new harshness in his tone.

Jaeger looked up from the voice-pipes. 'He's already there, sir.'

The motorboat ploughed into view across the lens, familiar faces he knew and respected leaping past his vision.

Leitner seemed to speak from miles away. 'It's afloat anyway. Good thing.'

Another voice said, 'The boat will tow it to the hoisting gear, sir.'

Was that all Leitner cared? Was it perhaps unimportant to him when so many men had died horribly just moments ago?

He gripped the binoculars harder as the motorboat's bowman clambered on to one of the plane's floats and hauled himself on to the fuselage. He wrenched open the cockpit and faltered. It must be a hundred times worse close to, Hechler thought despairingly.

Then he saw the man turn and signal. One dead.

She was alive. *Alive*.

He lowered his glasses to his chest and made himself walk slowly to the chart-table.

Around him, smoke-grimed and dazed by the cruel swiftness of destruction, the watchkeepers watched him dully.

Hechler said, 'As soon as the boat is hoisted inboard, get under way and alter course as prearranged.' He saw Gudegast nod. 'I want a complete inspection of hull and upper deck. We could have sustained some minor damage.' He touched the rail again. Even as he said it, he sensed that the *Prinz* would be unscathed.

He looked at Theil. 'Take over.' He half-turned to the rear-admiral. 'With your permission of course, sir?'

Leitner looked away. 'Granted.'

Bells jangled softly and the ship gathered way again.

Hechler hesitated at the top of the ladder to watch as the Arado was swung over the guardrails on its special derrick. The doctor and his assistant were there, and some men with stretchers. He hesitated again and looked into the bridge. His world. Now he was sharing it. Hopeless? Perhaps it was. But she was alive. Because of what she had done, they had all survived. He glanced at the admiral's stiff shoulders. He had made an enemy there, but it no longer mattered.

He nodded to Theil and then hurried down the ladder. This world could wait.

The *Prinz Luitpold*'s spacious wardroom was almost deserted. It was halfway through the first watch, and the officers who would be called to stand the middle watch were snatching all the sleep they could. Then the hand on the shoulder, the unfeeling voice of boatswain's mate or messenger, a mug of stale coffee if you were lucky, and off you went to the wretched middle watch.

A few officers sat in deep armchairs, dozing but unwilling to leave their companions, or quietly discussing the explosion which had destroyed the supply submarine and everyone aboard. One man suggested it was lucky they had pumped off most of the fuel. Otherwise both ships might have been engulfed in the same inferno. But most of them, especially the older ones, were thinking of the miles which were hourly streaming away astern. The ship had made a violent turn and was now heading south-east, further and still further from home. If they continued like this, even at their economical speed of fifteen knots, they would cross the Equator in two days' time, and into the South Atlantic.

Viktor Theil as the senior officer in the mess stood with his back to the bar, a glass of lemon juice in his hand. He was conscious of his seniority, the need to set an example at all times in a wardroom where the average was so low. His immediate subordinate, Korvettenkapitän Werner Froebe, tall, ungainly, and unusually solemn, clutched a tankard of something in one of his huge hands and asked, 'Do you think it went well today?'

Theil eyed him warily. An innocent enough question, but the delay in casting-off from the doomed milch-cow had been his responsibility. It could have been a criticism.

He replied, 'We saved the new plane anyway. Only superficial damage. Pity about the observer.'

Froebe grimaced. 'And the woman. Caught a splinter, I'm told.'

Theil swilled the juice around his glass. 'Could have been much worse.'

He looked at the red-painted bell on the bulkhead. Like an unblinking eye. As if it was watching them, waiting for them to relax, lose their vigilance even for a minute. Then the clamour would scream out here and in every watertight compartment throughout the hull. You never really got used to it.

Even in his bed at home, sometimes in the night – he gritted his teeth. He must not think about it. It would all solve itself. He tightened his jaw. But Britta would have to come to him. She had been in the wrong. He could see it. In the end he would forgive her. They would be reunited as never before.

Froebe watched him dubiously. 'I just hope they know what they're doing.'

'Who?' Theil wanted to finish it but something in Froebe's tone made him ask.

'I don't know. The staff, the high command, OKM, everybody who doesn't have to pick up the bloody pieces!'

Two of the very junior offices hovered closer and one said, 'At home, our people will know about us, and of *Lübeck*'s great sacrifice!'

Theil smiled. 'Of course. We are honoured to serve in this way.'

A figure moved heavily into the light. It was the doctor, jacket unbuttoned, his tie crooked.

He looked at them each in turn, his eyes tired. To Theil he said, 'There are ten casualties below. All doing well.'

Theil nodded. They were the men who had been cut or injured by falling debris on the upper deck after the explosion.

The same young officer exclaimed, 'They are lucky to be free of standing their watch!'

The doctor looked past him. 'The *Lübeck* didn't go down gallantly with guns blazing, by the way.' He returned his gaze to Theil. 'She was scuttled.'

Theil felt as if his collar had suddenly become too tight. Figures in nearby chairs were stirring and turning towards the small group by the bar. From torpor between watches the air had become electric.

Theil exploded, 'What are you saying? How dare you tell such lies in this mess!'

Stroheim gave him a sad smile. 'I was in the W/T office. One of the operators broke a finger when he lost his balance as the supply boat blew up. They were monitoring an English-speaking broadcast, from Bermuda it may have been. But that was what they said.' His voice hardened and he leaned forward, his eyes on Theil's outraged face. 'And something else to fill your pipe with. The Tommies and their allies are up to the Rhine, *do you hear me?*' He swayed and glared around the wardroom at large. 'Ivan is coming at us from the East, and *they're* up to the Rhine!' He looked at Theil again. 'Don't you see, man? We're on the bloody run!'

Theil snapped, 'Keep your voice down! How dare you spread – '

Stroheim made a sweeping gesture. 'What is the matter with everyone? It was in the W/T office! What are they in there, a separate navy, or something?'

Froebe interrupted unhappily, 'Easy, Doctor – this won't help!'

Stroheim removed his glasses and massaged his eyes savagely. 'Then what will, eh?' He stared at the sideboard at the end of the bar, Adolf Hitler's profile in silver upon it with the ship-builder's crest and launch-date underneath.

'All lies. Raised on them, led by them, and now going to hell because of them!'

Theil said sharply, 'I must ask you to come with me.' He could feel his grip returning, although his anger was matched by a sense of alarm.

The doctor laughed, a bitter sound. 'Follow you? Of course, *sir*. Does the truth disturb you that much?'

Froebe saw another figure rise from a chair and then slip through a curtained door.

It was the flag-lieutenant. He suppressed a groan. In about three minutes the admiral would know all about this.

The doctor moved after Theil and said mildly, 'Don't any of you get sick until I return!'

Froebe leaned on the bar and stared at the steward. 'You didn't hear that.'

The man bit his lip. 'No, sir.'

Froebe saw the curtain sway across the doctor's back. The poor sod was drunk too. God, what a mess.

Suppose it was true. If it was, would it make any difference if they held up another convoy, or two dozen of them, *really* make a difference in the end?

He thought suddenly of his wife and two children. Near the Dutch frontier.

He felt like a traitor as he gave silent thanks that the Allies and not the Russians would reach there first.

Hechler clipped the door behind him and stood inside the admiral's bridge. It was illuminated only by the light immediately above the main table against which Leitner was leaning, his hands flat on the chart.

'You sent for me, sir?'

Leitner glanced up. 'I like to know where you are. At all times, eh?'

Hechler watched him as he peered down at the chart again. He had expected Leitner to lose control, to scream at him. It was obvious that he must know about Theil and the doctor.

Hechler had been in his quarters when Theil had come searching for him, his eyes ablaze with anger and indignation. Hechler had closed the door to his sleeping cabin where the girl lay drugged and unconscious after being treated by the doctor. One of Stroheim's attendants had sat nearby, and Hechler had stood beside the bunk, not moving, hardly daring to breathe as he looked down at her. She seemed so much younger, like a child's face, eyes tightly shut, beads of perspiration on her upper lip and forehead.

A splinter had hit her in the side, just above the left hip. Stroheim had explained that she had lost a lot of blood, and a bone had been chipped, how badly he did not yet know.

Hechler had turned down the sheet and stared at the neat bandages, a small red stain in the centre. She was dressed in a pyjama jacket, and he pulled it across her breast, one of which was exposed in the bunk light.

He remembered the touch of her skin against his fingers as he did so. Burning hot, like some inner fire, or fever. Otherwise, apart from bruising from her harness when she had made a desperate attempt to steady the aircraft as it had smashed down in a deep trough, she was unmarked. It was a miracle.

He thought of Theil's outrage, and Stroheim's apparent indifference. He was still not sure what he would have done, but the telephone had called him here. It might give him time.

Leitner was saying, 'Leutnant Bauer just brought me a new batch of signals. I have been working on them, plotting what we shall do.'

Hechler studied his glossy head and waited. So it was Bauer.

He said abruptly, 'He is one of my officers, sir, and as captain I expect to be informed of every signal which affects this ship.'

Leitner looked up, his eyes cold. 'His first responsibility is to me. I will decide – '

Hechler could feel the armoured sides of the bridge closing in, just as he could sense his rising anger and disgust.

'So it's true about *Lübeck?*'

Leitner straightened his back, his face moving into shadow as he snapped, 'Yes, I knew about it. What had happened.'

'You told our people she had gone down in battle.'

Leitner replied, 'Do not adopt that tone with me. It was the right decision. Afterwards, they can believe what they like!'

'I can't believe it.'

Leitner smiled gently. 'Because Rau was another captain, is that it? Death before dishonour? I can read you like a book. You've not changed, you with your outdated ideals and fancies!'

Hechler met his eyes. '*Graf Spee* would have fought back. Her captain was ordered to scuttle too. It did more damage than losing the ship to the enemy. It was madness.'

Leitner banged his hand on the table. 'I believe he shot himself after that, eh? Hardly the act of a *gallant captain!*'

He moved back into the shadows, his voice barely under control. 'I will not be questioned. I command here, so remember it. And if that idiot Theil cannot keep order in his own wardroom, and shut the mouth of any foul, defeatist rumour, I will have him removed!' He strode about the small bridge, his shadow looming against the grey steel like a spectre. 'God damn it, I could order a man shot for such behaviour!' He swung round and said, 'After all I did for him, the ungrateful bastard!'

Hechler said, 'He brought the doctor to me, sir.'

'And I suppose you gave him a pat on the back! He can do no wrong, not one of *your* officers, oh no! Ingratitude, that's what it is. I am betrayed on every side – '

'I'm sure he acted as he thought right, sir.'

'Not before half the ship's officers heard what Stroheim said.' Leitner paused by the table, his chest heaving with exertion. 'I should have known, should have overridden your belief in the man, damn him. No wonder his bloody wife was taken away – '

He paused at that point, his eyes staring, as he realised what he had said.

Hechler pressed his hands to his sides. 'When was that, sir?' He leaned forward. 'I must know!'

Leitner ran his fingers through his hair and replied vaguely, 'When we were at Vejle.'

All that time, while Theil had gone around the ship like a man being driven mad by some secret worry, Leitner had known.

'What had she done?'

Leitner took his calm voice as some kind of understanding. 'She had been making trouble. Her parents were arrested. Terrorists, I expect.'

'Is she in prison, sir?'

Leitner's gaze wavered. 'The Gestapo took her.' He looked at the chart without seeing it. 'That's all I know.'

Hechler thrust his hand into his pocket and gripped his pipe. He felt sick, unable to believe what he had heard. *Gestapo*.

Leitner picked up a telephone and added, 'Well, you wanted the truth, Dieter. Sometimes not an easy thing to share, is it?'

'Does Bauer know about it?'

'Yes.' It sounded like *of course*.

'Anyone else?'

Leitner smiled very gently. 'Only you.'

Leitner spoke into the telephone and asked for the navigating officer to be awakened and sent to the bridge.

He put down the telephone and said, 'The war goes on, you see. Within the week we shall carry out an attack which will throw the enemy into utter confusion.'

'Are you going to tell me about it, sir?' He was surprised that he should sound so level. If he had had a Luger in his hand instead of a pipe he knew he could have killed him.

'When I have decided.'

'Then I should like to leave, sir.'

Leitner watched him by the door. 'It is up to you whether you tell Theil about his wife. The ship comes first, you told me so yourself. If Theil is told, what good can it do? He is like the rest of us. A prisoner of duty until released, or killed. As it stands, stupid as he may be, he is a competent enough officer. I will not tolerate interference with my plans because of him, or anyone else, do I make myself clear?'

'Perfectly, sir.'

'Then you *are* dismissed.' He bent over the chart again.

Hechler opened the door and groped his way through the darkness, the night air clammy around him.

On the forebridge all was quiet, the men on watch intent on their various sectors, although Hechler guessed that Theil's confrontation with the doctor would by now be common knowledge.

He thought of the men he commanded. The ones who had trusted him, who had listened to Leitner's passionate speech about the *Lübeck*. Her sacrifice, he had termed it. Rau must have been ordered to scuttle his ship by no less than the Führer. Was there no room left for honour?

He knew Theil was waiting for him, could see his dark outline against the pale steel.

Theil said in a fierce whisper, 'I have sent him to his quarters, sir.'

'Good.' Hechler walked past him. 'I will have a word with him in the morning.'

Theil persisted angrily, 'He was raving about the *truth* all the time! Why should we be told everything, when security must come first! I did not believe him anyway – we would have been informed if – '

Hechler did not hear the rest.

What would you do with the truth, I wonder? If I told you here and now that your wife had been taken by the Gestapo?

He looked over the screen and allowed the spray to refresh his face. She was probably in some terrible prison. She might even be dead. God, it did not bear thinking about.

Theil finished, 'Duty first, I say. The truth can wait.'

Hechler slipped into the chair and touched his arm. 'If you say so, Viktor.'

It was as if Theil had decided for him.

12

━━ ━━ ━━ ━━ ━━ ━━

Doubts

Konteradmiral Andreas Leitner appeared to shine as he stood in the entrance of the conning-tower and waited for Hechler to receive him.

'All present, sir.' Hechler touched the peak of his cap and noted that Leitner was dressed in white drill, with a freshly laundered cap-cover to set it off.

Inside the conning-tower it was already stiflingly hot despite the fans, and the sunlight which cut through the observation slits seemed to add to the discomfort of the ship's heads of department who were crowded around the chart-table.

Leitner stepped over the coaming and nodded to his subordinates. For the next few moments at least *Prinz Luitpold* would be in the hands of her junior officers.

They were all there, Theil, beside the towering Gudegast, Froebe, and Kröll, even Stück, immaculate in a white boiler suit and somehow out of place. Oberleutnant Meile, the stores officer, who could at any time tell you how many cans of beans or sausages were being consumed per every nautical mile streamed, and of course Bauer, the smooth-faced communications officer.

Hechler saw the new doctor's shape wedged in one corner, as if he was trying to stay out of sight.

Leitner cleared his throat and glanced at his side. 'Very well, Helmut, we will begin.'

Hechler saw Gudegast raise an eyebrow at Froebe, and the latter's brief grin. Leitner's familiarity with his flag-lieutenant was unusual in public.

Hechler felt their interest as the aide laid a new chart on the table. It was covered with arrows and estimated positions where Leitner had plotted the ceaseless stream of information gathered by the W/T office.

He thought of the hasty Crossing the Line rituals that morning as the ship had reached the Equator, the makeshift ceremony on the forecastle while the anti-aircraft guns had sniffed at the clear sky, and every lookout had scanned his allotted piece of ocean. There was no carrier within a hundred miles, nor had any more submarines been reported. But the spies and the intelligence network which had been built up into an efficient world-wide machine during the past ten years or so, could not be expected to have all the answers.

Hechler had been on the bridge and had watched the boatswain, Brezinka, dressed in a false beard of spunyarn and a flowing robe made of bunting. His cropped head had been topped by a convincing crown, as he had challenged the cruiser's right to enter his domain. The rough ceremony was like a tonic after the strain and uncertainty, and even the young officers who were subjected to the 'bears'' rough handling and ducked in a canvas bath, took it all in good part.

He thought of the girl who was confined to his own quarters, of his last, short visit there. She had been propped on a bank of pillows, dressed in another pyjama jacket which Stroheim's assistants must have found somewhere. She had greeted him with a smile; once again it had been an awkward greeting. Not as strangers this time, but like those who have been parted for a long while. 'Are they taking care of you?' Even that had sounded clumsy. He had wanted to tell her how he had touched her, had later sat on the bridge chair and thought about her, when the words had flowed so easily through his mind.

She had smiled and had tried to struggle up on her elbows. He had seen the sudden pain in her eyes, and helped her to be comfortable again.

She had said, 'You came to me when I got back.'

'Yes. We were all so proud of you.' He had looked at his hands. 'I was very proud. I thought when I saw the damage – '

She had reached out and their hands had touched. 'I knew you'd wait for me. Somehow I thought you'd pick me up.'

She had lain back, her hand still against his. 'How is the plane?' she had asked.

Then they had laughed together. As if it mattered.

Hechler looked up as Leitner's voice brought him into the present.

'It has been confirmed that the major convoy of enemy troops is going ahead.' He waited for his aide to rest a pointer on the chart. 'Around Good Hope, then escorted all the way to Gibraltar to change to an even larger protective screen with all the air cover they need.' He eyed them calmly, and Hechler wondered if the others were thinking of the doctor's outburst about the *Lübeck*, the Allied successes in France and Holland. Equally, if Leitner was searching for doubt or disloyalty amongst them.

Hechler glanced at Theil. He looked very calm, but the hands which gripped the seams of his trousers made a lie of his composure.

Leitner continued, 'If the British have a weakness it is their overriding interest in protecting life rather than the materials of war. They do not seem to realise that without such materials, they can lose everything, including the lives of those they intended to defend. It is a false equation, gentlemen, and we shall prove just how futile it is.'

The pointer moved on past the Cape, where the Atlantic met the power of the Indian Ocean.

'In moments of crisis, whole armies have been forced to a halt by the inability to keep up a supply of fuel. Even our own forces in Russia have often been in a stalemate because of holdups, flaws in the supply-line.'

Hechler thought of the great battleship *Tirpitz*, confined in her Norwegian fjord while her fuel had been earmarked for the tanks on the Eastern front. Because of her inability to move, the British midget submarines had found and crippled her. It was unlikely she would ever move again. Hechler still believed that the precious fuel would have done far more good in *Tirpitz*'s bunkers than in a squadron of snow-bound tanks in Russia. She was the greatest warship ever designed. If she were here now, they could have taken on the troop convoy and destroyed it, no matter what escorts were thrown against them.

Leitner said, 'There is just such a convoy, two days behind the troopships. A fast one, of the very largest tankers.' He allowed his words to sink in as the pointer came to rest on the Persian Gulf. 'It was assembled here. Twelve big tankers. Think of them, gentlemen. The life-blood of an army!'

Then his tone became almost matter-of-fact, bored even, as he said, 'Except for any unforeseen factor there would be little chance of surprise. My information – ' his gaze rested only lightly on Hechler ' – is that the enemy has no idea where we are at present, nor how we are obtaining our own fuel supply.' He nodded slowly. 'Planning, gentlemen – it far outpaces sentiment and outmoded strategy.' He jerked his head at his aide. 'Show them.'

The pointer rested on a mere dot in the Atlantic, just north-west of Ascension Island.

Leitner watched their faces as they all craned forward. 'The island of St Jorge.'

Gudegast said, 'A rock, nothing more. Like a pinnacle sticking up from the ocean bed.'

Leitner gave him a thin smile. 'I shall ignore your scepticism. You are, after all, more used to trading your wares around the sea ports than practising the arts of war, eh?'

Gudegast flushed, but when he opened his mouth to retort, Froebe touched his arm.

Hechler saw it, but doubted if anyone else had noticed the warning.

Leitner said, 'There is a Cable and Wireless station there which was built just before the outbreak of war.' His eyes flashed. 'Before we were forced as a nation to defend ourselves against British Imperialists and the dictates of Judaism!'

His aide said nervously, 'The wireless station has a powerful transmitter, more so even than those in the Falklands.'

Hechler asked, 'Shall we destroy it, sir?' He felt he had to say something, if only to snap the tension, to release his officers from being addressed like unreliable schoolboys.

'I spoke of *surprise*.' Leitner was very relaxed. Only the eyes gave away his triumph, the sense that he had them all in the palm of his hand. 'Provided we are not detected or attacked by some untoward enemy vessel, I intend not to destroy that radio station, but to capture it!'

They all stared at each other, their incredulity giving way to surprised grins as Leitner explained, 'We will *fly* our landing party ahead. By this method the enemy will have no chance to warn their patrols and raise the alarm. Down here, in mid-Atlantic, it would be the last thing any sane man would be expecting.' He turned his face very sharply to Hechler. 'What do you say?'

Hechler pictured the lonely Cable and Wireless station. An outpost in the middle of nowhere. No real loss to the enemy if some long-range U-boat surfaced and shot down the radio masts. But absolutely vital if they could signal the *Prinz*'s whereabouts.

Hechler said, 'Capture it and make a false signal.'

Leitner said, 'Yes. When – er, we are ready.'

He sounded irritated, disappointed perhaps that Hechler had not waited for a full explanation of his plan.

Hechler said, 'It is a wild chance.' He looked at Theil's blank face. 'And I think it might just work.'

What did it matter now anyway? Any risk, almost, was justified this far from base. Keep the enemy guessing, leave no set or mean track, and then they would continue to hold an advantage. A final confrontation could be avoided if their luck held out.

Leitner said, 'We will have another conference tomorrow.' He eyed them for a few seconds. 'Early. I will not abide laggards in this command!'

He swung on his heel and left the conning tower.

Gudegast exclaimed, 'Aircraft? Better them than me!'

Theil crossed to Hechler's side. 'What do you really think?'

Hechler looked at the chart. If they failed to mount a surprise attack it would be an open invitation to every enemy squadron and patrol to converge on the tiny island of St Jorge. Hechler pictured the *Lübeck* as she must have been, heeling over, her guns silent while the enemy watched her final moments.

Suppose a signal was handed to him? The order to scuttle rather than meet an honourable fate; what should he do? What *could* he do?

He said, 'It is a daring plan, Viktor. It would mean leaving some volunteers on the island. For them, the war would be over, but we will cross that bridge when we come to it. After the war they might be heroes.' He watched for some sign of a smile or even disagreement. But Theil said fervently, 'For Germany. *Any* man would volunteer!'

'Perhaps.' He heard Gudegast give a snort of anger at something Froebe had said and when Theil turned to listen he watched his profile. Did he suspect, he wondered? Surely no man could love someone and not feel her anguish, her need?

For all their sakes, the ship had to come first. And yet, had he been informed earlier, when Leitner had not been aboard, would he have told Theil about his wife?

Suppose it had been Inger?

He saw the doctor making for the door and called, 'I want to talk to you.'

The doctor faced him warily. 'Sir?'

'Come to the bridge. I should like to ask you something.'

Theil watched them leave and ground his teeth. Thick as thieves, even after what had happened.

It was because of that girl. How could the captain behave so stupidly? Any officer, let alone one given command of a ship like this, had to be above such things. He stared after the others as they hurried away to their various departments. It was all so unfair. *I should have command here.* Perhaps it had all gone wrong a long time ago without his knowing? Britta may have said or done something indiscreet. It would go on his record, not hers. He clenched his fists together until he felt sick with the realisation. It had been her fault. When the war was over, he would be overridden by younger men; he might even be discharged! He thought of the friendly way Hechler had spoken to the doctor.

A new strength seemed to run through him. This was his chance to show Hechler, to prove to everyone what he could do, how much he was worth.

Gudegast rolled up his chart and watched his superior grimly. What was the matter with everybody, he wondered, if they could not see that Theil was cracking up?

He glanced at his watch. He would work on his charts and then retire to his cabin. The painting was coming along well. He gave a great sigh. Gerda was probably fixed up with another man already. He grinned. The painting would have to do instead. But for once he was unable to lift his apprehension.

Hechler felt the arm of his chair dig into his side, remain there, and then slowly withdraw as the ship swayed upright again. They had reduced speed to twelve knots and the *Prinz* was finding it uncomfortable. She was more used to slicing through every kind of sea with her cutaway Atlantic bow.

Despite the clear blue sky it was chilly on the open bridge after the heat of midday. The sun looked like a solid bronze orb, and was already laying a shimmering cloak down from the hard horizon line. Hechler turned up the collar of his watch-coat and saw his reflection in the glass screen. Hat tugged over his forehead, the old grey fisherman's sweater protruding through his heavy coat. Not everyone's idea of a naval officer, he thought.

A seaman handed him a mug of coffee and another to the doctor who had joined him, somewhat uneasily in that corner of the bridge. Hechler said, 'It will be another clear day tomorrow.'

'Is that good, sir?' He watched Hechler's strong profile. A face with character and determination. No wonder Erika Franke was so interested. She had not said as much, nor had he asked her directly, but Stroheim knew enough about women to recognise the signs.

Hechler sipped the coffee. It must have been reheated for a dozen watches, he thought. But it was better than nothing.

'It could make things easier for our pilots.' He thought of the girl in his bunk. It might have been Leitner's intention to send her with the others, perhaps with a film camera as her sole protection. She had at least been spared that. He thought too of his answer. Another clear day might also bring an unexpected ship or aircraft, detection and the beginning of a chase.

Hechler added abruptly, 'You were stupid to speak as you did in the wardroom. I should punish you, but – ' He turned in the chair and glanced at the doctor curiously. '*But*, that word again.'

Stroheim smiled awkwardly. 'Perhaps I was wrong. I'm sorry. But I was angry at the time, incensed. Not that I could do anything.'

Hechler turned away to watch the horizon as it began to slope to the opposite side once more. *In another moment he will ask me what I think, if what he heard is true.*

He said, 'You are a non-combatant, but out here you are at risk like the rest of us.'

Stroheim made himself look at the ocean and shivered despite his thick coat.

He would be glad when night fell. The ship became more dominant, invulnerable, just as his own quarters and sick-bay had become personal, an escape.

He watched the bronze reflection and knew he would never be at home on the sea. Up here, on one of the highest points in the ship, it was all the more obvious. A vast, shark-blue desert, endless in every direction, horizon to horizon, so that the great ship seemed to shrink to something frail and unprotected. He thought of Gudegast, a man he liked although the navigator fought off every kind of close contact. He was at home out here, could find his way as others might grope through a city fog.

A man of peace, no matter what he proclaimed openly. A true sailor, not a professional naval officer like Theil and most of the others. He glanced at Hechler again. And what about the captain? One who was not of any mould he knew. A loner, who accepted leadership without question.

Stroheim asked, 'Do you ever have doubts?' For a moment he thought he had gone too far, that the small contact was broken.

Hechler swung round in the chair, his eyes very blue in the strange light.

'Doubts? What do you think? You are the expert, surely!' He became calm again, angry perhaps that his guard had been penetrated so easily. 'My day is full of them. I must question the weather, my resources, the strength and weakness of every man aboard. The ship is like a chain. A weak link can cause disaster.'

He forced a smile. 'Satisfied?'

Stroheim grinned. 'I am glad you are in command. I hate the sea, but if I must be here, then so be it.'

Hechler did not look at him. 'You are a man of the world. While I have been at sea, learning my profession, you have seen and done many things. You must have found the war very difficult.'

Stroheim replied, 'I thought at first it was the end of life as I had known it. You on the other hand would have seen the war as a culmination of things, a suitable theatre to practise the arts of battle, to exercise all that training.' He looked at the captain's profile again. 'But I learned to live with it. People always need doctors.'

Hechler heard the bitterness. 'I know you were in trouble with the authorities.'

Stroheim grimaced. 'The whole world seems to know that.'

He recovered from himself and added, 'But I am a good doctor, surgeon too. Otherwise I would be in field-grey on the Russian front instead of here on a cruise.'

'You see, I am ignorant of that kind of life.' Hechler waved his hand over the screen. 'This is what I know best.'

Stroheim's eyes gleamed behind his gold-rimmed glasses. The captain was working round to something which was troubling him. He had experienced it many times, the patient in his plush consulting room, the roundabout approach to what was really the problem.

Hechler glanced round at the watchkeepers, familiar faces, men and boys who trusted him.

He lowered his voice. 'I knew someone who got into trouble, too. He was arrested, in fact.'

Stroheim held his breath. 'Easy enough to do.'

Hechler did not seem to hear. 'I was wondering, what sort of process does it involve?' He changed tact immediately. 'Here, in my command, justice is swift but I hope fair. I would never punish a sailor just to prove my authority. I am the captain, that is all the proof they need. The rest is up to me.'

Stroheim made himself look abeam where some large fish were leaping from the swell and flopping down again. He could feel Hechler watching him, could sense the importance of his casual questions. 'It depends on which security force is involved.'

Hechler said, 'Suppose it was at the top, the Gestapo. I mean, they have a job to do, but they must surely tread carefully too?'

Stroheim clenched his hands in his pockets. Gestapo. The *bottom*, he would describe them.

He said tightly, 'They are scum.' He felt the same recklessness as when he had spoken to Theil of the British broadcast. 'They are a machine for creating terror.' He faced Hechler suddenly and said, 'If your friend is in their hands, he can expect as much mercy as a heretic facing the Spanish Inquisition!' He turned away and stammered, 'I – I am sorry, sir, I had no right – '

He started as Hechler gripped his arm. 'Do not apologise. I asked for your help. You gave it.' He retained his grip until their eyes met. 'I have been in the dark.'

Feet clattered on ladders, and the watchkeepers shifted their bodies about, impatient to be relieved so that they could go below to their other world.

Stroheim flinched as Hechler said, 'I will not *ask* you this other question.' He tried to smile, but his eyes were very still and cold. 'You knew my wife. She had come to you for an abortion before, but this time you could not help.'

Stroheim stared at him. 'You knew?'

'*Guessed.* She came to my ship as you know. I should have realised why she had come, I ought not to have had *doubts*, eh?'

Stroheim said quietly, 'You would not be the first one to be deceived, Captain. She would have claimed that the child was yours.'

Hechler looked away. How could anyone hate the sea?

He said, 'Thank you for your company.'

Stroheim moved away as Kapitänleutnant Emmler, the assistant gunnery officer, clumped on to the bridge to take over the First Dog Watch.

As he reached the internal companion ladder he heard Hechler call after him. He turned and said, 'Captain?'

Hechler merely said, 'Between us.'

Stroheim nodded, suddenly moved by the man's quiet sincerity. 'Of course. Until the next time.'

Hechler faced the ocean again and wondered why he had spoken so freely with the doctor.

He had not needed to demand an answer from him about Inger, it had been plain on his face. But in his heart he had also known it, and that was what hurt the most.

The tiny cabin was more like a store or ship's chandlery with a place to live and sleep. There were shelves, jam-packed with wire strops, spare lashings and blocks. Mysterious boxes were wedged beneath the bunk, and the air was heavy with paint, spunyarn and tobacco smoke.

Rolf Brezinka sat cross-legged on the bunk, a huge pipe jutting from his jaw. The cabin was very hot, the air ducts switched to a minimum flow, and he wore only his singlet and some patched working trousers. As boatswain he stood alone, between wardroom and petty officers' mess. One of a dying breed, he often said, a man who could turn his hand to any form of seamanship, who could splice wire or hemp with equal skill, and who knew the ship's hull like his own battered face.

Opposite him, a cigar jammed in one corner of his mouth, was Oskar Tripz, the grey-haired petty officer. They were old friends, and although both had given most of their lives to the navy, they had each served in the merchant service between the wars, and more to the point in the crack Hamburg-Amerika Line.

When Brezinka had been drafted to the *Prinz Luitpold* he had pulled strings to get his old comrade and fellow conspirator posted to her too. The strings he pulled were unorthodox, but carried no less power than the brass at head-quarters.

'It's asking a lot, Oskar.' *Puff, puff.* The big, crop-headed boatswain eyed him grimly through the smoke. 'We've taken a few risks, but I don't know about this one.'

Tripz grinned. At first he had thought of ignoring it, of telling young Stoecker some cock-and-bull yarn to set his mind at ease. Then, the more he had thought about it, the less of a risk it had become. Those cases contained loot, there was no other word for it. Tripz had served in a destroyer in the Norwegian campaign and had seen senior officers shipping their stolen booty back to Germany. They came down like an avalanche on any poor sailor who so much as lifted a bottle of beer without permission. It was all wrong. Leitner must be in it up to his neck, although a ship was the last place Tripz would have stored it, unless he could not trust anybody.

He said, 'Suppose we're wrong? Maybe all the boxes are full of papers, secret files and the like.' He could see that Brezinka did not think so either. 'If we are, we'll drop it right there.'

Brezinka removed the pipe and shook it at him. 'You bloody rogue!' He grinned. 'How *could* we have a look-see? The place is guarded, day and night, and we don't want half the ship's company getting involved. I'm an old bugger, but not ready for the firing party just yet, thank you very much!'

'Nor me.' Tripz rubbed his chin. 'The only time the place is left without a sentry is –'

The boatswain frowned. 'I know. When the ship is closed up at action stations, you in your turret, and me in damage-control. No, mate, it just won't work.'

Tripz sighed. 'What about Rudi Hammer?'

The boatswain stared incredulously. 'Mad Rudi? You must be as crazy as he is!'

Hammer was a petty officer with the damage-control party and on the face of it, the obvious choice. He was no boot-licker, not even a Party member, and although he said very little, was liked by almost everyone, perhaps because of his eccentricity. His hobby was glass. He was determined to retain his skills as a glazier, in spite of all his mechanical training, and nothing could deter him. His divisional officer had had him on the carpet several times about scrounging glass and cluttering his mess with it; he had even taken him in front of Theil because of it. Glass was dangerous in a confined space, especially if the ship was suddenly called to action.

It made no difference. Some hinted that Rudi Hammer's apparent dedication was his way of staying sane, not the other way round.

Brezinka persisted, 'You couldn't rely on him, Oskar, he might blow the whole plan to the executive officer.'

Tripz shook his head. 'He hates officers, you know that, Rolf.'

'But, but – ' Brezinka grappled for words. 'It makes me sweat, just thinking about it. No, we'd best forget the whole idea.'

Tripz said, 'If Rudi has any doubts, you know who he goes to?'

The boatswain swallowed hard. 'Well, *me*.'

'Exactly.' He leaned over to stub out the cigar. 'I'll put it to him. The rest is up to you.' He knew that his friend was wavering. 'Look, Rolf, we've been through a lot together. Remember the time we sold that fishing boat to a Yank, when it belonged to the harbour master?'

The boatswain grinned sadly. 'It would have meant jail in those days, not the chop.'

'They'll dump us when this lot's over. Like last time. I don't want to end up on the scrap heap, begging for bread, do you?'

Brezinka nodded firmly. 'No. You're bloody right, old friend. Let's just have a peep at the boxes.' He winked. 'Just for the hell of it.'

They both laughed and then solemnly shook hands.

'Mad Rudi it is.'

She lay as before propped up on pillows, her face pale in the bunk light.

Hechler heard Stroheim's orderly leave the cabin and after a slight hesitation sat down beside the bunk.

She watched him and said, 'You look tired.'

He saw that she had placed her hands under the sheet. In case he might touch one, he thought.

'How are you feeling?'

She smiled. 'The motion is awful. I was nearly sick.' She saw his concern and added, 'I'm feeling better. Really.'

Hechler heard the dull clatter of equipment, the buzz of a telephone somewhere. Perhaps for him. No, the red handset by the bunk was silent. Mocking him.

He explained how the ship was moving slowly to reach their rendezvous at the right time.

She listened in silence, her eyes never leaving his face.

'Don't you get tired of it?' She reached out from beneath the sheet and gripped his hand. 'It never ends for you, does it?'

He looked at her hand, as he had on the bridge that first time. Small but strong. He found he was squeezing it in his own.

'You know about the plan to fly off our Arados ahead of the ship?'

She nodded. 'Yes. The admiral came down to see me.' She seemed to sense he was about to withdraw his hand and said, 'No. Stay like this, please.'

Hechler grimaced. 'I am behaving like an idiot again.'

She returned his grip and smiled at him. 'A nice idiot.'

He asked, 'Can it be done?' He had pictured the two pilots missing their way, flying on and on before they fell into the sea.

She seemed surprised, touched that he should ask.

She replied, 'Yes, they could find it. After that – '

Hechler pushed it from his thoughts and said, 'I want you to be well again very soon.' He studied her face, feature by feature. 'My little bird belongs up there, where she is free.' He smiled and added, 'I wish – '

She saw his hesitation and asked softly, 'You wish I was not here, is that it? You are going to fight, sooner or later, and you are afraid for me?' She tried to raise herself but fell back again. 'Do you think I cannot tell what is going on in that mind of yours? I have watched you, listened to what your men say, I gather fragments about you, because it is all I have!' She shook her head against the pillow. 'Don't you *see*, you stupid man, I want you to *like* me!' She was sobbing now, the tears cutting down her cheeks and on to the pillow. 'And I look a mess. How could you feel more than you do?'

Hechler placed his hand under her head and turned it towards him. Her hair felt damp, and he saw a pulse jumping in her throat, so that he wanted to press her tightly against him and forget the hopelessness of it, the drag of the ship around them. He dabbed her face with the corner of the sheet and murmured, 'I dare not use my filthy handkerchief!' He saw her staring up at him, her lips parted as he continued quickly, 'You do not look a mess. You couldn't, even if you wanted to.' He touched her face and pushed some hair from her eyes. 'And I do like you.' He tried to remain calm. 'More than I should. What chance – '

She touched his mouth with her fingers. 'Don't say it. Not now. The world is falling down about us. Let us hold on to what we have.' She pulled herself closer to him until her hair was against his face.

'You came for me. I shall never forget. I wanted you to know.'

It was more than enough for her and he could feel the drowsiness coming over her again as if it was his own.

He lowered her to the pillow and adjusted the sheets under her chin. In the adjoining cabin he heard the orderly humming loudly, a warning perhaps that the doctor was on his rounds.

Then he bent over and kissed her lightly on the mouth.

A telephone buzzed in the other cabin and he turned to face the door as the white-coated orderly peered in at him.

'The Admiral, sir.'

Hechler nodded and glanced down again at her face. She was asleep, a small smile still hovering at the corners of her mouth.

Hold on to what we have.

He found he could accept it, when moments earlier he had believed that he had nothing left to hold on to.

13

Revelations

Acting Commodore James Cook Hemrose trained his binoculars towards the oncoming cruiser and watched as she started to swing round in a wide arc, in readiness to take station astern of the *Pallas*.

It should have been a proud, satisfying moment. The newcomer was the third ship in his squadron, the *Rhodesia*, a graceful vessel armed with twelve six-inch guns. Fast, and fairly new by wartime standards, she was commanded by Captain Eric Duffield, a contemporary of Hemrose; they had even been classmates at Dartmouth. Hemrose grimaced angrily. That felt like a million years ago.

He saw the diamond-bright blink of her signal lamp, heard his chief yeoman call, 'From *Rhodesia*, sir. Honoured to join you.'

Hemrose would have liked to send a witty reply, but the moment had soured him. Duffield would hate being ordered here, to serve under his command. They had always been rivals. Even with women.

He snapped, 'Acknowledge.' It was strange, these *Mauritius* Class cruisers were in fact slightly smaller than his own ship, but they appeared larger, more rakish.

The destruction of the convoy by the German raider had been hard to take, when so many warships were out searching for her. But it had put an edge to their purpose; he had felt it too when he had visited the New Zealander, the *Pallas*. A spirit of determination, a need for revenge.

Now there would be a sense of disbelief, anti-climax even, with the obvious prospect of being returned to general duties. He tried not to face the other important fact. It would also mean dipping his temporary promotion. He ground his teeth. *For all time.*

He lowered his glasses and watched the new cruiser continuing to turn in a great display of creaming wash. The weather was quite faultless. Clear blue sky, sunshine to display *Rhodesia*'s square bridge and raked funnels, her four triple turrets. When Duffield had finished buggering about, getting his ship perfectly on station, he would doubtless make another signal. To say he was sorry that the hunt was over. Meaning exactly the opposite.

Hemrose saw the commander hovering nearby and said, 'What time is our ETA at Simonstown?'

The commander watched him doubtfully. Hemrose had been even more difficult since The News, as it was termed in the wardroom. He could sympathise with Hemrose, although in secret Commander Godson was not sorry to be spared from crossing guns with a ship like *Prinz Luitpold*.

'We go alongside at sixteen hundred tomorrow.'

Hemrose had thought about it until his brain throbbed.

They had received a lengthy signal from the Admiralty, and an even longer top-secret intelligence report. It was quite plain. He should swallow his disappointment, even his pride, and accept it. A United States submarine had made a brief emergency signal to announce that she was in contact with the raider. There had been a shorter one, too garbled to decode properly. It was her last word.

When US warships had finally reached the search area, they had found nothing for a full day, except for a two-mile oil slick, and some cork chippings of the kind used in a submarine's internal paintwork to diminish condensation. Then later, as another darkness had closed in, one of the ships had picked up some human remains. To all accounts there had been little enough to discover in the grisly fragments, except that they were German.

The American submarine was known to have collided with a freighter which had failed to stop after their brief contact. The US commander had signalled that he was returning to base only partly submerged because of the damage to hull and hydroplanes.

Hemrose had considered the signals with great care, and had called the New Zealand captain, Chantril, across for a conference.

The Kiwi had accepted it philosophically.

'So the Yank got in a lucky salvo. Beat us to the punch. But it cost him dearly for doing it.'

Hemrose slumped in the bridge chair and said, 'Get a signal off to Simonstown, Toby. The squadron will refuel on arrival. But *lighters*, not alongside.' He slammed his hands together. 'I want to be ready for sea at the first hint of news.'

The commander opened his mouth and closed it promptly. It was obviously going to drag on until the boss accepted the inevitable. He ventured, 'They won't like it, sir.'

Hemrose slid from the chair and snapped, 'Plotting team in the chart-room, chop chop. I've got a *feeling* about that bloody German.'

In the cool shadows of the spacious chart-room Hemrose glared at his team. A mixed collection, he thought. But he had to admit that they had done well in their new role. Even the chaplain, who had devised a special file of sighting reports and information from neutral sources. It had all come together far better than he had dared to hope. Until the news about the submarine.

He knew they were watching him, gauging his temper. That suited him. He had always found that fear was the best prop to naval leadership.

The navigating officer had updated the charts daily, adding known convoys, escort groups, and isolated strangers in the vast sea area which touched two continents.

Even the progress of a solitary hospital ship was noted. They were always at risk. A U-boat commander might put one down because he had not taken the time to identify the markings, or the brightly lit hull at night-time. Or another, who was on his way back to base, might do it because his search for victims had been ill rewarded.

117

Hemrose pictured his German captain. No, he was not the sort to sink a hospital ship with its cargo of sick and wounded survivors. Hemrose held no admiration for Hechler whatever. He did not even know much about him, other than the intelligence reports and some newspaper articles, but he knew his worth as a fighting sailor. He could still remember the ship reeling over to the aggressive mauling of those eight-inch guns. Hechler was a man who took risks, who would not damage that reputation by killing wounded men.

He said, 'What do we know, gentlemen, *really* know?' They remained silent and he added, 'Some Jerry remains were picked up but we cannot be certain they were from *Prinz Luitpold*. Or if they were, she might be damaged, steaming away to put it right, preparing to come back into the fight when she's good and ready.'

The navigating officer, a fresh-faced lieutenant who had proved his ability even to Hemrose's satisfaction, said, 'My guess is the latter, sir. She was damaged, and is making for home base again.' He looked at the others as if for support. 'And why not? She's wiped out a convoy and other ships besides – she'll likely get a hero's welcome if she makes it back to Norway or wherever.'

Hemrose nodded, his heavy features giving nothing away. 'Good thinking, Pilot. In which case the Home Fleet will catch the bugger this time.' He looked round. 'Ideas?'

The chaplain cleared his throat. 'But suppose the raider is still at large, sir. Where will she go next? How does she find fuel?'

'Fucking good question.' He saw the chaplain wince at his crude comment, as he had known he would. 'She'll likely go for the big troop convoy, although my guess is that she's left it too late. The escort has already put down two U-boats, and they've not lost a single ship as yet.'

The navigating officer tapped the chart. 'There's the iron-ore convoy, sir. It should be near the Falklands about now.' He lifted the chart to peer underneath. 'Two more off Durban, both destined for the UK, and of course the fast oil convoy from the Gulf.'

Hemrose pictured the network of convoy routes in and out of Britain. In two great wars those same lifelines had almost been cut. Had that happened, the country, and therefore her dwindling allies would have been brought down. So many times, the convoy losses in the Atlantic had outpaced their ability to build replacements. It had been a raging battle from the first day, and the casualties had been awesome. Yet still men went back to sea, again and again, with only a handful of clapped-out escorts to protect them or die too.

He tried to picture himself in *Wiltshire*, a lone raider like Hechler's ship. *At large*, as the chaplain had described it. He would. But the man of God had a point about fuel supplies. It had to be something big before *Prinz Luitpold* could run for home. Iron-ore? He peered at the chart, his shadow across it like a cloud. Once it could have been vital, but not now. Not unless Mister Hitler pulled another rabbit from his hat. The Russians were still advancing, and the Allies were about to burst across the Rhine. It was still almost too hard to believe after all the retreats and stupid mistakes.

The Durban convoys then? He examined the navigator's typed notes. Times, dates, weather, and already some hint of the escort. He said bluntly, 'I'd go for the big prize.' He thrust the upper charts aside. 'The oilers. Still the most valuable convoy, no matter what the newspapers blather about.'

The commander said, 'It would be a terrible risk, sir.' He flinched under Hemrose's red-rimmed stare. 'For the krauts, I mean.'

'Of course it would.' He stood back and decided he would have a Horse's Neck in a few moments to settle his thoughts. 'He could get cut off on the wrong side of the Cape of Good Hope if he decides to go looking for the convoy too soon.'

The commander said, 'But if their lordships and the C-in-C have already considered this, then surely – '

Hemrose beamed at him. Godson's stupidity was somehow reassuring. He had not missed the fact that none of them had further suggested that the *Prinz Luitpold* had been destroyed, or that they were all wasting their time.

He nodded, his mind made up. 'Did you signal Simonstown?'

The commander sighed. 'All agreed, sir.'

Hemrose rubbed his hands. 'Captains' conference immediately we anchor.'

The navigator looked up from the chart and asked simply, 'But if we're wrong, sir?'

Hemrose did not reply at once. 'You mean if *I'm* wrong, Pilot?' They all laughed politely.

Hemrose picked up his cap and studied it. It would look good with another row of oak leaves around the peak, he thought.

He said, 'My wife won't like it a bit.'

Not one of them realised that he actually meant it.

Korvettenkapitän Josef Gudegast stood with his hands on his hips and waited for the two Arado pilots to scribble a few more notes on their pads. It might be another warm day, but the dawn air in the conning tower was cold and dank. The massive steel door purred open on its slide and Gudegast saw the captain framed against a dull grey sky.

'Nearly ready, sir.'

Hechler glanced at the two pilots who had sprung to attention. 'At ease.' He knew Gudegast would take care of everything. He had done it often enough, but the pilots had to be certain of their orders. Both float-planes had been stripped of unnecessary weight, and would carry no bombs.

As Leitner had replied testily when this had been mentioned, 'We want to use the radio station, not blow its bloody mast down.'

He was up there now on his bridge, impatient, eager to get moving.

Hechler went over it again. Both aircraft would land in a tiny sheltered strip of water, and the landing party would go ashore without delay in rubber dinghies. The planes would be packed like cans of sardines, he thought. He lingered over the officer in charge, Oberleutnant Bauer. An obvious choice as he was a communications specialist. But he had done very little field training, so a good petty officer had been selected as second-in-command. Eight men in all, excluding the pilots. The intelligence reports were definite about the radio station. It was never fully operational and reliable reports stated that it was about to be adapted as a giant radar beacon. The invasion of Europe had made that an unwanted luxury. There were only three men on that lonely pinnacle of rock. Gudegast had said, 'What a way to fight a war. The poor bastards might never be told if it's over, or who's won!'

Theil had snapped at him, 'The war will end for *them* if they try to sabotage the station!'

Poor Theil, he was looking more strained, with deep lines around his mouth.

Hechler said, 'Met reports are good.' He looked at each of the fliers and recalled Leitner's angry outburst when he had suggested that the new Arado should be sent, and so keep a fully operational one on board, just in case.

Leitner had shouted, 'That is defeatist talk, Captain! For a man of action you seem beset by caution! The new plane will be employed *when I say so*!'

He too seemed more on edge. The prospect of action, the apparent lack of enemy signals. It was like steaming into an impenetrable fog.

Hechler glanced at the bulkhead clock. 'Five minutes.' He nodded to the pilots. 'Good luck.' He recalled his letters to the parents of the men lost in the Baltic. Their faces already wiped from his memory. He resisted the urge to shiver.

He made his way to the forebridge, and noted the lookouts and gun crews huddled together at their defence stations.

There goes the captain. He could almost hear the whispers. *Does he look worried?*

He waited for a seaman to wipe the moisture from his chair and then climbed into it.

Korvettenkapitän Werner Froebe had the morning watch, his face red in the chilled air, his huge hands wrapped around the gyro-repeater so that it looked no larger than a coffee cup. Young Jaeger was nearby, ready to relay orders, watching and learning. He seemed to have become suddenly mature after the lifeboat, and the convoy.

Hechler thought of their two survivors. The aged boatswain was still in a kind of daze, and Stroheim said that he rarely paid attention to anything that was happening. The other one, the young mate called Ames, had made a complete recovery. Hechler pictured the drifting corpses. If anyone ever got over that sort of experience.

Theil joined him on the gratings, his fingers busily adjusting his powerful binoculars.

Hechler glanced at him. 'After we find the convoy, Viktor, we can turn for home. Fight our way right through the British Fleet if need be.'

The first Arado coughed into life and he tasted the sharp tang of high-octane fuel. Surprise was everything. It was unlikely that the crew of the radio station would even guess what had hit them. After all, it had never happened before.

A phone buzzed and the seaman who picked it up yelled, 'Ready, sir!'

Hechler could imagine Leitner peering down from his armoured nest. But he did not turn to look. 'Go!'

The plane roared along the short catapult, dived clumsily towards the water, rallied and then climbed away from the slow-moving ship.

Voices muttered by the starboard ladder and Jaeger said, 'Visitor, sir.'

Hechler glanced across in time to see Theil's frowning disapproval and a signalman's quick grin.

She crossed the bridge very carefully, her hair rippling over her coat collar while she rested on a stanchion for support. Hechler took her hand and guided her to the chair. Once, he glanced up to Leitner's bridge and thought he saw the admiral's cap move back quickly out of sight.

He asked, 'How are you?' He noticed the way she was holding her side and wondered why she had come. All those ladders, and she was still weak from losing so much blood.

She settled down on the chair and tucked her chin into a scarf. 'The doctor said it was safe.' She watched the second Arado as it roared away from the side, the camouflage dull against the dark, heaving water. 'I feel better already.'

Hechler heard Froebe say, 'The camera is cranking away, I see! God, we'll all be film stars yet!'

Hechler looked at her and found he was able to shelve his immediate problems. The next fuelling rendezvous. The convoy. The cost in ships and men. Perhaps after that, Leitner would be content. He ought to be.

He offered, 'You look fine. You've got your colour back.'

She looked at him, and for a few moments it was like a bond, a physical embrace although neither of them had moved.

A seaman called, 'From W/T office, sir. They are monitoring a broadcast and request instructions.'

Hechler nodded. 'You go down, Viktor. It may be nothing, but we need all the news we can get.'

He thought of Froebe's sarcastic comment, and then of the supply submarine's hideous end. Leitner had said originally that the women of the camera crew would be transferred to the supply boat with their cans of film. The milch-cow had been due to return to base to replenish stocks of fuel. He did not imagine that the two women would be very pleased at being made to wait for another rendezvous, with the prospect of a battle beforehand. With luck, the risk of damage should be minimal. All the enemy's heavy escorts were with the big troop convoy, and other units were still sweeping to the North for some reason. It was likely that valuable though it was, the convoy of oil tankers would rely on speed and a small, local escort until the last long haul to Biscay and beyond.

She was still watching him, her tawny eyes very bright in spite of the misty dawn reflections.

She said, 'It is like going on and on for ever.' She placed her hand on the rail below the screen so that it was just inches from his.

Another voice called, 'Lost contact with aircraft, sir.'

'Very well.' Hechler looked at her hand. It was almost a physical pain. But it was no longer ridiculous, even though any kind of future was nothing more than an idle dream.

She dropped her voice. 'Do you still miss her?'

Hechler stared. 'No. I – I'm not sure. To say I have wasted my other life beyond this ship, is like a betrayal – a deep hurt.'

The words seemed to burst out of him, yet he could not recall ever being so open with anyone. Like being stripped naked, left without any defences.

She said, 'I know what you're thinking, Dieter. You are wrong. I think all the more of you because of your frankness, your sense of honour.'

Hechler was only half aware that she had called him by name, that for just a few seconds her fingers had rested on his wrist.

She added, 'I have never met anybody like you.' She withdrew her hand and shrugged. 'Will you make me say it? Would you despise me if I told you?'

He looked at her. The figures around the bridge seeming to mist over like moisture on metal fittings.

He heard himself say, 'I will not make you. Let me say it, no matter what the rights and wrongs are.'

She said, 'We can decide.'

'Yes.' He looked away, afraid she would change her mind because of his inability to find the words. 'I want you.' It sounded so flat, so crude that he looked at her, expecting to see anger, or contempt. He was shocked by the happiness in her eyes, a new brightness there like the moment in his quarters.

She whispered, 'It's all I needed to hear. I've known there was something, I think from the beginning.' She shook her head as if she barely believed it. 'We must talk.'

Jaeger said, 'W/T office, sir.' He held out the telephone, his eyes on the girl.

'Captain?'

It was Theil. 'It was just some Brazilian radio station, sir.' He sounded petulant, as if he thought a junior officer could have been sent to deal with it.

Hechler looked at the horizon. The light was strengthening all the time. He tried to picture it in his mind. One hundred miles to the Cable and Wireless outpost. They should have arrived by now. Give them another five minutes, then full speed ahead. The *Prinz* would be there in three hours. By that time – he glanced at the chair but it was empty. He looked at Jaeger who said, 'She went below, sir.' He sounded very calm, but his young face asked a million questions. Something to tell his hero father about, if they ever got home again.

He heard Theil, humming quietly in his ear. A nervous sound. Hechler said, 'Never mind, Viktor. Check it through. You might glean something, eh?' He put the telephone in Jaeger's hand. 'Ask the navigating officer to come here.' He smiled, glad of something to distract him as he saw Gudegast already present, stripping off the canvas cover from the ready-use chart-table after a quick glance at the clear sky.

'What do you think?'

Gudegast stuck out his lower lip so that his untidy beard sprouted over his uniform, mottled with grey like frost on a bush.

'Now, sir.'

Hechler nodded. The W/T office would have picked up any alarm call from the island if the mission had gone rotten on them. There was always the chance of course that the two pilots had lost their way. He saw Gudegast's expression and knew it was less than likely.

'Take over. Full speed. Warm radar, and tell the Gunnery Officer to muster his landing party.'

Hechler would not be able to step ashore. Nothing was safe any more. But it would have been like a release to tread on firm ground again. With her. Her fingers inside his. Just a few moments of make-believe. He had said it to her. *I want you.* He examined his feelings, and the words seemed stronger than ever. It was true. He climbed into the chair. She had been loved, perhaps even married. He took another glance at his thoughts. Nothing changed. It was not a dream after all.

Theil watched the stooped shoulders of the radio operators, and listened to the endless murmur of morse and static over the speakers. The junior officer in charge, Leutnant zur See Ziegler, stared at him anxiously and said, 'I am not certain, sir. My superior has left no instructions – '

Theil glared. 'I'll deal with it!' He gripped the handle of Leutnant Bauer's private office and then rattled it angrily.

Ziegler stammered, 'It's locked, sir.'

'I can see that, you dolt!' He knew he was being unreasonable but somehow he could not contain it. Perhaps seeing Hechler with that girl had done it. He was married. What was he thinking of?

'Give me the key!'

The young one-striper wrenched open a desk and handed it to him. Theil saw that it had a red tag on it. To be used only in a final emergency. He ground his teeth. It was unlikely that anyone would bother about coloured tags with a ship on her last nose-dive to the bottom.

He slammed the door behind him and slumped down in Bauer's chair. It was curious that he had never set foot in here since the ship had been handed over by the builders. A secret place. A nerve centre.

He was growing calmer again and took several deep breaths.

There was a framed photograph of a young naval officer on the desk. Theil picked it up and grunted. It was Bauer himself. Typical of the man. He thought of Stroheim's outburst in the wardroom, the stares of the other officers while he shot his mouth off about some enemy propaganda. Naturally the British would claim all sorts of victories for themselves and their allies. They would hope for fools like Stroheim to listen in and spread the poison.

There was another key on the tag, a much smaller one.

Theil listened to the busy radio-room beyond the door. Back to normal, each man thinking of the one-striper's embarrassment when he had been told off. Serve him right, he thought savagely. We all went through it – he pushed the key into a steel drawer and held his breath as it clicked open.

He was the second-in-command. In battle he stayed with damage-control, whereas Hechler usually stood firm on the open bridge and disdained the massive armour plate of the conning-tower. Theil had thought about it often. He guessed that many officers in his position would consider the very real possibility of stepping into a dead man's shoes.

Even Leitner might fall in battle. Theil suddenly saw himself returning to his home in Schleswig-Holstein, to be decorated by the Leader.

His hand faltered on a pale pink folder with the eagle crest and stamp of naval intelligence emblazoned on the cover. He flicked it open and felt his heart stop. His own name was at the top. Serial number, rank, date of commission, everything. There was his original photograph when he had joined this ship. His fingers felt numb, unable to turn the page. He wanted to lock the drawer, leave now, and to hell with the Brazilian broadcast. There was a freshly typed signal flimsy under the first page. His eyes blurred as he scanned the bottom first where Leitner's signature had been counter-signed by Bauer.

The name at the top was Britta's. Apart from a file reference there was little else except for the line which stood out like fire. No *further action by naval intelligence. Subject arrested by Gestapo.*

Theil did not remember locking the desk drawer, or even groping his way from the office.

The young officer snapped to attention and said, 'Nothing more from that station, sir. I – ' He stared after Theil as he blundered past him and out of the W/T room.

Theil fought his way to the upper deck and clung to the safety rail by a watertight door for several minutes.

Britta arrested? It could not be. For an instant he was tempted to rush back there and read the file again. But it was true. It had to be.

Britta arrested. He squeezed his eyes tightly shut to find her face as he had last seen her. But all he could see was the empty house and dead flowers, the neighbours watching behind their curtains, the doctor's calculated advice.

He wanted to scream it out aloud. They all knew, must have done. Leitner, and that crawling Bauer. He thought of Hechler, his mind reeling like a trapped animal. He would know too, had probably been told weeks ago.

He allowed his mind to rest on the Gestapo. He had always avoided contact with them like most people. Secrecy had not always worked, and he had ignored that too.

But he had heard things. Torture, brutality for the sake of it. He thought of her face, her pleading eyes, the bruise on her body after she had tried to find out about her parents.

Gestapo. It was not just a word any more. It was death.

The ship began to shake and quiver around him and he knew they were increasing speed towards the tiny islet.

What should he do or say?

He turned his face this way and that, clinging to the rail as if he might otherwise fall.

Britta was dead, or was she even now screaming out her pleas to her torturers?

'No!' His one cry was torn from him, but rebounded against the iron plate as if it too was trapped and in agony.

14

'Auf Wiedersehen . . .'

Oberleutnant Hans Bauer strode down the steep, rocky slope and stared at the two float-planes as they lifted and swayed in the swell. They were safe enough, moored with their small anchors, and each with its pilot still aboard in case the sea should get up.

Bauer stood with his feet planted apart, his fine black boots setting off his uniform to perfection. The heavy pistol at his waist, like the silk scarf thrown casually around his throat, gave him a dramatic appearance, or so he believed. He had enjoyed every moment of it, the culmination of surprise and excitement when the two rubber dinghies had been paddled furiously ashore and his men rounded up their prisoners.

It had gone almost perfectly, but for one unexpected development. There had been two extra people at the radio station. He now knew they were mechanics who had been left here for some maintenance work.

Bauer considered what he would say to the rear-admiral. Leitner would give him the praise he was due for his quick thinking. He shaded his eyes to watch the cruiser's shortened silhouette as she headed towards the small islet, only her bow-wave revealing the speed she was making through the water. After she had topped the hard horizon line in the early light she had seemed to take an age to gather size and familiarity, he thought. He went over the landing, the exhilaration giving way to sudden alarm as the two additional men had appeared. Yes, Leitner would be pleased. He frowned. He was not so sure about the captain.

He turned, his boots squeaking on the rough ground, and surveyed the desolated station. A long, curved corrugated building which the British called a Nissen hut, and two radio masts, one small, the other very high and delicate. It was a wonder it could withstand the gales.

He saw two of his men, their Schmeissers crooked in their arms, and congratulated himself on his choice. Hand-picked, and all good Party members. It was right that they should profit by this small but obviously vital operation.

Closer to the building lay a corpse, covered by a sheet which was pinned down by heavy rocks.

One of the visiting mechanics. He had seen the landing party, and had turned, blundering through his astonished companions, and run towards the building. To send a message, a warning, or to sabotage the equipment, Bauer did not know even now.

He remembered his own feeling as the heavy Luger had leaped in his grip, the man spinning round, his eyes wide with horror as he had rolled down the slope kicking and choking. The second bullet had finished all movement. After that, the others had crowded together, shocked and frightened, seeing only the levelled guns, the sprawled body of the dead man.

Bauer had told them to obey each order without hesitation, and after the building had been thoroughly searched, the radio transmitter checked for demolition charges, they had been locked in a storeroom and left under guard.

Bauer adjusted his cap at a more rakish angle, rather as the rear-admiral wore his. Such a fine officer, an example to them all.

He saw the petty officer, a grim-faced man called Maleg, coming down the slope, two grenades bouncing on his hip. He was not one of Bauer's choice for the raid. He thought of Theil who had detailed the man for the operation. Bauer was suddenly grateful he had never cultivated Theil as anything more than a superior officer. He had had everything within his grasp, and had been stupid, instead of taking full advantage of his position. He owed everything to the Fatherland, everything. How could such a man become involved with a subversive, a traitor? He should have known his own wife better than anyone. He sighed. Instead –

The petty officer saluted. 'About the burial, sir?'

Bauer eyed him coldly. 'The prisoners will do it. It should dampen anyone else's foolishness!'

Maleg stared past him at the distant cruiser. They had found no weapons, no demolition charges either. Even the prisoners were harmless civilians. It was all the lieutenant's fault, but any aftermath would be shared amongst them. Bauer had enjoyed killing the man, he decided. Given half a chance he would have gunned down all the rest. Maleg knew about officers like Bauer. Why had he been the one to get saddled with him?

Later as the prisoners stabbed at the rocky ground with picks and spades, Bauer entered the makeshift radio station and looked with disdain at the garish pictures on the walls, the nudes and the big-breasted girls in next to nothing. Decadent. How could they have hoped to win the war, even with the Yanks as allies?

He pictured his family home in Dresden, the paintings of his ancestors, proud, decorated officers. A heritage which was a constant reminder of his own role and his promising future. Leitner had promised him an immediate promotion with an appointment to the naval staff as soon as they returned to a safe harbour. Bauer was not so blind that he did not know about the rear-admiral's relationship with Theissen, his flag-lieutenant, but nothing could mar his qualities as a leader and an inspiration.

Maleg watched him and was glad that the ship was getting nearer. The *Prinz* was something he could understand and work in. He had good comrades in the petty officers' mess. He sniffed at the aroma of fresh coffee from the hut's spindly chimney. It was quite amazing. They had proper coffee and piles of tinned food which he had almost forgotten. He would take some back with him to the mess, he thought. He tried not to dwell on an old newspaper called *Daily Mail* he had found in the sleeping quarters. He could read English fairly well, but even if he had not been able to, the war maps and photographs with their screaming head-lines would have told him anyway. The Allies were said to be through France and Belgium, and the only German resistance was in isolated pockets in Brittany and the Pas de Calais. The sites of the rockets and flying-bombs, the much-vaunted secret weapons, were said to be overrun, their menace removed for all time. It could not all be true. There was mention of some 400,000 German troops being taken prisoner. That could not be accurate, surely?

And the newspaper was not new. What had happened while they had been attacking the convoy? He considered himself to be a good petty officer, and he had destroyed the newspaper before the others could see it.

He looked round as he heard Bauer reading crisply from a small prayer book while the others stood leaning on their spades. Maleg wanted to spit. Kill a man, then send him off with full respects. He watched as Bauer threw up a stiff Nazi salute, then pocketed the prayer book with the same detachment he had shown when he had reholstered his Luger.

The spades moved again and Bauer marched towards the hut.

He said, 'Duty is duty, Maleg, no matter what.'

The petty officer sat down on a rock and waited for one of the men to bring him his coffee.

Suppose. The word hung in his mind. Just suppose they lost the war. It was unthinkable of course, but if the *Prinz* was down here in the South Atlantic, what then?

He turned and peered out at the ship, which in the last minutes seemed to have doubled in size.

Hechler would get them home somehow.

The first Arado was being hoisted up from alongside, many hands reaching out to boom it away from the hull as the ship dipped heavily in the surrounding current.

Leitner had come down to the forebridge, and his cigar smoke drifted over the screen like perfume.

Leitner said, 'Like clockwork. What did I tell you, eh?' He was almost jocular. 'God, what a coup it will be.'

Hechler trained his binoculars on the lonely station. They would land a small party with two of the ship's wireless telegraphists. They would have all the right codes, and even if they had been changed by the enemy, no one would question their one frantic call for help. Several things could go wrong, of course. A vessel might unexpectedly arrive on a visit to the islet. If that happened, a prearranged alarm signal would be made, and the *Prinz* would be on her own again. Or the fuel convoy might be delayed or rerouted. That was so unlikely it could almost be discounted.

What else then? They might meet with enemy warships, be held down to an engagement until heavier forces arrived to join the battle. He had gone over the rendezvous points with Gudegast; there were three possible choices, and the supply submarines would be on station whatever happened.

He glanced at Leitner. The admiral was nobody's fool, and would want to return to Germany as soon as the next convoy was destroyed. They might fall upon other ships on the return passage, small convoys, single fast-moving troopers too.

There was a blackout on Allied radio communications, or so it seemed. The enemy must be puzzled about their sources of fuel supply, and it was likely that all other convoys in the Atlantic had been laid up in their ports until the raider's position was verified.

Hechler was a practical sailor but had never ruled out the value of luck. Theirs simply could not last, and he had often imagined some special task force fanning out from Biscay for a sweep south in pursuit. They would have carriers, or at least one. Just a single sighting report was all the enemy admiral needed.

Feet clattered on the ladder and Theil entered the bridge, his eyes concealed by dark glasses.

He said, 'I've sent a double anchor party up forrard, sir, and given orders to break the cable if need be.'

Leitner's shoulders shook in a small chuckle. 'More caution, eh?'

Theil ignored him. 'Have you selected the men to remain on the islet, sir?'

Hechler looked at him. 'I have spoken to the doctor, Viktor. Three are still in sick-bay after being thrown from their feet.'

Theil replied, 'I have their names, sir. I did think they were malingering.' His voice was quite flat and toneless.

Hechler turned so that Leitner should not hear. 'Are you all right?'

Theil straightened his shoulders. 'I am.'

Hechler nodded. 'Good. We can land the two survivors also.'

Leitner turned. 'When they are picked up eventually, nobody can say we were not humane!' It seemed to amuse him.

Theil stared past him. 'A man was killed over at the radio station.'

Hechler exclaimed angrily. 'When? Why was I not told immediately?'

Leitner said, '*I* was informed. You were busy anchoring the ship, remember?'

Hechler recalled Bauer reporting aboard when a landing party had been sent to relieve him. An hour ago? It seemed like minutes.

Theil had a hand to his chest as if he was in pain but dropped it as he explained, 'Bauer shot one of the mechanics.' He waited and added harshly, 'A civilian.'

Leitner swung round again. 'In God's name, man, what do you expect? I will not have our people put at risk for any reason! Bauer acted as he thought fit. I will uphold his decision. Millions have died in this war, and millions more will follow, I have no doubt!' He was shouting, ignoring the men on watch nearby. 'One bloody shooting is not my paramount concern, thank you, *sir*!'

Theil eyed him blankly from behind the dark glasses.

'Evidently, sir.' He turned and hurried from the bridge.

'Now what the *hell* was that all about?' Leitner grinned, but his eyes remained like cold glass.

Hechler thought he knew Theil. Now he was not sure of anything. He said, 'Nobody wants to see non-combatants killed, sir. I'll grant that it may have been necessary in this case. However – '

Leitner sniffed. '*However* sums it up, I think!'

Hechler was suddenly sick of him, even of Theil. When the latter discovered – he raised his binoculars to watch the party on the beach to hide his sudden apprehension. Suppose Theil already knew? How could he? As captain he had been told nothing until Leitner's anger had let the news spill out about Theil's poor wife.

Strain, combat fatigue, the yearning for a command of his own, of this ship most of all – moulded together they could have this effect on him.

Leitner said, 'You can speak to the men you have detailed. It will come better from you.' He was calm again, but as their eyes met Hechler could sense the spite in his casual remark.

Tell them you are leaving them behind. Why? For Germany? Would it be enough this time? He gritted his teeth. It was all they had.

He said, 'Tell the sick-bay I am coming down.'

Jaeger picked up a handset and watched him walk past.

Command – was this what it meant? Was this what it might do to the man who held it?

Leitner snapped, 'Don't gape! Do as you're told! By God, I intend to produce a full report on all this when we get back to Germany!'

A messenger called nervously, 'Camera team request permission to come to the bridge, sir.'

Leitner moved away from the side and loosened the collar of his white tunic.

'Of course.' He glanced at the others, Gudegast brooding by the chart-table, the petty officer of the watch, young Jaeger, and the rest of those subservient faces.

'All honour will be shown to this ship, gentlemen. A film which our children will remember!'

Gudegast watched him march to the rear of the bridge. Children? The admiral would have no problems there, he thought.

The ship was still in a state of immediate readiness, if not at action stations. On the petty officers' mess-deck, the air was hissing out of the shafts, compressed and smelling faintly of oil. The deadlights were screwed shut, and most of the watertight doors clipped home. The ship was stopped but only resting, and even the fans and muffled generators sounded wary and ready to switch to full power.

The small cluster of men at the end of the tables appeared to be engrossed in the one who was seated, his fingers busily arranging a pattern of coloured glass under an overhead light. Acting Petty Officer Hans Stoecker watched the man's hands working nimbly with the newly cut pieces of glass. Rudi Hammer was putting the finishing touches to yet another small box, a present perhaps for a wife or girlfriend. It was nerve-racking, unbearable, and yet Stoecker knew he must not break the silence. Opposite him, his grey head bowed with no outward show of impatience, Oskar Tripz also watched the box taking shape.

The fingers eased a fragment over and snipped a rough edge away. The man nicknamed Mad Rudi was pale in every respect, hair and lashes, even his skin; he was not far removed from an albino.

Stoecker tried not to think of that day when an unknown hand had given him the letter. The rest was a nightmare.

He glanced at the other petty officer named Elmke, a dour, humourless man whose only friend in the ship, it seemed, was Tripz.

Stoecker wanted to wipe his face. It felt wet with sweat. The sealed air perhaps? He knew otherwise. It was uncontrollable fear and disgust at what he had begun.

It had all seemed like a daring exploit when he had shared the letter with Tripz. He was friend and mentor all in one. But it had got out of hand. Even the boatswain Brezinka was implicated, and now Mad Rudi and Elmke.

He concentrated on the pattern of glass. What would his mother say, and his father when he found out? It had all been so simple, so right. As if it was a kind of destiny. Even meeting with Sophie. He turned the thought aside. She had been with Jaeger. An officer.

Tripz said, 'Well, come along, old fellow, spit it out!' He was grinning, but the tension was clear in his voice. 'We have to know, God damn it!'

Hammer put down the flat-jawed pliers he used for snapping off excess glass. 'I nearly broke that piece!' He shook his head. 'After the war they will need all the glaziers in the world to put the cities together again, you'll see!'

Tripz patted his shoulder. 'God, man, if it's true what we think, you can buy your own glass factory!'

Hammer smiled. He was always such a gentle, reserved man. In his petty officer's uniform he looked like an imposter.

He said severely, 'Well, it wasn't easy, I can tell you.'

Elmke said roughly, 'Come *on*, man!'

Tripz shot him a warning glance. 'Easy, Ludwig! Give him time!'

Hammer smiled. 'It is true. I opened just two of the boxes.' He spread his hands. 'Jewels by the thousand, gems of every kind. Gold too. A factory, Oskar? I could buy a whole town with my share.'

The others stared at each other but Stoecker felt as if his guts were being crushed.

They were speaking of a *share*. It was all accepted, decided even.

He heard himself say a little more than a whisper, 'But if we're found out?'

Surprisingly it was Hammer who spoke up. 'In this ship we can die in a hundred different ways, Hans. I do not believe in miracles. We have fought a just war, but we are losing.' He seemed surprised at their expressions. 'Face it, comrades, it is not so bad when we have discovered an alternative to oblivion, yes?'

Tripz produced a bottle of schnapps. Drinking on duty would cost him his rank, all of them for that matter.

Very solemnly he filled four mugs and they clinked with equal gravity together. 'To us.'

Only Stoecker felt that he wanted to vomit. But the nightmare had already grown in size and power. It had been too late when he had taken that letter.

Hechler walked along the port side beneath the elevated barrels of the anti-aircraft weapons, nodding occasionally to familiar faces, pausing to speak briefly with the petty officer in charge of a working party.

There was no difference from being here at this rock and out on the high seas. The great ocean was the enemy, and yet being anchored made him feel vulnerable, unprepared.

A rising plume of smoke from the funnel showed that Stück and his engineers were equally impatient to move. Men off duty hung about in groups, nervous and not far from their action stations.

A lieutenant crossed the deck and saluted. 'The boat is ready, sir.'

Hechler stared past him at the small landing party, three of whom were still showing signs of their injuries.

It had been a difficult thing to tell them what was required. Hechler knew better than to make a speech. About Germany, the great sacrifice that others had made already.

He had explained simply, 'It is for us, comrades. The ship.'

A senior wireless telegraphist was in charge, with one other assistant, while the remainder were from the sick-bay.

'I shall come back for you if I can.'

He had sensed their efforts to be brave, not to let him down. It was, he thought, one of the hardest things he had ever asked anyone to do.

He walked with the lieutenant to the side, where a motorboat was waiting to transfer the small party to the radio station and bring back the others. After that – he sighed. It was best not to think of how they would feel when they watched their ship speeding away to disappear eventually below the horizon.

They were assembled by the accommodation ladder. Hechler shook hands with each one. He had entrusted a letter to the senior telegraphist to hand to the British or whoever arrived. Under normal circumstances he knew they would be well treated. But with a civilian lying buried on the islet, the letter might ease the situation.

He saw the two prisoners already in the tossing motorboat. The old boatswain had stared at him blankly when he had told him he would soon be released. The other one named Ames had met his gaze, not exactly hostile, but strangely defiant. He had warned the senior telegraphist about him. He was probably safer off the ship, he thought. As a mate, he knew about navigation and would have the *feel* of the sea like Gudegast. You could not watch a man all the time unless he was in irons. He might have been able to escape and sabotage the steering gear or something else vital, even at the cost of his life.

He said, 'I shall send aircraft for you if I can. If not – ' He had almost shrugged but had seen the pain on their faces. 'It is the war. Our success rests in your hands.'

He looked round and saw the sunlight flash on binoculars from the upper bridge, and guessed that Leitner was watching each magnified face and reaction.

He thought of Theil. He should be here too. Something would have to be done before they met the enemy again. When their luck ran out.

Hechler saluted as they climbed down the side, one with a plaster cast on his arm swinging round to stare up at his messmates who waved to him. Suddenly, as if at a sign, one of the sailors at the guardrails began to sing. He had a rich, mellow voice, and as Hechler watched he saw many of his men leaning over the rails, their voices joining and rising above the sea, and the splutter of the boat below the ladder.

'*Auf Wiedersehen – until better days!*'

Hechler watched the boat until it vanished around the high bows then walked slowly aft. He remembered his brother Lothar joining with his fellow cadets and singing that same, lilting song when he had gained his commission.

'That must have been dreadful for you.'

He saw her standing by a screen door, one foot on the raised coaming. How long had she been watching he did not know, and yet in some strange way he had been aware of her.

'It was.' He stood beside her, shielded from the rest of the ship by the heavy, steel door.

She said quietly, 'If the war is won they will be free very soon. If not – ' She did not continue.

He took her hands in his. 'I have been thinking about you.' He felt her return the squeeze. 'Maybe too much. But I have not forgotten our words up there, in my eyrie.' He saw her smile.

She said, 'People, your men, think you are made of iron. An iron pirate, did you know that?'

He looked down at her, studying her mouth, imagining how it would feel trapped in his.

She watched his face, his indecision. 'But I know the *real* man.'

He said, 'After we leave here – ' He tried again. 'When we meet with the enemy – I want you safe. No matter what happens, I need to know you are spared the true danger. After the war – '

Her eyes left his face for the first time. 'I will not wait that long, Dieter.' She looked down and there was fresh colour in her cheeks. 'You think that is cheap, shameless?'

He touched her hair. 'No. I only feel shame for letting you say what I am thinking.'

The junior communications officer, Zeigler, appeared round the door and stared at them blankly.

Then he said, stumbling over his words. 'I have to report that the shore party has tested the signal, sir.' His eyes blinked quickly at the girl as he continued, 'No further enemy broadcasts intercepted.'

'Thank you.' They watched him march off and she said, 'We frightened him, poor boy.'

He knew he must go. 'Later on – '

She stepped back over the coaming, one hand to her side.

'I shall be there. Have no doubt of it.'

Hechler climbed to the bridge and walked to the fore-gratings. Voices hummed up and down the pipes, and messengers and boatswain's mates stood with handsets to their ears and watched the steam from forward as the cables clanked up and through the hawse-pipe.

'Stand by.'

Bells jangled and Gudegast said, 'Course to steer, one-three-five, sir.'

He heard someone murmur behind him, 'See the poor buggers on the beach, Max? I'd hate to be left – '

A petty officer snarled, 'I shall *personally* maroon you if I get the chance! *Stand to*, damn you!'

Hechler felt the sun warming his face through the toughened glass screen. The cable was coming in more quickly now. *Clank-clank-clank*. Would they ever drop anchor again? He smiled despite his anxieties. The Flying Dutchman. He smiled again and seemed to hear her voice. *Iron pirate*. The enemy probably had a less colourful name, he thought.

He craned forward and saw Theil with Leutnant Safer who was in charge of the forecastle, although in action he was quarters officer in Turret Anton. Theil had his arms folded, as if he was hugging himself. Perhaps when they got into open water again he would snap out of his mood.

How would I feel? It was strange that he did not compare Theil's wife's plight with Inger. He pictured Erika's face. Her defiance. And her defeat.

'Anchors aweigh, sir!'

Hechler glanced at the lieutenant of the watch. It was as if the man had had to repeat it before he had understood.

'Slow ahead together.' He felt the deck vibrate gently, the ugly hump of land begin to move past. 'Starboard ten.'

Gudegast crouched over the gyro to check a last fix on the tall aerial.

'Steady. Steer one-three-five.' He picked up the telephone and noticed it had been cleaned. 'Chief? This is the Captain. Revolutions for twenty-five knots in half an hour.'

Stück sounded surprisingly close. 'You told me.'

Hechler grinned. 'Getting old, Chief.' He put down the telephone and saw Jaeger talking with Stoecker, the youngster who should have taken his final exam for petty officer but for this raiding cruise. He was obviously worried about it, for his eyes looked quite red. Lack of sleep probably.

Theil came into the bridge. 'Anchor secured, sir. Hands dismissed.'

He stared round the bridge. 'I'm not sorry. Not in the least.'

'Is there something you want to tell me, Viktor?' He glanced past him. 'Now, while we're alone.'

'*I am worried about my wife.*' He seemed to be staring, although the dark glasses made it hard to gauge his expression.

'I can understand that.'

'Can you?' Theil watched two sea-birds rise above the screen, their raucous cries suddenly loud and intruding.

He added calmly, in an almost matter-of-fact tone, 'You didn't have to consult with the doctor about the landing party, sir. I had it in hand you know.'

Hechler tugged out his unlit pipe and jammed it in his mouth. 'It was my responsibility.'

Theil nodded very slowly, his dark glasses like two sockets in a skull.

'I see that, sir. A commanding officer must shoulder every burden where it concerns those who have to trust him.' He saluted. 'I must go to damage control and exercise the fire parties.' He added vaguely, 'Might help.'

Hechler made to climb into his chair but walked instead to the opposite side.

Theil was right. *I must tell him.* But Theil's words, his erratic behaviour, held him back, like a warning.

He turned and saw Gudegast watching him from the compass platform. The navigator dropped his gaze immediately, but not before Hechler had seen the concern there. Did he believe that Theil was falling apart? Even his bitter comment about asking the doctor. He was still angry about the scene in the wardroom, and Leitner's offhand indifference.

He raised his binoculars and trained them over the quarter towards the radio tower, but it was already blurred and indistinct. He thought of the unknown seaman's words. *I'd hate to be left.*

Korvettenkapitän Froebe, the executive officer, stamped on to the gratings and saluted.

'Well?' Hechler felt the warning again but could not recognise it.

Froebe shifted his long, ungainly legs.

'I hate to bother you, sir, but one of my divisional officers has made a complaint. He has threatened – '

Hechler stopped him. 'Nobody threatens you, Werner. You are part of my authority, a most important one.' He saw the words go home, some relief on the tall officer's features.

'The communications officer – '

Hechler kept his face impassive. It would be Bauer. A man of great conceit. He had certainly displayed no remorse over killing the civilian.

Leitner had given him his blessing. Was that all it took, after all? *I did my duty, nothing more.*

Froebe continued, 'He claims that the second-in-command entered his private office after forcing the watch-officer to give him the key.'

It hit Hechler like a steel bar.

So that was it. It was so obvious he could not understand how he had missed it. He had even ordered Theil to go there himself.

'You have told me, Werner. Leave it with me, eh?' He smiled, but his mouth felt like stiff leather.

Froebe bobbed his head, satisfied and relieved.

'And tell Bauer to mind his manners. Tell him from me.'

He heard Froebe clattering down a ladder and then bit hard on the pipe-stem. Theil knew. Who would blame him? What might he do?

When the sun dipped towards the empty horizon he was still sitting in the chair, and his questions remained unanswered.

15

Middle Watch

Gudegast crouched over the chart-table and rubbed his eyes to clear away the weariness. It was two in the morning, but he could not sleep, and wanted to make sure he had forgotten nothing. He read slowly through his neatly written notes and paused again and again to check the calculations against his two charts. The ship was quivering violently beneath him, but he had grown used to that. She was steaming at twenty-eight knots, south-east, over an unbroken sea.

On deck it was easier to understand with a ceiling of bright stars from horizon to horizon. Here in the chart-room, it was all on paper. Noon sights, and careful estimations of tide, speed and weather. It was vaguely unnerving, with only the chart lights for company, but for a while longer he needed to be alone.

He tried not to think of a hot bath, scented with some of that Danish stuff he had picked up in Vejle. So long ago, he thought wistfully. He scratched himself beneath his arm as he pictured the voluptuous Gerda in her little house above the fjord. There would not be many baths from now on. Water was strictly rationed, and it would get worse unless they returned home. Home? Where was that?

He heard feet scrape against steel and guessed that the watch was changing its lookouts yet again. An empty ocean outside, and yet in here you could see the inevitability of the embrace, the savagery of the approaching battle.

It would have to be a salt-water shower. He grinned into his beard. He must be getting soft as well as old. In the merchant service, where the owners counted and begrudged every mark spent, you got used to faulty fans, bad food, and machinery which went wrong at the worst moment. It had taken him a long while to get used to the navy, its extravagance at the taxpayer's expense.

The door slid open and he turned with an angry challenge on his lips. Instead he said, 'I've been over it all again, sir.' He watched Hechler by the table, his body shining in an oilskin. So he could not sleep either. *If I were captain* – he stopped it there. Gudegast would not have taken command of a warship if she were ballasted with gold bricks.

Hechler compared the charts. 'At this rate, fifty-seven hours.' He pictured the desert of ocean, their solitary ship heading swiftly on a converging course. There had been no signals from Operations Division, and silence in this case meant that the convoy was on course, and should now be around the Cape and steering north-west. Fifty-seven hours was too long. He peered closer at the pencilled lines and crosses. To increase speed would dig deeply into their fuel supply. To risk a late confrontation might invite disaster. He said, 'Thirty knots.'

Gudegast regarded him gravely. The cruiser could go faster, but she was not on sea trials, nor was she within reach of help if something failed.

Hechler smiled. 'I have just spoken with the Chief.' He saw him in his mind, cautious as ever, but quite confident. 'He agrees.'

Gudegast watched him, feeling his disquiet. 'After this, we can refuel at one of the rendezvous.'

Hechler glanced at him and smiled. It had sounded like a question, a challenge.

'My admiral favours the second rendezvous, 2,500 miles to the west.'

Gudegast dragged the second chart closer. The bright cross marked the exact grid position only; dates and times were safely locked in Hechler's safe.

Gudegast pursed his lips. 'The last thing the enemy would expect.'

'What you really mean is, we could be heading further north to the other rendezvous, and cutting off some 900 miles, right?'

Gudegast showed his teeth. 'Something like that, sir.'

'Fuel economy is not always the answer.'

Gudegast picked up his parallel rulers. 'I'll work on it for a while. An alternative might come in handy.'

Hechler nodded. 'I shall be increasing speed in two hours when the watch changes. Let me know what you find in your search.' He paused, one hand on the door clip. 'But get some sleep. I depend on you. You know that.'

The door slid shut and Gudegast stared at it with quiet astonishment. He both liked and respected the captain, but he had never thought that his feelings had been returned.

He grinned and turned back to his charts. He would do a sketch of the captain at the first opportunity. Just him with the ocean behind his back. It was something to look forward to.

Hechler did not remember much about leaving the chart-room, nor did he feel the usual guilt at not being on the bridge or in his little sea-cabin.

The charts, Gudegast's finality over the converging ships, had cast a cloak over all else. There was nothing, could be nothing beyond this ship, he told himself. Even if his suspicions about Theil were correct, he could not reveal it now or Leitner would have him arrested, humiliated and disgraced before everyone. God, it was bad enough as it was. Theil loved the *Prinz* as much if not more than all of them. He would not do anything to destroy that loyalty. But if the shock of his wife's arrest had acted as a twist of guilt, he might not even be the man he had once known.

He almost smiled. He was the one who had told Theil about a captain's responsibility.

An armed sentry stiffened at attention as he clipped a watertight door behind him. He stared at the passageway with its shaded emergency lights, the blank-faced doors, the racks of fire-fighting gear laid out like an omen.

Hechler walked past the sentry and knew the man was staring after him. It was strange but he did not care. Not about that anyway. The whole ship had probably made up its mind long ago. Then he paused and listened to the movements about him, the gentle rattle of equipment, the shiver of metal as the great ship sliced through the water. Nearly a thousand souls were contained within her graceful hull. Men as varied as Theil and Gudegast, young Jaeger and the acid-tongued Kröll. On and on forever, she had said. With a start he realised he was standing outside the door of his own quarters. Perhaps he had known what he was doing, or had he allowed his heart to steer him?

He felt it pounding against his ribs, a terrible uncertainty which made him hesitate and stare at himself like a stranger. Tomorrow was the day which would tell. After that, their future could only be measured by hours and by luck.

But that was tomorrow.

He tapped the door and opened it.

The day-cabin was in total darkness and he saw her sitting beside the bunk in the adjoining one, staring towards him so that the door's rectangle stood out like an intimate photograph.

She wore his dressing gown, the one with his initial on the pocket, which his brother had given him on that last birthday together. It was shabby, but he would never part with it.

He walked towards her as she said, 'I have worn it several times.' She moved her arms beneath it. 'It helped.'

He rested his hands on her shoulders and drew her to her feet. They stood together for a long while until he pulled her against him. She did not resist, nor did she respond as he stroked her hair, and pressed his hand against her spine.

He murmured, 'I had to come, Erika.'

She lowered her face against his chest. 'I *willed* you to be here, with me.' She leaned back in his arms and studied his face. 'Welcome to our new home.'

She smiled, but he could feel the tension like a living thing, the nervousness which stripped away her outer confidence. Hechler sat her down on the bunk and knelt against her, his head pressed into her body. He felt her hand in his hair, moving back and forth, gentle and yet demanding, speaking for both of them.

She said softly, 'You won't stay, Dieter. I know you can't.' When he tried to look up at her she gripped his neck and held him more tightly.

'No. Hear me. You said you wanted me. We cannot wait.' He tried to free himself but her arm was like a band around his head. 'I – I feel so shy now that I have said it. But it means so much – ' He took her wrist and lifted his face to watch her, to share the emotion her eyes revealed.

Hechler said, 'I love the way you are.' He felt her shiver as he untied the dressing gown and pulled it open. He kissed the warm skin and then dragged the dressing gown down until her shoulders, then her breasts were naked. He kissed her hard on each breast, felt her gasp as he pressed each nipple in turn with his lips, until neither of them could stand it.

He laid her on the bunk and undressed her. It was without gentleness, but she reached out to help him, until she lay watching him, her naked body shining in the solitary light above the bunk.

Hechler did not even glance at the telephone above them – it could shatter their moment with the ruthless power of a torpedo. He saw the livid scar on her side, as if some beast had sunk its jaws into her body. She seized his head as he placed his mouth over the wound.

It seemed as if life was compressed into a single moment. There had been nothing before, and ahead was only uncertainty like an empty horizon.

He wanted her so much that it hurt, and yet he needed this moment to last forever. Even when he took her limbs, stroked and kissed them, or ran his fingers around and deep into the dark triangle of hair, he clung to each precious second as if it was the last. She was no longer passive, she was dragging at his clothing, pulling him over and against her until she could find and hold him.

For just a fraction of time more they looked at each other, their faces almost touching, and then, with her hand urging and guiding him into her, they were joined. Then, as they fell together, with love and in passion, Hechler knew that no matter what lay ahead, life without her would be pointless.

Hechler slumped in the tall chair, his face stinging with salt and spray, his ribs seemingly bruised by the pressure of his ship crashed through the long Atlantic swell. Was it lighter? Were those millions of stars smaller? It was said that only at sea, on an open bridge, could a man truly understand the reality and the power of God.

He rubbed his eyes with the back of his glove and heard a man move with alarm. It could be no fun to stand the middle watch with your captain always present. He thought of the friendly glow of the reading light above the untidy bunk in his sea-cabin. At any other time he would have dived into it, fully dressed, needing a shave as he did now, not caring for anything but escape. Not this time. He had wanted to stay awake, had needed to, in case he lost something of those precious moments.

It was so clear in his mind, her body thrusting against his, her cry of pain, the instant pressure of hands on his shoulders when he made to draw away. He had hurt her. It had been a long time. How right. The same for them both.

He touched his face and decided he would have a shave. He looked into the black shadows below the chair, both happy and shamed. His face must have been as rough as the clothes which he had worn, when he had felt her beneath him, sensed her legs spread out and over the side of the bunk. He could not recall anything like it, so complete, like a frankness which had pitched all barriers aside. And afterwards it had remained between them. More than just a bond, far more than a momentary passion for sex.

He glanced at the lieutenant of the watch; it was Ahlmann again.

Hechler wanted to touch himself beneath the oilskin, as if he was still sharing it. For he could still feel her. As if it had just happened.

Figures moved behind him and he heard the boatswain's mate of the watch ask politely, 'Some coffee, Captain?'

Hechler glanced down at him and nodded. Whatever it was, it would taste like champagne.

He said, 'I shall go to my sea-cabin for a shave afterwards.'

He peered at his luminous watch. When the time came to increase speed and alter course perhaps for the last time before – he did not dwell on the possibilities. They were all behind. Only this moment was real and important.

He thought of the small landing party he had left at the Cable and Wireless station. What would they be doing? Playing cards, writing letters, something sailors usually did without the slightest knowledge of when they would be sent on their way, let alone read by their loved ones.

His mind strayed to the convoy. It would make a big hole in the enemy's fuel supplies. For how long? Two weeks – ten? Even a few days could make all the difference to the embattled armies while they waited for winter, their most needed ally.

He thought of the meeting in Kiel with von Hanke, the way he had looked at him when he had disputed the German army strength on the Russian Front. An oversight? It seemed hardly likely. In his great command bunker was the Führer also deluded by the maps and victorious arrows and flags? Could it be that *nobody* dared to tell their leader the terrible truth? That half of his finest divisions were buried by their thousands in the mud and snow of Russia? It was stupid to think of such things. The ship was only a part of the whole; nobody, not the General Staff, Donitz, not even the Führer could see the complete picture.

Someone coughed behind him and several voices whispered pleased or sarcastic greetings to the morning watch as they changed places with those who had stood the past four hours.

Froebe stooped beneath the chart-table's protective hood and spoke briefly with Ahlmann and his junior assistant. Then he stood up, glanced at the captain as if to ascertain whether he was awake or dozing and said, 'The watch is relieved.'

Feet shuffled on wet steel, and the smell of coffee drifted amongst the newly awakened officers and seamen like a welcome drug. Between decks the watchkeepers threw themselves into their blankets, some in hope of sleep, others merely to find solitude when surrounded by so many.

Thoughts of home, worries about shortages there, bombing, the next leave and the last one. It was all part of a sailor's life.

In the great engine-room and adjoining boiler-rooms the men on watch in their blue or white overalls shouted to each other or sang their bawdy songs, all unheard in the roar of machinery, but to one another. The duty engineer officer stood on his shining catwalk beside the little desk with its telephone and log book. Old Stück would be down again soon. He had led all of them from the moment the first machine parts had been installed in this great hull. And yet he trusted nobody completely when important orders had to be executed.

The engineer officer, whose name was Kessler, could feel his shoulders ache as he gripped the rail with his gloved fingers. He felt the ship, too, thundering around and beneath his feet. She was the finest he had known. He grimaced. Down here anyway. What he had heard about their gallant admiral hardly inspired anyone. Kessler stared at the quivering bilge water far below the catwalk, blue-green in the harsh lights; it reminded him of the Christmas tree at his home as a boy. The first glimpse of it on that special morning, the presents, his father's huge grin. He had made himself go there on that last leave. The house had gone completely. He had known about it of course, just as he had sensed Hechler's compassion when he had seen him after the town had been bombed; he had asked for leave when the RAF had gone after the ball-bearing plant there. But as Hechler had explained, had there been a dependant, a wife, children, then perhaps –

The captain had been right, of course. But Kessler had gone home all the same when his time for normal leave had come up.

He still did not know what he had expected, a gap in the houses, all that was left of his boyhood and his family memories. It had not been like that at all. The whole street had gone, and several on either side of it too.

He squeezed the rail until his fingers ached. Would he *never* get over it?

The telephone made a puny rattle above the chorus of engines and fans.

He pictured Hechler up there in the open bridge, the air and the ocean which seemed endless.

He said, 'Ready, sir.'

Over his shoulder he heard Stück's voice and turned to see his figure framed against the bright pipes and dials, almost shining in a fresh suit of overalls.

'The Old Man?'

Kessler glanced at the shivering clock. 'Yes, Chief.' Stück was even earlier than usual. But Kessler was glad without knowing why.

Stück leaned his buttocks against a rail and folded his arms. He could see through the haze of steam and moisture, and his keen ears told him more than any log book.

He looked at the lieutenant and guessed what his assistant had been brooding about. He toyed with the idea of mentioning it, but sentiment found little comfort in lip-reading, in competition with their sealed, roaring world.

His eyes came up to the dials above the deck as a bell rattled again, and the three speed and revolution counters swung round with expected urgency.

Stück grinned and pretended to spit on his hands. His lips said, 'Come on, Heinz, feed the beast, eh?' Seconds later, the three great shafts gathered speed, so that even the men on watch had to make certain of a ready handhold.

Stück watched the mounting revolutions. A thoroughbred.

Here we go again.

Theil lay on his back and felt the increase of speed creating a new rhythm as it pulsated through the bunk and into his body. He had tried to sleep, but had been wide awake since he had left the bridge. His eyes felt raw, and despair dragged at his mind and insides like some creeping disease.

If he went to the admiral and pleaded for him to make a signal through the next refuelling submarine, would it make any difference? He knew immediately that it would not. Leitner could have told him about the arrest before the ship had weighed anchor, might even have intervened on his behalf. He did not want to, did not care; it was that simple.

Theil rolled on to his side and stared desperately at his clock. He would be called by a messenger very soon, then he would have to put on an act again, or go mad under this terrible weight. The ship was beginning to shake more insistently, so that objects in his cabin clattered together, as if to drive him out. Very soon now the ship would need him more than ever before. But for that sure knowledge he knew he would kill himself. Over the side in the night watches, lost in seconds in their ruler-straight wake. Or a pistol to the temple, a moment's fearful uncertainty – then nothing. The thought of the pistol which hung from his bunk made him violently angry, sick with it, until every limb trembled like the ship.

He saw himself in that cabin again, Bauer's stupid, handsome face exploding like a scarlet flower as the bullet smashed him down.

See if *he* could take it as well as he could shoot an unarmed civilian.

The thought brought no comfort. Unarmed civilian, like Britta. Perhaps she was released now, back at their house, putting right the damage to her beloved garden.

He buried his face in the pillow and found that he could not stop himself from sobbing aloud.

Two cabins away, Oberleutnant zur See Willi Meile, the stores and supply officer, lay on his side and stared at the naked girl who was clutching her breast and gasping with exhaustion.

Meile was no fighting soldier, his world was food and drink, paint and cordage, everything which fed and sustained his ship.

He had worked on one of the camera team ever since she had come aboard. She was certainly no beauty, but she was young and had a fine body. To Meile it was like being in heaven. Nothing like it had happened before, nor could occur again.

The executive officers and U-boat commanders had all the glamour. They were more than welcome to it, he decided. It was said that half of Hamburg was owned by ex-pursers of the Hamburg-Amerika Line, just as naval bases like Wilhelmshaven were profitable investments for retired supply officers like Meile.

No, after the war, those who controlled the food and drink would be the new heroes.

He leaned on one elbow and felt her breast. He had left lights switched on as he did not want to miss anything. Her bare shoulders were quite red in places where he had squeezed, even bitten them. She gasped out that she could take no more. 'You are more than a man – ' The rest was silenced as he kissed her hard on the mouth, his hand reaching for her, exciting her despite all exhaustion. Neither of them noticed the sudden increase of engine noise, nor considered what it might mean.

Meile dragged her wrists over her head and held them tightly. He said, 'Don't fight me. I'm going to take you. *Now!*'

In the next cabin, young Jaeger switched on his light and squinted at his wristwatch. He would not wait to be roused, but would have a shave before they tested action stations to start another day. He thought he heard the girl's stifled cry through the thick steel and shook his head. That Meile was like an animal where women were concerned. He tried not to think of the gentle Sophie; it was wrong even to picture her in his mind with all that was going on in the next cabin. The sooner they dropped the three women off in the next rendezvous supply-boat, the better. He thought of Hechler's face when he had been speaking with the girl pilot. No, perhaps not her.

He stood up and felt the carpet tremble beneath his bare feet. Then he looked at the disordered bunk. It was not so difficult to see Sophie here after all.

On the opposite side of the ship the girl gathered up her things and pushed them unseeingly into a small grip. She would return to her allotted cabin, which she shared with one of the camera girls. Like Jaeger, she switched on some lights and stood, swaying to the heavy motion in front of a bulkhead mirror. Where he adjusted his uniform before going to speak with his sailors. She pouted at herself. Or, in the past, leave to see his unfaithful wife.

She opened her shirt and watched herself touch the scar on her side. It still hurt. Her hand drifted slowly across her skin as his had done. She could still feel him; her body was both elated and sore from their need for each other.

She had not realised how it was possible to be both loved and possessed, to feel victor and conquered at the same time. She buttoned her shirt and looked very slowly around the empty cabin. She would not come back again. Not ever, unless they were together.

She heard quiet movements from the captain's pantry. Poor Pirk, his servant and guardian angel. In some strange way, his acceptance of her here had seemed like a blessing.

She supported herself in the doorway and listened to the mounting rumble of power. Like something unleashed, which would never be cowed until satisfied, or destroyed.

Her fingers rested hesitantly on the last light switch. She would remember everything. The rasp of his clothes against her nakedness, the thrust of his body which was like love and madness together.

The cabin retreated into darkness and she closed the door.

As she walked past the dozing sentry at the end of the passageway she knew she would regret nothing.

16

━━ ━━ ━━ ━━ ━━ ━━

The Signal

Peter Younger, one-time radio officer of the SS *Radnor Star*, drew his knees up to his chin and shaded his eyes with one hand. He was still unused to being on dry land again, and for hours after his arrival with the small party of German sailors he had been light-headed, unsteady on his feet like some dockside drunk. When the raider had weighed anchor and had headed away from the tiny islet Younger had almost expected that each minute was to be his last. He had seen the rough grave, and had heard what had happened from one of the station's crew. It was curious, but the resident crew had been as withdrawn as the Germans from him, and of course Old Shiner. He glanced at the white-bearded boatswain who was sitting with his back to a rock, facing the sun, eyes closed. He could be dead, he thought.

He idly watched one German who was strolling up and down the slope, a machine-pistol dangling from his shoulder. Younger had heard the senior rating telling him off for not wearing his cap; it was absurd, when you knew you would soon be changing places with your prisoners.

Mason, the man in charge of the small station, had whispered to him that the place was no longer properly operational. So no regular monitoring or signals would be missed or expected. The enemy had worked it out very well. The man had said that when the German operator made his false signal, someone on the receiving end might realise it was not the usual telegraphist. He had added somewhat condescendingly that only a radio man would understand that. Younger had contained his impatience and irritation. *You can say that again*, his inner voice had answered.

Younger had decided not to share his plan with anyone just yet. The station crew seemed too dazed and shocked by what had happened to their companion. Cowed was putting it mildly, he thought angrily. The Germans would not want to kill anyone for no purpose. If the British or American warships arrived to find more graves, they might forget the Geneva Convention, so far from home, and take their own revenge. The krauts would think that anyway.

It would have to be after the false signal and without giving them time to destroy the transmitter. Younger had measured up the distance he had to cover, had even selected the sailor he would overpower to reach the radio-room. The German sailor in question was often on guard duty; he was apparently useless as a cook or anything else with one arm in plaster. He could not therefore carry more than a pistol, and he usually kept that buttoned in his holster. And why not? They had no means of escape, nowhere to run to. They were all prisoners now. He tried to gauge their feelings, those of the senior operator in charge anyway. He could see him now, standing by the ladder to the radio-room, his cap dangling from one hand as he shared the frail sunlight.

He was young but prematurely bald, a fact made more obvious by the dark hair on either temple. He was a thoughtful-looking man, introspective, with the sensitive features of a priest. He was probably brooding on his own predicament, which had been thrust on him in the name of duty.

Younger licked his lips and tried to relax his body, muscle by muscle. When he considered what he intended to do he was surprised at his strength and conviction. There was no fear at all. He thought of the torpedo which had blasted the old ship apart, men screaming and on fire, others being carried away by the suction to the same Atlantic grave.

This would be for them. The Old Man, Colin Ames, all of them.

With a start he realised that the old boatswain had opened his eyes and was watching him without recognition. His eyes were washed-out blue, so pale in the glare that they were like a blind man's.

Younger smiled. 'Okay, Shiner?' He wondered if he knew where they were. How they had got here.

The boatswain opened and closed his hands. They lay on the rock beside him, as if they were independent of their owner.

He said huskily, 'Wot time we goin' to eat, Sparks?'

Younger shot a quick glance at the two Germans, but neither had noticed.

He hissed, 'Don't call me that, mate!'

The eyes did not blink. 'You're Peter Younger, that's who.' He nodded, satisfied. 'Sparks.'

Younger sighed. 'Ames is dead. I've taken his place.' He could feel his plan running out like sand. 'The krauts wouldn't let me within a mile of this lot if they knew.' He gripped his arm fiercely. Through the ragged jersey it felt like a stick. 'Help me. To even the score for the lads and the old *Star*, eh?'

He saw understanding cloud the pale eyes for the first time. He said shakily, 'All gone. The lot of 'em. Jim, Colin, and – ' he stared round, suddenly desperate – 'where's – '

Younger gripped his arm and said quietly, 'It's all right, Shiner. The cat didn't feel anything. He's buried with the lads now.' He watched the sentry's shadow reaching across the rough slope. 'Because of these bastards.'

The old man closed his eyes. 'Dead, you say?'

Younger looked down. *Please help me. In God's name, help.*

He said aloud, 'It was a U-boat. But they're all the same. The crew here don't understand like we do. They seem to think a war's for someone else to fight.' He steadied himself, knowing he would break down otherwise. 'Will you give me a hand?'

'Just tell me what to do, Sparks.' He smiled but it made him look ever sadder. 'Sorry, I mean *Mr Ames*.'

Younger sat back on his haunches. It was suddenly crystal-clear what he would do. As if he could see it happening in slow motion, something already past.

He considered what the man Mason had told him about one operator being familiar to another. He had always known it, and the radio officer who had taught him had described how you could often recognise the sender before the actual ship was identified.

Did that mean Mason or one of the others would make the signal to keep in with their captors?

It made him sweat to think of it. The raider was off to attack the biggest prize yet. It must be really important to leave some of their own people behind. None of them seemed to know where the attack might be launched. In case they were captured and interrogated before the raider could make good her escape. The stark picture of the drifting lifeboat, the moments when he had been almost too terrified to open his eyes when he had drowsed over the tiller. They had all been waiting for him. The nightmare had never gone away. They had died one by one, mostly in silence with a kind of passive acceptance.

It would not be much, but his actions might help to save other helpless merchant seamen. He hoped his old mother would find out that he had died this way. His dry lips cracked into a smile. Might get the George Cross. Something for his Dad to brag about down at the Shipwright's Arms.

Another shadow fell across them. 'We eat soon.' It was the senior operator, apparently the only one who spoke English. He would, of course.

'Thanks.'

The German glanced down at the old boatswain. 'He okay?'

Old Shiner did not open his eyes. 'Right as bloody ninepence, ta.'

The German turned away. That last sentence had thrown him.

He walked down to the water's edge and stared at the dark water. It shelved away steeply after that. Just a pile of rock in the middle of nowhere, he thought.

His name was Ernst Genscher and his home was in Leipzig. It would be cold there now. Winter always came early to that city. He tried to see it as in his boyhood, the spires and fine buildings. Not as on his last leave. The bomb debris, Russian prisoners working to clear the streets of corpses and rubble. The prisoners had looked like human scarecrows, and had been guarded by units of the SS. He thought of his divisional officer, Leutnant Bauer. They had never got on together. He smiled bitterly. That was why he had been detailed for this final job. Bauer would have been right at home in the SS.

How much longer would the war last, he wondered? He and the others would end up in some prisoner-of-war camp in England or Canada. It might not be too bad. It was like their situation here in this damnable place, he thought. Neither side wanted to antagonise the other in case the wrong one came out victorious.

He thought of his companions. They were more worried than they admitted. Some even expected the *Prinz* to come back for them. A tiger had never been known to come back to release a tethered goat.

Genscher replaced his cap and smiled at his earlier show of discipline with the sentry.

He looked at his watch. He would send the signal in a few hours' time, just before sunset. His priest's face brightened into a smile.

It was somehow appropriate.

The three captains sat in Hemrose's deep armchairs and held out their glasses to be refilled.

Hemrose crossed one leg over the other and plucked his shirt away from his body. The air was hot and lifeless, and even with the scuttles open it was hard to ease the discomfort. The glass seemed steady enough, Hemrose thought, but it smelled like a storm. It was all they needed.

He watched his steward pause to take Captain Eric Duffield's glass to be topped up. *Rhodesia*'s captain was a big, powerful man, whose face had once been very handsome. A bit too smarmy for Hemrose's taste. Always excelled at sport and athletics. Not any more, Hemrose thought with small satisfaction.

He had forgotten how many Horse's Necks he had downed, nor did he care much. It was getting more like a wake than a relaxed drink in harbour with his captains, with a good dinner to follow. They would not be *his* captains much longer. He shied away from the thought.

With an effort he stood up and crossed to the nearest scuttle. The lights of Simonstown glittered on the water like a swarm of fireflies, while here and there small boats moved through the dusk between the anchored warships. It could be peacetime, he thought. Well, almost.

He heard Duffield say, 'Good place to settle down, South Africa. I'd think about it myself after this lot's over, but you never know.' Hemrose gritted his teeth together. He meant that he would be staying on in the service, promoted probably to end his time in command of a base, or with a nice staff job in Whitehall.

The New Zealand captain, Chantril, replied, 'We've not won the bloody war yet.' His accent took the edge from his words. He was feeling it too. The chance to meet and destroy the raider. Become a part of the navy's heritage.

Hemrose turned and signalled to his steward. 'I still can't believe it, you know.'

Duffield smiled. 'Believe or accept? There's a difference.' Hemrose ignored him. 'A whole ship gone west, not even a scrap of wreckage discovered?'

Chantril said, 'It happened to HMS *Sydney*. Her loss is still a mystery.'

Duffield glanced at his watch. He could not wait to eat up and go. Get back to his own ship and tell them all how Hemrose was taking his unfought defeat.

He said, 'The backroom boys at the Admiralty know more than they let on.'

Hemrose glared. 'Bloody useless, most of them!'

Duffield coughed. 'We'll probably never know.'

Hemrose pushed a strand of hair from his eyes. He was getting drunk. 'That Jerry is still around. I'll stake my reputation on it.'

The others remained silent. They probably considered his reputation had already slipped away.

'I've had my team working round the clock,' Hemrose pictured the charts, the layers of signal pads and folios. All for nothing. 'We had a damn good try anyway.'

They both stared at him. It was the nearest he had ever come to an admission of failure.

The thought of sitting through dinner with them made Hemrose feel slightly sick. Chantril was all right, a real professional, but tonight was not the time. He had a letter to write to Beryl, and a report to complete for the Admiralty. After that, he could almost feel the carpet being dragged from under him. Perhaps they would both accept an excuse, go back to their ships instead –

He looked up, angry and startled, as if he had spoken aloud.

'Well, what is it now?'

The commander nodded to the seated officers and then handed a signal pad to his superior.

Hemrose had to read it twice, his face shining with sweat, as if he had been running.

He said slowly, 'From Admiralty, gentlemen. Thirty minutes ago a signal was received from the Cable and Wireless station on St Jorge.' He could tell from Duffield's expression he hadn't a clue where that was. 'It reads *Am under attack by German cruiser*.' He lowered the pad and eyed them grimly. 'There was no further transmission. We may draw our own conclusions.'

Chantril exclaimed, 'I know the place! Christ, it's nor'-east of Ascension. What the hell is he – '

Duffield said, 'And all the time – '

Hemrose remained grave and under control even though he wanted to yell out aloud. It was like having a great orchestra or band pounding into your ears, shutting out all else but those vital words.

He said, 'Yes, all the time we thought the German was destroyed.' He could not resist it. 'Some of us, anyway.'

Chantril stood up and knocked over a glass without even seeing it.

'What is he trying to do?'

Hemrose smiled gently. '*Do?* Who really cares? He probably intended to carry out a last attack before running to some friendly South American bolthole, *Graf Spee* all over again. *Kapitän Hechler* – ' he spat out the name ' – will know that heavy forces are to the north of him.' He nodded. 'He will head south after this, then scuttle, whether *he* likes it or not.'

'Can we rely on that signal, sir?'

Hemrose looked at him and beamed. 'What? Can you doubt your *backroom boys* at the Admiralty? Tch, tch!' It was like a tonic.

Commander Godson shifted from one foot to the other. The signal had knocked the breath out of him. It was like opening a door and expecting to meet an old friend, only to be confronted by a maniac.

Hemrose looked at him, but saw his own expression as it would be remembered after this day. Grave and confident.

'Make a signal to Admiralty, Toby. *The squadron is leaving without delay.*' Thank God he had insisted on fuelling from lighters; it would have taken another hour to clear the port otherwise. He took his time to look at the gold wristwatch which Beryl had given him.

'Pipe special sea dutymen to their stations in one hour.' He looked at the others as poor Godson fled from the cabin. 'Another drink, eh?' He grinned. '*Afore you go*, as the man said.'

He watched their faces, each man thinking of his own ship's readiness for sea. Hemrose added gently, 'Call up your ships from here.' He recalled the *Rhodesia*'s great display of speed and swank when she had joined the squadron. 'I don't want to leave here alone!'

Later he said, 'It must be fate. I knew we were destined to meet. Right from the beginning. I always knew.' He glanced round the cabin affectionately. 'Settle the score.'

At the prescribed time, as watertight doors were slammed shut and men bustled to their stations for leaving harbour, Hemrose mounted the *Wiltshire*'s bridge and looked towards the lights of the shore. The raider had not allowed for anyone making a last desperate signal, any more than they would expect three British cruisers to be ready, and in the right place.

In his mind he could see the chart, south-west. Close the trap which the German had sprung on himself.

He touched his cap to Godson as he reported the ship ready to proceed.

It was no longer just a remote possibility. There soon would be two lines of oak leaves around his peak.

It was a proud moment. There should be a band playing.

He turned and looked at the chief yeoman of signals.

He said, 'Make to squadron, Yeo. *Weigh anchor and follow father.*'

The sort of signal they always remembered. He could not stop grinning. The fact that Duffield would hate it, was a bonus.

Hechler came out of his dream like a drowning man fighting up for a gasp of air.

Even as he propped himself on one elbow and jammed the telephone to his ear he knew what it was. The only surprise was that he had been able to sleep at all.

It was Froebe. 'W/T office has reported the signal, sir.' He sounded cheerful. 'Right on time.'

Hechler stared around the tiny sea-cabin, his things ready to snatch up, the place in total disorder.

'Thank you. You know what to do.' He thought of the wild dream which had been driven away by the telephone's shrill call. Her nakedness, her desire, the way she had writhed beneath him as if to postpone the conquest.

He said, 'I'll be up shortly.' He hung the phone on its cradle above the bunk and wondered what she was doing now. Thinking, but not regretting? Hoping, but not allowing it to reach out too far. He slid from the bunk and suddenly craved a shower. Even that was already too late.

He thought of the senior operator, Genscher, he had left on the islet. He had obeyed orders, no matter what he thought about the need or the futility of it.

Even now the signal would be flashing around the world. The raider had been verified and slotted into one section of this great ocean. Brains would be working overtime as staff officers rearranged their thinking and defences, like drawing the strings of a huge bag. Except that the *Prinz* was nowhere near the small islet, and was speeding in the opposite direction.

Hechler deliberately stripped himself to the waist. The narrow door opened slightly and he saw the faithful Pirk peering in at him with a steaming bowl of water for his shave. He had understood. But Pirk always had. Ice, sunshine, bombardments or dodging enemy aircraft, Pirk's world ran on quite different lines.

The telephone rang again and Pirk handed it to him.

Hechler said, 'Captain?'

This time it was Theil. 'Exercise action stations, sir?'

'Not yet.' He thought surprisingly of Nelson. 'Let them have one more good meal. It may be the last for some time.'

Theil grunted. 'Dawn attack, sir?'

'Yes. As planned, Viktor. Let me know when the admiral is on his bridge.'

He turned to the mirror and touched his face. As she had done. 'It's going to be a very long night, old friend.' But Pirk had left. He lathered his cheeks with care and thought of each last detail. The Arados would have to be prepared well before dawn. Every station and gun-mounting checked and visited by a senior officer. The last meal for some time. Forever, if things went badly wrong. He searched through his mind for flaws. His landing party had played their part. Now it was up to them. He grimaced at his image in the mirror. At one time he had nursed doubts. He had imagined then that the enemy had some secret strategy which neither he nor Operations had recognised.

Now he knew differently. There was no secret plan. Once again, the *Prinz Luitpold*'s luck had won through.

Shortly after midnight Hechler made his way into the bridge. That last cat-nap had driven the tiredness away. Or was it the prospect of action?

In the darkness figures moved towards him, or held motionless at their positions. As if they had never shifted. It was a beautiful night, bright stars, and a deep, unbroken swell again. Gudegast had already reported that there might be rain with a south-easterly wind. He never sounded as if he trusted the signalled broadcasts as much as his own intuition.

Leitner's pale outline glided through the watchkeepers, and Hechler could smell his cologne as he groped his way to the forward part of the bridge.

'A good beginning,' he said calmly. 'They'll not forget this day.'

Hechler was glad when the admiral had departed for his quarters. To prepare himself, or to share the last hours with his aide, he did not know or care.

As the time dragged on, the weather began to change. It grew much colder, and the steep swell became visible on either beam as a rising wind broke the crests into ragged, white lines. The *Prinz* was built for this kind of weather, and as she dipped her forecastle until spray burst over the stem or spouted through the hawsepipes she seemed almost contemptuous.

More signals came in a steady stream. It must be strange for those far-off operators, Hechler had thought many times, to send off their instructions and messages, while the recipient had no way of risking an acknowledgement.

Operations Division sent one signal about a small Polish cruiser squadron leaving Simonstown. Agents there must have started a chain of messages almost as soon as the Tommies had hoisted their anchors.

It was hardly surprising, he thought. Germany had many friends in South Africa. When the Kaiser had been forced to surrender in the Great War, it was said that black flags had been raised over Johannesburg to show where their true feelings had lain.

Hechler said: 'Action stations in ten minutes.' He felt his pockets in case he had forgotten anything. He remembered as he had left the sea-cabin how he had seen Inger's familiar picture in the drawer. He had looked at it for the first time without feeling, even bitterness.

'Tell the supply officer to keep the galley on stand-by. I want soup and coffee sent around every station until the last moment.'

A winch clattered loudly and he knew the aircraft handling party were at work with the first Arado preparing for launching. If the launch misfired, the plane would be left to fend for itself. He thought of the girl's own aircraft, dismantled and folded into its nest. A last display for the camera? Or did Leitner have some other scheme in mind?

Gudegast stood beside his chair. 'Time to increase to full speed in twenty minutes, sir.' He sounded calm enough.

'Good.' Hechler peered at his Doxa watch. 'Sound off.'

The alarm bells clamoured throughout the ship, followed by a few thuds as the last of the heavy doors were clipped home. Voice-pipes and handsets muttered around the bridge, an unseen army.

'Anton, Bruno, Caesar and Dora turrets closed up, sir!'

'Secondary and anti-aircraft armament closed up, sir!'

From every gun, torpedo and magazine the reports came in.

Hechler pictured his men within the armoured hull. Down in the sick-bay, Stroheim and his assistants would be waiting, their glittering instruments laid out, waiting for the pain and the pleading.

As it must have been at Coronel and Falklands, at Dogger Bank and Jutland. Hechler jammed his pipe between his teeth and smiled. Trafalgar too probably.

He heard himself ask, 'What about Damage Control?'

Froebe replied, 'Closed up, sir. Some delay over a lighting fault.'

Theil was there entrusted with saving the ship if the worst happened. Or taking command if the bridge was wiped out.

'The admiral, sir.'

Hechler took the handset. 'Sir?'

Leitner said, 'I want another flag hoisted today. See to it, eh?'

He meant another rear-admiral's flag.

Hechler said. 'Ship at action stations, sir.'

'I shall come up presently.' The line went dead.

Hechler said to the bridge at large, 'I'm going to the plot.' He walked to the ladder as Gudegast picked up a chart and followed him. He could visualise it clearly in his mind. Training, experience, skill. He heard Froebe telling a signalman to fetch another flag and take it aft. He wondered if the camera would record that too.

While their captain climbed to the conning tower, the men throughout the ship went grimly about their preparations. Ready-use ammunition in place, magazine lifts sliding smoothly up and down their shafts, gun crews testing training and elevation gear, the gleaming breeches open like hungry mouths.

Above them all, Kröll the gunnery officer sat in his small steel chair and adjusted his sights while he studied the radar repeater. His team, hung about with stop-watches, earphones and the tools of their trade, watched him, keyed up like athletes under the starter's gun.

The most junior member of the fire-control team, Acting Petty Officer Hans Stoecker, stared at his empty log, one hand wrapped around his telephone.

They had all worked together so long that there were no hitches, nothing to bring Kröll's wrath down on them.

It was like a small self-contained world. Essential to the ship's firepower, but entirely separate, so that when the heavy guns roared out, they too seemed like something apart.

He tried not to think of Rudi Hammer's mild features just as the bells had sent them all racing to their action stations.

He had smiled almost shyly and said, 'A very good time for our little plan, yes? Everybody minding his own business!'

They would be found out. Stoecker gripped the telephone with both hands, his eyes misty as he stared at the log book. It was madness, a lunacy which would cost them their lives.

The speaker intoned, 'Main armament, semi-armour piercing shell, *load!*'

Stoecker felt his seat tilt under him as the helm went over. The ship was increasing speed. Sometimes it felt as if their steel pod would tear itself away from the bridge superstructure as every strut and rivit shook violently in protest.

Kröll twisted round in his chair and glanced at the intent figures below him, lastly to Kapitänleutnant Georg Emmler, the assistant gunnery officer. Together they held the reins. Beyond here, quarters officers, gun captains, and even individual sailors strapped in their rapid-fire automatic weapons, waited for the word. *Bearing, range, target.*

Kröll bit his lip. Another convoy. One day he would get his chance to pit his skills against a powerful enemy warship.

'Loaded, sir.'

Kröll scowled. Ten seconds too long. He thrust the watch into his pocket. He would soon put that right.

On the bridge once more Hechler looked at the stars. Fainter now. He felt spray cutting his face, heard it pattering over the chart-table's canvas cover to make puddles in the scuppers.

A voice said, 'First-degree readiness, sir.'

The galley was shut; the cook and his assistants would be sent to help damage-control and the stretcher parties.

Hechler gripped the rail below the screen and stared into the darkness.

They should hold the advantage with the convoy framed against the dawn.

149

The escort had not been identified, which meant that it was nothing important. They were holding that for the next leg. He looked at the stars. But that would be denied them.

'Port fifteen!' Hechler heard his order repeated, almost a whisper, lost in the clamour of fans, the great writhing bank of foam which surged down either side.

'Steady! Steer zero-four-zero!'

The bows plunged into a deeper trough than usual and the sea boiled up and over the forecastle as if a broadside had fallen silently alongside.

As the ship turned, the two big turrets below the bridge trained across the starboard bow. Without turning Hechler knew that the two after ones, Caesar and Dora, were also swinging round in unison, until all four guns were pointing on the same bearing, the long muzzles like wet glass as they steadied over the side and the great surge of spray.

The sea was still in darkness, so that the leaping crests looked like birds, swooping and falling to appear elsewhere in another guise.

'Admiral's on his bridge, sir.'

'Very well.' Hechler tightened the towel around his neck as more heavy spray burst over the screen and pattered against their oilskins.

Leitner had made a suitably timed entrance. Hechler thought of the girl. She had shown no fear, but being sealed below behind massive watertight doors would test anybody.

Somebody whispered and was instantly rebuked by a petty officer.

Hechler kept his binoculars sheltered beneath the oilskin until the last moment to keep them dry. But he had seen what the lookout had whispered to a companion.

A thin pale line, like polished pewter, cold and without colour. Dawn, or nearly so. Hechler thought suddenly of his father. How he had described the horizon of that other war. It had been first light on the parapet of his trench. That had been the full extent of his world in that horrifying arena in Flanders.

'*Radar – bridge!*'

They all tensed.

Then the speaker continued, 'Target in sight. Bearing Green four-five. Range twelve thousand!'

Hechler tugged his cap more firmly across his forehead. The peak was wet and like ice.

He stood up and let the spray dash over him as he peered towards the starboard bow.

They had found them. Now it was up to Kröll.

'*Open fire!*'

17

Blood for Blood

The paired explosions from the after-turrets were deafening, and with the wind thrusting across the starboard quarter, the down-draft of acrid smoke made several of the men duck their heads to contain their coughing fits.

Hechler held the binoculars on the bearing and watched the tiny pale feathers of spray as the shells fell on the horizon. Harmless, without menace, although he knew that each waterspout would rise to masthead level. The explosions sighed through the water and faded again.

The speaker said, 'Twelve ships in convoy, estimate three escorts.'

Froebe called from his bank of handsets, 'W/T office reports signals from enemy, sir.'

'*Shoot!*' Kröll sounded quite different over the speaker, his words drowned by the immediate response from all four turrets.

Hechler watched the sky. After the previous days it looked threatening. There was cloud there too. He imagined signals beaming away to the enemy's supporting squadrons and to London.

He tensed; a bright flash lit up the horizon and several of the ships for the first time. They looked low and black, but in the spreading glow of fire he could just determine their course and speed.

The speaker again. 'One escort hit. Sinking.'

Hechler could picture the gunnery team's concentration on the radar screens. One tiny droplet of light falling out of station, dropping further and further astern of the fast tankers. It would vanish from the screens altogether.

The guns roared out again. Surely the tankers would scatter soon? He held his breath as a straddle of shells fell across one of the ships below the horizon. She was instantly ablaze, but it was made more terrible by distance as the fire seemed to spread down from the horizon, like blood brimming over a dam.

'*Shoot!*'

Hechler waited and winced as the eight big guns thundered out.

'Slow ahead!' He crossed the bridge and saw a signalman watching him, a handlamp at the ready.

'*Now!*' The first Arado lifted from the shadows and circled quickly round and above the mastheads.

'*Shoot!*'

The whole bridge structure shook violently and Hechler had to repeat his order to the engine-room to resume full speed. He would launch the second plane if there was time.

Someone was yelling, 'Another hit! God, two of them are on fire!'

Hechler glanced round to silence the man, but all he saw was Leitner's second flag breaking out from the mainmast truck, the only patch of colour against the sky. It was raining more persistently now, but even that tasted of cordite. It was hard to believe this same sky had been full of stars.

Hechler moved across the bridge, half-listening to crackling static as the Arado pilot reported back to the ship.

It was a sea of fire. The great shells must have come ripping down out of the darkness without the slightest warning. He saw lazy balls of bright tracer rising from the sea and guessed that the Arado was already near the convoy. How slow it looked. How deceptive. He hoped the pilot had his wits about him.

'Convoy breaking up, sir!' Kröll's voice cut through the murmur of orders and instructions behind him. It was as if the fire-control position, the pod, was alive and speaking of its own free will.

Kröll added, 'Two lines diverging, sir.'

Hechler lowered his glasses and wiped them with fresh tissue.

'Acknowledge.' He pictured the convoy; they would need no encouragement to break away. *We must close the range.*

'*Shoot!*'

'*Cease firing!*' It was Kröll but he sounded momentarily confused.

Hechler picked up the fire-control handset. 'Captain. What is it?'

Kröll must have been leaning away to study his radar; when he spoke he seemed angry, as if he no longer trusted what he saw.

'A ship turned end-on, sir. Rear of second line.'

'Wait!' Hechler pushed his way aft and into the tiny steel shack which had been added to the bridge to house a radar repeater alongside that of the sonar. He bent over the screen and as his eyes accustomed themselves to the flickering symbols he saw the complete picture as seen by *Prinz Luitpold*'s invisible eye. The diverging ranks of ships, and then as the scanner swept over them, the motionless blobs of light, ships burning and dying in the spreading flames. Then he saw the isolated echo. A large one which had until now been mistaken for one of the tankers. But it was much bigger and was not standing away, but coming straight for the *Prinz*. Hechler had to force himself to walk back to the bridge.

'Can you identify it?'

Kröll sounded very wary. 'There are no major warships listed with the convoy.'

Hechler turned away. 'Carry on. Tell the conning tower to alter course. Steer zero-six-zero!'

The bridge quaked again as the after guns bellowed out, their bright tongues lighting up the rain-soaked superstructure and funnel. A figure stood out in the flashes and Hechler heard Jaeger call, 'Captain, sir! Message from Arado pilot! The ship is a merchantman!' He hesitated, baffled. 'A liner!'

For an instant longer Hechler thought she might be a hospital ship, one which was trying to keep clear of the convoy, or which had been damaged and was out of control.

A figure in shining oilskins brushed Jaeger aside and Gudegast exclaimed, 'Steady on new course, sir. Zero-six-zero.' He clung to the safety rail, his body heaving from exertion.

Hechler said, 'Do you know what it is?'

Gudegast nodded jerkily. 'It was in the recognition despatches, sir. Oh, yes, I know her all right!' He ducked as the guns fired again. Flashes rippled along the horizon. Kröll was ignoring the solitary ship in case the heavy tankers might escape.

Gudegast stared at him, his eyes wild in the reflections. 'She's the old *Tasmania*. Used to come up against her when she did the Scandinavian cruises in the thirties.' He pounded his fist on the rail and shouted, 'They've made her an Armed Merchant Cruiser, for Christ's sake!'

Hechler snatched up the handset. 'Gunnery Officer! Shift target to the big liner – she's the *Tasmania*, armed merchant cruiser!'

'Immediately, sir.'

Gudegast was staring at him. 'She won't stand a chance! You know what they're like. No plating at all and just a few guns from the Great War!'

Hechler called, 'Warn the secondary. armament, then call up the Arado.'

He swung on Gudegast and said, 'Have you forgotten the other AMC's, man? *Jervis Bay*, an old cargo liner, but she held off *Admiral Scheer* nonetheless! An old merchantman too, set against a battleship! She was sunk, she knew it was hopeless when she turned to face the *Scheer*, but by God, her sacrifice saved her convoy, and *don't you ever forget it!*'

He turned back to the screen as the four forward guns edged round, paused and then fired in unison.

The sky was brightening, although with all the smoky rain it seemed to have taken them by surprise. Hechler watched the exploding shells, the ice-bright columns of water. Then he saw the oncoming ship. In her dull paint she still looked huge, with her three tall funnels overlapping as she turned still more to steer towards the heavy cruiser. The next salvo fell right across her path, and for an instant, Hechler thought she had been hit.

Jaeger called thickly, 'She mounts eight-inch guns, sir!'

It was ironic. The same armament as the *Prinz*, in size and numbers only.

'Speed?'

Jaeger replied. 'Twenty-eight knots maximum, sir.' He faltered as the after turrets fired, paint flaking down from the upper bridge fittings because of the blast. 'In peacetime.'

Hechler stared at her dull shadow while he wiped his glasses again. They were on a converging course, approaching each other at the combined speed of some sixty miles an hour. Old she might be, and to all intents she could not survive, but just one lucky shot was all it took to delay them, while the convoy clapped on speed to escape. Spectators would remember this day if they were fortunate enough to survive.

'*Shoot!*'

A straddle. The liner was hidden by falling spray, and at least one shell had smashed into her unarmoured side and exploded deep inside the hull. It was like a glowing red eye.

Hechler heard Jaeger shout, 'That should stop her!'

Gudegast seized his arm. 'Take a good look, *boy!*'

Jaeger stared with disbelief. 'She's hoisting flags to each mast!'

Gudegast stared past him at Hechler's shoulders, shining in the grey light as the rain bounced down on them.

'They're *battle ensigns!* They sent the poor old girl to fight, and by God she's about to!'

'*Shoot!*'

It was a controlled broadside from all four turrets, the heavy shells straddling the tall hull, and blasting one of the outmoded, stately funnels overboard, like paper in a wind.

Jaeger gripped the chart-table as it tried to shake itself from his fingers. He wanted to screw up his eyes as a great scream of shellfire shrieked over the bridge and exploded in the sea, far abeam.

He wrote in the log. 'The enemy opened fire at – ' The rest was a blur.

Hechler turned to watch the falling spray. 'Tell our pilot to take a fly over that ship. He might get a lucky hit.'

He did not let himself blink as two flashes lit up the liner's side. Her armament was divided out of necessity. At most she could train only three or four guns at a time.

He bit his lip as Kröll's next salvo erupted on her waterline. Smoke and fire seemed to roll across the waves, and he guessed that one shell had burst deep inside her.

But she was firing back, the old guns sounding strangely hollow when compared with the *Prinz*'s.

A messenger handed him a telephone, his face ashen as a shell screamed past the bridge.

It was Leitner. 'What is the matter with your gun crews!' He was almost screaming. '*Kill them! Stop that ship!*'

Hechler handed the phone to the seaman and watched a livid flash fan out from beneath the liner's bridge. A mast was falling, but the white battle ensigns still seemed to shine through the rain, and her bow-wave was as before.

Froebe shouted, 'She's on fire aft, sir! What's holding her together?'

Hechler let his glasses fall to his chest. The range was dropping rapidly so that she seemed to tower over the sea like a leviathan.

He said, 'I shall have to turn to port. It will give our spotters a chance.' It would also expose the whole broadside to the enemy, but speed was essential now. It was all they had.

'She's slowing down!' A man's cheer was cut short as the liner's two most forward guns fired together. It was all confused, and even the thundering crash of the explosion was muffled.

Half-deafened by the shell-burst Hechler dragged himself along the rail to the starboard side. A man was screaming, his face cut to ribbons, and Hechler saw that most of the glass screen had been fragmented by the burst. There was a lot of smoke, and he could smell the stench of burning paintwork and cordite.

'Steady on zero-six-zero, sir!' The voice-pipe from the wheel-house was unattended and Hechler saw a petty officer lying dead against the flag lockers. There was not a mark on him, but his contorted face told its own story. Hechler thrust a man into his place.

'Tell the wheelhouse to remain on course.' He slipped on blood and trained his binoculars on the other ship. She was listing badly, flames bursting through her side as if from jets. The last internal explosion had found her heart.

'Engine-room request permission to reduce speed, Captain!'

'What is it, Chief?' Hechler pressed the phone under his cap.

Stück's voice was very steady. 'Pump trouble. Nothing we can't fix. I'm still waiting for reports. That last shell – '

Hechler did not wait. 'Half speed, all engines.' A massive explosion rolled across the water, and fragments of steel and timber rained down until every trough seemed full of charred flotsam.

A man cried, 'She's going!'

Some smaller shells exploded close to the capsizing ship, and Hechler snatched up the gunnery handset, suddenly remembering Gudegast's despair. 'Shift target to the convoy!' It was not a rebuke for the gunnery officer, but it sounded like one.

The two forward turrets were already training round, seeking their targets. But the ships were scattering in several directions; each one was a separate attack.

In the armoured conning tower Gudegast had his face pressed against an observation slit. The *Prinz* had been hit, how badly he did not know. He could hear the intercom chattering, the stream of demands and orders as the damage-control parties swung into action. Gudegast had felt the explosion come right through the deck plates. As if they had hit a reef. Now all he could see was smoke, some small running figures by a dangling motorboat, cut in halves as it hung from its davits.

All he could think of was the sinking liner. The old *Tasmania*, of the Cunard White Star Line. He had seen her many times when she had been taken off her Atlantic runs to do some cruising in and around the lovely fjords of Norway. He had even been on board her once for an officer's birthday.

He could see her clearly, so different from his own timber ship. Spotless, well-laid decks, passengers drifting about with cameras, the elegance, the style of the liner and what she represented. He watched, sickened, as she rolled heavily on to her side, another funnel tearing adrift. There were more explosions, and Gudegast thought for a moment that Kröll was still directing guns on her.

He shouted wildly, 'Leave her! She can't hurt you now! Leave her alone, you bloody bastard!'

His assistants watched anxiously from the rear, their eyes glowing in the reflected explosions through the narrow slits.

Gudegast pressed a button and felt icy rain on his face as the massive steel door slid to one side.

He clambered out on to the little catwalk and then without realising what he was doing, removed his cap.

A ship had just been destroyed because fools had sent her to war.

He wiped his face with his sleeve. And she died with that same old dignity he had always admired so much.

Peter Younger knelt on the floor of the storeroom where the prisoners had been locked up for the night, and pressed his eye to a hole in the wall where a bolt had rusted away.

It was early morning and he heard some of the German sailors calling to each other. He found it hard to tell if they were angry exchanges or not.

Old Shiner sat with his narrow shoulders against the wall, idly watching the young radio officer's eyes in the filtered sunlight. 'They're makin' a bloody row,' he said irritably. 'Couldn't sleep 'cause of it.'

Younger ground his jaws together as he concentrated on his tiny view of the station.

He said, 'They broke open a stock of booze, that's what all the racket's about.'

He should have guessed that something of the sort might happen. As soon as the false signal had been made, the prisoners had been herded together. It was as if the Germans had to let off steam, now the reality of their position was out in the open. Celebrating their part in the plot, or commiserating together at the prospect of early captivity he did not know, but he cursed himself for not taking precautions.

Mason, the man in charge of the station, dropped down beside him.

'It's too late then?' He sounded wary after Younger's outburst during the night, when he had told them what he was going to do. Mason had asked then, 'How do you know all this anyway?' Younger had exploded. 'We were bloody prisoners aboard the raider, that's how!'

He said, 'I must try. There's still a chance we might save a few lives, or call our blokes down on the krauts.'

Old Shiner said, 'If they don't open the bloody door I'm goin' to drop me trousers right now!'

Younger closed his eyes and thrust his forehead against the warm metal until he could think properly again. Poor old Shiner was halfway round the bend. He looked at Mason. 'When the guard unlocks the door we'll grab him and get his gun.'

Old Shiner remarked, 'Accordin' to the Geneva Convention we should 'ave proper toilet arrangements. I seen it in a book somewhere.'

Mason stared at him. 'God Almighty!'

Younger persisted, 'Are you with me?' He nearly said, *or are you like your chum over there who sent the signal under the German's supervision?* But he needed Mason. He was the only one now.

Mason nodded unhappily. 'It'll be the end of us, you know that?'

Younger shrugged. 'I'm not going to think about it.'

He stood up and walked to the corrugated door. The others would probably let him get on with it, watch him gunned down to join the dead mechanic.

Like the shutter in a camera he saw the drifting lifeboat for a split second. The patient, eyeless faces. The very horror of it. He glanced at Old Shiner. Poor bastard. He had been torpedoed and sunk so many times it was a wonder he was still breathing.

Mason said quietly, 'I'll *try*.' He sounded terrified, as if he could barely get the words out.

Younger touched his arm. 'Once inside the transmitting-room I'll have a signal off before you can blink.' He was amazed he could speak so confidently, when he had not even seen inside the place. It might already be out of action, smashed by the Germans after raising the trick alarm. He decided against that. Germans or not, they were all sailors. No sailor was ever keen to sever a possible lifeline.

Mason exclaimed, '*He's coming!*' He pressed himself to the wall and whispered, 'Jesus!'

Younger tested the weight of the makeshift club in his hand. It was a length of firewood, probably left at the station for the winter months. It was not much, but the guard might be half-cut from the night's drinking. He thought of the balding senior operator. Obviously his sense of discipline was no longer shared by his companions. He held his breath until his temples throbbed as the man fumbled with the padlock and tried several times to insert a key. Younger heard him curse, and the clatter of the padlock as it fell on the rock floor.

Please God, let it work! He flung his weight against the door, it flew back and thudded heavily against the guard's skull as he stooped down to recover the padlock.

It all happened in seconds, and yet it lasted forever. The man's face squinting up in the sunlight, blood seeping down his face from the blow, then jerking back as Younger slammed his sea-boot into his gaping jaw. He did not recall how many times he brought the heavy piece of wood down on his head, but it was running with blood and torn skin as he threw it aside and wrenched the sub-machine gun from the man's shoulder.

Then he was running towards the rough ladder, expecting at any second to hear a challenge, feel the agony of a bullet between his shoulders. He heard Mason panting behind him, sobbing and muttering to himself as he followed.

At the top of the short ladder Younger turned for a quick glance. The shutter again. The sprawled sailor, and some terrified faces peering from the storeroom. Younger felt his heart breaking as he looked at the sea. So vast and impersonal, and suddenly without hostility.

It was all over. His ship, his friends, everything.

With a cry he kicked open the door and saw the German with the plastered arm staring at him, a mug of something in his free hand. Several things happened at once. The German lunged for his holster, which was dangling from a chair; Younger squeezed the trigger, but stared aghast as the gun remained silent. *Safety catch.* He fumbled for it, dimly aware that the German had dragged out his pistol, and that Mason was on his knees behind a packing case, burbling incoherently and in tears of terror. Something blurred across Younger's vision and he saw a heavy iron bar smash down on the man's plastered arm to crack it like a carrot. The German dropped his pistol and fell to the floor, his lip bitten through as the pain exploded in his shattered arm.

Old Shiner, his washed-out eyes blazing wildly, stepped further into the room and swung the long bar once more. It must have taken all his strength, but the German lay quite still, probably dead. Old Shiner tossed the bar aside and snatched the sub-machine gun from Younger and snorted, 'Yew'm never took a DEMS course like me. 'Ere, I'll keep them buggers off!'

With a gasp Younger sat down before the transmitter, his heart pumping as with a purr of power he switched it on. It was not so different from the one he had trained on. He dashed the sweat, or were they tears, from his eyes, and concentrated every fibre on the key. He knew most of the abbreviated codes issued by the navy. They needed to in Atlantic convoys, with ship after ship falling out of line, falling astern for the wolves. He blinked hard. Like *Radnor Star*.

He pressed the headphones over his ears and managed to hold the new sounds at bay. Sudden shouts, the blast on a whistle.

He came out in a rush of sweat. *The signal was already being acknowledged.* He grinned uncontrollably at the key. *You're the one who's too late, Baldy!* He was thinking of the senior operator, who probably wondered what the hell was happening.

There was a rattle of machine-gun fire and a line of holes punched through the wall, so that dusty sunlight cut across the room like thin bars.

Old Shiner had the door open just an inch and the room filled with smoke as he fired a long burst down the slope.

'Got one o' the buggers!' He was laughing as he crossed to the opposite side. Neither of them even noticed that Mason, the unwilling volunteer, had already been killed by the first shots.

Younger heard Old Shiner cursing as he snatched up the other German's pistol. He must have emptied a whole magazine in one go.

Younger winced as more shots crashed through the room and some exploded the dials and fuses at the top of the transmitter.

Too late. Too late. The words seemed to deafen the clatter of small arms fire, the occasional heavy bang as Old Shiner took a potshot at someone below the building.

More crashes, and the transmitter went dead. Younger threw the earphones on the bench and swung round. '*We did it!*' But the old boatswain did not hear him. He sat lopsided against the wall, blood seeping through his tattered jersey. His eyes were tightly closed, like those last moments in the lifeboat.

A window shattered and he stared without comprehension at a heavy cudgel-shaped object as it fell at his feet. He had not, of course, ever seen a German hand-grenade before.

His mind had just time to record that Old Shiner even had his arms cradled, as he had been when he had nursed his cat, when the grenade exploded and there was only darkness.

There was less smoke now and Hechler guessed that the fire-fighting parties had doused most of the flames between decks.

Voice-pipes chattered incessantly until Froebe shouted, 'Damage-control, sir!'

Hechler jammed the telephone to his ear while he watched the dead petty officer being dragged away. The man with the glass-flayed face had already gone; only his blood remained, spreading and thinning in the steady rain.

Theil said, 'A fluke shell, sir.' Someone was screaming in the background. 'A shot in a million.'

Hechler watched the smoke spiralling above the broken screen.

'Tell me.'

Theil explained in his flat, impersonal tone. One of the armed merchant cruiser's last eight-inch shells had plummeted down to pierce the battery deck between the bridge and Turret Bruno. As Theil had said, it was a chance in a million. It had struck the air shaft of a mushroom ventilator and been deflected through the armoured deck before exploding against a magazine shaft. Sixteen men of the damage-control party there had been killed. In such a confined space it was not surprising. But it was a double disaster. The explosion had severely damaged the training mechanism of Turret Bruno. Until the damage could be put right, the whole turret was immobile. It could not even be trained by manual power.

Hechler considered the facts as Theil described them. The engine-room was confident that all pumps would be working again at full power within the hour. Casualties elsewhere were confined to the bridge, and two seamen who had been putting out a small fire below the funnel. They must have been blasted over the side without anyone seeing them go.

'Report to me when you have completed your inspection.'

Froebe whispered, 'The admiral, sir.'

Leitner seemed to materialise on the bridge like a white spectre.

'What the *hell* is happening?' He glared through the trapped smoke, his shoulders dark with rain. 'I am not a bloody mind-reader!'

Hechler looked at him coldly. 'B Turret is out of commission, sir. We've lost nineteen men killed, and three injured.' He glanced at the blood. It had almost been washed away now. 'One man was blinded.'

'*I do not hear you!* What are you saying?' Leitner strode from one side to the other, his shoes crunching over broken glass. 'We have lost the convoy – don't you understand anything?'

Hechler looked up as Froebe called, 'New course is two-three-zero sir.'

Hechler said. 'We have to turn, sir. Radar reports three tankers sunk and two, possibly three escorts as well.'

'*I don't care!*' Leitner was beside himself with rage, and did not even notice the astonished watchkeepers around him. 'Three tankers! A pinprick! We should have taken the whole convoy.'

Jaeger waited for Leitner to rush to the opposite side and stammered, 'W/T office has picked up a signal from the radio station, sir.'

Hechler eyed him calmly, although his nerves were screaming.

'Well?'

'They are not sure, sir. But it seems as if another operator has disclaimed the first signal. Now there is only silence.'

'Steady on two-three-zero, sir. All engines half-speed ahead.'

Leitner was suddenly facing him, his face streaming with rain.

'What was that? Am I to be told nothing by these idiots?'

Hechler replied, 'The information will doubtless have been sent to your bridge, sir.' He tried to contain his patience, when all he wanted to do was discover how badly the *Prinz* was damaged.

'It means that somebody on St Jorge took over the transmitter. Had it been any earlier we would have had to abandon the whole convoy. I – '

Leitner thrust his face so close he could smell the brandy. 'I don't want your snivelling excuses! I'll have those men courtmartialled and shot, and I'll personally break the officer responsible for the landing party!'

Hechler stood back, sickened. 'It was a risk. We knew it. It might have been worse.'

'*Worse? Worse?*' Leitner waved his arms at the bridge. 'I don't see that! A relic of a merchant ship stood against *Prinz Luitpold*, and because of someone's incompetence we had to withdraw! By God, Hechler, I'll not be a laughing-stock because of it! Do you know what I call it?'

Hechler pressed his hands to his sides. He wanted to hit Leitner, to keep on hitting him. A laughing-stock, was that all he saw in it? Men killed, and this fine ship isolated and at bay because of his haphazard orders.

'I call it cowardice! In the face of the enemy – what do you think of *that?*'

'I can only disagree, sir.'

'Can you indeed.' He stared around the bridge. 'There are some who will live long enough to regret this day!' He stormed off the bridge and Froebe hissed, 'I'm no coward, damn him!'

Hechler ignored him. 'Recall the Arado. Tell W/T to monitor every signal. We have roused a hornet's nest.'

He looked round, surprised, as sunlight broke through the dull clouds. 'And I want the navigating officer here at once.'

There was no point in wondering about the hand on the transmitter. It was probably as dead as the men trapped below when the shell had exploded amongst them.

A messenger handed him a telephone. Leitner's voice was quite controlled again. It could have been someone else entirely.

'We will rendezvous at the *second* grid-point. It will be safer than heading north right away.'

'Very well, sir.' *Why don't I argue with him? Tell him that we are wasting sea miles and precious time. Steer north and take the risk.* It would be 900 miles closer to home. But even as he thought it, Hechler knew it was fruitless. Leitner was unstable in his present mood. All he could think of was their failure to destroy the whole convoy, the effect it might have on his own reputation. He had made it quite clear that he would see that all blame would rest elsewhere. On the captain's shoulders, no doubt. Hechler was quietly surprised that the realisation did not touch him.

What they had achieved this far, they had done well. The courage and sacrifice of that one old liner had shifted the balance, from offensive to the need for survival. That was war. It was also luck.

He heard Gudegast's seaboots crunching over the glass and turned to face him.

'You've heard about St Jorge?'

Gudegast met his gaze, troubled and wary. 'Yes, sir. The whole ship has.' He seemed to expect anger, even dismissal.

Hechler said quietly, 'You were right, Josef. She *was* a fine old lady.'

Gudegast's bearded features softened, 'No, I was a fool to question your actions. It was not my place to speak as I did.'

Hechler looked up at the rain. A man had died here, another had been blinded, just feet away. *It could have been me.*

He said, 'My guess is that the Tommies are on their way to St Jorge, or were until that last signal was sent. It will give us some sea-room, I think. Maybe our admiral is right to head for the second rendezvous. It will keep us out of the air patrols, and I think that the hunters will be expecting us to head for the North Atlantic without further delay.'

Gudegast shrugged. 'Home then, sir.'

'Yes. But we'll not reach Germany again without a fight.'

Theil entered the bridge and eyed them grimly. 'I have done my rounds, sir.'

Hechler nodded. 'Tell me the worse, Viktor.'

Theil looked at the broken screen. He had heard the blinded man screaming before he had been silenced by Stroheim's staff.

'One of my petty officers, Hammer, is trapped in the empty, ready-use room, sir. The mechanism was broken in the explosion.'

Gudegast said, 'But he should not have been in there surely?'

He saw the petty officer in his mind, a mild man, yet one who always seemed to be against authority in his mad desire to keep stocks of glass in any vacant space.

Hechler said, 'I have the key in my safe, Viktor.'

Theil faced him. 'Yes. And the admiral had the other. I am fully aware of the security arrangements in this ship. I – ' He seemed to check himself with a real effort.

'Well, he's trapped inside. With the admiral's boxes.'

It would have to be solved, but against what had happened it seemed trivial.

He would go round the ship as soon as the Arado had been hoisted inboard. With more and more enemy ships being homed either towards the broken convoy or the silent radio station, they would need all their eyes to avoid discovery.

'See what you can do.' Hechler looked at each of them in turn. 'And thank you.'

He felt utterly drained. Yet he must inspect the immobilised turret, see his heads of department, and bury their dead.

He thought of the girl's face so close to his own, the need to see her. It might be the last time.

He thought too of the unknown hand on the transmitter key, and the captain of the old ocean liner as she had charged to the attack. His men could and would fight like that. He pictured Leitner's insane fury and felt a sudden anxiety.

The legend and the luck were no longer enough.

18

No Hiding Place

Acting Commodore Hemrose moved restlessly to the starboard side of the *Wiltshire*'s bridge and fastened his duffle coat more tightly. The rain was getting heavier, he thought irritably. They could do without it.

He peered through a clearview screen and watched the long arrowhead of the cruiser's forecastle begin to shine through the darkness. Dawn soon. He felt like rubbing his hands but it was too wet for that. Since leaving Simonstown the three ships had maintained almost their full speed, and each had been closed up at action stations since midnight. Exciting, exhilarating, it was much more than either, Hemrose thought. Gone was the boredom and the nagging suspicion that the German raider was cocking a snook at them. For two days they had pounded through the heavy ocean swell, gun crews exercising without all the usual moans. This time it was in earnest.

Hemrose could picture his ships clearly despite the darkness. The *Rhodesia* was half a mile astern, while the light cruiser *Pallas* was way ahead in the van. If the

German's radar was as good as the experts had implied, it was better to have the smallest ship in the lead. The *Prinz Luitpold* was a powerful and formidable opponent, but they would dart in to close the range, singly, while the others maintained covering fire to halve the enemy's resources. Hemrose thought of their old Walrus flying boat, the Shagbat as it was affectionately known in the navy. One engine, a *pusher* at that, with a ridiculous maximum speed of 130 odd miles per hour. But it only needed one sighting report, and the ancient Walrus could do that just as efficiently as any first-rate bomber.

Hemrose glanced at his bridge staff. The first lieutenant and officer-of-the-watch, the navigating officer, two junior subbies, and the usual handful of experts, signalmen and the like. As good a ship's company as you could find anywhere, he decided.

He licked his lips and tasted that last mug of cocoa, *pusser's kye*. It had been laced with rum, his chief steward had seen to that. Just the thing to meet the dawn.

He heard the OOW answering one of the voice-pipes, then turned as he said, 'W/T office. Chief telegraphist requests permission to come up, sir.'

'*What?*' Hemrose dug his hands into his damp pockets. 'Oh, very well.'

The chief telegraphist was a proper old sweat. Not the kind to make fruitless requests when at any moment they might make contact with the enemy.

The man arrived on the bridge and paused only to nod to his messmate, the Chief Yeoman of Signals.

'What is it?'

The man had a signal pad in his hand but did not seem to need it.

He said, 'From Admiralty, sir, repeated Rear-Admiral commanding Force M.' He swallowed hard. 'The signal from St Jorge was a fake, sir. The northbound tanker convoy is under attack by the raider. HMS *Tasmania* is engaging.'

Some of the others had heard what the chief petty officer had said and were watching Hemrose, waiting for him to explode. Hemrose was surprised that he should feel so calm. And yet he had never expected this to happen. Not in a thousand years.

The chief telegraphist added, 'Also, there was one further transmission from that radio station, sir. Someone there was apparently trying to warn us.'

Hemrose looked up sharply as the first lieutenant murmured, 'Brave bastard!'

'Get the commander up here.' He had to think, but all he could see was the convoy, the shells ploughing amongst those heavily laden oil tankers. 'Call up the squadron. Remain on course. Reduce to cruising speed.' He hated to add, 'Fall out action stations. I'll speak to our people presently.'

'More kye, sir.' His chief steward had appeared by his side.

'Thanks.' He tried to grin, but his face felt rigid. 'I bloody need it.'

Godson clattered up the ladder and exclaimed, 'I just heard, sir. Bad show.'

Is that what you really think? Aloud Hemrose said, 'We'll be getting our marching orders soon, hence the signal repeated to Force M.'

Godson remained silent. Force M was one of the fleet's powerful independent groups, a battle-cruiser, a big carrier, with all the support and escorts they needed. It would be the end of Hemrose's little squadron. He would become a small fish in a much grander pool. Godson hated himself for being pleased about it. But it would be a whole lot safer.

The navigating officer murmured, 'When it's convenient, sir – ' He hesitated as Hemrose turned towards him.

Hemrose said, 'We shall maintain this course for the moment, Pilot.'

Godson offered, 'Someone will have to lie off St Jorge and pick up the Germans if there are any.'

Hemrose said harshly, 'Well, not me. Leave that to some errand-boy!'

His sudden anger seemed to tire him. He said, 'I shall be in my sea-cabin. Call me if – ' He did not finish it.

Alone in his cabin abaft the bridge he lay fully clothed, staring into the darkness.

When the telephone rang he snatched it up and snapped, 'Well?'

It was Godson. 'Signal from Admiralty, sir.' He cleared his throat as he always did when he was about to face something bad. 'The Armed Merchant Cruiser *Tasmania* has been sunk. One escort reported seeing a shell-burst on the raider. Most of the convoy has survived. We are to await further instructions.'

Hemrose slumped down again. Poor old *Tasmania*. It must have been the last thing her captain had expected too. He clenched his fists with sudden despair and anger. What was it he had learned when he had been a cadet at Dartmouth? *God and the Navy we adore, when danger threatens but not before.* How bloody true it had been proved over and over again in this war. Pleasure boats and paddle steamers used for mine-sweeping, Great War destroyers fighting the Atlantic and anything the krauts could fling their way. And it would be the same in any future conflict. Spend nothing, but expect a bloody miracle, that was John Citizen's battle cry.

He heaved himself up and stared at the luminous clock. What was the matter with him? Was he so overwhelmed by the German's trick that he had missed something so obvious? No ship as good as *Prinz Luitpold* would be deterred by the second signal from St Jorge. Not at that stage, with helpless tankers falling to her broadsides. The old AMC had scored one hit, they said. Well, it might only take one. It must have been bad enough to make Hechler break off the action.

He seized the telephone and heard the OOW reply, 'Bridge, sir?'

'Get me the commander.'

Godson sounded alarmed. 'Something wrong, sir?'

'*Tasmania* hit the raider, Toby. The *Prinz Luitpold* must be in trouble.'

Godson stammered; 'One shell, sir – well, that is, we don't know – '

'Shut up and listen. I want the attack team mustered in the chart room in ten minutes.'

There was no comment and he snapped, 'Are you still there?'

Godson replied weakly, 'Are you going after the raider again, sir?'

Hemrose touched his face. He would shave, and meet his little team looking refreshed and confident.

He said, 'We needed a bit of luck, Toby. That poor, clapped-out AMC may have given us just that.'

Godson persisted, 'The Admiralty will probably decline to – '

'Don't be such a bloody old woman.' He slammed down the phone.

It was so obvious he wanted to shout it at the top of his voice. The US submarine had been damaged, but had fired at the raider because her skipper had never seen such a target. But his torpedoes must have hit something else, hence the remains of German corpses and a massive oil-slick. The so-called experts had acted like a ship's lookout who saw only what he expected to see. It must have been another submarine. He wanted to laugh, when he recalled it was the poor chaplain who had first put the doubts about the raider's fuel supply in his mind.

It had to be that. But just because it had never been done before, nobody, not even Duffield's back-room boys had even suspected it.

God, the enemy must have been planning all this for months, and everything, even the RAF's recce reports over the Norwegian fjords, had been fooled by one ruse after another.

The door opened. 'I've brought you your shavin' gear, sir.' The steward showed his teeth. ''Ad a feelin' you might be askin' for it.'

Hemrose stared at himself in the mirror. He could still be wrong. There was nothing really solid to go on. But it was all he had. They would go right through every report and signal. If they found nothing they would do it all over again until they did.

Nobody had really considered submarines before. The Admiralty and intelligence sources had concentrated on checking lists of so-called neutrals, especially those in South American ports, where a supply ship might have been waiting for a rendezvous.

Later in the chart-room Hemrose explained his thoughts on the raider's performance.

'Hechler had that convoy on a plate. He'd knocked out the escort, and picked off the first tankers like fish in a barrel. But for the old AMC he would have polished off the whole boiling lot.'

The young navigating officer said, 'If he's damaged, he'll also need fuel.'

Hemrose nodded. 'Good thinking. When his bunkers are topped up he'll make for safe waters again – my guess is Norway.' He added grudgingly, 'Even with the Home Fleet and Force M on the alert he's the sort of captain who might just pull it off. If he sails safely into port after cutting our blockade in both directions he would do far more good for German morale at home than by wiping out that convoy.'

Godson said, 'The Germans have been using the big supply submarines in the South Atlantic for two years, I believe.'

Hemrose waited silently, seeing his hazy ideas forming into a possibility on their faces.

The first lieutenant said, 'They work to a grid system, don't they?'

Hemrose smiled. 'Check all the U-boat reports in that area, ours and the Yanks.'

Hemrose rocked back on his heels. He was already heading into disaster, so where might this additional risk take him?

'Then make a signal to *Pallas* and *Rhodesia*. I'd like to see the captains before we begin.'

Godson wilted under his stare but asked, 'And Admiralty, sir?'

'Balls to their lordships, Toby! I was given this job and I intend to see it through!' He glanced at the chaplain. 'And thanks to our warlike padre here, I think we may be on the home stretch!'

Hemrose walked out into the daylight and lifted his face to the rain.

It was hard to accept that within two hours he had risen from despair to optimism.

As he passed the forward funnel he saw the ship's crest bolted to a catwalk. Beneath it was her motto in Latin. Hemrose's red face split into a grin so that two Oerlikon gunners peered down with astonishment to watch him.

Translated, their motto was *Count your blessings.*

It was not much, but it was a start.

Leitner looked up from his littered desk and eyed Hechler for several seconds.

'You wish to see me?'

Hechler nodded. He wondered how Leitner could leave the upper bridge to spend time in his spacious quarters. The cabin was unusually chaotic, with clothes strewn about, and a life-jacket hanging on the door.

Hechler said, 'We have just buried the men who were killed, sir.'

Leitner pouted. 'Yes, I felt the ship slow down.' Some of the old edge returned to his tone. 'Not that she's exactly a greyhound of the ocean at the moment!'

'The engine-room expects the pumps will all be working at full pressure soon.' They had said that yesterday, but this time Stück seemed quite confident. 'It's B turret that worries me.'

'You? *Worry?*' Leitner put down his pen and regarded him calmly. 'After their performance with the convoy I'd have thought the whole gunnery team should be *worried!*'

It was pointless to argue, to explain that the single shell from the *Tasmania* had been a fluke shot. Anyway, Leitner seemed so preoccupied he would only have challenged that too.

Hechler said, 'The rendezvous with the supply-boat, sir. I am having second thoughts. At this reduced speed we will meet the milch-cow on her final day in the prescribed grid. After that we may not find the time to refuel before we turn for home.'

'I had considered that, Dieter.' The sudden use of his name was also unexpected. 'But we still stick to our plans. I intend to transfer the camera team to the submarine. They can make their own arrangements when she reaches Germany.' He sounded vague, almost disinterested.

'And the woman pilot?'

Leitner gave a small smile. 'Ah, yes. The lovely Erika. I am afraid she has not earned *her* release just yet.' He dragged a chart from beneath a pile of papers. 'The rendezvous is here, right?'

Hechler bent over the desk. Why go over it again? All he could see were the lines of flag-covered bodies, the rain sheeting down while he had read the burial service. Then the signal to the bridge to reduce speed, the last volley of shots, and the seamen rolling up the empty flags for the next time. Faces and groups lingered in his mind, like little cameos of war itself. A young seaman wiping his eyes with his sleeve and trying not to show his grief at the loss of a friend. The camera crew filming the funeral, a petty officer staring at them, his eyes filled with hatred and disgust. Leitner should have been there. It was the least he could do. And he had seen the girl too, her coat collar turned up as she had gripped a stanchion below two manned anti-aircraft guns and watched him, listening to his words as he had saluted, and the pathetic bundles had splashed over the side.

Hechler had been kept busy with hardly a break. Now, in the sealed cabin it closed in like a blanket. He was dog-tired at a time when he needed to be at full alert.

Somewhere overhead one of the Arados was testing its engine.

They were off the shipping lanes, and as far as Bauer's telegraphists had been able to determine, all enemy forces had been directed either to the convoy or further north. OKM Operations Division had been silent. It was as if the *Prinz Luitpold* had already been written off as a casualty, left to her own resources.

Hechler closed his fingers. One more cargo of fuel and he would be able to assess their immediate future. If they avoided the enemy Kröll and his artificers would repair the turret's training mechanism. Otherwise all their main defences would be down aft.

Leitner did not look up from the chart, and some of his sleek hair fell forward like a loose quill. It was so unlike him that Hechler wondered if the last engagement had broken his faith.

Leitner was saying, 'Now about my boxes, hmm?'

Hechler thought of the petty officer who was still trapped. The damage control section had told him that the door was buckled, and it would have to be cut away with torches. There was an air vent, so the luckless Hammer was in no danger. Yet.

'They are working on the door, sir.'

Leitner did not seem to hear. 'That man had a key. He must have stolen it or made it. He is a thief, a menace to this ship, a traitor. I intend that he shall stand trial as soon as he is freed.' He raised his eyes suddenly. '*I want that door open.*' His eyes hardened. 'It can be done, *yes* or *no*?' He swung round. 'What now?'

Theil stood in the entrance, his cap dripping with rain.

'The door won't move, sir. The engine-room is supplying some heavier cutting gear – '

Leitner screamed at him, 'Don't come here with your snivelling excuses! I want the door forced open immediately! Blow it down with a limited explosion!'

Hechler stepped between them. 'It could kill Hammer, sir. In such a confined space – '

Leitner glared at him wildly. 'It will save him from the firing squad! He was spying on me, and he's not the only one! Must I repeat everything? Blow it open!'

Theil looked at Hechler, his face pleading. 'He's one of my men!'

Leitner was breathing hard. 'I have no doubt of that!'

Theil faced him. 'What exactly do you mean, sir?'

Leitner stared at him, astonished. 'Are you questioning me or my orders?'

Hechler snapped, 'I would like to remind both of you that we are in some danger.' To Theil he added, 'Wait outside. I'll deal with this matter.' As the door closed he said, 'How dare you accuse my officers of plotting against you?' He could not stop himself. 'You are supposed to offer leadership to this ship's company, not act like some sort of god!'

Leitner's jaw hung open. It was as if Hechler had struck him, or screamed some terrible curse.

Hechler continued flatly, 'I intend to fight this ship back to Germany, and to do that I need the trust of every man aboard. Respect, not fear, *sir*, is what we survive on.' He watched him coldly. 'Or we go under.'

Leitner dragged out a spotless handkerchief and slowly dabbed his lips.

'So that is your attitude?'

'It is.'

He waited, half expecting Leitner to call to the sentry and put him under arrest. A Luger lay on the table nearby. He might even drag that out and shoot him in his present unstable mood.

Leitner nodded jerkily. 'I shall remember this. Now get that door open and have that man arrested.'

Hechler stepped away from the table. Leitner had again become very calm. It was unnerving.

Leitner continued, 'Let me know when you are increasing speed to this rendezvous.' He was pointing at the chart, but his fingers were nowhere near the pencilled position. 'I shall be receiving the final instructions shortly. When I do – ' He looked away. '*Leave me!*'

Hechler stepped out of the cabin and found Theil waiting.

'You think I knew, don't you?'

Theil gaped at him. 'I – I don't understand.'

'You love this ship, Viktor. I know that. In a matter of days, maybe hours, we shall be called on to fight, against odds. I shall need your loyalty then, and so will the *Prinz*.'

He looked away, unable to watch Theil's despair as he said brokenly, 'She was arrested by the Gestapo. I was not told. The house was empty.' The words were spilling from him in a torrent. 'If I hadn't read that file – '

Hechler said gently, 'It was too late to do anything when I found out about it. We were under enforced radio silence, you know that. It may not be as bad as you think – ' Their eyes met and he knew it was pointless to go on. Even if the Gestapo had made a mistake, it was unlikely they would admit it. What was one more life to them?

Millions had perished. He thought of the unknown hand on the morse key at St Jorge, the men he had buried, the petty officer who had died without a mark on him. He looked around at the grey steel. They could still break through. He touched Theil's arm and this time he did not drag away. It was already too late for him.

'I am the captain of this ship, Viktor, and many people probably think I am too remote, too secure to watch minor events under my command. But I have seen and heard things. I will not allow this ship's reputation to be smeared.' His eyes were hard. 'By anyone.'

Theil touched his cap. 'I'll do what I can.' He swallowed hard. 'I wasn't certain – I – '

Hechler walked out to the open deck; it was like sharing a terrible secret to see the tears running down Theil's cheeks. He felt suddenly sickened by it. By Leitner's inconsistent behaviour, his malice and his instability. But more by his own uncertainty. Like a man who has been given a weapon he suspects is faulty.

'You walk alone, Dieter?'

She stepped from beneath the same gun-mounting, her cheeks glowing from wind and rain.

167

He faced her and wanted to fold her in his arms, forget everything but this moment.

'I need to talk, Erika.' He knew some of the seamen were watching him. It was like a farewell at a railway station. Alone within a crowd. No words until it was too late to utter them.

'I know.' She gripped his arm. 'I was afraid.' She shook her head so that her damp hair bounced on the fur collar. 'No, not of war, of the fighting and the dying. But afterwards. I thought you might think it was a momentary lapse, a need which we both shared, but only for a moment.' She gripped him more tightly. 'I want you for myself.'

He smiled down at her, the other faces and figures fading into distance. 'I shall never give you up.' He turned as a messenger bustled up to them and saluted. 'From the bridge, sir. The engine-room can give full speed now.' His eyes flickered between them.

'Tell the bridge to wait. I am coming up.' He looked at the girl's eyes, hung on to what he saw, needing her to believe him, to trust him, no matter what happened.

He said, 'I love you, Erika.' Then he stepped back and saw the way she lifted her chin. It was as if they had both found a strength they had not previously recognised.

As he vanished up the ladder to the forebridge she whispered aloud, 'And I you, dearest of men.'

The deck began to tremble and she watched the wash rise up alongside as once again the bows smashed into the sea as if they despised it. She walked slowly below the high bridge structure and saw the black hole where the shell had plunged through to explode between decks. It was all so unreal to see and feel the enemy right here amongst them. She thought of Hechler's features as he had read the burial service, his strong voice raised above the laboured roar of fans, and the hiss of rain across the armour plating. She smiled sadly. *The iron pirate.* She could not see more than a day ahead, and she guessed that most of her companions felt much the same. But after this precious moment she knew she would find him again, that she could love nobody else.

The following morning, with less than an hour left of the prearranged rendezvous time, they made contact with the giant submarine. Men lined the guardrails as it surfaced, the water streaming from the casing and squat conning-tower, many of the onlookers remembering the other submarine's savage end, and wondering if this one's commander even knew about it.

Theil, megaphone in hand, watched the lines being fired across, the engineering party ready and waiting to sway the huge fuel hoses inboard and connect them to the bunkers.

He kept seeing Hechler's face, the sadness he had shown when he had confronted him about Britta.

Nothing seemed to matter any more. If they reached home there was nobody waiting for him. Anyway, Leitner would make certain he would climb no further in the navy. If they met with the enemy, he might at least save the ship.

He waved his megaphone to the boatswain's party at the guyropes and tackles.

Either way, only Leitner could win. He stared so hard at the swaying wires and ropes between the two ill-matched hulls that his vision became blurred. Leitner had known all about Britta. He could have made a signal when they were still in safe waters, if he had wanted to help.

Theil was suddenly quite calm. He knew what he was going to do.

The pilot of the *Wiltshire*'s twin-winged Walrus was a young Wavy Navy lieutenant. Despite what other Fleet Air Arm officers said about his antiquated flying-boat he had grown extremely fond of it.

He was singing silently, his voice lost in the throaty roar of the Pegasus radial engine which hung above the cockpit like some ungainly cradle, and watching patches of blue cutting through the cloud layer, like a sea on a beach.

The three other members of his crew were peering down at the ocean, where occasionally their inelegant shadow preceded them as they tacked back and forth over a forty mile line.

Rumours had spawned in the cruiser's wardroom at a mounting rate. Ever since it had been announced that the German's presence at St Jorge had been a clever ruse, and then that the Admiralty was ordering Hemrose to withdraw and join up with Force M. A new buzz had spread through the ship before the old one had been found true or false.

How vast the ocean looked from here, he thought. Nothing, not even a hint of land. It was a vast grey-blue desert, broken here and there by tiny white ridges, and dark troughs which from the sky seemed quite motionless.

A great ocean, with nothing ahead but the winding coastline of South America. He chuckled. And that was 500 miles away. Hemrose would have to give in soon, he thought. He had pushed his luck too far with the Admiralty this time. Old Godson would be pleased. He was scared of his own shadow.

His observer and navigator climbed up beside him and switched on his intercom.

'Time to turn in five minutes, Bob. Then one more sweep to the south and back to Father.' He peered at the endless terrain of water.

'The Old Man's not going to like it.'

The pilot eased the controls and glanced quickly at the compass. The news from Europe was amazing, advances everywhere. Only the coming of winter would slow things down now. He had been at school when the war had started, and the navy, temporary or not, was all he knew. It would probably carry on in Japan afterwards, he thought.

It was strange, but he had never dropped a bomb or fired one of their elderly Vickers machine-guns in anger. Just up and down lines of convoyed ships, or scouting like this ahead of the cruiser.

It would have been a nice thing to remember. 'What d'you reckon, Tim?'

His companion grinned. 'No chance. The Old Man's dropped a right clanger this time!'

They both laughed into their mouthpieces and then the pilot looked again and gasped, 'Christ, Tim! *It's her!*'

The old Walrus leaned over, the engine protesting shakily as he thrust the stick hard against his knee.

It was not a silhouette like the ones in their charts and manuals. It was a flaw in the sea's face, a hint of shadow, solid and somehow frightening.

'Quick! Back to Father!' They clung on as the Walrus tacked into a low bank of cloud with as much dignity as it could manage.

There was so much the pilot wanted to know and to recognise. He could have risked flak and worse by going nearer, but he knew what Hemrose would say if he disobeyed orders.

He felt his friend punching his shoulder and stared at him, his eyes suddenly bright with understanding pride as he shouted, 'Never mind the bloody fleet, Bob! Just remember this day! *We found the bastard!*'

Had the Germans seen them? It no longer mattered. They had indeed done what everyone else had failed to do. In all this ocean, it was a bloody miracle!

They both fell about laughing when they realised that neither of the other crew members as yet knew what had happened.

Aboard their ship Hemrose sat nodding in the noon sunlight, his cap tilted over his reddened face.

The Chief Yeoman of signals steadied his telescope and said, 'Signal from *Pallas*, sir. *In contact with your Walrus*. Message reads.' The yeoman licked his dried lips. '*Enemy in sight!*'

Hemrose slid from the chair, feeling their eyes on him. As if he had just parted the Red Sea.

'Make to squadron, Yeo. *Increase to full speed*.' He saw the yeoman watching him too, his eyes asking a question. They had been together a long time and Hemrose did not disappoint him.

'Hoist battle ensigns!'

19

Last Command

Hechler stood on the bridge wing and watched the huge submarine manoeuvring abeam. The sea seemed to flood between them, as if both vessels were stationary. Hechler knew differently, could sense the group of junior officers who had been summoned by Froebe to the bridge to study the formidable art of ship-handling. The supply-submarine had all her work cut out to maintain proper buoyancy and trim as the big hoses began to quiver like oily snakes, and the first of the precious fuel was pumped across.

Theil was with the boatswain on the maindeck, his megaphone or one hand slicing the air to control the seamen at the guy-ropes and wires.

'Revolutions seven-zero.' Hechler heard the order repeated behind him and pictured the intent group far below his feet in the armour-plated wheelhouse.

'*Stop starboard!*' He watched narrowly as the bows straightened up again, and the channel between the hulls became even.

'Slow ahead all engines.' He gripped the safety rail and leaned right over, the rain slashing across his oilskin, although he barely noticed it.

He loved to feel the might and power of the ship beneath him, as if he was holding her, as a rider will control a wilful mount. He saw a lamp blink from the conning tower and resisted the urge to smile. He knew already what the brief signal would ask.

'Signal, sir. *Request send boat with passengers.*'

'Negative. Tell the commander to break out a rubber dinghy.' It would be a lively crossing between the cruiser and the submarine even when controlled by hand-lines and tackles. He knew the camera team was already mustered by the guardrail, their cans of film safely protected in heavy bags. If he had one of their own boats lowered, the submarine might be tempted to break away and dive at the first suggestion of danger. Her commander would know this of course, but it was always worth a try.

He craned still further across the rail and saw one of the camera girls clinging to Meile, the supply officer, in a tearful embrace. Some of the sailors were grinning at them, and one hidden soul gave an ironic cheer.

Whatever happened from now on, it would be done without the benefit of a filmed record, he thought.

He said, 'Tell the wheelhouse to allow for the drag. Ease to port. Hold her there!'

The big submarine would not have a smooth passage home, he thought. All the long haul up to Iceland and around through the Denmark Strait before the ice came down. Then over to Norway, following the coastline to the narrows which guarded the way into the Baltic. What would they find when they finally reached Kiel, he wondered? It would be a prime target for the Allied air forces, and all the flak in the world could not hold out against such odds. He could picture his last visit there without effort.... He called sharply, '*Half astern starboard!*' He counted the seconds as the drag of one screw took effect. 'Slow ahead starboard!' He wondered if the fledgling one-stripers had noticed that his attention had drifted for those few vital seconds. He saw Theil peer up at the bridge; he of all people would know how simple it was to veer too close and grind into the supply-boat. Or to drag away, snapping lines and hoses and covering the sea with fuel.

He heard Froebe lecturing to the young officers. Hechler took a deep breath. Close thing.

A messenger called, 'Half completed, sir.' He had the engine-room handset pressed to one ear. 'Another thirty minutes.'

Hechler waved his hand without turning. There were no hoses immediately below the bridge, and he pictured the luckless petty officer, the one they called Mad Rudi, locked in his steel prison. It was still not clear how he had got there, or why, and communication between him and the working party outside was limited to a series of frustrating exchanges with hammer-taps on the heavy door.

Leitner's order to blow it open was absurd. The compartment was next to the forward flak switch-room, while beyond that was one of the great bunkers, still full and untapped.

The right gun, then the left in Turret Bruno lifted a few degrees, and the whole structure gave a drawn-out groan, as if steel were grating on steel. The turret remained motionless. Only one shell had found its mark, but the effects showed no sign of improving. Kröll was fuming with anxiety and impatience and had every artificer from his department hard at work to clear the training mechanism. No, even a controlled charge to open Hammer's prison would be courting disaster. Like a man tossing a lighted cigarette into a barrel of gunpowder.

Leitner had not thought fit to discuss this further setback, but had sent Theissen, his aide, to enquire about progress.

The man obviously knew nothing of his admiral's original intention. To offload his mysterious boxes into the submarine, perhaps? If so, why bring them this far?

He heard Gudegast rumbling away in the background, pointing out the behaviour of wind and sea and their effect on two tethered hulls.

He recalled Gudegast's outburst over the old AMC. It added to the man in some way, as if he had always managed to keep his real self hidden in the past.

The boatswain walked towards the forecastle, his arm gesturing to some men with heaving lines. Brezinka knew just about everything that happened in the ship. He would certainly know the truth about Hammer.

Hechler tried not to think of the girl, how she had looked when he had blurted out his true feelings for her. He knew he would never forget. He screwed up his eyes and concentrated on the taut or slackening wires, the way that the sea was breaking over the submarine's nearest saddle-tank.

He had to see her again. Was it so hopeless that it must remain just an incident, like so many thousands in wartime?

And what of Theil? Fretting, hating, nursing his despair, which was as deep as any wound. Which would last? His love for the ship, or the inner madness that would in time destroy him?

'Radar – bridge!' The speaker made the young officers peer up with alarm.

Hechler seized the handset. 'Captain speaking.'

'Aircraft at Green one-five-oh! Moving left to right, extreme range.'

A dozen pairs of powerful glasses swivelled round and a man exclaimed, 'I saw a flash, sir!'

Hechler kept his eyes on the submarine. 'Keep watching!' He dared not hand the con to one of the others.

Froebe said, 'It's gone into some clouds, sir.' He sounded interested but nothing more. 'Dead astern now. Target moving very slowly.' He swore silently. 'Lost it again.'

The speaker intoned, 'Secondary armament stand by!'

Hechler wanted to turn, but snapped, 'Cancel that order!'

Gudegast joined him and together they stared down at the supply-boat's great whale back. The dinghy had been warped alongside and he saw one of the women being guided or dragged to the open forehatch. The sooner the passengers were safely below and the hatch slammed shut, the happier the commander would be.

Gudegast said, 'Maybe it didn't see us, sir?' He sounded doubtful.

Hechler considered it. A small aircraft, over 500 miles from land – it had to be hostile. Everyone had reported it as being very slow. He felt the dampness of sweat beneath his cap. Had it been from a carrier, it would have been swift, and soon to be joined by others.

He replied, 'It saw us all right. Might be a neutral.' He shook his head, dismissing his own assessment. 'My guess is that it's a float-plane of some kind.' He felt Gudegast sigh and added, 'I intend to assume it's from a warship, but not a carrier.'

Gudegast gave a chuckle. 'That's something, I suppose.'

Theissen appeared on the bridge companion ladder. 'I have been sent to enquire about – '

Hechler said bluntly, 'An aircraft, presumed hostile. If the Admiral wishes to know why I ordered the gun crews to stand down, please tell him that I would prefer that the enemy thinks we did *not* see him.' He watched the hoses throbbing across the lively wash of trapped water. 'I intend to complete oiling.'

As the man hurried away Gudegast asked quietly, 'What then, sir?'

Hechler was picturing the immediate chart in his mind. Soon the submarine would vanish. The ocean would be a desert again.

'Warn the first Arado to prepare for launching.' He waited for the big navigator to pass the order. 'My guess is that an enemy ship,' he hesitated, 'or *ships*, are close by. I'd say one hundred miles maximum. That plane will be going to its superior officer with the haste of hell. No radio, in case we pick him up – he'll be depending on surprise.'

Gudegast murmured, 'You saw all this in a few seconds, sir. I admire that very much. Gunnery patrol would have had every weapon with that range banging away in one more moment!'

Hechler smiled. 'You used to carry timber as you have often told me. I have always done this, since I was a boy. It is my life.'

'Arado ready, sir.'

Hechler said, 'See the pilot and give him a course. I want him to find the enemy and report back to me.'

Gudegast watched his profile. It would be a suicide mission. He was glad he did not have to make such decisions.

Hechler turned his attention to the other vessel. At best, the other ship would be in sight before sunset. If the enemy stood off to await reinforcements to ensure their kill, it might offer time enough to alter course, lose them in the darkness. With their far-reaching radar they had an edge on the enemy. But for it, he would never have known about that speck in the clouds, the slow-moving aircraft.

One thing was certain, no battleship or battle-cruiser had been reported in this area as yet. They were all to the north, employed with the convoys or protecting the supply lines as more and more of their troops flooded across the English Channel and into France. He bit his lip. Into Germany.

So it had to be a cruiser. He viewed his unknown adversary from every angle. If they could hold him off, or cripple him without sustaining more damage to the *Prinz*, they could still break through. Once their intentions were known, the British in particular would pull out all the stops. He remembered when the battleship *Bismarck*, the greatest warship ever built except for the trapped *Tirpitz*, had gone down with all guns firing. But it had taken the whole of the Home Fleet to find and destroy her. Revenge gave an edge to every commander, he thought. Their own sister-ship *Prinz Eugen* had slipped through the blockade then; so could they!

He heard men stand to attention and Froebe's whispered warning. Leitner moved through the bridge, his uniform soaked with rain. He stared at the submarine, his eyes listless. 'How much longer?'

'Ten minutes, sir.'

Some of the visiting one-stripers ducked as the Arado roared from the catapult and lifted above the bridge like a huge eagle on floats.

Hechler glanced quickly at the admiral. He had expected another outburst as to why the plane had been launched without his first being told.

Leitner merely grunted. 'Taking a look, eh?'

'It seems likely we'll have to increase to full speed, sir.' Hechler watched him in brief snatches while he never lost his hold over the ship. 'As soon as it's dark I shall – '

Leitner shrugged. 'The Führer will be watching us. We must not break that faith.'

He moved away and moments later, left the bridge.

Gudegast passed him on the ladder, but he knew the admiral had not even seen him. He whispered to Froebe, 'What did you make of that?'

Froebe spread his big hands. 'He knows we shall fight, Josef. He feels sick about it, and so would I in his shoes.'

Gudegast eyed the captain's intent shoulders. Thank God he was in command, he thought fervently. There had to be a way out. They had done the impossible, sunk, burned and destroyed to the letter of their orders. What was there left?

He clenched and unclenched his fists. In a few moments now the submarine would slide beneath the waves and they would stand alone. He found himself hating it and all its kind. They, more than any other weapon, had brought horror and brutality to the sea. In a few months they had trodden down all the time-won lessons and the code of the brotherhood of sailors, which had once meant more than anything. It was never a perfect world, and some wars were inevitable. But that kind of cruelty would never be forgotten. He glanced up at their flag, like blood against the jagged clouds. Because of them, they were all branded the same.

'Ready to cast off, sir. Engine-room reports fuelling completed.'

Hechler straightened his back. 'Pass the word. Stand by, all lines. Warn the wheelhouse.'

He turned and glanced beyond the bridge, past the raked funnel and Leitner's command flag.

Come what may. He was ready.

'New course, zero-one-zero, sir.'

Hechler loosened his collar. The rain, thank God, was moving away.

'Full revolutions.' He stared astern, his hand to the peak of his cap as if at a salute. But there was no sign of the big supply-submarine. It was as if she had never been.

The clouds were much thinner too. Fine for the flak crews, not so good for their Arado, wherever it was.

He felt the ship trembling more urgently and pictured the engine-room dials misting over to the thrust of the three great screws. The wake was rolling away on either quarter, stiff and almost silver against the shark-coloured sea. If only –

He took a telephone from one of the boatswain's mates.

'Captain.'

It was a lieutenant with the damage-control party.

'The compartment is almost open, sir!' He sounded jubilant, as if nothing else mattered. 'Hammer is still all right.'

Hechler smiled grimly. 'Thank you. Stay with him.'

He shaded his eyes again to watch the sea which seemed to be rushing to meet them, as if he should feel some kind of impact before it parted and sliced away on either beam.

He said, 'Check Turret Bruno. I want a full report.'

As if to mock him, the left gun in that turret lifted like a tusk and then depressed again.

He heard someone say, 'There goes the admiral's crawler.' He did not have to look to know it was Bauer, the communications officer. No one seemed to like him, even less so since the incident on the island.

Hechler beckoned to Gudegast. 'Call communications and try to discover what has happened to our aircraft.' He saw Froebe watching him, gauging his own fate perhaps.

Hechler moved restlessly around the bridge. Horizon to horizon, shining and empty. It made him feel vulnerable, as if he was suddenly stripped naked.

'The admiral sir.'

He took the handset. 'Sir?'

'I have had an important signal, Dieter.' He sounded emotional. 'Direct from our Führer. Germany is expecting great things from us – ' He broke off with a curse as the intercom cut through.

'Aircraft, bearing Green four-five!' A pause, then, 'Disregard, friendly!'

Someone muttered hoarsely, 'About time too!'

Hechler held up his hand. '*Silence on the bridge!*' Apart from the wind through the halliards and superstructure it was suddenly still.

Gudegast whispered, 'Gunfire.'

Every glass was raised yet again, and even men on the gun sponsons crowded to the rails to stare at the empty sky.

Then they saw the long trail of smoke before they could identify the Arado. The smoke lifted and dipped behind the plane like a brown tail, and Hechler saw the drifting tracks of shellfire which told their own story. The pilot must have dared too much and had gone too close to the other ship, or had been trapped by her main armament.

'Stand by on deck to retrieve aircraft!'

Hechler tried not to lick his lips as he watched the Arado's desperate progress. Lower and lower, until he imagined he could see its blurred reflection on the sea's face.

He said, 'Tell damage-control what is happening. I want a side-party with scrambling nets immediately!'

It would mean reducing speed, stopping even, but he could not just leave these men to drown after what they had done.

Someone was using a hand-lamp. So they had been badly mauled, hit with flak enough to knock out their radio.

The senior signalman opened his mouth but Gudegast said, 'Signal reads, *enemy in sight to north-east.*' They were all watching him. '*One destroyer.*' He winced as the plane dived and almost hit the water before rising again like a dying bird. '*Two, repeat two enemy cruisers!*'

Froebe said tersely, 'Damage-control, sir.'

Hechler dropped his binoculars to his chest as the Arado lifted towards the sky, staggered and then exploded in a livid, orange ball of fire.

'Tell them to dismiss the side-party.'

Jaeger offered him the telephone, his face ashen.

Hechler watched the smoke as it clung to the heaving water, and pictured the fragments drifting to the ocean's floor like ashes.

'Sir?'

He had to hold the telephone away from his ear as Leitner yelled, '*Two* cruisers and a *destroyer*! So much for your reckoning, damn you!'

Hechler said sharply, 'There are people here, sir. We just lost some brave men!'

'Don't you dare to interrupt me! The Führer entrusted me with a mission!' He slammed down the handset, and Hechler looked at Gudegast with a wry smile. 'Not pleased.'

Minutes later Theil appeared on the bridge and stared wild-eyed, as if he could barely speak.

Hechler faced him, his patience almost gone. 'This had better be urgent!'

Theil swallowed hard. 'Is it true, sir? I have just been ordered to load these boxes aboard the spare Arado!'

Hechler grappled with the words, his mind still lingering on that last hopeless message. Three ships, but one only a destroyer. There was still a chance.

He said, 'Tell *me!*'

Theil recovered with considerable effort. 'The admiral's aide told me personally. I had just reported that we have forced open the compartment. The boatswain and his men did it. I sent Hammer to the sick-bay. Then I got this order!'

It was all suddenly so clear and simple that Hechler was surprised he could accept it so calmly.

'Then do it, Viktor.' He lifted the telephone from its special rack, half-expecting there would be no reply.

Leitner said, 'Under these circumstances I have no choice. Neither have you. My instructions are to fly immediately to the mainland. The fight goes on.'

Hechler saw the others staring at him, officers, seamen, young and not so young. All seemed to have the same stunned expression. Disbelief. Astonishment. Shame.

'And my orders, sir?'

Leitner shouted, 'You will take immediate steps to prevent this ship from falling into enemy hands! Close the shore and *scuttle her!*'

Gudegast murmured, 'Dear Christ!'

Hechler put down the telephone and looked at Theil. 'Load the aircraft and prepare for launching.' His voice was toneless. 'Then report to me.'

Theil stared at him despairingly. 'Not you too? You of all people!'

Hechler regarded him gravely. 'We do not have much time left.'

As Theil turned in a daze he added softly, 'No, Viktor. *Not me!*'

He was not sure if Theil heard him. He was not certain of anything any more. He crossed to the bridge wing and watched the crane dipping over the catapult, the brightly painted Arado suddenly perched there, as if this moment was a part of destiny.

He heard her voice on the bridge ladder and said, 'No visitors!' But she knocked Jaeger's arm aside and ran towards him. '*I won't go!* Do you hear? I won't run away because of that coward!'

He caught her and held her, his eyes looking beyond her as he said, 'Slow ahead all engines.'

Then he said, 'I am ordering you to leave.' His voice was hoarse. He tried again. 'I should have guessed, Erika. A hero's return, or a hiding-place in Argentina. You will take him.' He pressed her against his body. 'I have to know that you at least are safe.'

She sobbed into his coat, her face hidden. '*No!* Don't force me!'

Hechler said, 'I need my remaining Arado. Please go now, my dearest Erika. *Please*, my men are looking to me.'

She stood back, her face very controlled despite the unheeded tears on her cheeks.

Then she said quietly, 'You'll not scuttle, Dieter? That's what you're saying?'

He did not reply directly. 'I shall never forget.'

Then he turned away. 'Escort her to the plane.'

He did not look again until she had left the bridge. He heard the Arado's engine roar into life, saw Theissen holding his cap in place, his face creased with dismay as he realised for the first time he was being left to fend for himself by the man he admired, perhaps even loved.

'*Radar – bridge!*' The merest pause. '*Enemy in sight!*'

Hechler barely heard the babble of instructions to the main armament. He strode to the wing and saw Theil by the catapult, then watched with surprise as Theissen was pushed up into the cockpit behind the girl.

'What the *hell* – !'

Froebe called, 'From damage-control, sir! The door to the admiral's bridge has jammed! A power failure!'

Hechler stared at the brightly painted plane, then very slowly lifted his cap high above his head.

With a coughing growl the Arado bounced from the catapult and lifted away from the ship, its wings glinting in the glare.

'Full ahead, all engines!' Hechler watched the Arado until it turned away and headed towards the western horizon.

Froebe said huskily, 'The admiral demands to speak with you, sir.'

Hechler recalled Theil's face. He alone must have cut the power from the damage control to seal Leitner in his own bridge.

'Starboard twenty!' Hechler removed his oilskin and tossed it behind a flag locker.

'My respects to the admiral, but I have to fight a battle.'

When he looked again the tiny plane had vanished. And yet he could still feel her pressed against him, still feel her anguish like his own when they had parted.

He said, 'We shall share our victory, but I'll never share his dishonour!'

177

Gudegast regarded him soberly. His one regret was that he had not yet begun the painting. Now he never would.

Hechler levelled his glasses with difficulty as the bridge shook to the vibration.

'Steady on zero-five-zero, sir.'

Hechler took the engine-room handset. 'Chief? Captain here. I need everything you can give me.'

'Can I ask?' Stück sounded faraway as if he was studying his dials.

'We are about to engage. Three ships. Do your best.' He hesitated, knowing that Stück wanted to go to his men. 'If I give the word – '

Stück's voice was near again. 'I know, sir. I'll get my boys on deck, double-quick.'

Hechler turned away and plucked at the grey fisherman's jersey. It was quite absurd but he wished he had changed into a clean shirt and his best uniform. The others nearby saw him grin and were reassured. But Hechler was thinking of the little admiral. What Nelson would have done.

The speaker intoned, 'Range fourteen thousand. Bearing steady.'

Two cruisers in line abreast to offer their maximum firepower. Hechler could see them as if they were right here. The destroyer was slightly ahead; they would sight her first.

He heard Kröll's clipped tone, caught in the intercom to give another small picture of their world high above the bridge.

'Anton, Caesar and Dora will concentrate on the cruisers. Warn flak control to expect enemy aircraft, spotters, anything.'

Hechler glanced around the open bridge. He might be forced to go up to the armoured conning-tower, but he would hold out as long as possible. He had been brought up on open bridges, where he could see everything. When their lives were in the balance it was even more important that his men should see him.

Kröll again. 'Large cruiser at Green one-oh.' A brief pause. 'She's opened fire.'

Hechler found that he could watch like any spectator as the enemy salvo exploded in the sea far off the starboard bow. A leaping wall of water which seemed so slow to fall. The wind was whipping it towards them, and he could imagine that he tasted cordite. Death.

'Second ship's fired.'

Someone laughed in the background, a nervous, unstable sound, and Kröll's deputy silenced the man with a sharp obscenity.

'Main armament ready, sir!'

Hechler watched the two forward guns swing across the side, at odds with the jammed barrels of Turret Bruno. Aft, the other turrets were already lining up on Kröll's directions and bearings. Hechler jabbed the button below the screen and seconds later the six big guns lurched back on their springs, the roar and earsplitting crashes punching at the bridge plating like giant battering rams.

More enemy salvoes fell and churned the sea into a maelstrom of leaping waterspouts and falling spray.

More seconds as the layers and trainers made their last adjustments.

'*Shoot!*'

The deck jumped beneath the bridge and a huge column of smoke burst over the side while patterns of falling debris were lost in seconds in their rising bow-wave.

The voice-pipes settled down into a staccato chorus, reporting, asking, pleading.

Hechler heard the taut replies from his bridge team. More like robots than men.

'Send stretcher bearers. Fire party to torpedo TS. Report damage and casualties.'

Froebe shouted, 'One hit, sir. Under control.' He ducked as another salvo screamed over the bridge and exploded far abeam.

'*Port fifteen!*' At this speed the ship seemed to tilt right over before Hechler's calm voice brought her on course again. The din continued without a break, giant waterspouts rising and fading astern as the *Prinz Luitpold* tore towards the enemy, her own guns firing more slowly than the enemy's. Hechler knew that Kröll was marking every fall of shot, making certain that his crews concentrated on their markers and did not allow them to fall into the trap of a pell-mell battle.

'Direct hit on left ship!' Someone cheered. 'Still firing!'

A great explosion thundered alongside so that for a few moments Hechler did not know if they had received a direct hit in return. As the smoke filtered downward he felt rain on his face, and was grateful that the clouds had returned. If they could keep up a running fight until dusk . . . He winced as two shells exploded inboard and a huge fragment of steel whirled over the bridge to plough down amongst some men at a Vierling gun. He stood back from the screen, tasting bile in his throat as he saw a seaman hacked neatly in two halves before pitching down amongst the bloody remains of his companions.

'*Another hit!*' The speaker sounded excited. 'Left ship is losing steerage way!'

Hechler wiped his face. 'Tell them to concentrate on the heavy cruiser to the right!' Kröll needed no telling, and as if to show its revived determination, Turret Bruno began to swivel round until it was trained on the same bearing as its twin.

'*Shoot!*'

All four guns recoiled together while the after-turrets followed immediately.

'*Short!*'

Hechler swung round and saw Leitner, hatless and staring, as he groped his way across the bridge. Theil must have returned the power and released him.

Leitner seemed unaware of the danger, and barely flinched as Kröll's trigger released another shattering salvo from all four turrets.

'You treacherous bastard! *You trapped me!*'

He peered around and coughed in the billowing smoke.

'I'll see you praying for death! It will be denied you!'

Hechler ducked as steel splinters shrieked and clattered around the bridge. *Another hit.* He tried to listen to the garbled reports, picture his men at their action stations in magazines and turrets; tending the boilers or just clinging to life.

He shouted, 'Don't lecture me! This is my ship! You are the traitor, Andreas Leitner!' He seized him violently, all caution and reserve gone in the din and thunder of gunfire. 'You were going to run like a bloody rabbit when you found you weren't your own propaganda hero after all!'

'*Captain!*' Jaeger was holding out a telephone, his face white as a thin scarlet thread ran down his hairline.

Hechler grabbed the phone. It was Gudegast.

'We should alter course now, sir.'

'Very well.' Hechler slammed it down. 'Hard a-port. Steer – ' He ran to the compass repeater and wiped dust and chippings away with his sleeve. 'Steer *zero-one-zero.*' It would leave the badly damaged ship where she could not interfere and allow Kröll to concentrate on the enemy's heavy cruiser. '*Steady as you go!*' He saw a great column of water shoot up by the port quarter and felt the bridge jerk savagely as another shell slammed down near the quarterdeck. As if by magic, black, jagged holes appeared in the funnel, while severed rigging and radio wires trailed above the bridge like creepers.

'Request permission to flood Section Seven, sir?'

Hechler could imagine Theil down there with his team, watching the control panel, the blinking pattern of lights as one section after another was hit or needed help.

The main armament was trained almost directly abeam, their target hidden in smoke and distance.

Hechler dragged himself to a safety rail and squinted to clear his vision.

Small, sharp thoughts jerked through him. She would be on her way to safety. Five hundred miles was nothing to her. He wanted to shout her name. So that she would hear him. Like a last cry.

The hull shivered and flames seared out of the deck below the secondary armament. Men ran from their stations, some with extinguishers, others in panic, and one screaming with his body on fire.

'A straddle!' The voice almost broke. '*Two hits!*'

Hechler clambered above the rail and waited for the smoke to funnel past him. He had to hold his breath to stop himself from choking, but he must see, must know.

Then he caught a misty picture in the powerful binoculars, like a badly distorted film.

The big enemy cruiser, so high out of the water, was ablaze from stern to bridge, and both her forward turrets were knocked out, the guns either side smashed or pointing impotently at the clouds.

A voice yelled, 'The pumps are holding the intake aft, sir!'

'Casualties removed and taken below!' He pictured Stroheim with bloodied fingers, his gold-rimmed glasses misting over in that crowded, pain-racked place. In his wildness he pictured the scene with music playing, Handel, from Stroheim's dusty stack of records.

A shell ploughed below the bridge and more splinters smashed through the thinner plating by the gate. Two signalmen were cut down without a sound, and Froebe clung to the gyro compass, his eyes bulging in agony as he gasped for air. There was a wound like a red star punched in his chest. Hechler reached for him, but he was dead before he hit the gratings.

Hechler yelled, 'Take his place, Jaeger!' He shook the youth's arm. 'Move yourself! We'll beat the Tommies yet!'

He saw the incredulous stare on Jaeger's face, and guessed that he must look more like a maniac than the stable captain. But it worked, and he heard Jaeger's voice as he passed another helm order, quite calm, like a complete stranger's.

Kröll's intercom croaked through the explosions. 'Both cruisers have lost way, sir. Shall I engage the destroyer? She now bears Red four-five!'

Hechler wiped his streaming face. Exertion or rain he neither knew nor cared. The destroyer would stand by her consorts; she was no longer any danger. By nightfall . . . he swung round as men ducked again and the air was torn apart by the banshee scream of falling shells.

For a split second Hechler imagined that another cruiser had got within range undetected. He knew that was impossible. Then the salvo fell across the ship in a tight straddle, the shells exploding between decks, while others brought down rangefinders and the mainmast in a web of steel and flailing stays.

Hechler expected to feel pain as he struggled to the opposite side. Even as he levelled his glasses again he knew the answer. The flaw in the picture, which even Kröll's instruments had overlooked.

The destroyer had zigzagged through a smoke-screen, although there was already smoke enough from gunfire and burning ships, and had fired a full broadside into the *Prinz*. Hechler coughed painfully. Except that she was no destroyer. She was a light cruiser, which nonetheless had the fire-power to do real damage if only she could get close enough. Her two heavier consorts had seen to that.

Another scream of falling shells and this time the full salvo struck them from funnel to quarterdeck.

Hechler gripped the rail, could feel the power going from his engines as Stück fought to hold the revolutions steady.

Gudegast had appeared on the bridge and was shouting, 'Engine-room wants to reduce speed, sir!'

'*Half ahead!*' Hechler watched the two forward turrets swing round, hesitate and then fire, the shockwave ripping overhead like an express train.

There was no response from the after-turrets. The last enemy salvo had crippled them.

'*One hit!*'

The light cruiser was zigzagging back into her own smoke-screen, one yellow tongue licking around her bridge like an evil spirit. 'Tell the gunnery officer – ' Hechler wiped his eyes and stared up at the control position. It was crushed, like a beer can, riddled with holes despite the thick armour.

'Transfer fire control – ' He watched, sickened, as dark stains ran down Kröll's armoured cupola, as if the whole control position was bleeding. Which indeed it was.

Throughout the ship, men groped in darkness as lights were extinguished or passageways filled with choking smoke. Others clung together behind watertight doors which would now remain closed for ever.

In his sick-bay Stroheim put down a telephone and shouted, 'Start getting these men on deck!' The smoke had even penetrated down here, and spurted through doors and frames like a terrible threat.

Deeper in the hull Stück clung to his catwalk and watched his men stooping and running through the oily steam, like figures in hell. The three massive shafts were still spinning but he would have to slow them still further. Was it to be now?

Like this, he wondered? He felt the hull lurch as more shells exploded close by. His instinct told him they came from a different bearing, and he guessed that one of the damaged cruisers was rejoining the battle.

The two forward turrets were still firing, but more slowly under the local control of their quarters' officer.

There were fires everywhere, and not enough men to carry away the wounded, let alone the dead.

One man lay where he had fallen from a ladder, after Kröll had sent him to Turret Dora to discover the extent of the damage. Acting Petty Officer Hans Stoecker sprawled on his back, his face tightly pinched as if to protect himself from the unbroken roar of gunfire and internal explosions. Even the deck plating felt hot, and he wanted to call out for someone to help him. Each time he tried, the agony seared through him like a furnace bar, but when he attempted to move his legs he could feel nothing.

A bent-over figure slithered down beside him. It was the grey-headed petty officer, Tripz.

He made to cradle his arm under the young man's shoulder, but as a freak gust of wind drove the smoke aside he bent lower still. There was little left of Stoecker below the waist, and he tried to protect him from its horror.

He gasped, 'We did it, Hans! All that gold and jewellery! *We did it!* We'll all be rich!'

Stoecker sobbed as a single shell exploded against the bridge superstructure and sheets of steel drifted overhead like dry leaves. 'I – I did – not – mean – to – ' He clutched the other man in a pitiful embrace. His eyes blurred with agony, so that he did not see the cruel splinter which had just killed his comforter.

Stoecker lay back, the pain suddenly leaving him as he pictured his mother, and the girl called – he tried to speak her name but the effort was too much, so he died.

There were more corpses than living men on the forebridge and Hechler stared down at himself as if expecting to see blood. He was untouched, perhaps so that he should suffer the most.

Gudegast arose, shaking himself from a collapsed bank of voice-pipes, dust and paint flakes clinging to his beard as he stared around like a trapped bear.

Hechler heard Theil on the handset. 'Come up, Viktor. Tell your assistant to take over.'

He turned and saw Leitner standing in the centre of the bridge.

He screamed, '*Where is Theissen?*'

'He went in the plane with your boxes!'

Hechler wondered how he could find words even to speak with him.

Leitner held out a canvas pouch and shook it wildly.

'These are mine! All that's left! Someone broke into my boxes, damn you!' He flung the pouch down in a pool of blood which was quivering to the engines' beat as if it was trying to stay alive. '*See?*'

Hechler watched as jewelled rings and pieces of gold scattered among the blood and buckled plating. So that was it.

He heard himself answer, 'So it was all wasted?'

'Not quite, you *bastard!*' The Luger seemed to appear in his fist like magic and Hechler knew he could not move aside in time.

All around him men were dying, or waiting to be struck down. Because of men like Leitner. He felt suddenly sickened and cheated. No wonder Leitner could never understand his ideals, his love for a ship, her loyalty.

A voice shattered the sudden stillness. '*Torpedoes to port!*'

The explosions were merged into one gigantic eruption, so that it seemed to go on and on forever.

Hechler was vaguely aware of objects crashing past him, the sounds of heavy equipment tearing adrift and thundering through the hull between decks.

His mind was cringing but all his skill and training tried to hold on, just long enough.

The light cruiser must have darted in to launch her torpedoes while her battered consorts had kept up a ragged covering fire.

He knew without hearing a single report that it was a mortal blow. Corpses were moving again, returning to life perhaps as the deck tilted over.

Gudegast hopped and limped towards him, his eyes blazing as he exclaimed, 'Thought you were done for?'

Hechler hung on to his massive shoulder. How long had he been unconscious? He could recall nothing beyond the great gout of fire as the torpedoes had exploded alongside.

The admiral lay on his side, his tongue protruding in a crude grimace. One hand still held the Luger; the other was like a claw as it reached out for the scattered fragments of his fortune.

Gudegast aided the captain to the bridge chair. 'He's dead, sir.'

He watched the anguish on Hechler's profile. There was no point in adding to his pain by telling him that he had seen a bullet hole in the middle of Leitner's back. Someone must have gunned him down deliberately as he had aimed at the captain, when the torpedoes had abruptly ended all their hopes.

'The enemy's ceased fire, sir.' That was Jaeger, a bloody handkerchief pressed to his forehead.

Hechler heard the distant shouts of men on the deck below and Gudegast said, 'When I thought you were – '

Hechler held his arm. 'You ordered them to clear the lower deck?' He nodded painfully. 'Thank you, Josef. *So much.*'

Would I have done that, he wondered? Might more of my men have been made to die?

Now he would never know.

The deck gave a terrible lurch and the chart-table shattered into fragments.

Gudegast said, 'I'll pass the word, sir.'

Hechler shook his head. 'No. Let me. I must do it.'

He clung to the screen and saw the nearest enemy cruiser for the first time. Her fires were out, and her turrets were trained on the *Prinz* as she began to heel over very, very slowly.

Hechler raised his hand to the men nearest him. 'Abandon ship!' The words to wish them well choked in his emotion and he heard Gudegast mutter, 'Come on, sir. We'll still need you.'

Hechler tried to stand, but when he gripped the rail he found that he was staring not at the enemy but straight down at the littered water. Floats, broken boats, corpses, and swimmers, some of whom trod water to watch as the heavy cruiser began to roll over.

Hechler knew he had hit the sea, and that his lungs were on fire when hands seized him and dragged him into a crowded float. Someone cried, 'Here's the Captain!'

Hechler hooked his arm round Gudegast's shoulder and heard him murmur, 'Come *on*, old girl, get it over with, eh?'

It was like a great bellow of pain, an indescribable roar, as with sudden urgency the *Prinz Luitpold* lifted her motionless screws from the sea and dived.

Hechler struggled upright on the float and watched the maelstrom of flotsam, the tell-tale spread of oil.

They were still a long way from home.

But those who survived would speak for many years of the *Prinz*.

He stared up at the first, pale stars.

The Iron Pirate. The legend.

Epilogue

The train was moving very slowly as if weighed down by the packed humanity which crammed every seat and compartment. Hechler was glad he had been able to find a place by a window, although it was so gloomy beyond the misty glass he could see very little.

It was hard to believe that the journey was nearly over, that the long train was already clanking through the outskirts of Hamburg.

Prinz Luitpold had begun her life in this port. It all seemed so long ago. He glanced at his companions, mostly in army field-grey, like the rest of the train, creased, worn-out, huddled together for warmth and comfort.

It was about noon, but it could have been evening, he thought. Winter already had its grip on the countryside. He stirred uneasily as his mind explored the past like a raw wound. A year since that day in the South Atlantic when the *Prinz* had lifted her stern and had dived. So many familiar faces had gone down with her; too many.

The survivors had been gathered into the British ships, and Hechler had found himself aboard the light cruiser *Pallas*, the one which had fired the fatal salvo of torpedoes.

It was strange, but he had sensed no elation amongst the victors. It had been relief as much as anything. He had learned snatches of the final action, of the British commodore being killed by the *Prinz's* first straddle, and the New Zealander's initiative in pressing home the attack despite an overwhelming adversary.

Hechler had been separated from his men, then from most of his officers.

Some he knew had died in the cruiser's final moments. Kröll directing his guns, the taciturn Stück, dying as he had lived with his engines roaring around him when the torpedoes had burst in on him and his men.

Hechler had managed to stay with Gudegast, even after they were transferred to a fast troopship with an armed escort, to be landed eventually in the port of Liverpool.

He had seen young Jaeger for a while, but once in England Jaeger had been sent to an officers' prison camp somewhere in the south.

Gudegast had told him of Theil's last appearance, all that anyone had seen of him. As the ship had taken on her final list, with men pouring up from the smoke and fires between decks, several of the survivors had seen Theil returning below, as if going to his quarters. Hechler had asked if he had seemed to be in a great hurry? Perhaps he was trying to retrieve some small item of value from his cabin before he abandoned ship with all the others.

Gudegast had shaken his head. 'They said he was just walking. As if he had all the time in the world.'

A way out. Remain with the ship he loved, which was finally being taken from him. Now they would never know the truth.

Hechler thought of the months as a prisoner-of-war. He gave a faint, wry smile. *In the bag*, as his British captors termed it.

The camp had been in Scotland, a bleak, lonely place, shared mostly with embittered U-boat commanders.

Hechler had been interrogated several times, on arrival, and later by officers in civilian clothes who were described as being from Naval Intelligence.

They questioned him mostly about the incident at St Jorge, and whether he considered that as captain he was solely responsible for the shooting of the civilian mechanic. Bauer was probably the only one who knew the whole truth of that, but he had been blasted to fragments with the rest of his staff early in the engagement.

After that, nobody took much interest in him. Gudegast was good company, and when they were not walking around the wire fences and looking at the varying colours of the heather, Gudegast would be busy with his paints and sketches. He obtained all the materials he needed by offering to do portraits of the guards. It was an amicable arrangement.

Then one day Gudegast was ordered to leave for another camp in the south.

It had been a sad unemotional farewell. They had survived too much for anything more.

He had asked Gudegast what he would try to do after the war.

The big man had plucked at his beard. 'Back to the sea. It's all I know.'

Before he left he had handed Hechler a small roll of canvas.

'For her,' he had said awkwardly. 'You'll meet her again, don't you fret.'

Then he had marched away with some others, and Hechler had saluted without knowing why.

After that it had been a matter of waiting and enduring. Christmas, with local children gathering outside the wire to sing carols. One of the U-boat officers had killed himself shortly afterwards. Hechler had withdrawn even further from his companions. They seemed alien; their war was not one he had shared, and he wished that Gudegast was still with him.

He often thought of the others, men like Brezinka who had survived, and the doctor Stroheim who had last been seen tying his own life-jacket to a badly wounded seaman. The quiet hero.

Then the time when the guards had fired their weapons in the air, and all the lights had been switched on.

Hechler had accepted the end of Europe's war with mixed feelings. The time seemed to drag, and yet he almost dreaded his release. He had written to Erika Franke several times at the two addresses she had left for him, but had received no reply.

His head lolled to the monotonous clank-clank-clank of the wheels and he stared through the window as some great white humps of land. He saw the khaki uniforms of British NCO's who were directing some tractors and a great army of German workers. He realised with a chill that the humps were all that was left of buildings, whole streets, now mercifully covered with the first snow of this bitter winter.

Someone said, 'Nearly there! Home sweet home!' Nobody else spoke. One man, an infantry captain, was dabbing his eyes with a soiled handkerchief, another was trying to pull his threadbare coat into position. Home? There was not much of it left.

Hechler thrust his fingers into his pocket as if to reassure himself that his pipe was still there. In his other hand he held the parcel which contained Gudegast's gift. It was a small portrait of himself, not aboard ship, but with some Scottish heather as a background. So typical of Gudegast, he thought.

He felt his stomach contract as he realised that the train was suddenly running into the station. Again there seemed to be wreckage everywhere, the platform roof blasted open like bare ribs against the dull sky.

He sensed a new tension all around him. Most of the soldiers had only just been released; many had come from the Russian Front, gaunt, despairing figures who rarely even spoke to each other. The train stopped with a final jerk and slowly at first, then with something like panic, the passengers spilled out on to the platform.

Here and there were signs of occupation. Station direction boards in English with regimental crests on them. The bright red caps of the military police, khaki and air force blue, voices and accents Hechler had taught himself to know while he had been *in the bag*.

He stared at the barrier beyond the mass of returning German troops. Police, service and military, a British provost marshal smoking a pipe and chatting with a friend. Further still, an unbroken wall of faces.

He came to a halt, his heart pounding. Was this freedom? Where was his courage now?

A solitary German sailor, the two ribbons whipping out from his cap in the chill breeze, dropped a package and Hechler picked it up.

'Here!'

The sailor spun round and snapped to attention.

Hechler handed him the parcel, and they both stared at one another like strangers. Then the man gave a slow grin, and reached out to shake his hand.

The saluting, like the war, was finally over for both of them.

The girl, Erika Franke, stood by one of the massive girders which supported the remains of the station roof and watched the train sigh to a halt.

It was the third one she had met this day, and her hands and feet were icy cold. Or was it the awful uncertainty? Not knowing? As each train had trundled into the station to offload its cargo of desperate, anxious servicemen she had seen the reactions of the crowd, mostly women, who waited there with her. Like her. She looked at the noticeboards which had once recorded the most punctual trains in the Reich. Now they were covered from top to bottom with photographs, some large, others no bigger than passport pictures. Addresses and names scrawled under each one. It was like a graveyard.

Now as the first hurrying figures approached the platform gates and the line of military policemen, she saw many of the same women surge forward, their pitiful pictures held out to each man in uniform.

'My son, have you seen him?' To another. 'He was in your regiment! You *must* have known my man!'

She wiped her eyes, afraid she might miss something.

A young British naval lieutenant with wavy stripes on his sleeve asked, 'You all right, Fräulein? I've got a car outside if – '

She shook her head and replied politely, 'No, thank you.'

A woman in a shabby coat with two photographs held up in front of her pushed past a red-capped policeman and asked that same question. The soldier brushed her away; he did not even look at her. He seemed embarrassed, afraid that he might recognise someone he had left in the mud with a million others.

The girl watched the other wave of figures coming through the gates. Not many sailors, this time. She would come back tomorrow.

She remembered his letters, bundled together, when she had finally returned home. It was all like a dream now, and the last flight to Argentina, an impossibility.

She recalled the moment when she had climbed down from the Arado and into a waiting launch. She had felt nothing but a sense of loss. Even when German consulate officials had opened the boxes to find them full of broken fragments of coloured glass, she had thought only of Hechler, with every minute taking him further away, perhaps to his death.

Leitner's aide had had hysterics when he had seen the broken glass. She had heard him shout the name of a petty officer called Hammer. Whoever he was, he must be a very rich man if he was still alive.

The woman with the two photographs pressed forward. 'Please, sir! Tell me, *please*! Have you seen my boys?'

The man stopped and took the photographs.

The girl felt her heart stop beating. It was Hechler. For a long moment she stared at him without moving, taking in every precious detail. The lines were deeper on either side of his mouth, and there were touches of grey beneath his cap. He was wearing that same old fisherman's jersey under his jacket. He seemed oblivious to the cold.

Hechler said quietly, 'I am sorry, my dear, I have not seen them. But don't lose hope – ' He looked up and saw her and the next instant she was wrapped in his arms. He did not even see the woman staring after him, as if he had just performed a miracle.

How long they clung together, neither of them knew.

She whispered, 'It had to be the right train!' She ran her hand over him as if to reassure herself he was real. She saw the loose threads on his right breast where the Nazi eagle had once been, and looked up to see a new brightness in his blue eyes.

He said, 'I knew I'd find you, my little bird. Somehow – '

Some British sailors were waving and cheering as some of their companions boarded another train. Hechler put his arm around her shoulders and they walked out into the drifting snow.

Once he glanced back at the station and the jubilant British sailors.

Then he squeezed her shoulders and said softly, 'Like us, they're going home.'

IN DANGER'S
HOUR

For my Kim,

for all the help

and all the love

you freely give.

Life to be sure is nothing much to lose,
But young men think it is, and we were young.

Engraved on a memorial in the Old Naval Cemetery
at Vis in the Adriatic, in 1944.

A different battleground: the same sacrifice.

Author's Note

Minesweeping . . . a war without glory, where death lurked beneath the sea or floated from the air. A war without mercy or discrimination. The mine was impartial and gave no warning.

The men who fought this lonely battle did so knowing it was an essential one. Every day each channel had to be swept, otherwise the country's lifelines were clogged and the vital cargoes could not move.

They were a mixture of young men and old sailors; many of the latter had spent much of their lives trawling for fish, most of the others had been school-boys before the war.

To keep the sealanes open, four hundred minesweepers, 'the little ships', paid the price, and nearly five thousand officers and men died doing it.

D.R.

1

Officers

The sky above Dover harbour was a clear washed-out blue, so that the afternoon sunshine gave an illusion of warmth and peace. Just an occasional fleecy cloud drifting on a fresh south-easterly breeze, but none of the too-familiar vapour trails which betrayed the silent air battles, the pinpoints of flame as friend or enemy fell into the Channel.

It was April 1943, only a few days old, and the harbour, like the weather, appeared to be resting. There were not many warships of any size moored to the jetties; most of them went to safer harbours, *round the corner* as the sailors termed it, in the Thames or Medway, or in the East Coast base of Harwich.

Here there was little peace for long. Sneak raids by fighter-bombers, or the deafening arrival of the great shells fired from Cap Gris-Nez to land in the town or amongst some coastal convoy as it scuttled through the Channel.

Lying side by side at one wall were two fleet minesweepers, their ensigns and Jacks lifting and rippling in the breeze to make bright patches of colour against the drab grey and camouflage dazzle paint. They were twins, and to a landsman might appear to be small, foreshortened frigates.

Straight-stemmed, with a spartan superstructure of bridge and solitary funnel making them look businesslike, only the clutter of minesweeping gear and derricks right aft on the cut-down quarterdeck marked them apart from any of the escort vessels.

There was no visible sign of life on board. Sunday afternoon, and make-and-mend for the duty watch, a chance to snatch some rest after weeks of sweeping the deadly mines, often within sight of the French coast.

Dover Castle with its bombproof headquarters beneath stood guard over the harbour and its approaches. For at this point the enemy were just twenty miles distant – a jarring thought, if anyone still needed reminding.

In his cabin in the outboard fleet minesweeper, Lieutenant Commander Ian Ransome unclipped a scuttle and opened it to let the weak sunshine play across his face. It was good to be leaving the long nights behind, even if the risks might be extended accordingly. He narrowed his eyes to study that part of the town which was visible from his cabin. A defiant, battered place on the very elbow of Hellfire Corner, as the newspapers named it. His mouth moved slightly in a smile. *Shit Street* was the sailors' nickname. The smile made him look younger, like a shadow passing away.

He saw his reflection in the scuttle's polished glass and ran his fingers through his hair. It was dark, and although not originally curly it had somehow become so. Too many days and nights up there on an open bridge, in salt spray and in all weathers. He turned and looked at his cabin. Small, and yet spacious compared with his tiny hutch behind the bridge, where he could snatch an hour and still be ready instantly when the alarm bells tore a man's heart apart.

He saw the calendar propped on his little desk and it all came crowding back again. The fourth of April 1943. He had been in command of this ship, his ship, for one year exactly.

He stared round, his ears seeking some familiar sound to distract him. But the ship was quiet, with only the far-off murmur of one of the Chief's generators to give a hint of life.

Ransome sat down at the desk and stared at the clip of signals which had awaited their return to Dover. He had known they would be in harbour for this day. They would have shared a solemn drink in the wardroom, perhaps invited some of the old hands to enliven the occasion.

His reefer hung carelessly from the only other chair, the two-and-a-half wavy lines of gold lace on its sleeves. The Royal Naval Volunteer Reserve. A wartime navy; the amateurs who were now the true professionals. On the jacket's breast above the pocket was a single blue and white ribbon. The Distinguished Service Cross. For gallantry, they had said. He smiled again, but it was sadder than before. For surviving, was nearer the truth. He pulled up the sleeve of his grey fisherman's jersey and studied his watch. Nearly time. It made him feel sick. Uneasy. Perhaps a year was too long in any ship. Or was it the job? He had gone into minesweepers almost immediately after entering the navy at the outbreak of war.

He reached out and opened a small cupboard, so that the untouched bottle of Scotch seemed to wink at him in the reflected sunlight. He had been hoarding it for today.

He toyed with the idea of pouring a glass right now, and to hell with everything. Later perhaps. He might even invite the skipper from their sister ship *Ranger* aboard to join him. Even as he considered it he knew he would not.

He began to fill one of his pipes with fierce, jabbing thrusts from an old jar he had found in a junk shop at Plymouth.

Nobody had been to blame. It had happened before. Others would die because of that momentary distraction. Lack of vigilance? Who could tell?

It was often said that the danger from sudden air-attack was at its greatest when a ship was making for harbour.

They had been doing just that after weeks of sweeping, with let-ups only to refuel and take on extra ammunition. No matter how skilled his men had become there were some who had been thinking of a run ashore, a brassy pub behind the blackout curtains where just for a few hours they could dream or make-believe.

David Rule had been an excellent first lieutenant in every sense. He had never tried to gain popularity by being soft, but even at the defaulters' table he had usually managed to end the day without malice.

Ransome knew he had not always been easy to work with; he had been at it a long time. In war even six months could be an eternity, and Ransome had been sweeping mines for three years. That was when he had not been needed for escort work, for picking up convoy survivors and anything else a senior officer might dream up. But Rule's cheerful disposition, impudence when he thought it was needed, had made them into an unbreakable team.

Ransome looked at the ship's crest on the white bulkhead. HMS *Rob Roy*, built by John Brown's on Clydebank just two years before the Germans had slammed into Poland, built when men cared about their craft, before ships were flung together, almost overnight it seemed, to try and balance the horrific toll in vessels and men alike. He nodded, as if David was here with him, as they had intended it would be.

Together they had made the little *Rob Roy* the best sweeper in the group.

It had been an early dawn when the sweep had put up a mine. Ransome had peered aft from the open bridge as Rule's sweeping party had slowed the winch, and a boatswain's mate had passed the word that the drifting mine had snared a wreck, or part of one. God knew there were enough wrecks littering the seabed on the approaches to every harbour.

Just a minute or so with every eye on the mine's bobbing, obscene shape, a signal lamp stabbing from the ship which now lay resting alongside, so that the shattering roar of a diving aircraft had made several believe that the mine had exploded. Out of the clouds, perhaps returning from a sortie over the mainland; they would never know. The rattle of machine-guns and cannon fire, then another roar of power as the plane had climbed away to the clouds, heading for home.

They had not even time to track it with the Oerlikons, let alone the main armament. It was over in seconds and David lay dying, his blood thinning in the spray boiling over the stern as they increased speed away from the mine, which was dispatched by marksmen on the trawler that always followed astern when they were sweeping.

Mercifully he had died before the ship had berthed alongside. The cannon shell which had cut him down had blasted off his shoulder and half of his face. Nobody else had received so much as a scratch.

The telephone jangled sharply on the desk, and Ransome had to pull his thoughts together, to accept that the ship was connected to the shore switchboard.

It was a woman's voice, a Wren from the S.D.O.

'Lieutenant Hargrave will be joining *Rob Roy* as expected, sir.'

Ransome stared at the ship's crest. He must get over it. A new first lieutenant? So what?

The voice said, 'Are you there, sir?'

Ransome pushed back his unruly hair again.

'Yes. Sorry.' What was she like, he wondered? 'Too good a lunch, I expect.'

She laughed. 'All right for some, sir.' The line went dead.

Ransome tried again. He stared at himself in the small mirror beside his bunk. Shadows beneath his eyes, lines of strain which seemed to tighten his mouth. He leaned closer and touched his sideburns. White hairs. He straightened his back and tried to grin at himself. He noticed that the grey eyes did not smile back at him.

He sighed. Aloud, he spoke to the small cabin. 'Not surprised. I feel bloody ancient!'

Ian Ransome was twenty-eight years old.

Lieutenant Trevor Hargrave returned the salutes of two passing seamen and swore silently under his breath. He carried a heavy suitcase in one hand and had his respirator haversack and steel helmet slung from the opposite shoulder. Even sailors who normally went to great lengths to avoid saluting anybody seemed to take a delight in doing it when an officer had his hands full.

Hargrave was tall and had even features and blue eyes which had made several of the Wrens at the base watch him as he passed. He shivered slightly as he looked at the moored vessels, and an idling Air Sea Rescue launch about to get under way from one of the jetties. His deeply tanned face told its own story. He had been back in England for six months, but even now in April it seemed bitterly cold after the glistening expanse of the Indian Ocean and South Atlantic.

He thought of the powerful cruiser which had been his home for over a year. She had been employed as a main escort for long-haul convoys, most of which carried troops and all the equipment and vehicles they might need when they were finally delivered to their theatre of war. Simonstown, across the ocean to Ceylon or down to Australia and New Zealand. They were there just in case a commerce raider, or some death-or-glory German cruiser, broke out to savage the convoy routes before she was run to earth. Just one major enemy unit could tie down convoys for weeks; even the rumour of one was bad enough.

But all in all they had seen little of the real war. Lines of deep-laden merchantmen, sometimes with an escort to provide air cover for the dicey part where ocean-going submarines, German and Japanese, might be at large.

It was as if the war had been held at arm's length. The cruiser reacted accordingly, and there was little difference in her ordered world from the days of peace. Mess dinners, banyan parties on the islands, even some regattas when they had been down-under with the Aussies.

He thought of his dismay when he had gone to London to protest about his new appointment. A *minesweeping course*. He could still see the contained amusement on the commander's face in the dusty Admiralty office.

He had tried to discover his father's whereabouts but had met with a stone wall. The Western Desert, Scotland – nobody knew or would tell him. At the back of his mind he nursed the suspicion that his father was behind it somehow.

Hargrave stopped and looked along the old stone wall. The course was over. It was not next month. It was now.

He felt the breeze flapping at his blue raincoat. Everything looked tired and run-down. Like the town with its bombed houses and boarded-up shops. And London with its wailing sirens and shabby people, ration queues and uniforms everywhere. He had never seen so many foreign servicemen. Free-French, Norwegians, Polish, Dutch – the list was endless, as if to record the enemy's total oppression of Scandinavia and Europe.

His eyes narrowed as he saw the two fleet minesweepers. At this angle they were almost bows-on to him. As if they were resting, leaning against each other for support.

His gaze rested on the outboard one and he felt his heart sink still further. He had read all he could about HMS *Rob Roy* but seeing her in the frail sunshine was still a shock.

He saw the scars on her paintwork. Coming alongside in the dark, or manoeuvring against another vessel to take off survivors probably. Hargrave knew quite a lot about *Rob Roy*'s history. She had even been to Dunkirk where she had made several trips, returning home each time loaded with exhausted soldiers.

He saw her pendant number, J.21, painted on her side, the thin line around her single funnel which marked her as the senior ship in the flotilla. It gave him no comfort at all.

He went through the details once again in his mind. It had not taken him long to gen up on the ship; after all, she was not exactly a cruiser. Two hundred and thirty feet from stem to low stern, 815 tons with an armament of two four-inch guns, two Oerlikon twenty-millimetre cannon and a few heavy machine-guns. He began to walk along the edge of the wall towards her; the nearer he drew the smaller she seemed to get. And yet crammed into her neat hull she carried a total complement of eighty officers and men. It did not seem possible.

He reached the steep brow which led down to the inboard ship. He saw her name was *Ranger*, built in 1937, the same as *Rob Roy*. The year made him start. How would he have felt about the navy had he known this would happen?

He had applied for the submarine service when the time had come to leave the big cruiser. Apart from his other qualifications he was a good navigator, and on the long hauls and across those far-off oceans he had had plenty of opportunity to extend his knowledge and make full use of the ship's chartroom.

After a brief interview his request had been turned down. His own captain had merely informed him that he had been considered unsuitable for submarines. What the hell did that mean? As soon as he had this appointment sorted out he would apply again and make certain he saw the right people. He was being childish and he knew it. Destroyers then? He stared down at the minesweeper's deck and saw the sentry watching him with mild curiosity. He did not move to help him with the suitcase, however.

As Hargrave clambered down the steep brow and saluted, the sentry tossed up a careless acknowledgement. For some reason it irritated him.

Hargrave snapped, 'I'm going across to *Rob Roy*.' He looked meaningfully at the slack webbing belt and heavy pistol holster. 'Aren't you going to ask for my identity card?'

The sarcasm was lost on the gangway sentry. 'You're *Rob Roy*'s new first lieutenant.' He hesitated and added as slowly as he dared, '*Sir.*'

By the time Hargrave had crossed the deck to the other side his arrival had been noted. Both the quartermaster and gangway sentry were ready and waiting for him.

Again the salutes, then the quartermaster said, 'I'll 'ave yer case put into yer cabin, sir.'

Hargrave looked around. She seemed crammed with equipment and loose gear. But the two boats, one a whaler, looked smart enough, and the ship's bell was freshly polished.

The quartermaster's words made him turn. 'I'd better hold on until the first lieutenant has cleared out his own stuff,' he replied.

The man eyed him curiously. 'All done, sir.'

'Well, thank you.'

The seaman gestured towards a steel door. 'Wardroom's through there, sir. Time for tea.'

I could use something stronger, Hargrave thought bitterly.

As soon as he had stepped over the lobby coaming the quartermaster said to his companion, 'Bit stuck-up, eh?'

The seaman grinned. 'The skipper'll 'ave 'im fer breakfast.'

The quartermaster rubbed his chin worriedly. 'I 'ope so.' He added, 'Never thought I'd ever miss an officer, but the old Jimmy was a good bloke.'

They lapsed into silence and waited for the watch to change.

Hargrave climbed down a steep ladder and found a white-coated petty officer checking a list against some tins of biscuits.

He gave a lop-sided grin. 'Arternoon, sir. I'm Kellett, P.O. steward. I looks after the captain an' the wardroom.' Again the grin. 'In that order, so to speak. Care for some char, sir?'

Hargrave nodded and pushed the heavy green curtain aside before stepping into the wardroom.

Like most small ships it was divided in half, if necessary by another long curtain. To starboard was the dining space with a bulkhead sideboard and pantry hatch beyond. A faded photograph of the King was hung above it. Hargrave noticed that the glass was cracked. On the opposite side the place looked snug, but again it was a cupboard after a cruiser's wardroom. Bench seats and some padded chairs, their red leather worn but well polished, enjoying being without the canvas covers normally used at sea.

A letter rack, a glass-fronted case of revolvers and a tiny fireplace with a club fender completed the fittings.

Hargrave looked at the officer who was sitting propped against the side, his jacket unbuttoned to reveal a none-too-clean sweater. He was an RNVR lieutenant but his appearance made Hargrave stare longer than he normally would. He was very fair, and his lashes looked almost white against the deepset brown eyes. A lean, high-cheekboned face, like one in an old portrait.

The lieutenant put down a dog-eared copy of *Men Only* and returned his gaze. It was almost physical. Even insolent.

'I'm Philip Sherwood, Render Mines Safe Officer, a new addition to the senior ship.' It seemed to amuse him. 'They feel safer with me aboard.' He nodded casually to another figure slumped in an armchair whom Hargrave had noticed. The officer was relaxed in a deep sleep, his mouth wide open like a hole, and Hargrave saw with disgust that his false teeth were in a glass beside one which still held some gin. The man was old and unhealthy-looking, with a heavy belly poking over his belt. He was quite bald, and appeared to have no neck at all.

The lieutenant explained in the same soft voice, 'Yonder is Mr Alfred Bone, our Gunner (T).' He smiled gently. 'Aptly named, don't you think?' When Hargrave remained silent, he said, 'He and the Chief are the ancient mariners – the rest of us just *feel* that way.' He smiled as the sleeping warrant officer groaned noisily. 'Means well, but as ignorant as shit.'

'Do you always discuss your fellow officers in this vein?'

Sherwood replied abruptly, 'Usually.'

The petty officer entered with a tray of tea cups and the Gunner (T) jerked into life as if responding to some silent signal. In two deft movements he downed the flat gin and replaced his dentures. He saw Hargrave and muttered thickly, 'Welcome aboard.' He looked even older awake.

The curtain moved aside and a figure in a white overall peered in at them. 'I'm John Campbell, the Chief.' He made to offer his hand but saw it was smudged with grease so withdrew it. 'You'll be the new first lieutenant?'

Hargrave moved to the club fender and studied the ship's crest above the empty grate. It was very suitable for a ship of her name. A lion's head wearing an antique crown with the MacGregor's motto, '*Royal is my race*', beneath.

Hargrave knew he had made a bad start without understanding why. He recalled something he had read as a boy, how the Campbells had seized the lands of the MacGregors and driven them out.

He faced the others and said, 'You must feel out of place here, Chief?'

Campbell sipped his tea. 'I manage.'

The petty officer fussed around as if he sensed the coolness amongst his charges.

'I'll take your coat, sir.'

Hargrave slipped off the raincoat and reached out for a cup. The others stared at the straight stripes on his sleeve.

Sherwood gave a soft whistle. 'God, a bloody regular!'

Hargrave swung round and noticed for the first time that Sherwood wore a medal ribbon he did not recognise. He recalled how he had described himself, the R.M.S.O. They were the ones who defused mines when they fell ashore or in harbours.

He decided to ignore Sherwood's comment. 'Weren't you ever scared doing that job?'

Sherwood picked up his book. 'You only feel fear when there's an alternative.' The pale lashes closed off his eyes.

The Chief, a commissioned engineer with a lifetime's experience and skill symbolised by a solitary gold stripe, said awkwardly, 'There are two subbies in the mess, er, Number One.' He seemed to falter over the title, and Hargrave felt that Sherwood was watching him again.

The Chief continued, 'Bob, or should I say *Bunny* Fallows is the gunnery officer, and Tudor Morgan assists with navigation. There is of course our Mid, Allan Davenport.' He gave a tired smile. 'Green as grass.'

Sherwood spoke from behind his book. 'And all bloody hostilities-only, except for the two ancient mariners here. I don't know *what* the Andrew's coming to.'

Seven officers who would eat, write their letters, laugh or weep in this small confined space. There could not be many secrets here.

The petty officer named Kellett said, 'Beg pardon, sir, but the Captain would like to see you right away.'

Hargrave picked up his cap and smoothed his hair, still bleached by the sun.

As he left the wardroom he heard Campbell exclaim, 'One of these days, Philip, you'll say something you'll be made to regret.'

'Until that day – ' Hargrave did not hear the rest.

The petty officer steward said, 'This way, sir. Don't worry about your cabin. I'll get anything extra you need.'

He pointed to a door labelled *Captain*, a few yards from the wardroom. Further along past a watertight door Hargrave heard the clatter of crockery. Petty Officers' Mess most likely. Little steel boxes welded together into one hull.

Kellett brushed a crumb off his white jacket and said quietly, 'This ship's been through a lot just lately, sir. Some of 'em 'ave got a bit on edge.' He dropped his eyes as Hargrave looked at him. He repeated, 'Been through a lot, all of us.'

The tannoy squeaked and then a boatswain's call shattered the stillness.

'D'you hear there? Duty part of the watch to muster! Men under punishment fall in! Fire parties to exercise action in fifteen minutes!'

Hargrave nodded to Kellett. At least that was the same everywhere. He rapped on the door. Perhaps when he had done a tour of the ship he might feel differently.

But try as he might he could not dispel the picture of the cruiser's impressive wake as she ploughed beneath the stars of the Indian Ocean.

'Enter!'

Now for the next step. He thrust open the door.

After his first meeting with Ransome on that sunny April afternoon, Hargrave often asked himself what he had expected. Perhaps all, or maybe none of the things he saw as he stepped into the small cabin with his cap jammed beneath one arm.

Hargrave did, of course, know something about his new captain and had told himself that he did not care about serving under an officer whom Sherwood might sarcastically describe as *hostilities-only*.

Ransome had spent most of his war sweeping mines and had won a D.S.C. somewhere along the way. The vessel he had commanded prior to *Rob Roy*, a veteran of the Great War, had hit a mine one night in the North Sea. She had lost most of her forecastle and should have gone to the bottom there and then. But with a last bulkhead shored up and weeping at every rivet, Ransome had somehow got her back to port. In six months that ship had been repaired and with a new company had carried on with her sweeping. Three months ago she had hit another mine and had blown up with a terrible loss of life. Bad luck? Or was it that Ransome no longer stood on her bridge?

As Ransome cleared some files from the spare chair Hargrave studied him guardedly, and took time to glance around the cabin to glean any extra information about the man upon whom he might depend for his next step to a better appointment.

Ransome was younger than he had expected – an alive, interesting face, tired perhaps, but it did not conceal the man's alertness, a sudden warmth as he smiled and gestured to the chair.

'Take a pew. Sorry about the mess. All a bit of a rush.' He looked at the deckhead as feet thudded somewhere. The fire parties getting ready for another night in harbour with a good chance of an air-raid or two. There would be a moon tonight. The bombers' favourite. Ransome continued, 'You've been thrown in at the deep end, I'm afraid. I've seen your report from the minesweeping course – you did well, I think. Bit of a change after a cruiser, I suppose.' He did not anticipate an answer. 'You'll soon settle down. I think you may have met some of the wardroom?' His eyes came up, level and unmoving, like a marksman adjusting his sights. 'Good bunch for the most part.'

'The RNVR lieutenant, Sherwood – ' Hargrave tried not to blink as the eyes studied him without emotion. 'I just wondered – ?'

'Not what you've been used to, I expect.' The eyes dipped and Ransome began to refill the pipe he had been holding as Hargrave had entered. 'Sherwood is extra to complement, but he's an experiment of sorts. The Germans are using more delicate ways of making our job nasty. We need an expert who can strip down a mine or a fuse and perhaps save time as well as lives.' He watched

Hargrave through the smoke as he held a match over the bowl. 'He's a brave man, but there are limits to what anyone can stand. He needed to get back to sea, and for that I'm grateful.'

'That medal, sir.'

'George Cross.' Ransome sat back and watched the smoke drift towards the open scuttle. 'Sat on a bloody great magnetic mine and defused it.'

Hargrave remembered Sherwood's hostility. 'I suppose a lot of his sort – '

'His sort?' The grey eyes levelled again. 'I should have mentioned. The mine was alongside some fuel tanks.' He leaned forward suddenly. 'And if you're bothered about serving with temporary officers you'd better tell me right now. I need a first lieutenant badly.' His eyes hardened, like the sea's colour before a storm. 'But not that badly. This is a crack flotilla, and I intend to keep it that way!'

Hargrave looked away. 'I only meant – '

Ransome pushed his fingers through his unruly hair. 'Forget it. It must be harder for you. Rank hath its privileges. Using it on you is not my style.' He grinned. 'Normally, that is – '

He turned sharply as someone tapped at the door. Hargrave could not see who it was but Ransome stood up and said, 'Excuse me. One of the hands. I'm packing him off home.' He stared at his pipe, which had gone out. 'His family was killed last night in a raid on London. I had the job of telling the poor kid this morning.' He walked past the chair and as he opened the door, Hargrave caught a glimpse of a very young seaman, dressed in his best uniform with a gunnery badge in gold wire on his arm. He was very pale, like a frightened child.

He heard Ransome say, 'Well, off you go, Tinker, the coxswain's fixed it up for you.'

Hargrave heard the youth give a sob, and then Ransome went out and closed the door behind him.

Hargrave looked around the cabin, and tried to picture the cruiser's captain dealing with a situation like this. He could not. Instead he examined the cabin piece by piece, while his ears recorded sounds and directions beyond the steel plating which would soon be familiar to him.

There were several pipes on the desk, and a handwritten letter from somebody. His glance moved to the bulkhead where a smaller version of the ship's crest was displayed. In a frame nearby was a pencilled drawing. An oilskin bag of the kind sailors used for money and documents in case their ship was sunk lay beneath it, and Hargrave somehow knew it was for the picture.

He studied it more closely. It portrayed a young man in sweater and slacks sitting with his back to a partly built hull. There was another craft in the background. A boatyard somewhere. The young man held a pipe in his hand. As he had just seen him do. It was little more than a sketch, but it told him a lot. A framed photograph of a young midshipman was on the opposite side. It looked exactly like Ransome as he must have been, but it was not him.

The door swung open and then slammed shut.

Ransome sat down heavily and stared at his pipe. 'Jesus Christ, how much more can we take of this?'

He glanced at the photograph. 'My kid brother. That was taken at *King Alfred*.'

He smiled suddenly; the mood changed again. 'A million years ago. He's a full-blown subbie now!'

For those few seconds Hargrave saw them both. The boy and the sketch, like one person.

He said, 'I was looking at the drawing, sir.'

'Oh, that.' Ransome dragged some papers across the desk. 'I'm going to be away all day tomorrow. Lieutenant Commander Gregory,' he gestured with the unlit pipe, 'he drives *Ranger*, will take over as senior officer in my absence. I've left all the notes on the rest of them, two smaller fleet minesweepers and the trawler. They're at sea with a group from Portsmouth. A joint exercise. But we shall remain here to complete a few repairs. Unless the country is invaded, or a new delivery of Scotch is announced, in which case we shall slip and proceed to search for it!'

He became serious. 'I'd also like you to go over the charts. We don't carry a navigator as such, it's mostly up to you and me.'

Hargrave felt on safer ground. 'I was assistant pilot before – '

Ransome eyed him for a few seconds. 'Thousands of miles of ocean, right? If you were a mile out at the end of it, you'd soon correct it, I expect?'

'Yes, sir.'

Ransome nodded slowly. 'On this job thirty yards is all you'll get.' He let his words sink in. 'Further than that,' he slapped out the loose tobacco into his palm, 'you're bloody dead.'

He changed tack again. 'Your old man is a rear-admiral, I believe?'

Hargrave nodded. 'I went to see him.'

Ransome looked at his pipe and decided to change it for another. *I'll bet you did*, he thought. Hargrave was much as he had expected, although he had been surprised that a regular officer should have been sent to replace David. Unless – Hargrave had been found unsuitable for submarines. That was hardly surprising, in that elite service within a service. Did someone high up, his father for instance, see the minesweeper as a chance of a quick promotion?

'I suppose you wanted a destroyer?'

The shot made Hargrave flush but Ransome grinned. 'I know *I* did. The last thing I wanted was the chance of getting my arse blown off minesweeping.' He gestured vaguely. 'But it's important. I expect you've had that rammed down your throat at the training base until you're sick of it. But it's true. Without us, nobody sails. If we fail, the country will be squeezed into defeat. It's that simple. The swept channel runs right around these islands, an unbroken track, into which the enemy throws every device he can dream up. Tyne, Humber, Thames, from Liverpool Bay to the Dover Straits, we sweep each and every day, no matter what. There's no death-or-glory here, no line-of-battle with flags and bands playing.' His eyes fell on his brother's picture and he felt his muscles contract. In his last letter Tony had been full of it. Appointed to the Light Coastal Forces. A motor torpedo boat. God, his mother would love that.

He added, 'We sweep mines. It's a battle which started after Dunkirk and will never stop until – ' he shrugged. 'God alone knows.' He made up his mind and wrenched open the little cupboard, and placed the whisky bottle and two glasses on the desk.

Hargrave watched as he broke the seal. His stomach was empty, he had been on a train for hours, but something made him understand that the drink was more than a gesture. It was important to Ransome.

Ransome tilted the whisky around the glass. 'Well, Number One?'

Hargrave smiled. 'I'll try and be a good one.'

'You'll do better than that.' He frowned as the phone rang and he snatched it up even as voices and slamming doors vibrated through the hull.

He said quietly, 'Signal from the tower. The bastards have just opened fire.'

Hargrave found that he was on his feet, his hands clenched at his sides. It was like being naked, or left as a helpless decoy.

Ransome said, 'They spot the flashes from Cap Gris Nez. It takes just over forty seconds for the shells to arrive.'

Hargrave looked down at him and saw that the glass in Ransome's hand was empty.

The roar when it came was like a shockwave, as if someone had beaten the side of the hull with a battering ram.

Ransome waited; there were four explosions somewhere on the far side of the town.

He said, 'The flashes are the only warning. At sea you can sometimes hear the fall of each shell, but *after* it's gone off.' He poured another glass of neat Scotch. 'Bastards.'

There were no more explosions but when Hargrave looked through the scuttle he saw a far-off column of smoke rising across the clear sky. Like a filthy stain. There would be more grief now. Like the young sailor called Tinker.

He picked up his glass. The whisky was like a blessed relief.

'May I ask where you will be tomorrow, sir?'

Ransome was staring at the photograph of his brother.

'Your predecessor's funeral.'

Hargrave looked at the door but sat down as Ransome said, 'Please stay. I'm celebrating. I've had this ship for a year today.'

He held out his glass and waited for Hargrave to clink it with his.

Ransome said quietly, 'I wish – '

Hargrave saw the brief blur of despair in the grey eyes. Like something too private to share. He waited but Ransome said, 'Here's to David.' Hargrave guessed it was his predecessor.

Ransome felt the neat whisky burning his throat but did not care. He never drank at sea, and only rarely in harbour. After tomorrow, David, like all those other faces which had been wiped away, would fade in memory.

He thought of the youth called Tinker, his wretched tear-stained face as he had listened to him, needing him. A travel warrant, a ration card for his journey home. Except that there was no home any more. Like a beautiful ship as she hits a mine and starts to roll over. An end to everything.

He looked hard at his glass. 'I – I don't want to go. But I must. He was my friend, you see.'

Later, as Hargrave unpacked his belongings in his new cabin, he thought about the interview.

No, it was not what he had expected. Nor was Ransome like anyone he had ever met before.

As darkness fell over Dover Castle the air-raid sirens wailed, and people everywhere went to the shelters or huddled beneath stairs with their loved ones and their pets.

Aboard the fleet minesweeper *Rob Roy*, Ian Ransome sat at his desk with his face on his arms and slept for the first time in weeks.

2

━━ ━━ ━━ ━━ ━━ ━━

. . . and Men

Lieutenant Hargrave was not the only replacement to be joining the fleet minesweeper *Rob Roy* before she was once again ordered to sea.

On the following Monday afternoon with a fine drizzle making the moored ships gleam like glass, Ordinary Seaman Gerald Boyes stood on the wall and stared across at the ship he was about to board.

The leading patrolman who had escorted him from the gate pointed with his stick and said importantly, 'Good record. Swept more mines than you've 'ad 'ot dinners, my lad.'

Boyes nodded, but was too polite to suggest that the harbour wall was probably the closest the leading patrolman had been to the sea.

Boyes was a slim, pale youth of eighteen. He had a kind of frailty which now, as he stared at his new home, was at odds with his set expression of determination.

At school he had been something of a dreamer, and usually his thoughts had been on the sea and the mystique of the Royal Navy. His parents had smiled indulgently while his mother had set her hopes firmly on a local bank where Boyes's father had worked for most of his life. While many of the people he knew in the unassuming town of Surbiton on the outskirts of South London had been stunned by the swiftness of events, Boyes had seen the declaration of war as something like a salvation.

Throughout his boyhood, at a respectable grammar school which his father occasionally mentioned had 'been worth all the money it cost' him, Boyes had found his escape in magazines, the *Hotspur*, the *Rover* or the *Adventure*. There was rarely a time when they were without a story or two about the navy, the officers of the dashing destroyers in particular.

Boyes had volunteered for the navy as soon as he was seventeen. His mother, having seen his determination, had been tearfully proud. 'You'll soon be an officer, you see, Gerry.' He hated being called Gerry. 'With your background and education, they'll be crying out for your sort.'

The training to begin with had been hard, but always Boyes had seen his guiding light beyond the discipline and the foul language which at first made him blush to the roots of his hair. Until he realised that it was his innocence which was really the target. He watched the occasional appearance of the officers. Some seemed positively elderly, brought back from retirement, and others with the single wavy stripe on their sleeves seemed like young lords of creation.

His mother had been right about one thing. He had been officially listed as a C.W. candidate, a potential officer, and sent to sea for three months in a sleek, brand-new destroyer. Another world again, working alongside tough, experienced seamen who for the most part had left him in peace with his so-called posh accent, even tolerated his efforts to fit in. At the end of three months, spent mostly in and around Scapa Flow in readiness to escort and protect the huge battleships there, he had been sent to Hove in Sussex, where he would begin his officer's training after a brief series of interviews. He had been wildly excited, and had even met some of the boys who had joined up with him, several from his own district at home. It had all ended there. It was still almost impossible to grasp. It was so brutal, so unfair.

The senior officer had merely said, 'You may get another opportunity later on.' He had looked genuinely sorry for the pale-faced youth with the feverishly bright eyes. 'We need volunteers in this war. We can't all be officers, you know.'

Back home for a few days before returning to the barracks for drafting to another ship. His mother had been upset. Or had she been humiliated, shamed because of his failure? His father had muttered sternly, 'Their mistake, son, not yours.' None of it was much help. Boyes had returned to R.N.B. Chatham and almost immediately had heard about the growing demand for men in the minesweeping service.

As a petty officer at the drafting office had cheerfully remarked, 'Good for you, lad, join the navy and see the world. Volunteer for minesweepers and see the next!'

With unbelievable dedication Boyes had entered the minesweeping course at the shore establishment, HMS *Lochinvar*. The need to prove himself, or to lose himself in danger, he neither knew nor cared.

He examined his feelings as he stood on the harbour wall, the light drizzle bouncing off his cap and oilskin, his kitbag leaning beside him in a puddle.

How did he feel? Not afraid, nor even elated. Just glad to be *moving* again, doing something which would wipe the shame away. He had heard the old hands talking about minesweepers. True guts, they said. 'You wouldn't get *me* in that bloody regiment – '

Boyes turned, but the leading patrolman had gone. He gathered up his kitbag, little suitcase, gas mask and the joining chit which he had produced several times on his way here to prove what he was doing and why. The train had been delayed for several hours because an air-raid had caused a derailment somewhere. He had been crammed in the overloaded train with sleeping soldiers and sailors, the air thick with tobacco smoke and crude jokes.

Boyes made his way across the brow to the inboard ship. It was high-water, and the crossing was reasonably safe.

The gangway sentry pulled his bag aboard for him and grinned as Boyes explained that he was the new replacement.

He said, 'Never 'ave guessed, would we, Bert?'

The quartermaster pointed to *Rob Roy*. 'Shouldn't join 'er, matey, they're killing 'em all off!'

They both laughed as if it was a huge joke.

Boyes eventually arrived on the other ship's wet deck and saw a chief petty officer watching him from beside the quartermaster's little folding desk.

'Well, nah, my son? What are all we then?'

He had a Cockney accent you could sharpen a knife on, although Boyes did not understand that. But he did recognise the crossed torpedoes and wheel on the man's lapels, his air of jovial authority. He was the coxswain, a kind of god in every small ship-of-war.

'Ordinary Seaman Boyes, sir.'

The coxswain's heavy brows came together to make a dark bridge across his battered nose.

'Not *sir*, my son. Call me Cox'n. I run this ship.' He grinned. 'Me an' the Old Man, that is.'

He became businesslike. 'You're in Three Mess.' He gestured to a seaman by the guardrail. 'Take 'im down. Then bring 'im back to me to get 'is part of ship, an' that.'

Boyes eyed him thankfully. There was something reassuring about the coxswain. His face looked as if it had been in many brawls, but his eyes were steady and not unfriendly.

Chief Petty Officer Joe Beckett, the *Rob Roy*'s coxswain, asked offhandedly, 'Age?'

'Eighteen, si – I mean Cox'n.'

'Gawd. Another wot's too young to draw 'is tot. Makes yer sick.'

Beckett watched the slight figure being led to the forecastle. Already lost. He frowned. Not for long. Not in this ship. There was no room for passengers.

He saw the new first lieutenant approaching and toyed with the idea of avoiding him around the funnel, but sighed and stood his ground. Between them they had to manage the ship. He thought of the new lad, Boyes, sent to replace a seaman who had gained promotion and been drafted to an advanced course ashore.

The navy was like that. All comings and goings. He glanced aft towards the shining new paint where the previous Jimmy-the-One had been cut down. All goings for some.

Joe Beckett often considered his own entry into the navy. A London Eastender from Hackney, he was one of seven children. It was a bloody wonder his mum and dad had found the time, he thought. His dad was more in prison than out of it, and two of his brothers had begun thieving at Marks and Spencer's and Woolworths almost as soon as they had got their first pair of boots. They were likely as well known at the Hackney nick as his father by now.

So Joe Beckett had joined the navy at the age of sixteen. He had done well, despite several demotions and *bottles* at the defaulters' table in one ship or another. He was now thirty-six, one of the *old bastards* as they called him behind his back. It was a joke when you thought about it. His upbringing had been hard and without too much love. But it had taught him to take care of himself, as his face and scarred knuckles showed if anyone was stupid enough to challenge his authority. Now, as coxswain, he was as high as he would rise. Here in the fleet minesweeper he ran just about everything. A word in the right ear could shift a man from a miserable look-out position to a snug station elsewhere. Over half the ship's company were too young to draw their rum. That was a bit difficult. Rum and tobacco, 'ticklers', were the currency of the lower deck. He almost smiled. Not far different from the nick after all. And as coxswain he was also responsible for discipline, a sort of judge and policeman in one. How his old dad would have liked that!

At action stations, entering or leaving harbour, and at any other occasion when his seamanship and hard-won knowledge were required, Beckett was on the wheel, thick and thin. He had been sunk once, wounded once, and three times recommended for a decoration. Like Christmas, it was always still coming.

He watched the new first lieutenant as he paused to speak with Mr Midshipman Davenport. Unlike some of the regulars, Beckett admired the Wavy Navy reservists for most of the time. Many of them, like the RNR ex-trawler skippers, were professional seamen, and others, like the Old Man now, had done something before they joined up. Were not too proud to chat about that other world which had probably gone forever.

He was not happy about the new Jimmy. Strait-laced, and from a bloody cruiser at that. Beckett had been an A.B. in a heavy cruiser, had been weighted off for punishment for pitching a petty officer over the rail. Fortunately it had been in Grand Harbour, Malta, where you were more likely to be poisoned than drowned. Cruisers, like the carriers and battlewaggons, were floating barracks. Not for Joe Beckett. He scowled as he saw the white flash of Davenport's winning smile. Beckett had decided within a week of the midshipman's joining the ship that he could well be the reason for himself being disrated, busted as low as was possible.

Even when he considered it calmly over his tot, Beckett had reached the conclusion that if Davenport had sailed with Bligh in the *Bounty* the mutiny would have happened a bloody sight earlier.

He touched his cap in salute as Hargrave approached him.

''Ad a good tour, sir?'

Hargrave brushed down his sleeves. 'Been right over her, stem to stern.'

The midshipman drew closer. 'I could show you the radar, sir?'

Beckett tried not to look at him. *A real little prick.*

He said, 'Watch out fer wet paint, sir.'

Hargrave frowned at a smear of grey on his trousers. '*Thanks.*'

Beckett added, 'New ratin' 'as just joined the ship, sir. I've put 'im in Mr Morgan's division.'

Their eyes met. 'I'd like to be told first, Swain.'

'You wasn't 'ere, sir.' Beckett met his gaze coldly. 'We was one short, so to speak.'

The tannoy snapped the tension.

'D'you hear there! D'you hear there! *Up spirits!*'

Beckett tucked his clipboard beneath his arm and watched Hargrave walk briskly towards the bridge, the midshipman falling into step to keep up.

'Stand fast the 'oly Ghost!' he muttered. 'By Christ I've never needed a bloody tot more!'

The Chief and Petty Officers' Mess was about the same size as the wardroom, although less conventional. There was a small bar at one end where a seaman in a white jacket was acting as messman, and ranged behind it were souvenirs from various pubs scattered from Leith to Gibraltar. Beer mugs, ashtrays stamped with pub or brewery names, photographs of various groups at darts matches, regattas or just a good booze-up. There were a few dazzling pin-ups too, one even signed by a well-known madam in Gosport.

Beckett sat at the mess table which had been cleared of their supper, a meal of baked beans, tinned sausages, and great wads of toast made with fresh bread from the town – a real luxury.

He glanced at his companions. He and Dai Owen the C.E.R.A. were in fact the only members rated as chief petty officers. The rest were petty officers, heads of various departments, the backbone in any class of warship. Masefield, the P.O. sickberth attendant, known as Pansy, the closest thing to a doctor carried in *Rob Roy*, was bent over a letter from his mother, one delicate hand shading it from the others, like a schoolboy in an exam. Topsy Turnham, a dark-chinned, stocky figure with twinkling blue eyes, was the chief boatswain's mate, the *Buffer*, a direct link between the seamen and the first lieutenant. He was poring over some photographs of a full-breasted girl he had found somewhere. Beckett smiled grimly. He did not know how the Buffer managed it. He was married and had a home in Chatham, but always seemed to have his feet under the table with some bit of crumpet wherever he was based. A stoker P.O. lay snoring gently in his bunk behind a half-drawn curtain; otherwise the mess was empty. Kellett was doubtless fussing around his wardroom, and the others were ashore until midnight.

Beckett gazed at a mug of beer on the table. The lull before the night's storm. He would be almost glad to be at sea again. You felt so bloody helpless stuck in harbour, and the Jerries only twenty miles away. About the same distance as Margate. It didn't do to look at it like that.

It was a good mess, he thought. They had their bad moments, but that happened in any small ship where you lived in each other's pockets. But in bigger ships you found all the brains, whereas in *Rob Roy* the other key jobs were carried out by leading hands, just kids, some of them.

Beckett looked up sharply. 'Turn up that radio.'

The messman obliged so that the cool, precise tones of the BBC announcer intruded into their small, private world.

'And yesterday our forces advanced still further westwards along the Libyan coast, supported by units of the Mediterranean Fleet. Some pockets of resistance were dealt with on the outskirts of Tripoli, but the advance continues.' The announcer's voice reminded Beckett of Hargrave. He could have been describing a cricket match. In his mind's eye Beckett could see it clearly. He had taken part in the evacuation of the army from Greece and Crete in the bad days. Ships sunk on every hand, exhausted soldiers, no air cover. A real foul-up. He had seen the battleship *Barham* explode and turn turtle after a U-boat had penetrated the destroyer's screen and fired a salvo of torpedoes. *Barham* had been Beckett's first ship before the war. When he had been an O.D. like Boyes. He gave a sad smile. Well, not really like him.

His friend the C.E.R.A. glanced at him across the table. 'Remembering, Joe?'

'Yeh.' He downed the beer and signalled the messman. 'Turn that stuff off, or find some bloody music!' He faced his friend. He liked Owen, a man with a dark intelligent face, the engine-room's centre-pin. A bloody good chap. He smiled again. For a Welshman.

He said, 'I'm almost scared to think about it, Dai. These advances in North Africa. After all the setbacks and losses. Can we really be on the move this time?'

Owen shrugged and glanced at the bulkhead clock. Soon time for engine-room rounds. It would never do to let the Chief get there before him.

He said, 'Well, at this rate, Joe, we'll have Rommel's bloody Afrika Korps with their backs to the sea before the month's out. There's nowhere else for the buggers to go, see?'

Topsy Turnham folded his photographs and placed them in his wallet.

Beckett said, 'You should keep a bloody filing-cabinet for all your bits of skirt!'

Turnham beamed. He was quite ugly when he smiled.

'Jealous, swain? I can't 'elp it if they finds me irresistible now, can I?' He was a Londoner too, from Stoke Newington, not that far from Beckett's manor.

Masefield glanced up from his mother's letter. 'What's the new Jimmy like?'

Beckett shrugged. 'Not your type, Pansy. Real old school tie.'

Owen grinned. 'Might be *just* his type then, see?'

Beckett conceded, ''E knows 'is stuff all right. You couldn't catch 'im out on the nuts and bolts of the ship. But I dunno, Taffs, 'e's no *warmth*. A proper cold bastard.'

Owen changed the subject. 'The Old Man's at the funeral today then?'

'Yeh. I 'ate burials.' He reflected. ''Cept at sea o' course. That's different. A bit of spit an' polish, a few words and splash, old chummy's gone for a last swim. A good tot and a tuck-in afterwards, well, you can see the point o' *that!*'

The tannoy intruded. 'D'you hear there! Air-raid warning Red. Short-range weapons crews close up. Duty part of the watch to muster.'

'*Sods!*' Beckett groped for his cap and a full packet of duty-free cigarettes. ''Ere we go a-bloody-gain!'

The mess emptied except for the P.O. sickberth attendant and the sleeping stoker.

A few minutes later the sky above Dover and beyond was lit up by bursting flak like hundreds of bright stars which touched the clouds and made them glow from every angle. The crump-crump of anti-aircraft guns from the batteries on the cliffs and inland, and then the sharper clatter of cannon-fire as some of the ships joined in the barrage. Whenever there was a lull they could hear the familiar drone of bombers, passing over, perhaps for London again.

Beckett disdained a steel helmet, a *battle-bowler*, and tugged his cap more tightly across his forehead.

The Jerries might be nearly thrown out of Africa, he thought savagely, but maybe they hadn't heard that at this end of the war.

Ordinary Seaman Gerald Boyes sat at the mess table and looked around his new home. Number Three Mess was a grand name for one scrubbed table with a bench on one side of it, and the cushioned lockers opposite which fitted against the ship's forecastle plating. There were the usual shelves packed with attaché cases, cap boxes, and life-jackets in easy reach, and two sealed scuttles, tightly closed against the darkness outside.

At the head of the table, Leading Seaman Ted Hoggan, the acting gunner's mate and killick of the mess, was engrossed in darning a seaboot stocking, his eyes screwed up with concentration. Some hammocks were slung, their owners, mostly watchkeepers, apparently able to sleep despite the blare of music from the tannoy and the noisy conversation from the mess opposite, where a game of uckers was in full swing.

Hoggan eyed Boyes thoughtfully. 'You can sling yer 'ammock over there on them 'ooks, lad. Young Tinker is ashore for a spot o' leaf.' He gestured with the seaboot stocking to a small oval hatch in the deckhead where Boyes had struggled down with his bag and hammock. 'When Action Stations goes you fly up that ladder like a bat from 'ell, see?'

Boyes nodded. He had changed into a sweater and overalls, apparently the rig except for those on watch in harbour. If anything it made him feel more of an intruder. The other seamen who lounged about writing letters, yarning, or watching the uckers game, wore overalls scrubbed and cleaned so often that they were pale blue, almost white in the harsh deckhead lights. Boyes's were still dark, regulation colour. He concentrated on the leading hand, a real-life seaman. Tough, with a wind-reddened face, and a snake tattooed around one thick wrist.

Hoggan had returned to his darning. 'Just keep yer nose clean, an' do wot you're told. If you wants to know summat, ask *me*, got it? Don't 'ave no truck with the officers.'

'Why is that, er, Leading – '

'Call me 'ookey.' He tapped the killick on his sleeve. 'You're Gerry, right?' He did not see Boyes wince. 'Well, there are officers and officers, Gerry. Some are better than t'others, of course, but deep down they're all bastards.' He gave a slow grin. 'I should know. My boss is Mr Bloody *Bunny* Fallows, the gunnery officer 'e calls hisself. Nice as pie one minute, the next, phew! Specially when he gets pissed.'

A seaman who was stitching a new leather sheath which he had fashioned for a formidable-looking knife, said, 'Which is all the bleedin' time in 'arbour!' He glanced casually at Boyes. 'You a C.W. candidate?'

Boyes flushed. 'Well, no, actually.'

'No, *actually*,' the other man mimicked him and brought grins from the others until Hoggan said quietly, 'Leave it, Sid.'

The seaman shifted along the bench and touched Boyes's sleeve. 'No 'arm done.' He grinned. 'You're not old enough to draw a tot yet?'

Boyes shook his head. It was a question he was asked quite a lot.

'Well, you come round for sippers tomorrow, eh, Gerry?'

Hoggan watched them, pleased they had accepted the youth. It was not his fault, the way he spoke.

He said, 'Yeh, meet Sid Jardine, a *real old sweat*, eh? Must be twenty-one at least! Roll on my bloody twelve!'

Boyes wondered when it would be prudent to sling his hammock. He was not very good at it yet. Even in a big destroyer there had not been room enough, especially for a C.W. candidate, a potential officer.

He glanced with interest at his companions. Most of the mess were ashore, on a 'short run' as Hoggan had explained. They might return aboard by ten o'clock either in silence or fighting drunk. After ten they would arrive back with an escort of the naval patrol. Boyes wondered what his mother would make of these men.

'*Tea up!*' An elderly seaman with three stripes on his sleeve banged down the ladder with a huge fanny of tea.

Hoggan put down his darning. 'Teaboat's alongside!'

What sort of craft was that, Boyes wondered?

The old seaman glanced down at Boyes and then filled a cup of typical sailors' tea, almost yellow in colour from tinned milk, and so much sugar you could stand a spoon in it.

''Ere, this one's free, son!'

The sailor called Jardine exclaimed, '*Free*, Stripey? Do my ears *deceive* me?'

Another called from the opposite mess, 'Better keep your overalls on in your hammock when that old bugger's about!'

Boyes had heard much the same banter before. He took the sweet, sickly tea and thanked the three-badged sailor for it.

He did not care any more. He was accepted. The rest was up to him.

The chief petty officer Wren from the Welfare Section stood beside the khaki-coloured car, and watched the young sailor called Tinker as he stared at the ruined house which had once been his home. She was a severe-looking girl, with her hair set in a tight bun beneath her tricorn hat. It was not that she did not care, but she had seen too many broken homes and shattered marriages to let it reach her any more.

She said, 'The bomb hit the front of the house.' She gestured with her cardboard file. 'There was a whole stick of them right across three streets. They were both in bed. They wouldn't have felt anything.' She watched his silent anguish. 'I checked with the A.R.P. people and the Heavy Rescue chaps.' He gave no sign and she said, 'The police too.'

Tinker stepped amongst the rubble and peered up at one bare wall. The same striped wallpaper, a pale rectangle where one of his pictures had hung. Next to his old toy-cupboard. His eyes smarted again. His own little room.

The rest of the housefront lay at his feet. He heard the car engine turning over behind him and clenched his fists tightly. Bloody cow, couldn't wait to be off! What did she know?

Something like panic gripped him. He had nobody, and nowhere to go! It was like a nightmare. All the fear and tension of minesweeping was nothing by comparison.

He said quietly, 'I had to see it.'

She nodded. 'Very well. The salvage people have all the recovered property in store in case – ' She did not finish it.

Tinker remembered a time, one month after he had joined *Rob Roy*, when they had sighted an airman in a dinghy. He had turned out to be a German, shot down in the Channel, and almost overcome by exposure and exhaustion.

Tinker had been one of the hands to go down a scrambling-net and pull the airman on board, who had fetched him coffee laced with rum. He clenched his fists tighter until the pain steadied him.

'I wish I'd killed the bastard!' he whispered.

He heard footsteps on the fallen fragments and the Wren call sharply, 'Not this way, sir!'

Tinker swung round, hurt and bewildered by the intrusion. He stared and thought his heart had stopped completely.

Then he was running, his cap fallen in the dust as he threw himself into the arms of a man in heavy working-clothes. '*Dad! It can't be!*'

The chief petty officer Wren gaped at them. 'But I was told you were dead! They said you were both in bed!'

The man clutched his son's head tightly against his chest and stared fixedly at the remains of his house.

'She was in bed right enough! But the other bastard wasn't me!'

He lifted his son's chin. 'Pity I wasn't here in time. Come, we'll go to Uncle Jack's.' He turned the youth away from the house. 'But then it seems I was never here when I was needed.'

The Wren watched them walk away without a backward glance.

Her driver said, 'Wasn't your fault, Miss. There's more to this bloody war than bein' blown up.'

She slid into the car and adjusted her skirt.

It sounded like an epitaph, she thought.

3

No Safe Way

Lieutenant Commander Ian Ransome sat behind his small desk and tried to relax his mind. The cabin looked bare as it always did prior to leaving harbour. Books secured on their shelves, his gramophone records carefully wedged in a drawer with newspaper between them. It was a trick he had learned after his first collection had been broken when a mine exploded almost alongside. He was dressed in his old seagoing reefer; the wavy stripes on the sleeves were so tarnished they looked brown in the glare of the desk-lamp.

Outside it was early morning, with a lively chop in the confined waters of the harbour. He felt the deck tremble gently and knew the Chief was already going over everything with his assistant engineer.

The tannoy again. 'D'you hear there! Special sea dutymen to your stations! Close all watertight doors and scuttles, down all deadlights!'

Another departure.

The cabin even felt different. It always seemed as if you were leaving it behind like part of the harbour. Until *Rob Roy* berthed or anchored again, the minute sea-cabin abaft the wheelhouse would be his refuge. He wore his favourite roll-necked sweater, his trousers tucked in his old leather seaboots. Fresh socks, some of the thick ones his mother had made. It might keep her mind off the other side of the war which had taken her two sons to sea.

Ransome patted his pockets although he barely noticed his usual precaution. Pipe and tobacco pouch, plenty of matches. He glanced at the cabin door behind which hung his duffle-coat and cap, binoculars, and a newly laundered towel to wrap around his neck.

His glance fell on the drawing of himself which Hargrave had remarked upon. It all came crowding back as it had yesterday at poor David's funeral. The weather had been bright and fresh at the Hampshire village where the family lived. Ransome had not met any of them before. It was strange, he thought. War was like that. Someone who became a true friend, a bond as close as love; yet when he had been smashed down by cannon-fire it made Ransome realise he knew so very little about him.

The tannoy squawked, 'D'you hear there! All the port watch, first part forward, second part aft! Stand by for leaving harbour!' A brief pause; Ransome could hear the boatswain's mate's breathing on the tannoy. He sounded cold. 'Starboard watch to defence stations!' More noise this time, thudding feet, the dull bang of another watertight door or hatch. Men hurrying to familiar metal boxes. Not looking at each other just yet. Probably thinking of their last letters home. Like his own which had gone with the naval postman an hour ago.

He tried not to think about the funeral any more and imagined Hargrave as he coped with his new ship getting under way, or the curious stares from the men who were still remembering David in his place. So many things. But it did not work.

There had been several women of varying ages, most of them in black. David's father had been there, but had not looked a scrap like him. Another surprise: David's mother had apparently remarried. That explained it. The clergyman had spoken of David's sacrifice; several people had been quietly weeping. There were two others in uniform, both aircrew from the RAF who had apparently been at school with David. They had looked uncomfortable – embarrassed perhaps? They had most likely been to too many funerals in their trade. The next time . . .

He unhooked the drawing of himself and held it to the lamp. The rest of the cabin was in darkness, the deadlights screwed shut when he had been roused with a cup of tea by Kellett, the P.O. steward.

It had been after the funeral, the coffin hidden by freshly dug earth, a man rolling up a borrowed Union flag. Handshakes, David's mother murmuring something to him. 'So glad you were here, Commander.' It had sounded so formal, but he had said nothing. Was she really glad, or would she be thinking of her dead son, wishing he and not David had been the unlucky one this time?

The girl had been with her family. A slight figure with her long hair in a pigtail which hung down her school blazer.

Ransome's heart had given a leap. It was impossible, and yet – He studied the drawing again, remembering exactly how the girl had walked into his father's boatyard in Fowey, her sketch-pad under her bare arm, pausing to ruffle the head of Jellicoe the cat, who had been drowsing in the summer sunshine on an upturned dinghy. Like the girl at the funeral, she must have been about thirteen then. He slipped the picture into the oilskin bag and laid it beside his gloves.

But the schoolgirl had turned to stare at him when David's mother had been speaking. She had not been at all like Eve. He almost heard her name again in his thoughts.

How could she be? That had been in that other world before the war, when every summer had been full of sunshine and promise. The last time he had seen her had been in the summer of '39. He bit his lip. Four years back. In war it was a bloody lifetime.

The telephone above his bunk gave a sharp buzz. The one on the desk had gone, in a drawer too probably. Symbolic. The link with the land was cut. Almost.

He picked it from its cradle. 'Captain . . .?'

It was Sub-Lieutenant Morgan, his Welsh accent very strong over the wire. He had entered the navy by a roundabout route, and had first been in the merchant service where he had obtained his ticket. He had transferred to the navy and had started all over again. He was a junior sub-lieutenant, and yet was qualified in navigation and watchkeeping, and could in time have a command of his own. He would be hard to replace.

'Signal, sir. *Proceed when ready.*'

Ransome asked, 'What's the forecast?'

'Freshening wind from the south-east, sir. Not too bad, isn't it?'

Ransome smiled and put down the handset. He said that about every sort of weather.

The desk was throbbing more insistently now and he could picture the other minesweeper alongside, the complicated mass of wires and fenders which still held them both netted to the shore.

Hargrave would be down soon. What did he really think about his new job?

He thought of that last meeting with the girl called Eve. She and her parents had come to Cornwall to a cottage over the water in Polruan. They apparently borrowed it every year from a friend. He knew it was ridiculous of course, he still did, but he had always looked forward to the school holidays when people filled the villages and seaports, or hiked across the cliffs and moorland. Always she had brought her sketch-pad with her. Shy at first, they had become close while she had told him of her ambition to become a proper artist. He could see her clearly in her faded shorts and shirt, her long dark hair tied back from her ears, her eyes watching him while he had explained about building boats. The yard was owned and run by Ransome's father, who had moved there in the twenties from a smaller Thameside yard. Fowey with the village of Polruan on the opposite side of the little estuary had been exactly what he had wanted for his craft, for his two sons to follow in his footsteps, although Tony had still been at school then himself. Ransome felt the old twinge of jealousy he had known when he had seen his brother walking and chatting with the bare-legged girl. The same age; it had seemed natural and yet . . .

He stood up, angry with himself for allowing the memory to unsettle him. He *was* ridiculous. God, he was ten years older than she was.

He thought of the girl at the funeral; she had been standing as Eve did when she was trying to fix a subject in her mind's eye for her sketching.

Ransome always remembered that last meeting. He had been driving a potential buyer for one of his father's fishing boats to the station in the yard's pickup van, and had met Eve with her parents waiting with their luggage. The holiday had been cut short. Ransome had not been sure which had surprised him more.

Her parents had not been unfriendly but had kept their distance. He had been surprised that Eve had not told him her father was a clergyman; or that she was leaving on that day.

She had been in her school uniform, something he had not seen before, and he knew she was hating him seeing her like that, embarrassed, when they had always shared each other's company like equals.

Her father had said, 'I expect the next time we meet, whenever that may be, you will be married, eh?'

Ransome had seen the girl look away, her mouth quivering. The schoolgirl again.

The train had whistled in the distance and Eve's mother had said, 'So we'll say goodbye, Mr Ransome. Ships in the night.' She had watched her daughter, had been aware of her bitter silence.

'Say goodbye to Mr Ransome, dear – '

She had held out her hand solemnly. 'I shall never forget – '

Her father had peered at the incoming train. 'Ah me, holiday friendships – where would we be without them?' He had been eager to go.

Ransome had watched the porter putting the luggage in the compartment. He had felt his mouth frozen in an idiotic smile. What did he expect? And yet his heart had been pleading. *Please don't turn away. Look at me just once.*

Eve had swung away from the door and had run towards him, then she had reached up and kissed his cheek, her inexperience making her skin flush like fire.

'Thank you . . .' She had stared at him, searching his face, her eyes already pricking with tears. 'Think of me sometimes . . .' He had never seen her again.

There was a tap at the door and he snapped, 'Yes!'

Hargrave stepped over the coaming, his eyes wary.

Ransome sighed. *He'll think I'm rattled already. Halfway round the bend.* 'All set, Number One?' He saw Hargrave flinch, as unused to the title as he was to giving it to someone other than David. He also noticed he was wearing a collar and tie.

'Both parts of the port watch ready for leaving harbour, sir. Starboard watch closed up at defence stations.' He forced a smile. 'I hope I've remembered everything.'

Ransome unwound, muscle by muscle. It was a whole lot harder for Hargrave, he thought. He would learn. Or else.

He slipped into the duffle-coat and dragged his cap tightly over his unruly hair. 'Would you like to take her out?'

He saw it all on Hargrave's handsome features. Uncertainty, knowing that every eye would be watching him. Knowing too that he could not refuse. It was probably unfair, but they had to start somewhere.

Hargrave nodded. 'I'd like to, sir.'

Ransome glanced around the cabin. Would he ever set foot in it again? He thought of David, the earth rattling on the plain coffin. It was over.

He slammed the door.

'We'll do it together, Number One.'

Ordinary Seaman Gerald Boyes groped his way aft along the guardrail, his feet catching on unfamiliar ringbolts and other unmoving projections.

He looked at the sky and the fast clouds and shivered despite his thick sweater. He had slept well, wrapped in his hammock with the other gently swinging pods, and had not awakened once, even when the returning liberty men had crashed down the ladder, banging their heads against the hammocks and giving a mouthful of abuse to anyone who objected.

The other hands in the quarterdeck party to which Boyes was assigned stood around the coils of mooring wire and the huge rope fenders which were ready to supplement those already hung between the two steel hulls.

It was not like the mess, he thought. Here he recognised no one. He saw the quarterdeck officer, the squat and formidable Mr Bone, hands on hips as he discussed something with his leading seaman. Boyes tried to mingle with the other vague shapes, better still, disappear. He told himself not to be so timid. Tomorrow and the day after he would get to know all of them. The ship's company of the destroyer where he had done his sea training had been double that of *Rob Roy*'s.

A seaman lounging against the steel door beneath the after four-inch gun straightened up. He had a handset to his ear, but stood to attention as he acknowledged the call from the bridge. 'Aye, aye, sir!' He looked for Mr Bone. 'Single up to back spring and sternrope, sir!'

Boyes was almost knocked off his feet as the figures were galvanised into action.

Guttridge, the leading seaman of the quarterdeck, a swarthy-faced young man with curling black hair, snapped, 'Cut them lashings off!' He peered at Boyes, 'You're new!' It sounded like an accusation. 'Well, shift yer bloody self.'

Boyes fumbled with the lashings around the nearest mooring wire, and his cap fell to the deck.

Mr Bone was old and ungainly but he was across the quarterdeck in a flash.

'*You* – what's yer name?'

Boyes stammered it out.

Mr Bone growled, 'One of *them*, are you.' He bustled away.

Boyes heard yells from forward as the other wires were let go from the ship alongside. He felt lost and humiliated, and sensed some of the others grinning at him.

A familiar voice said roughly, ''Ere, put these gloves on, *Gerry*.' It was the seaman called Jardine who had mimicked him in the mess. 'There's often loose strands in these moorin' wires. Don't want you to 'ave yer lily-white 'ands damaged, do we?' Then he chuckled. 'Don't mind the Gunner. He don't like nobody!' He pulled out the fearsome-looking knife Boyes had seen him measuring against his new sheath and expertly cut away the spunyarn lashings. 'One day he'll tell you all about 'ow he was a hero at Jutland.' He lowered his voice as Mr Bone bustled past. 'Jutland? It was a bloody picnic compared with what this tub went through last year.' He did not explain.

The deck began to tremble and Boyes saw the backspring rise up and tauten like an iron rod.

Leading Seaman Guttridge, called Gipsy by his friends, exclaimed, '*Jesus*, what's the Old Man up to?'

Another voice said, 'It ain't him. It's the new Jimmy takin' us out.'

Mr Bone snapped, 'Slack off the spring! Stand by sternrope!' He gestured into the gloom by the boat davits. 'Chief Bosun's Mate! More fenders down aft! Chop-bloody-chop!'

The Buffer appeared with some extra seamen and Jardine grinned. 'Poor old

Buffer, he won't like that, gettin' a bottle in front of the lads! I 'spect he was out on the batter again last night, the randy old sod!'

Boyes watched the Buffer hanging over the guardrail to point where the extra fenders were to be placed as the hull began to angle away from the *Ranger*, so that the two sterns seemed to be opening like one great hinge.

Jardine said, 'See?' He watched happily as the Buffer snarled at a seaman for not putting the right hitch on a fender.

'If you lose that fender, you'll spend the rest of the war payin' for it!' He certainly sounded out of sorts.

Jardine nodded. 'Anything in a skirt. Like a rat up a pump, 'e is.'

It was still too dark for him to see Boyes blush.

The communications rating called, 'Let go sternrope!'

Men ran amongst the jutting objects, the wire clattering inboard behind him where it was overpowered and lashed down like an endless serpent.

The hull was still swinging out, and when Boyes glanced up towards the bridge he saw the first lieutenant leaning right out to watch the remaining mooring wire.

No matter what, he thought. I'll be like that one day.

Froth and spray burst up around the low stern and Jardine said, ''Ere we go again then.'

'Let go aft, sir!'

Mr Bone watched the last wire snaking inboard through its fairlead and snapped, 'Take this message to the first lieutenant.' He thrust out a folded piece of paper to Leading Seaman Guttridge. 'We need a new wire afore we comes in again. Might as well break it out of the store now, right?'

Guttridge showed his teeth in a grin and looked even more like a gipsy.

He gestured to Boyes. 'You – Useless Eustace! Take it to Jimmy the One!'

Jardine winked. 'Take if off yer back, Gerry. They don't mean no 'arm.'

Boyes hurried along the side deck, watching out for more obstacles until he reached the first ladder to the bridge. He felt that he understood what Jardine meant. They might use the way he spoke or his lack of experience as a butt for their jokes. Sooner or later they would turn to another newcomer. Either way, they had accepted him.

'Where are *you* going?'

Boyes gripped the ladder to prevent himself from falling as the hull heeled unexpectedly to a sharp turn. It was the midshipman, whom he had not seen before.

'I've been sent to the bridge, sir.'

A shaft of frail sunlight broke through the clouds and brought out the colour of the dazzle paint on the bridge. But Boyes could only stare at the frowning midshipman.

He exclaimed, 'Good heavens, it's *you*, Davenport!'

It was amazing, he thought dazedly. Davenport was about his own age, and they had been at the same school in Surbiton, in the same class for most of the time.

Davenport looked as if he had been hit in the face. He seized Boyes' arm and dragged him past the starboard Oerlikon mounting where a seaman gunner was already strapped in his harness and testing his sights against the land.

Davenport asked wildly, 'What are you doing here?'

It was such a ridiculous question that Boyes wanted to laugh.

He replied, 'I was drafted – '

Davenport did not let him finish. 'You failed your C.W., did you?' He hurried on like an actor who has only just been given his lines. 'I can help you. But if they know we grew up together, I shall have to keep out of it.'

He straightened his back as a petty officer hurried down the ladder.

'And call me *sir*, next time!' Then he gripped his arm again, his voice almost pleading. 'Really, it will be better for your chances.'

Then he lowered himself to the deck and Boyes stood there unmoving while he took it all in. A friend in the camp? He doubted it; in fact he had never really liked Davenport at school. All the same . . .

He reached the bridge and handed the paper to a boatswain's mate. The latter said, 'I'll see Jimmy gets it. Things is a bit fraught up 'ere at the moment.'

Boyes took a lingering glance around the open bridge. The rank of repeaters and telephones, a leading signalman with his glasses trained on the tower ashore, a look-out on either side, some officers grouped around the compass platform, the occasional murmur of orders up and down the wheelhouse voicepipe.

An officer in a soiled duffle-coat, his binoculars dangling from his chest, brushed past him. Then he hesitated. 'Who are you?'

Boyes recalled Mr Bone's tirade and answered cautiously, 'Ordinary Seaman Boyes, sir.'

The officer nodded and gave him a searching glance which Boyes could almost feel. 'Oh yes, the replacement.'

He unexpectedly held out his hand. 'Welcome to *Rob Roy*.' Then he walked aft to peer down at the quarterdeck.

Boyes whispered to the boatswain's mate, 'Which one is that?'

The man laughed. 'That's the Guv'nor. The Old Man.' He nudged him roughly. ''E won't shake yer 'and again if you meet 'im across the defaulters' table.'

Boyes barely heard him. The young officer was the *captain*.

Boyes's day was made.

'Cox'n on th' wheel, sir!' Beckett's voice sounded harsh as it echoed up from the wheelhouse directly below the bridge.

Ransome nodded to the vague shapes of the watchkeepers, then made his way to the tall, wooden chair which was bolted to the deck behind the glass screens.

Around and beneath him he could feel the vessel moving restlessly against the other minesweeper alongside, caught the acrid downdraught of funnel-gas as the wind buffeted the bridge.

It was darker than he had expected, the sky still grey beyond the fast-moving clouds.

He settled himself in the chair and tightened the fresh towel around his neck. He recalled something his father had said on mornings like this. *Spring in the air – ice on the wind.*

Voicepipes muttered around the bridge and he watched as familiar figures and faces took on personality. Shapeless in duffle-coats, but he would know any one of them in pitch-darkness.

The leading signalman, Alex Mackay, his cap fixed firmly to his head by its lowered chinstay, binoculars to his eyes as he watched the harbour for unexpected signals. They would be unlikely to get any, Ransome thought. As soon as they quit harbour they faced death in every mile. But you had to accept that. Accordingly, the minesweepers' comings and goings were taken for granted. *Routine*.

And if the air cringed to a sudden explosion and you saw one of your group blasted to fragments, you must accept that too. The navy's prayer, 'If you can't take a joke you shouldn't have joined', seemed to cover just about everything.

Standing by the wheelhouse voicepipe's bell-shaped mouth, Lieutenant Philip Sherwood stood with his gloved hands resting on the rail below the screen, one seaboot tapping quietly on the scrubbed gratings. He gave the impression that he was bored, indifferent to anything which might be waiting outside the harbour.

Sub-Lieutenant Tudor Morgan, the assistant navigator, crouched on the compass platform, using the spare moments to examine the gyro repeater and take imaginary 'fixes' on dark shapes ashore.

Ransome glanced round towards the *Ranger* alongside, pale blobs of faces watching while the hands stood at the guardrails handling the mooring wire and fenders, ready to cast off.

Above *Rob Roy*'s bridge their most valuable addition, the radar lantern, like a giant jampot, glistened in overnight damp or drizzle. It was their 'eye', all-seeing but unseen. Not even a dream when *Rob Roy* had first slid down into salt water some six years back.

Ransome wanted to leave the chair and prowl around the bridge as he always did before getting under way, but knew Hargrave would take it as a lack of confidence. He saw the heavy machine-gun mounting abaft the funnel swivel round, the six muzzles moving in unison as its crew tested elevation and training. The two four-inch guns and a single Oerlikon on either side of the bridge completed their *official* armament. Ransome recalled Hargrave's surprise when he had seen some of the sailors cleaning an impressive array of light machine-guns which ranged from Vickers .303's to a couple of Bren guns. The previous skipper had taken *Rob Roy* to Dunkirk and had helped to rescue several hundred soldiers. When Ransome had assumed command and had asked the captain much the same question as Hargrave, he had replied, 'The army seemed to forget their weapons when we landed them in England.' He had given a wink. 'It seemed a pity to waste them, eh?'

Feet clattered on a bridge ladder and Ransome heard Sherwood mutter, 'God, I didn't know it was a black tie affair! A bit formal, what?'

Ransome shot him a glance to silence him and saw Hargrave taking a last glance at the forecastle deck where he had been speaking with Bunny Fallows, who was standing in the eyes of the ship near the bull-ring while he waited for Hargrave's order.

Ransome wondered what Hargrave thought of the sub-lieutenant. A temporary officer he might be, but he could not be faulted at his job. Beyond that he was a bloody menace, Ransome had decided. He was one of his small team he would not be sorry to lose.

Fallows would be waiting for just one seaman to make a mistake, and his clipped, aristocratic voice would be down on the man's head like a hammer.

Fallows was really two people. At sea he was the perfect officer, with both eyes firmly set on the next step up the ladder of promotion. In harbour he often drank too much, and had been warned several times for abusing the hands when he could barely stand. As Campbell, the Chief, had once wryly commented, 'On the bridge he's a real little gent. When he's awash with booze I seem to hear the accent of a Glasgow keelie!' It was unusual for Campbell to make personal remarks about anyone. He certainly had Fallows' measure.

The loud hailer on *Ranger*'s bridge gave a shrill squeak, then Ransome heard the unmistakable tones of her captain, Lieutenant Commander Gregory. A good friend over the months they had been sweeping together, but one would never really know in a hundred years.

'Did you have a party last night?'

Ransome glanced at Hargrave as he spoke to Morgan while they stooped over the hooded chart-table. It *was* taking Hargrave far too long. *Rob Roy* should have been through the gate by now. Even to mention it would throw him off balance, and might discourage him from asking advice when it could prove to be vital. For all of them.

The magnified voice added, 'I suppose your ship is aground on gin bottles? I can give you a wee push, if you like!'

Some of *Ranger*'s seamen grinned broadly.

Lieutenant Sherwood muttered, 'Stupid bugger!'

Hargrave crossed the bridge. 'Ready to single up, sir.' He seemed oblivious to the banter alongside.

'Carry on, Number One.' He tried to settle down in the chair. It was a strange, uncomfortable feeling he had never experienced before. It was like having an unknown driver take the wheel of your new car.

'Single up to backspring and stern rope!'

The dark figures came to life on the forecastle, and Ransome heard the scrape of wires along the steel decks, the throaty bark of the Gunner (T), Mr Bone, from the quarterdeck, his personal domain when the ship moored or got under way.

'Stand by wires and fenders!' Hargrave looked even taller on the starboard gratings as he watched the activity on both ships. He was going to pivot the ship round, using *Ranger*'s hull like a hinge. There was not enough room ahead to make a simple turn. Men scampered aft with extra fenders, and Topsy Turnham, the Buffer, could be heard threatening death to anyone who scored the new paint. 'Stand by!' Hargrave gestured to Morgan. 'Warn the wheelhouse!'

Ransome leaned forward to watch the ship's forecastle deck, like a pale spearhead in the feeble light.

Bunny Fallows cupped his hands. 'All clear forward!'

Hargrave glanced briefly across the bridge at Ransome, but he did not turn. Hargrave waited for his breathing to steady. 'Slow astern port.'

The deck responded instantly and a steady froth of disturbed water surged away from the stern. The remaining spring took the strain, the Buffer and a leading seaman watching the wire tightening as the ship put all her weight against it. Turnham growled, 'Slack off there!' Or, 'Watch that bloody fender, man!' The bows began to swing outwards away from the other ship, from which came a muffled, ironic cheer.

Wider and wider until the two ships angled away from each other at about forty-five degrees.

Ransome cleared his throat, and knew that he was gripping his unlit pipe so tightly that it might snap unless Hargrave stopped the ship.

Hargrave called, 'Stop engines! Let go aft!'

'All clear aft, sir!' The boatswain's mate holding the bridge handset licked his lips. He must have been sharing Ransome's anxiety.

Hargrave nodded. 'Slow ahead together. Port twenty.'

Ransome did not raise his voice. 'Back the port engine, Number One.'

Their eyes met and Ransome smiled. 'I know from near misses that this corner is tighter than it looks.'

Hargrave lowered his mouth to the voicepipe but kept his eyes on Ransome. As if he wanted to see what he really meant, or if it was a criticism.

'Slow astern port!'

Back came Beckett's reply. 'Port engine slow astern, sir. Twenty of port wheel on!'

The ship moved very slowly beneath the shadow of the wall, whilst in the shadows astern the other minesweeper was already casting off her lines, her screws churning the water brilliant white against the weathered stone.

Ransome nodded. 'I've got her, Number One.' He moved to the voicepipe. 'Slow ahead together. Follow the markers, Swain.'

He looked at Hargrave. 'Best to leave it to the man on the wheel. Joe Beckett is the best there is. You can lose precious minutes by passing and repeating orders.' He touched his sleeve. Hargrave's jacket felt like ice. 'That was well done.'

Hargrave stared at him. 'Thank you, sir.'

The tannoy intoned, 'Hands fall in for leaving harbour! Attention on the upper deck, face to starboard!'

When Ransome looked again, *Ranger* was in line directly astern, her hull beginning to shine as the light grew stronger. The seagoing ensign, patched, tattered and grubby from funnel smoke, flapped stiffly from the gaff, and already most of the wires and heavy rope fenders had vanished, stowed away until the next time.

Ransome raised his powerful glasses and studied the undulating silhouette of the land. South-east England, which had had just about everything thrown at it. Blitzed, bombed, shelled, and nearly starved on more than one occasion when the convoys had been cut to ribbons in the Atlantic long before they had been close enough to face the lurking hazards of enemy mines.

'But not invaded.'

'*Sir?*' Hargrave looked at him.

Ransome glanced away. He had not realised he'd spoken aloud.

He said, 'It's never stopped. We sweep every day, whether there's anything to sweep or not.' He smiled sadly as he remembered the ladies in black at the funeral, the schoolgirl in her blazer with a cardboard gas-mask container hanging from her shoulder. 'For as the King once said, how else do you know there's nothing there?'

The bows lifted and made the uneven lines of men on forecastle and quarter-deck sway like drunken sailors waiting for the liberty boat. It was as if the sea was already groping into the harbour to find them. To take them back where they belonged.

Ransome moved the gyro compass repeater and found he no longer wanted to talk. But he said, 'Fall out harbour stations. We'll exercise action stations and test guns in fifteen minutes.'

He heard Morgan whispering behind him. When to make the first turn. The course to steer. The latest wrecks to be checked against the chart. Above their heads the radar kept its silent vigil, and once into deeper waters the Asdic would begin to sweep the darkness beneath *Rob Roy*'s pitted keel.

Ransome had seen it so many times, and yet it was always new. He smelt cocoa, 'kye' as the Jacks called it, and felt his stomach contract. He had slept like the dead, and was regretting the whisky it had taken to do that for him.

As he stepped down from the compass platform his hand brushed against the picture in his duffle-coat pocket. If anything went wrong this trip, he would still have that.

He tried not to think of the funeral, and of the boy called Tinker he had sent on compassionate leave.

A young seaman appeared at the top of the ladder, and was speaking with the boatswain's mate. A new face.

Behind him he heard Hargrave ask, 'Are the hands always dressed like that when we leave harbour?'

Morgan made to reply but Sherwood's voice was sharp and incisive.

'What, no swords and medals, Number One?' His voice was quieter as he swung away. 'It's not a cruiser. There's no safe way in this job!'

Ransome frowned. There was bad friction there. He would have to do something about it. But first he crossed to the young seaman, who had apparently carried a message to the bridge.

'Who are you?' It was not much, but it was the best he could do.

In line ahead the two fleet minesweepers pounded out of the harbour, their tattered ensigns making them appear strangely vulnerable.

They were back in the war.

4

Battleground

Ransome half-turned in his chair and took a steaming cup from the boatswain's mate. Eight-fifteen. It was tea this time. As he sipped it, feeling its hot sweetness drive away the last of the whisky, he watched the horizon as it tilted slowly from side to side as if to slide *Rob Roy* back towards the land. It looked as if it was going to be a better day after all, he thought. Still heavy patches of cloud, but the sky above was blue, and when he looked towards the land he saw sunshine on the cliffs, the light reflecting from house windows. Bed-and-breakfasts in those far-off days, now billets for the army, every man doubtless aware of the enemy's nearness. It looked peaceful for all that, except for a cluster of barrage balloons, probably towards Walmer and Deal. Like basking whales, placid in the sunlight.

He felt the deck lift and dip down again, and found that he was on edge with a kind of eagerness to see the rest of the flotilla again. Actually it was only half the full group, as the fleet sweepers were working in these waters mainly to back up the many other vessels, ex-fishing trawlers, and the even smaller motor mine-sweepers, *Mickey Mouses* as they were nicknamed.

When the whole flotilla of eight ships was together they carried the Senior Officer aboard. Now he had to be content with his office ashore, a gaunt, former holiday hotel which had had its windows blown out so many times they used plywood and sandbags instead.

He smiled as he thought of the Senior Officer Commander Hugh Moncrieff, a proper old salt from the Royal Naval Reserve, was always good company, but Ransome was glad that his trips to sea in *Rob Roy* were rare these days. For he had been in command of this ship until handing over to Ransome. Even during the simplest manoeuvre you could feel Moncrieff's eyes everywhere, no doubt comparing, remembering how he would have performed it. Moncrieff had begged to be returned to a seagoing appointment so many times that even the Flag Officer Minesweeping was getting nasty about it.

Ransome glanced around the bridge. Hargrave had the forenoon watch, and was busily checking the chart. Davenport the midshipman was beside him, supposedly learning from his betters. He was unusually silent, Ransome thought. Sub-Lieutenant Morgan was staring ahead, ever watchful. The others, the signalman and two lookouts, also kept their eyes outboard, back and forth, their glasses sweeping an allotted arc, while overhead the radar, which had already reported the rest of the flotilla on a converging course, watched for anything they might miss.

The ship was at defence stations, with the short-range weapons permanently manned, and the remainder of the hands working about the upper deck, whilst aft the minesweeping party were busy preparing the float and otter for lowering once the sweep was begun. He could picture Mr Bone directing operations, although it would be Hargrave's job when they started in earnest. What had got Bone into sweepers, he wondered? They did not normally carry a torpedo gunner, so he must have volunteered. A hard, unyielding man who should have been at home with his grandchildren.

Hargrave stood beside him. 'Alter course in five minutes, sir.'

'Very well.' Ransome groped for his glasses as he saw some men on the fore-castle pause to peer across the port bow.

Hargrave said, 'When I came on watch some of the off-duty hands were hanging about, a few even sleeping near the funnel for warmth.' He shrugged. 'I'd have thought they'd be glad to use the extra messdeck rather than that.'

Ransome raised himself in the chair and levelled his powerful glasses. The tide was on the turn so it was closer to the surface, like a slimy, abandoned submarine.

'Take a look, Number One.'

Hargrave fetched his glasses from the chart table and stared hard on the bearing.

Ransome watched his profile. 'That's a destroyer, HMS *Viper*, an old V & W class from the Great War.' He remembered the nausea when he had first passed near the submerged wreck; the sea was even shallower then. He had been in his first minesweeper, an old Grimsby trawler with an RNR skipper who seemed to feel his way about the Channel by the smell of it.

Ransome heard himself say, 'She hit a mine and went down in fifteen minutes.'

He waited for Hargrave to look at him. 'You mentioned the hands' "rig of the day" when we left harbour, right? And just now you wondered why they prefer to shiver on deck rather than go below? The *Viper*'s commanding officer was a thoughtful man. He sent half his company below to change into their number ones for a run ashore. They would waste less time that way. You can see how near home she was when the mine caught her.' He did not hide his bitterness. 'For weeks we had to pass that wreck, and at low water, until the Royal Marine divers could hack their way into her you could see their faces at the scuttles, arms moving in the water as if they were still trying to get out. Those old destroyers had no escape-hatches then, and the scuttles were too small to climb through.'

Hargrave lowered his glasses. It was as if he had seen it for himself.

'I – I'm sorry, sir. It answers both my questions.'

Later, as the other ships lifted from the sea, Leading Signalman Mackay climbed to the bridge and took over from his assistant. It was as if he knew. A lot of the old hands were like that. Men like Beckett, and the chief boatswain's mate. They were always nearby when their extra skill might be needed.

Almost at once a diamond-bright light began to blink across the grey, heaving water.

Mackay was using his old telescope. It had been his father's; he in turn had been a chief yeoman of signals in the peacetime navy.

'From *Firebrand*, sir. *We were getting lonely.*'

Ransome watched the rising pall of smoke as the leading ships drew nearer. *Smokey Joes* they called them, and no wonder. More veterans from the other conflict, and just about the only coal-fired warships still afloat.

He said, 'Make to *Firebrand*. *Take station as ordered.*' His mouth softened only slightly. '*Follow father.*'

Hargrave was watching him. 'Your last command was one of those, sir?'

Ransome nodded. He could still feel the devastating impact when the mine had caught them halfway along the side of the forecastle. It was like being pounded senseless although he could not recall hearing any sound of the explosion.

He answered slowly, 'Yes. The *Guillemot*.' His eyes were distant while he studied the other minesweepers as they started to turn in a wide arc. 'Good ships in spite of the coal. They could manage seventeen knots like *Rob Roy*, with a following wind anyway.' He smiled, the strain falling away. 'And we never lost a man.'

Hargrave watched, feeling his hurt for the ship which had gone down under another captain. They had picked up only two. He thought, *You never lost a man, you mean.*

Ransome raised his glasses and waited for the third vessel to harden in the lenses.

He said, '*Firebrand* and *Fawn* are twins, but the rearmost ship is *Dryaden*, an ex-Icelandic trawler.'

'I gather they're a bit cramped, sir?' He suddenly did not want Ransome to stop, to shut him out as he had that morning.

Ransome studied the *Dryaden*'s perfect lines, her high raked stem and a foredeck which would ride any sea, even a hurricane.

'This one is a thoroughbred, Number One, not like my old tub. They just threw out the fish and pitched us in. Not like *Dryaden* at all. She was taken from the Icelanders when our patrols caught her smuggling diesel and stores to U-boats.' He nodded again. 'A fine piece of shipbuilding.'

Hargrave remembered the pencil drawing in Ransome's cabin.

'Was that your line, sir?'

'My father owns the yard. I was beginning to get the hang of designing boats.' He heard the girl's voice as if she had called out on the wind. *Show me what you do. Please.*

He said, 'Fix our position again, then make the turn, Number One.' He waved towards the salt-smeared glass screen. 'We lead, the others follow in echelon.' Ransome forced a smile. 'Just like you learned in training, eh?'

'What about *Dryaden*, sir?'

His eyes hardened. 'She drops the dan buoys to mark our progress. They call her the *blood-boat*. No need to stretch the imagination for that, is there?'

As Hargrave returned to the chart Ransome listened first to the radar reports, then to the starboard look-out as he called, 'Fast-moving craft at Green four-five, sir!'

The short-range weapons moved their muzzles on to the bearing until the gunnery speaker barked, 'Disregard! All angels!'

Ransome watched the low hulls as they flung up great wings of creaming spray. M.T.B.s, back from the other side, making for their base, probably Felixstowe. How many had they lost?

He tried not to think of Tony, always the one in a hurry. Falling from a horse, capsizing a sailing-dinghy, everything was a great game to him. He listened to the throaty, animal growl of engines. He would find this a very different kind of game.

He heard the leading signalman say contemptuously, 'There they go, the Glory Boys!'

Ransome turned. 'Maids-of-all-work maybe.' His voice had an edge to it. 'We're just the charwomen, so let's bloody well get on with it!'

He slithered from the chair, angry with himself and knowing why, angry too at the hurt on Mackay's open features.

He leaned over the voicepipe. 'Cox'n?'

'*Sir?*' As usual, Beckett was ready.

'Half ahead together!'

Beckett repeated the order, then. 'Both engines half ahead, sir. Revolutions one-one-zero.'

Ransome moved to his gyro repeater and stared through the V-sight while he steadied the compass with the azimuth circle.

He said, 'Starboard ten.'

He ignored Beckett's voice in the pipe as he watched the bright flickering colour of the dan buoy's flag creep across the sight. 'Midships.' He licked his lips. *I must not get rattled.* Bad memories meant death. '*Steady!*'

Beckett would be down there peering at his steering repeater as it ticked round in the sealed wheelhouse.

'Steady, sir, course zero-two-zero.'

Ransome could just make out the next dan buoy's flag beyond this one. The breathing-space.

'Steer zero-two-two.'

He straightened his back. 'Pipe the minesweeping party aft, Thomas!' To Hargrave he said, 'Ready?'

Hargrave tugged his cap over his forehead. At least he had discarded his collar and tie, and wore a white sweater instead.

'When you are, sir.'

Ten minutes later Ransome hoisted the signal *Out sweeps to starboard.*

As the leading signalman and his mate watched the flags streaming out from the yard Ransome said simply, 'Didn't mean to bite your head off, Mack.' He turned to watch the other ships acknowledge the signal and so did not see Mackay's pleasure, or Midshipman Davenport's disapproval.

Ransome searched the sky too. If it was fine for sweeping so was it for aircraft. Originally one of the minesweepers had hoisted a tethered barrage balloon in case they were pounced on by a single fighter or dive-bomber.

It had its drawbacks. For it had acted as an accurate marker for the German guns across the Channel.

He thought of Hargrave's face when he had told him about the sunken destroyer *Viper.*

Feet clattered on the deck below, while heavy gear was dragged aft by the Buffer's party. At the big winch the P.O. stoker and Mr Bone would be watching the sweep-wire, hoping or dreading as the mood took them. Hargrave was with experts. He should be all right.

He climbed on to his chair as Morgan took over the watch.

And why not? You shouldn't have joined etc. etc.

The boatswain's mate put down his handset.

'Sweep's out and runnin', sir!'

Ransome dug out his pipe. Now the waiting game began. Petty Officer 'Topsy' Turnham banged the palms of his thick leather gloves together and said cheerfully, 'Sweet as a nut, sir!'

Hargrave watched the fat, torpedo-shaped float with its little flag cruising jauntily through the water. He had to admit that it had gone much more smoothly than he had dared to hope. He glanced round at the sweeping party as they secured their gear yet again without the need for any comment or order from anyone. And that was the real difference, he decided. On the minesweeping course they had all been novices. For every manoeuvre ashore and afloat they had constantly changed places with one another, taking, then giving orders, enduring confusion and caustic comments from their instructors.

In *Rob Roy* the business of putting out the sweep-wire had gone like clockwork. First the heavy Oropesa float, which had required manhandling clear of the side while it was lowered outboard. All available men were piped aft to assist, and Hargrave knew that any error of judgment could mean at best a crushed hand, or someone's arm pulped between the float and the ship's side. Next the otter-board, a clumsy device which looked something like a farm gate, with toothed and explosive wire-cutters, and finally, at the end of the Oropesa sweep and closest to the hull, was the *kite*, which like the otter would hold the sweep-wire beneath the surface at the required depth and veer it some forty-five degrees out and away from the ship's quarter.

Now, as the black balls were hoisted to masthead and starboard yard to show any stranger which side the sweep was dragging, *Rob Roy* and her consorts were on station in an overlapping line, in echelon.

The ship felt heavier in the water, which was not surprising with five hundred yards of stout wire towing astern.

Hargrave said, 'How is it in rough weather, Buffer?'

The petty officer rubbed his chin with the back of his glove. It made a rasping sound.

'Dicey, sir. It's when th' wire snares somethin' you gotta be all about. You can't *see* nothin' in a drop of roughers, and the bloody thing can be right under yer counter before you knows it!'

He winked at the petty officer stoker who was controlling the powerful winch.

'Old Nobby 'ere was blown right off 'is last ship.' He raised his voice above the din. 'Blew the ruddy boat right out of yer 'and, didn't he, Nobby?'

The other P.O. gave a grim smile. 'Coulda been worse,' was all he said.

Hargrave thought of the disciplined world of the cruiser. It was impossible to compare with this one, amongst men who never seemed to take death and disaster seriously. Not openly at least.

Hargrave returned his gaze to the Oropesa float as it appeared to bound across the water like a pursuing dolphin. He had seen the incoming M.T.B.s, just as he had watched a flight of Spitfires when they had lifted from the land like hawks, before taking formation and heading towards France and the enemy. They were fighting, hitting back.

'And we keep this up all day, Buffer?'

Turnham glanced at him, enjoying the officer's despair. 'Aye, we do, sir. Up this way, drop our dan buoys in case some careless geezer decides to take a short cut through the swept channel an' misses it like, then back to do it all over again.'

Hargrave wanted to remain silent and not display his uncertainty by asking questions. But the Buffer was a professional seaman, and a regular of the old style, although you would hardly think so to see him in his patched jacket with its faded red badges, and a cap which looked as if he slept in it.

He persisted, 'And at night?'

Turnham gestured savagely at a seaman who was casually coiling some wire.

'Not *that* way, you numbskull! Like I showed you!' He seemed to realise what Hargrave had said. 'Well, sometime we 'ave to sweep at night.' He grinned at a sudden memory. 'We 'ad some Yankee brass 'ats visitin' the flotilla a while back, and one of 'em says we'll soon 'ave the know-how to sweep in pitch-darkness.' He shook his head. 'The Old Man gives 'im a saucy look an' says, we bin doin' that for months, *sir*.'

Hargrave knew that the Buffer was quite a bit older than Ransome. Old Man did not seem to fit.

The leading seaman called, 'All secure, sir.'

Turnham nodded. "'E's a good 'and, sir. Bit too much mouth, but knows sweepin' inside out.'

Hargrave heard feet on the deck and saw the gunnery officer striding aft with one of his men hurrying to keep up.

Bunny Fallows would take some getting used to, he thought. Like now, for instance. He was wearing a bright balaclava helmet on his trim red hair, and on the front of his headgear he wore a large knitted rabbit. It seemed out of character for an officer who spent his time trying to be more pusser than any gunnery officer at Whale Island. At the same time Hargrave sensed that if Fallows was no good at his job the *Old Man* would get rid of him. It was an odd mixture.

Turnham had seen his glance, and had guessed what he was thinking. He would have liked to add his own twopennyworth, but he knew better than to push his luck. Nobody on the lower deck, and in the petty officers' mess in particular, had any time for Fallows. A good woman would snap the little bugger in half.

Instead he said, 'We're due for a spot of leaf soon, sir.'

It was the first Hargrave had heard of it. 'Really?'

Turnham almost licked his lips. 'Six days up the line with a nice little party.' His eyes gleamed at the prospect. 'Beats cock-fightin' anytime!'

Hargrave turned and looked up at the bridge as the signal lamp began to flash towards the other ships.

He said, 'They've sighted wreckage ahead.'

Turnham strode aft and called to his team. 'Stand by on the winch, wreckage ahead!'

The leading hand called Guttridge eyed him with surprise. 'I always thought you said you can't read morse, Buffer?'

Turnham showed his teeth. 'Can't neither, Gipsy. But the new Jimmy can!'

The telephone buzzed in its case below the gun and the communications rating called, 'From the bridge, sir. Wreckage ahead!'

Turnham grinned even wider so that he looked like a small ape. 'We *knows* that, sonny! The first lieutenant told us!'

Hargrave dug his hands into his pockets and looked away. He did not belong here. He must not allow himself to fall into the trap. And yet he knew that Turnham's obvious pleasure at knowing something before being told by the bridge had made him feel just the opposite.

The wreckage was no hazard to the sweep-wire; it was all too small and scattered for that.

Turnham watched the pathetic remains drift down either beam: broken planks, some charred, a few lifebuoys, great disconnected patches of oil, and a solitary deckchair.

He said, 'Last convoy that went through, I 'spect, sir.' He shaded his eyes and added, 'No dead-uns though, thank Gawd. We got no room for corpses in this ship. The convoy's tail-end Charlie would 'ave picked 'em up.'

The watches changed, soup and sandwiches were carried to the gun crews while the work continued with a new dan buoy to mark each section as they swept it.

Planes passed occasionally overhead, some of them probably hostile, but today nobody was interested in the staggered line of minesweepers.

Hargrave knew that he was being watched by the men working around him, and tried not to show any emotion or surprise when he saw the extent of this largely unknown war. The masts and upperworks of so many ships which had been mined, shelled or torpedoed in sight of safety. The wrecks were marked on all the charts, but seeing them like this was totally different from a dry correction in A.F.O.s. Some had tried to struggle into the shallows to avoid blocking the swept channel, others had run amok, on fire and abandoned, to line the channel like gravestones.

Turnham occasionally pointed out a particular wreck which *Rob Roy* had tried to help, or from which they had taken off survivors.

Hargrave was stunned to find that he felt cheated, as if all the promise and training at Dartmouth, and later when he had served in two different cruisers, had been a complete waste of time. That until he had joined this slow-moving, poorly armed ship he had seen nothing and done nothing of any use.

Wrecks, stick-like masts, and mournfully clanging green buoys to mark those which lay in deeper water – it was a battleground, no less than the broad Atlantic.

The communications rating called, 'From the bridge, sir. Take in the sweep.'

Hargrave looked at him without seeing him. *All we do is clean up the mess, and leave the fighting to others.*

By dusk they had swept the channel six times without finding a single mine. For Hargrave it had been a long, long day – and his first lesson.

Ian Ransome wriggled his muffled body against the back of his bridge chair and began to wipe the eyepieces of his binoculars for the hundredth time. It was bitterly cold on the open bridge and against the moonlit rim of a cloud he could see the starboard look-out's hair ruffling in the wind like grass on a hillside. Like most of the watchkeepers, the look-out disdained to wear any form of headgear. Some sailors swore that it hampered the faint sound of danger, and others hated to wear their steel helmets anyway, no matter what Admiralty Fleet Orders had to say about it. Some six months back *Rob Roy* had been under a surprise attack from an aircraft, and their only casualty had been a seaman whose nose had been broken by his companion's helmet rim as he had ducked for cover.

Ransome fought back a yawn. It was three in the morning or thereabouts, and the ship was still closed-up at action stations. At night their duty was to patrol the swept channel, not to look for mines but to watch out for any stealthy intruder or aircraft trying to drop them.

The worst part was over. An hour back they had received and acknowledged the brief challenge of the eastbound convoy's wing escort. It was amazing when you thought about it. One convoy forging around the North Foreland, with no lights, hugging one another's shadows like blind men, and they would soon pass another convoy coming down the east-coast. Because of the narrowness of the swept channel between land and their own huge minefield, the convoys would have to gridiron through each other. No lights, and only a few with radar, and yet Ransome could recall only one serious collision.

He listened to the slow, muted beat of engines and pictured Campbell and his men sealed in their brightly lit world. Almost everyone else was above decks, huddled around the gun mountings and shell-hoists, trying to keep awake, praying for the next fanny of steaming kye and some damp sandwiches.

Fawn and *Firebrand*, the two Smokey Joes, had returned to base to re-bunker; they would be back on the job tomorrow.

Now, at reduced speed, *Rob Roy*, followed by the vague blur of *Ranger*'s silhouette with the Arctic trawler *Dryaden* somewhere astern, continued their patrol in the area known as Able-Yoke, a huge triangle off the North Foreland which commanded the approaches to both of the major rivers, Thames and Medway.

The eastbound convoy's escort commander had reported one straggler, an elderly collier in ballast. He could not spare anything to watch over her, so she must make her own way into the Medway once she was *round the corner*, if she could not complete her repairs in time to rejoin the convoy.

There was a faint blink of light from the shaded chart-table and Ransome heard Sub-Lieutenant Morgan explaining something to the new replacement, Ordinary Seaman Boyes. He was in his division, and Morgan obviously thought he would be better employed at action stations helping with charts than fumbling around an unfamiliar ammunition hoist. Boyes was obviously keen and intelligent, and even though his chance of a temporary commission had been dashed by the bald comment, *Lacks confidence. Unlikely to make a suitable candidate*, he might have something to offer on the bridge.

Lieutenant Sherwood was officer-of-the-watch, although Ransome liked them to change round regularly so that they knew each other's work. *Just in case*. It did not do to dwell on it.

Sherwood was speaking into the voicepipe now.

'Watch your head. Steer one-nine-oh.' Then there was Beckett's harsh reply.

Sherwood was a strange man. He shied away from close relationships. Poor David was the only one who had got along with him, and then not too close. He was a loner in more ways than one. His parents and sisters had been killed in the first months of the war during an air raid. Although he never mentioned it, Ransome guessed it was his reason for his dedication to his work, and why he had volunteered for the most dangerous assignment of all in the first place.

Midshipman Davenport's voice echoed up another pipe from the automatic pilot in its tiny compartment within the wheelhouse.

'Plot – Bridge?'

Sherwood grunted. 'Bridge.'

'C–7 buoy abeam to starboard, one mile, sir.'

'Very well.' Sherwood peered round for Morgan. 'Get that?'

All as usual. Ransome wanted to walk about and restore the circulation and warmth to his limbs. But any movement might break their concentration. And yet if he stayed in the chair he might nod off. It had happened before.

A feeble light winked abeam, one of the buoys still marking the channel. Many were extinguished for the duration, and even the helpless lightships had been strafed by enemy fighters so that most of them were withdrawn from station. Those which remained were a godsend, and were presumably left alone because they also aided the enemy.

It felt as if the ship was without purpose and direction as she moved slowly into the darkness, an occasional burst of spray her only sign of movement. There were destroyer patrols, old V & Ws like the poor *Viper*. Sloops and others from years back, even peacetime paddle-steamers which had carried carefree passengers from Brighton to Margate were employed in the grim work of minesweeping and inshore patrols.

Why were they never prepared?

'Radar – Bridge!' Surprisingly it was Hargrave's voice.

Ransome picked up the handset. 'Captain.'

'I think we've picked up the straggler, sir. Green four-five, two miles.'

Ransome said, 'Keep me posted, Number One.'

They should have spotted the straggler earlier; doubtless in one of the new destroyers they would have done. But here in the channel, with shadows and static bouncing off the land, they were lucky to see anything.

So Hargrave was using his time to familiarise himself with the ship's defences. It was a start.

Ransome said, 'Prepare recognition signal, Bunts. Warn "A" Gun.'

He heard Fallows's sharp voice acknowledging the order from the bridge and pictured him near the gun in his ridiculous balaclava.

The other convoy would be heading along the Suffolk coast about now. Full hulls destined for other ports to be offloaded into heavier ships for the next part of the obstacle race. The Atlantic, the *killing-ground* as the sailors called it, or deeper to the south – the Indian Ocean, anywhere.

The convoy might wait for a night-time dash through the narrow seas, or if they were fast enough might risk the daylight, aircraft, Cap Gris Nez guns and all.

Ransome slid from the chair and moved to the opposite side of the bridge. Shafts of pain shot through his legs with every step and he swore silently while he waited for the cramp to go away. He stood on the steel locker which held the spare signal flares so that he was able to train his glasses above the smeared screen. He felt the wind across his cheek, the rasp of the towel, now sodden with spray, against his neck.

No sign of the straggler yet. And yet the moon was up there, glinting around some of the clouds, making an occasional silver line on the horizon.

Above the bridge, Hargrave crouched over the senior radar operator's shoulder and stared at the revolving, misty shaft of light until his eyes throbbed. Like a badly developed film shot underwater, he thought. Little blips and smudges abounded, but he had already taught himself to recognise the unchanging outline of the coast, unchanging except that it quivered in the strange light as if about to disintegrate.

Booker, the operator, said, 'With the new sets, you can pick out individual buoys no matter what back-echo you get.' His voice was gentle, a New Zealander from Wellington. How had he found his way here, Hargrave wondered?

Booker added, 'Watch the ship, sir.' He gestured with a pencil. 'She's almost up to that buoy now. Better tell the Old – I mean the captain.'

Hargrave hesitated. 'The buoy looks too big.'

Booker chuckled. 'It's marking a wreck, sir. Upperworks of the tanker *Maidstone*.' He glanced at his clipboard of wrecks and unusual marks in the channel, so that his eyes shone green in the twisting phosphorescent glow. 'Why, sometimes at low water – '

He broke off as Hargrave snatched up the handset. 'Radar – Bridge!'

It seemed to take an age for Ransome to answer.

'Sir, the wreck buoy at Green four-five. We've picked up the upperworks . . .'

Ransome sounded calm. 'Impossible, Number One, it's high water now – '

Then Hargrave heard him shout, 'Starshell! Green four-five! Range four thousand yards!'

Booker stared at the set, then he exclaimed, 'Jesus, sir! It's moving!'

The E-boat must have been idling near the wreck buoy, taking its time after the convoy had passed, neither wishing to be seen nor to engage. The unexpected arrival of the lonely straggler must have taken the E-boat completely by surprise, as with a crashing roar of power it surged away from the buoy, ripping the night apart with its Daimler Benz engines.

Ransome pounded the rail with his fist. '*Open fire!*'

The gun below the bridge recoiled violently and seconds later, with the echo of the explosion still rolling across the water, the starshell cast its blinding light across the scene, making night into day. It was all there, the rising jagged wash of the E-boat as it increased speed away from the land, twin splashes when two torpedoes hit the water and tore towards the helpless collier.

'All guns open fire!'

The air cringed to the rattle of Oerlikons and machine-guns, the vivid balls of tracer lifting away from the ship and then from *Ranger* astern to plunge down on the fast-moving E-boat.

The explosions were dulled by distance, but the giant waterspouts that shot up alongside the collier told their own story.

'Radar – Bridge! E-boat steering oh-seven-zero! Losing contact!'

Ransome thrust his hands into his pockets as the moon broke through the clouds, so that when the starshell died they would miss nothing. The collier was going down fast, the single, spindly funnel tearing adrift and lurching over the side with one of the loading derricks. They could hear her anchor cable running out, the explosions had probably done that, and in the arctic moonlight Ransome saw the rising wall of smoke and steam. One torpedo at least must have found the old ship's engine-room. Nobody would get out of there. He thought of Campbell; he would be listening, understanding better than anyone. Scalded to death as the sea roared in.

Ransome shook himself. 'Scrambling nets at the double! Signal *Ranger* to stand off and cover us!' He craned over the voicepipe, his eyes on the reflected ripple of flames as the other ship caught fire.

'Swain! Close as you can! Dead slow both engines!'

'Aye, aye, sir!'

He heard the tiny rattle of the ceasefire gong and imagined the E-boat racing away like an assassin. Forty-two knots against *Rob Roy*'s maximum of seventeen. He felt the bitterness welling up inside him.

'Stand by to come alongside starboard side-to.' He watched the other ship loom from the darkness, the familiar crackle of flames, tiny pathetic figures running, but to where? At least she wasn't a tanker. The whole sea would be ablaze by now.

He leaned over. 'Starboard a point, Swain. *Steady* now.'

He heard Hargrave beside him. 'Well done, Number One.' He kept his gaze on the other ship as men ran forward with the Buffer to wedge fenders into place for the impact. It would have to be quick.

'I – I'm sorry – '

'Don't keep apologising. You saw a flaw in the picture.' Hargrave had obviously been expecting to be blamed in some way.

Ransome said tersely, 'Stop together! Port ten!'

The ship was towering above the starboard anchor now. They could all smell the fire, the charred paint, even hear the jubilant roar of inrushing water. A ship dying.

'Get up forrard, Number One. Fast as you like. She's going to roll over. Haul those poor bastards on board!'

Minutes dragged like hours, and a fire-fighting team dashed into the bows as flames licked over the fairleads and made some of the seamen leap to safety.

To Sherwood, Ransome said, 'The E-boat was lying low. You know what that means?'

Sherwood's pale features shone with the orange light from the fires, his eyes like twin flames.

'She was dropping mines, sir.'

Ransome craned over the screen and saw Hargrave signal with his hands.

He snapped, 'Half astern together! Wheel amidships!'

Slowly at first and then with sudden desperation *Rob Roy*'s screws thrashed the sea into a surge of foam as she backed away from the sinking collier.

Ransome heard the thunder of heavy equipment tearing adrift and smashing through the hull, saw the old bows rise as she began to turn turtle. Whoever had been left behind would stay with her.

Hargrave clambered into the bridge. 'Eight survivors, sir. Two badly burned. The P.O.S.B.A. is coping with them.'

They both watched as the ship dived in a welter of leaping spray and acrid smoke. She did not have far to go, and hit the seabed with such a crash that it felt as if the minesweeper had run aground.

Ransome said, 'Stop together.' To Sherwood he added, 'Resume course and speed.' He looked at Hargrave. 'All right?'

'One of them was nearly burned alive, sir. How can they – ' He broke off as a dark figure handed Ransome a signal flimsy.

Ransome held it beneath the chart table's hood and said quietly, 'We shall begin sweeping at 0500, Number One.' He watched Hargrave's astonishment. 'What did you expect, a medal?'

He looked at the rising welter of flotsam from the vanished collier.

'All part of the job. Now take over while I try and outguess the Krauts.' He hesitated by the chart table. 'Nothing moves until we say so. If that's any comfort, Number One?'

Hargrave heard someone retching and knew it was young Boyes.

They had been in action just moments ago, tracer tearing the night apart while a ship had blown up before his eyes. Now even the moon had gone into hiding, ashamed perhaps for all of them.

Again it was like being cheated. There would be no call to arms, men facing their front to defy the enemy.

Just the cold signal. *Begin sweeping at 0500.*

Hargrave stepped up beside Ransome's tall chair and leaned against the screen. Below by 'A' Gun he could hear a man whistling as he sponged out the muzzle.

Afterwards he thought it was like a lament.

5

▬ ▬ ▬ ▬ ▬ ▬

Next of Kin

The weeks which followed Hargrave's arrival on board *Rob Roy* were an unending test to his ability and patience as first lieutenant. The strain of minesweeping was double-edged.; day after day the routine never changed, sweeping from first light to dusk and often patrols during the night. And yet while there was both boredom and frustration the anxiety of waiting for the unexpected was always there.

Four days at sea, then perhaps one or two in harbour, when tempers flared, or the gripping, suppressed fear erupted into drunken fights ashore, with the inevitable queue at the first lieutenant's defaulters' table the next day.

Convoys threaded their way back and forth through the narrows and around the newspapers' beloved Hellfire Corner. The enemy continued his relentless attack by air, by E-boats, and by bombardment. Men, usually cheerful, disappeared on compassionate leave to return red-eyed and despairing. In some ways it was wrong to have them back, for their private grief, the loss of a wife or family, made them slipshod in a job where carelessness could mean sudden death.

Only from that other war in the Middle East came daily news of success and advances where before there had been retreat and chaos.

The almost legendary Eighth Army, which had been the last line to stand between Rommel's crack Afrika Korps and the conquest of Egypt, had never stopped hitting back. The infantry must have marched and fought all the way from El Alamein, following the coast through Libya and on into Tunis itself. There had been no stopping them. Now, if the news reports could be believed, the enemy's retreat had turned into a rout. The once unbeatable German desert army was hemmed in near Cape Bon. After that, there was nowhere else to go but across the water to Sicily or Italy. All those months, famous names of places like Tobruk and Benghazi, which had changed hands so often it was said that the wretched inhabitants kept pictures of both Churchill and Hitler in their cafés until they were certain who was the victor, were a part of history.

Hargrave watched the resentful faces across the defaulters' table. One of them had been the young seaman Tinker who had returned from leave overdue after fighting a losing battle with the M.P.s. Joe Beckett, the burly coxswain, had told Hargrave in private, "'E's a fine lad, sir, never no trouble, but you know 'ow it is, like. 'Is dad was always away puttin' up aircraft 'angers, and his mum was 'avin' it off most of the time with an A.R.P. bloke.'

Hargrave had replied, 'It's no excuse. You should know that, Cox'n.'

Beckett had glared back at him. ''Cause I'm a reg'lar, is that wot you mean, *sir*?'

'Partly. And because you are expected to maintain discipline too!'

They had barely spoken since.

The lower deck buzz about leave, or *leaf* as Topsy Turnham called it, proved to be faulty, so that when the news did come it ran through the whole ship like a tonic.

Hargrave heard it first from the captain when he mounted the bridge to take over the forenoon watch.

Ransome was leaning back in his chair, as if he never left it, letting the warm breeze ruffle his hair, his grubby duffle-coat wide open while he stared up at the sky. It was strange to be steaming ahead of their consorts with no tell-tale black balls hoisted, or the Oropesa float skimming above the water far out on the ship's quarter.

Somewhere to port lay the great expanse of the Thames Estuary, but the land in the early sunshine was merely a purple blur. No Channel guns to watch and estimate their positions, and some chance of an early warning of any sort of air attack.

Ransome greeted him with, 'What it is to feel the sun, Number One!' He stretched his arms and gave a huge yawn. In those few seconds he looked like a boy again, Hargrave thought.

'And another thing.' Ransome groped in his pocket. 'Just had a signal. The flotilla is to enter Chatham Dockyard at the completion of the next sweep. Just think, a proper refit for once!'

Emotions chased one another across Hargrave's features. A chance to see his father perhaps, to obtain a transfer, a different appointment somewhere.

'That's good news, sir. I hope it reflects on the defaulters' table.'

Ransome wedged his pipe between his teeth and regarded him gravely. 'There's responsibility on both sides of that table, Number One.' He changed his mood with the subject. 'I might have guessed why the Boss is taking us out of Able Yoke. We'll be nice and close to Chatham on this sweep.'

Hargrave tried to concentrate on what he was saying. *Rob Roy* and the others had been ordered to sweep another sector of the war channel, to the east of Shoeburyness. There had been no explanation, and Hargraves thought it was more likely because they were short of sweepers as usual, rather than caring about *Rob Roy*'s proximity to Chatham for a refit.

Ransome said, 'I want to begin the first sweep at noon. Make a signal to that effect to the group.'

'Something up, sir?'

'A fast southbound convoy. The RAF are laying on a bit of hostility over the other side to keep their minds occupied. So it's obviously important. Put the word about the ship, although I expect most of the lads knew of the leave before I did. It may not be a long break this time so make sure that the ones with the farthest to go leave first. The rest of us can have local leave, so take every case on its merit. But no defaulters' grudges, Number One.' He watched him, his eyes level. 'All right?'

Hargrave nodded and climbed on to the compass platform to check the course which required to be steered in this powerful offshore current. He saw Morgan watching him, the way he dropped his eyes when he saw him.

Hargrave gestured to the signalman. 'Write this down, Bunts. To *Ranger*, repeated to the rest of the group –'

He looked at the glassy swell as it tilted the hull more steeply in the path of the sunshine.

They dislike me for my ideas on discipline, do they? The sooner I'm off this damned ship the better!

In the wheelhouse beneath Hargrave's feet, Ordinary Seaman Boyes was carefully polishing the glass of the automatic plot table. By day, the thick black-out curtains which separated it from the rest of the bridge were lashed up to the deckhead. It made the place seem larger, and with the windows and scuttles clipped open Boyes sensed a new atmosphere, relaxed and cheerful.

Reeves the chief quartermaster, a ruddy-faced leading seaman with two good conduct badges on his sleeve, watched the tape of the gyro-repeater as it ticked a fraction this way or that, to be corrected effortlessly by his hands on the wheel. On either side of him a telegraphsman stood by his engine-room and revolutions speed control, but they were chatting quietly, telling jokes but careful not to stand too close to the voicepipe's big bell-mouth.

By the opposite door which opened on to a bridge wing, Topsy Turnham the Buffer was expertly splicing a signal halliard and muttering fiercely, 'Bloody green 'orns, they don't team 'em nothing'!' But he obviously enjoyed showing off his skills.

The chief quartermaster asked casually, 'Wot you doin' when we gets leave, Buffer?'

Turnham's eyes twinkled. 'Nice little party up the line, I got.' He did not see the others exchange winks. 'Tender as a boiled owl, she is –'

Boyes listened while he concentrated on his polishing. *Sharing it.*

'I shall come back a new man!'

'Make sure she don't give you summat else to bring back with you, Buffer!' They all joined in the laughter until Hargrave's voice echoed down the pipe.

'Less noise in the wheelhouse! Report to me, Reeves, when you're relieved!'

Reeves lowered his head. 'Christ Almighty!'

Turnham scowled and straightened his battered cap. 'Leave Jimmy to me. I've just about 'ad a gutful of *'im!*'

One of the telegraphsmen grinned. 'Ain't that the truth?'

Dead on noon the four fleet minesweepers hoisted their black balls and took station on the leader, like sheep responding to a familiar shepherd.

The sky remained clear, and apart from the deep unbroken swell, the sea was without malice.

Boyes went to the bridge to join Sub-Lieutenant Morgan by the chart-table, while Lieutenant Sherwood took several fixes from the gyro-compass to make certain *Rob Roy* was exactly on course. Boyes took it all in, from the clatter of Leading Signalman Mackay's Aldis lamp, to the regular reports from the W/T Office, or from the quarterdeck as the sweep streamed away on the starboard quarter.

Most of all he watched the captain as he moved occasionally from side to side, or levelled his glasses on the next astern. *Ranger* had signalled that she had lost a dan buoy overboard and had requested time to recover it. Now she too had her sweep in the water, but was following astern of the two coal-burners. At this slow speed, that same black smoke would come gushing on to *Rob Roy* once they turned to sweep in the opposite direction.

Mackay had remarked to a boatswain's mate, 'Just about due for a bloody refit, the lot of us, me especially!'

Ransome had thrown off his duffle-coat and was sitting sideways on his chair. He saw Boyes watching him and said, 'Settled in?'

Boyes nodded and blushed. 'Aye, aye, sir.' He grew redder as Morgan grinned and Sherwood exclaimed softly, 'Another admiral, no less!'

Ransome smiled. 'Ignore it.'

Boyes was stunned at being spoken to like this, and the fact that even Sherwood, a man who was said to be a bit 'round the bend', seemed able to accept his presence.

He replied, 'Yes, sir I – I'm still not quite sure what happens when the sweep goes out, but – '

The look-out yelled, '*Mine*, sir! *Green four-five!*'

The others ran to the side, glasses trained, all humour gone.

'Make a signal to the group, Bunts! *Mine to starboard!*'

He ignored the clatter of the lamp's shutter, the bright stabbing light of the next ship's acknowledgement. Flags soared up to the yard, and Boyes could feel the tension like a vice closing around his heart and lungs.

'Clear the lower deck!' Ransome raised his glasses again. 'Tell the Gunner (T) to check all watertight doors.'

Sherwood said tightly, 'Must have just broken adrift. There's still some cable on it.'

A voice murmured in the pipe. 'Cox'n on the wheel, sir.'

Ransome watched the mine; in the powerful lenses it was huge and obscene. It was within the scope of the sweep-wire, but might well pass over it somewhere in the middle. 'Signal *Dryaden* to open fire as soon as the mine's clear.'

He saw Boyes staring at him, his eyes filling his face.

'Your question, Boyes. *This* is what happens.'

Boyes was to remember that for a long time to come.

Down aft with his sweeping party Hargrave hung over the guardrail and stared at the mine. It was imagination but it seemed to be swinging towards *him*.

Turnham said, 'Stand by on the winch, Nobby!' Then to Hargrave he added sharply, 'Clear the quarterdeck, sir?' It did not sound like a question.

Hargrave nodded and heard the leading hand telling the others to move into the shelter of the superstructure.

Turnham said, '*Fawn*'ll put a few shots into the bloody thing. If not, the blood-boat'll fix it.'

He shaded his eyes to look up at the signal halliards. No order to withdraw sweeps. With a drifting mine so close it could be fatal.

Hargrave felt his mouth go quite dry, like a coat of dust. He could not tear his eyes from the mine, half-submerged, turning slightly to reveal its pointed horns. Just a playful touch from one of those and –

The mine seemed to hesitate, then spiralled round in a complicated dance. Someone called, 'It's free, sir!'

Turnham saw the first lieutenant give a great sigh. Do him good, he thought savagely. Nearly shit himself that time.

Hargrave did not even know or care what the Buffer thought at that moment.

He was remembering his first meeting with Ransome, his crisp comment about accuracy of navigation. *Thirty yards. Further than that you're bloody dead.* He could almost hear his voice as he watched the mine dropping slowly astern. With the ships in echelon, *Fawn*'s overlapping sweep would either pick up the drifter, or marksmen would do the job. Some mines made a fantastic exploding column of water; others, once punctured by small-arms fire, sank in silence to the seabed.

Mackay's lamp began to stammer again from the bridge.

Hargrave turned to read it. What happened next was blurred, unreal like a nightmare.

The explosion flung him from his feet, so that he collapsed over the depth-charge rack with the Buffer on top of him.

He struggled frantically to his feet, vaguely aware that the winch was hauling in the sweep, that the ship was leaning forward, sliding from a great wave-crest which seemed to be thrusting them through the water like a surf-board.

He stared wildly at the ship astern. Through belching smoke he caught a brief glimpse of buckled plates and dangling frames; her bows had completely gone, torn off by the force of the explosion. She was already dropping back, the other ships fanning out to avoid a collision.

The tannoy bellowed, 'Away sea-boat's crew! Stand by scrambling nets!'

It was already too late. Hargrave found that he was bunching his fists so tightly that they throbbed with pain while he stared at the stricken ship. One of their own. The front of the bridge was caved in like wet cardboard, and he knew that the threadlike scarlet lines down the plating were in fact blood. Everyone on the bridge must have been wiped out.

The communications rating shouted, 'Bridge, sir!'

Hargrave took the handset, his whole body quivering, out of control.

'This is the captain.' He sounded miles away. 'Take in the sweep. I have told *Ranger* to take charge. Go with the whaler and see what you can do.'

Hargrave wanted to scream. *For God's sake, why me?* He did not recognise his own voice. 'Very well, sir.'

On the bridge, Ransome returned the instrument to the boatswain's mate. He saw Sherwood's pale features, the way he was staring astern like someone stricken by fever.

Ransome said, 'The mine's remaining cable must have snared something and pulled it into *Fawn*'s side. She was an old ship.' He wanted to shrug, but felt too drained to move. 'She stood no chance.'

As if to confirm his words Mackay called, 'She's going, sir!'

Ransome walked to the gratings and stared at the other vessel's blunt hull as it began to rise up in the midst of her own wreckage. The bows had dropped completely off, and her forepart, what was left of it, was already hidden. The funnel was still gushing smoke as if she was at full speed, while her abandoned Oropesa float wandered aimlessly nearby as if it had suddenly gone blind.

He saw the whaler pulling through the smoke, Hargrave standing in the stern-sheets, the Buffer at the tiller.

Huge bubbles, horrific because of their size, began to rise around the sinking hull, where men thrashed about in oil and coaldust, and others floated away as if asleep.

Ransome had known her captain, Peter Bracelin, a mere lieutenant, very well. He was to have been married in the summer.

There was a great sigh from the watching seamen and stokers as with a sudden lurch the *Fawn* dived, her unused Carley floats and rafts tearing free when it was already too late to help anyone.

Ransome said, 'Stop engines.' He looked at Sherwood. 'Pipe the motor-boat's crew away; it'll save time. Some poor bastards might still be out there.'

Sherwood watched him, his pale lashes covering his eyes. 'And then, sir?' He already knew the answer.

Ransome walked to his chair and seized it with both hands.

It could have been us. It should have been.

He said, 'We will carry on with the sweep, what else?'

Sherwood gave what might have been a smile.

'Indeed, sir. What else.'

When Ransome made himself look again there was only the usual slow whirlpool of filth and debris to mark the passing of another victim.

He said, 'Tell W/T to prepare a signal for their lordships.'

He watched the whaler pause on the swell, willing hands reaching down to drag some gasping survivors to safety.

Tomorrow or the next day there would be the usual curt communiqué in the newspapers, one which would only affect a few people when compared with the whole, mad world.

It would end in the usual way. *Next of kin have been informed.*

Ransome ran his fingers through his hair and felt his mind cringe.

It's not enough, he wanted to shout. But then, it never was.

Commander Hugh Moncrieff RNR, the flotilla's Senior Officer, slumped in the other chair and watched Ransome pouring brandy and ginger ale into their glasses.

Around them the little ship murmured with unusual sounds, strange voices of dockyard maties and their foreman, equipment being winched or dragged aside with tackles. One scuttle was blacked out by part of the basin wall, beyond which Chatham dockyard sprawled out towards the barracks.

The four ships had entered the basin this morning after the usual tortuous manoeuvring through the yard. It looked more like a scrapyard than one which worked day and night to repair and patch up the ravages of war, Ransome thought.

He sat down and pushed a glass towards Moncrieff. 'Sorry it's a Horse's Neck, sir. There's not a drop of Scotch aboard until I can have a word with the supply officer.'

Moncrieff sat back and pretended to study the glass. It was a bit early in the day for both of them, but what the hell. He watched the strain on Ransome's face, the dark shadows beneath his level grey eyes.

'Cheers!' Moncrieff said. He was a thickset, heavy man with a circlet of pure white hair around his tanned head. His reddened face was a mass of wrinkles, with deep crow's-feet around his eyes. Dressed in his naval reefer jacket with its three intertwined gold stripes, with a bright patch of medal ribbons above the breast pocket, he looked every inch the old sea-dog. You would have known him for that even if he'd been wearing a pin-striped suit in the City.

Moncrieff said, 'Got a fast car as soon as I read the signal. Bad show about *Fawn*. Still – ' He did not finish it.

Ransome tasted the brandy's fire on his tongue. He felt that it was his first time off the bridge for years. He had not even found time to bath and change before Moncrieff had bustled aboard.

Ransome glanced at the envelope he had put aside for Moncrieff. The full report. He supposed it would be filed with all the others, and then forgotten. In war it was best to forget.

Moncrieff said, 'You've done wonders with *Rob Roy*.' He nodded firmly. 'Smart as paint. I see you've not been able to get rid of that rascal Beckett?' He kept his right hand deep in his pocket while he lifted his glass with the other. 'What about this Hargrave chap?'

Ransome smiled wearily. 'Settling in, sir.'

Moncrieff frowned so that his twin white brows were joined like a rime of snow.

'Bloody hope so.' He looked round the cabin. 'God, I do miss her.'

He had shown less emotion when his wife had died, Ransome thought.

Moncrieff was one of those men you rarely heard about. He had been everywhere and done just about everything. A deck officer in the Union Castle Line, he had fought pirates in the Malacca Strait when he had been a mate aboard some clapped-out tramp steamer, had sailed in the Fastnet Race, and had been in so many obscure campaigns that even his medal ribbons seemed a part of a world long gone.

'Anyway.' He made up his mind. 'I'm putting *Ranger*'s captain in charge during the leave period. He was the last commanding officer to have any decent time ashore.'

Ransome thought of Lieutenant-Commander Gregory, *Ranger*'s captain. He had hurried aboard within minutes of docking in Chatham, just ahead of Moncrieff.

He had said, 'But for that bloody dan buoy, *Ranger* would have been astern of you, as always.' He had looked round despairingly, which was rare for him. 'God, it would have been us!'

Ransome had replied, 'We all think that, James, every bloody time. So forget it.' He smiled sadly. He was a fine one to talk.

Moncrieff saw the small smile. It did not reach his eyes, he thought. A man would only stand so much. Command of any ship, battle-cruiser or M.L., took its own toll of a man's last resources. This small offering of leave might do the trick. It must help anyway.

Moncrieff asked, 'Where will you go, Ian?'

Ransome shrugged. 'Home, I suppose. I've not had much time with my parents since I got *Rob Roy*.'

He did not want to talk about it. He asked, 'Are you going to tell me why we're here, sir?'

Moncrieff's bright eyes twinkled and almost vanished into folds of crow's feet.

'Cheeky bugger, Ian.' He offered the empty glass. 'Fill this up, eh?'

Ransome did as he was told. In some ways Moncrieff was more like a father than his Senior Officer. But God help him if he had bumped the dock wall as they had moored. He had seen Moncrieff's keen stare as he examined the ship for possible damage, *neglect*, he would call it.

Then Moncrieff said, 'It's Top Secret, of course.' Their eyes met.

Ransome waited, wondering how he would react, preparing himself.

Moncrieff said, 'It's the Med. We're going to need a lot of fleet minesweepers out there. So that's what this overhaul is all about. You'll not get much opportunity later on.'

'That's nothing new, sir.'

They both smiled. Then Moncrieff added, 'In *Rob Roy*'s case, it'll mean a couple of new gun mountings. Two pairs of Oerlikons instead of the two singles, and a few other bits and pieces. No need to bother your head about that just now.'

Ransome pictured it. More guns meant extra hands. The ship was already overcrowded, they all were.

'You and *Ranger* will be carrying doctors too.'

Ransome nodded slowly. Doctors were rare in small ships. He said, 'We're going to invade, sir? The other way round for a change?'

Moncrieff frowned. 'I've said nothing. Keep it to yourself, but yes, I think an invasion is in the wind. Sicily is my guess.'

There was a tap at the door and Hargrave poked his head around the curtain.

'Come in, Number One.'

Moncrieff nodded. 'How d'you do?' As usual he did not remove his hand from his pocket to take Hargrave's as he made a half-attempt to offer it.

Ransome marked his expression. He would see it as a snub, or rudeness from another reservist. In fact, Moncrieff rarely showed his hand except to throw up a casual salute. He had lost his three middle fingers in an air attack at Dunkirk. His hand was like a crude pair of callipers. It was fortunate that he was left-handed anyway.

Moncrieff said bluntly. 'You think sweeping a bit of a let-down, eh?' Then he shook his head. 'No, your C.O. *didn't* tell me anything. I guessed it.'

He warmed to his pet theme. 'There was a time, when this war started, when reservists were outnumbered by the regular navy. Looked down on in some ships, I would say. Well, as you now know, that situation has fortunately changed. All these young men you work with joined up for one thing only, to fight the Hun – not to make a nice comfortable career for themselves, right?'

'I didn't see it like that, sir.'

'Good.' Moncrieff glanced at his empty glass. ''Cause if you did, I'd remind you that but for these Wavy Navy chaps and old codgers like meself, Mr bloody Hitler would have run up his flag over Buck House two years ago!'

Ransome felt sorry for Hargrave and asked, 'What did you want, Number One?'

Hargrave took the question as a lifeline. 'It's the base padre on the telephone, sir.' He looked at Moncrieff. 'About a service for *Fawn*.'

Moncrieff struggled to his feet. 'Yes, I forgot. I suppose it won't hurt to have a few words with God. Can't help poor Peter Bracelin though.'

He turned and stared at Ransome. 'You've earned a rest, fifty times over, Ian. So use it. Lose yourself. Leave this little lot to me.' He held out his uninjured hand and shook Ransome's very gently. 'And don't worry about *Rob Roy* either. She's my next of kin now.'

They went on deck together and watched a khaki ambulance pulling away from the brow. The last of *Fawn*'s survivors who had died while the ship had headed up the Medway.

All told, *Fawn* had lost thirty of her company.

They had all worked together for many months, a lifetime in any war. They would be sadly missed. So would *Fawn*. Ransome saluted as Moncrieff strode heavily across the brow. *Poor old Smokey Joe.*

He said, 'Get the people away on leave, Number One. The cox'n and leading writer will help you. They know what to do.'

'I was wondering, sir – '

Ransome watched him calmly. *Invasion.* It was like seeing it in bright painted letters a mile high. The *where* didn't much matter. They only had to care about the *how.*

He said, 'I'm afraid you'll have to forget it, if you were about to ask me about leave, Number One. I need a good officer here in my absence. And well, let's face it, Number One, you've only been aboard a dog-watch. Right?'

Hargrave gave a rueful grin. 'Understood, sir.'

I doubt that, Ransome thought. He said, 'It's ten days. I'll see what I can do for you.'

That evening Ransome left the ship. It felt like no other time. The emptiness, the stillness, the voices and daily routine already like another memory.

He waited in the dusk and looked down at her. Tomorrow she would stand upright in dry-dock.

Ransome turned and walked quickly towards the gates. But that was tomorrow.

6

━━ ━━ ━━ ━━ ━━ ━━

Up the Line

The train from Waterloo's mainline station seemed to wait for ages before it eventually moved off. Unlike the first part of the journey from Chatham when the train had been filled mostly with sailors, this one was crammed almost to bursting point with a strong proportion of all three services.

Gerald Boyes was fortunate and had a window-seat, although with anti-blast netting pasted across the glass it made little difference, except that he was only being squashed from one side. It was a corridor train, and that too was packed. Boyes noted that he had not seen a single civilian climb aboard, or maybe they had been no match for the wild stampede of servicemen, partly rushing to avoid losing a precious minute of their leave; also by sheer weight of numbers some had hoped to crash through the handful of military policemen and railway inspectors to prevent anyone from discovering they had no tickets.

There had been a brief hit-and-run air-raid on London, someone said. Another complained that the train was too overloaded to move. Boyes glanced at his companions; curiously they were all sailors although he did not know any of them. It never failed to amaze him that they could sleep instantly, anywhere, and without effort.

He had seven days' leave. His stomach churned with both excitement and uncertainty at this unexpected break. He had tried to sleep on the slow, clattering journey from Chatham through the Medway towns and finally to London. It was different from the last leave when he had been so full of hopes for his chance of getting a commission. He could still feel his mother's disappointment, as if it was some kind of slur on her and the family. But the events of the past weeks had changed him, although he could not understand how. When he had tried to sleep on the train he had found no peace, but had relived the terrible moment when he had seen *Fawn* explode and disintegrate. The survivors hauled aboard, some coughing and gasping, black with coal-dust and oil, others horribly burned so that he had wanted to look away. As a boy he had always imagined that death in battle had dignity. There had been none there on *Rob Roy*'s deck as Masefield the petty officer S.B.A. had knelt amongst them, working with dressings and bandages, his expression like a mask.

One badly wounded man had looked up at Boyes when he had carried fresh dressings from the sick-bay.

His face had been scorched away, with only his bulging, pleading eyes left to stare at Boyes. For that brief moment Boyes had felt no fear. He had wanted to help the dying man without knowing how. The Gunner (T) had dragged a bloodstained cloth over the man's face and had barked, 'Can't do nothin' more for this one.' But even he had been moved by it.

Boyes glanced down at his uniform. Next time he would find a way of buying a proper, made-to-measure jumper and bell-bottoms like the real sailors wore. He turned his cap over in his hands after making sure that he was the only one awake. He had rid himself of the regulation cap tally with the plain *HMS* embroidered in the centre. He held it so that it caught the afternoon sunlight even through the dirty, net-covered window. In real gold wire, he had bought it from *Rob Roy*'s leading supply assistant, whom the others called Jack Dusty for some reason.

He felt a shiver run through him. *HM Minesweeper*. Pride, a sense of daring, it was neither. Or was it?

The corridor door jerked open even as the train gave a sudden lurch and began to move from the station.

Boyes glanced round and saw a girl in khaki peering in, a second girl close behind her.

She said, 'No seats here either. God, my feet are killing me!' She glanced along the sleeping sailors. 'Looks as if they've all died!'

Boyes stood up, clinging to the luggage rack as the train tilted to the first set of points.

'Take mine.'

The girl in the A.T.S. uniform eyed him suspiciously, then said, 'A proper little gent, eh?' She gave a tired grin and slipped into his seat. 'I'd give you a medal if I had one.'

Boyes struggled out into the corridor where men clung to the safety rail across each window, or sat hunched on their suitcases. The lavatory door at the end of the corridor was wedged open and Boyes could see some soldiers squatting around the toilet, shuffling cards with grim determination.

'She wasn't kidding either. Poor Sheila has been on the move for days.'

Boyes faced the other A.T.S. girl for the first time. She was wearing battledress blouse and skirt, her cap tugged down over some dark, curling hair. She was pretty, with an amused smile on her lips, and had nice hands, both of which she was using to grip the rail as the train gathered speed.

'Had a good look, sailor?'

Boyes felt his face flushing uncontrollably. 'Sorry, I – '

Her eyes lifted to his cap and she gave a silent whistle. 'Minesweeping – is that what you do?'

He nodded, his skin still burning. 'Yes.' He wanted to sound matter-of-fact, casual even. 'It's just a job.'

She wrinkled her nose. 'I can imagine.'

She had very nice eyes. Not blue, more like violet. She was older than he was, he decided. By a year or two. But who wasn't?

She asked directly, 'You going back?'

He shook his head. 'No. Some leave.'

'Lucky you. I've just had mine.'

She had an accent he could not place. He asked carefully, 'Where do you come from?'

'Well, Woolwich actually.' She watched him challengingly. 'Where did you think, then?'

'Sorry – '

She gripped his arm. 'Don't keep apologising. It's the way I talk. Like you – we're different, OK?'

Boyes was losing his way fast. 'Your family – what do they do?'

She watched him again. He was just someone to pass the time with. They would never meet again. And yet she knew he was not like anyone she had met. Not because he had given Sheila his seat, or because of his careful, posh accent. She shied away from it. Not again. It was too soon.

'My dad's on the docks. Makes good money with the war on, and that. Most of it goes against the wall, but that's life, right?'

'Can I ask, where are you going?'

She shrugged. 'In the park, near Kingston. Know it?'

He nodded. 'My home's in Surbiton. Quite close.'

She said, 'I belong to an ack-ack battery there. God, I wish I was in the bloody

Wrens. I'd give anything to see the sea every day instead of a lot of randy gunners and the deer!' She laughed. 'Did I shock you?'

'N – no. Of course not.' He stared through the window. It was not possible. They were almost there.

He stammered, 'I'm Gerald Boyes. Maybe we shall – '

She touched his arm, then dropped her eyes. 'I'm Connie.' She peered past him and said, 'I must wake her up. We're getting off here too.'

The next moments were lost in confusion as the train came to a halt and disgorged a living tide of uniforms on to the platform.

She said quickly, 'I've only been here a month. I was in North London before. I suppose you know your way around in these parts?'

The other girl exclaimed, 'Where's my bloody cap?'

The girl called Connie laughed and pointed to her respirator haversack. 'In there, you goof!'

Sheila said, 'I see they've sent the old Chevvy to fetch us.'

She stood discreetly away as Boyes said, 'Here, this is my address. If you ever want – '

She stuck the piece of paper in her blouse pocket. 'You're a real card, you are!' But her eyes were suddenly warm, vulnerable. 'Maybe. We'll see, eh?'

The two girls hurried away towards a camouflaged lorry where some others in A.T.S. uniforms were already sorting out their bags and parcels from home.

Boyes walked slowly down the slope from the platform. Apart from all the uniforms it had not changed much. Shabbier, but so was everywhere else.

He would walk the rest of the way to his home, steeling himself as he went up St Mark's Hill, just as he had that morning on his way to school when he had been dreaming of being accepted for early entry into the navy.

He had known that church on the hill for most of his life, and had sung in the choir there because of his mother's insistence.

But that morning it had been quite different. When he had passed the last houses he had looked for the church tower and steeple, a landmark thereabouts. There had been nothing but the steeple left standing; a German bomb had wiped the rest away. It had felt like an invasion, like being assaulted by something obscene. He shivered, as he had done when the *Fawn* had finally dived to the bottom.

Then he gripped his case and walked into the sunlight. He turned once to stare after the lorry but it had already swung out on to the main road, and he thought he could hear the girls singing some army song.

A real girl. And she had liked him.

He caught sight of himself in a shop window and tipped his cap to a more jaunty angle.

Home is the sailor.

Lieutenant Philip Sherwood paused on the steps of the club and waited for his eyes to grow accustomed to the darkness. He breathed deeply like a farmer returning to the land; even in wartime it was still London. Bombed, battered and rationed, with traffic groping up St James's Street towards Piccadilly, the night sky already criss-crossed by early searchlights, nothing seemed able to take away its personality.

He half-smiled. Like the old club he had just left, where he had dined alone in the high panelled room with its portraits of stern-faced bankers and businessmen.

His father had put his name down for membership years back when he had left school for Cambridge. His grandfather had been a member there too.

Just now he had asked an elderly servant if the club had ever been bombed.

The man, in his Pickwick-style brass-buttoned tailcoat, had given a wry smile while he had glanced at some equally old members who were sleeping in their chairs, faces hidden by their newspapers.

'It is my belief, Mr Sherwood, Hitler wouldn't dare!'

Mr Sherwood. Even that sounded old and quaint. Sherwood was twenty-six and had been in the navy since the beginning. His father had wanted him to wait a while. The business would not function without a younger head in the boardroom. Anyway, the war would be over by Christmas. That was four years ago.

In the club's elegant entrance hall hung one huge chandelier, unlit now because of the black-out and power cuts. But it was a chandelier which had once been the pride of London's clubland.

It had been made, or *built* as they called it in the profession, by one of the oldest chandelier companies, Sherwood's.

It had gone during the first devastating fire-blitz on London. They had all been there, that was the worst part, his father, mother and two sisters, helping after hours, to pack some of the antique, priceless pieces which would be sent into the country for the duration. The whole street had been demolished, and the blaze had been so terrible that the firemen had been unable to fight near enough to save anyone still inside.

It was still hard to accept that life could change so completely and remorselessly. Sherwood had left the affairs of his family in the hands of a solicitor who had been his father's friend and a cousin from Scotland he hardly knew. He could not face going back to the family home outside London in the quiet suburbs. Sherwood's had always kept a small flat in Mayfair, for foreign buyers and the like. By some miracle it had so far avoided both the bombing and being commandeered for some deskbound warrior from Whitehall, so Sherwood stayed there whenever he was able to reach London. To many people the city was a rambling maze; to Sherwood it was sheer escape, and could have been a desert island for all the notice he took of those around him.

An air-raid siren began its nightly wail, rising and falling above the growl of the traffic, with barely a passer-by glancing at the sky. It was all too commonplace. To think about it could bring nothing but dread and despair. You just kept going.

Sherwood could see beyond the thousands of servicemen of so many nationalities who thronged the cinemas, pubs and dance-halls in search of momentary enjoyment. He saw instead the people, as they went about their daily affairs almost unnoticed. People who set out each day for the office or shop by any form of transport left running after a night's air-raid, not even knowing if the place of work would still be standing when they reached it. And at the end of their stint, returning home again, with that same gripping fear that it too might have been wiped away in their absence.

They were the real heroes, he thought. Without their courage under fire, all the sea battles and tanks in the world could not keep this island going for long.

He thought suddenly of Hargrave, their first meeting in the wardroom. *Confrontation.* His question about fear, his own reply about its only coming when there was an alternative. It was terribly true, but how could anybody like Hargrave understand?

Sherwood knew he was being unreasonable. Once he had tried to contain it. Now he did not care any more.

After his family had been killed he had returned to his ship and straight away had volunteered for mine disposal. He had been in *Rob Roy* about nine months. He had not expected to be alive this long when he had first volunteered for what they called the most dangerous work in any war.

His mind lingered on fear. That was the strange part. With him it was no act. He really did not feel it. He had supposed that one day he would either crack up completely as some had done, or make a stupid error which in the blink of an eye would have solved everything.

A dark figure seemed to slide from a doorway and he heard a girl say, 'Hello, love, d'you feel like a go?'

Sherwood quickened his pace, angry at the interruption, the intrusion into his solitude.

She insisted, 'Anything you like, and I'm clean!'

Sherwood caught the scent of strong perfume and sweat.

He snapped, 'Bugger off!'

She yelled after him. 'You stuck-up bastard! I hope they get you!'

Sherwood swung round. '*What did you say?*'

He heard her high heels tapping on the pavement as she ran into the jostling figures and disappeared.

Sherwood walked on more slowly, his hands deep in his raincoat pockets.

Perhaps he should have gone with her. He almost laughed out loud. Probably end up in Rose Cottage, as they called the officers' V.D. hospital.

He looked up and saw the tiny pinpricks of bursting flak. Soundless from here. The searchlights were groping across some clouds; it all seemed quite harmless, unreal. It was south of the Thames somewhere.

A voice said, ''Ere we go again. Let's find a shelter.'

The crowd seemed to be thinning, and Sherwood found himself walking past the Ritz, beside Green Park. He had often walked there with his sisters.

He clenched his fists together in his pockets. *Leave it. They've gone. You can't bring them back.*

Crump – crump – crump – the familiar sound of shell-bursts, nearer now. More casualties, more smashed debris where streets had once stood and survived the years.

Like the times when he had been sent to deal with the parachute mines dropped on congested towns and seaports. Every street was always cleared beforehand. Just the *Unexploded Bomb* sign, his rating assistant, and utter desolation. As if every living thing had been spirited away.

He had never got over the feeling that he was intruding. The *Marie Celeste* atmosphere of meals from precious rations left steaming on tables, letters half-read or partly written. Mantelpieces with their framed pictures of dear ones in uniform. Sons, husbands, lovers. And always below the tell-tale damage, the huge, deadly mine hanging from its parachute.

Intrusion. That summed it up better than anything. What war was all about.

A voice said sternly, 'Just a moment, sir.' A policeman in a steel helmet stepped from his little sandbagged observation post. Sherwood peered at him through the gloom, saw the helmet reflect a couple of the shell-bursts. It was strange, but you never got used to seeing a London bobby in a tin hat.

'Yes?'

The constable said, 'Air-raid, sir. There'll be some shell splinters dropping about soon. It's not safe to walk the streets. Your cap won't stop the stuff.'

Sherwood thought of the ships he had watched being blown up or strafed, of *Fawn* and her broken, pathetic survivors.

He replied, 'It's the war, I expect.'

He walked on and the policeman muttered to himself, 'Another bloody hero!'

By the time Sherwood reached the street where the company flat was installed he had guessed that the raid was heading further away, to the City or East London perhaps.

He heard the far-off crash of bombs and the familiar rumble of collapsing buildings. As he climbed the stairs to his flat, the streets came alive with other sounds. It was like a mad symphony, he thought. The clamour of fire-engine and ambulance gongs, taxis roaring down side-streets, not with passengers this time, but towing small pumps as a part of the auxilliary fire service. It was as if the whole of London was putting its weight against the enemy. Nobody was spared. And yet when another smoky dawn laid bare the ruins, these same ordinary people would go about their daily tasks. *Make the best of it.*

Sherwood threw his cap on the bed and prepared himself for the night. He took a bottle of gin from the cupboard, one glass and a rare lemon he had brought from the ship.

Then he hung his jacket on a chair and glanced around the flat. As it was in Mayfair, he supposed it was worth a fortune. But it was for visitors who came and went without caring too much about the decor. It was dull, without personality.

He swallowed half a glass of neat gin and bit back a cough. Then he switched off the lights, opened the black-out curtains across the window, and seated himself in a comfortable chair to watch the progress of the raid. He heard the occasional clink of a splinter on the roof or in the street and thought of the policeman's warning.

Another ambulance dashed through the unlit street, its bell clanging violently. Some terrified soul would awake in a hospital bed. He grimaced and took another drink. Or not, as the case might be.

He did not remember falling asleep, but awoke with a jerk, his mind clearing instantly despite the gin, his reflexes tuned like those of a wild animal.

For a brief moment he imagined the building had been hit by a bomb or an incendiary. There were fires flickering beyond the window, and he heard a sudden crash and knew that was what had awakened him. But the glow of fires was several miles away. The noise seemed to be from the flat next door. He drew the curtains, then something fell against the wall and he heard a woman cry out; then a man's voice, blurred and indistinct, but full of menace.

Sherwood ran from the flat, wishing he had picked up a weapon. It must be a robbery, or some burglar who had been disturbed on the job. He had had no idea that the other flat was occupied. He stood breathlessly on the landing, gauging the distance as he stared at the closed door.

Then with only the briefest thought of the consequences he hurled himself at it. It flew open, the lock flying across the room so violently that the two occupants froze stock-still, like figures in a waxworks.

Sherwood was used to making up his mind in a split second. It did not need a genius to work out what had been happening. An army officer's tunic with red staff tabs on the lapels lay on the floor, and the bedside table was filled with bottles and a soda syphon. The scene was set.

Sherwood looked first at the man, a big, wild-eyed individual in khaki shirt and trousers, his eyes almost popping with surprise, then fury as he realised what had happened.

The woman lay propped against the wall, one leg bent under her, her blouse torn from one shoulder, a smear of lipstick or blood beside her mouth as if she had been hit, and hit hard.

Sherwood took it all in. She was very attractive, and half out of her mind with terror. He also noted she was wearing a wedding ring.

She called, 'Help me, *please*!'

Sherwood found that he was so calm he wanted to laugh. And it was not the gin.

He asked. 'Whose flat is this?'

'What the hell is that to do with you?' The man lurched towards him. 'I'm living here, and – '

Sherwood reached out and helped the woman to her feet. 'Are you all right?' But he kept his eyes on the army officer.

She thrust her foot into a shoe which had fallen under a chair.

'I came because he was going to tell me about – ' She hesitated. 'About my husband – '

The man glared and then laughed. 'She *knew* what it was all about!'

He seemed to realise that Sherwood was partly dressed in uniform. 'You a bloody sailor?'

Sherwood said quietly, 'Go next door. It's open. Just walk in. You'll be safe there until the raid's passed over – '

'Don't you bloody dare to burst in here giving orders! When I've finished with you – ' He got no further.

Sherwood lashed out hard and hit the man in the stomach. It was like exploding a bag, he thought. He just folded over, retching and choking, his face contorted with agony.

Sherwood said, 'You shouldn't drink so much, *old chum.*' He picked up a chair and smashed it across the reeling man's shoulders, so that pieces of wood and fabric flew in all directions.

He was aware of two things. That the young woman was pulling at his arm, pleading with him to stop. The other was that he knew he wanted to go on hitting the man until he was dead.

She did not resist when he guided her to the flat next door.

He said, 'Make yourself comfortable. I'll try to get a taxi, or walk you home if you like.' He heard the man lumbering around in the other room, the crash of glass and the loud flushing of a toilet.

He said, 'See? He'll live.' He watched her as she sat in the chair by the window. 'Do you want to tell me about it?'

She was not listening, but trying to drag her torn blouse across her shoulder.

Sherwood picked up her coat and bag where she had dropped them when he had slammed the door. Perhaps the man in the other flat was telling the truth, that she had gone there for a bit of fun, which had got out of control. She was quite pretty, he thought, about his own age. He gropped for a handkerchief and dabbed the corner of her mouth. She winced but did not pull away.

She said in a small voice, 'I lost my husband some time ago.' She was staring at her hands, anywhere but meeting his eyes. 'In the Western Desert.' She spoke in clipped sentences, like parts of an official communiqué. 'He was in the infantry. First they said he was missing. Then they discovered he had been – ' She looked away. 'Killed in action.'

'I see.' Sherwood sat very still opposite her, the blood-stained handkerchief held between them like a talisman. 'Go on.'

'I'd met Arthur – ' her voice hovered on the name. 'The man next door, when his regiment was in Dorset, my home. He knew my husband, and quite recently he telephoned me to tell me he was stationed in London, that he had discovered something about my husband's death.'

Sherwood nodded. He had noticed that at no time had she revealed her husband's name. As if just to speak it aloud after what had happened would destroy even a memory. It was all she had now. So he was not alone after all.

'So naturally I – I came up on the train. He'd said that there would be others here – ' She looked up suddenly and stared at him.

'I thought you were going to kill him.'

Sherwood smiled. 'Wish I had, now.'

'I intended to find a hotel, you see.'

Sherwood considered it. The raid seemed to have moved on, but the A.A. guns were still cracking away, the emergency vehicles as loud as ever in their combined protest.

'You'll not be able to find anywhere now.' He studied her impassively. 'Stay here.' He saw her eyes widen with alarm and added, 'No problems. This is a flat owned by my father's company.'

'Suppose he found out?'

'He's dead.' Sherwood stood up suddenly. 'They're all dead. So you see – ' He looked back at her and saw that she was crying without making a sound.

'I'm sorry, I didn't realise – '

Sherwood hear the man groan again through the wall. *I'll bet his bloody wife doesn't know what he's up to.*

Sherwood said, 'Look, I'll tell you what. You sleep here tonight. I can doss down in the chair, or find somewhere else if you'd prefer.'

She stared at the wall. 'No. After what you did, I – '

Sherwood waved her words aside. 'Tomorrow we'll go out for breakfast. I think you can still get a good one at the Ritz. There's nothing here.'

She was looking at the wall again. 'What about him? Won't he call the police and get you into trouble?'

'I wouldn't think so, not him. It might make too much of a scandal.' He tried to hide his bitterness. 'And trouble is no stranger to me anyway.'

'I don't know what you must think.'

He said gently, 'I *think* you are a very pretty lady, but too vulnerable for the likes of *Arthur* next door.'

She kicked off her shoes and Sherwood felt a pang of envy for the man who had known her, who had died in the Western Desert. He could even envy the scheming bastard next door who had tried to rape her.

She said, 'You're very kind to me. And thank you for what you just said.'

He smiled and held out his hand. 'I'm Philip Sherwood, by the way.'

She saw his jacket hanging from a chair. 'Navy. I'm so glad.'

He did not ask her what she meant. Perhaps it was because her dead husband who had loved and known her, but made the mistake of marrying in war, had been in another service.

Sherwood went into the tiny kitchenette while she used the bathroom. He heard her climb into bed. It must seem a far cry from Dorset, he thought. Suppose there was another air-raid? They might be found together, like poor Tinker's mother had been discovered.

He downed another glass of neat gin. *So nobody lives forever.*

The excitement, the strain of the past months, and the gin took their toll, and within minutes he was fast asleep, slumped across the kitchen table.

He did not hear the wail of the *All-Clear*, nor did he feel the girl come to the kitchen and cover his shoulders with a blanket.

They had both learned a lot about themselves; if not each other.

7

'When Are You Going Back?'

Ian Ransome paused outside the boatyard gates and removed his cap to allow the lively Channel breeze to drive away the discomfort of the journey. There was a hint of haze above Gribbin Head where it thrust itself out into the sea like the bastion of some ancient fortress: a sign of an early summer perhaps.

He turned and looked through the sagging wire gates, then up at the big board which stated, *Edward Ransome and Sons, Boatbuilders.* The sign was flaking, and Ransome felt a touch of sadness for his father. He was carrying on as best he could, and from the din of saws and hammers within the yard, there was more than enough work to do. *Edward Ransome and Sons.* Now, one was sweeping mines, the other doing heaven knew what with torpedoes and deadly cannon-fire.

He walked through the entrance and stared in wonderment at the activity on every hand. Not graceful yachts or stocky fishing-boats, but hulls that looked more like giant egg-boxes than anything that floated.

A voice said, 'Bit of a come-down, eh, Mr Ian?'

Ransome swung round, then seized the rough hand of the yard's foreman, Jack Weese. Ancient yet timeless, as much a part of the boatyard as any frame or timber in it. Ransome knew he must be well into his late sixties, but he seemed exactly the same, as he had always looked. Heavily built, his shoulders rounded by stooping over every sort of craft from dinghy to ocean-racer, he was wearing a spotless white apron, and of course his cloth cap. The latter was occasionally changed at Christmas-time when one of his offspring presented him with a new one.

Weese said, 'Landing-craft – infantry jobs.' He eyed the nearest with distaste, his eyes wrinkled against the glare. 'Bloody things. Still, it's a living.'

'I didn't know you were building them, Jack?'

Weese shrugged and eyed him keenly. 'Bless you, Mr Ian, they're throwing 'em together all the way from here up to Lostwithiel. For the Second Front, whenever that's going to be.'

Ransome fell into step beside him while Weese pointed out the various stages of construction, and all the strange faces who had been brought to work on the landing-craft.

'They don't know what an apprenticeship is,' he said scornfully. 'Just give 'em a hammer and nails, that's about their style!' He added, 'You look a bit bushed, if I may say so.'

Ransome smiled. 'As you say, Jack, it's a living.'

They paused by a small jetty and Ransome asked, 'Where is *Maggie May*?'

She was an old tug, very small, which his father had used first on the Thames, then down here for local jobs, towing timber to the yard, or moving craft to difficult berths. Like Jack, she was a part of it from the beginning.

He recalled his mother's horror in what Churchill referred to as 'the Dark Days' when she had discovered that the elderly tug was missing from the yard.

One of the local coastguards had told her, 'Mr Ted's gone to sea in the old girl, Missus. You know he's always wanted to.'

Ransome recalled the touch of pride and love he had felt when the news had reached him.

His father had taken the little tug with some of the fishermen from Fowey and Polruan, and of course Jack Weese, to a place over the other side called Dunkirk. It was still a miracle they had survived, let alone brought off some fifty soldiers in two trips.

Jack Weese said quietly, 'Your lot have taken her *for the duration*. I hope they looks after her.' He sounded like a man who had lost an old friend.

Ransome nodded. 'What about my – '

Weese cheered up and grinned, his eyes vanishing again.

'Your *Barracuda*? God, I've fought harder for her than me bloody pension!'

They walked through the litter of rusting metal and wood offcuts until Ransome saw the long hull resting on stocks, her deck and upperworks covered by patched tarpaulins.

Barracuda had been his dream. She was a big motor-sailer of some forty-six feet, one he would cruise in, and if necessary live aboard when the time came.

When not working on plans for his father and learning more about the craft of boat-building, Ransome had spent his spare time and the long summer evenings working on his boat. The hull had been overhauled, and some of the inside accommodation completed when Ransome had been called to make use of all the training he had done with the peacetime RNVR. She had stood here ever since, and Weese had indeed fended off the greedy approaches of the Admiralty agents who toured the ports and harbours around Britain in search of vessels which might be thrown into naval service. A sort of press-gang, as Weese put it; not to be tolerated in Fowey.

The agents had insisted on taking *Barracuda*'s two diesel engines for war service in some harbour-launch or other, but the hull was still safe.

Weese watched as he crouched under the canvas awning, reliving all those dreamy days when he had come here. Ransome ran his hands along the curved planking. Old, but a proper boat, a thoroughbred. The girl had come here to watch, to sit with him, or just to sketch. He straightened his back, and looked across the harbour to the village of Polruan on the opposite side. The little houses banked street upon street, the pub by the jetty where the tiny ferry chugged back and forth. He had taken her to the pub once. She had been too young to go inside, but they chatted together on the benches near the jetty. A slim, sprite-like girl with long hair who had put away a Cornish pasty from the pub as if it was a mere crumb. He remembered her eyes while she had listened to him; her bare knees had usually been scratched or grubby from exploring the water's edge and this same boatyard.

'Memories, Mr Ian?'

'A few, Jack.'

Weese waited for him to re-tie the tarpaulin. 'When are you going back?'

Ransome grinned. Everyone said that, as soon as you came on leave. 'A week. I can spare that.' His inner voice said, *I need it.*

Weese said, 'Mr Ted's over in Looe Bay today. He'll be here before dusk.' He watched Ransome's profile. 'A freighter was torpedoed off the Knight Errant Patch a week back. There's some quite good timber washed ashore. Pity to waste it.'

Ransome slapped his shoulder. 'Years ago you would have been a wrecker!'

He hesitated, then asked suddenly, 'You remember the kid who used to come here in the school holidays? She sketched things – pretty good too.'

Weese nodded. 'I remember her. Her dad turned out to be a Holy Joe, didn't he?' His eyes became distant. 'She *did* come here again.' He was trying to fit it into place, so he did not see the sudden anxiety in Ransome's grey eyes. 'Same cottage as the other times.' He bobbed his cap towards Polruan. 'Your brother, Mr Tony would know. I think they went to a dance together over at St Blazey when he joined up.'

Ransome replaced his cap with care and tried to stifle his disappointment. *What is the matter with me?* Eve would be Tony's age. But it hurt him all the same.

'I'll go up the house and see my mother.' He groped in his gas mask haversack, which contained several items but no respirator, and handed a tin of pipe-tobacco to him. 'Duty-free, Jack. Have a good cough on me!'

Weese took it but watched him uncertainly. He had known him all his life, first on the Thames, then here in Cornwall.

Some of the lads had commented on it at the time. Cradlesnatching, that kind of remark. Weese had not realised that it had gone any deeper.

And now this. He studied Ransome as if for the first time. He was the same person underneath. Friendly but reserved; he had been quite shy as a boy compared with his young brother.

Now look at him, he thought. Fighting the bloody war, a captain of his own ship, but still just the same uncertain kid who had wanted his own boat.

He said, 'I reckon Vicar'll know. They were as thick as thieves during that last visit.'

'Thanks, Jack.' He turned towards the houses. 'I'll see you tomorrow.'

Weese shook his head. 'By the old *Barracuda*, no doubt!'

Ransome clipped the haversack shut and wished he had brought Eve's drawing with him. It was all he had, all he was ever likely to.

As he walked slowly past the familiar houses bathed in the afternoon sunshine he thought about the torpedoed freighter, the casual way Weese had mentioned it. So even here, the war was never far away. Right now some U-boat commander might be picking his way through a minefield, his periscope's eye watching this green sweep of land. Thinking perhaps of his own home, wherever that was.

His mother looked older, he thought, but hugged him with her same vigour.

'You've no meat on your bones, son! They don't feed you enough!'

Ransome smiled. Another misunderstanding, he thought. It was said that the cooks in Chatham Barracks threw away more spoiled food every day than the whole town got in rations.

She was bustling about, happy to have him home. 'I'll soon take care of *that*!'

Ransome saw the two photographs on the mantelpiece above the old fireplace where they burned logs in the winter, and his father had told unlikely ghost stories.

'Heard from Tony, Mum?'

She did not turn but he saw her shoulders stiffen. 'A few letters, but we did hear from one of his friends that his flotilla . . . whatever you call it, has gone to the Mediterranean.'

Ransome tried to remain calm. So much for security.

She was saying, 'I thank God the war's nearly over out there.'

Ransome groped for his pipe. The Mediterranean was about to erupt all over again. How could he even hint that *Rob Roy* would soon be going there too?

She turned and studied him. 'How is it, dear? As bad as they say? I think of you both all the time – ' She bowed her head, and he took her in his arms to comfort her as her bravery collapsed.

Later that evening as Ransome sat at the table and faced an enormous dinner with his parents, the war intruded once again.

His father had switched on the wireless to hear the news. It was all much the same as Ransome had heard before he had left the ship. Until the very end when the urbane tones of the BBC announcer made the brief announcement.

'The Secretary of the Admiralty regrets to announce the loss of His Majesty's Minesweeper *Fawn*. Next of kin have been informed.'

It was a long time before anyone spoke. Then his father said flatly, 'She was one of yours, Ian? I'm so sorry.'

As night closed in over the little harbour Ransome mounted the stairs to his room and stared at the fresh curtains, which his mother must have made for his visit so that it would always look as if he had not really been away.

He had changed from his uniform into his oldest shirt and flannel trousers and lay on the bed for a long time, the window open to listen to the breeze, the querulous muttering of some gulls who slept on the roof.

He thought about the *Fawn*, of another gathering somewhere with more women in black to mark that curt announcement.

Perhaps he would sleep again and dream of the sun across his back while he worked on the boat's hull. Maybe in the dream she would come once again.

Lieutenant Trevor Hargrave sat at Ransome's little desk and leafed half-heartedly through the latest batch of signals and A.F.O.'s. Wrecks and minefields to be re-checked or inserted on the charts, new regulations about the issue of Wrens' clothing, revised designs for ship-camouflage, instructions for firing parties at service funerals. It was endless.

He listened to the muffled chatter on the tannoy speakers, the obedient gales of studio laughter, another comic programme to give a lighter side to the war.

It was strange to feel the ship moving gently again after being propped in dry-dock, her decks snared by electric cables and pipes while the dockyard completed a hasty overhaul of the lower hull before refloating her. Tomorrow she would be warped out to the gunwharf for re-ammunitioning, and for further inspections by the armaments supply officers and fitters.

Now at least they were a ship again, the deck empty of boiler-suited dockyard workers who seemed to spend more time idling and drinking tea than working.

As Campbell had dourly commented, 'If it's not screwed down, the buggers will lift it!'

The whole fleet knew about survival rations looted from Carley floats and boats while a ship lay in the dockyard. There were worse stories too, of dead seamen trapped below after being torpedoed, being robbed of their watches and pathetic possessions before they could be cut free from the mess.

Hargrave glanced around the cabin until his eyes settled on the drawing. It was unsigned, and yet he had the feeling that Ransome's unwillingness to discuss it meant there was much more behind it.

The ship's company were either on home leave, or ashore locally, leaving only a small duty-watch on board for safety's sake. Tomorrow the next batch would be packed off to their wives and mothers. More the latter in this youthful company, he thought.

He toyed with the idea of going to the wardroom. Bunny Fallows would be there, the Chief too probably. The rest were away. Even Mr Bone, whose home was in nearby Gillingham, was absent.

Hargrave decided against it. Campbell was friendly enough but kept very much to himself. Fallows, well – he stopped his thoughts right there.

The tap at the cabin door was almost a welcome relief. It was Petty Officer Stoker Clarke, a tough, dependable man who was said to have survived the sinking of his last ship by being blown bodily over the side after the explosion had sent most of his companions to their deaths. He was the only petty officer aboard, with Leading Seaman Reeves, the chief quartermaster, to assist him.

'What is it, P.O.?'

Clarke stepped warily over the coaming and removed his cap.

'It's Ordinary Seaman Tinker, sir.'

Hargrave picked out the youthful sailor's resentful face from his thoughts.

'Not back from leave again? I told the commanding officer that – '

Clarke shook his head. 'No, he's back aboard, sir. He's requestin' to see you, *Personal*.'

Hargrave said, 'I'll see him when I take requestmen and defaulters tomorrow, after we've cleared the dock.'

Clarke eyed him stubbornly. 'He says it's urgent, sir.'

'What do *you* think?'

Clarke wanted to say that he would have kicked the lad's arse clean through the bulkhead if he had not respected his anxiety. But he said, 'I wouldn't have bothered otherwise, sir.' He made to leave.

Hargrave snapped, 'I've not finished yet!'

'Oh?' Clarke eyed him calmly. He had suffered too much, gave too much each day to conceal it, to put up with officers like the Jimmy who always seemed to want to go by the book. 'Thought you had, sir.'

'Don't be impertinent.' He knew he was getting nowhere. 'So fetch him in now, all right?'

Clarke withdrew and found the young sailor waiting in the passageway. In his best uniform he looked even more helpless, he thought. Tinker was a good lad, always cheerful and willing to learn. Or he had been once. The whole ship knew about his mother playing open house while Tinker's dad was away. Nobody joked about it. There were too many men in the navy who might be wondering about the faithfulness of their loved ones at home. Especially with all the Yanks and hot-blooded Poles running about the country.

'He'll see you.' Clarke straightened Tinker's neatly pressed 'silk' which was tied beneath his blue collar. 'Keep yer 'air on, my son. Just tell 'im what you told me, an' no lip, see? Or you'll end up in the glasshouse, and you won't like *that*!' He gave his arm a casual punch to ease his warning. 'I wouldn't like it neither.'

Tinker nodded. 'I'll remember, P.O.'

He stepped into the cabin and waited by the desk. The first lieutenant looked much younger without his cap, he thought.

Hargrave glanced up at him. 'Well, what's wrong?' It sounded like *this time*.

Tinker said, 'My dad, sir. He's been out of his mind since – since – ' he dropped his eyes. 'If I could be with him. Just a few more days. I'd make up for it later on, I promise, sir.'

Hargrave sighed, 'But you've just had leave. Would you make another man give up the right to go home so that you can get extra time in his place?'

Tinker was pleading. 'Able Seaman Nunn has offered, sir. He's got nowhere to go, not any more.'

Hargrave frowned. Another undercurrent. A home bombed, or a wife who had been unfaithful.

He said, 'You see, it's not in my province to offer you something beyond the bounds of standing orders. Perhaps later on – '

The boy stared at the carpet, his eyes shining with tears and suppressed anger. 'Yes, I see, sir.'

256

Hargrave watched him leave and grimaced. Tomorrow he would telephone the welfare section and speak with the Chief Wren there, unless –

He almost jumped as the telephone jangled on the desk.

He snatched it up. 'Yes? First lieutenant.'

There were several clicks, then a voice said, 'Found you at last, Trevor!'

Hargrave leaned forward as if he was imagining it.

'Father? Where are you?'

The voice gave a cautious cough. He probably imagined there was a Wren on the switchboard listening in to their conversation.

'Next door at R.N.B. Thought you might care to join me for dinner. There are a couple of chaps I'd like you to meet. Very useful, d'you get my point?'

'It's just that I'm in charge here.' He stared around the cabin as if he was trapped. 'The captain is – '

'Don't say any more. Have one of your underlings take over. God, it's only spitting-distance away, man!'

It was unlike his father to be so crude. He must have been drinking with his friends. Hargrave felt a surge of envy, the need to be with career officers senior enough to free his mind from the drudgery and strain of minesweeping.

His father was saying, 'If any little Hitler tries to get stroppy, just tell him to ring *me*.' He gave a husky chuckle. 'But to ask for *Vice*-Admiral Hargrave now!'

Hargrave swallowed hard. 'Congratulations, I mean – '

'I'll tell you at dinner. Must dash.' The line went dead.

Hargrave leaned back, his hands behind his head. It was not all over after all. Strange, he had not expected it would be his father who would ride to the rescue.

Outside in the passageway Petty Officer Clarke said, 'Well, we tried, Tinker. Be off to your mess, eh?'

Clarke watched the slight figure move to the ladder. Poor, desperate kid. He glanced at the door and swore savagely.

With some alarm he imagined that he had uttered the words aloud because the door opened immediately and the first lieutenant strode from the cabin.

He saw Clarke and said, 'I shall be ashore, at R.N.B., this evening. Sub-Lieutenant Fallows will do Rounds with you.'

'Aye, aye, sir.' He tried again. 'About young Tinker, sir.'

'Look, it's over and done with. Young he may be, but he knows the score as well as any three-badgeman. So there's an end to it, P.O.!'

He stroke aft towards his quarters.

Clarke nodded slowly. 'That's *bloody right*, sir. 'E comes to you for 'elp and you tells 'im to sling 'is 'ook. While you go an' stuff yerself in the barracks ward-room!' If only the coxswain was here, he thought. He'd have probably sent the kid ashore without asking anybody's permission. But he was the only one who might get away with it.

Clarke went to his mess and said to the sailor on duty, 'Get me a wet. I don't care wot, I don't much care 'ow. Just get it!'

The man did not bother to remind the petty officer it was only four in the afternoon.

Clarke called after him, 'An' you can join me! I don't feel like sippin' alone just now!'

The sailor came back with a jug of what Clarke guessed was hoarded tots.

He felt better already. 'Ta, very much.'

The man grinned. 'I just 'eard that Mr Bunny Fallows is gettin' tanked up already.'

Clarke paused in mid-swallow. 'Christ, I'd better get down aft and bit sharpish. Jimmy's ashore tonight.'

He found Fallows in the wardroom, squatting on the padded club fender by the unlit fire, a large drink in his hand, his face almost as red as his hair. He was just a youngster, probably not even twenty-one. God, he'll look like something from Skid Row when he gets to my age, Clarke thought.

'Yes, what is it?'

Clarke wished that the Chief, his own boss, was here. He never got in a flap, never pushed his stokers to do what he had not done himself a million times.

'The first lieutenant's compliments, sir, and – '

Fallows gave a knowing grin. 'Come on, man, spit it out! This is not a court-martial, y'know!'

He was already losing his posh accent, Clarke noticed. He thought, *It's a pity it's not yours*. He said, 'He's going ashore this evening, sir.' He watched the glass empty in one swallow. 'I'm to do Rounds with you, sir.'

Fallows considered it for several seconds. 'Righty-ho, can do! Got fuck-all else on tonight anyway.' He tapped his nose with the empty glass. 'But tomorrow, that's something else, eh?' He gave a little giggle.

Clarke breathed out with relief. Drunk or sober, he could handle the red-haired subbie. He had expected him to fly into a rage like he often did. That was something he could not manage, not after the Jimmy's behaviour.

He withdrew and heard Fallows yelling for the messman.

Later after a hearty supper of shepherd's pie and chips, Petty Officer Clarke was sitting alone in his mess, a glass at his elbow while he wrote a letter to his wife in Bromley.

The chief quartermaster tapped at the door and said, 'The first liberty men are comin' off, P.O. Seem quiet enough. Shall I tell the O.O.D.?'

'Hell no, I'll come up meself.' He reached for his cap and heavy torch. The latter was useful in a darkened ship; it also came in handy to pacify a drunken liberty man.

He added, 'Our Bunny's smashed out of 'is mind. God knows what the Jimmy will have to say.'

Reeves grinned. 'Who cares, eh?' They walked out on deck. It was almost dark, with gantries, ships' masts and funnels standing against the sky like jagged black shadows.

The men returning early from local leave would either be broke or disillusioned by Chatham's shabby hospitality. A sailors' town, where landladies charged them good money for the privilege of sleeping three in a bed with a cup of weak tea and a wad of bread and dripping before they plodded back to the barracks. Men serving in ships preferred to come back early. Like *Rob Roy*'s people; she was their home.

Leading Seaman Reeves said, 'I was a bit surprised about Tinker.'

'I wasn't.'

'No, I mean that Fallows allowed him to go ashore after what you said.'

'*What?*'

The chief quartermaster fell back a pace. 'Thought you knew, P.O.!' He forced a smile. 'No skin off your nose. Bunny is actin' O.O.D.'

Clarke looked away towards the brow as the first lurching figures groped across.

'I wasn't thinkin' of that. It's the kid I'm bothered about.'

Reeves shrugged. 'Well, you told him, so did Ted Hoggan the killick of his mess. So wot else can you do, I asks you?'

The liberty men glanced around on the darkened deck to make sure there was no officer present, then made their way forward to their messdeck. One said thickly, 'That bird you picked up, Fred – she was so *ugly*! I know you've never been fussy, but God, 'er *face*!'

The other man mumbled, 'You don't look at the bloody mantelpiece when you poke the fire, do you? Well then!'

Reeves groaned, 'Sailors, I've shot 'em!'

It was nearly midnight when Hargrave eventually returned on board. It had been something of a triumph to share the evening with his father's friends. Both were flag officers, and one was well known for his appearance in the press and on newsreels.

Even the thought of returning to *Rob Roy* had seemed unimportant.

His father had spoken to him privately before he had left barracks.

'Ours is a true naval family, Trevor. Things might have been different in the ordinary way, but we must think of the future, eh?'

By 'things' Hargrave knew he had been referring to the fact that he had had three daughters. He was the only male to follow in the family footsteps.

'War is terrible, we *know* that, Trevor. But when it's over, all these other chaps will go back to their proper jobs again – the navy will be just a memory, an experience in which they will be proud to have made a contribution.' He had leaned forward and tapped his knee, his breath smelling hotly of brandy and cigars.

'So we must use the time to benefit ourselves, and of course the service. It's why I want you to get a command, not bugger about in a damn great cruiser, don't you see? You were found unsuitable for submarines, and I can't say I'm sorry about that, and you've not time to make up the experience anywhere else but in small ships like *Rob Roy*. As a regular executive officer you stand out. Be patient, and I promise you a chance to walk your own bridge within months!'

Like speaking with the two flag officers, it was as if Hargrave had been lifted a few feet higher than he had been before. Provided he could stay in one piece, and that applied in any ship, he would have his father's promise to sustain him.

To his surprise he found the Chief alone in the wardroom drinking black coffee.

'I thought you were staying ashore for the night, Chief?'

Campbell looked at him coldly. 'Lucky I changed my mind then, isn't it?'

'What's happened?'

Campbell stood up and walked to the fireplace. 'I had to do Rounds. It's not my job, Number One.'

'Look – ' Hargrave could feel his irritation rising. 'This isn't a bloody trade union, not yet anyway! Any officer should be capable of – '

'It's not a question of being capable.' Campbell faced him angrily. 'This ship has a fine reputation, everyone knows that. I came back on board to find the Acting-O.O.D. smashed out of his mind, spewing his guts up over the side, and the officer responsible ashore at the barracks! So be good enough not to lecture *me* about capability!'

Hargrave snapped, 'I think we've both said enough.'

The Chief strode to the door. 'And Ordinary Seaman Tinker's adrift, by the way.' He vanished, leaving the curtain swirling in his wake.

Hargrave sat down heavily. 'Bloody hell!' He saw the messman watching from the pantry hatch. 'Horse's Neck!'

'Bar's shut, sir.'

'Well, *open it!*' He stared hard at the deckhead. Nothing must spoil it. Tinker had deserted. Perhaps it was inevitable. He would speak with Petty Officer Clarke about the facts.

He took the glass from the messman. 'Thanks.'

The man eyed him anxiously. 'Mr Fallows's mess chits, sir.'

'What about them?'

'He's not signed for his drinks.'

'I see.' The distinguished faces of the admirals at dinner were already fading, out of reach. 'Leave it to me.'

Just a few more months and all this would be behind him. Tomorrow he would sort out Mr Bunny Fallows. But that could wait.

A command of his own. It was still uppermost in his thoughts when he fell asleep.

Ian Ransome stared at his reflection in the mirror and automatically adjusted his tie. The house seemed so quiet, as if it was waiting for him to go.

His father stood by the door, one arm around his wife's shoulder.

He said, 'Six days, Ian. That's all you've had.'

Ransome watched his own expression in the glass as he might a face across the requestmen's table.

He had worked hard on *Barracuda*, and the weather had remained fine, so that each night, after going over to The Lugger for a pint with his father, he had fallen into bed, and had slept undisturbed. Something he had not believed possible.

Then there had been the telephone call. He was required on board. He had made his last visit to the boat, had touched the smooth hull with affection, even love.

Old Jack Weese had watched him. *It's breaking his heart*, he had thought. *For once, he doesn't want to go back.*

Ransome wanted to tell his parents all about it, but he knew he would crack up if he did, and that might finish his mother.

Now, in pressed doeskin uniform with the single blue and white medal ribbon, a crisp clean shirt which his mother had washed and ironed for him, he was back in the role again. The naval officer. The captain of *Rob Roy*.

His mother said again, 'Surely someone else could manage while you were away, dear?'

His father tried to change the subject. 'I'll run you to the station in the van. It'll not be breaking the patrol rationing regulations. I've got some gear to deliver there.'

Ransome looked round the room, half expecting to see the old cat Jellicoe. But he had long gone, and was buried with the other pets in the special place they had chosen as youngsters.

He recalled the same feeling when he had left his day cabin to go to the bridge on that day. Then too he had glanced around. *Was it the last time?* As it had been for *Guillemot* and *Fawn?*

He faced them and smiled. 'Off then. Might be back before too long.'

His mother watched him. 'I've packed some sandwiches for you.'

'Thanks.' He gazed at them fondly, despairingly. Going back. *I don't want to go.*

He thought of the telephone call, the unknown voice of an officer at Chatham.

It had been discovered early in the morning. A young seaman, doing extra work as a man under punishment, had been inspecting the air-raid shelters, checking each one to make certain that all the light bulbs were working. He had apparently run gasping to the main gates to call the officer of the guard, nearly beside himself with terror.

He had been standing on a bench in one of the long, underground shelters when he had felt someone watching him.

He had turned to stare into the face of Ordinary Seaman Tinker. He had been hanging from an overhead girder.

Ransome said, 'Don't forget to write.'

He kissed his mother and walked from the house, without looking back.

8

Full Day

Commander Hugh Moncrieff sat behind his desk in a temporary office above the dockyard and puffed heavily on his pipe.

'It was good of you to come, Ian. When did you get in?'

Ransome stood by a window and felt the sun's warmth on his face. He did not feel tired now, but it would hit him later in the day. He watched an elderly destroyer in a nearby basin, stripped of almost everything as she underwent the indignity of a hasty refit and a conversion to a long-range convoy escort. Once a sleek destroyer which age and service had overtaken. Now sans everything. A great cloud of red rust hovered over her eyeless bridge, and the air quivered to the thud of rivet guns.

He replied, 'Early morning, sir. There was a raid on Plymouth yesterday. All the trains were in a real potmess.'

He thought of Hargrave standing across his desk in his small cabin; he had looked strained and unusually pale, as if he had not slept since Tinker's death.

Moncrieff said slowly, 'I half-expected you'd ask me to get Hargrave trans-ferred.'

'It was not entirely his fault, sir.' Was that really what he thought? 'Circum-stances, bad luck, a bit of everything. I'd not see him damned because of that.'

'Thought you'd say as much – hoped so anyway. We lost two more sweepers while you were on leave. On the East Coast run. So we'll be shorter still of experienced officers and men.'

Ransome smiled. 'That's one way of looking at it, sir.'

'The *only* way, Ian. If we go on like this – ' He did not finish it. Instead he brightened up and said, 'The flotilla's being made up to full strength, one extra in fact.'

'Oh?' Ransome turned and looked at him. 'Newcomers?'

Moncrieff tapped out his pipe. 'Both foreigners so to speak. One from the Free Dutch navy, the other Norwegian. Both pretty experienced I'm told. I'll let you have all the guff later on today.' His eyes gleamed. 'Still top secret, but you'll be moving westward as soon as the leave period is completed.'

'May I ask where, sir?'

'You may not.' He chuckled. 'I've laid my hands on some Scotch for you, by the way. It should be aboard *Rob Roy* by now.'

He became serious again. 'That boy Tinker. He'd probably have done what he did anyway.'

'I know that, sir. But he needed to talk – '

'And you blame yourself for not being there. God, Ian, you drive the ship, you're not a wet nurse for everyone in her! Tinker's a war casualty as much as any other. When I think of some of the things that go on while we're at sea it makes me heave!'

Ransome smiled. 'Now, about these extra people?'

The old sea dog grinned hugely. 'Safer ground, eh? Well, you're getting a doctor. So is *Ranger*. There'll be four extra hands for gunnery, and I have to tell you that a new sub-lieutenant is supposed to be arriving today too.'

Ransome stared at him. 'What shall I do with them all, sir? Stuff them in a magazine hoist?'

Moncrieff pulled a huge dog-eared ledger towards him and frowned. Ransome guessed that he had probably been fighting off his other captains with equal determination.

'Your midshipman, Davenport, will be leaving in a few months when he gets his first stripe, won't he? The new sub will be doubly useful then. I see that at least two of your leading hands are due for promotion, and several others are awaiting advanced courses ashore.' He wagged his pipe at him severely. 'At this rate you'll be glad of every experienced Jack you can hold on to. They're building a whole new bunch of sweepers to replace the losses, and *they'll* be bleating for trained hands too. Supply and demand – it all amounts to that, my young friend!'

Ransome looked out of the window again. He was right of course. More ships, new faces, but the same deadly war to prepare them for.

He pictured Fallows as he had seen him an hour ago. Very grave-faced but quietly confident. He knew very little about Tinker's death, if he had, etc. etc. – No, Tinker had not approached him about leave, and in any case he had been given to understand that the first lieutenant had already refused it.

Ransome wondered about that, but Fallows had lost no time in clearing his own yard-arm.

'Still brooding, Ian?'

Ransome smiled at the dusty glass. Old Moncrieff could read his mind. It would be good to have him along when they left for the Med.

'Oh, I was just thinking, sir.'

'The first lieutenant went over to R.N.B. to meet his father, *Vice*-Admiral now, no less! Something anyone of us might have done. There was after all, science's latest triumph, the telephone, if things got out of hand.' He tapped his thick fingers with the pipe-stem. 'The Chief was aboard, so was Sub-Lieutenant Fallows, and the Gunner (T) was due back in the early morning. There was the duty-part of the watch, plus a very experienced P.O.'

Ransome looked at him fondly. He had certainly done his homework. 'I know, sir. I suppose it's my failing.'

Moncrieff glanced meaningly at the clock. 'I've got to see *Dryaden*'s C.O. in a minute. But I shall say the same to him, and I'm sending his chief stoker away on a well-deserved course for promotion, and he won't care much for that either!' He held out his left hand. 'Your failing, Ian?' He looked at him searchingly. 'It's what makes you the best I've got.'

By the time he had returned to the ship Ransome had decided to speak with Fallows again, to try and fit in the missing piece.

He waited on the dockside for several minutes as he studied his little ship, his gaze taking in the new double-mountings of twenty-millimetre Oerlikons, an extra winch down aft and a powerful-looking derrick which had replaced the old one. New paint, even a different motor boat in the davits; they had certainly pulled out all the stops. Probably Moncrieff, he decided.

He walked quickly down the steep brow and saluted, then glanced at the duty-board by the quartermaster's lobby. Apart from Lieutenant Sherwood and the Chief everyone appeared to be aboard.

He nodded to the chief quartermaster, the ruddy-faced Leading Seaman Reeves, the public's idea of the true sailor, with his silver chain and call tucked into the deep V of his jumper.

'All quiet, Q.M.?'

Reeves watched him warily. 'Very, sir. The new doctor's aboard, and the extra subbie will be joinin' this afternoon, earlier than expected.'

Ransome looked directly at him. 'What about Tinker?'

He shifted his feet. 'We're all sorry about 'im, sir. Nice kid, 'e was, too.'

'What do you think happened?'

'He requested to go back on leave to be with his dad, sir, his old woman bein' dead, like.'

Ransome waited. 'And?'

'Well, it was refused, sir. Like I told the first lieutenant after it was reported, I was on the gangway when Tinker went ashore. I asked 'im about it, and he said it was local leave, he wasn't in the duty-part of the watch, y'see, sir. He told me that Bun – I mean Mr Fallows gave him permission.'

'And you didn't think to check on it?'

Reeves swallowed hard. 'It was a bit difficult – ' He saw Fallows's scarlet face when he had gone down to the wardroom later to tell him what had happened. P.O. Clarke had been with him.

The sub-lieutenant had been beside himself with fury, and barely able to stand.

'How *dare* you speak to me like that? Stand to attention when you address an officer, damn you!'

In fact Fallows had been the only one unable to stand upright.

'I did not *see* this wretched fellow Tinker, nor did I give him fucking permission to go ashore, *see*?'

Reeves had been amazed to hear his voice. Like one of their Scottish stokers on a binge.

Ransome nodded, 'How was he dressed? Did he say anything?'

Reeves frowned. 'I saw that 'e was carryin' nothin' but 'is gas mask, sir.'

'Which was why you imagined he was going on a local run ashore?'

Reeves faced him. 'There was somethin', sir. He said, "They don't really care, do they?" or somethin' like that, sir.' He dropped his eyes under Ransome's grey stare. 'I – I'm just sorry I can't 'elp any more, sir.'

Ransome looked up at the tiny masthead pendant above the radar jampot.

'I think you have, Reeves. Now put it out of your mind, O.K.?'

Reeves stared after him and exclaimed, 'Christ, what a bloke!' He looked at his hands, expecting to see them still shaking. Young he might be, but the skipper knew every bloody thing in this ship!

When stand-easy was piped, the tea-boat was already passing out mugs of tea in exchange for pence or barter, soap perhaps for the dhobying firm who would wash a sailor's blue collar better than any housewife, tobacco or 'ticklers', and of course *sippers* of rum from those who were old enough to draw their tot.

Around the scrubbed table of Number Three Mess, the seamen sat in quiet contemplation. They sipped their sickly tea and watched Ted Hoggan, the killick of the mess, as he placed the dead sailor's few personal effects on the table. It was not much, Boyes thought as he sat wedged between Jardine and a seaman named Chalky White, who had developed a nervous tic in one eye over his months of minesweeping. A new cap with gold wire inscription, a pusser's knife or 'dirk' as they were known, a hand-made ditty-box from which Hoggan, as their senior, had removed some personal letters and a photograph of Tinker himself as a boy at HMS *Ganges*.

It was the first time Boyes had come up against something like this. He could sense its importance in the faces around him, tough, hardened ones for the most part, who had seen and suffered experiences he could only guess at.

Jardine leaned over and whispered, 'We'll raise a few bob from this lot, see? Then we 'as somethin' to remember the lad by, an' 'is people will 'ave a bit to put towards – well, *things*.'

Boyes nodded and opened the flap on his belt where he kept his money.

Jardine saw the ten-shilling note and said fiercely, 'Not that much, Gerry lad! It's a sort of token. Not a time to show off 'ow much you got.'

Hoggan tapped the table. 'Well, mates, this here is a pretty good ditty-box – what do I hear?'

And so it went on until the table was cleared. Boyes sat staring at the knife which he had bought for two shillings. It was exactly a twin of his own, and yet it seemed special, had belonged to a boy like himself whom he had seen only for a few minutes before he had walked away from life.

Leading Seaman Hoggan tipped his tin on to the table and counted the contents with great care.

'Four pounds, one an' a tanner, lads.' He looked at each of them in turn. 'What d'you think?'

Someone said, 'His old woman's gone west, 'ookey, an' to all accounts 'is dad 'as 'it the jar since.'

Boyes looked at their expressions, half-expecting them to laugh or dispute such a casual summing-up, but they were all deadly serious.

Hoggan nodded. 'My thoughts too, Dick.' He scraped the coins into 'is tin again. 'We'll keep it – ' he glanced at his world, Number Three Mess. 'For the next one of us, eh?'

They all nodded and emptied their mugs as if it was a kind of salute.

Hoggan looked at Boyes and gave a sad grin. 'Learnin' somethin', kid?'

Boyes nodded. 'Yes, thank you, Hookey.'

Nobody mimicked him this time.

Hoggan patted his arm. 'You can take Tinker's locker an' sling yer 'ammock on 'is 'ooks from now on, Gerry.'

Boyes stared around at the others and did not know what to say. Such a simple thing, some might say, but to Boyes it was like being awarded a medal.

To close the proceedings the tannoy bellowed, 'D'you hear there? D'you hear there? Out pipes, hands carry on with your work!'

Tinker had been popular in the mess, indeed throughout the whole ship. But Boyes somehow knew that his name would not be mentioned again.

Rob Roy's officers stood or lounged around the small wardroom and waited for lunch, the event of the day.

Lieutenant Hargrave sat in a well-worn leather chair and stared at a copy of the *Daily Mail*, although he found that his eyes remained unmoving more often than not.

He was still dazed by Ransome's acceptance of his report. He had missed out nothing, had even admitted that he blamed himself for keeping Tinker from going ashore.

Ransome had listened without interruption and had said, 'You'll know better next time. If it's any consolation I think he might have done it anyway. In view of your full, and I believe honest report, I think you acted correctly.'

It was probably the closest they had ever been, Hargrave thought. But he had no doubt of Ransome's attitude if anything like it occurred again.

He glanced at the others, standing with drinks in their hands, bored with their stay in the dockyard while they waited for the rest of the leave party to return.

The Chief had just come in; he was wearing his best uniform, quite unlike his seagoing rig of boiler-suit or an ancient reefer with ragged and tarnished lace.

Bone the Gunner (T) sat massively on the fender and contemplated a large tankard of beer, his bald pate shining in the deckhead lights. For although they were out of dry dock, the scuttles were still masked by the jetty wall and *Ranger* on the outboard side.

Hargrave stared at Fallows until the sub looked at him, flushed, and glanced away. As well he might, Hargrave thought. He was even drinking tomato juice. At least Sherwood was still ashore, so there would be no friction for a while. Hargrave's eyes sparked with sudden anger. *If he comes the old soldier again I'll cut him down to size, hero or not.* He heard the midshipman's incisive voice as he discussed his prospects of promotion with the Chief.

Campbell kept his alert face impassive. 'I suppose being an old-school-tie type, you'll soon be up the ladder, eh, Mid?'

Davenport sighed. 'Well, it *helps* of course. My father wanted me to go into the army.' He added vaguely, 'One of the household regiments, actually.'

Campbell glanced at Hargrave, then walked across to him. 'Drink, Number One?'

They eyed each other like duellists, then the engineer said, 'If you will forget it, I can.' He lowered his lanky frame into another chair and signalled to Petty officer Kellett. ''Nother Horse's Neck, or whatever it is, for the first lieutenant!' He regarded Hargrave curiously. 'What did the Old Man say?'

Hargrave put down the newspaper. 'Nothing much.' His own surprise was clear in his voice. 'In his place I think I'd have hit the roof.'

The Chief grinned. 'Well, you ain't, *sir*!' He raised his glass. 'To a new start, wherever it takes us.'

Hargrave leaned forward. 'Have you heard something?'

Campbell glanced across at Davenport, who was trying to interest Fallows.

'Sometimes I feel I'd like to beat the shit out of that pompous little snob!' He seemed to recall the question and tapped his nose with his glass. 'I've got friends over in the stores. They're breaking out shorts and fair-weather gear for the flotilla.'

Hargrave smiled. 'In that case it could be the Arctic.' They both laughed.

At that moment Sub-Lieutenant Morgan, who was O.O.D., drew back the curtain and entered with another young officer wearing a single wavy stripe on his sleeve.

Hargrave stood up to greet the new arrival. 'Sub-Lieutenant Tritton? I'm the first lieutenant.'

He had noticed that both Morgan and the newcomer had been in close conversation when they had entered the wardroom. They must have known each other elsewhere. The navy's way.

Tritton looked around. A pleasant, youthful face, with a ready and innocent smile.

'I'm glad to be here, sir.' He glanced at Morgan. 'I was a snotty in his last ship. One of the reasons I volunteered for minesweepers, as a matter of fact.'

Fallows said irritably. 'Don't swing the lamp yet!'

Bone peered across his beer. 'What's yer name?' For the Gunner (T) he was being remarkably friendly; his trip home must have done him some good.

'Actually, it's Vere.'

Bone nodded sagely. 'That's a queer sort of 'andle to 'ave!'

Tritton looked at his friend. 'Most people call me Bunny.'

Hargrave heard Fallows choking on his tomato juice and said, 'Welcome to *Rob Roy*.' He added. 'Funny, we already have a Bunny in the mess.'

'Really, sir?' Tritton's eyes were like saucers. 'Well, of course we do breed quite quickly.'

Morgan slapped Fallows on the shoulders. 'All right, Bunny? Cough it up, eh?'

By the quartermaster's lobby Beckett heard the laughter and thought suddenly of Tinker. *Heartless bastards.*

The Buffer hurried along the side-deck and beamed at him. He looked even more like a monkey, Beckett thought.

'Time for yer tot, Swain. I'll tell you about the party I picked up when I was up the line.'

Beckett grinned. 'Why not?' Tinker was forgotten.

Lieutenant Philip Sherwood wrenched open the door of a First Class compartment and stared with distaste at the occupants. He tried the next, where to his surprise there was a corner seat by the corridor. In the navy you learned to cherish privacy, even lying on a table with your cap over your face.

He slumped down and turned up the collar of his raincoat. It was early morning, with the clattering, lurching journey to the Medway towns and Chatham still stretching ahead.

It had been cool, icy even when he had left the flat in Mayfair. For once no sirens had split the night apart, and the barrage balloons, floating high above the beleaguered city, shone in faint sunlight, although on the ground it was still as dark as pitch. Sherwood had left early so that he could walk all the way to Waterloo. He had not realised how out of condition shipboard life had made him. He thought of the woman he had left sprawled across the bed, sleeping as if she was dead. Maybe when she awoke, she might wish she was.

Sherwood closed his eyes as an air force officer smiled across, as if he was about to open a conversation.

Sherwood thought of their night of passion. He was still not sure how it had begun. In her case it had been a release probably. He had taken her to hotels and restaurants she had only heard about. Even a red-tabbed general had turned to stare when a head-waiter had called Sherwood respectfully by name. It had reminded him of the staff officer he had knocked down with a chair. He still could not believe that he had changed so much.

Working within a hair's breadth of self-destruction, defusing mines and sometimes huge bombs with delayed-action booby traps, he had taught himself to empty his mind of everything but the job, and the one after that. Even of fear, for himself and for others.

It had simply happened. He could place no time or exact reason. That final evening they had walked back to the flat, across Berkeley Square, then along Hill Street.

She had not spoken about her dead husband, and he had said nothing further about his family.

Once she had caught him looking up at a chandelier in one hotel restaurant, and he had found himself telling her about the company.

She had watched him closely as if she had been trying to remember every feature of his face.

'What will you do when the war's over, Philip?'

He had heard himself say, 'Over? It'll go on for years and years. I try not to think about it.'

Once their hands had touched across the table and he had found himself holding her fingers, as her husband must have acted.

Perhaps that had done it, he thought.

When they had returned to the flat last night they had stood in the centre of the room without speaking.

Then he had remarked, 'No sirens yet. We'll get a good sleep for once.'

She had been unable to look at him. 'Don't sleep in the kitchen. Not tonight, Philip.' That was all.

He had held her without yearning, lifting her chin to look into her eyes, to see a pulse beating in her throat like a tiny, trapped creature.

It had started like a brushfire, and had ended with them both sprawled naked and breathless across the bed. He had hurt her; she had not had a man since her husband had gone overseas. She had cried out in pain and in a wild desire which neither of them had expected. Just once, when she fell asleep on his shoulder, she had spoken his name. *Tom.* It was a secret Sherwood knew he would keep.

Later he had stood by the window and waited for the first hint of morning. The clink of a milkman's basket, a policeman's boots on the pavement below. Men and women had died, probably in their thousands, while they had been making love in this room, he had thought. But that had been somewhere else.

He thought desperately, *I must not see her again. I can't. Any connection now would make me careless and unaware.* It might also break her heart.

Her name was Rosemary. It was better to leave now, brutally and finally. They had had their precious moment, both of them. In war that was rare indeed.

Ransome leaned on one elbow and plucked his shirt away from his chest. With the deadlights screwed tightly shut for another night alongside the dockyard wall the air felt clammy and unmoving, in spite of the deckhead fans and a breeze from the Medway.

He stared at the pile of ledgers and files through which he had worked with barely a break, but could find no reward in what he had done. As if the day had been empty.

Dockyard reports to check and sign, signals to read, orders from the Staff Officer Minesweeping, from even higher authority at the Admiralty, which all had to be examined; *translated* was a more apt description.

Dockyard foremen had come and gone, and his own heads of departments, from the first lieutenant to Wakeford the leading writer, once a physics master at a grammar school, had all visited this cabin to increase or diminish his workload.

Now it was done. Even a personal letter to Tinker's father, although he wondered if it could make any difference to him. Had he acted correctly with Hargrave? No matter what he had told old Moncrieff he still felt some lingering doubts.

But the other rumour was now a fact. *Rob Roy* and the flotilla would soon be heading for the Mediterranean, to a real war, where it would take every ounce of skill and endurance to carry out the work for which this class of warship had been designed. It would not just be 'putting up with it', a conflict of boredom punctuated occasionally by stark and violent death and destruction. It was no time to start changing the team around. He had met the new sub, Tritton, a likeable youngster who probably saw the dangerous grind of sweeping mines as something glamorous. Fallows might have to leave soon when his promotion was announced. He might end up as somebody's first lieutenant. Better them than me, he thought. *But he did know his job.* In war that was vital, at the top of the stakes. In another year, there would be even more eager, barely trained amateurs filling gaps left by the Fallows of this world.

He thought about his brief meeting with Surgeon Lieutenant Sean Cusack RNVR. He had not been what he had been expecting. If small ships were fortunate enough or otherwise, to carry a doctor, they were usually little more than medical students with stripes on their sleeves. He pictured Cusack as he had sat opposite him that afternoon in the other chair. In his thirties, with dark, almost swarthy features and the brightest pair of twinkling blue eyes he had ever seen.

He had said in reply to Ransome's question, 'I got fed up with the R.N.H., and one damned barracks after another. I am in the navy, so why not a ship, I asked myself?' He had chuckled at Ransome's surprise. 'It's the Irish in me, I suppose.' Then he had said with equal candour, 'There'll be a lot of stress in a job like this one, eh?'

He had sat back in the chair, his head on one side like a watchful bird. It had made Ransome feel defensive, unguarded.

He had replied, 'I suppose that's true. You tend to think death is the only enemy, that you can cope with all else, like a sort of god. When you discover you can't, it leaves you raw. Vulnerable.'

'Like the boy Tinker I've been hearing about.' The blue eyes had barely blinked. 'Perhaps I could have helped. I have some experience in that field.'

Ransome had made some excuse and the new doctor had departed.

He reached down to the cupboard and took out one of Moncrieff's bottles of Scotch. He poured a full measure and added a dash of soda. The first today. What would Cusack have made of that, he wondered?

The ship felt quiet and still, with only occasionally footsteps on deck, and the creak of rope fenders between the hull and *Ranger* alongside.

A full flotilla, with more new faces, different characters to know and understand.

They might be working with the fleet, taking part in an invasion which must not fail. If it did, all the sacrifices which had left a bloody trail from Dunkirk to Singapore, Norway to Crete, would be wasted. There would be no second chance. If they put a foot back into Europe, no matter where, it must advance. Otherwise it would not be a question of a retreat, or a *strategic withdrawal* as the war correspondents optimistically described them. It would mean an inevitable defeat. He thought of his parents as he had seen them on his last leave. No, it must not fail.

There was a tap at the door and the doctor looked in at him, his eyes everywhere as he took in the piles of papers and files which filled the desk and part of the deck too.

'And there's me been enjoying myself with my new comrades, sir!'

'What is it, Doc? Your cabin not to your liking?'

Cusack stepped into the light. 'I'm such a fool. I completely forgot in all the excitement of joining the ship today!' He held out a letter. 'This was given in my care at the gates, to hand to you. To be sure, you'd have got it faster if they'd entrusted it to a blind man!'

He watched as Ransome took the letter and examined it without recognition.

Cusack said, 'A woman's hand, I'll wager, sir.' He nodded. 'I'll be off to finish unpacking and to put my *strange* S.B.A. straight on a few facts of life.'

Ransome looked at the handwriting. It was addressed correctly, c/o G.P.O. London, but the writer had upgraded his rank to Commander. Somebody's wife or mother trying to dodge the rules and red tape, he decided.

He said, 'Thanks, Doc. One thing before you go.'

The doctor's eyes fell hopefully on the Scotch but Ransome asked, 'Are you from the north or the south of Ireland?'

Cusack pretended to be offended. 'No true Irishman comes from the *North*, sir!' He withdrew quickly.

Things might be very different with him around.

Ransome glanced at the bulkhead clock. An early night, a drink in *Ranger*, or a walk along the wall to clear his thoughts.

Orders would be arriving tomorrow.

He looked at the unopened letter and noticed it was postmarked Plymouth.

Something made him reach for his knife and he slit it open.

First he turned the neatly written letter over and then he felt a chill run down his spine. It was signed, *Sincerely, Eve Warwick*.

The ship, his worries, everything seemed to fade as he read it, very slowly and carefully. He should have known, although he had never seen her handwriting before; ought to have guessed, even though he had never trusted too much in fate.

Sentences stood out from each page as if lit from beneath. *I have thought about you since we last met. Worried about you more than I could tell anyone. I went to see your funny boat. Imagined us sitting there in the sun, and you answering all my daft questions. I saw your brother Tony –*

Ransome raised his glass to his lips but it was empty.

I wanted to know what you were doing, how you were –

Ransome reread it a third time. He could see her smile, her sadness too. Hear her voice in the writing.

Once or twice he glanced up at the drawing on the bulkhead. She was in Plymouth where her father was now a canon. He stared at the date. It had taken several days to reach here.

He sat bolt upright in the chair, recalled how the train had been held up by another raid on Plymouth.

They were used to them down there. Like Coventry and London, Portsmouth and Liverpool.

But he could not push the anxiety from his thoughts. Now he knew what it felt like to worry about someone who was as much under fire as any serviceman.

He examined his feelings, and was surprised but grateful that he no longer felt foolish because of his – he hesitated over the word. *Love* – how could that be?

Eventually, the question still unanswered and the letter lying open in the lamplight, Ransome took time to fill a pipe of tobacco.

It had been a full day after all.

9

Victims

The three weeks which followed the minesweepers' departure from Chatham were the busiest and probably the most maddening Ransome could remember.

The ships steamed west through the Channel, dodging a sudden and concentrated bombardment from the Cap Gris Nez guns and arriving eventually in Falmouth. There they joined up with the rest of the flotilla, the first time they had all been together for months.

Apart from the newcomers, the Dutch minesweeper *Willemstad* and the very useful additional heavy trawler *Senja* from the Free Norwegian navy, the other ships were quite familiar. But in the time they had been apart, transfers, promotion, even death in a few cases, meant different faces and minds to contend with.

Commander Hugh Moncrieff, true to his fearsome reputation, kept his brood hard at it during every hour of daylight, and quite often during the night watches. They steamed around Land's End and into the Bristol Channel where Moncrieff threw every exercise and manoeuvre in the book at them, and many which he had apparently dreamed up on the spot. He was in his element. He even cajoled the C-in-C Western Approaches to lend him a submarine on one occasion to break through the flotilla's defences in the role of a U-boat.

With half of their number still sweeping, the rest of them had carried out repeated attacks on the submarine until she eventually surfaced to make the signal, '*You've given me a headache. I'm not playing with you any more!*'

Each ship's company must have cursed Moncrieff until his ears had burned, but Ransome had felt the old pride coming back, the feeling perhaps that the minesweepers were no longer the drudges of the fleet.

It must have been even more difficult for the two foreign captains, he thought. Both the Norwegian and the Dutchman were skilled and experienced, but had been used more for local escort work than chalking up kills in the minefields.

Moncrieff had remarked on one occasion, 'No matter, Ian, they've got the edge on the rest of us.'

Ransome knew what he meant. Like all the servicemen who had left their countries in the face of German invasion, they wanted only to fight, to free their homelands, and rejoin those they loved.

It was hard to imagine how it must feel, to know that a wife or family was in occupied Europe or Scandinavia. If news of their work alongside the Allies reached the Gestapo there was little doubt of what might happen. The bang on the door before dawn. Humiliation, agony, oblivion.

The flotilla even found time to work with the army, covering landing craft in a mock invasion along the Welsh coast, repeating signals for a mythical bombarding squadron.

As Beckett had complained, 'Gets more like a bleedin' circus every day!'

Then, when even Moncrieff was apparently satisfied, the flotilla returned to Falmouth.

Ransome had written a letter to Eve Warwick, but either there had been no time for her to reply or she had had second thoughts. In Falmouth, he decided to telephone her at the number shown on her letter. He presumed it was a vicarage, and waited, rehearsing like a teenage midshipman, planning his exact words should Eve's mother or father pick up the telephone.

In fact, he was unable to make any contact. He thought again of the air-raids, and called the switchboard supervisor.

She had said wearily, 'The telephone at that number is out of action.' When he had persisted she had snapped, 'There *is* a war on, you know, *sir*!'

Curiously, it had been Moncrieff who had unknowingly presented a solution.

'I've been summoned to the C-in-C's office at Plymouth, Ian.' He had attempted to conceal his rising excitement. 'Bit of a flap on apparently. I was asked today about our readiness to sail. I told them, God help any of my skippers who isn't!'

So the rumour was gaining even more substance. Moncrieff added, 'The real thing this time. I want you to come with me. As my half-leader you might find the trip useful. You're used to the blood-and-guts of war; down in the command bunkers they see all that as mere statistics.'

Ransome had left Hargrave in charge. He had not warned him about responsibility again. If he had not learned his lesson, he never would now.

Hargrave had asked politely, 'Is something on, sir?'

'Yes, Number One. I can't tell you yet, but if you've any mail outstanding I suggest you take some time to deal with it.'

Perhaps Hargrave already knew; maybe his father had told him?

Moncrieff had been provided with a staff car and Wren driver for the trip, and as they roared through narrow lanes then on to the main road to St Austell, Ransome was conscious of the closeness of the home where he had spent just six days of his leave.

Moncrieff must have read his thoughts. 'I shall be a couple of days at least with Staff Officer Intelligence, Ian. You could take some time off. It might be a long while before you can again.'

Ransome had experienced something like guilt. *I might never come back at all.* He knew that he could not leave this time without at least trying to see the girl. But he said, 'I might take you up on that, sir.' It only made him feel more guilty.

Moncrieff slept for most of the journey, waking suddenly as the car pulled into a roadside inn where he had arranged for them to take lunch. The Wren driver declined the invitation to join them and Moncrieff said, 'Pretty little thing.'

Ransome thought he had never looked so wistful.

They reached Plymouth in time for tea, and while Moncrieff went off to make his number with the staff officer on duty, Ransome took advantage of his freedom to begin his search.

As he made his way through the city he was appalled by the extent of the damage. Great areas of buildings wiped out, streets marked only by their chipped kerbstones and pavements, the rest a blackened desert where people had once been born, gone to school and learned to fend for themselves.

An air-raid warden directed him to Codrington House, the address she had given, and had assured him that it had missed the bombing. *So far.* Ransome had asked him why he should be so certain that one particular building amongst so many had survived.

The man had regarded him curiously. 'Well, it's a sort of halfway-house – like a hospital, isn't it?'

A taxi eventually took him there. It must have been quite beautiful in its day, with a long, gravelled drive curving amongst fine oaks to a pillared entrance, and a fountain around which cars, and at one time, carriages made their entrances and exits.

Now the grass was untended and the walls flaking, while the fountain was still filled with dead leaves. The once-impressive entrance was almost hidden by sandbagged barriers.

A woman of severe appearance in a grey costume watched him enter and asked, 'May I help?' It sounded like *what do you want?*

Ransome was at a loss. 'I understood that the Warwick family lived – '

She changed instantly, removing the mask and replacing it with welcome. 'Oh, Canon Warwick? Of course! Is he expecting you?'

'Well, no – ' Ransome glanced round as three women in dressing-gowns accompanied by a tired-looking nurse crossed the great hallway. What is this place?'

She studied him, her eyes moving from his single medal ribbon to the rank on his sleeves. He looked far too young for both, she thought.

'Canon Warwick has an official role here as well as his religious duties.' She waved her hand as the little procession vanished into another door. 'Evacuee children, bombed-out families, people who have lost everything and everyone – ' She shrugged. 'I don't know what we would do without him.'

'If I could leave a message – '

'Nonsense.' She picked up a telephone. 'He's in the building. What name is it, please?'

The girl spoke from the entrance doors. 'It's Lieutenant Commander Ransome, Mrs Collins.'

Ransome swung round and stared at her. How long she had been there he did not know. Like those times in the boatyard. Watching. Listening to his words.

She did not move as he strode toward her, and only when he put his arms around her shoulders did she show any emotion.

'I can't believe it. Your letter. Now you.'

He kissed her on the cheek, conscious of her warmth, the touch of her hair against his face. Like that other impetuous kiss when he had seen her leave. For the last time.

He said, 'Sorry about this, Eve. It was just a chance, so I took it.'

She slipped her hand through his arm and guided him towards the door again. The birds were still singing, and there was sunlight clinging to the treetops.

He wanted to look at her properly, but she held to his arm as if to prevent just that.

She said, 'I've dreamed about this. I wanted to write.' She shrugged. 'I was a bit afraid, I think. But when I got your address I made up my mind. I sat with the paper in front of me for hours.' She swung round and faced him, her hands in his. 'I was frightened you might have changed. When you answered my letter I knew – ' She reached up and touched his hair. 'You look wonderful.' The slight catch in her voice gave away the lie.

He said, 'I've thought about you so much. My little girl in shorts and pigtails.'

She smiled. 'Not any more.'

Ransome studied her slowly. It *was* like a dream. Four years, and yet she was not so different. She wore a shirt and overall trousers, the latter daubed with dried paint.

She said, 'If I'd only known – ' She ran her hands across her forehead to brush away some strands of hair. 'I'm a mess!' Then she laughed, with relief, or with joy, perhaps both.

'How long can you stay? I am sure they'll ask you to when – '

There was a footfall at the top of the steps and her father hurried down to meet him.

'It is *good* to see you, Mr Ransome – or should I call you Captain?'

He looked older, his face drawn to give him cheekbones where there had been none.

Ransome shook his hand. 'I hope you don't mind, Canon?'

'Call me Simon, eh?' He looked around at the trees and some more aimless figures. 'One does what one can of course.' He did not continue.

Instead he said, 'You must eat at our table. Things are a bit chaotic here, have been since the vicarage was destroyed. But still, God's work cannot wait for the war-damage repairs, eh?'

He looked at his daughter. 'You are a bit flushed, dear. Go and tell them we have a guest for dinner.'

Ransome tried to protest, but it was to no avail.

They walked together across the coarse grass where there had once been an elegant lawn. Canon Warwick wore a long black cassock with a small crucifix hung about his neck. His eyes were everywhere, probing, almost fanatical.

'It's been bad here?'

Warwick considered it. 'Bad enough. It is an unending flow of people, searching for hope, loved ones, refugees in their own way as much as those who clogged the roads in Holland or Greece.'

He changed the subject. 'Not married yet? That does surprise me.'

Ransome looked away. *I love Eve. I always have, and always shall.*

But he said, 'There's never enough time for anything these days.'

Warwick seemed satisfied. 'Eve's been a real blessing since her mother – '

Ransome started. 'She's not – ?'

Warwick tucked his hands into his cassock and shook his head. 'Betty had a lot of bad luck, poor dear. First the vicarage was bombed and she had a slight stroke. Then later on she was in the town at her stall – she helps the W.V.S., you know, selling tea and buns to the sailors, that kind of thing. There was a hit-and-run raid, and a bomb fell near to her little stall. Most of the servicemen who were queuing to be served were killed or badly maimed. It really upset her. She's still not herself.'

Ransome pictured the dead servicemen. It had probably upset them too.

He asked quickly, 'What does Eve do?'

'My daughter?' He smiled gently. 'She shares her love of art with some of the patients here. But maybe you didn't know she could paint and draw?'

Ransome thought of the picture in his cabin. 'Yes, I knew.'

'It's worthwhile work.' He nodded to emphasise it. 'If she left to join one of the services, I'd be in a sorry state, I can tell you.'

'Is that what she wanted to do?'

Warwick did not seem to hear the question. He said, 'I'll show you the kitchen garden – we are almost self-supporting here.'

It was a difficult meal, Ransome thought. And yet he would not have wanted to be anywhere else.

Eve's mother, a frail, vague lady who seemed to laugh a lot, but looked very near to tears when she did so, fired questions at Ransome from start to finish.

And all the while he was conscious of the girl who sat opposite him, her eyes rarely leaving his as he tried to paint a picture of his ship, of *Rob Roy*'s people. Although he answered her questions they were all directed at the girl named Eve.

The canon's wife looked fondly at her husband. 'He is so busy, Mr Ransome. He never spares himself for the good of others.'

Warwick jerked from his thoughts. 'Which reminds me. I have two hospital visits to do tonight.' He glanced at the clock. 'May I offer you a lift, Commander?'

Suddenly Ransome felt the girl's shoe press against his foot, saw the sudden anxiety in her dark eyes.

He heard himself reply, 'It's all right. I'm at the R.N.B. Devonport tonight at least. I can manage.'

Why was it he could not bring himself to call him Simon as he had requested?

'Well, if you're sure – ' He fumbled for his watch. 'I've asked the porter to attend to the black-out, my dear.' He smiled at his wife, but his eyes said that he was elsewhere. 'I'll be off then. Very nice to meet you again after all this time, er – ' Then he was gone.

Ransome helped the girl to clear away the table. To Mrs Warwick he said, 'A fine meal. Made me feel really at home.' But she had fallen asleep in her chair.

In the kitchen, which appeared to be stacked with every kind of ration from powdered milk to corned beef, she faced him.

'I'm sorry. You didn't hate it too much, did you?'

He held her at arms' length. 'Of course not. *I* was sorry to hear about your mother. Your father feels it badly.'

'Oh, you noticed?' She studied him sadly. 'Many wouldn't.'

He tried to laugh it off. 'Believe me, my girl, when you command even a little ship in this man's navy, you either learn fast about folk or you go under!'

She did not smile. 'What you said – am I really *your* girl? Like it was, all that time back?' She shook her head so that her long hair flowed across her shoulders. 'I'm not a child any more. Please don't treat me like one.'

Then she pressed her face into his jacket and shook; the sobbing seemed to burst out of her in a flood.

He tried to pacify her, stroked her hair, held her against him, but it was to no avail.

Between sobs she whispered, 'You mustn't laugh, but I have always loved you. I dreaded seeing you in case you had met someone else.' She leaned back and stared at him, blinking tears from her eyes. 'You haven't, have you?'

'No. Of course not.' It came out so simply it was as if he had shouted his love from the housetops.

He added, 'I'm a lot older than you –'

She hugged him and shook her head again. 'I'm nineteen. Two days ago. So you see, I'm catching you up!'

They walked into another garden, the dishes abandoned.

It was a starry night, with a warm breeze to ruffle the leaves. Somewhere a wireless set or gramophone was playing a lilting Spanish tune, and a small night creature ran through the grass; searching for food, trying not to become it.

In the darkness it seemed somehow natural, he thought. His hand on her waist, her head against his arm.

As they walked he told her more stories about the people he served with. Moncrieff, the ancient mariner; Sherwood who had been with a famous firm which had built chandeliers. He left out the pieces about Sherwood's grief, which was slowly driving him mad. About Hargrave's ambition, for himself rather than the ship, of Midshipman Davenport who bragged to everyone about his upper-class upbringing, when in fact he had been to the same modest grammar school as young Boyes. Or about Fallows who had probably been the last link with life when Tinker had killed himself. Now Fallows was the haunted one because he could remember nothing at all about what had happened.

Above all, he told her nothing about the danger they faced every time they went to sea. Danger and death were things they knew about in Plymouth. For centuries. Since Drake had routed the Armada, and Nelson had sailed for the Nile, since the little *Exeter* had sailed home to Plymouth after beating the German *Graf Spee* into self-destruction. And now the bombing. Even here, on the outskirts, amidst the ageless oak trees you could smell the rawness, the scorched and shattered buildings. Oh yes, they knew all about that.

She said softly, 'We didn't choose the time, Ian. It was held out to us. *For* us.' She looked up at him, only her eyes reflecting the stars. 'It was not our choice!'

As if to some silent signal they both turned and looked through the trees towards the house. It was in darkness with all the black-out shutters and curtains in place.

She said, 'I'll have to go in soon.' The words were dragged from her. 'Mother doesn't like to be alone if the sirens start. Everyone goes down to the shelters now.' He felt her shiver and tightened his grip on her shoulders. 'I don't know if I'm really doing any good here.'

'I'm quite sure you do.' They walked across the grass again and he said, 'I'll be at the Royal Naval Barracks all tomorrow, maybe longer. My boss is having a few meetings with the top brass.'

'Can I ask where you'll be after that?'

He looked away. 'Overseas. For a while. I shall write as often as I can.'

'Yes, *please*.' Her voice sounded husky. 'Tell me your thoughts. Share them with me.'

They stood by the gates and Ransome wondered if he would find a taxi. Otherwise, it would be a long hike back to the base.

She said, 'I'm not afraid any more, Ian. It seems so right. I feel as if a great weight has been taken away. You can't possibly know.'

She looked along the drive. 'I must go. She'll come worrying otherwise.'

Ransome turned her towards him. 'I wish it was broad daylight. I want to look at you all over again.'

She tilted her head, then wiped her cheek with the back of her hand. 'Kiss me. *Please*.'

Ransome touched her mouth with his. A quick, innocent kiss, like that time at the railway station.

She said softly, 'I'll get better.' She stepped away. 'I'll make a fool of myself any minute.'

Ransome turned once and thought he saw her standing beside the gate's tall pillar. Then she was gone.

He walked down the road, hearing the breeze in the trees, catching the first breath of the sea as he topped the hill. *Waiting*. Always waiting. Like a great force which could be evil or kind as it chose for the moment.

He did not have to walk for long; a jeep full of military policemen pulled up beside him.

One redcap asked, 'Where are you goin', chum?' Then, as he saw the gleam of gold lace, 'Care for a ride, er, sir?'

They dropped him at the gate of the barracks and vanished into the night in search of drunks or deserters.

Ransome found his small room, his shaving kit and spare shirt still packed on the bed. There was a flask too, some of Moncrieff's Scotch.

He sat on the bed and thought about her face across the table, the warmth of her lips, the strange sense of fate or destiny which they both felt, and no longer challenged.

If he stayed another night he would try to take her out somewhere. Away from the sea, from people. Just walk and talk as they had once been able to do.

He looked at the flask and smiled. He no longer needed it.

The Staff Officer, Operations, an RN commander, greeted Ransome warmly.

'Good of you to call, Ransome. I feel I already know you pretty well. You and your flotilla have made quite a mark on the map!'

He sent for tea and biscuits and gestured towards a huge wall-chart of the Mediterranean.

He said cheerfully, 'Nice not to see any bloody swastikas on the North African coast any more, eh?'

Ransome waited while a neat little Wren brought a tray of tea to the room.

The S.O.I. said, 'It's to be Sicily, but I think you already know that?' He stood up and walked to the chart. 'Combined Allied invasion, with a vital role for the supporting squadrons.' His finger moved to Gibraltar. 'We've got quite a fleet here already. Big chaps, all of them. It will be no surprise to you that they can't even move an inch without you clearing the way for them. How does it make you feel – proud?'

'Useful, sir.'

'The main supporting flotillas will be combined, so that there are no foul-ups like we've had too many times in this war. Like the rest, you will have to be ready to change roles at a moment's notice. We must get the "brown jobs" on to dry land, Ransome.' He eyed him grimly. 'If they get thrown back this time, well – ' He sipped his tea instead of spelling it out.

He continued after a glance at the clock. 'A flag officer has been appointed solely for that task.'

Somehow Ransome knew who it was going to be.

The commander said, 'Vice-Admiral Hargrave. Good chap, knows his stuff.'

Ransome thought about it. It should not make any difference who it was. Yet somehow he knew that it did. He wondered where Moncrieff was, why he was not sharing this meeting.

'So be prepared for sailing orders, Ransome. You'll be routed with a convoy, that's about all I can tell you.' He grinned and looked human. 'About all I know!'

'Will Commander Moncrieff still be our senior officer, sir?'

The man pouted his lower lip. 'I was coming to that. Moncrieff is a fine sailor, but – '

Ransome stiffened in the chair. It would break his heart.

'He's used to the home patch, the War Channel, moulding a lot of fishermen into minesweepers. The Med is different. The flotilla will be commanded by a small destroyer, a headquarters ship which can direct and divert as the occasion arises.' He softened his voice. 'Commander Moncrieff will be in control until Gibraltar. That's it, I'm afraid.'

Ransome did not remember much else of the interview. He found a lieutenant waiting for him by the operations room, who explained that Moncrieff had already returned to Falmouth. A car was provided for Ransome, and a signal had already been sent to the flotilla to announce his time of arrival there. So there would be no walks away from the sea.

Moncrieff wanted to be alone, to face up to the decision in his own way.

The same Wren was leaning against the staff car, and opened the door for him as he approached.

He tried to smile. 'Home, James.'

She studied him and liked what she saw. She knew all about Ransome; most of the girls at the Wrennery did.

Past the saluting sentries and the neat sandbags, Ransome watched her gloved hands on the wheel as she steered the big Humber with reckless enthusiasm around a convoy of army lorries.

'How long have you been in the Wrens?'

She puffed out her cheeks and blew some hair from her eyes.

'Six months, sir. Does it show?'

'No. I was just thinking of someone.'

She grimaced. *Pity.* She said, 'My brother's in *Ranger*, by the way, sir.'

He looked at her. 'Who?'

'The subbie, John Dent.'

A face fell into its slot. A navy within a navy. Like a family, with its own pride and pain like any other.

They reached Falmouth in record time. The girl was still staring after him as he walked towards the jetty where a boat was waiting.

Hargrave was standing with the side-party as he climbed up from *Rob Roy*'s motor boat, the 'skimming-dish', while the boatswain's mates split the air apart with their shrill calls.

It was the one part of the job he had never got used to, or took for granted.

Hargrave saluted. 'Welcome back, sir.' He looked relaxed and pleased about something.

As they walked towards Ransome's quarters Hargrave said, 'Orders have just arrived, sir.'

Ransome smiled. The S.O.I. must have known that even as they were talking together. *In case I got killed on the road, perhaps?*

Hargrave added, 'Commander Moncrieff is aboard. Sorry, sir, I forgot.'

'How is he?'

Hargrave was surprised at the question. 'Er – much as usual, sir.'

So he had said nothing.

Moncrieff was sitting in the cabin, his legs crossed while he thumbed through an old log-book.

He looked up and shrugged. It made him look as if he was in pain.

'He told you?'

'Yes, sir. I can't say how bad I feel about it.' He watched the disfigured hand resting on the open log, like a pair of crude callipers. It was his old log. When he had still been in command.

'The admiral is probably right. I'm too old for new tricks. I'm a sailor, not a bloody robot. No doubt the new senior officer will have it at his fingertips. Conferences and meetings all the time, that kind of caper.' He smiled at some old memory and added, 'You know what I think? From the ashes of today's conferences will arise the phoenix of tomorrow's fuck-ups!'

Then he said, 'Your orders are here. You're under twenty-four hours' notice. I'd like to see all the commanding officers this evening, sometime in the dog-watches. I don't want to make a *thing* of my immediate future. We've still got to reach Gibraltar, you know.'

'I understand.' He looked at the clock.

Moncrieff grinned. 'I thought you'd never bloody well ask. Yes, young man, I'd relish a large drink *right now*!'

Ransome glanced round the cabin. He was glad Moncrieff would be using it on his last passage in *Rob Roy*. Ransome would spend most of his time on the bridge or in his sea-cabin there.

It would be bitter for Moncrieff all the same, no matter how he tried to disguise it.

Later, with the other nine commanding officers packed into the wardroom, he had seen no weakening in Moncrieff's aggressive enthusiasm or his ability to tell all of them what he needed from them; what he expected.

Moncrieff said afterwards, 'I'll be ashore tonight, Ian. See you an hour before we leave harbour.' He studied him thoughtfully. 'You're looking better. You'll tell me why, when you want to, I expect.'

By eight bells that evening every man in the flotilla had been told about sailing orders. Bags of letters would be going ashore in the morning, all carefully censored, just in case. Like the humorous posters you saw in canteens and bars. *Be like dad, keep mum!* Or a sailor shooting his mouth off to his girl-friend with a barely disguised Hitler or Goering crouching under their table.

After North Africa, the Germans and their Italian allies would be expecting an attack. They could not guard the whole coastline from Greece to France. But just one hint . . .

There was a tap at the door. Hargrave stepped in and asked, 'I was wondering, sir, would you join us in the wardroom? They would all appreciate it.'

Ransome smiled. 'Of course. We may be a bit busy later on.' He would go ashore and telephone from there. His parents too.

He glanced up as Leading Telegraphist Carlyon hovered outside the open door. 'Come in, Sparks.'

To Hargrave he said, 'After you've had your meal, Number One, all right?'

Neither of them noticed Carlyon's stricken expression.

Ransome took the signal flimsy from the telegraphist's hand.

Hargrave smiled. 'Don't tell me it's cancelled after all.'

Ransome reread the neat printing. It was like hearing a voice.

He said quietly, 'It's my brother. He's been reported missing, presumed killed.'

He recalled her voice. Was it only last night? *It was not our choice.*

Hargrave looked at Carlyon and jerked his head. As the rating left he asked, 'What can I do, sir?'

Ransome thought of the boatyard. His parents must have been told about the same time as he had been with Eve.

He replied, 'You're doing it right now.' He glanced at the old personal log which Moncrieff had left behind.

'I've seen a lot of people just lately whose lives have been knocked about.' But in his heart he was screaming. *Not Tony. Not him, for Christ's sake.* His voice was flat and unemotional as he said, 'We still have a war to worry about. Deeper than that, we have *this ship* and the eighty-odd people who depend on us because they have no choice either.'

Hargrave watched him, stunned by it. Unable to think clearly.

'I – I'll tell the others, sir.'

'*No.* I'll come down as I said I would.' He stared at the slip of paper which had changed everything. 'It's nobody's fault.'

Hargrave tried not to glance at the framed photograph, of a midshipman who looked so like Ransome. Just a boy. It made the war stamp right into the cabin like a monster.

Ransome looked up from the desk. 'Just leave me a while, Number One. I've a couple of phone calls to make.'

As the door closed silently behind him the ship seemed to withdraw too.

He remembered his stupid jealousy when Tony had taken her to a dance, of his perpetual eagerness to get the most out of life. He picked up the telephone, and after a lot of clicks he was connected to the switchboard ashore.

What shall I say to them? They'll expect me to come home, when I belong here, now more than ever . . .

I must speak to Eve. Tell her I can't see her until . . .

He ran his fingers through his hair and stared at the signal until his eyes stung. Aloud he said, 'Oh dear God, *help me!*'

The operator coughed. 'The number's ringing for you, sir.'

It happened all the time, every day. Others had had to cope with it. If he could not contain his despair he was not fit to command. Men would die, and it could be his fault because –

He heard the familiar voice in his ear and steeled himself.

'Hello, Dad, I've just heard about Tony . . .'

10

To the Deep

Ordinary Seaman Gerald Boyes gripped the ready-use chart-table for support and watched as the side of the upper bridge dipped steeply in the heavy swell. It was as if the great shark-blue procession of rollers was climbing over the ship before *Rob Roy* skittishly lifted her stern and pitched over on the opposite beam. It was all so new and breathtaking he could barely drag his eyes from it.

The bridge was filled with all the usual watchkeepers, but no one seemed to be paying him much attention. He had cleaned the chart-table, sharpened the navigator's pencils and checked the bulb in the tiny, hooded bracket which by night was concealed by a canvas screen. It was halfway through the forenoon watch, the little ship lifting and plunging, hanging motionless for seconds or so it appeared, before attempting a different position.

Boyes glanced at the captain's chair in the forepart of the bridge behind the glass screens. It looked wrong to see it empty. Ransome was always there, had been for the long four days from Falmouth into the vastness of the Atlantic before joining up with an impressive convoy.

Boyes had sensed new excitement and tension as the ships had been rounded up like sheep, chased and harried by powerful fleet destroyers before forming into columns for the long haul to Gibraltar. Boyes, in his duty of acting-navigator's yeoman, felt privileged to pick up the rumours which circulated every watch amongst the élite on the bridge.

It was a convoy to rouse anyone's attention, he thought, but the escort had been equally exciting. A heavy cruiser as well as the destroyers, and bang in the middle, a carrier. Not one of the big fleet ones, like the famous *Ark Royal* or *Illustrious*, but a stubby escort-carrier. A merchant ship's hull with a wooden flight-deck, a *banana boat* as some of the old hands called them. But the little escort-carriers had changed the whole face of every convoy lucky enough to enjoy their protection. No longer were there great areas of ocean where air-cover could not reach or be provided.

A Focke-Wulf condor, one of the huge long-range maritime bombers, had found the convoy the second day out. But the sight of three Seafires being scrambled from the carrier had soon sent the enemy racing for home. Whereas before, these same aircraft would circle a convoy, day in, day out, just beyond the range of the guns, and all the while homing U-boats on to a helpless target.

They had not seen another enemy plane after that incident.

The ships in convoy were all big ones, including two troopers, ex-liners, and several fast freighters, their decks and hulls crammed with tanks, crated aircraft, and other vehicles. No wonder they had taken such precautions. Far out into the Atlantic, zigzagging ponderously in response to irate signals from the commodore, then around Biscay and south into warmer waters. Some of the sailors, especially those on the open bridge, were already sporting healthy-looking tans.

Boyes glanced at his companions. Lieutenant Sherwood was the O.O.W., with the new sub, Tritton, assisting him. Leading Signalman Mackay was studying the *Ranger*, which was steering a parallel course some four miles away, the rest of the minesweepers divided between them in two lines.

It was strange to see the ocean so deserted, Boyes thought. Just yesterday the convoy had increased speed and had gone on ahead. Each ship had been capable of much greater haste than the sweepers, but they had all kept together until the worst part of the passage was astern.

By glancing at the vibrating chart Boyes knew that neutral Portugal lay some two hundred miles across the port beam; they should be passing the invisible Lisbon about now. It was the furthest he had ever been in his life.

He looked at the empty chair again. Everyone knew about the captain's brother. Occasionally Boyes had watched him, had found himself searching for some sign of grief or anxiety. He had discovered nothing but a remoteness, something respected by the other officers.

He thought about the radar plot beneath his feet in the wheelhouse. The chief quartermaster, Reeves, was on the wheel, while Beckett was down below somewhere dealing with some requestmen. It never seemed to stop. Midshipman Davenport always managed to avoid him. It was as if they belonged to a separate society. Difficult at any time in the two-hundred-and-thirty foot hull.

He found himself thinking back to his leave again. His mother saying how she had seen young Davenport in his officer's uniform. *So smart, so dashing.* She could have had no conception just how much it had hurt.

And then, out of the blue, had come *the great adventure.* One evening when he had been having tea with his parents the telephone had rung.

Boyes's mother had bustled away, and his father had murmured, 'If it's another bridge-party I shall really do some extra fire-watching to get out of it!'

But she had returned, her eyes questioning, even suspicious. 'It's for *you,* Gerry.' It had sounded like an accusation. 'A girl!'

Boyes had hurried to the door. Over his shoulder he had heard his father ask mildly, 'Who was it, dear?'

'Someone who met our son. Sounded rather common – '

Boyes had not even noticed.

The girl named Connie had sounded very easy and matter-of-fact over the phone. Boyes had had virtually no experience of girls apart from the school dance once a year. His arrival on the lower deck of a fighting ship had made him flush with embarrassment, even if half what the others said was true.

She had said, 'You're not doing anything then?'

'N – no – ' he had imagined his mother listening through the closed door. 'I'd been hoping, actually – '

She had laughed. 'You naughty boy!'

He had felt himself flushing all over again.

'What about the pictures? There's a good one on at the Regal – '

When he had remained tongue-tied she had added, 'But if you've something better – '

'No. I'd love to.'

'In an hour then.' The adventure had begun.

The cinema had been packed, mostly with servicemen and their girls, so that when a cracked, much-used slide was thrust across the screen to announce that an air-raid warning had been sounded, there had been a great bellow of protest. 'Get it off!' Plus whistles and derisive laughter. She had leaned against him in the cinema, until halfway through the main film when he had put his arm around her shoulder.

As the light blazed from the screen, he had seen her looking at him. Surprised? Curious? But then Boyes knew nothing about women.

Afterwards they had walked to the square in Kingston where the army had thoughtfully sent a truck for its army girls, a sort of liberty boat to get them back to camp safely.

They had stood in a shop doorway, and to hurrying passers-by it was just another sailor on leave with a girl in khaki. To Boyes it was something else. But he had had a sense of disappointment, not in her but in himself.

He had asked desperately, 'May I see you again, Connie? *Please*?'

She had watched him, her eyes bright despite the black-out.

She had expected the usual wrestling-match in the cinema, a groping hand, the sense of shock when it touched her. Boyes was different. God, he was so different.

'You've never had your own girl, have you?'

He had hesitated. 'Not before.'

She had wanted to hug him. To weep for his innocence, his old-world sense of honour.

'I'm free tomorrow, if you like.'

They had met in the warm afternoon, and had gone into a pub by the river for a drink. He had told her about the navy, about the ship, and all the while she had watched him, her bright lips around the straws in her port-and-lemon, her other hand close to his across the table. She had taken him to another cinema, a smaller one than the Regal, one which had been known as a flea-pit in his schooldays. It had been practically empty, and she had led him to the back row of seats. They were in pairs.

She had whispered, 'Must have been a right lot of lovers in your neck of the woods, Gerry!'

During an interval he had blurted out, 'I'm off tomorrow, Connie.'

She had straightened up, her eyes suddenly anxious.

'Already? I thought – '

He had said, 'I've loved being with you so much. I can't tell you.'

She had waited for the lights to dim. 'Kiss me.'

He had tried, but had pressed his face into her hair. 'Sorry.'

She had stood up. 'Keep my seat warm. I'm going to the Ladies.' She had reached out and touched his mouth. 'It was sweet. Just needs a bit of practice.' But she was not making fun of him.

For a time Boyes had imagined she had left by one of the fire-exit doors, but then he saw her hurrying up the aisle and felt her sink down beside him. He put his arm round her and kissed her again. She had her hand behind his neck and had pulled him against her, so that their mouths were locked until she opened hers and touched his tongue with hers. She had taken his hand and moulded it to her body. Her tunic had been unbuttoned, and he had felt the fullness of her breast through the shirt, her heart thumping as if to break free.

She had spoken into his ear. 'I got rid of the army-issue in the Ladies.'

He slipped one of the shirt buttons open and touched the bare skin beneath. Then another button until he had held her breast in his hand, the nipple hard between his fingers.

She had been gasping, 'Don't stop, Gerry! Oh, for God's sake!'

He had felt her reaching for him in the same wild desperation, finding and gripping him until he could barely control himself.

When they had finally left the cinema and made their way to the same square where the army lorry was waiting, he had hugged her again.

She had pushed him away, her voice breathless, 'Not here! Not like those others! Next time –' She had kissed him hard on the mouth, then had run through the night to the throbbing lorry.

Afterwards he had realised that he could not remember the name of the film or anything about it.

Sometimes now he would touch himself as she had done, and relive the moment when he had slipped his hand into her open shirt.

'*Ranger*'s calling us up, sir.'

Mackay's voice shattered his dream and made him stare around the bridge like a stranger.

The leading signalman's mouth moved in time to the diamond-bright signal lamp across the heaving swell.

'*Wreckage in the water at one-six-zero degrees*, sir.'

Sherwood nodded. 'Better tell the captain.'

'I'm here.' Ransome strode from the ladder and climbed into his chair to reach for his binoculars. 'What was that bearing?'

Mackay called, 'From *Dryaden*, sir. *Shall I investigate?*'

'Negative.' Ransome ignored the clatter of the Aldis lamp. 'Alter course to close. Inform *Ranger*.'

'What's up?' Moncrieff lurched heavily across the bridge. He looked as if he had just woken up.

'Wreckage, sir.' Ransome looked at him as if expecting an argument. *Dryaden* was better suited for these tasks. The point of her being here at all.

But Moncrieff merely said, 'Right-oh.'

Boyes dodged aside as Sherwood crouched over the gyro repeater.

'Port ten. *Steady*. Steer one-six-five!'

Up the voicepipe came Beckett's harsh acknowledgement. 'Course one-six-five, sir.' He had taken the wheel without being called.

Boyes made himself small in case anyone ordered him from the bridge. Another drama. And he was part of it.

Ransome said, 'Full revolutions.'

Boyes saw Sherwood glance at the captain's back, the slightest rise of one eyebrow. But that was all.

As the revolutions mounted the ship headed slightly away from her consorts so that Boyes was able to see them from a different angle. Third in line, *Fawn's* sister-ship *Firebrand*, an old Smokey Joe, was puffing out black clouds against the clear sky. It had caused quite a lot of friction with the convoy's escort commander, until Moncrieff had seized the loud hailer and had told him to mind his bloody manners.

Hargrave had appeared on the bridge now, and raised his glasses to peer over the screen at the drifting spread of flotsam. Remnants from another convoy perhaps?

Ransome tried to lean back in the chair and relax his mind and body. Why had he taken *Rob Roy* from the formation when the trawler could have managed? Moncrieff would have been justified to question his decision.

It was a distraction. Anything better than the brooding, the regrets, the pain. He knew it was getting into him more deeply, had noticed how careful the others had been to make themselves scarce or busy when he was near. It wasn't their fault, as he had tried to tell the first lieutenant. But it still didn't help. He felt himself leaning forward again, the old dryness at the back of his throat.

'Half ahead together.' Would anyone ever be able to sum up the cost of the war at sea? Ships and men, material and hopes, the very balance of fate for friend and enemy alike.

Hargrave asked, 'What do you think, sir?'

Ransome raised his powerful glasses again. It was all too familiar. Drifting timbers and odd fragments of canvas, packing-crates, an upended lifeboat, the whole sea littered with it. He trained his glasses on the capsized boat. He could just make out the port registry, Liverpool, painted on the hull. There was a lot of scum around the planking. It had been wandering with the aimless currents for a long time, probably weeks, the last reminder of a ship, perhaps a whole convoy which had fallen foul of a U-boat pack.

He heard a look-out remark, 'Not much left in that lot!'

He snapped, 'Well, keep looking! Any clue might be useful later on!'

He turned away, sick inside, angry with his inability to stay calm.

Sherwood said, 'There's a raft, sir. Red four-five.'

Ransome found it, his glasses taking in the scene as if he had actually been there. The roar of a torpedo, perhaps more, the sudden confusion, a shock of despair as the ship went over. This vessel may have been carrying explosives, and had been blown apart before the boats could be got away. Just the one raft. Low in the water, barely rising up to challenge each roller or trough. There were three figures on board. Spreadeagled across it, tied there like some grisly warning to those who risked the Western Ocean.

'Slow ahead together.' Ransome slipped from the chair and stood on the gently vibrating gratings. 'Send the sea-boat away, Number One.' Their eyes met. 'Tell the doctor to go too.'

'What is it, sir?'

Ransome wiped his glasses with a piece of tissue. 'Nothing. You go across with the boat, will you?'

Hargrave walked away and soon the tannoy barked, 'Away seaboat's crew!' Then, 'Slip the gripes, stand by for lowering!'

Ransome turned back to watch the little raft. Must have been quite a big ship to carry some naval personnel. He held the glasses fixed on the sprawled shape of the officer whose outthrust arm splashed in the sea alongside. Strained and sodden, but the single gold wavy stripe on the sleeve told its own story. The other two were seamen; one had lost a leg, and appeared to have been lashed to the raft by his companions.

'*Out pins! Slip!*' The whaler dropped smartly on to *Rob Roy*'s falling bow wave and veered away from the side on the boatrope. As it was cast free, the oars dipped and sliced into the water, and Ransome saw Hargrave standing upright in the swaying sternsheets while Surgeon Lieutenant Cusack crouched beside the coxswain, the sunlight touching the scarlet cloth between his stripes like blood.

It would not be a pretty sight. Ransome glanced around at the others and saw the new sub, Tritton, fingering his own sleeve, as if he had seen himself lying there. Leading Signalman Mackay too, his expression a mixture of pity and hate. He had served in the Atlantic and knew the score well enough. Sherwood, eyes partly hidden by his pale lashes, his jaw very rigid as he watched the compass. And the youngster Boyes, who had been staring at the flotsam until he felt his eyes on him. Ransome nodded to him. It was all he could offer. And yet Boyes seemed to symbolise everything as clearly as a bursting starshell. They all expected him, their captain, no matter how young and unprepared, to hold every answer.

Moncrieff said thickly, 'Not a nice job at any time.'

Ransome watched the whaler's oars still, the bowman reaching out warily with his boathook as the raft lifted sluggishly, then surged against the hull. They would hold their breath, pretend it wasn't really happening, while someone reached over and cut away the identity discs from those poor, broken corpses who had once been like Mackay and Tritton. *Like me.*

Someone, somewhere would have received a telegram, *Missing, presumed killed.* The three discs would wipe away any last hope for those who still believed in such things.

He said angrily, 'Signal the whaler to tow the raft alongside!' He knew he was speaking harshly, but could not contain it. 'At least we can remember them properly, for God's sake!'

And so it was to be.

It was the first time Ransome had been off the bridge for days. It felt like an eternity as he climbed down the two ladders, past the new Oerlikon mounting and grim-faced look-outs, and then along the side-deck past the whaler, now hoisted snugly in the davits again, the wetness of its recent excursion already dried in the sunshine. How different it all looked from down here, he thought. The men off-watch, clinging to stanchions and life-rafts similar to the one they had cast adrift to remain with all the other flotsam of war. Faces watched him, some sad, some stony, all familiar to him like his own family.

It was the same as all the other times, and yet not the same at all. The three shapes by the break in the guardrails, no longer without privacy or dignity, but safe under the ocean flags. He heard a snapping sound and saw Cusack pulling off some rubber gloves. Leading Seaman Hoggan was standing with the burial party, the snake tattoo very obvious around one thick wrist as he whistled silently to himself. Two faces by the engine-room hatch, Campbell the Chief, and Nobby Clarke, his petty officer, who knew all about losing a ship. Sub-Lieutenant Fallows, his mouth a thin line as he took charge of the party. He never wore his woolly rabbit any more, Ransome had observed. He was like a different person who was trying to find himself.

Ransome looked first to seaward where *Dryaden*, which oddly enough had the most modern Asdic in the group, ploughed around them protectively, the sunlight flashing on levelled glasses on her superstructure. Then he glanced up to *Rob Roy*'s bridge and saw Hargrave craning over the side to watch him, silhouetted against the sky.

Ransome removed his cap and opened the little book. It was so creased and worn he wondered why he had not obtained a new one. The three identity discs seemed to stare up at him.

That was why it was different. They were some of their own. Probably part of a naval gun-crew carried aboard a big merchantman. This was for all of them. *For us.* He made himself face it. *For Tony.* As he read the familiar prayer he glanced up occasionally as if to test his own strength, his own resolve.

He saw Able Seaman Nunn who had lost everyone in his family gripping the lines by the open guardrail, his face expressionless. Only his eyes told it all. Young Boyes sent down from the bridge with an extra flag, his face screwed up while he held on to the new knife which hung from his belt; beside him the tough seaman Jardine with an arm around the boy's shoulder.

No, he could not let any one of them down. Especially not now.

He glanced up at the bridge and instantly the last tremble of power began to die away.

Ransome read the last part from memory.

'We commend unto thy hands of mercy, most merciful Father, the souls of these our brothers departed, and we commit their bodies to the deep . . .'

The rest was blurred, wiped away. As he replaced his cap he saw that the deck was cleared, the flags being folded again. There was the clang of telegraphs, and as if emerging from a brief rest, *Rob Roy*'s screws beat the sea into an impatient froth once more.

While Ransome made his way forward to the bridge ladder he pictured the three little bundles sinking slowly into eternal darkness. The sea was two and a half thousand fathoms hereabouts. Undisturbed.

When he reached the upper bridge he walked to the chart-table and saw that Hargrave had marked the burial for future reference.

Moncrieff was slouched in his chair. He watched him thoughtfully.

'Feel better now, Ian?'

Ransome faced him. 'Much.'

He was the captain again.

11

Gateway

Ian Ransome gripped the rim of the motorboat's canvas dodger as the little hull bucked wildly over another craft's wash. The spray across his face was surprisingly cold despite the full, hazy sunshine, and it helped to drive away the strain of marshalling the minesweeping flotilla to their various buoys.

The whole anchorage appeared to be filled with ships, moored, anchored, or tied alongside one another at the mole, so that it gave the impression they might never be able to move again. Above it all, the towering bulk of Gibraltar made even the capital ships appear almost insignificant.

Ransome glanced at the ships as the boat tore between them. Famous names, battleships and cruisers he had read about as a boy, some he had even served aboard in the peacetime RNVR days during his annual training. He thought it unlikely that there had been such a gathering of naval force before. The troopships and ungainly landing-craft too, all bedecked with lines of khaki washing hung out to dry like drab bunting.

This was naval power, the machinery it took to sustain an invasion.

A long barge crossed the motorboat's bows and he heard Able Seaman Suggit, the skimming-dish's coxswain, swear between his teeth. The launch bore the markings of a rear-admiral. Nothing must stand in his path. No wonder leaders who held the real authority could not afford to consider men as individuals. Ashore they were flags on a map. At sea just a marker with your ship's name on it. To show that you were at least still afloat.

Like sweeping mines, he thought. You never knew what effect you were having on the whole panorama of war. You worked at it, you mourned when a friend blew up and men burned before your eyes. And yet in the front line you could still afford pity.

The coxswain said, 'There she is, sir!'

Ransome saw the anchored destroyer immediately. HMS *Bedworth*, one of the small, speedy Hunt Class destroyers which had been created at the outbreak of war to fill the gaps left by peacetime neglect and reductions. They carried no torpedoes and were used mainly for escort and patrol work. For their size they were heavily armed with four-inch and multi-barrelled weapons, and the *Bedworth* even mounted a single pom-pom right in the eyes of the ship, a bow-chaser which could singe the whiskers of even the fastest E-boat. The little Hunts had an impressive speed of thirty-two knots. She would run rings around her brood of minesweepers, he thought, but then who didn't?

'*Bows!*'

The bowman raised his boathook and held it above his head as the *Rob Roy*'s only motor boat scudded round and headed towards an accommodation ladder.

He wondered if Moncrieff was still aboard, or, as in Plymouth, if he had already left without a word.

A flight of Hurricanes roared low overhead and Ransome imagined the Spaniards across the water in Algeciras watching every movement, using a one-sided neutrality to keep their German friends fully informed.

Gib in peacetime had been a favourite calling-place for the fleet. A sailors' port then, today it would seem like Aladdin's Cave to the youngsters who made up most of the ships' companies that came here.

Ransome thought of his own company. Hardly any of them had been out of home waters before. Gibraltar never changed, with its blazing lights and garish cafés, its tiny shops and stalls filled as always with junk. To these young sailors it would seem like the treasures of the Orient.

It would be packed with servicemen now more than ever before. Like the Great War when the troopships had assembled here before the bloody carnage of Gallipoli. *The Rock.* Who held it, commanded the gateway to the Mediterranean.

The motor boat's engine coughed and went astern as the hook swept down on to the accommodation ladder to bring them together.

Ransome ran lightly up the side, feeling sweaty and out of place when he was confronted by the white-clad side-party, the O.O.D. in shorts that looked as if they had just been washed and ironed.

The lieutenant saluted. 'Welcome aboard, sir. We watched you enter harbour. Yours is a job I'd prefer to see from a distance.'

Ransome followed him to the quartermaster's lobby. Just a small hard-worked destroyer, some forty feet longer than *Rob Roy.* And yet in a strange way she felt twice as big.

He heard Moncrieff's voice before they even reached the door marked *Captain.*

'I don't give a bloody toss what they say, whoever *they* are, I think it's a damn stupid – ' The rest was cut off as the lieutenant tapped on the door.

Another voice spoke. '*Come!*'

The lieutenant grimaced at Ransome. 'Good luck, sir.'

Ransome knew a fair amount about the new S.N.O. *A bit of a goer*, everyone said, an officer who had seen most of his service in destroyers, and latterly working with Combined Operations right here in the Med.

Ransome adjusted his expression and stepped into the cabin.

Commander Peregrine Bliss, DSO, Royal Navy, was young for his rank. He had a square, eager face and dark curly hair which with his deeply tanned skin made his eyes stand out like chips of blue glass. He thrust out his hand, his eyes crinkling as he gave a wide grin. 'At last, Ransome. Been dying to meet up with you. Take a pew.'

He glanced at Moncrieff. '*We've* been having a discussion.' Like the man, his speech was lively, like a sea breeze. Ransome could picture him without any difficulty at all, conning his destroyer through some hazard or other, his men hanging on his every word.

Ransome sat. 'I came immediately, sir. I have all the reports you asked – '

Bliss waved a sunburned arm. 'Hell, that can wait. We're on the move right now. Can't you feel it in the air?'

Moncrieff exclaimed angrily, 'I think it stinks!'

Ransome noticed for the first time that Moncrieff held a large tumbler in his good hand; it was almost empty.

Ransome looked away. God, what was the matter with him? It was only nine in the morning!

Bliss saw his glance and beamed. 'What about a Horse's Neck, eh?'

Ransome forced a smile. 'Not for me, sir. The sun isn't over my yard-arm at this hour, I'm afraid.'

Bliss nodded, his eyes amused. 'Good show.'

Ransome tried to stay calm. Bliss had no glass, nor had he any intention of joining Moncrieff or anyone else for a drink. What was the point? A little test to see if the new boy was up to it?

Ransome tried again. His nerves were worse than he had imagined.

He said, 'My people have been working hard together, sir. By August we shall have it off to a fine art.'

Moncrieff opened his mouth but Bliss snapped, 'My turn, I think!'

To Ransome he continued, 'There's been an advance of plans. The invasion of Sicily, Operation *Husky* as it is codenamed, will begin on July 10th.' The smile expanded into a confident grin. 'It will succeed.'

Ransome said, 'Two weeks' time?' He watched the grin and recalled when he had read to Tony about the Cheshire Cat in *Alice*.

Bliss nodded. 'This flotilla, and all other inshore forces involved, must ensure that the heavy supporting squadrons are on station to offer covering fire before the first landing-craft drops its ramp!'

A hundred details seemed to scramble through Ransome's mind. He sensed that Moncrieff had been protesting on their behalf; he also had the strong feeling that this was the original date as planned. The high command may have thought that security and the shortest notice possible to risk the news leaking out, was of more value than preparing the ships for what lay ahead.

Ransome said, 'We'll just have to manage.'

Bliss regarded him with some amusement. 'I like it, Ian. May I call you that?' He hurried on, 'Just two days on dry land, and we'll have the Krauts by the short and curlies!'

Ransome relaxed slightly. He had noticed that Bliss rarely appeared to wait for, even to expect an answer. But he was a live wire, right enough. He was disturbed to find that his sadness for Moncrieff was changing to pity. Where would his Phoenix fit in now?

There was a tap at the door and a sub-lieutenant glanced in at them. Like the O.O.D., he was an RNVR officer, so Bliss had no prejudice there at least.

'I beg your pardon, sir, but the commander's boat is already alongside.'

Bliss nodded. 'Very well.' He thrust out his hand to Moncrieff. 'I do hope we meet again, old chap.'

Ransome stared. Quite apart from the obvious insincerity he could scarcely believe what he had heard.

'You're not leaving *now*, sir?'

Bliss explained smoothly, 'There is apparently a shortage of places in available aircraft. Their lordships are keen for Commander Moncrieff to take over his new appointment without any delay.'

Moncrieff lumbered to his feet. '*New appointment*, Ian. It's a supply dump in Orkney!' He dropped his eyes and stared blindly at his maimed hand. 'A bloody stores clerk!'

Bliss had turned away to peer through a gleaming scuttle.

Ransome said quietly, 'I'd hoped to lay something on for you, sir. After all this time. To leave like this – '

Moncrieff gripped his hand. It was like a vice. 'No more, Ian – I can't take it, y'see.' He groped for his cap with its cherished peak of oak leaves. 'Just tell the others – ' He seemed to regain some of his old power and added fiercely, 'Tell 'em I'm *proud* of them!' The power faded; Ransome saw it dying in his eyes as he added huskily, 'Look after the ship, eh? My old *Rob Roy*.' They walked to the door and Bliss and Ransome saluted as he clambered down into a harbour-launch alongside.

While the boat surged away towards the white buildings ashore Moncrieff looked back only once. But he was staring at *Rob Roy*.

Bliss said absently, 'Last of his kind, I shouldn't wonder.'

Was it meant with contempt, Ransome thought?

He replied calmly, 'No better way to be remembered, I'd say, sir.'

Bliss made no comment until the 'skimming-dish' sputtered back to the accommodation ladder. He stood with his feet wide apart, his strong fingers interlaced behind his back as he stared gravely at the mass of assembled ships.

'You will meet the new vice-admiral tomorrow, Ian. He will want to speak with you, and your other C.O.s of course.' He turned suddenly and fixed him with a blue stare. 'But I command the group now and my head will be on the block if just one captain screws this up. Am I making myself clear?' Again, he did not wait. 'I am, how do you say, *unused* to failure.'

He saluted as Ransome climbed back into the motor boat. He had disappeared before the bowman had even cast off.

All the way back to *Rob Roy* Ransome tried to accept Bliss for what he appeared to be. A man of courage and ability; his record said all that and more. He knew what it was like to fight the enemy at close quarters and it was obvious that that experience plus his training as a regular officer made him a perfect choice for this task.

He was ruthless too; his attitude to Moncrieff and the hint of his displeasure if anyone else *screwed things up* left little to the imagination. But then you could not fight this kind of war with a book of naval etiquette.

It was something else. Ransome watched the ships passing on either side, guns being swivelled round in their turrets, seamen and marines working on deck and in the various superstructures. Like some vast iron hornet's nest waiting to be unleashed.

He nodded to himself. *That was it.* Bliss made it all sound so personal, as if nothing and nobody would be spared to make his part of the operation a success.

Ransome smiled inwardly. In the navy, that was not unique.

Later, as he was sitting in his cabin, Hargrave came to see him. Ransome glanced up and nodded to the other chair. He felt different now in his clean shirt and shorts. Like someone playing a part. As for Hargrave, he looked almost a stranger in white, although he was obviously quite used to it.

Ransome said, 'I should like you to organise a party for tomorrow, Number One. If you're short of anything, I'll sign a couple of magic chits for you to take to the Base Supply Officer!'

Hargrave watched him curiously. It was not just a change of uniform, he thought. He could picture Ransome's face right here in the cabin as he had read out the signal about his brother's death, and again when the three bodies had been tipped over the side.

If it was an act, it was very convincing. Or was he really able to put things like that to the back of his mind in the name of duty? Hargrave had had all that rammed into him from early boyhood as a cadet in the Royal Naval College at Dartmouth. He had actually believed it, just as his father had insisted he would, given time. But never once, from midshipman to lieutenant, had he ever expected to see it as a physical presence. He was seeing it now, and from a man who had been a civilian until the outbreak of war.

Ransome saw the look and thought he could guess what he was thinking.

He touched a sheet of notepaper on the desk. 'This was waiting for me.'

Hargrave nodded. 'The guardboat brought it shortly after you'd left, sir.'

'It's from the vice-admiral's secretary, no less. In it he "suggests" that a party given by us might be the best and most informal way for the admiral to meet our commanding officers.'

Hargrave replied quickly, 'My father said nothing of it to me, sir, and that's the truth.'

'Thank you. I never doubted it. But it *sounds* like a command all the same, so lay on the party, right? It might be the last for quite some time.'

He gave Hargrave a thoughtful glance. '*It's* been brought forward. Two weeks from now. Top Secret, but you should know in case – '

Hargrave stared at him. He had never considered it from that angle. That Ransome might be unable to retain command, that he could be injured, even killed, before the invasion began. He felt the sweat trickling down his spine. Surely that wasn't what his father had meant about a ship of his own.

Ransome said, 'Arrange shore leave for all but the duty-part of the watch, Number One.' He was formal again. 'I believe there are two men requesting to see me?'

Hargrave nodded. How did he know that already? 'Bad news from home for both of them, sir. I don't see what we can do about it now.'

Ransome half-smiled. 'I can *talk* to them. It's the least I can do.'

Hargrave stood and made to leave. 'The Chief wishes to discuss the new pumps with you, sir.'

'Ask him to come now, will you?'

As the door closed Ransome leaned back and massaged his eyes. It never ended. He thought of Bliss's words. *I command this group now.* He should have added, 'And don't you forget it!' Ransome recalled too when he had obtained his own first command, the poor old *Guillemot.* He had looked up the meaning of command in his dictionary. It had been quite an ancient version and one definition had been, 'To demand with authority.' It fitted Bliss rather well.

It was evening by the time he had dealt with with Chief and his problem of spare parts for the new pumps, seen the doctor about a seaman whom he had put ashore with the first signs of gonorrhoea, and finally made several operational signals both to the Admiralty and to the Flag Officer Gibraltar. He felt drained. The one redeeming fact about the luckless rating sent to the V.D. clinic was that he was a new hand, who had joined the ship at Chatham. He would certainly miss the invasion anyway, and might well end up in the glasshouse as payment for a few moments of doubtful pleasure.

He smoked his pipe, took a glass of Scotch and listened to one of his Handel records. The liberty boats squeaked their fenders alongside to mingle with the jubilant chatter of shore-going sailors, then came the pipe to clear up messdecks and flats for Rounds.

At times like these he was grateful for his privacy. He pictured Moncrieff arriving in England. No ships to visit, to be part of. How would he cope? Ships were all he knew, all he had left.

Eventually he knew he was ready. Very carefully he opened his writing-case, the one his mother had given him for his last birthday, and picked up his pen.

It was easier than he had dared to hope. It was not like writing to her. It was as if she was here, listening to him, or sitting with her bare legs tucked beneath her chin in the old boatyard where it seemed as if the sun had always shone.

My dearest Eve, We did not have that walk together which I had promised for us, but I walk with you every day, and we are together . . .

Apart from Sub-Lieutenant Fallows, *Rob Roy's* wardroom was deserted. Even the old hands like Bone and Campbell who had little to say in favour of the Rock's attractions had gone ashore, and aboard *Ranger* tied alongside the situation was the same.

Fallows decided that he would go ashore tomorrow, perhaps before the wardroom party. He glanced down at the single stripe on his shoulder strap and considered his future. A second ring very soon now, but what then? You needed a push, a friendly word in the right places, and Fallows was not so much of a fool that he did not know his own unpopularity. But it had not been easy for him. He had nothing but determination and guts. Even the captain had seemed satisfied with his work and would have to say as much in his personal report.

He thought of the others. Bone and the Chief did not count, but young Morgan would do well because of his navigation qualifications if nothing else. Even the newcomer Tritton – just thinking of his name made Fallows burn with anger and humiliation. *Bunny* Tritton. He too seemed so full of confidence. Fallows had never got to know Sherwood, but then he suspected that nobody ever really *knew* him. On the face of it he should have had everything. He felt envy replacing his anger. Sherwood came from a prosperous family, should have had the world at his feet even after his family had been wiped out. *Suppose my own family were killed?* Fallows swallowed his neat gin and coughed. He did not need to seek an answer, not if he had been in Sherwood's shoes. Sherwood had known the life Fallows had only dreamed about. Cruise ships, and luxury yachts, good hotels and women probably eyeing him whenever he passed; Fallows could imagine it all. With his background, and especially when he had tempted death to gain the George Cross, second only to the VC, he could have found a safe and comfortable billet anywhere he chose. And after the war, he would never have to work again.

Fallows avoided thinking of Hargrave. He had sensed his disapproval, dislike even, from the start. Another one who had it made, no matter how things turned out. A naval family, his father a flag-officer, and right here in the Med to offer a leg-up as soon as it presented itself – no, he would get nothing out of him.

He saw the duty messman watching him. He was a seaman-gunner named Parsons who chose to act as a steward rather than work another part of ship when not employed on 'A' Gun. As gunnery officer, Fallows had been instrumental in getting him what was both a soft number and a lucrative one.

'Another gin, Parsons.' Fallows never said *please* or *thank you* to a rating. He thought it was beneath him.

Parsons fetched the bottle and, while he measured the gin, watched the ginger-haired sub-lieutenant as a milkman will study a dangerous dog. The big shindig would be tomorrow. They would be working fit to bust, he thought. Ted Kellett the P.O. steward would have all his work cut out. He couldn't be everywhere at once. With the place packed with officers all downing free gins it would always be possible to fake a few records. There would be some bottles going spare, unaccounted for, and Parsons always knew where he could sell duty-free at the right price for a nice, handy profit.

He put down the glass. So Bunny was drinking again. That was something. He was a bastard, one of the worst Parsons had known, but he had eyes like a bloody hawk when he was sober.

Parsons began warily, 'I was wondering, sir, if we could clear up the accounts before the party?'

Fallows frowned, his train of thought disturbed. 'What d'you mean?'

Parsons had been a pub barman before the war in Southampton. Like the milkman and the dog, he could usually spot the signs. He said in a wheedling tone, 'It's not me, sir, you know that, but the Jimmy the One has been riding all of us a bit over the mess bills, an' things.'

'*And?*' Fallows stared at him. He had not taken a real drink for so long it was making his mouth and tongue numb.

'Well, sir, you didn't sign your mess chits – '

Fallows slammed down the glass. 'What the bloody hell are you yapping about? I always pay my bills – ' He contained his anger and asked sharply, 'When was this anyway?'

'In Chatham, sir. You'd been working very hard, and Jimmy the One landed you with extra duty – '

Fallows smiled gently. 'Don't crawl, man, it doesn't impress me!'

Parsons licked his lips. 'There's ten quid to cover, sir.'

'*What?*' Even Fallows lost his practised calm. 'At duty-free prices, how the hell could that happen?'

Parsons persisted; it was all or nothing now. 'It was the night when young Tinker came down to see you, sir, when you told him – ' He did not go on. There was no need to.

Fallows stood up and dragged at his short-sleeved shirt as if it was clinging to his body.

'I told him what?'

Parsons watched him. Just for an instant he had thought he had gone too far, chosen the wrong moment. But now . . . He said, 'Tinker asked to go ashore, sir, because of what had happened.'

Fallows sat down heavily on the club fender and pinched the crown of his nose between finger and thumb as he tried to remember, to make the picture form in his mind.

It was like a terrible nightmare. You knew it was bad, and yet you could never make any sort of form or sense out of it. He *had* been plagued by some vague, distorted memory about Tinker.

Parsons added, 'You shouted at him, sir.'

Fallows looked up. 'Did I?' The admission seemed to stun him. 'Then what happened?'

Parsons could scarcely believe it, but the old in-built caution flashed its warning. Like the drunk in the bar who takes one too many, who picks up a bottle, thirsting for blood.

'You were worn out, sir, like I told you. You shouldn't have been on duty that time.'

Fallows nodded like a puppet. 'That's right. I do remember. Number One – ' He checked himself just in time, and asked curtly, 'What did I say to Tinker?'

Parsons took a deep breath. 'You told him he was *not* going ashore, that he was a disgrace to the ship and his uniform. Things like that.'

Fallows eyed him like a man who has suddenly lost his memory, afraid of what he might be or do. 'There's more?'

'You told him that his mother was an effing whore, sir, that it was the best thing that could have happened to her.'

Fallows stood up and walked to the side and back again. He felt sick, trapped by the nightmare he could still not recognise or break.

He said, 'I have to do Rounds in a moment.' He looked vaguely at the letter-rack. 'First I must go to my cabin.'

'About the money, sir.'

Fallows fumbled with his wallet. 'How much was it, ten pounds?'

Parsons took the notes. They were damp from the officer's sweat.

'Thank you, sir. We've all got to stick together in some things.'

But Fallows had thrust open the door of the officers' heads and Parsons heard him vomiting helplessly.

He folded the notes inside his paybook and smiled.

'Bloody little bastard!' He poured himself a tall measure of brandy and swallowed it in one gulp. As he topped the bottle up carefully with water he added savagely, 'Now you'll know what it's like to bloody well crawl, *Mr* Bunny!'

Unexpectedly, Vice-Admiral Hargrave stepped from the brow which crossed to *Ranger*'s deck and touched his cap to the ramrod stiff side-party. He paused to listen to the music, the muted buzz of voices from the wardroom skylight, and said, 'Sounds like a good party, Ransome.'

Ransome said, 'Sorry about the reception, sir. You caught us all on the hop, I'm afraid.'

The admiral smiled. 'I didn't expect a guard and Royal marines band – I happen to enjoy informality!'

Ransome looked at the slender figure who followed the admiral across the brow. Like the admiral, she was all in white, the only touch of colour being the blue of her shoulder-straps; a second officer in the W.R.N.S.

'This is Second Officer Rosalind Pearce, by the way, my flag lieutenant and guardian angel.' He laughed loudly.

How like his son he was, Ransome thought. A bit heavier, but the same good looks, and the added confidence of age.

He looked at the girl. She was tall, almost the same height as her admiral, with dark hair showing beneath her neat tricorn hat, and serious eyes which were probably blue.

The vice-admiral added, 'She wanted to see all you rough, sea-going types anyway – another experience, eh?'

They glanced at each other. Ransome could detect a closer relationship, the sense of understanding.

He said, 'I'll lead the way, sir.'

The wardroom was packed, and the guests overflowed into the passageway and at least one neighbouring cabin.

Hargrave pushed through the throng and then saw his father. 'Welcome aboard, sir!'

Ransome saw his eyes shift to the girl.

Vice-Admiral Hargrave made the same introduction and again they looked at one another. Ransome suspected that the admiral said the same thing quite often. Explanation, or defence, he wondered?

Hargrave beckoned to a perspiring messman with a loaded tray.

'A bit of a mixture.'

She said, 'That one looks nice,' but her eyes were on Hargrave.

Comparing, perhaps?

Ransome turned as a messman took the admiral's heavily oak-leaved cap from him. There was true difference. The thinning hair, the deeper lines around his mouth and eyes. His immaculate white-drill uniform with its double row of decorations did not hide the slight belly either.

The vice-admiral nodded to the officers nearest him and said, 'At last we're shifting my H.Q. to Malta, Ransome. Exciting, eh? After all the disappointments and the blockades, we'll be back where we belong.'

The girl remarked, 'I'll not be sorry to leave that cavern under the Rock they loosely *describe* as our present H.Q.'

The vice-admiral grinned hugely. 'You wait till you get to Malta, my girl! That dismal tunnel at Lascaris may be bombproof, but it's like living in a sewer, believe me!'

Hargrave asked, 'How long have you served with my, er – with the admiral?'

She regarded him thoughtfully. In the hard deckhead lights her eyes were violet, very relaxed, like a cat's.

'Six or seven months, I think.' She had a low, well-modulated voice. Very self-assured.

A boatswain's mate appeared in the door and gestured to the first lieutenant.

'What is it?' Hargrave was irritated at the interruption, just as he was confused. His father had never mentioned the girl before. She was quite stunning, with the looks of an actress, and, he guessed, an intelligence as sharp as anyone he had ever met.

The seaman called above the din, ''Nother guest, sir! A civvy!'

The vice-admiral chuckled. 'Good old Jack, never changes, thank God.' He added, as he reached for a passing drink, 'My guest actually – you'll like him. He's Richard Wakely. Heard of him?'

Who hadn't? Right from the early days, the Phoney War as it was called by those who did not have to fight it, Richard Wakely had been a household name. As a BBC roaming journalist he had brought every aspect of the war to Britain's firesides. When England had stood quite alone he had rallied every heart with his stirring words. Even before Dunkirk he had toured the front lines of the British Expeditionary Force, and visited the unbreachable Maginot Line, where he had enthralled his massive audience when he had described the nearness of the enemy in the Siegfried Line; the *Huns* as he had called them. He had disappeared after Dunkirk for a time, and had carried on his broadcasts in the USA.

Then when Britain stood firm and her friends and allies rallied from all parts of the world, Richard Wakely came back. From a Lancaster bomber above Berlin, or in the Western Desert even within range of German snipers there, he had told his listeners what it was like, regardless of the risk to himself.

It seemed strange that such a famous figure was about to enter their tiny, private world in *Rob Roy*.

The vice-admiral turned aside so that nobody else should hear. 'I want you to meet him because the people at home need to be told about your war for a change. Just be natural.' He added sharply, 'I didn't know *he* was coming too!'

Ransome saw Commander Bliss enter with the man he knew was Wakely. He heard the admiral mutter, 'I thought he was at that damned meeting!'

The girl replied indifferently, 'Must have finished earlier, sir.' She watched him, gauging his mood.

Ransome watched Bliss being greeted by the admiral. What was it? Something from the past? He had assumed that Bliss was his choice; now he was not so sure.

Ransome took Wakely's hand and shook it. It was surprisingly soft and limp.

Wakely looked a lot like his pictures. Tall, heavily rather than powerfully built, with wispy fair hair and a round, plump face.

'I am really looking forward to this, Commander Ransome!'

Bliss asked, 'Have I missed something, sir?'

The vice-admiral shrugged. 'Mr Wakely has agreed to keep us company while he gathers material for his next series of broadcasts.' He lowered his voice although it was quite unnecessary as the noise, which had faded at Bliss's entry, had mounted again. '*Operation Husky.*'

Wakely gave a childlike smile, 'All the way to Europe's soft underbelly, as Winston calls it!'

Bliss nodded approvingly. 'You honour us, Mr Wakely. I've often listened to your broadcasts.'

Wakely sipped what looked like an orangeade and blinked modestly. 'Then the honour is all mine, believe me.'

Bliss nodded again, this time to Ransome. 'Everyone here?'

'All the commanding officers anyway, sir.'

The vice-admiral dabbed his mouth with a handkerchief. 'I'd like to speak with them now.'

Bliss was saying, 'We'll do all we can to make you comfortable in *Bedworth* – '

Ransome held up his hands and the conversation began to die away once more. It was unfortunate because the vice-admiral's voice was made to sound unnecessarily loud.

'Richard Wakely is sailing with *Rob Roy* as it happens. It's all about minesweeping, and bloody time too if you ask me!'

Ransome saw Lieutenant Commander Gregory, *Ranger's* CO, chain-smoking as usual, nudge his companions, Stranach of the *Firebrand*.

Hargrave had placed himself beside the Wren officer again. They made a handsome pair, Ransome thought. Did he think so too? Or was he pondering on his father's morals, his mother and sisters in England?

Vice-Admiral Hargrave announced, 'You will be sailing very soon now to play an important part in a moment of history. Sicily is a stepping-stone and the pace will be hot and demanding. Our success will mean the opening of the Second Front, with all that that implies, and the end result, with God's help – '

Ransome saw the Wren officer's perfect mouth quiver very slightly in what could have been a smile.

Vice-Admiral Hargrave concluded, ' – will be the eventual defeat of our enemies!'

They all applauded and the vice-admiral said softly to the girl, 'Pretty good, eh, Ross?' She nodded and clapped her hands with the others.

Ransome felt suddenly grateful as the admiral glanced at his watch. It was bad enough to have Bliss here with his face like thunder without the others sensing a rift between their superiors as Gregory had obviously done.

The vice-admiral seized a few hands. 'Malta, then. We shall all meet again before too long.' He smiled at Richard Wakely. 'I have some more people waiting to hang on your every word!'

Wakely shook Ransome's hand, his eyes distant. 'I'm getting the *feel* of it already.' He nodded firmly. 'I'm never wrong.'

Ransome accompanied them to the brow and wondered why the vice-admiral had chosen to board *Rob Roy* via *Ranger*. Perhaps he never threw away the chance to see and be seen.

The Wren officer turned to face him.

'It's been a pleasure, Commander.'

Ransome felt her gaze like an inspection. Outwardly cool and composed. But the admiral's use of her first name told a different story.

He returned to the wardroom and found Bliss in deep conversation with several of the commanding officers.

To Hargrave he said, 'It went well enough, I thought.'

Hargrave plucked at his shirt. 'All these people. Every mother's son seems to know about the invasion.'

Ransome thought about the peacetime Budget, when it was always touted as a total secret until the actual announcement in the House of Commons. And yet as his father had pointed out many times, there were hundreds who must have known the 'secret'. The secretaries, the financial advisers, and all the printers who produced the final budget papers. Like Second Officer Pearce and her staff, these officers and God alone knew how many others in Whitehall. There was no such thing as a true secret.

Bliss made his excuses and left. He seemed calm enough but his eyes were angry, like the moment he had been curtly put right about Wakely.

His boat was waiting on the outboard side and Bliss paused to say, 'If you have any problems, tell *me*, right?'

Ransome nodded. *Before telling the vice-admiral*, he might just as well have said.

Bliss added, 'So your Number One is the admiral's son?'

'Yes, sir.' It was a sounding remark. Bliss knew just about everything. Perhaps he and the vice-admiral were too much alike.

There was a commotion in the wardroom and Bliss said shortly, 'I'm off. Before the high jinks begin. Best to get it out of their systems now, eh?' It sounded vaguely like a threat.

Ransome paused by the wardroom where Petty Officer Kellet was hovering outside the curtained entrance.

He said anxiously, 'I'd like to offer you one of my special cocktails, sir.'

Ransome took the hint. 'Trouble?'

Kellet shrugged. 'Storm in the teacup, sir.'

Beyond the curtain, Lieutenant Philip Sherwood clung to the back of a chair and stared glassily at the mass of figures which filled the place. He had missed Bliss by seconds, having boarded *Ranger*'s deck from a passing launch.

He looked tousled and crumpled and there was a wine stain on his shirt, like dried blood.

'Well, well, well! A celebration or a wake, which must it be?'

Hargrave made no step forward but Campbell touched his arm. 'Leave it, Number One. He's never been like this before.'

Sherwood beckoned to a messman and took a glass from the tray without even looking at it.

'I am sorry I missed the party, I was elsewhere – ' He swallowed the drink and swayed against the chair for support.

Someone called, 'For Christ's sake take it easy, or you'll spill a drop!' Another said, 'Don't anyone light a cigarette near him or you'll blow up the ship!'

Sherwood ignored the laughter and stared around with haunted desperation.

He said in a surprisingly clear voice, 'If we are mark'd to die, we are now to do our country loss: and if to live, the fewer men, the greater share of honour – '

He almost fell and then pivoted round as Ransome entered the wardroom.

Sherwood made a mock bow. 'Oops. I – I am so sorry, *dear* Captain, but I am slightly pissed – '

Surgeon Lieutenant Cusack stepped forward and caught Sherwood as he fell.

To the others he said, 'I think his party's over.'

Ransome looked round their faces, so different and yet suddenly bonded together, sobered by Sherwood's rambling quotation, which he had delivered like a prophesy.

As captain he was just another guest here in *Rob Roy*'s wardroom. It was not the time or the place to make a stand on Sherwood's behaviour. He had not seen him like it before, and tomorrow he would have to put it all behind him. Otherwise . . .

He nodded to the others and left the wardroom, but even when he reached the companion ladder there was still no sound to mark his departure.

He opened his cabin door and switched on the light. It seemed to shine directly on Tony's face.

Sherwood was not the only one, he thought. Nor would he be the last once they were through the gateway.

Chief Petty Officer Joe Beckett tilted his cap further over his eyes and stared up at the Rock, the strange shimmering haze which swirled around the summit like smoke.

The Buffer stood beside him watching the last of the NAAFI stores boats alongside, another taking aboard the final sack of letters from *Rob Roy* and *Ranger*.

Beckett said, 'Any more for the Skylark, Topsy?' He glanced at some of the seamen in their clean shorts and white tops. 'Soon be their old scruffy selves again, eh?'

The Buffer nodded. 'Big White Cheese come aboard last night, I 'ear?'

Beckett grinned. 'Yeh, an' you bloody missed it, scuttlin' about the Rock like a randy dog, no doubt!'

The Buffer shrugged. 'I've seen more admirals than young Boyes over there 'as 'ad 'ot dinners!'

Beckett savoured it. 'But 'e 'ad 'is Wren officer with 'im.' He blew a kiss. 'I'd rather be on 'er than the middle watch, I can tell you!' His grin faded as he took on his stern coxswain's expression.

'An' wot are all we, then?'

All we was one small, slightly built sailor who was being unceremoniously manhandled over the brow from *Ranger*, his frail body almost buried by hammock and kitbag, attaché case and gas mask respirator. His uniform was new and did not fit very well.

The Buffer gave a theatrical groan. 'Must be twelve years old, eh, Swain?'

'No more, and that's the truth!'

He beckoned the small figure over. 'Wot's yer name, son?'

'G – Gold, sir.'

'*Gold*, is it? Wot're you, a four-by-two or summat?'

It was all quite lost on the newcomer, who looked as if he might burst into tears at any moment.

Beckett relented slightly. 'You must be the replacement for whatsisname.'

The Buffer showed his monkey teeth. 'The one wot got a dose of clap!'

'Don't shock the lad, Buffer!' He looked severely at the sailor. 'Last ship?'

'This is my f-first, sir.' He peered around the busy deck, clattering winches, order and purpose, none of which he could recognise. 'I – I was supposed to be joining a c-cruiser, s-sir.'

The Buffer stared outboard. 'A stutter too, that all I bleedin' need!'

Beckett touched the youth's shoulder and felt him jump.

'No sweat, Gold. You'll soon settle in, though as you can see with yer own mincers, this ain't no bloody cruiser!'

Boyes walked past and Beckett seized him like a straw. ''Ere, Boyes, take this lad to Number Three Mess and get 'im fixed up.' He winked. 'Veteran like you should know wot to do, eh?'

Boyes helped the new hand gather his kit. The deck was beginning to tremble, and there was a stronger trail of smoke from *Rob Roy*'s single funnel.

Getting ready to slip from the buoy, Boyes shivered and glanced up at the bridge as if expecting to see the captain. But there was only a solitary signalman who was flashing his Aldis towards the shore.

'This way.' He picked up the hammock and led Gold towards the forecastle.

The Buffer shook his head. 'No experience. *None*. Wot do they expect us to do?'

Beckett made a few notes in his book about Gold's future. The machinery had already take over.

He said abruptly, 'Try an' keep the poor little sods alive, that's wot!'

Boyes recalled his own despair when he had entered the lower messdeck. Now, with almost everyone aboard and standing up in the small, confined space, it was a picture of utter chaos.

Men were changing into the rig-of-the-day as all the ships would have to look right and pusser when they left harbour, not merely for the F.O.I.C.'s sake but also the ever-watchful Spaniards. Some were trying to cram a last souvenir into lockers or kitbags.

Leading Seaman Ted Hoggan appeared to be the only one seated, at his usual place at the head of the table, apparently undisturbed by the packed bodies all around him, a rock in a tideway.

Boyes said, 'I'll show you where to put your gear. You'll not have a place to sling your hammock, of course. There aren't enough hooks in this mess.'

Gold nodded, then flinched as the tannoy squeaked and the boatswain's call shattered the air. 'D'you hear there! Special sea dutymen to your stations! *Away* motor boat's crew!'

Able Seaman Suggit, his mouth spurting crumbs, pushed up the ladder, cursing through his food. 'Bloody officers! Always want something!'

Boyes got to the table and waited for Hoggan to look up.

'New one for the mess, Hookey.'

Hoggan eyed the newcomer without any change of expression. 'You've put 'im in the picture, Gerry?'

Boyes nodded. 'I think so.' He turned to Gold. 'First sound from *that* bell, and you drop everything, run like hell for your action station, right?'

He did not see Able Seaman Jardine, the one who wore a wicked-looking knife in his hand-made sheath, give a broad wink, nor Hoggan's acknowledgement.

Jardine said, 'Take the advice of an *old sweat*, my son.' He clapped Boyes round the shoulder as he had beside the burial party. 'He'll see you right – '

He might have burst out laughing but the tannoy made them all look up.

'All hands! Hands to stations for leaving harbour! Stand by wires an' fenders!'

Hoggan thrust a partly darned sock into his locker and grabbed his cap.

He watched Boyes leading the new seaman up the ladder and smiled sadly.

'Here we go again – ' But he was alone; the messes on either side of the deck were empty.

12

One of Their Own

Sub-Lieutenant Tudor Morgan lifted his face from the wheelhouse voicepipe and squinted into the fierce glare. 'Steady on zero-four-five, sir!'

Ransome crossed to the opposite side of the bridge and grimaced as his bare arm touched the steel plating. It felt like an oven door.

He levelled his glasses above the screen and watched the flotilla taking station again for the next sweep, the hoisted black balls showing they were trailing their wires to port.

Their formation keeping was so good now that they could all have been connected by a cable, he thought. He moved the glasses along the echelon of dazzle-painted hulls, the occasional flash of colour from the little flags on their scurrying Oropesa floats. Then Ransome trained his glasses directly astern. How unreal it all looked. More like an ocean than the approaches to Malta. They had begun sweeping at dawn as they had the previous day; now it was halfway through the forenoon watch. There was no horizon, and the great expanse of water was like pale blue milk, rising only slowly in a shallow swell. The sky had no colour at all, and the sun, although covered by haze, shone brilliant white like a furnace bar.

The men working aft with the sweep wire or employed about the upper deck were almost naked, their bodies either brown or uncomfortably reddened in these unfamiliar surroundings. So different from the North Sea and the English Channel, Ransome thought.

It was almost impossible to believe that the purple blur barely visible astern was actually Malta, that these very waters had been fought over continuously since the retreat from Greece and the start of the real desert war against Rommel. The seabed was littered with wrecks, ships of every size, from carriers to tiny sloops, even China River gunboats which had been sent to bolster up the embattled fleet and had soon paid the price for it. Ships of Rudyard Kipling's navy against Stuka dive-bombers, E-boats, and crack Italian cruisers.

And now it was as if the war had never been. In the first dawn light they had headed past a vast fleet of minesweeping trawlers, of the kind which had kept the channels open around Britain since the beginning; many of them were veterans of that war, of Dunkirk and the ill-fated Norwegian campaign.

Ransome had been standing on the bridge, his first cup of tea in his hands as they had pounded through the scattered fleet of trawlers. It had reminded him of a picture his mother still treasured, of a Japanese fishing flotilla with Fujiyama in the background. The same unlikely sea and mist, the ships like models above their own seemingly unmoving images.

Rob Roy was steering north-east; the coast of Sicily lay about forty miles away. Just months ago this area had been dominated by the Luftwaffe, the killing-ground for any vessel which had dared to make for Malta with food and supplies.

Overnight, or so it seemed now, all that had changed. Malta was relieved, new airstrips had been hastily laid there by the Americans so that daily fighter patrols could be maintained.

He heard Sherwood speaking with Morgan as they pored over the chart-table together. A good team now that they were at sea again.

Sherwood had apologised for his behaviour on the night of the party. Ransome had left it at that. Whatever had happened to throw Sherwood off balance seemed to be under control once more. That was part of his trouble. He held himself stretched out like a wire. He only appeared to be content when he was working.

Ransome looked aft to the quarterdeck and saw Richard Wakely with his cameraman speaking with Hargrave beside the new winch. He saw him smile as he put on a steel helmet, then point, squinting at the sky, while his cameraman recorded the moment. Even without using his binoculars Ransome could sense the first lieutenant's embarrassment as the little act continued. Necessary probably, but somehow cheap against those sailors who were watching, who had seen the real thing far too often. Was that the real reason for Vice-Admiral Hargrave's insistence that Wakely should be in *Rob Roy*? So that his own son could get some of the limelight, if any was ever left by Wakely?

Ransome crossed to the forepart of the bridge and trained his glasses ahead. The sea was empty, rising and falling so slowly, as if it was breathing. Nothing. Not even a gull or a leaping fish.

But there were mines here, or had been until this massive sweep had been mounted. British, Italian, German, it was a veritable deathtrap for any ship too large to avoid them. Yet many had braved the minefields; submarines had crept through that silent forest of rusty wires with their obscene iron globes, to carry aid to Malta. They had had to lie submerged in the harbour throughout the day to avoid air attacks which could be mounted in minutes from both Sicily and the Italian mainland. Then at night they would unload their precious cargoes of fuel and ammunition, tinned food, and anything else they could cram into their hulls. Even their torpedo tubes had been used to carry vital supplies although it left the submarines without teeth for the hazardous journey back to base. Many did not make it.

Rob Roy alone had put up twenty mines in these waters so far; *Ranger* had swept three more than that. If you were lucky it was a whole lot easier than in the Channel, with its troublesome currents and fierce tides. Here at least it was non-tidal, and if you picked up a mine – Ransome did not continue on that train of thought.

He said, 'Another hour?'

Sherwood looked at him. His hair was even more bleached by the sun.

'Near enough, sir.' He glanced at the glistening water. 'Surely they must know what's happening?'

Ransome nodded. Probably what every Jack in the flotilla was thinking. The enemy, silent and unseen, must have known for weeks what to expect.

He replied, 'Four days from now.' He thought about the pack of intelligence reports and plans in his cabin safe. The sea was empty, and yet from Gibraltar and the battered North African ports where *Rob Roy* had refuelled, and from

Alexandria in the Eastern Mediterranean, the huge fleet of landing-ships and their protectors was massing for this one-off assault on Sicily.

He added, 'They're probably more worried than we are.'

Richard Wakely appeared on the bridge ladder, his round face dripping with sweat.

'What a day, eh, Captain?' He mopped his feathers with a spotted silk handkerchief. 'Just a few more shots in case the light changes, I think.' He beamed to the bridge at large. 'I don't want to leave anything out!'

Sherwood had replaced the dark glasses he often wore on the bridge.

'You must have seen quite a lot of different types of action.'

Wakely smiled gravely. 'That's true, I suppose. I've been lucky.'

Sherwood asked, 'Did you ever run across a Brigadier de Courcey in the Western Desert, sir?' He seemed suddenly very intent. 'Alex de Courcey?'

Wakely mopped his throat vigorously. 'Can't say I have. But then I meet so many, y'know.' He looked at Sherwood for the first time. 'You know him?'

'Friend of my late father, actually. They used to shoot together.'

'I see.' He turned away. 'Must be off. Still a lot to do.' He called for his cameraman. 'Where *are* you, Andy?'

When he had gone Ransome asked quietly. 'What was all that about?'

Sherwood removed his glasses and polished them with his shirt. His eyes looked bitter.

'He knows who I'm talking about, right enough, or he should. Alex became a staff officer after he was promoted out of the tanks. He told my father all about Richard Wakely in the early days in France when he was a tank commander.'

'I take it you don't care much for him?' Ransome added sharply, 'Come on, spit it out, man!'

Sherwood glanced briefly at the nearest bridge look-out. The man was crouching by his mounted binoculars, his eyes protected from the glare by a frame of deeply tinted glass. He was apparently out of earshot.

'Wakely's a phoney, a complete fraud. Never went near the front line the whole time. After Dunkirk he shot off to the States to protect his precious skin.' He faced Ransome and gave an apologetic smile. 'That's what he said.'

Ransome climbed on to his chair and winced from the contact.

'You are too cynical by half.'

Sherwood glanced at the ladder as if he expected to see Wakely there, listening.

'That famous broadcast from El Alamein.' He shook his head. 'I'll bet he did it from his suite at Shepheard's in Cairo!'

They both turned as Leading Signal Mackay shouted, 'Signal from *Dunlin*, sir! *My catch, I think*!'

Ransome strode to the opposite gratings and steadied his binoculars against the slow roll.

He watched the stab of *Dunlin's* signal lamp, the bright hoist of flags breaking from her yard.

'Signal *Dryaden* to close on *Dunlin*.'

Ransome ignored the clatter of the signal lamp, the stir of excitement around the bridge. *One more time. Should be all right*. He shifted his glasses on to the graceful Icelandic trawler and saw the mounting white moustache of her bow wave as she increased speed, her marksmen already up forward in readiness to dispense with yet another would-be killer.

'There it is, sir! *Dunlin's* quarter!' There was an ironic cheering from aft and Ransome wondered if Wakely's cameraman was recording the moment.

Leading Signalman Mackay was using the old telescope, his lips moving silently as he spelled out another signal.

'From *Scythe*, sir. *Senior Officer closing from the south-west*.'

Ransome waited for *Dryaden* to forge ahead until he could train his glasses astern again.

So Bliss was moving up to join them. He had been content to stay with the main force of minesweeping trawlers until now. A compliment or a snub, it was hard to say.

'From *Bedworth*, sir!' Mackay braced his legs wide apart. '*Aircraft approaching from the north*!'

Ransome let his glasses fall to his chest. 'Acknowledge.' His mind seemed to click into place, to remind him of Sherwood's earlier words. *They must know what's happening.*

He said, 'Inform the first lieutenant, recover sweep immediately.'

He stared at the red button below the screen, the metal around it worn smooth by all those other emergencies.

They might think he was losing his grip. Going round the bend at last. Plenty had.

He vaguely heard a cheer, then the rattle of small-arms fire as *Dryaden*'s marksmen punctured the released mine and sent it on its way to the bottom.

Too careful, or like the ill-fated *Viper*'s captain had been, too bloody confident for his own good?

He did not realise he was speaking aloud as he exclaimed! 'They can think what they bloody well like!' Then he pressed down the button and heard the shriek of alarm bells coming up the rank of voicepipes.

'*Action Stations! Action Stations*!'

The calm was shattered, the momentary interest of a mine made harmless forgotten, as the barebacked figures scampered to their stations, groping for anti-flash gear and helmets, making sure their lifebelts were tied loosely around their bodies.

All down the line the alarm was picked up, and Ransom felt the hull shiver as the new winch hauled on the sweep wire like an angler with a giant marlin.

'Short-range weapons crews closed up!'

'Coxswain on the wheel!'

'Main armament closed up.' The latter was Bunny Fallows' voice on the intercom, his Scots accent strangely noticeable.

So many reports for so small a ship.

Ransome dragged his white-covered cap from beneath a locker and tugged it across his ruffled hair.

'From *Bedworth*, sir. *Do not engage*.'

Sherwood muttered. 'Must be some of ours after all.'

Ransome felt chilled despite the unwavering heat. If there was such a thing as instinct, he had never felt so certain.

'Aircraft, sir!' Red one-one-oh! Angle of sight – '

Ransome gripped his glasses until they hurt his fingers; he did not hear the rest. Did not need to.

There they were, not just two or three, but maybe a dozen or more, strung out against the empty sky in a fine curve, catching the sunlight like chips of bright glass.

'*Start tracking!*'

Sherwood was watching the tiny slivers with his binoculars. Young Morgan looked up from the chart-table. 'Heading for Malta, d'you think?'

Sherwood did not turn. 'Not this time. It's us they're after.'

Ransome said, 'Signal *Dryaden* to drop dan buoys *now*.' Someone would have to complete the sweep after this was over. He watched the leading aircraft, still without shape, as it began to turn, until it appeared to be flying straight towards him.

'Warn the engine-room. Full revs when I give the word.'

Richard Wakely's voice broke through the chilled concentration.

'What the *hell's* happening?'

Sherwood still did not take his eyes off the plane.

'Some good shots are coming up, sir. We are about to be attacked.'

'Alter-Course signal from *Bedworth*, sir. *Steer zero-nine-zero in succession.*'

Ransome nodded. 'Bring her round.' It had been a near thing. If Bliss had not had a change of heart the whole flotilla might have ended up in a minefield with their sweeps snug and useless on deck.

'*Here they come!*'

'*Full ahead together! Starboard twenty!*'

Ransome felt the gratings bounding under his shoes. They were going to attack from astern, and use the sun's glare to best advantage. Pictures flashed through his mind. The old instructor who had said, 'Always watch out for the Hun wot comes out of the sun!' Of David down aft where Hargrave was, the suddenness of his death, the women in black, and the girl who had looked like Eve.

He closed his mind against all of them. This was his purpose for being. Nothing else must matter now.

'Midships! *Steady!*'

He saw Morgan crouched behind the gyro repeater, a boatswain's mate cocking one of the old stripped Lewis guns they had 'borrowed' from the army. Even the cook would be down there with the damage-control party or helping the doctor. There were no passengers in *Rob Roy*.

He thought suddenly of Moncrieff and his last words about the ship he had loved above all others.

Ransome pounded the rail beneath the screen as the revolutions continued to mount in time with the increasing vibration.

'Come on, old girl – for him if not for me!'

Of course the enemy knew. No minesweepers meant no invasion, not until they were ready to repel it.

Wakely called, his voice shrill, 'What shall I do, for God's sake?'

Sherwood smiled as he picked up the parallel rulers, which had jerked to the deck from the shaking chart-table.

'What about a nice hymn, sir?'

*

The wheelhouse seemed to shrink as the door was clipped shut, and all but the slitted observation panels slammed into place.

Boyes wedged himself in a corner by the plot-table, his eyes everywhere as he tried to form a picture of what was happening, what had begun with the sudden scream of alarm bells.

Midshipman Davenport was leaning over the plot and making some adjustments for a new chart. His shirt was plastered to his spine by sweat, and Boyes could see it dripping on the chart from his face. Beckett was on the wheel as usual, the quatermasters manning the engine and revolution telegraphs. A messenger crouched by the emergency handset, and through the bell-mouthed voicepipe by Beckett's head Boyes could hear much of what was said on the upper bridge.

He heard the captain call for full speed, the deft movements of the waitings hands near the wheel, then Beckett's harsh reply, 'Both engines full ahead, sir!'

Faintly through the open intercom he heard Fallows' voice. 'All guns load with semi-armour-piercing – '

Then the captain's intervention, curt but seemingly untroubled.

Fallows mumbled, 'Sorry, sir, I mean high-explosive!'

Beckett turned aside from the voicepipe. 'Poor old Bunny's lost 'is bottle!'

Boyes whispered, 'How many, d'you think, er, sir?'

Davenport peered at him, his eyes wild. 'How the hell should I know? Just shut up and wait for orders!'

Boyes found to his astonishment that Davenport's tirade left him unmoved. At the same instant he realised he was unafraid. That really did surprise him.

The captain's voice sounded different; he was speaking directly to the engine-room.

'I know that, Chief, but I want everything you've got. *Now.*' There was the merest hesitation, and he was heard to add, 'Bale out if I give the words. No heroics, right?'

Davenport opened and closed his fists, his voice thick with disbelief. '*Bale out?*'

Leading Seaman Reeve clung to a shuddering telegraph and said cheerfully, 'Better swim than fry, sir!'

Right aft by the second four-inch gun, Lieutenant Hargrave shaded his eyes in the glare to watch the damage-control party taking cover, the Buffer calling out last minute instructions.

It was getting harder to hear anything clearly. The wake frothing up from the racing screws had risen level with the deck, and spray surged over the sides as if they were sinking by the stern. He saw the other ships astern, some making too much smoke, others almost lost in haze and drifting spume. He saw *Bedworth*, her yards alive with flags, turning in a wide sweep, showing all the grace of a thoroughbred as she displayed her streaming deck, the guns already pivoting round to track the target.

He said aloud, 'There they are, Buffer! Port quarter!' He felt a catch in his throat. 'God Almighty!'

The Buffer sucked his monkey-teeth and watched the tiny, glinting aircraft through slitted eyes.

He saw 'Gipsy' Guttridge, gunlayer on the four-inch, looking down at him, like a member of some forgotten monastic order in his anti-flash hood. As he turned his controls effortlessly in his strong hands he was singing quietly to himself, the words set against a well-known hymn.

> 'Six days a man shall work
> as long as he is able,
> and on the seventh shall scrub the deck
> and holystone the cable – '

They grinned at one another and the buffer called, 'That's bloody true, Gipsy!'

The gunnery speaker crackled into life, 'Aircraft starboard quarter! Angle of sight three-oh!'

The gunlayer and trainer spun their polished wheels and Gutteridge muttered, 'I just 'ope Bunny's got *that* bloody right!'

The speaker again. '*Barrage – commence – commence – commence!*'

Hargrave watched the other ships astern open fire, the sky suddenly filled with drifted balls of dirty smoke, then as the leading aircraft burst into view above their mastheads, the livid tracer and the steady thud-thud-thud of pom-poms added their weight to the barrage.

'*Shoot!*'

The four-inch recoiled violently and the breech was wrenched open, streaming cordite fumes before the shock-wave had receded.

'Gunlayer, target!' Then, 'Trainer, target!' And another sharp explosion cracked out towards the aircraft.

Hargrave heard a tremendous explosion, felt it punch against the hull like a ram, and saw a column of water beginning to fall. It looked as if it was right beside the third minesweeper, but they were still afloat, following in a sharp turn as *Rob Roy*'s rudder went over for a violent zigzag.

An aircraft just seemed to materialise right over Hargrave's head. It must have dived low after dropping a bomb, and he saw the stabbing flashes of its machine-gun fire, and gasped as the Buffer grabbed his arm and pulled him against the hot steel.

'Watch out, sir! That bugger's taken a real dislike to you!'

Hargrave tried to smile, but his mouth felt like leather. He saw the twin-engined plane roaring away ahead, pursued by bright balls of tracer, and one very near-miss from 'A' Gun. He even saw the black crosses, so stark on either wing, streaks of oil near the open bomb-bay doors.

He took a grip of himself. 'Nobody hurt?'

The Buffer pointed. 'They're attacking from both sides, sir!'

Hargrave saw Kellett, the P.O. steward, still wearing his white jacket, hurrying to the opposite side, a Bren gun cradled in his arms as he squinted at the sky.

The Buffer sighed. 'Where's the bloody RAF now that we need 'em?'

'*Shoot!*'

Hargrave winced as another plane roared down through the gunsmoke. His ears throbbed as if they would never hear again, and his eyes felt raw from the constant firing.

Brrrrrrr! He heard the harsh rattle of machine-gun fire, and stared at the advancing feathers of white spray until the metal clanged and cracked across the deck like a rivet-gun.

One of the damage-control party was down, kicking wildly, blood everywhere, so bright and unreal in the hazy glare.

The Buffer yelled, '*Get that man!*' He glanced at Hargrave. 'You be okay, 'ere, sir?' Then he was gone, his stocky figure pushing men where they were needed, pausing to restrain the wounded seaman as 'Pansy' Masefield, his red-cross satchel bouncing from one hip, appeared from nowhere.

'Nasty, Pansy.' The buffer grinned at the wounded man, whose eyes were filled with dread, like a terrified child's. 'But we've seen worse, eh?'

Masefield glared at him then beckoned to his assistants. 'Take him to the *real* doctor, chop-chop!' Then he patted the wounded man's face and said gently, 'You'll be fine, Jenner. I've stopped the bleeding.'

The hull swayed as the wheel went over again, and a great shadow swept above them like some nightmare seabird.

The Buffer looked for Hargrave. It was as if he had never moved. He turned to the plane again, even saw the bomb as it tumbled untidily from its belly.

He watched it with tired resignation. Why here, he seemed to ask. Why now?

From his position on the upper bridge Ransome saw the bomb too. '*Hard a-port!*' He gripped the voicepipe as the wheel went over and the ship seemed to reel to the thrust of screws and rudder.

'Thirty-five of port wheel on, sir!'

He heard men gasping and slipping as *Rob Roy* continued to pivot round, and he thanked God, not for the first time, that she had twin screws.

The bomb, which seemed to fall so haphazardly, suddenly righted itself and appeared to gather speed as it hurtled down while the plane, a Messerschmidt 110 fighter-bomber, bellowed low over the bridge, cannon-fire and machine-gun bullets raking the forecastle while the Oerlikons continued to pursue it with tracer.

The explosion felt as if the ship was being lifted bodily from the sea, and for a few seconds Ransome feared the worst, and prepared to stop engines before his ship charged headlong for the seabed. Then the towering column of water from the explosion fell. It was like something solid, as if the ship had been engulfed by a tidal wave.

He heard himself coughing and retching, trying to keep on his feet as water surged through the bridge and crashed to the deck below. As he wiped the spray and stinging salt from his eyes he saw a fireball suspended in space, then droplets of flame breaking away, to speckle the sea's face with bright feathers.

As his hearing returned he heard men cheering, and realised that the ME 110 must have been caught in the cross-fire even as the bomb had exploded so near to the ship.

Voicepipes crackled on every side and Ransome looked quickly to make certain his small team was still intact.

Sherwood was hanging on to the gyro repeater while Morgan was groping for the remains of his chart and scattered instruments. Leading Signalman Mackay was peering at his telescope and saw Ransome's glance. 'No damage, sir, thank God!'

The ship or his precious telescope, it was hard to tell.

'Bring her back on course!' Ransome wiped his sodden binoculars and peered astern. The aircraft were gone, the edge of their attack blunted at the sight of their companion's horrible end.

Cease-fire gongs were ringing, and he saw figures emerging from cover, as if dazed by their survival.

'Report damage and casualties.' Ransome looked at the sea ahead, the small fragments of the ME 110. There would be no survivors.

'First lieutenant for you, sir!' The boatswain's mate had put down his stripped Lewis, and Ransome noticed that there were several empty magazines by his feet.

'Captain here.'

'No damage, sir.' Hargrave sounded muzzy, a hundred miles away. 'One casualty. Ordinary Seaman Jenner. Not serious.' He hesitated. 'You all right, sir?'

But Ransome handed the telephone to the boatswain's mate and raised his glasses again.

The cheering had died away and some of the gun crews had left their stations to line the guardrails and watch.

Like a crude memorial, Ransome thought later. The forward section of a minesweeper seemed to rise amongst the others, pointing towards the white sun, the sea boiling around the hull like steam. Huge, obscene bubbles and a spreading blanket of escaping oil fuel. A ship dying. One of their own.

Morgan said huskily, 'It's *Scythe*, sir.'

Mackay called, 'From *Bedworth*, sir. *Senja will search for survivors.*'

Ransome nodded as he watched the upright hull, feeling the pain, wanting her to go, to get it over with. He could see her young captain, a mere lieutenant who had held the command for four months. Was he alive, he wondered? If so, how could he get over it?

'No damage below, sir. Engine-room request permission to reduce speed.'

'Very well. Half ahead together. Signal *Bedworth* and tell them what we're doing.' He spoke without emotion, as if he had none left to give.

Feet scraped on the ladder and Rickard Wakely, his eyes almost bulging from his head, dragged himself into the bridge.

'Is it over?' He stared round, his chest rising and falling as if he was about to have a seizure.

Ransome said, 'For some reason it is.' He steeled himself as the broken ship began to sink very slowly, stern-first, tiny figures struggling in the filth of oil and worse while the big Norwegian trawler *Senja* manoeuvred almost against the wreckage.

Ransome gritted his teeth together. They should have had air cover, but perhaps there was none to spare after all, or it was all being used to protect the troop convoys. The same German ME 110's had probably made a strike against those minesweeping trawlers they had seen in the dawn light.

Someone let out a sob as *Scythe* seemed to drop very suddenly from view. They heard several dull explosions, and more flotsam burst to the surface as if to torment further the gasping survivors.

Ransome turned his back and looked at the ship.

That violent turn had saved her. *This time.* Otherwise he and all the rest of them might be out there trying to keep afloat; waiting to die.

He saw Sherwood's eyes, Morgan's honest features twisted in pity and despair,

Mackay gripping his telescope, his eyes smarting but not from the sun. *One of their own.*

The Buffer appeared on the bridge, his battered cap hiding his expression.

'Beg pardon, sir, but Jimmy – I mean the first lieutenant is askin' for orders. I think our phone 'as gone dead on us, like. The Gunner (T) 'as got one of his torpedomen on the job.' He looked around until his glance settled on Wakely.

'They've gone 'ome, sir.' He barely hid the contempt in his voice.

Ransome could feel the shock and despair closing its grip on all of them. It was often like that.

'Orders, Buffer?' He dragged out his pipe and prayed to God his fingers would not shake as he tamped down a fill of tobacco. 'We shall resume sweeping to port in fifteen minutes. What did you expect?'

Their eyes met, each man in his own way needing the other.

The Buffer grinned. 'From you, sir, nothin' but the best!'

Ransome looked away. They had come through again.

Nothing but the best.

13

Husky

The tiny chart-room which adjoined Ransome's sea-cabin was unbearably sticky and humid. Condensation ran down the sides and dripped from the deckhead to add to the discomfort of the officers who were squeezed around the table.

Ransome glanced through the solitary open scuttle. The light was strange, the sky like smoky bronze. He waited for the deck to lift, to roll uncomfortably to starboard in a steep corkscrew motion. Anyone with a weak stomach would know it by now, he thought.

It was like a warning, an omen. From first light the weather had started to deteriorate with a wind strengthening from the north-west. It was unusual for July – the one flaw in all the planning and preparations for Operation Husky.

It was now late afternoon and the wind had risen still further, so that the angry, choppy sea had changed to a parade of crumbling rollers.

How could they hope for any sort of success? With a heavy sea running many of the landing-craft would never reach their objectives in time; some could be swamped with terrible loss of life.

He glanced up at their intent faces. Hargrave, more tanned than any of them, always clean and tidy no matter what was happening. Sherwood, eyes hidden by his pale lashes, examining the chart with its transparent overlay of Ransome's secret orders, the coloured markers which had to be translated into action – into results.

Sub-Lieutenant Morgan, his body swaying easily to the sickening plunge and roll, had his pad already half-filled with notes. As assistant navigator he was directly involved. Surgeon Lieutenant Cusack was also present, his intelligent features and keen eyes recording everything. Beyond the bulkhead, voices murmured from the duty watch, clicks and groans of steel under pressure, the endless stammer of morse and static from the W/T office.

Ransome said, 'The first landings are due to take place at 2:45 tomorrow morning.' He felt his words move around the chart table like a chill breeze through reeds. Not some hazy plan any more, some grand design, but right here, and just ten hours away.

Sherwood said, 'They'll have to call it off, sir.' He looked up, his eyes searching. 'Won't they?'

Ransome pointed at the chart. 'Every flotilla and convoy is assembling at this moment to the east and south of Malta. It involves hundreds of ships, thousands of men. The RAF and the American Air Force have been pounding the enemy airfields and defences for weeks. Everything was set fair – the High Command allowed just twenty-four hours to cancel the whole operation or give the go-ahead.' He heard the wind howl around the super structure, the blown spray lashing the bridge like a tropical downpour. It made a mockery of all the plans and hopes. 'If this wind holds out, the Americans making for the southern shore will be hard put to get their landing-craft in position.' His hand moved to Sicily's south-eastern coastline. 'Here the Eighth Army will land with the Canadians on their left flank. The Royal Marine Commando will go ashore to the left of the Canadians slightly earlier than H-Hour to seize vital objectives which otherwise might cover the landings.'

Hargrave rubbed his chin. 'I can't see it going ahead, sir.' He looked at the open scuttle and the strange, angry place. 'It would be a shambles.'

Ransome nodded. 'It could be a greater one if they try to cancel Husky at the last moment, Number One. There would be even more confusion, some might not even get the signal on time and attack without knowing they were unsupported. And if the assault was delayed for another day, the landings would be ragged, ill-timed. I think most of us know what that would mean.' He let his words sink in. 'The Met people were caught with their pants down, but then so were the enemy.' He forced a smile. 'It's not much, but it's all we have. Our role is to give a close support to the first wave of landing-craft under cover of a bombardment from the heavy boys.' He glanced at Cusack. 'You'll be dealing with the wounded if there are any – troops, sailors, anyone we pick up.'

Cusack nodded. 'I thought there was a catch in it.'

Sherwood smiled. 'Ain't that the truth!'

The others relaxed slightly. Ransome pictured those on watch, Fallows and young Tritton, Bone and Campbell, and all the rest. They had no say in any of it. They obeyed. It had to be enough.

Hargrave asked, 'When shall we know, sir?'

Ransome looked at the bulkhead clock. 'There will be airborne attacks on certain objectives, gliders and parachutists all with precise instructions on their objectives. They will be taking off from their bases in Tunisia this evening. After that – ' He did not need to finish.

Instead he said, 'This is just a small ship, a minute part of what might be a great campaign. Most of our people are little more than boys. I'll bet that fifty percent were still at school when Hitler marched into Poland, and even after that.

Give them all you've got. They deserve it.' He dragged a folded signal pad from his hip-pocket and flattened it on the chart.

'This is part of a signal from the C-in-C, Admiral Cunningham. I think you should hear it.'

He read it slowly, very conscious of the wind's deathly moan, the stillness around the table, the ship around all of them.

'On every commanding officer, officer and rating rests the individual and personal duty of ensuring that no flinching in determination or failure of effort on his own part will hamper this great enterprise.'

He looked up, expecting some witty cynicism from Sherwood or Cusack, but it fell to the young Welshman, Morgan, to say what they were all really thinking.

He said simply, 'Like Trafalgar in a way, see? Nothing grand, just the right words – ' He fell silent as the others looked at him.

Ransome said quietly, 'Tell your departments. I want, no, I *need* them all to understand – '

They filed out and Ransome sat for some time before opening his oilskin pouch and adding the last lines of the letter she might never read, or after tomorrow might never wish to.

Then he made his way to the upper bridge and watched the sea curling back from the bows, the spray bursting through the hawse-pipes and flooding the scuppers. Huddled shapes in oilskins, sweating despite the constant soaking, men at their guns and look-out stations. Men he knew.

The rest of the flotilla were like ghost ships in the bursting wave-crests and driven spray, the formation smaller now without *Scythe*. Already that seemed like a month ago instead of days. And tomorrow – what then? He saw *Bedworth* butting diagonally across the waves, her forecastle slicing through the troughs so that her solitary bow-chaser appeared detached from the rest of the ship as the foam surged around it.

He heard angry voices, the sharpness of resentment from men who were busy enough trying to prepare themselves for tomorrow. Richard Wakely stormed across the bridge, his shirt plastered to his body like another skin, oblivious to his hair, which was all anyhow in the blown spray.

'What are you doing, Captain?' He peered across the smeared screen. 'That's *Bedworth*!'

Ransome looked at him, feeling neither anger nor pity. 'It is.'

'I want – ' Wakely clung to a stanchion as the bows dipped again, and water thundered past 'A' Gun and along either sidedeck. 'I demand to be transferred to that ship at *once*!' When Ransome remained silent he shouted, 'You sent that injured sailor across to her! Don't deny that!'

Ransome thought of Ordinary Seaman Jenner. He had left the bridge to see him swayed over to the destroyer lashed in a stretcher. He might well lose his left foot. it depended how soon *Bedworth* had been able to transfer him to one of the big transports. But he would live. Ransome had taken his hand and had been shocked to hear the youngster plead despairingly, 'I don't want to go, sir! I'm with me mates here!' All that had happened, and he still wanted to stay in *Rob Roy*.

The memory touched his mind like a hot wire and he said sharply, 'He actually asked to stay aboard, Mr Wakely, did you know that?' He saw some of the watchkeepers turn to listen but did not care. 'God, I'd have sent you with pleasure, believe me, but the S.N.O. thought otherwise!' He waved his arm across the dripping metal, only then aware that he had forgotten to put on an oilskin. 'You wanted to see our war – well, that is precisely what you will be doing!'

Wakely stared at him as if he could not believe his ears. 'You don't know what you're saying! I'll see that you regret this!'

Ransome turned away. 'I hope so. That will mean that we've both survived. *Now get off my bridge.*'

He heard feet slithering down the ladder and then Hargrave coughed politely. 'I think he got the message, sir.'

Ransome breathed out slowly, and wiped his streaming face with his forearm.

Then he stood up on the gratings and held the top of the screen with both hands.

He said, 'Feel it? The wind's started to drop, Number One.' He had his head on one side like old Jack Weese did in the boatyard when he was gauging the day's weather.

He swung round and looked at the glistening bridge. It was like hearing a voice. The ship, perhaps?

He said, 'So it's on. No turning back.'

'You knew, didn't you, sir?'

'I'm not sure. Just a feeling.' He shrugged and repeated, 'Not sure.'

Leading Signalman Mackay watched the *Bedworth* just in case she might want to talk. He had heard every word, and earlier had seen the skipper leave his bridge to see the lad Jenner over the side.

Of course he knew. That was why *Rob Roy* was still afloat when so many others were so much scrap.

It made him feel better, and he began to hum a forgotten tune to himself.

By the time darkness finally closed over the flotilla the tension had become like something physical. Reports and requests whispered up and down the voicepipes and telephones, like nerve-ends; and in each ship those ends led directly to her captain.

Ransome made himself remain in one corner of the bridge where he was within reach of the voicepipes, but able to watch the faint outline of *Ranger*, which was steering about two cables to starboard.

Bedworth had ordered the fleet minesweepers to form two small columns, with the big trawlers following up astern.

Ranger's outline was little more than a jagged edge of lively spray around her stem, the occasional glassy shine of her hull as she rolled in a deep trough.

An hour earlier they had passed a slow-moving formation of landing-ships, butting through the choppy seas like huge, ungainly shoe-boxes. They were the first they had seen, and it was still hard to accept that the sixty miles of water between Malta and Sicily was probably packed with landing-craft, transports and heavily armed escorts.

Landing-craft of any size were difficult to handle even in calm seas. What it must be like for them in this wind, which had still not completely died, did not bear thinking about. They had had little chance to operate and manoeuvre together before as they had been needed for the build-up of men and stores, tanks and armoured fighting vehicles. Most of them were commanded by youngsters, RNVR officers like Sherwod and Morgan, who were standing side by side near the chart-table.

And what of the troops, Ransome wondered? Many of them must surely be sick from this savage motion, and in no fit state to charge ashore into God alone knew what the Germans had waiting for them. The tank crews would be in no doubt. When exercising with the army along the Welsh coast Ransome had heard a tank commander explain exactly what happened if one of their number would not start, or broke down at the moment of disembarking.

He had said with all the casual experience of a 23-year-old, 'You just shove the poor bugger ahead of you into the drink!'

'Radar – bridge.'

'Bridge?' That was young Tritton, the other Bunny, facing up to something he could barely imagine.

'*Bedworth* is taking up station astern, sir.'

Ransome nodded. 'I heard that.' Bliss was preparing to place himself in the best strategic position, where he could watch the supporting craft as well as the landing-ships when they eventually gridironed through to the beaches.

Ransome fixed the picture of the chart in his mind. He had studied it until he thought he could draw it blindfold.

As if to jar at his nerves the radar reported, 'Headland at three-five-zero. Ten miles.'

Ransome peered at his watch. 'Shut down all transmissions. This weather seems to have kept the Eyetie patrols in their beds, but the R.D.F. will still be working.' Somebody, probably Mackay, gave a chuckle. It was something.

Sherwood called, 'That will be Cape Passero, sir.' He sounded pleased. 'Right on the button.'

Ransome wished he could smoke his pipe. *Rob Roy* was leading her little pack and might be the first to come under fire. It was still better than groping blindly astern. The night could play cruel tricks on the watchkeepers. You would stare at the ship ahead so hard that it would vanish like a mirage. You might panic and increase speed to catch her, only to see her looming up beneath your stem. Terrible moments with the added knowledge that the vessel astern of you might well be charging in pursuit, her bows like a giant cleaver.

Ransome pictured his men around the ship. Hargrave down aft to oversee the guns there and take charge of damage-control. He would doubtless prefer to be here on the bridge, but the old lesson of too many eggs in one basket was never more true than in a ship at action stations. Mr Bone, grim and resentful, and no doubt clicking his dentures, would be ready to assist with anything but an act of God. And beneath all of them, Campbell with his team, sealed in their oily, thundering world, protected from the sea or a torpedo by steel plate little thicker than plywood. Fallows brooding over his mistake during the air attack; Cusack in the wardroom with his senior S.B.A., Pansy, waiting, probably as young Morgan had pictured it, as they had off Cape Trafalgar, their instruments rattling impatiently.

He thought too of Midshipman Davenport, with Boyes, manning the plot-table in the wheelhouse. Two boys from the same school, but a thousand miles distant from each other. After this, Davenport would be ready to pick up his first ring. But not in *Rob Roy*, which was just as well.

Sherwood said, 'Time sir.'

'Very well.' Ransome crossed to the central voicepipe.

'Revolutions for half-speed, Cox'n.'

He could picture Beckett without effort, even though he had never seen him at the wheel. Part of his own strength, like Campbell and the horny Buffer.

'Revolutions one-one-zero, sir.'

Ransome made to move away but asked, 'All right down there, Cox'n?'

He heard a laugh. 'Yeh, sir, like bugs in a pusser's blanket!'

Ransome moved to his chair and leaned against it, feeling the deck shiver and sway with each thrash of the screws.

Less than ten miles. The enemy's coastal batteries could doubtless shoot this far.

He looked up at the stars as they flitted between the pale clouds. Like that moment at Plymouth, he thought, the darkened outline of Codrington House through the rustling trees. Her mouth against his, his arm around her shoulders. Would she know what he was doing? Could the fate or whatever it was which had brought them together, tell her that too?

'*Aircraft*, sir!'

Ransome swung round. 'Bearing?'

'Not certain, sir!' The man was swinging his powerful nightglasses in a full arc. 'P'raps I was wrong, but it *was* a sound.' He nodded firmly, 'I'm sure of it, sir.'

Ransome touched his arm as he passed him. The seaman was one of the best look-outs. It was why he was here on the bridge.

Sherwood joined in. On every ship heads would be twisting round, men dragging off helmets or woolly hats so that their hearing would not be distorted or tricked.

Sherwood suggested quietly, 'Bombers?'

Ransome stood away from the side and cupped his hands behind his ears. 'Shouldn't be. Wrong direction.' He stared at him through the darkness. 'Those gliders we heard about?'

Sherwood shook his head. 'No, sir. Too far out. They're supposed to be letting them off their towlines somewhere in a fifty-mile drop area inland, according to my notes.'

'Aircraft, sir!' The seaman lurched back from his night-glasses, and no wonder.

It was like some great bat, black against the stars and reaching out across the slow-moving ship as if about to seize her from the water.

Someone shouted, 'For Christ's sake, they've released them in the wrong place!'

Ransome felt his face stiffen as the huge glider passed directly overhead, the air rushing over its wings like a great wind through a forest. There was another glider directly behind it, swaying wildly as its pilot realised what had happened.

The strong headwind, a last-moment miscalculation, or inexperience; it was all too late now.

They heard the first glider smash into the sea, even saw the white spectres of spray as one of the wings was ripped away by the terrible impact. Ransome tried not to see it in his mind. The airborne troops packed inside, loaded down with weapons and equipment.

Tritton's voice broke into his thoughts. 'First lieutenant, sir!' He sounded shocked out of his wits, and huddled down as another glider tore overhead and then dipped heavily towards the water.

Ransome asked, 'What does he want?' When Tritton remained silent he shouted, '*Pull yourself together*!'

Tritton replied in a small voice, 'Requests permission to lower rafts and scrambling-nets, sir.'

Ransome turned away, his mind cringing as another glider hit the waves and flopped over in a great welter of spray. Men were dying, drowning, not knowing why or how.

He heard himself say, 'Denied! We are here to support the landings, not search for those who lost their way!' He did not recognise his own voice. 'One of the trawlers will carry out a sweep.'

Sherwood watched him, feeling his anguish and sharing it, perhaps for the first time.

Morgan whispered, 'God, what a decision to have to make!'

Sherwood saw some tiny pinpricks of light, far away abeam. Lifejacket lamps. A common enough sight to sailors. But to those poor devils it must be a moment of horror.

'Flare, sir! Dead ahead!'

Ransome stared across the screen and saw the red flare drifting like a drip of molten steel.

He wanted to think about it, what it meant; the Royal Marines already ashore, or the Germans at last facing the reality of attack. The bridge suddenly lit up, as if a giant torch had been directed over it. Faces and fittings stood out but left the rest in darkness. The horizon astern flashed again, like lightening or a great electric storm. Ransome waited, counted seconds as they did at Dover. Then he heard the far-off roll of heavy gunfire and almost simultaneously the express roar of shells passing overhead.

Whooooosh! Then the tell-tale blink of lights from the land as the first great salvoes found their mark.

Ransome tugged his cap more firmly across his forehead and stood high on the gratings. Falling further and further astern now, the abandoned airborne soldiers – those who had survived the crashes – would hear the huge shells ripping above them from the invisible bombarding squadron, and would know they had been forgotten.

It was a madness, more terrible this time because he could not control it, but the smashed and abandoned gliders were made suddenly meaningless.

'*Slow ahead together*!'

They were committed. In minutes now the first landing-ships in this sector would be passing to starboard.

Their madness was about to begin.

Hargrave clung to the shield of the after four-inch gun and tried not to blink as the horizon flared up again and again. It was still dark, and yet in the regular flashes the fragments of the whole stood out like parts of a crazy dream.

He recalled hearing Ransome's voice in the background when he had told poor Tritton his decision. Hargrave accepted it was the right one but still wondered if he would have done the same. He had seen the great gliders hurtling out of the sky, some hanging on longer than their companions before smashing down into the sea.

Why should it seem different from any crashing aircraft? Men died every day. Hargrave rejected the argument immediately. What must those soldiers have been thinking when they realised the inevitable? All the training and preparation wasted? Or small, precious moments like the last farewell on some railway station or garden path? A wife, a child, a lover?

He winced as another massive salvo thundered overhead. There were battleships as well as cruisers back there. The navy he had been bred for. Great guns, order and discipline. The old flagship *Warspite*, the darling of the Mediterranean fleet, would most likely be adding her voice to the onslaught, and dropping her salvoes of some nine tons a minute on targets she could not even see.

The gun crew started to cheer as the pale silhouettes of landing-craft began to slide past beyond *Ranger*'s station abeam.

Hargrave snapped, 'Keep silent!', feeling their resentment but knowing that any second the communications rating might be passed an order from the bridge.

Between the thundering roar of heavy gunfire they heard the armada thrusting ahead, the choppy water surging against their blunt bows and ramps while the smaller, infantry landing-craft followed close astern as if afraid they might lose their way.

Once, just once, Hargrave heard the sound of bagpipes. What brave, crazy soldier could find the wind to play at a moment like this, he wondered? The next salvo blotted out the sound and Hargrave pictured the tanks lined up behind their steel doors, the air choking with fumes as they revved their engines. In the smaller, boxlike craft there would only be flesh and blood, eyes staring from beneath their helmets, bayonets fixed, legs braced for the moment of impact.

The Buffer appeared below him. 'I've spread the fire parties about.' He watched the lieutenant and wondered. 'Good idea of yours, sir.'

Hargrave had the great desire to yawn despite the gunfire. He dared not. Others had often told him it was the first sign of fear.

Gipsy Guttridge wiped his gunsight with his glove. 'Gettin' lighter already!'

The Buffer grunted. 'I remember once when I was in Sicily afore the war – ' He broke off as the sea exploded in a towering spire of water between the two lines of minesweepers. '*Strewth*!'

The spray drifted across the deck and Hargrave spat out the taste of cordite.

The enemy had woken up at last.

The next pattern of shells fell to port. Hargrave gripped a stanchion as the wheel went over, and the deck began to shake to an increase of speed.

He peered astern and saw *Dunlin* following her leader while the others remained shrouded in darkness.

The communications rating had his headphones pressed against his ears and did not realise he was shouting.

'Why don't we shoot! Can't we 'it the buggers?'

Gipsy Guttridge twisted round on his little seat and gave him a pitying glare. 'Wot, with *this*?' He slapped the breech. 'Like a fart in th'wind against that lot!'

More explosions threw up great columns of torn water. Against the dull sea they looked like solid icebergs. They seemed much closer, and Hargrave guessed they were around the headland now, and felt the change in the motion as the sea levelled off.

He saw dark orange flashes from the land, the occasional glitter of tracer. Too soon for the landings, so it must be the commando, or maybe some of the airborne who had found their objectives after all. Shells continued to whimper overhead but only daylight would measure their success.

Someone muttered, 'I just 'ope they know wot they're doin'!'

Gipsy Gutteridge grinned. ''Ear that, Buffer? Pathetic, ain't it? I seen more blokes killed by *our* admirals than the bloody enemy?' He looked defiantly at Hargrave's back, but the lieutenant did not rise to it.

Turnham said, 'Stow it, Gipsy, enough's enough!'

Hargrave was staring at the pale stars, the way they seemed to leave part of the sky in the darkness. He felt his heart begin to thump. It was the land, not an illusion. The high ground beyond the beaches which pointed north to Syracuse. They were that close. He gripped a stanchion as hard as he could while he assembled his thoughts. All the while, one stood out in his mind, like a voice yelling in his ear. If the captain fell today, he would be in command. *Can I do it*?

The Buffer seized his wrist. '*Down*, sir, for Gawd's sake!'

Hargrave watched the glowing ball of light as it tore across the sea barely feet above the water.

His mind had time only to record that it was a flat-trajectory shell, probably fired by an anti-tank gun of some kind, when it hit the ship like a giant hammer.

A man shouted incredulously, '*Didn't explode*! Went straight out the other side!'

Hargrave watched the second shell and waited for their luck to run out.

14

━━ ━━ ━━ ━━ ━━ ━━ ━━

Who Is the Brave?

Chief Petty Officer Joe Beckett shouted up the voicepipe, his eyes concentrating on the gyro repeater tape, 'Steady on zero-three-zero, sir? Both engines full ahead!'

Nobody else in the wheelhouse spoke now and the men at the telegraphs watched Beckett's hands on the polished spokes, and drew comfort from his strength while the hull quivered to the shock of falling shells.

Beside the plot-table Boyes gripped a fire-extinguisher bracket, as much to be doing something as to retain his balance. The ship felt as if she was moving at a tremendous speed, even though he had heard the others say often enough that she could barely manage eighteen knots with a following wind.

He stared at the others, their eyes and expressions illuminated only by the compass and indicator lights, although like the tense figures near him he had already noticed that the sky was lightening outside the bridge, the observation slits pale instead of black.

Beckett said between his teeth, 'Reckon they've landed by now, poor sods!'

Leading Seaman Reeves murmured, 'Don't feel all that bloody safe meself!'

Beckett roared, 'Close that door, you stupid oaf!'

The starboard door clanged shut again, and Boyes found himself forced painfully into his shrinking corner as Richard Wakely and his cameraman Andy crowded inside the wheelhouse.

Wakely peered anxiously round in the darkness. 'What's *happening*?'

Beckett bit back an angry retort and twisted the wheel a few spokes to hold the line steady on the gyro repeater.

It would do no good to take it out on Wakely, he thought. He was a *celebrity*, everyone knew that, and civvy or not could make a lot of trouble if he wanted to. He felt his stomach muscles tighten as the hull bounced to another explosion. Big shells from some Kraut shore battery. He gave a bitter smile. Or their own bombardment falling sort of the target. He thought of Wakely again. *Shit-scared.* But how could that be, after all he was supposed to have done? Or was that just a line of bull, the sort that old Goebbels and Lord Haw-Haw gave out on the German radio?

Midshipman Davenport stared at Wakely. 'We're under fire, sir!'

It was meant to come out like it did on the films, but Davenport sounded near to breaking-point.

Wakely looked at the plot-table, then at the other figures near the wheel. 'If they're landing troops now, why are we still being fired at?'

Beckett snapped, '*Listen*! – ' he nodded his head at the voicepipe. 'Up there on the bridge, they can tell you better than I can!'

Andy the cameraman unslung his heavy leather case. 'I'm going to get some shots as soon as it's light enough.' He was a small, rat-like man, everybody's idea of the downtrodden male, but there was no doubting his determination as he reached for one of the door-clips. He grinned. 'See you all later, gents – least I *hope* so!' Then he was gone.

Wakely exclaimed, 'Thinks he knows everything. Just because he was in Manchuria and the Spanish Civil War he imagines that – ' He broke off and ducked as a voice came down the pipe. '*Tracer to port!*'

Boyes felt the hull jerk as the shell struck the side like a fiery bolt. He did not know it, but the shell punctured the plating as if it was water and ripped across the upper messdeck and cracked through the opposite side without exploding.

Wakely cried shrilly, '*Get me out of this!*'

Beckett glared briefly at the midshipman. 'Keep that lunatic quiet, *Mr* Davenport! It's bad enough without 'im!'

The second shell hit the port wing of the bridge and ricochetted from the Oerlikon mounting before smashing into the wheelhouse. The rest, to Boyes at least, was unreal, a moment rendered motionless in time, as if his own world had stopped.

He realised that the shell had rebounded from two sides of the wheelhouse before exploding in a vivid white glare. He knew he was on his knees and thought he was screaming, the sound muffled by deafness. He felt the bite of broken glass in his fingers and knew the plot-table had been shattered to fragments; his shorts were sodden, and he wanted to cry out, to die before the agony came. He guessed from its sticky warmth that it was blood.

Beckett hung on to the wheel, his mind ringing to the explosion. In the beam of light from one of the repeaters which had had its shield blown aside, he saw Leading Seaman Reeves sliding down the steel plates, eyes wide and staring, his slow progress marked by blood until he hit the gratings and rolled over. Even in the poor light and trapped smoke he saw the hole in his back. It was big enough to put your boot inside.

Beckett felt a pain in his thigh and then the spread of fire running up his side.

But he did not fall, and the pain did not weaken his voice as he shouted, 'Wheelhouse – Bridge!'

Then Ransome's voice, very near, his lips against the bell-mouth. 'This is the captain!'

Beckett dashed sweat from his eyes and steadied the spokes as the lubber's line seemed to bend away from the gyro bearing.

'Men wounded down 'ere, sir!' The splinter in his thigh seemed to twist like a branding iron and he gasped, ''Oly shit! Sorry, sir, but I can't tell wot's up!'

Ransome called, 'Help on way. Can you hold the wheel?'

'Sir!'

'Bring her round. Steer three-five-zero.'

Beckett nodded. Was he the only one alive?

Boyes staggered to his feet, his mind clearing, sobbing uncontrollably as he realised that he was all right but for a cut hand. Wakely was pressed against the side, his fingers interlaced over his head, moaning and gasping, but apparently unhurt.

One of the telegraphsmen was on his knees and had turned over the messenger by the emergency telephone. He croaked, 'Bert's bought it, Swain.' His control cracked, 'Jesus, he's got no face left!'

Beckett snapped, 'You okay, Boyes?'

But Boyes was trying to drag Midshipman Davenport into a sitting position. It had been his blood which had soaked his shorts; in the strange light it looked black, solid.

'It's Mr Davenport!' He felt close to tears as he tried to make him comfortable. First Aid books had told him nothing about this. Davenport must have taken a shell fragment in the back, which had thrown him across the cowering Wakely and had consequently saved his life. He was probably dead. Boyes stared at him, the familiar features twisted into a mask, like the face of someone who had suddenly aged.

Beckett said, ''Old on, Boyes! Stiff upper lip, ain't that wot they say where you comes from?'

The door crashed open and Surgeon Lieutenant Cusack stepped over the broken table, his eyes taking it all in, his shoes skidding in blood.

He saw the man on his knees. 'Can you manage?'

The telegraphsman hung his head like an exhausted swimmer. 'Just about.'

Cusack nodded and turned away from the chief quartermaster's slumped corpse; only Reeve's bulging eyes held in a small beam of light seemed to cling on to life.

He saw Boyes and snapped, 'Don't lay him down.' He ripped open Davenport's shirt and threw it aside like a butcher's rags. 'In my bag. Two shell dressings!' He watched Boyes and added, 'You're doing just fine.' They both ducked as heavier shells thundered into the sea nearby, and they heard the falling water sluice over the bridge superstructure.

Cusack tilted Davenport's naked body forward and then pressed a heavy dressing over the wound. To Boyes he said, 'Here, tie these tapes. My hands are too bloody.' His eyes glinted as he looked up at Beckett's tall figure. 'You're a bit damaged too, Cox'n.' He shook his head. 'But you'll never break. Not you, man!'

Boyes said despairingly, 'Can't we lay him down now, sir? He's still breathing.'

Cusack listened to feet clattering up a ladder, someone hacking away broken fittings brought down by the shell. He answered quietly, 'You're a friend of his, are you, son?'

Boyes nodded without knowing why. 'We were at school together.'

It should have sounded stupid, Cusack thought grimly, with all hell breaking loose, and the ship liable to be straddled at any second. But it seemed to make all the sense in the world.

He said gently, 'He's dying. Drowning in his own blood. Stay with him. I'm needed elsewhere.' He tossed another dressing to the injured telegraphsman. 'Tie that on our man of steel, eh? I'll send someone as soon as I can.'

He touched Boyes's shoulder as he left. 'It'll not be long.'

Davenport opened his eyes and stared at Boyes for several seconds.

Boyes said, 'It's all right. I'm here. You were wounded when – ' He realised for the first time that Wakely had somehow disappeared. 'When you were saving Richard Wakely's life.'

'Did I?' His head lolled on to Boyes's shoulder. 'Can't feel much. Never mind.' He tried to laugh and blood ran down his chin.

Boyes mopped it away with a rolled signal flag. 'Easy. You'll soon be safe.'

'Safe.' Davenport tried to look at him. 'Next time – ' He broke off and groaned. 'You see me.' He was starting to struggle, as if he had suddenly understood but would not accept it. 'Sub-lieutenant, eh?' He closed his eyes, 'Oh, dear God, *help me*!'

It was several more seconds, while the ship tilted this way and that, and voices echoed from above and below like demented souls, before Boyes realised that Davenport had died.

Beckett called hoarsely, ''Ere, lend me a 'and, young 'un! You're the only bloke in one piece!'

The door was wrenched open again and the Buffer, an axe gripped in his hand, stared at the scene without speaking. The great daubs of blood, the buckled plates where the shell had ricochetted around the wheelhouse before exploding as it had been designed to do inside a tank, and lastly at his friend hanging on to the spokes, one leg tied with a reddened dressing.

'Jesus, Swain, you managin' to 'old on? I'll get one of the lads from aft to relieve you!'

Beckett grinned at him fondly. 'Fuck off, you mad bastard. Get on with your own job fer a change!' He gestured to Boyes, 'Me an' young Nelson is doin' very well!'

The Buffer showed his monkey teeth. 'Come round for sippers arter this lot, my son!'

Beckett retorted through his pain, 'He ain't old enough.'

The Buffer became serious for the first time. 'In my book 'e bloody is!'

Beckett said, 'Take the wheel fer a sec, Boyes.' He eyed him grimly. 'You *do* know wot to do?' He saw him nod. 'I'm goin' to fix this poor sod's bandage before things 'ot up again.'

Boyes cleared his throat and called up the voicepipe.

'Wheelhouse – Bridge!'

Sherwood answered immediately, his tone sharp, as if he expected the worst.

Boyes blinked tears from his eyes. 'Relieving the wheel, sir! Ordinary Seaman Boyes!'

Behind him he heard Beckett call, 'only time they care is when they think you're bloody dead!'

Sherwood gave a brittle laugh. Beckett had a very carrying voice.

He said, 'The enemy has shifted target to the beaches. Hold her on three-five-zero until you're told otherwise.'

Boyes watched the gyro tape until it appeared to mist over. He felt sick and faint, his whole being rebelling against the touch and stench of death.

Above all he was conscious of a great feeling of pride.

Ransome trained his glasses above the screen and saw the land looming in the early dawn light, the sea criss-crossed with the wakes of other craft while closer inshore tall columns of water showed a regular concentration of artillery fire.

'Starboard ten.' He craned over the screen and stared down at the port Oerlikon mounting; as it was pointing uselessly towards the quarter, the bright scar where the shell had smashed into it surprisingly sharp in the pale light. The Oerlikon gunner was squatting on the step massaging his head with both hands, seemingly oblivious to what was happening around him.

Ransome had called down to him immediately after the second shell had exploded beneath his feet in the wheelhouse, but the seaman had merely shrugged and spread his hands with disbelief. His guns were knocked out of action and yet miraculously he had been left untouched, apart from his headache.

Hargrave clambered on to the bridge, his face and arms streaked with dirt.

'Three killed and two wounded by splinters, sir.' He sounded out of breath.

Ransome waited as another massive salvo thundered overhead to burst somewhere inland. He could see the smoke now against the brightening skyline, like something solid which would never disperse. Fires too, with the more livid stabs and flashes from small-arms fire and mortars.

Ransome already knew about those who had died. It seemed incredible that anyone could have survived down there. The youngest and the most seasoned, Boyes and Beckett. If it was true what he had heard about Wakely it seemed a pity that others had fallen when he had done nothing to help them, but whimpered only for his wretched skin.

Hargrave said, 'Sorry about young Davenport, sir.'

They faced each other, each knowing that few people in the ship, if any, had liked the midshipman.

But he had tried, and with his eighteenth birthday hardly behind him, it was a bitter way to end everything. In his heart Ransome knew that in days, provided *Rob Roy* was spared, few would remember his name. Only at home in England – he closed his mind like slamming a door.

'Did you check the other damage?'

'Yes, sir. The messdeck was barely marked. No need to plug the holes at this stage. Too high above the waterline.'

They both looked up as two flights of fighter-bombers, their RAF roundels like starings eyes in the strange light, screamed low overhead towards the land.

Perhaps the most marked change of all, Ransome thought. Air-cover, and plenty of it. Not sitting ducks – not this time.

Morgan looked up from a voicepipe. 'R/T signal from *Bedworth*, sir. *Two mines adrift to the south-west.*'

Sherwood grunted. 'Not surprised after that gale.'

Ransome nodded. 'Signal *Dryaden* to investigate. Right up her street.'

Hargrave smiled sadly. 'Pity to get your bum blown off by a drifter at this stage of an invasion.'

Sherwood's eyes widened in surprise. 'Did I hear a *joke* from our first lieutenant?' He strode over and offered his hand. 'I salute thee!'

Ransome watched the unexpected gesture, the way Morgan and even young Tritton appeared to relax, while Leading Signalman Mackay gave a great grin.

Bedworth's signal lamp glittered across the water and revealed the great rolling bank of smoke which covered the slow moving landing-vessels like a blanket.

Mackay read, 'From *Bedworth*, sir. *Detach vessel to assist landing-aircraft which is out of command.*'

Sherwood murmured, 'Bliss likes to make signals, that at least is obvious.'

Ransome said, 'Signal *Dunlin* to assist. We will support her if required.'

A loud bang, familiar to all of them, made the air quake. *Dryaden* had found and destroyed one of the drifting mines.

Ransome watched *Dunlin* alter course away from *Rob Roy*'s straight wake and head towards the mass of landing-craft closer to the beach. As the light hardened it looked as if there was an impossible tangle of vessels with neither order nor purpose, landing-craft thrashing sternfirst from the beach, their box-like hulls higher now without their tanks and other vehicles, while others pushed ahead, following darting motor-launches with their bright pendants to mark their passage to a prescribed landing-place.

The gunfire was getting louder, and Ransome felt the air quiver to an unbroken artillery duel somewhere to the right of the beach. Probably the road to Syracuse, known to be heavily defended by crack German troops. If the English Army could not break their line of defence the rest of the invasion would be left in stalemate.

'Half ahead together!' Ransome levelled his glasses again. There appeared to be fighting everywhere, grenades, tracer, with a fiery backdrop of falling bombs as the RAF and American planes battered away at the enemy's support lines and gun emplacements.

Hargrave murmured, 'I'll never forget this.'

Ransome did not lower his glasses, but watched as *Dunlin* swung broadside on near a large landing-craft.

'You still here, Number One?' he smiled. 'It's something I never thought I'd see either, as a matter of fact.'

The Buffer appeared on the bridge. 'Wheel'ouse cleared, sir. I've put two 'ands in there to 'elp the cox'n.' He sighed. 'But you know wot '*e*'s like, sir, won't budge from that wheel!'

Ransome stiffened as two watersprouts shot up from the sea near *Dunlin*.

'*Hell*! They've got her ranged-in!' He beckoned to Mackay. 'Signal *Dunlin* to stand off immediately!'

More explosions made the sea boil and leap in bright columns through the drifting smoke.

Sherwood shouted, 'One of them hit the landing-craft, sir!'

Morgan called, '*Dunlin's* captain for you on R/T, sir!'

Ransome ducked down and snatched the speaker from the boatswain's mate.

'Obey that order and *stand away*!' He pictured the man's face, one more lieutenant like *Scythe*'s C.O., called Paul Allfrey. He came from the Isle of Wight.

'I can't sir!' His voice ebbed and flowed through the roar of explosions. 'The L.C.T. is full of wounded! Must get a two-line rigged!'

Just when you thought that death was elsewhere. Ransome snapped, 'Affirmative. We will assist you.' He ran back to the forepart of the bridge again. 'Signal *Ranger* to assume command. Then make a signal to *Bedworth. We are assisting.*'

He stared down at the side-deck and saw the corpses being lashed down under some bloodstained canvas. He knew them all. Reeves especially. A good man who had been hoping to take a petty officer's course.

'Get down there, Number One. The Buffer and the Gunner (T) will assist you. A towing job is never easy, and we've not much time.'

'*Oh God*!' Morgan clutched the rail and pointed as *Dunlin* took a direct hit just abaft her squat bridge. She was smaller than the other minesweepers, and the shell seemed to tear her upperworks apart in one blinding flash of fire. Falling debris, her mast and radar lantern hurled over the side and the sea pock-marked with falling fragments. Two more columns shot up in a tight straddle, and even above the roar of gunfire they heard the grating crash of splinters gouging through steel.

Hargrave had gone, and Ransome watched the gap between the ships narrowing.

'Cox'n?' he raised his eyes level with the glass screen. 'Bring her round to port. Hold her on a bearing with the L.C.T.'s stern.' It cut out the confusion of too many helm orders, and Beckett, injured or not, knew *Rob Roy*'s behaviour better than anyone.

'Slow ahead together!'

He heard shouts from aft, the grate of wires being manhandled along the deck.

Mackay lowered his telescope. 'From *Ranger*, sir. *Good luck.*'

Two more shells fell close to *Dunlin*, but it was impossible to measure the damage. *Dunlin* had stopped completely, and Ransome saw half of her motor boat dangling from the shattered davits. There was a lot of smoke, flames too, shooting from the foot of her single funnel. An old ship built for the Kaiser's war. It was asking a lot from her. Too much.

He thought of *Ranger* taking the trouble to make that short but so-important signal. Like old comrades, twins. He thought too of the Wren driver who had told him about her brother, a subbie, who was in *Ranger.*

Ransome strode across the bridge and gripped Tritton's arm. 'Take over the voicepipe.' He looked at him until the young sub-lieutenant met his gaze. 'I need to be where I can watch things.' He shook his arm gently. 'Don't worry about being scared. Most of us are, sometime or another.' He watched his words taking effect, hoped they would stay uppermost in his mind the next time, and the time after that.

Tritton nodded. 'Yes, sir. I'll do my best.'

Ransome pictured the scene as it must have been in the wheelhouse when the shell had burst into it. He was glad that young Boyes had come through. It was very important for some reason, as if he had become a mascot.

He listened to Hargrave shouting to his party. Thank God they did have good air-cover today, because he guessed Hargrave had stripped most guns of their crews to manhandle his tow-line.

Leading Signal Mackay said, 'I've got my bunting-tosser ready to pass messages aft if need be, sir.'

Their eyes met. Parts of a machine. The family. The Job.

'Good thinking. We'll try and tow her from her stern – it seems the bow door may be damaged.' He made himself take a few more seconds. 'You can shift your gear after this lot's over.' He saw the man's frown of surprise and added, 'Into the petty officers' mess.'

Sherwood grinned at him. '*Cheers*, Yeoman!'

Ransome leaned over the screen once more, glad he had told him. In minutes they might all be killed, but at least one man would know what he thought of him. Like poor Davenport, clinging on to his first gold stripe even in the presence of death.

'Stop together! Slow astern starboard!' He saw Leading Seaman Hoggan running across the forecastle, a heaving-line coiled and ready in his big hands. Once bent on to the tow-line they could get the L.C.T. moving until she was clear of danger.

A deafening bang rocked the bridge and Ransome saw a bright tongue of flame punch through *Dunlin*'s side.

Ransome shaded his eyes to watch the heaving-line as it snaked over the L.C.T.'s square bridge, where several seamen were waiting to seize it. He could feel *Dunlin* burning, the heat on his face like a noon sun.

Sherwood said flatly, 'She's going.'

Morgan called, 'Tow's going across, sir!'

Another explosion boomed against the hull and Ransome saw tiny figures jumping into the sea, some clinging to injured comrades as their ship erupted into flames from bridge to quarterdeck. That big explosion must have been deep in her engine-room. No one would walk away from there.

'Ready, sir!'

Ransome stared across at Tritton, his pale face framed against the smoke and fires of a dying ship.

'Slow ahead together.' He turned to watch the towing-wire rising from the water. '*Stop both engines*!' he bit his lip, made himself ignore the other mine-sweeper as she began to settle down, buried by fire.

'Easy now. Tell the Cox'n, minimum revolutions!' If they parted the wire now, the L.C.T. and then *Rob Roy* would fall under those guns. The towing-wire rose and tightened again. Ransome was banking on the L.C.T. being empty but for the wounded.

He watched, holding his breath, but the wire remained taut like a steel rod.

'Slow ahead together.' He glanced at Sherwood. 'Tell the Doc to stand by. They may not have one over there.'

Tritton swallowed nervously. 'Wheelhouse reports helm answering, sir.'

Ransome nodded and strode to the gyro repeater. 'Bring her round. Steer one-three-zero.' He smiled at Tritton's strained features. 'You can do it. Just like *King Alfred*, eh?'

A duller explosion rolled over the water and when Ransome glanced across he saw *Dunlin*'s keel rolling towards the sky, the screws stilled at last as she began to slide under amongst the struggling survivors.

Mackay licked his lips. 'From L.C.T., sir. *Have two hundred wounded on board. God be with you!*'

Sherwood said harshly, 'Put it in the log. *Dunlin* sank at . . .' He glanced away. 'Was it *worth* it?'

Ransome watched the L.C.T. yawning untidily astern and pictured the helpless wounded who had fallen almost before the landings had started.

He said to the bridge at large, 'For them it was.'

Ransome stood on a flat rock, and shaded his eyes to watch the motorboat as she zigzagged through a small brood of L.C.T.s to make her way back to *Rob Roy*. He felt strange, unsteady, standing on dry land, seeing his ship at anchor again for the first time since the invasion had begun.

Then he looked around the littered beach and marvelled that anybody had ever got further than the shallows. This same beach, which had been mined and covered by deadly cross-fire from several concrete emplacements, was a hive of activity, with shirt-sleeved soldiers digging and levelling the shell and mortar craters while the sappers laid fresh tapes to show the safe tracks for tanks and lorries, which arrived in a regular procession from incoming landing-craft.

In three days they had forced the enemy back, and as expected the Eighth Army had borne the worst of it, but had still managed to take Syracuse on the evening of the first day, and two days later the port of Augusta which gave the navy a useful base, a foothold from which future operations could be launched.

But the other side of the story was plain to see. Half-submerged landing-craft, pitted with holes or completely burned-out, abandoned tanks, and the tell-tale reminders of bayonetted rifles with helmets resting on them, to mark where some of the attackers had fallen.

The war made itself heard as it raged without let-up towards Catania, below the brooding presence of Mount Etna. But it was at a distance, and the regular sorties of aircraft which roared above the various beaches should make certain it remained so.

After that first day when *Rob Roy* had towed the damaged L.C.T. to the more experienced care of a fleet tug, the flotilla had been kept busy on duties which ranged from depth-charging a suspected enemy submarine, Italian or German it was never discovered, to carrying out more wounded, and keeping the beaches clear of obstruction.

They had suffered no further casualties, but there had been no slackening of vigilance, so that when not needed for duty the hands had fallen exhausted on deck, the memory of *Dunlin*'s end still stark in their minds.

Richard Wakely and his resourceful cameraman Andy had seen none of the aftermath. A gleaming launch had arrived from one of the big cruisers while *Rob Roy* had been unloading more wounded into a hospital transport vessel, and Wakely had departed without another word. Off to another theatre of war perhaps, later to enthrall his audiences on the wireless and in the newspapers? It was unlikely he would ever forgive what had happened in *Rob Roy*. It certainly seemed as if what Sherwood had said about him was not just a rumour.

The cameraman, on the other hand, had taken a few moments to say his farewells. To the men he had watched and photographed in action, the petty officers' mess where he had been quartered, and lastly the bridge where he had apparently shot some of his best film.

'So long, Captain. Stay lucky. It would have been a privilege to meet you even if we'd stayed in dry dock the whole time!'

A small, undistinguished figure, yet somehow head and shoulders above the man he worked for.

An army lieutenant-colonel was squatting on a shooting-stick, smoking a cheroot. He smiled amiably.

'Come to stretch your legs, Commander?'

Ransome saluted. 'It still looks a mess here, sir.'

The soldier watched his men chattering to one another as they worked beneath the cover of some mobile A.A. guns. 'It'll take weeks to sort it all out. There are so many Italians deserting from their old ally and surrendering to us, or scampering off in civvies, I reckon Jerry must be browned off with the whole bunch of 'em!'

He turned as Sherwood sauntered along the beach, his hands in his pockets. 'You've got a good lad there, a great help until our experts came.' He smiled, some of the strain passing from his face. 'He caught some of my chaps in a bombed church just up the beach. You know how it is, looking for souvenirs. There was a dead Jerry in there, one arm sticking out with a really tempting watch strapped on it. One of my lads was about to 'commandeer' it when your lieutenant arrived. He apparently tied a line to the corpse, ordered my soldiers outside – much to their irritation according to the sergeant-major – then he pulled on the line.' He spread his hands. 'The stiff was booby-trapped. Blew down the church wall. Near thing!'

Sherwood joined them and gave a tired salute. 'Your own bomb-disposal blokes are there now, Colonel. Should be okay.'

Ransome watched him. That close to danger and yet Sherwood seemed so calm, almost disinterested. It was unnerving.

The lieutenant-colonel said, 'Anyway, I just wanted to thank you for all you've done in the past days. It will come officially, no doubt, *through channels*,' he became grave, 'but you and I understand. We do the job when the planners have finished theirs.' His gaze strayed around the beach, remembering, holding on to the images, the faces of those he had known and would never see again.

'No matter what, we made it come true, Commander. Together.'

Ransome slowly filled his pipe. 'I'll pass the word, Colonel.' He watched his hands and expected them to start shaking now that it was over. When had he last slept? When would he again?

'Well, well, we've found them at last!'

Ransome turned and saw a small procession of soldiers, most of whom were wearing Red Cross brassards and carrying stretchers. The officer who had spoken was a major, his face still smudged from the dawn action, his eyes red-rimmed as if looking through a mask.

The major said to his companion, a lieutenant, 'I just *knew* the British would have someone who smoked a pipe!'

They were Canadians, some of those who had landed to the west of Cape Correnti.

They all solemnly shook hands and grinned at each other.

Ransome handed over his pouch and both Canadians took out their pipes.

The major said, 'I'm going to be greedy, Commander. Most of the guys smoke fags, and all our pipe tobacco was lost in the attack.' He shook his head with mock sadness. 'That was a real disaster, I can tell you!'

The colonel said, 'This is Lieutenant-Commander Ransome, by the way. His ship towed out those wounded on the first day.'

The major studied him curiously. 'Ransome?' He turned to his lieutenant. 'Hey, Frank, why does that name ring a bell?'

The lieutenant paused, his unlit pipe halfway to his mouth. 'You know, the partisans.'

The major nodded. 'That's right. We flushed out some Sicilian partisans who'd been hiding from the Jerries up in the hills. Bandits more likely. They came to my boys so as not to get shot up by mistake.'

Ransome stood motionless and despite the unwavering, dusty heat, felt like ice.

The major continued, 'Just a coincidence, of course, but they'd been hiding some kid from the Krauts – a young officer some fishermen picked up a while back – '

Ransome gripped his arm. 'Where? Which one?'

The major did not understand but sensed the urgency, the quiet desperation.

'Go and get him, Frank.'

Ransome watched two stretcher-bearers descend the slope to the beach.

The major added, 'The partisans say he was wounded and they got a doctor from some village. He had to operate immediately, but had no anaesthetics apparently – ' He broke off as Ransome ran along the beach.

'What is it?'

Sherwood said quietly, 'Don't ask. Just pray.'

They lowered the stretcher to the ground and Ransome dropped to his knees beside it.

With the greatest care he pulled the blanket down across a heavy, stained bandage, and gently brushed some sand from his brother's hair. Then, oblivious to the watching eyes, he put his arm round Tony's bare shoulders and hugged him for several moments, quite unable to speak.

His brother opened his eyes and stared at him, first without recognition, and then with disbelief.

Ransome whispered, 'You're going to be all right, Tony, I promise. *All right!*'

Sherwood said, 'It's his kid brother. Reported killed. He carried it with him day and night, but most of us never saw it.' He watched Ransome cradling the boy's head against his shoulder. 'We were all too busy thinking of ourselves.'

The lieutenant-colonel said, 'Leave them another minute, then take him along with the others to the field dressing-station.'

The Canadian major held a match to his pipe. 'And I thought they said miracles were out of fashion, eh?'

15

Aftermath

Lieutenant Trevor Hargrave turned and touched his cap as Ransome climbed up from his sea-cabin.

'Starboard watch at Defence Stations, sir.' He waited while Ransome walked to the gyro repeater and wiped it with his glove before adding, 'Course is zero-seven-zero, revolutions for eleven knots.'

Ransome stretched his arms and fought the desire to shiver.

'Very well, Number One.' It was eight o'clock in the morning, with the forenoon watchkeepers scattered throughout *Rob Roy*'s private world, at their weapons or in the engine-room. Ransome had donned an oilskin over his old duffle-coat and had wrapped a dry towel around his neck, and yet he was still cold. Too long on the bridge; or perhaps he had been foolish to snatch a few moments to be alone in his sea-cabin, to enjoy the luxury of piping-hot shaving water, and a mug of Ted Kellett's strong coffee. His face felt raw from the razor and he questioned the sudden need, the importance attached to shaving on this particular day.

He moved to the chart-table and saw Sub-Lieutenant Morgan step aside for him.

Surely there should be a feeling of relief, of joy even at returning home?

He turned the page of the ready-use log while he held it close against the shaded lamp bulb. Eight o'clock in the morning, but it was almost as dark as night. He saw Sherwood's writing at the close of the previous watch. The last day in November 1943. Perhaps time and distance were already making that other war seem unreal, the memories of Sicily and the months which had followed blurred, like mixed images.

Two months after the fear and excitement of watching the first troops surge ashore, the Allies had launched their second invasion, Operation Avalanche, on the Italian mainland, first on to the bloody beaches of Salerno, and later in a daring pincer-movement at Anzio. The enemy had been more than ready that time and every yard of the way had been fiercely contested. New weapons in the shape of glider-bombs had appeared over the landing-sites; controlled by parent aircraft they had been homed on to the heavier warships, many of which, including the battleship *Warspite*, had suffered casualties and damage. Another ship, the American cruiser *Savannah*, had received a direct hit, which had penetrated a turret and burst deep inside her hull, causing serious flooding and over a hundred casualties. The Germans, no doubt aware of their Axis ally's desire to declare a position of either neutrality or surrender, threw in everything they had with a total disregard for the rules of war. Two hospital ships, *Newfoundland* and *Leinster*, were bombed, although they were brightly lit to display their identity and purpose; the former sank with a heavy loss of life.

But *Rob Roy* and the remainder of her flotilla played no part in the Italian invasion. With her consorts she returned to the nerve-racking job of sweeping the channels and approaches around Malta, to make it safe even for the heaviest warships and transports once more.

Several minesweeping trawlers had been lost, but *Rob Roy*'s depleted flotilla seemed to recover the luck which had failed them when *Scythe* and *Dunlin* had gone down.

The orders to return to England had come unexpectedly. Even Bliss, who had dashed on ahead of the convoy in *Bedworth*, had seemed at a loss. The Mediterranean war was by no means over, and even now there were reports of the Allied armies being bogged down both by bad weather and reinforced German divisions, with little hope of an early victory. The flotilla had paused at Gibraltar to effect brief repairs before joining a small homebound convoy in the role of additional escorts, and Ransome had walked around his ship, sharing her tiredness as well as his pride in the part they had all played.

He glanced at Hargrave, his features deeply tanned against the dull backdrop of mist and drizzle, and the white scarf which showed above his oilskin. When he spoke to Morgan or one of the watchkeepers, his breath streamed from his mouth like smoke. The change in their circumstances was all around them, to the senses as well as the mind.

The convoy had dispersed northwards towards the Irish Sea. Just to think of it made Ransome's heart miss a beat. All those miles; the air-attacks, the frantic alarm bells in the night, the roar of mine and bomb, and now they were here at the gateway of the English Channel. Some five miles abeam was the ageless Wolf Rock lighthouse, which meant that the mainland of Cornwall was only about twelve miles distant.

He could feel it in the heavy rise and fall of the hull, the drifting spray and drizzle across the glass screen. Cold, chilling right to the marrow. The English Channel in winter.

He thought of Tony, remembering yet again that terrible moment of uncertainty and fear when he had turned down the blanket and had clutched his body against his own. Tony would be safely in hospital now. It had been a close thing; the wound in his side had been from a jagged shell splinter and was infected despite all that his rescuers could do. He had existed with the partisans in a small cave and had lived mostly on goat's milk and fish. It was all they had, and they had given it freely.

As far as Ransome had been able to discover, his brother was the M.T.B.'s only survivor. Perhaps one day Tony would be able to tell him what had happened.

Ransome climbed into his bridge chair and thrust his numbed fingers into his pockets.

After losing the convoy they had slowed down while *Firebrand* had carried out makeshift repairs to a stern-gland. Creeping along in the darkness there had been few who had not cursed the elderly minesweeper and her defects. For whatever was happening in Italy, the Germans were very active in the Atlantic, and on passage by their slow roundabout route they had sighted several abandoned wrecks and large patterns of flotsam. Convoys, or a solitary ship caught in a U-boat's crosswires: an insect in the web.

Ransome tried to ignore the spray and rain which ran down his face to soak into the towel. Coming back to another war, or to the one which they had left just months ago? Little was changed at home, he thought, except for one vital factor. Midget submarines, X-craft as they were called, had managed to penetrate deep into a Norwegian fjord where they had found and attacked the last great German battleship *Tirpitz*. The most powerful warship in the world, sister to the ill-fated *Bismarck*, she had remained the one real threat to the British fleet. While she lay in her heavily defended lair, protected by booms and nets, she was a menace to every convoy on the open sea. Heavy units of the Home Fleet were tied down in harbour or at Scapa Flow, just in case she broke out to ravage the supply lines with her massive armament.

A few midget submarines had achieved what others had attempted, and had laid their charges beneath her while she lay at anchor. Nobody knew for certain the full extent of the damage, because several of the tiny X-craft had been lost, and the surviving crews had been captured. But she might never move again. David and Goliath, with the odds somewhat worse, Ransome decided.

He thought of his orders for *Rob Roy*, to proceed to Devonport dockyard in company with *Ranger* to carry out a refit and overhaul. The others were being scattered to different yards where there was room for their needs.

Ransome considered his ship's company and how they had all been changed in some ways. Perhaps being far away from home, most of them for the first time, fighting alongside the real fleet, the big ships with their towering superstructures and battle ensigns. Strange and new. Their world had been grey seas and small ships, stubby trawlers and lean destroyers, tramp steamers and the Glory Boys of Light Coastal Forces. England under attack, shabby, rundown, defiant. A few Mediterranean skies and hot suns would work miracles here, he thought.

Plymouth. Where he had last seen her. Would she still feel the same? Was it wrong of him even to hope she would need him as much as he did her?

He had written to her whenever he had found the time, but had received no more letters from her. He was certain she would have put her thoughts on paper as he had tried to do in his own letters to her. They were probably following *Rob Roy* around the Mediterranean, to Malta and Alexandria and to North Africa. Minesweepers stood pretty low on the Fleet Mail Office's priorities.

'Char, sir?' The boatswain's mate handed him a heavy mug. Thick and sweet, the way only sailors could make it.

And how had it affected *him*, he wondered? Had he risen above the strain, the constant decisions, the need to exercise authority when his heart had directed otherwise? Would she see that in him too?

And he thought of the ones who would not be bothered either way. He had written to Midshipman Davenport's parents, and to the other men's families. Would it ever help? They might even blame him in some way for their lost ones.

Dunlin had been luckier than many, and had had just seven men killed. When Ransome pictured the final explosion that had blasted out her guts, it seemed like another miracle. Her young captain, Allfrey, from the Isle of Wight, had not been one of the survivors.

He heard feet on the deck below and knew that some of the men off watch were at the guardrails, looking for the land, seeing it as it would be, each to his own.

He thought of Sherwood's story, how he had demonstrated his chilling skills yet again with the booby-trapped German, of the cheerful Canadians enjoying their pipes once more, perhaps still unaware of what they had done for him. The lieutenant-colonel sitting on his shooting-stick, and the mad piper in one of the landing-craft; the lines of wounded waiting to be lifted from the beaches, suddenly so young and frail without their weapons and helmets.

The one extraordinary feature was the enemy. As in the war at sea, they had not seen the Germans at all. Always at a distance, ringed by fire, or laying down barrages of utter destruction.

He heard Morgan speaking into a voicepipe and knew he was talking to the plot below their feet. The youngster Boyes doing Davenport's job.

It was some beacon picked up on the radar, to be marked and compared on the chart. A link with home.

Ransome slid from the chair, aware of the stillness, the mist and drizzle. Shipboard noises, muted but for the creak of wet steel, the regular bleep from the Asdic compartment.

He glanced over the screen at the crouching lookouts, shining in their oilskins, their breath like Hargrave's. The port Oerlikons had never worked again to Fallows' satisfaction after being hit by the anti-tank shell. One more job for Devonport, 'Guz' as it was affectionately nicknamed.

Familiar shapes and outlines in the grey gloom. The hard man Jardine; Leading Seaman Hoggan, one of the stalwarts in this elite company; A.B. 'Chalky' White, who had a nervous tic in his eye; Gipsy Guttridge and all the rest. How did they feel? Ransome remembered Morgan's comparison with Trafalgar before the invasion. But there were no proud pyramids of canvas this dull morning to excite and warm the hearts of the watchers on the shore, had there been any. Not this time. Just eight small ships, tired and streaked with rust, dented from numerous encounters with jetties and mooring buoys, often in pitch-darkness.

Ransome looked up at the single funnel with its usual lick of smoke trickling abeam. He recalled what Commander Moncrieff had said after their last handshake.

He felt a lump in his throat. Well, they *had* taken care of her. One more time, *Rob Roy* was coming home.

Lieutenant Philip Sherwood withdrew his head and shoulders from the shielded chart-table where he had been peering at a signal pad and said, 'From C-in-C Plymouth, sir. Details of berthing tomorrow morning and arrangements for tonight.' He added as an afterthought, 'The dockyard ordnance people are coming aboard sometime in the forenoon.'

Ransome turned in his chair and winced. It was even colder, and beyond the bridge it was pitch-black, with only their sluggish bow wave to break the darkness.

A long day, and a strangely tense one, he thought. Only when they closed with the land to pass the Lizard, while the air was heady with the daily rum issue and some curious smells from the galley funnel, did he accept the reality of their return.

Then north-east with his own home, Fowey, somewhere to port, shrouded in gloom and mist; until like a disembodied island, the headland of Rame Head, guardian of Plymouth Sound and marked by a solitary winking buoy, passed finally abeam.

It was a nuisance to have to wait for morning, another day before he could take the ship into the dockyard. But it was a difficult entrance, past Drake's Island and through the narrows, a hard passage even in broad daylight.

'Tell Fallows about the gunnery thing.'

Sherwood nodded and resumed his position in the forepart of the bridge. It was odd about Bunny Fallows, he thought. He barely spoke to anybody these days; it could not still be pique over Tritton and Morgan's little joke. It was something much deeper, which gnawed away at him from within like a disease. Not fear then? It seemed unlikely. Fallows did not have the imagination to feel that kind of emotion. Sherwood pushed him from his thoughts and trained his glasses astern. *Ranger* was somewhere in their wake, the only one still in company. The rest were on their way to Chatham and Harwich, Rosyth and Tynemouth. Repairs, a lick of paint – then what?

He heard Morgan speaking quietly to the signalman. Would it mean a breakup of this company? Promotion, courses in various shore establishments, drafts to other ships to make way for green youngsters like Gold, and Boyes, who no longer seemed so youthful.

He glanced at Ransome's shadow framed against the glass screen. As if he never moved. *Rob Roy* and *Ranger* each carried a Render Mines Safe Officer. It was fortunate that the other R.M.S.O., like himself, held a watchkeeping certificate. It made the officers' watches on the bridge less of a strain, spread out instead of four hours on and four off without let-up. But the captain was always here. Everyone who visited the ship remarked how young he was to hold a command. Sherwood had told more than one, he bloody well needed to be young to keep from splitting into halves.

He shied away from thoughts of the girl he had met in London. Rosemary. But she often came into his mind when he was unprepared and vulnerable. He was all that and more just now. He was coming home – to what? A big bank balance which he had done almost nothing to create, property which was filled with memories, and a background which was worth very little in a fighting war.

He recalled her question. *What will you do after the war?* And his own cynical reply.

He might leave *Rob Roy*; he was surprised that the idea seemed almost painful. Once he had believed it did not matter, that he could not care less. In that at least he must have changed. Ransome had probably done it. He remembered that moment on the Sicilian beach when he had understood Ransome's own anxiety, shared it; afterwards he had thought it was like being privileged to do so.

Even if he did not see her again, he might give her a call. He owed her an apology for the way he had acted after – again he closed his mind to it.

I must not think like this. Next week, or the one after, he might be called to examine some new enemy technique, a booby trap designed only for the likes of him. He smiled as he thought of the soldiers' resentment when he had ordered them from the bombed church. Their embarrassed grins afterwards, their stammered thanks for saving them from being killed or maimed. It did no good to think that some of those same men were probably dead anyway by now.

A slight shadow crossed the bridge and he heard Morgan report, 'Ordinary Seaman Boyes, sir.'

Then he heard Ransome say, 'I want you on the plot full-time, Boyes.'

A flurry of snow sifted over the screen and a look-out muttered, 'Jesus! Roll on my doz!'

Ransome continued, 'You've done well.' There was some mumbled response from Boyes. 'I shall see it goes in your papers.'

Boyes stared at the captain's silhouette, oblivious of the snow which froze on his eyelids and lips. In a small voice he whispered, '*Papers*, sir?'

He tried to remember each word as Ransome replied, 'I think you should have another go, Boyes. A proper interview at least. How do you feel about it?'

Boyes could scarcely speak. It was everything he wanted, and yet to his amazement his first reaction was one of disloyalty to the men who had helped and guided him in the brutal kindness of the navy's lower deck.

'T-thank you very much, sir.'

Ransome said, 'We'll be entering the Sound within the half-hour, so get your charts tidied up. The dockyard maties will doubtless want to see Malta's efforts to repair your plot-table, eh?'

Boyes climbed down the ladder and saw Morgan's white teeth set in a grin as he passed. *Another go.* He had not really had one before. What would his mother have to say about *that*?

'All the port watch! First part forrard, second part aft, stand by for entering harbour!'

Boyes gripped the rail of the bridge wing, buckled by the shell which had cracked around the wheelhouse, killing, *killing*. He still found it hard to sleep; it haunted him like a nightmare which had no beginning or ending.

Leading Seaman Reeves, his eyes bulging with horror as if he had seen the shell coming, Davenport lolling against him, trying to laugh, and coughing out his blood while it drowned him. And the towering figure of the coxswain, tough, outspoken and unexpectedly kind. He still limped a bit from his wound, but was more afraid of being put ashore than any momentary pain.

When he had first come aboard he had been almost too frightened to speak. Bursts of anger born of strain, foul language and stories of conquests on runs ashore, blondes, barmaids and waterfront toms. They had been baiting him, testing his reactions. And yet at the sea burials it had been Sid Jardine who had put his arm over his shoulders while in their different ways they had shared the same grief.

If the captain could push his papers through it would mean leaving all this, and he knew that nothing would ever be quite the same again. As *Rob Roy* picked her way between the blinking buoys until she was met by a fussy harbour launch, there were others in her company who did not share Boyes's feelings.

Leading Seaman Gipsy Guttridge had been able to keep his wife out of his mind while the ship had been in the Med. Now he was back, and as he waited with the quarterdeck party amongst the well-used coils of mooring-wires, springs and rope fenders, he wondered what he would do when he faced her again. A laughing, bright-eyed girl with dimples. A friend had written to him once to tell him she was having it off with a pongo from the local army camp. He had confronted her with it but it had ended in passion in bed. And there had been another letter waiting for him at Gib, from the same 'friend'.

The Buffer brushed past and rasped, 'Jump about, old son, you look shagged out!'

Guttridge glared after him. It never seemed to bother the Buffer. If half of it was fact, he'd screw anything. He gripped the guardrail and turned his face into the freezing snowflakes.

When I catch whoever it is, I'll do for them both!

Alone at the wardroom table Sub-Lieutenant Fallows chewed half-heartedly on some corned-beef hash. He stared at the tablecloth, still soiled from the previous meal, then poured himself another mug of black coffee.

He could not remember needing a drink more. He swallowed hard; he could almost hear it being tipped into a shining, clean glass. What should he do? He glanced up as the messman padded through the wardroom. It was madness to feel guilt, or was it fear? But it was not Parsons; he would be on the forecastle for entering harbour.

I must have been out of mind to give him money. Fallows pulled out a tin of duty-free cigarettes and gestured to the messman to clear the table.

Parsons had explained that he would soon be leaving the ship, to go on an advanced gunnery course at Whale Island and pick up his leading rate. They would never see each other again.

Fallows wiped the sweat from his forehead although the wardroom was almost cold.

He should have seen it. Stood firm and stamped on the little bastard when he had first brought up about Tinker.

Fellows glanced at the single, wavy stripe on his seagoing reefer. He had not liked Davenport because he imagined he came from a better background than himself, but he understood how he had felt about getting on in the navy. Take the chance while it lasted. When he became a lieutenant he would feel more secure, and then – he stubbed out the cigarette and lit another without noticing. Parsons had asked for a loan at first, then another to tide over his domestic problems until he had completed the gunnery course.

He thought suddenly of his father in Glasgow, a belligerent, sneering drunk who had barely worked for years and had made all their lives hell.

'You'll never get anywhere with those stuck-up bastards! I know you too well, you'll fall in yer own shit before you get what you want!'

Nobody knew or cared what it had cost him to get where he was, or what that piece of tarnished gold lace represented to him. And despite all his care to cover up his humble background he had allowed a crawling rat like Parsons to sneak under his defences.

The last time they had been alone Parsons had explained in a hurt, wheedling voice, 'I feel as much to blame as you, sir. I should 'ave spoken out – an' wot if someone asked me about it sometime, wot then, eh?'

Who could he have turned to? Now of course it was all stark and clear. He should have gone to the commanding officer there and then. It might have damaged his chances of promotion, but it was better than admitting he had bribed a rating to conceal the truth, for that was exactly how it would look in the cold eyes of a court martial.

Fallows lived on his meagre pay and had no other funds. He had got into debt several times with his mess bills, and had borrowed at first to square the accounts.

With Parsons constantly pressing him – he shuddered; the word was *blackmail* – he had been forced to do some deals with a friend he had met in Alexandria. They had been at *King Alfred* together, but his friend had failed to become an executive officer. He had ended up as a paymaster-lieutenant in the naval stores there.

Dockyard paint which until then had meant nothing to Fallows. It was merely slapped on by the ship's company or men under punishment whenever there was a spare moment.

But in Alexandria any kind of naval stores were big business. All Fallows had been required to do was sign for something which in fact was never delivered to the ship.

He had told himself a hundred times that Parsons was too implicated to cause any more trouble for him. He was a vindictive and unpopular man in the ship, but there were always those who would believe his story.

Surgeon Lieutenant Cusack entered the wardroom and slumped down in one of the battered chairs.

'You can smell the land!' He watched Fallows curiously as he remained pensive and silent. 'There were times when I thought I'd never see green grass again.'

Fallows stood up and looked at him without understanding. 'I must go.'

Cusack leaned back and stared at the deckhead, picturing the work above as wires scraped on steel, and seaboots thudded past the sealed skylight.

It had been an experience, and he knew he did not want to go back to hospital until it was over. He thought of the men he had come to know, their hopes, and perhaps above all their secrets. Cusack smiled grimly. He had a brother who was a priest in Galway; perhaps he would be more use here than a doctor.

Above them all Ransome stood high on the bridge step and stared down at the activity on deck. Merely shadows and shouts of command, but he knew *Rob Roy* blindfold if need be.

Water thrashed in the darkness and he saw one of Devonport's ancient paddle-wheeled tugs standing by, her bridge and forecastle white with driven snow.

'Stop port!' He heard Sherwood repeating the order, the instant response from the engine-room. 'Slow astern port!'

He watched, dashing the snow from his eyes as he gauged the slow swing of the stern towards the stone wall.

'Sternrope's made fast, sir!' That was Morgan.

'Headrope's being hauled over now, sir!'

'Stop port, slow astern starboard!' He pictured the hands hauling the rebellious wires and securing them to their bollards. The deck rocked, and he heard the call for more fenders as they came reluctantly alongside. 'Stop together!'

He heard Hargrave's voice from the forecastle as he supervised the mooring. 'Out springs and breasts!'

Through the snow Ransome saw the blink of a signal lamp. A greeting, fresh orders; he was too tired to care.

'All secure fore and aft, sir!' Sherwood was looking up at him through the snow, his cap white against the wet steel.

'Ring off main engines, if you please.'

The deck shuddered and fell still as a low shadow passed slowly abeam, while the wary tug thrashed round with the ease of a London taxi. It was *Ranger* following their example.

Mackay called, 'Unusual signal, sir.' He controlled a chuckle. 'From the Wrens at the Signal Tower. *Welcome home.*'

Ransome stepped down. 'Tell them thanks, from all of us.'

But he was thinking of Eve. It was as if she had spoken those words just to him.

16

Lifelines

Commander Peregrine Bliss, DSO, Royal Navy, tossed his oak-leaved cap carelessly on to a locker and sat down in Ransome's other chair.

'All quiet, Ian? He looked bright-eyed and fresh, his powerful hands resting in his lap as if unused to inactivity.

Ransome nodded. The first day in Devonport dockyard and it had been a full one. People to see, at least five tours around the ship with various dockyard officials and other experts, not least the business of getting the major part of the ship's company away on leave again. It was only months since their last leave, but it felt like years.

He replied, 'They say at least three weeks, sir. There's apparently quite a queue for repairs or boiler-cleaning.' He recalled Hargrave's face when he had left the ship. Hargrave was changed in some way, perhaps more than he had realised. He had seemed uncertain, and could almost have been reluctant to leave *Rob Roy* now that the chance had arrived. Ransome wondered if it was because of his father and the lovely second officer named Ross Pearce. When they all got back there would be more changes waiting for them.

Ransome said, 'I know I have to stay aboard, sir, but I *could* let Lieutenant

Sherwood go. One officer for occasional duty is enough for me, and I do have *Ranger*'s Number One at my beck and call.'

Bliss examined his fingers. 'I sent word for Sherwood to stay.'

He looked up and flashed a white smile, like an impish schoolboy, but for his eyes. 'For a day or so. After that, well, it'll be up to you, of course.'

Ransome glanced at the list of names on his desk, a copy of the one he had already sent on board *Bedworth* for Bliss's consideration. He guessed he had not had time to read it yet. Bliss probably wanted Sherwood to transfer to another ship. Experienced watchkeeping officers were like gold, RNVR, or not. Once again Bliss proved him wrong.

'I read your summary of people for promotion and so forth. To some I can agree, others will have to wait.' He saw Ransome's expression and added, 'You can take it higher of course, but – '

Ransome said, 'There will be several overdue for advancement this time, sir.'

Bliss went off at a tangent. 'I see that you've started papers for Ordinary Seaman Boyes. I gathered he was washed out the last time?'

'He was not properly examined, sir.'

Bliss grinned. 'In *your* opinion. We must trust these training chaps. Surely they know their stuff.'

Ransome glanced down the list, seeing their faces, knowing them like his own family. He said flatly, 'I have put Boyes down for a Mention in Despatches.'

Bliss answered, 'Saw that too. Good thinking. No promotion board could very well turn down an interview with a chap who has a M-i-D, eh?' He threw back his head and laughed. 'God, you are a crafty one, Ian. I'd have done the same myself!'

He glanced around the cabin and nodded, suddenly grave. 'Stout little ships. If I couldn't drive a destroyer I'd have one of these old ladies any day.'

'About Lieutenant Sherwood, sir – '

There was a tap at the door and Bliss said casually, 'Hope you didn't mind, Ian. A bit high-handed maybe, but I sent my snotty to dig him out when I came aboard.'

Their eyes met. A challenge. A threat.

Ransome called, 'Enter!'

Bliss said, 'Good show. I can explain to both of you together. It'll save time, eh?'

Sherwood glanced round for a chair and then leaned against the closed door. It was as close to showing his irritation at being summoned by Bliss as he could demonstrate.

Bliss regarded him impassively. 'I *know* you, Sherwood. Your record, and it's damn good.'

Sherwood sounded surprised. 'Thank you, sir.'

Ransome watched the pair of them. Sherwood was beginning to lose his Mediterranean tan already. It was strange that he always looked so pale, his skin, his hair, his lashes. Even his eyes, which were watching Bliss. Like a cat's, Ransome thought, deciding whether to purr or lash out with its claws.

'You've done some useful work in the flotilla too.' He wagged a finger. 'There isn't much I don't know.'

The guard came down. 'Really, sir.'

Bliss turned to Ransome. 'Fact is, Ian, we've found a new German magnetic mine.' He said to Sherwood without facing him, 'I believe you had a go at one last winter?'

Ransome saw the lieutenant nod, his defences falling slightly as his intelligent features recorded some memory – the mine, or another before it.

Bliss said, 'They found it in the Thames Estuary while we were in Sicily. Commander Foulerton said it was a more sophisticated version.' Then he did turn to Sherwood again. 'You know the name, I see?'

Sherwood nodded, a lock of fair hair dropping over his forehead. 'He was at HMS *Vernon* when I was there, sir. Taught me everything I know. A fine man.'

Bliss smiled gently. 'A regular officer too.' The smile vanished. 'Well, now we've found another one of the bastards, near Portland Bill, provided it hasn't blown up yet. It's being kept a close secret – we mustn't let Jerry know we've got one.' He glanced briefly at Ransome. 'Not yet anyway.'

In those flashing seconds Ransome saw Sherwood's face change again. As if he had seen a ghost.

Ransome said quickly, 'I don't see why we should – '

Bliss snapped. 'I can't send *Ranger*'s R.M.S.O., he's not got Sherwood's experience. Might just as well trundle some heavy-footed soldiery along!'

Sherwood asked quietly, 'You're asking *me* to go?'

Ransome interrupted, 'What about this Commander Foulerton – what does he suggest, sir?'

'Well, there you have it, Ian.' Bliss looked at Sherwood, his eyes hard. 'He was killed while he was handling the one in the Thames Estuary. The only information is what he passed over his telephone to an assistant. They had to keep his death hush-hush.'

Sherwood said softly, 'Christ!'

Bliss added, 'I wouldn't ask, but – '

Ransome picked up his pipe. Portland was one of the most important naval harbours on the South coast, about seventy miles from here.

He persisted, 'But he'd be doing other duties on board, sir. He'll need an assistant – '

Bliss didn't shift his gaze from Sherwood. 'I'll get somebody. I can't order you to go, Sherwood.'

Sherwood turned his cap over in his hands. He replied, 'You just did.' His eyes glittered in the deckhead light.

He looked at Ransome. 'I'll get my gear, sir. I don't want to take anyone I don't know. If Leading Writer Wakeford agrees I'd like him, please.'

Bliss stared. 'That's your writer, Ian – what does he know about it?'

Ransome was equally baffled but was determined not to show it. There was something so compelling and yet so sad about Sherwood that he knew there was no room for doubt.

Sherwood said calmly, 'Leading Writer Wakeford was an excellent physics and chemistry master in a good public school, or didn't you know that, sir?' He did not hide his contempt. 'But they said he was too old for a commission. What is he? Thirty-two? Not too old to get his arse blown off in bloody minesweepers, though!'

Bliss ignored the outburst, or perhaps he was so relieved that Sherwood had agreed to go that he had not noticed it.

Ransome nodded. 'Send for him.' He pictured the quiet leading writer who had acted as his helper, secretary, and shadow all the while he had been in *Rob Roy*. A withdrawn, gentle man.

Sherwood said, 'I've often discussed mines with him. He's got a very retentive mind.' He gave a bitter smile. 'But the navy doesn't seem to care too much about such trifles.'

Ransome nodded to him. 'I'll see you before you leave.'

As the door closed he said, 'I must disagree with you on this, sir.'

'*Why?* Because you know him, or because you need him here?' He watched him curiously. 'Or maybe it's because you think he's over the top already, too far gone to cope.' His tone hardened. 'I can't lament over personalities, Ian, not any more. God Almighty, I've seen enough youngsters get the chop – so have you. It's the bloody war, man, it doesn't help to look over your shoulder or to care too much. I *know*. I've been there and back a hundred times. He's probably the best man for the job, and right now he's the *only* man we've got available.' He leaned forward to emphasise each point. 'The Met people have promised good weather, or the best you can expect in winter. If the wind drops still further, Sherwood will have a fair chance. *But we must know!* The Allies will attempt to invade France next year, you can bet on it. With the Italian campaign slowing down to a crawl, they'll have to launch the landings whether they want to or not. Any secret weapon Jerry can create we must master before it drops in our laps.'

'I'd like to be there with him.'

Bliss's expression softened. 'I expect you would. But I need you here. I shall go with him. I know he hates my guts – better that than you worrying about him, eh?' He relaxed and smiled. 'Besides which, our vice-admiral, who, like the sick and needy, is always with us, will expect it.' He stood up and seized his cap. 'I'll go and rouse the driver.'

Ransome followed him out to the darkened deck. The first full day. What a way to end it. So Bliss had known all along that Sherwood would go; he had even laid on a car for the fast drive to Weymouth and Portland Bill.

They paused by the quartermaster's lobby and Bliss observed.

'It'll look good for the flotilla too, think of it that way!' Then he was gone.

Sherwood arrived eventually carrying a small bag. He had changed into old blue battledress and rubber boots, which Ransome knew he always wore on these dangerous assignments.

Sherwood glanced up at the sky. 'No more snow, then. That's good.' He sounded very cool. Almost disinterested. He faced Ransome and added quietly, 'Thanks for trying to put a spanner in the works.' He shrugged. 'It'll all be the same in a thousand years, I expect.'

They heard steps on the steel deck and Leading Writer Wakeford hurried into view.

'He agreed then.'

Sherwood smiled for the first time. 'Glad to go. You work him too hard, sir.'

Wakeford peered at Ransome and said, 'Sorry about this, sir, short notice, but I've done all the files you needed for the dockyard and – '

Ransome gripped his arm. It felt like a bone through his raincoat sleeve.

'Just take care of yourself. I can't manage without you.' He stood away. 'That goes for you both.' He saluted. 'I want you back as soon as possible.'

Sub-Lieutenant Morgan, who was staying aboard as O.O.D., watched them go and said, 'Your writer left some letters, sir. It's as if he knew.'

Ransome shivered. There was no point in asking about Sherwood. He had nobody to write to. He doubted if he would anyway. There had been grief enough in his young life.

He said, 'It looks as if your promotion may be delayed a while.'

Morgan stared into the darkness but the two figures had vanished.

'Suddenly it doesn't seem that important, see?' He shook his head. 'It's always just around the next corner, isn't it, sir?'

He did not explain but Ransome knew exactly what he meant.

The Reverend Canon Simon Warwick stood with one hand resting on the huge stone fireplace and stared thoughtfully into the flames of a cheerful log fire. It gave only an illusion of warmth however, for this room, like all the others in Codrington House, were too vast to heat easily. Once away from the fireplace and the winter intruded like a chill breath.

He glanced at his wife, who was sitting with a local lady dressed in the uniform of the Women's Voluntary Service, of which Betty had been the most active member until the bombing.

Sometimes it was difficult to pick up the threads of God's reasons and reasoning, he thought.

The two women were checking their lists of promised gifts offered by local shopkeepers and farmers for the Christmas raffle.

Warwick was already thinking of Christmas, of how hard it would be to decorate this rambling house and brighten things up for the ebb and flow of evacuees and homeless people who stayed here.

But he was finding it hard to concentrate. He could hear the clatter of plates and cutlery from the dining-room where two evacuee volunteers were laying the table for dinner. He hoped the W.V.S. lady would leave before any of his guests arrived. He knew it was an uncharitable thought, just as he knew the reason for his inability to concentrate on Christmas.

But for the sound of cheerful chatter and clink of crockery, he knew he would hear Eve's voice from the draughty hallway, where the private telephone was situated.

He frowned. Seeing her face in his mind, the young lieutenant-commander, so self-assured, who seemed to think of little but his ship and the war. He had said a lot, but their eyes when they met across the table had told another story. Warwick had felt it then, something akin to jealousy, more like a suitor than a father.

She had answered the telephone herself. Warwick shied away from the thought which touched his mind like a raw nerve. Would he have summoned her, had he answered Ransome's call first? Or might he had made some excuse? It would only postpone, rather than prevent it. But the thought remained, unanswered.

The W.V.S. lady stood up and snapped her handbag shut. She was a square, competent woman, a local magistrate, and the widow of an old major-general who had died in the neighbouring village.

She thrust out her hand and said, 'Goodbye, Canon.' Her handshake was like her heavy shoes, firm, sensible.

Betty played uncertainly with her necklace.

'Well, er, – I'll see you to your car.'

Warwick bit his lip. They were old friends, but he knew Betty had nearly revealed that she had forgotten her name.

The door opened and Eve walked in. She wore her heavy fisherman's jersey, and her favourite trousers with the paint smears.

She hugged her arms across her body and shivered. 'I'm like ice!'

Betty smiled at her. 'How is he, dear?'

Eve looked fondly at her mother. 'He's all right, Mummy.' She dropped her eyes. 'I – I think he's had a bad time.'

The W.V.S. lady exclaimed, 'What's this, Betty? A secret love? I must say, I'm not surprised, what?'

Warwick said, 'He's someone we used to see when we were on holidays, before – ' He did not go on.

The woman said knowingly, 'I see. Well, well!'

She crossed the room and put her hands on the girl's shoulders. 'He's a lucky boy!'

She replied, 'He's a man, not a boy. He commands a minesweeper.' It sounded like defiance, a defence against the trite summing-up and her father's constant refusal to accept that she had feelings.

Once her mother would have helped and understood. Now she seemed to wander, lost in her own thoughts, which nobody could share any more.

She said, 'I'm going up to have a bath and – ' She looked down at her daubed trousers and remembered his smile when he had seen them, how he had recalled those other times in the boatyard, reminded her without making her relive them as a young girl, but as an equal. 'And change, I suppose.'

Warwick tucked his hands into his cassock. 'Good idea. Don't be long. Early supper tonight. In case there's a raid on Plymouth.'

The W.V.S. lady was still watching Eve, her flashing eyes when she had spoken out. Such a quiet girl, who rarely mixed. But something had changed her. It would make a new topic at the bridge party on Saturday, she thought.

Eve closed the door behind her and leaned against it, hoping that the heavy fisherman's jersey had hidden the thrust of her breasts and her breathing, which had still not settled after speaking with him. A bad line, but they often were nowadays. She had sensed the change in his voice, the careful way he spoke, as if each word was precious to him.

But nothing could take the real happiness away. He was back, after all the months and the days, and the hours; his ship was in the dockyard. It might have been anywhere, in Scotland or in the North of England, but *Rob Roy* had come to Plymouth. He had not told her in so many words, and she had had the feeling that many ears were on the line, fingers waiting to snatch away the hissing, noisy connection. By mentioning the gardens around this old house, he had made her realise where he was.

He could not say when he would see her. There were 'things' which had to be done. Again, she had felt the same sense of anxiety, that someone he cared about was in danger.

She ran up the great spiral staircase to her room. She did not even see the flaking paint, the rough notices pasted to the wall which gave directions about the nearest air-raid shelters, what to do in a gas attack, how to deal with an incendiary if one fell through the ceiling.

She arrived in her room and stood panting by the window before drawing the heavy black-out curtains. There had been snow, but most of it had melted.

Perhaps he would be home for Christmas? She threw herself on the bed and pressed the old teddy bear against her face.

She thought of his brother, the irrepressible Tony, who was still in the naval hospital. *He* was to be home for Christmas; he had written to her, had told her about meeting Ian in Sicily. It had taken several attempts before she could control her tears and read it.

She had made a point of visiting Fowey to see his parents. His father had hugged her warmly and treated her like one of the family. His mother had kept a polite distance, playing much the same role as the Canon downstairs. She had gone to see his old boat, the *Barracuda*, and the foreman Jack Weese had pulled her leg about sailing off with her before young Master Ian got home for good. It could all have been so different. She closed her mind to the other thought. That it might still change.

She opened a drawer and took out his precious letters, and lastly the big newspaper article written by the celebrity war correspondent Richard Wakely. It was very much like the broadcast, so that when she read and reread it she heard his familiar voice describing the scene just as he had witnessed and shared it. The shrill scream of Stuka dive-bombers, the roar of ships exploding, the troops fighting their way up the Sicilian beaches.

Richard Wakely had been right there beside Ian. Could have reached out and touched him. Wakely's cameraman had taken several action pictures, and one of them had been of Ian.

He had been looking up at the sky, pointing with one arm while smoke rose behind him like an evil presence.

She looked at the picture now. *Oh, dearest of men, I love you so.*

Wakely had finished his broadcast like the article, with his usual flourish.

'Together, that young captain and I had looked into the face of death, and come through yet again.'

She had written to the newspaper and had asked if it was possible to purchase a copy of the print of Ian's picture. So far there had been no response.

She walked into her small bathroom and turned on the taps. She saw the unopened jar of bath salts by the window. They didn't make it any more. As the lady in the shop had said wistfully, 'I expect it's used for explosives now!'

Eve would save it, as she had – She felt her face flushing and left the bathroom. Then she did something she never normally did. She locked the bedroom door, and stood in front of the wardrobe mirror for several tormenting seconds, while the hot water hissed into the huge bath like a pool of lava.

Very deliberately she opened a flat drawer at the bottom of the wardrobe and took out the nightdress. She carefully removed the little sachet of rosebuds and rosemary although their fragrance remained in the fine white silk, as it had for the two years since she had bought it. She smiled and held it up against herself while she watched the image in the mirror and remembered. She had almost emptied her post office savings account to buy it, in the days before rationing had made such luxuries beyond the reach of all but the very rich and the black market. She had taken two buses to go to another district and withdraw the money, in case the local postmistress might tell her mother what she had done.

She made up her mind, and pulled the jersey over her head and slipped the trousers down to her ankles.

Her heart was beating painfully; she kept her gaze on her own reflected stare as she tossed her underwear on to the bed and stood quite naked, with the nightdress held up to her chin. She would not put it on until . . .

Two years she had had it. She had known then, and before that, that she had wanted him. If he had turned instead to another, she would never have married. She did not know how she was so certain. She just knew.

Her mother called, 'Will you be long, dear?'

She smiled and carefully folded the sachet inside the nightdress before slipping it into its special bag.

'Ten minutes, Mummy!'

She walked, naked, across the cold room and into the steamy embrace of the bath.

Soon. They would make up for all things lost. Together.

The big staff car seemed to be hurtling into complete darkness. With the headlamps almost blinded by the regulation shields to prevent them being seen from the air, objects loomed out of the shadows as if the driver had lost control.

Commander Bliss muttered, 'God Almighty, I'm glad she knows the road!'

She was a leading Wren from the C-in-C's staff at Plymouth, a small, wiry girl, who seemed to be enjoying the drive, a conflict between herself and the car.

Sherwood saw pale cottages, their small windows blacked out, crouched by the roadside, then gaps where the fields took over again, gaunt hedgerows which shone in the dipped beams from the melted snow, and once a horse staring over a gate, its eyes like bright stones in the glare.

Up to Exeter and away from the sea to Honiton in Devon, the windscreen wipers fighting a losing battle against the mud and slush thrown up from the road by other vehicles. Most of the latter were military, Sherwood noticed, huge lorries which seemed to fill the breadth of the unmarked road.

In the front seat beside the driver, Leading Writer Wakeford sat stiffly back in his swaying seat, and Sherwood got the impression he had both feet pressed against the floor – as well he might.

Sherwood kept thinking of Ransome's attempt to keep him from this unexpected assignment. He had heard about Wakeford's letters, which he had left in safe keeping, and wondered why he had not done the same. Just a note, a few words to try and explain why he had left her asleep, why he had not even written to her.

If this job went badly wrong . . . He glanced out of the streaked window so that he could avoid opening another conversation with Bliss. He seemed to speak of little else but The War, in capital letters. It was like being cooped up with the nine o'clock news, he thought.

The mine might easily explode. Something new could have been added. Bliss had stopped the car once to make a telephone call: when he had returned he had said that the mine was still intact. He had sounded almost relieved, as if it would have spoiled his record to lose it.

Sherwood thought of the girl called Rosemary, the way they had clung to one another, had demanded so much that they were totally spent.

A letter would have made it worse for her; that is, if she cared after what he had done.

He thought too of the men who shared his life in *Rob Roy*, a typical small ship's company. How long would they remember him if things went wrong? He forced a smile. Just a dog-watch, as the old sailors said.

He could picture some of them now, making their different ways to all points of the compass. The luckier ones would already be home, down at the local pub, or picking up the pieces of a broken marriage, discovering peace away from their messmates, from everything. Others might still be wondering what they would find. A gap where the house had once stood, sympathy, and a feeling of utter loneliness.

He thought of Rosemary again. She was alone. Could she remember her husband, the soldier called Tom? Had she been loving *him* on that last, desperate night in Mayfair?

Sherwood heard his bag rattle behind the seat as the car lurched over to avoid a man pushing a bicycle. The man shouted something after them and the little Wren murmured, 'Stupid sod. Trying to get his name in the papers.' She seemed to remember her senior passenger and added, 'Sorry, sir.'

Bliss replied cheerfully, 'Just so long as we get there, eh?'

Sherwood thought of the two bottles of gin he had in his bag, packed alongside his instruments. That was what he needed right now. Oblivion. He recalled his feeling of disbelief when Bliss had told him about Commander Foulerton. It did not seem possible that it could happen to him. He was a genius. A quiet, unassuming man who had known more about mines than any other human being, be they magnetic or acoustic, dropped from the air, or laid by any ship which could slip through the defences.

As Bliss had been quick to point out, Foulerton had been a regular officer. But he had not mentioned that he had been a ranker, who had joined the peacetime navy as a boy, and had got there by his own sweat and intelligence. These rare characters who had climbed up to the quarterdeck the hard way were the backbone of the navy. He thought of *Rob Roy*'s engineer officer, John Campbell, and poor old Bone with his dentures and his stomach troubles. They had to stand aside now and leave the medals to younger men, but without them the fleet would never have put to sea.

He leaned forward, as if his mind had been triggered like a time-fuse.

'The sea. I'm sure I can smell it!'

The Wren called over her shoulder but fortunately never took her eyes from the twisting road.

'That's right, sir. That was Lyme Regis. We're in Dorset now. We should be there in an hour at this rate!'

Bliss said irritably, 'A few hours sleep then. I hope somebody has remembered to arrange our messing and accommodation.' When Sherwood remained silent he added, 'Well?'

Sherwood replied, 'I shall go to the place first.'

The Wren had up to then believed that Bliss was some kind of V.I.P. Now she knew differently. The young pale-faced lieutenant who rarely spoke or smiled was the one who counted for some reason. She had been told nothing, so it was obviously important.

Bliss said, 'It's up to you, of course – '

Sherwood stopped it there. 'So it seems.'

Sherwood touched the girl's shoulder and apologised as she jerked with alarm.

'Sorry.' He pointed ahead through the filthy windscreen. 'What's the next place?'

She said, 'Bridport, sir. We stop for a road-check usually, provided the army or the Home Guard haven't all gone to the pub!'

'I'd like to make a phone call from there.'

She seemed to sense the tension, the sudden determination in his tone. 'Know just the spot, sir.'

Sherwood took out his wallet and felt the small notebook in the darkness. Why had he taken her telephone number? What did he think he was doing?

They swept through a checkpoint, waved on by some vague, helmeted figures beside a sandbagged barrier.

Bliss said, 'We could have been bloody Germans for all they know!'

The Wren was glad it was too dark for Bliss to see her grin. She knew most of the personnel who mounted these checkpoints, and few of them would care to stop one of the C-in-C's own cars.

She exclaimed, 'Here it is now, sir.'

Sherwood felt the car slew off the road and saw a small inn, its weathered sign swaying slightly in the chill breeze. Like a scene from *Treasure Island*, he thought.

Bliss said, 'Don't be too long.' It sounded as if he was trying to reassert himself. 'I'll just go and pump the bilges while we're here.' He peered at his watch. 'Why not snatch a pint? It's still opening time, or near enough.'

Wakeford shook his head. 'Not tonight, sir, but thanks all the same. Tomorrow, well, now, that'll be different.'

Sherwood touched his shoulder and opened the door. Probably too close to the truth for comfort, he thought.

As the two officers left the car and separated in the darkness the Wren asked, 'What's it all about?'

Wakeford shrugged. 'That's Lieutenant Sherwood. The one who was given the George Cross, remember?' He saw her eyes widen in the pale oval of her face. 'He's gone to phone someone. Probably thinks it's his last chance.'

She looked away. 'You make it sound like the condemned man.'

Wakeford sighed. 'He is, in a way.'

Sherwood in the meantime had found his way into a bar which was barely furnished, with six farm labourers and two dogs the only customers.

The landlord looked at Sherwood without curiosity. His old battledress with the tarnished gold stripes on the shoulders implied he was up to something. That was nothing new along this stretch of coast. It was safer not to ask.

347

'Telephone, Skipper? Roight through therr – ' His accent was as West Country as Drake.

Sherwood sat on a small stool and held his book near a ship's lantern with an electric bulb shaped like an ancient candle. He dialled the number, then had to ask the exchange to help him. Then he had a crossed line, and he thought he heard a car door slam: Bliss displaying his impatience.

Sherwood tightened his lips. *Well, let him. He's not taking the risks.* A straight-forward bed-and-breakfast job for *him.*

A man's voice answered and Sherwood almost replaced the receiver. Then he remembered. She had said that she lived with her elderly parents.

'Er, could I speak to, er – Rosemary, please?'

There was a lengthy pause, as if the man was thinking about it.

He said, 'It's a bit late, y'know!'

Sherwood felt the desperation rising like a flood.

'I must speak with her!'

'Now just hold on, whoever you are. My daughter's not – '

There was a muffled sound, and he guessed the telephone had been covered by somebody's hand.

When she spoke the line was suddenly clear. It was as if she was right here beside him.

'Who is that?'

He tried to explain. 'I had to speak to you. To tell you – ' He got no further.

'Oh, Philip, where are you? I've been so anxious, so terribly worried. I thought you disliked me, that I'd done something – '

He said, 'Please. Listen to me. I have to leave right now. It's a job I must do.' Now that he had begun he could not stop. 'I'm not sure what's going to happen.' He heard her sharp intake of breath but hurried on. 'I just wanted you to know what you did for me, how happy those days together really were.'

She said, 'I know. I wrote to you several times, but – '

'They're still following me, I expect.' He heard the car toot its horn. 'I didn't want to hurt you, Rosemary, you've had enough, but I couldn't be so near to you without – ' He stared at the telephone, his eyes smarting. He was doing everything he had sworn not to do.

She said, 'Don't hang up. Whatever it is, wherever you have to go, please take care, for me if nothing else – I must see you again, Philip.' She waited and added, 'Are you still there?'

'Yes.' One word, and he could barely get it out.

'I shall never forget either – '

Sherwood murmured, 'Goodbye, darling girl.' He put down the telephone and two pennies beside it before walking back through the bar. They were all still in their places. Only one of the dogs had moved.

He climbed into the car without speaking.

Wakeford asked quietly, 'All right, sir?'

Sherwood watched the bushes gathering speed again. 'Yes. Now it is.'

He did not speak again until the car rolled to a halt and the sea opened up to greet him like an old enemy.

It took Sherwood only a few minutes to gather all the facts he needed. The mine's parachute had snared itself on some sunken boat, a local fisherman's apparently. The wind was still without much power, but there was a hint of more to come, snow too.

In the back of an army fifteen-hundredweight Chevrolet, its red-painted wings marking it as one of the Bomb Disposal Squad, Sherwood studied the map, his breath mingling with that of two sapper officers, and a lieutenant from the naval base at Portland.

The mine was too close to the Chesil Beach, that strange ridge of stones which ran parallel to the coast, right down to the northern part of Portland Bill itself. It was an eerie place even in daylight, the graveyard for many ships through the centuries, although some were said to have been lured here by wreckers.

Now, with the breeze sighing against the wet stones, and the knowledge that the mine was just offshore on a sandbar, it would make anyone's flesh creep.

Sherwood said, 'It's low water. This has to be done quickly. If the parachute breaks adrift, or the mine is thrown up on this beach, we'll not get a sniff at it.' The two sappers nodded together. They had probably defused enough bombs and mines in their time. They would not be here otherwise. One said, 'We've rigged the line for tomorrow.' Sherwood lowered himself to the ground and sniffed the bitter, damp air. Tomorrow might be too late. Why did he think that? Was it because he knew his nerve would not last until then?

'It's got to be now. I'll need two good lights.' He laughed to break the sudden tension. 'The black-out will have to put up with it!'

'What's all this about lights?'

Vice-Admiral Hargrave, followed by two aides, marched down the beach.

Sherwood murmured, 'God, it's getting like a flag-day!'

The vice-admiral studied the map and then said, 'You're right, Sherwood.' So far he had not spoken to Bliss at all. 'See that it's done.' One aide hurried away. To the other he snapped, 'Tell the police inspector to get on with the evacuation. Those cottages up there, and anyone else who might – '

Sherwood was crouching beside his bag. 'Get blown up, sir?'

The vice-admiral chuckled. 'Sorry about that.'

Sherwood took Wakeford's thin arm and led him away from the others. 'According to the map there's part of a concrete wall which the Royal Engineers built here as an exercise. Run the telephone line up to that and keep out of sight.'

'Yes, sir.'

Sherwood touched his lips; they were bone-dry. 'Look, I can't keep calling you Leading Writer Wakeford, now can I, under these sorry circumstances. What's your first name?'

Wakeford looked at the beach. 'Horace, sir. A name I have always detested.'

It was suddenly very necessary to find and keep close contact with this gentle man. He would probably be the last one to hear his voice; would need to write it all down, so that the next poor idiot – He persisted, 'What did the kids at school call you behind your back?'

Wakeford seemed to brighten up. 'Stinky, sir, because of my job.'

'So be it.' Sherwood handed him his cap. 'The inshore sounds are a nuisance. I must be able to hear.' He gripped his arm. 'Off you go. If I say the word, hit the deck sharpish!'

Wakeford stared at him in the darkness. 'If, I mean, sir, how long?'

Sherwood picked up his bag. 'If the fuse goes, there's usually about twelve seconds to play with.'

Wakeford watched him stride down the beach where more anonymous figures hovered at the water's edge, while some stood in the sea itself, holding a small rubber boat.

Sherwood saw the sappers paying out a field-telephone line while they waded through the shallows, pushing the boat ahead of them. Once the tide began to turn it would be too late yet again. As he held on to the boat and sloshed through the water with the others, Sherwood tried to remember everything he had learned about this type of mine. Packed with over fifteen hundred pounds of deadly hexanite. Enough to knock down several streets, or demolish a cruiser.

A sapper switched on one of the lights, and Sherwood could imagine the consternation on the shore. It was so close it was startling, lying half-submerged, the torn parachute vanishing into the shadows of deeper water. The mine was cleaner than usual because of the sea. The one he had dealt with before had been grimy with black filth from the exhaust smoke of the plane which had unloaded it. He could see the identifying letters and figures shining in the hard beam, the way it appeared to roll about in the current. But that was only a trick of the light – otherwise he would be dead.

'All right, Sergeant, take your chaps off now.' The men moved back into the surrounding darkness.

Sherwood felt the sea breeze like ice on his face. He had tried to make it sound encouraging for Wakeford's sake. Twelve seconds. Maybe. But here the real difference was that there was nowhere to run, no empty house, or garden wall, or as in one incident, pressed against a railway embankment. That one had exploded and he had seen two complete railway carriages fly over his head as if they were paper kites.

He tested the telephone. 'D'you hear me, Stinky?' He made himself chuckle, although he felt as if the breath was being strangled out of him.

'Yes, sir.'

'Write this down. It's a Type Seven. That's the only classification we have to go on so far.' He measured it with his eye, moving the light an inch at a time until the beam was shining beneath the slopping water. 'About nine feet six long, I'd say.' He paused to tug his bag clear of the water on to a small hump of sand. The sea sounds seemed so loud out here. The tiny purr of the fuse would probably pass unheard. Not that it would make any difference anyway.

'I've found the fuse.' He fumbled for his special callipers, the ones he used to prevent it from moving and coming to life. He wiped the spray, or was it sweat, from his eyes. The callipers locked on to the keeping ring which held the whole fuse in position.

Sherwood rocked back on his heels. 'There's something wrong.' He did not realise he had spoken aloud.

'What is it, sir?'

'Not sure.' He peered into the water again. Was his mind playing tricks or was it already deeper?

'It's too easy, Stinky. All I have to do is unscrew it, just like the earlier models.'

Wakeford said, 'Be careful, sir.'

Sherwood smiled despite his raw nerves. *Careful.* Commander Foulerton had died trying to defuse one of these mines. He was a true expert, a professional. Otherwise, this mine might indeed be one of the easy jobs. Lucky to have been washed clean by the sea, to have come to rest the right way up.

Sherwood moved slowly along the mine, his free hand feeling it as if it was alive.

He returned to the fuse again and touched the keeping ring with his fingertips. A few turns, and the whole thing would slide out. Not easy, but not impossible.

It was then that his hand began to shake as if he had a fever. He put the light in his bag and gripped his wrist with the other hand. *For Christ's sake, not now!* He tried again. If they were on dry land, he would risk attaching a tackle to the hoisting flaps. As if to mock him the wind ruffled his hair, and part of the sodden parachute floated against his thigh like a shroud.

There was no more time. His whole body was quivering. What he had always dreaded more than anything.

He picked up the lamp again and began another careful inspection. A voice seemed to jeer at him. *You're putting it off. It's over. Why not give the brute a kick and end it all right now?*

He tried to cling to fragments of memory, like a man caught in a dying ship's final whirlpool. Her voice on the telephone. When was it, one, two hours ago? Was that all?

He pulled out the special spanner he had had made for himself at *Vernon*. Foulerton had probably used the original one.

He stared wildly at his flickering reflection in the water. *Hoisting flaps!* It seemed to scream out at him so that he almost dropped the lamp.

He spoke carefully on the field telephone. 'Stinky. This mine has hoisting flaps. They stopped using them eighteen months ago.'

'I – I don't understand, sir!'

'Don't try, old son.' He recalled his words to the Canadian major in Sicily when Ransome had run to the stretcher. 'Just pray!'

He lined up the flap with the fuse, tightened his spanner around it and then stared at the low clouds.

Twelve seconds. He put his weight on it. Nothing happened at first, then it scraped away from its new paint and began to turn.

He gasped, 'It's under the flap, Stinky.' He let the lamp fall into the sea by his boot, which had now filled with icy water. Another turn, and another. How much time would he have to know what was happening?

He shouted, 'It's here, under the flap. I'm doing it now.' He inserted the callipers and began to turn. Suppose Foulerton had seen it too, and this was the real booby-trap.

He yelled, 'Well, it's too bloody late now, you bastards!'

The fuse slid into his fingers, and the sudden silence seemed to probe his ears like fingers. He returned to the original ring and inserted the callipers. Inside the gap there was the second fuse, now made harmless by his discovery. But for some warning instinct the mine would have exploded at the first or second turn of the keeping ring.

He heard Wakeford calling, 'Are you all right, sir? Please answer me!'

He bent over against the mine and gasped into the telephone, 'Come and get me out of this! I – I can't move!' He vomited over the telephone and hurled it into the water.

Men were running through the water towards him, then someone put his arm round his waist and a voice shouted, 'Here, lend a hand! The poor bastard's done his bit for the night!'

Then there was Wakeford on the Chesil Beach, although Sherwood did not remember how he got there. It was no longer empty, but dark figures ran and bustled in all directions.

Commander Bliss reached out and took his hand. It was like a piece of ice.

Bliss said, 'I wondered what you chaps did. Now that I know, I'd still like to be told *how* you do it! That was a bloody brave thing you just did.'

Sherwood tried to speak, but nothing made sense. He was shaking so badly he knew he would have fallen but for the others holding him. The Wren driver wrapping a rug over his shoulders, laughing and sobbing at the same time, the vice-admiral thumping the beach with a walking-stick and booming, 'Well, how about that, eh?'

Wakeford whispered, 'What is it, sir?'

'Just get me away from here. Somewhere I can use a telephone.' Then he fainted.

Bliss said, 'Call up *Rob Roy*. Tell her captain. He wanted to be told at once, though we were all expecting it would be tomorrow.' He glanced up at the clouds as the wind whipped his coat against his legs. 'Then it would have been too late, I fear.'

He watched some soldiers carrying Sherwood up the beach towards the road.

'I don't know how many of those damnable things that lieutenant has made safe, but I swear to God, that one will be his last.' He looked out at the black water as if expecting to see it lying there, as evil and as patient as ever, but there was only the faint gleam where Sherwood had lost one of his lamps in the water, and the sigh of a tide on the turn.

When Wakeford returned to the car he found Sherwood sitting in the back, the rug still around his shoulders, his face hidden in his hands.

The Wren whispered, 'He was just sick again.'

Sherwood looked up; in the darkness his eyes were like holes.

'Telephone?'

'D'you think you should, sir?'

'Please.' His voice was very small. 'Help me.'

They found a telephone at the police station where the news of the mine had obviously been a lively topic since it had been dropped by an enemy aircraft one night earlier. The German pilot had probably jettisoned it because he was caught in a barrage, or being pursued by night fighters. They would never know.

Tomorrow the sappers would haul the mine from the sea and then it would be the boffins' chance to examine it.

Sherwood found himself in a small office with pictures on the wall of wanted criminals and missing persons.

Wakeford got the number for him, handed him the telephone and then withdrew. He tried to smile at him, to offer some encouragement, but all he could think about was the sound of Sherwood's voice on the field telephone, like a man staring at the rope or a firing squad.

Sherwood heard her voice immediately.

She said huskily, 'Somehow I knew you would phone. I had to wait. To be sure. Tell me what to do.'

Sherwood tried to clear his mind. 'I want to see you. Now. I – I need to – '

She said quickly, 'Where are you? I'll come at once.'

He tried to laugh. 'The police have offered to drive me, you see.'

She said, 'I shall be here, waiting. Don't do anything, just come.'

But Sherwood could not reply this time. His defences had finally broken down.

17

——————

Reunions

Ian Ransome stamped his feet on the stone flags to restore the circulation and watched the snow falling steadily from a dull grey afternoon sky.

Every so often he turned and looked at the massive abbey and the groups of people who were making their way towards it.

Many of them were in the uniforms of all three services; in fact they outnumbered the civilians. Some were accompanied by girl-friends, others walked purposefully and alone. There was no saluting although the ranks varied from army privates to at least one group captain from the local air station.

Eve had chosen this place where they would meet for the first time since *Rob Roy* had entered the dockyard. That had been three days ago, with only their brief, sometimes anxious telephone calls to sustain them.

There was a concert being held at the abbey, musicians from Plymouth and some surrounding towns, plus a few in uniform. She had remembered that he enjoyed classical music, and had bought tickets for this one performance.

It was not just that. She had told him on the last telephone call, she wanted them to meet *on their own ground*. Perhaps she meant away from her usual surroundings, even her father? He had answered Ransome's calls twice and had been outwardly friendly, and yet Ransome felt his reserve; he was careful not to display too much warmth.

He glanced at his watch and saw the snow clinging to his sleeve. He thought of Sherwood, what Cusack had said when he had gone to see him.

The astute Irish doctor had described finding him in the care of the young woman to whom he had gone directly after the incident with the mine.

'Before he never felt fear, y'see, because he no longer *cared* about living. He thought that his life, in its deepest sense, was finished, with only some driving force keeping him going, a determination to hit back at the enemy in a field he knew better than most.' He had shrugged and downed another glass of Ransome's Scotch. 'Then everything changed. He and this woman found one another, though that part was left suitably vague for my benefit, I suspect. Philip

Sherwood did explain how it hit him when he was working on the mine. He thought of dying, and for the first time since his life had been smashed to pieces, he wanted, no, *needed* to live.'

Thank God Sherwood was not required for duty. He wanted to come back to *Rob Roy*, but Ransome knew inwardly that he was finished with his lonely encounters with mines and whatever the enemy could dream up, forever. Perhaps in his strange, distant fashion he wanted to share his change of fortune with the only people he really liked.

He heard a door closing behind him and felt a start of anxiety. Maybe she had changed her mind? Or she had been prevented from coming? A small bus rolled to a stop with slush dripping from its sides, and suddenly she was there, running towards him, her arms outstretched, oblivious to the other passengers and the grinning bus driver.

They clung together for a long moment, saying nothing, each reassured that it was really true.

Then she said, 'Shall we go inside?' She looked up at him, searched his face, and in those few seconds she saw it all. The shadows beneath his eyes, the small tight lines at the corners of his mouth. She wanted to keep on hugging him, to hold him as she would a child, and make the strain go away.

She asked, 'Perhaps you'd rather not? I – I mean they're not from Covent Garden or the Albert Hall. But I thought – '

Ransome put his arm around her shoulders and guided her into the ageless shadows of the entrance, where he shook the snowflakes from his cap on to the worn stones. 'I'd *love* to, Eve. I can't tell you – '

A wizened usher guided them to their seats in one of the pews. The place was quite cold, but strangely moving with its flickering candles and air of timeless strength.

She pressed against him while he spread his greatcoat over their knees like a rug.

She whispered, 'No heating. To save fuel.'

A man in an unfamiliar uniform touched Ransome's shoulder. 'Excuse me, sir, but would you let this party into your pew?'

Ransome had wondered why the rest of the pew had been empty when the abbey appeared to be packed.

A line of young RAF officers filed past them, silent, and looking neither right nor left. The highest ranking one was a flight-lieutenant. They were all about Eve's age.

As the last one attempted to pass he knocked a prayer book from its shelf, stooped down and then handed it to Eve with a mumbled apology. He had been a good-looking youth, but now half of his face had been burned away. Just like wax, with a gleaming glass eye to complete the mockery of his survival. The others were much the same, burned, mutilated, and somehow embarrassed.

Eve said, 'Thank you. There's not much room, is there, in such a big place.'

Ransome saw the young pilot stare at her. Astonished that anyone who looked like her could treat him as if he were normal. Perhaps he had once had a girl like her, before –

Ransome saw a tear run from his remaining eye before one of the others pulled his sleeve and said jokingly, 'Come away, Bill, she's in the navy's care!'

What did each hour cost them? Yesterday's heroes.

Ransome felt her fingers digging into his hand. But she did not speak this time.

He glanced around. The wounded pilots still had the same need as the other servicemen here, he thought. Like an oasis, to help repair what they had lost.

The orchestra made itself comfortable, and while a senior lay churchman made a ponderous introduction there were all the usual exciting if discordant sounds of musicians tuning up.

It was a mixed Baroque concert, the Telemann violin concertos, and after a freezing fifteen-minute interval, a selection from Handel's *Water Music*. Eve had even remembered that, and Ransome thought of his small and dwindling collection of Handel records in *Rob Roy*. Too many explosions and near-misses had done for most of them.

And all the while he was very aware of the girl beside him, her warmth, the scent of her long hair, and when he glanced at her profile, the memory of those other times. Was it wrong to hope in wartime? Could it even be fair to profess love when each day the odds against survival mounted?

Then the concert was over, and they were outside in the snow again.

'I have to get back.' He hated each word.

'I know.' She thrust her arm through his as they walked towards the bus-stop. 'You warned me.' Then she turned and looked at him. 'I'm so happy, Ian. Just to have you with me. I shall never forget this, the concert –' her eyes dropped. 'Those poor airmen. Everything. I feel a part of it now because of you.'

Ransome had already been told about Richard Wakely's broadcast and newspaper article. He should have guessed. Wakely's image was far more important to him than trying to score points off the men who had been there, who had seen him grovelling and blubbering for his own skin. Perhaps in its way his was a kind of courage too. Being in contact with events which could strike terror and revulsion into you when you did not have to, because of duty, or whatever sent a man to war . . .

The bus floundered through some deep puddles and they climbed on to it. It was about twenty miles to Plymouth and yet it seemed to pass in minutes.

When they reached the outskirts of the city it was pitch-dark, with only the falling snow giving any sort of life to it.

She said, 'Thank you for meeting me at Buckfastleigh.' She shivered, although not from cold. 'Sometimes when you spend your days in and around Christianity it can become oppressive.' She smiled and wrapped her arms around his neck. 'But never with you!'

Ransome gripped her and wanted to blurt out everything, as Sherwood had probably done. As he held her against him he was very aware that she was no longer the schoolgirl, and he knew she understood what he was thinking.

She said, 'When can we meet? Please make it soon. I've been so worried, I've tried to be with you wherever you were. Then seeing your picture, hearing how it was –'

He replied, 'I'll call you tomorrow. Things on board should be in hand by then. I'll have to go and visit my parents – Tony will be home too, with any luck.' He looked at her, then kissed her very gently on the cheek, feeling the snow melt on his lips. 'Will you come with me?'

She nodded. 'We can look at your funny boat.' She was almost in tears.

'Don't be sad, Eve. I love you more than ever, at least I would if that were possible. I don't want to share you with anyone.'

She touched his mouth with her fingers. 'I know. Once I didn't dare to admit what I was thinking about you.' She shook her head. 'No, don't look at me! I never knew I could feel that way, so utterly wanton.'

Another bus groped its way towards them. She said breathlessly, 'I want you, Ian.' Then she kissed him hard on the mouth and ran to the bus. He watched her wiping the condensation off a window with her sleeve to wave to him as the bus headed away towards Codrington House.

Ransome thrust his hands into his greatcoat pockets and walked slowly into the deeper darkness, his whole being clinging to those last words. *I want you.* No demands or conditions, not even a doubt, without knowing it she had already given him the greatest gift of all. Her trust.

When he reached *Rob Roy* there was an air-raid warning in progress, two seamen of the duty watch were under arrest for being drunk and disorderly in a dockside canteen, and Vice-Admiral Hargrave had been asking for him several times on the shore telephone.

Ransome listened to Morgan's report and then touched his arm. 'Deal with it, will you. Then come to my cabin and listen to some music.'

Sub-Lieutenant Morgan watched him go below and smiled.

Like the cat that found the cream, he thought. And about time too.

Ordinary Seaman Boyes felt his heart quicken as a camouflaged Bedford three-tonner rolled into the station yard and spilled its khaki occupants on to the slushy snow. For a moment longer, he thought she was not there, and realised just how much he wanted to see her again. Then he saw her, her face lighting up in a grin as she pushed through the soldiers and A.T.S. girls from her battery who had been given a lift into town.

It was hardly like the West End, but he guessed that anything was probably better than gaunt army huts in Home Park across the river from where the battery provided A.A. support for the sky above London.

She let him kiss her and stepped back to look at him.

'How long have you been back, then?'

'Two days.' It sounded like an apology. 'I had to see the parents of one of our people in *Rob Roy*.' He looked at her, his eyes pleading. 'He was killed at Sicily.'

She put her arm through his. 'Never mind, Gerry. I'm taking you to a party. It'll be warm at least, and more important, it's free.'

As they walked she glanced at him. He had changed in some way. Not matured, that would be too simple; if anything he had seemed more defenceless when he had blurted out about someone who had bought it at Sicily. His face held a kind of desperation, made him look older.

They crossed a street near the riverside of Kingston-on-Thames, with the massive chimneys of the power station standing against the dull sky like abandoned lighthouses. He did not know where she was taking him. He had hoped to be alone with her, and recalled his mother's tone when he had telephoned the army camp to ask for her.

She had warned, 'Don't get into any trouble, that's all I ask.'

His father had murmured soothingly, 'Don't worry, dear. He's home now, and to all accounts he's earned a bit of leave.' He might just as well have saved his breath.

Boyes thought of his visit to Davenport's home. It was as if the midshipman's body was still in the house. Everything was so still and deathly quiet.

They had been civil enough, but when he had left he had had the feeling that Davenport's parents resented his being alive while their son lay fathoms deep in the Mediterranean.

Davenport's father had asked just once, 'Did he suffer? Was he able to speak?'

Boyes had replied as truthfully as he could. 'He didn't feel very much.' He thought of Davenport clinging to the talisman of his promotion even as his life had drained away.

Davenport's mother had asked almost sharply, 'How could you know that?'

Boyes had got to his feet and had answered without hesitation, 'Because I was with him. He died in my arms.' Before, he would have stammered and felt in the wrong. That at least he had left behind.

The girl dragged his arm around a corner, an ordinary street of Victorian houses. It could have been anywhere.

She stopped outside one of them, 'Here 'tis. Might be fun.'

A gramophone was cranking out dance music, and she led him into the sitting-room where several others were already swapping jokes and making steady headway into crates of bottled beer. The owner of the house was apparently a local butcher, who did quite a bit of business with the army in Home Park. His wife, a lively looking girl with dyed blonde hair and wearing, surprisingly, a bright party dress, was obviously a good bit younger than her husband, but they both made Boyes and the girl called Connie very welcome.

There was Connie's friend Sheila with a bombardier from the battery, and a massive quartermaster-sergeant whose contacts with the butcher had opened the way for this and perhaps previous parties.

A leading aircraftman and his girl, related in some unexplained way to the host, made up the party.

Connie settled down on a sofa beside him and took two glasses of beer from the table.

'Cheers, Sarge!'

The quartermaster-sergeant beamed at her and touched his ginger moustache. He nodded to Boyes. 'Up the navy!' Then he turned to his host and thrust another full pint into his hands. 'Come on, my son, drink up! It'll put hair on your chest!'

Connie giggled. 'You'd think it was *his* beer he's being so free with!'

Boyes tried to remember how much he was drinking. He did not usually drink, and was too young to draw his tot of rum as Beckett had often reminded him. The thought of the coxswain and his friend the randy Buffer touched him like a hot wire. The shell screaming and ricochetting around the wheelhouse, men dying, Richard Wakely attempting to hide under the table where Davenport lay bleeding.

Connie saw his expression. 'What is it, Gerry?'

He shook his head, not wanting to spoil anything. 'Someone walked on my grave, that's all.'

She did not believe him but said, 'I'm just going to powder my nose.' She waited for his eyes to meet hers. 'Remember the last time, you naughty boy!' Then she was gone.

Boyes could not remember how long she had been away, and for one awful moment imagined she had become irritated by his mood and had left, perhaps with somebody else.

He stared around the room. All but a table lamp had been switched off; Sheila and her bombardier lay in one another's arms, her stockinged feet curled over his massive army boots.

The leading aircraftman and his girl were trying to dance without cannoning into the beer crates and empty bottles.

Boyes blinked. Surely they hadn't drunk all that? Then he saw the butcher and knew that he must have consumed the bulk of it. Their host lay propped in a corner, his mouth open, his shirt and waistcoat sodden with spilled beer. He was out to the world.

The leading aircraftman and his girl left without speaking, so that only the quartermaster-sergeant and the butcher's wife remained in the centre of the floor, slowly gyrating but barely moving to the beat of the music.

The sergeant had his arm around her waist and was pressing her against him, while she clung to his neck, her body swaying even when the record came to an end.

Boyes noticed that her party dress was caught in the sergeant's uniform, but when they turned slowly once again he realised why the hostess had her eyes tightly closed. The sergeant's other hand was thrust up beneath her skirt.

Connie opened the door softly and quickly turned over the record. She looked at Boyes and held out her hand. 'Sorry to leave you with this lot, but I had things to do.' She pulled him to his feet. 'They won't miss us.'

She led the way up the stairs to a narrow landing and asked, 'Home for Christmas, d'you reckon?'

'Don't know.' He noticed that she did not look at him, and had the same bright nervousness as that time in the cinema.

She opened a door and waited for him to enter. He saw her lock it behind them, then turn to watch his reactions.

'I don't think they'll be wanting their bed, do you, Gerry?'

Boyes felt his mind in a whirl. Mixed feelings of uncertainty, even fear, ran through him; he could not even speak.

Connie came towards him and held his blue and white collar with both hands.

She said, 'You'll have to help, Gerry. You sailors seem to wrap yourselves up like herrings in a barrel!'

He pulled his jumper over his head and tossed it on to a chair. When he tried to hold her she evaded him. He heard himself say, 'I'm sorry, Connie. I've never – '

She nodded very slowly. 'I *know*. That's why – ' She began to undress until she wore only her underwear and stockings.

She threw herself on the bed and watched him. 'I should be in pure silk, not army issue, for a moment like this.' She giggled.

Boyes sat beside her and touched her skin, then her breasts. She moved to make it easy for him, until she lay quite naked, surprised that she could feel shy while he finished undressing.

She rolled down the sheet. 'Slip in beside me. It's bloody cold in here.'

But still Boyes waited, without knowing why. A girl all of his own, her curly hair in disarray against the pillows, her breasts full and pink-tipped, as he had known they would be. He tortured his dazed mind a little longer, then climbed into the bed.

At any second someone might come banging at the door, no matter what she believed, but nothing save this moment mattered, nothing but his Connie.

She lay back and felt his hands exploring her breasts, then down into her hair and her smooth thighs.

If he kept this up, neither of them would hold out for long. She reached out and gripped him, felt his body quiver as if he had received a shock.

'Come, Gerry!' She murmured against his skin but retained her hold of him. It was his first time, she had always known it would be, but there was no hesitation or disappointment after all.

Lieutenant Hargrave walked quickly across the hotel lobby and looked around at all the uniforms. It was the first time he had returned to the Savoy Hotel since his father had given a dinner party here when he had got his first ring. God, how long ago that felt.

Hargrave had come from their home in Hampshire, the same place he had known all his life. In fact, he had been born there. Old, comfortable and dependable – even with the grounds dug into vegetable gardens, with pigsheds kept as far away from the house as possible, it did not seem to have changed.

The hardest thing to stomach had been the gardeners who joined in the country's craze to *Dig for Victory*, even to be self-supporting in some cases. All the gardeners were Italian prisoners-of-war, with a foreman who was apparently a conscientious objector.

When he thought of the ships he had watched go down, men wearing the same uniforms as *Rob Roy*'s company, choking out their lives while they drowned in fuel, it seemed unrealistic and unfair.

His mother had explained that the vice-admiral was staying in London again now that his headquarters had shifted back to England. To be ready for instant briefings, to advise Churchill, to send ships and men wherever they might be needed. He wondered if his mother really believed all of it.

At the Admiralty he had been politely informed that the vice-admiral was on tour, after his return from the West Country where he had witnessed Sherwood's success with the mine.

'You can leave your number, sir.' Which meant that they firmly believed that if Vice-Admiral Hargrave had intended anyone to know the address of his private billet, he would have told them himself.

But an old messenger had whispered, 'Your father often drops into the Savoy for a drink after he's finished here, sir.' His watery eyes had lit up as Hargrave had put a pound note in his fist. 'Why, bless you, sir.'

Unknown to Hargraves he often sold tit-bits of information to junior officers in this way.

'May I help you, sir?'

The concierge regarded him gravely. He probably thought this was no place for a mere lieutenant, a regular or not.

'I was looking for my father.' He felt some of the others in the lobby watching him. He was suddenly angry with them and himself. His father would feel at home amongst them, he thought, there seemed to be no one less than a brigadier in the place. He continued, 'Vice-Admiral Hargrave.'

The concierge's eyes did not even flicker. 'I think *not*, sir. But I shall enquire right away.'

A small page marched through the throng of uniforms carrying a card on a stick. It read *Air-Raid Warning in progress*. Nobody took any notice. It could just as easily have been an announcement about a telephone call.

'Well, this is a surprise, Lieutenant.'

He turned, still angry, then caught aback by the girl who was watching him, her lips slightly parted in an amused smile.

Second Officer Ross Pearce looked anything but an admiral's flag-lieutenant. She wore a long dress of dark blue silk, and there was a diamond clip below one shoulder which must have cost a fortune.

'I hope it is a *pleasant* one?' She pouted, and although she was obviously well aware of the watching, envious glances, she was equally able to ignore them.

Hargrave began, 'I came looking for my father.'

'Oh dear. Well, I'm afraid he's not here.' She touched her lip with her tongue. 'I am not permitted to tell you where he is.'

Hargrave said, 'Well, I thought you *would* know!'

Her smile faded. 'I can understand your feelings, I *think*, but I do not have to tolerate your rudeness!'

Hargrave stepped closer. 'I'm sorry. I didn't mean to behave like a ten-year-old schoolboy, really. Could we begin again?'

He expected another rebuff and was surprised at his own surrender.

She was tall, cool, and extremely beautiful.

He added, 'It was just that I was expecting – '

She nodded slowly, her eyes examining him without curiosity.

'As I said, he's not here.' She gave a small shrug. 'But join me, if you like. You can tell me about *Husky*.' She mentioned it so casually she might have been on the beach in Sicily. 'I'd like that. All the reports, the despatches coming every hour to our H.Q. in Malta – well, it's not like the real thing, is it?'

A waiter hovered near her elbow, 'Shall I lay the table for two then, m'lady?'

She smiled at him. 'Please.'

Hargrave was floundering. *My lady*. 'I'm sorry. I wasn't told.'

'Does it make any difference? Anyway, the vice-admiral probably thought it less irksome this way. He likes to feel dominant – but I expect you know that?'

Hargrave did not know what to say. Her direct, challenging manner was like nothing he had experienced. He was in awe of her after just a few minutes, and yet strangely stimulated, as if the reason for his being here no longer counted.

She eyed the menu and said, 'Afterwards we can talk about you, and the command you hope to get. How does that suit?'

Hargrave had the feeling he was getting into something which was already out of control.

*

Ransome sat on the well-padded arm of a familiar chair and felt the warmth, and yet the unreality of his homecoming. His father, back to the blazing log fire, was in his favourite old sports jacket with the leather patches on the sleeves; Jack Weese held a pewter tankard of cider in his fist while he listened to the conversation, the reunion of a family he loved like his own. His wife was in the kitchen helping to prepare the Sunday lunch, which from what Ransome had glimpsed through the door threatened to be a gargantuan one.

Occasionally he let his hand stray close to Eve's shoulder. She was sitting below him in the deep chair, and whenever she felt or sensed his hand close to her she would move slightly against it, or turn to glance up at him.

Ransome looked at his brother and wondered. Even after the months of treatment, and two operations to repair the damage left by a wound which had gone bad on him, he looked thin and very pale.

He was finished with M.T.Bs, he had already been told that. His first disappointment seemed to be behind him; now he was more concerned that the navy might find him unfit for any service at all. It seemed unlikely, but Tony had had plenty of time to brood about it, and what had done this to him.

He seemed as irrepressible as ever. He said, 'I mean, I'm fit enough – everything still works, as the bishop said to the actress!' He shot Eve an apologetic grin. 'Sorry!'

She retorted, 'No, you're not.' Then, 'Can you remember what happened yet?'

Tony stared at his empty glass. 'Not really. We were working inshore, the skipper was hoping to catch one of Rommel's transports slipping out of North Africa.' He tensed and Ransome saw his fingers tighten around the glass like claws. 'There was a flash right under the bows.' He was speaking so quietly that they could hear the wind swishing against the windows. 'The next thing I knew, I was in the drink. I don't recall much else. Just vague pictures. A boat, the fishermen who later turned out to be partisans. Then there was the little doctor they brought from their village. He did what he could. I'd be dead otherwise.' He glanced up and realised his mother was in the doorway listening. 'Sorry, Mum.'

'Did you see the doctor again?' His father was looking at him as he might when he had been a child.

Tony lowered his head, as Jack Weese leaned forward and took away his glass.

'The Germans shot the poor little bugger when they pulled out.'

Ransome said, 'I shall never forget that day on the beach.'

Tony seemed to shake himself, to be glad of the interruption. 'And what about you?' His eyes moved between them. 'What have *you* been up to?'

She spoke first. 'We went to the concert at Buckfastleigh.'

Tony grimaced. 'Classics, eh? Seeing *Fantasia* at the local cinema is as close as I get to that kind of stuff!'

But his eyes asked, *Are you in love? Have you become lovers?*

Eve turned and put her hand on his. Ransome could feel the others watching, just as he could sense her quiet defiance.

'The sun's out, Ian. Take me to see the boat, *please?*'

His mother called, 'Don't be too long. I'm dishing up in half an hour.' She beamed at her two sons. 'Officers or not!'

Ransome put a short oilskin coat about her shoulders before they left. There were always several such coats around the house, used by the family and boatyard workers alike.

Outside they were met by bright sunshine, cold and hard, the air crisply clean. There was even a slight vapour of steam rising from some of the canvas-covered boats in the yard, the winter sun drying out puddles of overnight rain.

He put his arm round her shoulders and together they walked through the rough, untended grass, past the familiar boatsheds and slipways, scattered pieces of rusting engines, bilge pumps and other discarded clutter.

They said nothing until they had gone to the lower slope of the boatyard where *Barracuda* stood apart from all the rest, covered from stem to stern by a black tarpaulin. That too was steaming slightly, and Ransome felt a pang of sadness. Was she a part of the impossible dream too? She might stay here forever, rotting away, forgotten.

Then she turned and looked at him, her long hair whipping across her mouth so that only her eyes were clearly visible.

'Something's wrong, Ian. What is it? Please tell me. Remember our promise – no secrets.'

He gripped her gloved hands, and wanted to hug her.

'The refit has been cut to a minimum. We're on the move again.'

She said in a small voice, 'Not home for Christmas?'

'Not this time.' Try as he might he could not raise the dullness from his voice. In war why was one day different from another? Well, *it was this time*. Four years of it, and he had never been at home for Christmas. It had not seemed that important before.

'*But why?*' The words were torn from her, so that she became the girl he had first met in this yard once again.

He thought of Lieutenant Commander Gregory's explanation when he had been told the same thing for *Ranger*. 'Can't give us a bloody minute, Ian. They think we're expendable, the whole damn lot of us!'

But he replied, 'We have to keep all the lanes open. With the war moving as it is, big ships will be sent where they're in the most advantageous positions.'

She hugged his arm with hers. 'For the Second Front?'

Ransome nodded. He glanced around the yard, remembering Jack Weese's contempt for the boxlike landing-craft they were building. There were only two half-completed ones here now. That was all the evidence they needed. The Allies were ready to move again, or soon would be when the weather improved. All the people who had been screaming and demanding a Second Front would get their wishes. How many more had to die to satisfy those who never endured the agony of battle?

She sensed his mood and faced him, her hands gripping his arms while she looked directly into his face.

'Nothing is going to keep us apart, Ian! Now it's my turn to help *you*.' She pulled him around the sleeping *Barracuda* and pointed across the estuary, towards the tiered houses of Polruan on the opposite side. 'We're not going to lose it now! Remember how my family used to stay at that cottage over there, every year? I used to think of nothing else, dream of the moment when I would be able to come and see you, show you my paintings and sketches. Once, I came but you were away training with the navy.'

'I didn't know, Eve.'

She did not seem to hear. 'I went back to Polruan and cried my heart out. My father probably thought I'd got myself into trouble.' She gave a laugh, so bitter that Ransome barely recognised it. 'How could he know even if he wanted to? That I was yours then, and I've never looked at another man!'

Ransome held her, felt her body trembling through the rough oilskin.

She said, 'You're a wonderful person, and you just haven't any idea, have you? The way you treat people, make them smile when there's precious little to grin about nowadays – it fills my heart. With love, with pride, everything!'

Ransome said, 'I was afraid to show how I felt about you. But you know now.'

Something in his tone made her turn towards him again, her eyes shining.

'I want to be married here, to be with you always, to come down the aisle knowing we both mean it, and when the church bells ring – '

Ransome held her more tightly. Even that was a brutal reminder. No church bells rang any more. Only if German parachutists were reported to be landing. Many bells had been sent to the war effort for scrap.

She was crying quietly against him, but said in a stronger voice, 'That's how it will be.' Then she moved away and stood on the edge of the slope, framed against the swirling current below, her hair streaming in the breeze. 'I just want to be with you.' She must have heard his steps through the wet grass and said, 'Not yet.' Her arm pointed across the Fowey River. 'I can see the cottage, next to the one with blue shutters. Is it empty?'

Ransome watched her shoulders, the way she was holding herself by force.

He said, 'Yes. Most of them were for holidaymakers. They're not suitable for the military either.'

Then she swung round, her eyes very large and bright, but not with tears anymore.

'One day, soon, could we – '

'Could we what?' He thought he knew, but dared not even imagine it.

She joined him on the slope and stood on tiptoe to put her face against his cheek.

'Have the cottage? Just for us? To make it come true?' She leaned back as he put his arms round her. 'It would be ours for just a while. Not some hotel room with all the remarks and leers. Just us.'

He pulled her closer. Was it her heart he could feel or his own?

'People will know. It's like that here.' When she remained silent he said, 'I must tell you, Eve, I don't know when it might be, but I would like it better than anything in this world.'

She walked towards the tarpaulined boat and reached up beneath the wet cover with her hand.

Ransome heard her say, 'Wish us luck, funny old boat.'

Then she ran to him again and whispered, 'Take care of yourself this time, dearest of men.'

Someone was calling from the house and Ransome said, 'Just in time. And yes, I shall take care.'

They walked back to the house, his arm around her shoulders as if it had always belonged there.

From the window Ted Ransome watched them coming down the path and asked, 'What do you make of it, Jack?'

'Fine pair.' Jack Weese raised his tankard in salute. 'God bring 'em luck!'

Tony, sitting in his chair, grinned, then winced as his savage wound made its presence felt again. He was rarely free of pain.

In his heart he had always known about Eve and Ian. He recalled with sudden clarity Ian's face, inches from his own, while he lay helpless on that damned stretcher.

It was hardly surprising, he thought, they were closer even than brothers.

As darkness closed in over Davenport Dockyard the rain returned, heavier than the previous night's, to make a mockery of the Sunday sunshine.

Sub-Lieutenant Robert 'Bunny' Fallows paused to fix his bearings, breathing hard, his head swimming after stopping at several bars. He had not gone on leave, although he was entitled to it. The idea of facing his home and all that it represented made staying aboard an easy choice, and as happened only too often he did not have the cash to spare for a hotel, something he had often dreamed about.

The blacked-out dockyard was always a trap for the unwary, drunk or sober, and Fallows had consumed too many gins to take chances on the maze of catwalks and bridges which separated the various basins from one another. The dark silhouettes of ships loomed out of the downpour, under repair or enjoying a complete overhaul as *Rob Roy* was supposed to have had. But all that was shelved. The minimum repairs possible, and already the dockyard workers had left the ship to work on something more important.

But Fallows, despite the ache behind his eyes and the sour sickness in his stomach, had other things uppermost in his blurred thoughts. That morning he had met Tudor Morgan and had been astounded to see he was wearing a second gold stripe on his working dress, several shades brighter than the old one.

He had been retained aboard instead of going on a long navigation course, but his promotion to lieutenant had unexpectedly come through all the same. Fallows still could not accept it. Although Morgan was a professional sailor who had started in the merchant service, their seniority was about the same, surely?

He grabbed a handrail and began to pull himself across another catwalk, on one side of him a yawning empty basin, the other containing the battered hull of a destroyer which had almost been sunk after an air attack in the Western Approaches.

He had confronted Morgan with it, but the young Welshman had merely suggested that the delay was due to some formality or foul-up along the line.

As he had drunk himself from bar to bar Fallows had considered it from every angle, until his mind throbbed like a drum. It had to be because of Tinker. That little bastard Parsons, who was leaving the ship anyway for a gunnery course and promotion to higher rate, must have told somebody. Spite, hatred, it did not really matter.

Fallows clung to a chain rail and stared up at the rain until it cleared his mind a bit.

Now they were going back to sea, to God alone knew what. Morgan promoted, while he remained a sub-lieutenant. Some of them would get a laugh out of that. Most of all his bloody father.

He saw a figure swaying towards him from another catwalk and he thought for an instant he was going mad.

Able Seaman Parsons straightened his back and wiped his mouth with his wrist. There was an acrid smell of vomit despite the steady rain: Parsons had also been drinking, saying various goodbyes to old shipmates before he left the flotilla for good to go on the course at Whale Island.

He saw Fallows and peered at him uncertainly. Then he bowed, his collar black with rain, so that his hat fell on the catwalk unnoticed.

'We shall say our farewells, eh, *Mister* Fallows?' He laughed, and almost threw up again. It was funny to see the officer's face. Even in the darkness he could make out the anger and the dismay.

Fallows exclaimed, 'You little bastard! After all I did, all I gave you!'

Parsons almost laughed, but said instead, 'Take it off your back, Bunny! All's fair in love and war, and you treated all of us like shit. *And* you know it!' When Fallows remained speechless, clinging to the rail for support, Parsons shouted, 'You're pissed, you useless git – but if one of *us* got tanked up you'd slap him in the rattle!' He leaned right over to get his eyes into focus.

Fallows said thickly, 'You told them what I said that night!'

Parsons could hardly believe it. 'Told *who*, for Chrissake? You were too drunk to say *anything* that night! Tinker never even spoke to you!'

Fallows wiped his face and yelled, '*You're lying!* I gave you money – '

Parsons sneered. 'So what?' He waved his arm over the dockyard. 'You'll remember me after this, eh?'

It was all a blur. Fallows stepped forward, intent only on hitting him no matter what the consequences might be. Parsons gave a high-pitched giggle and ducked away. The chain which joined two stanchions behind his back was only inches above the catwalk at its centre. Too late Parsons realised what was happening; the giggle changed to a shrill scream and he toppled backwards into the basin where the bombed destroyer shone in the rain like black ice.

Fallows peered wildly around, his mind reeling. He had heard no splash, nor even a cry for help, for unknown to him Parsons had hit the concrete knuckle of the dock as he fell and had probably been dead when he struck the water.

Fallows waited, the rain bouncing off his cap, trying to steady his thoughts, to stop himself running for help. Then after what seemed like an eternity he straightened his back and stared along the basin to the next berth.

He saw Parson's cap, lying where it had fallen on the catwalk. Fallows started to laugh, and for several minutes was unable to stop. Then he kicked the cap carelessly into the basin and continued towards his own ship.

18

Signals

'Flamborough Head bears three-three-zero, seven miles, sir!'

Ransome peered down at the chart on the bridge-table, his head and shoulder beneath the waterproof hood while he studied the pencilled fixes and bearings. He could feel the rain slashing across his buttocks and legs, hammering on his oilskin like pellets.

January in the North Sea again. Three shades of grey, all bleak and hostile. He rubbed his eyes and felt his elbows press on the table as the hull lifted and rolled drunkenly in a steep quarter sea. The North Sea never had the great storms of the Western Ocean, but this sickening, corkscrewing motion was in many ways much worse.

He heard Lieutenant Morgan rebuking the quartermaster in a fierce whisper for straying slightly off course. It was unusual for him to be on edge, but the whole ship had been like it since they had left Devonport without waiting for Christmas. That was almost exactly a month ago. Now as *Rob Roy* lifted and staggered at the head of her diagonal line of consorts, the Mediterranean barely more than a blurred memory.

Even the other events of the war seemed remote, as if they were no longer a part of it. On Boxing Day for instance, when they had been sweeping this same channel, the German battle cruiser *Scharnhorst*, the last of Hitler's major warships, was destroyed by the guns of HMS *Duke of York*. It was a terrible fight in Arctic conditions and in the midst of a snow blizzard. Enemy or not, *Scharnhorst* had always been admired by her enemies; her luck and skill had become part of naval legend. Without her lurking presence, more British warships could be spared for the buildup of an invasion fleet.

Important though that victory was, it barely touched the weary men of the minesweepers.

Ransome often thought of that precious moment beside the *Barracuda*. Her simple gesture when she touched the hull beneath the tarpaulin. Sometimes when he was snatching a few hours in his sea-cabin, the 'coop' as Kellett the P.O. steward called it, he would jerk wide awake, almost pinching himself to make her words become clear in his mind. That the cottage she wanted to call *ours* was not merely part of a taunting dream.

He withdrew his head from the chart-table and crossed to his chair, holding on to it, stamping his scuffed seaboots on the deck to make his circulation come alive. It reminded him of the time he had waited outside the abbey when –

He turned as Sub-Lieutenant Fallows clattered up the ladder and paused to look at the tossing whitecaps, the grey murk, no beginning or end, no horizon either. It was noon, and the watch was changing. That was another reason for the edginess, Ransome knew. There were several new faces in the ship to replace others who had gone to courses ashore, or to other ships where their experience would be vital amongst the stream of new recruits.

Sherwood was still ashore. Cusack had kept close contact with one of his colleagues, whom he telephoned whenever *Rob Roy* was able to take some time in port.

Sherwood would be coming back, but as Bliss had predicted, his work as an R.M.S.O. was over. As an experienced watchkeeper he was badly missed, and as a friend too.

Another face absent from the wardroom was the Gunner (T) Mr Bone. Ransome had seen him in the privacy of his cabin to inform him of the signal. Bone was being sent to a training depot, to instruct raw seamen in the business of minesweeping.

Bone was a hard man. He had shown neither pleasure nor disappointment. After all his years in the service his widowed mother had chosen for her fourteen-year-old son, it was likely he could not be surprised at anything.

'S'pose I'll get used to it. I'll miss the duty-free booze though.'

He had not been making a joke. Bone rarely did.

He surprised Ransome by thrusting out his spade-shaped hand and muttering, 'You've been a good captain, sir. I'd not get a better.' He had tried to grin. 'One thing, I'll not 'ave to muster the lads or 'ear that pipe "Out Sweeps" again, not in my lifetime!'

Another missing face was that of Pansy Masefield, the P.O. sick berth attendant. He had never really settled down after Cusack had taken over the ship's health and welfare, and had accepted his draftchit to a big hospital in Portsmouth without argument.

Ransome recalled how they had all tried to make their own Christmas a happy one. It had been an uphill task. *Rob Roy* and half of the flotilla had been sweeping this same channel from the Wash to Flamborough Head to keep open all the vital approaches to the Humber Estuary and the port of Hull.

He remembered the P.O. steward, Kellett, who always wore his hair plastered diagonally across his forehead anyway, donning a small false moustache and doing a lively impersonation of Adolf Hitler at the forecastle's 'Sods' Opera.' Leading Seaman Hoggan had sung *This Old Hat of Mine*, always a popular sailors' ditty, becoming bawdier and drunker by the minute and tossing his clothes aside until he was completely naked but for a lanyard upon which hung a bag of contraceptives.

The youngest, and by far the smallest member of the ship's company, Ordinary Seaman Gold, had stuttered his way through the part of playing the captain for Christmas Day, although one of Ransome's reefer jackets had reached almost to his knees.

It had all been compressed into a few precious hours while the ship was in harbour to refuel. *Rob Roy* had lain at a buoy, not even alongside in any contact with the land.

He heard Mackay speaking with the young signalman who had just come on watch. Mackay still wore the sailor's square-rig, but had the crown and crossed anchors on his sleeve now to show his promotion to petty officer. A yeoman of signals. It was unlikely that *Rob Roy* would be able to hold on to him once his full advancement had been confirmed. He would be greatly missed, as would his expertise.

Morgan was saying, 'Time to make the turn in seven minutes, Sub.'

It was not meant to be condescending. It was what a one-striper was usually called.

But Ransome had sensed the barrier between them, and it did not come from Morgan. He was openly delighted that his promotion had been posted without his having to take up another course.

'I shall be able to stay in *Rob Roy*, see?' He had stared around the wet, dismal bridge. 'I'd not want to go until I was ordered, sir.'

Fallows stood beside him now as they compared notes by the chart-table. He had got terribly drunk at Christmas, and Hargrave had threatened to take him in front of the captain, higher if need be. After that Fallows had improved considerably, and was making a great effort to keep out of the first lieutenant's way. He was more withdrawn than usual, his mouth turned down in a permanent frown.

'Forenoon watch relieved, sir!' Morgan touched the peak of his cap. 'I'll bring the new snotty with me in the dog-watches if I may, sir. He's got to start somewhere.'

Ransome smiled. Davenport's replacement was called Colin Piers. A round-faced eighteen-year-old who looked about twelve. Nobody had really had much time to either make him welcome or get his measure, as he had been horribly seasick almost from the day he had stepped aboard.

Ransome's request for Ordinary Seaman Boyes's C.W. papers to be started again had been granted, and the Mention-in-Despatches had been announced on the same day. Ransome had told him personally, and had been moved by the youngster's thanks and sincerity. He had made the right decision, and in his heart knew that many captains would not have bothered once the first decision had been made.

One thing was certain, Boyes was getting plenty of experience on chartwork and the radar plot machine, for with the new midshipman rolling about the ship with his face as green as grass, he was doing everything himself.

Fallows had walked to the forepart of the bridge, while his assistant Sub-Lieutenant Tritton stood by the voicepipes.

Tritton, young and inexpert as he was, had been forced to take over Bone's duties and part of ship. Thank God for the Buffer, Ransome thought. But what Tritton lacked in experience he more than made up for with his good humour, which kept the men he worked with grinning at some of his schoolboy jokes. He had been able to put the memory of the air attack behind him. It was the first, the most difficult step of all, and they had all been made to face up to it, one way or the other.

Ransome said, 'Tell the first lieutenant to take in the sweep.' He glanced at Fallows. 'Your department all buttoned up, Sub?'

Fallows half-turned, showing his profile, the red hair flapping beneath his cap like a bird's wing. He no longer wore his ridiculous rabbit.

'Yes sir. Able Seaman Norton has settled down quite well as trainer on "A" Gun. Quite well.'

Ransome glanced at him. It had been a surprise when Able Seaman Parsons had failed to return from shore leave. He had long requested the gunnery course at Whale Island, and it would be stupid to miss the chance because of overstaying his leave.

Ransome had expected a signal explaining that he had been taken ill, or had overslept in some sailors' boarding house. He smiled at the old naval excuse. *Slept at Aggie Weston's and never heard the bell, sir.*

The coxswain had been told that Parsons had gone off to celebrate his transfer with some old friends. Beckett had remarked darkly, '*Friends*, sir? A skate like that one don't 'ave no mates!'

But there had been no signal, so the police and provost department had had to be informed. It was a pity, but his chance of advancement had probably gone forever.

Ransome lifted his binoculars and trained them on the next astern; it was *Firebrand,* showing her bilge one moment, then her open bridge the next as she rolled steeply. The strange light made her bow wave and wash look dirty yellow. He lowered the binoculars slightly and saw Hargrave's wind-reddened face leap into the lens. He was first-rate at his job now, but always kept at a distance from his men. A hard thing to do in such a small ship; but he seemed to manage it.

'Sweep's secure, sur!' The boatswain's mate watched Fallows as he climbed to the gyro repeater. Everyone was busy, but the boatswain's mate, O'Connor, had a moment to relax. He was thinking of Christmas too. How he had been on watch while the ship lay at her buoy, and had listened to the carol singing on the messdecks, his insides protected from the bitter cold by two helpings of roast turkey and several tots of 'neaters'.

Like some of the others O'Connor had good cause to dislike Fallows – he had smelt his breath once, and accused O'Connor of drinking on watch. It had been a rare and unfortunate occasion for O'Connor that Fallows had been stone cold sober.

Fallows had taken him in front of the first lieutenant as a defaulter, with the result that he had lost his only good conduct badge, and had been given extra work as punishment. He had never forgotten.

At the Christmas party, Fallows had taken more than usual and had lurched on deck, without his jacket despite the wind and rain, and fallen dead drunk on a rack of depth-charges.

He had gone to rouse the officer, but as he had gripped his outflung arm he had been horrified to find that he wanted to tip him over the side. He had even levered the unconscious officer against the guardrails before he knew what he was going to do. Nobody would have noticed, and with a stiff tide running past the buoy, everyone would think Fallows had stumbled overboard.

A stoker had appeared through an engine-room hatch and had offered cheerfully, "'Ere, Pat, I'll give you a 'and to get the pig down aft again!'

Fallows had known nothing about it. O'Connor watched him balefully. *Would I have done it?* He was afraid of the answer.

Ransome said, 'Take her round, Sub.'

An oilskinned figure clambered into the bridge and handed Ransome a folded signal flimsy.

'Thanks, Sparks.'

He held it below the screen to shield it from the rain and spray and read it before the telegraphist's lettering began to run down the paper.

'They found A.B. Parsons. He was dead. Drowned apparently.'

He heard Tritton exclaim, 'The *turn*, Bunny!'

Ransome snapped, 'Starboard twenty!' He pushed past Fallows and peered across the compass repeater. 'What the hell's the matter? You've taken over the con many times by now, man!'

Fallows opened and closed his mouth. 'I – I'm sorry, sir.'

'Midships.' He heard the quartermaster's response. 'Steady.'

The quartermaster called up the voicepipe. 'Steady, sir! Course zero-seven-zero!' It was exact. They had done this channel so often it was hardly surprising.

Ransome stepped away and raised his glasses to watch the faint splash of colour as a fresh dan buoy was dropped by the trawler *Senja*.

Only then did he look at Fallows. 'You know the narrow margin, Sub. So in future just *watch it!*'

He was being harsh with someone who could not answer back. But *Rob Roy* and all her company were far more important than some bruised feelings.

He settled in his chair and said, 'Make the signal. *Out sweeps to starboard. Take station on me.*'

And so it went on, in weather so bad that it was hard to hold station on their set courses; and there was the additional fear they might not see a drifter if it came amongst them, its obscene horns hidden by the North Sea's steep waves.

He thought of Eve, of the letters she had written, of the ones which might be waiting when they returned to harbour to refuel and restock their provisions.

Fallows moved away from the chair and trained his glasses abeam. They had found Parsons. He must have been trapped under the bombed destroyer. Fallows had made himself walk back past the basin on the following day. Some men had been working on the damaged ship, but there was no alarm, not even Parsons's cap.

He had sweated about it for days. Suppose Parsons had dragged himself clear? Maybe a watchman had found him alive?

At Christmas it had become too much for him, and only Hargrave's fury had made him take a grip on his nerves.

Now it was all behind him. Parsons was really dead. They'd say he had fallen in by accident, drunk.

He felt the same insane grin cracking his jaws and had to grate his teeth together to prevent it.

It had all been a mistake, but Parsons was the one who had made it.

It was mid-February, while *Rob Roy* and *Ranger* lay alongside each other in Hull to refuel, that their private worlds were upset once again.

Ransome sat in his cabin reading a letter from Eve, while the ship stood at arm's length beyond the door, and routine flowed around him, leaving him momentarily alone. Heavy rain pattered on the decks and made thick silver bars across the scuttles, with only the occasional creak of tackles or a muffled shout to show that anything was actually happening.

Hull seemed an unhappy place to be, even when they had been at sea with barely a break. It had been bombed so many times that the place was barely recognisable. But the work went on, and it was said that the turnround of ships in the port was quicker than ever.

He put Eve's letter down as Petty Officer Kellett opened the door a few inches.

'Beg pardon, sir, but *Ranger*'s captain 'as come aboard.'

Lieutenant Commander Gregory strode into the cabin, nodding only briefly to Kellett. 'Sorry to barge in, Ian.' He dragged a tin of duty-free cigarettes from his pocket. 'Knew you wouldn't mind.'

Ransome watched him, the quick nervous movements of his hands as he lit another cigarette.

'What is it, Jim?'

Lieutenant Commander James Gregory tried to settle in the other chair and blew a thin stream of smoke to the deckhead.

'I'm leaving, Ian. That's what.'

Ransome waited. They had come through so much together. Their small, hardworked group of fleet minesweepers, each one a personality. They had watched others go down, those whose luck had run out. *Fawn, Dunlin* and *Scythe*, with other names they could scarcely remember. Ships and men torn apart in a war which was without glamour and beyond the headlines, yet one which was as vital today as it had been right from the start.

Gregory shrugged. 'It's all part of the scheme for a bigger support group for the next invasion. I'm to take over a new flotilla of motor minesweepers as senior officer. I shall have a free hand, with Bliss's blessing of course.'

Ransome asked, 'Are you pleased? It shows what they think of you – I agree, you're just the bloke for it. Somebody who knows what it's all about.'

Gregory glanced around the cabin; it was an exact replica of his own.

'I'll miss her, Ian.'

'I know. We'll all miss you too.'

Outside the tannoy bawled, 'D'you hear there! Cooks to the galley! Senior hands of messes muster for rum!'

Ransome grimaced. 'The right idea, I think.' He took out a bottle and two glasses. *Ranger* would not be the same without Gregory. He felt the same about losing her.

He pushed a full glass across the table. 'Cheers!'

Gregory drank some of it and swallowed hard. 'Christ!' Then he studied Ransome and said, 'You really don't know, do you?'

'Know what?'

'*Ranger*'s new skipper is Lieutenant Trevor Hargrave.'

Ransome stared at him with astonishment. 'No, by God, I didn't!'

Gregory smiled. 'I suppose I shouldn't care. I've served under skippers who thought that nobody could ever be good enough to take their places. All the same –'

Ransome refilled the glasses. He was losing Hargrave. A command of his own. He felt suddenly angry. The Old Pals' Act; it had to be. Hargrave's father had pulled strings. On the face of it, Gregory was being promoted, and as *Ranger*'s Number One was fairly new to the job, Hargrave might seem the logical choice. He was experienced, a good ship-handler, and even if he was new to *Ranger*, he was not to the flotilla.

The door opened and Leading Writer Wakeford peered into the cabin.

371

'Oh, sorry, sir. I'll come back later.'

Ransome saw the thick envelope in his hand and said, 'Bring it in.'

He watched as the Leading Writer laid the various items on the desk. He was as before, self-contained, studious, quiet. It was hard to see him crouched on the field telephone as Bliss had described it to him, speaking to Sherwood, waiting to write it all down, to hear his final words if the mine sprung its fuse.

Wakeford did not look at Gregory as he said, 'This one is about the first lieutenant, sir.'

It was the usual formal wording. 'Upon receipt of these orders you will etc. etc.'

Ransome looked up at his friend. 'Sherwood's coming back tomorrow. As first lieutenant.'

Gregory was still contemplating his own change of direction. 'That's a shaft of light, anyway.'

The big sealed envelope had been signed for by the O.O.D., Tritton. Ransome read it quickly. 'I think another enormous drink is in order.' Then he said quietly, 'We're moving to Falmouth in three days, Jim. Hargrave will assume command there.'

'Falmouth.' Gregory watched him thoughtfully. 'That's where I'm to take over the flotilla of Mickey-Mouses. Does that mean –?'

Ransome poured the drinks and shook the bottle. His stock was almost finished.

He replied, 'I think it does. It will be a work-up for the invasion. The big one.'

Gregory glanced at his watch. 'I'd best get back. I'll tell my lot in the ward-room. They'll all be gathering there for lunch anyway.'

He stood up, momentarily lost. 'I thought I'd end the bloody war in *Ranger*, does that sound potty? I know we have no say in these things, but I'm loathe to leave the old girl.' He met Ransome's questioning glance. 'No, not because of Hargrave. He'll probably do a good job. It's just – '

'I know.' It was like Moncrieff's last moments when he had relieved him. 'I'd be the same.'

When Gregory had gone, he took the bulkhead telephone from its bracket and jabbed one of the buttons.

He heard Kellett's chirpy voice reply, 'Wardroom!'

'Would you ask the first lieutenant to spare me a few minutes, please?'

He replaced the telephone and then straightened Tony's picture. He had written to him twice. That was quite something. Tony had never been a great letter-writer.

He was feeling much better, mainly, Ransome suspected, because he had been appointed to a destroyer which was still on the stocks and only half-built. It would be many months before he got to sea again. Their mother would be pleased about that.

Tony had written, *So I'm all right, big brother. To tell the truth I'd have taken the job running a NAAFI manager's boat rather than be beached!* He had ended by saying, *Eve's a lovely girl. You're so right for each other. I envy you.*

There was a knock on the door. It was Hargrave.

'You wanted me, sir?'

Ransome pushed the orders across the desk. 'You'd better sit down before you read this.'

He saw Hargrave's eyes moving slowly across the curt, unemotional wording. Even when he received his own for taking command they would lack any of the excitement they usually represented.

One thing was obvious, Hargrave did not know either. He was not that good an actor.

'But – but, I don't understand, sir.' Hargrave stared at him. '*Ranger* – she's our sister-ship.' He looked at his hands. Even that one word *our* was a thing of the past.

Ransome smiled grimly. 'I'll not tell you about the birds and the bees. You've learned well, considering it was not all that long since we were facing each other here for the first time. We are going to Falmouth again. Sail in *Ranger* and watch everything Gregory does. *Ranger* may be a twin, but her people are used to him and his ways. If we are going into Europe they'll need all their confidence. It's not time for the new broom syndrome.' He spread his hands in apology. 'Sorry. The birds and the bees win after all!'

Hargrave stood up. 'If I'm any good at it, sir, it will be your doing.' Then he almost lurched from the cabin.

Ransome sat staring at the closed door. *Into Europe.* How easy it was to say.

It was not like losing poor David. He had been a true friend, the closest he had ever had before or since joining the navy. He often saw him still. Those chilling nights in the bridge, booted feet on the ladder. Or a shadowy oilskinned figure hurrying aft when the order to prepare the sweep was piped. The women in black. The schoolgirl who had looked like Eve.

He picked up her letter again and thought of her writing it.

Dearest of Men – It feels so long since –

Ransome found that he could lean back and smile. He would telephone her this evening. Just to tell her he was coming. Without breaking the Official Secrets Act, of course.

He heard footsteps moving away and knew that Hargrave had been standing there, putting his thoughts in order, grappling with his change of fortune.

Hargrave was indeed thinking of nothing else. He walked right past the Buffer who was about to offer him a list of names, a rearrangement of the watch bill, his mouth already opened to speak.

As he strode aft the Buffer gaped after him. 'Gawd, Jimmy's like a whore at a christenin' today!'

He saw the new S.B.A., a small, pimply youth, leaning on the guardrail and staring down at the trapped water between the two hulls.

'Stand up straight! Never 'ang on them rails, sonny!'

'I – I thought – '

The Buffer roared, 'Leave thinkin' to 'orses, they've got bigger 'eads than you 'ave!'

He bustled away, the first lieutenant's behaviour forgotten. He usually felt better after he had offered someone a good bollocking.

Hargrave paused by the big winch and the Oropesa float, resting on its chocks like a faceless dolphin.

His mind kept returning to Ross Pearce, what she had said, the cool way she had outlined what she believed he needed. Like moving pawns on a board. Gregory's promotion to all intents and purposes and a ready opening in *Ranger*. It would probably mean a half-stripe, albeit lost again when the war ended. He stared round and up at the deserted bridge. What was the matter with him? Sherwood was right. The war might go on for years. Even if the invasion was a success it could drag on in stalemate. Then there was the Pacific and Burma. It seemed endless. None of the people he had seen today as requestmen or defaulters, working about the ship, or queueing impatiently for their rum issue, might be alive by then.

He was sure of one thing. He was completely infatuated with Ross Pearce. Without effort she had fenced with him, keeping him at a distance, giving no real hint of promise. He had met nobody like her. The more he had seen of her the less he could imagine his father having any more success than he had.

He looked across at *Ranger*. The sentry and quartermaster were watching him without apparently doing so. The buzz would be all through the ship. *Rob Roy*'s Jimmy was getting the Old Man's chair.

He thought of Ransome's quiet advice. *They'll need all their confidence.*

It was what he had been trained for. This was just the next step on the ladder. He might never know if his first command had been engineered, or influenced by his father. But it seemed likely. Ross's father was a viscount, and had a deep interest in service matters and stood on a House of Lords committee. What was good for Hargrave might easily turn out to be even more advantageous for his father the vice-admiral.

Shall I miss Rob Roy?

Only time would answer that.

The girl stood behind her mother and watched her reflection in the dressing-table mirror. She could hear the wind exploring the windows and sighing against the roof, but the rain had gone, and tomorrow was going to be a fine day, according to the postman.

The postman was old for the job, but had come back to work to help fill the gaps left by the younger men who had gone to war. He had his own special signal as he wheeled his red bicycle up the twisting driveway if he saw Eve waiting for him.

A wave if there was a letter from him. A thumbs-up if there was not. Meaning that there would be soon.

That morning he had given a wave.

He handed over a great pile of mail for Codrington House, all the usual replies to appeals, applications for jobs, offers of homes for the bombed-out and dispossessed. It never stopped. He had given her the letter in its familiar buff envelope.

'I reckon he's telling you he still loves you in this 'un, Miss Eve.' He pulled her leg quite mercilessly. His defence was that he was old enough to be her grandfather.

It was a lovely letter. They all were. She could hear his voice, see his grey eyes, touch his hand in every line.

He had telephoned as well. Another awful connection, but he had been lucky to get through at all.

He was coming south. To her.

Her fingers slipped on the comb as she completed setting her mother's hair, and their eyes met suddenly in the dressing-table mirror.

'What is it, dear?'

Eve smiled although it touched her deeply to see her mother like this. They had always been so close. She had been as much a friend and companion as mother.

'I had a letter this morning.' She watched for some hint of curiosity. 'From Ian.'

'Who, dear?'

Eve picked up a brush and touched up the sides of her mother's hair. She had always had such fine hair. How had they met, she wondered?

'Ian Ransome.'

She paused with her brush in mid-air. It was like a curtain being lifted, a light illuminating a darkened room. Her mother's eyes were as they were before. Clear, questioning, amused.

'You really love him, don't you, Eve?'

Eve nodded, almost afraid to move.

'Then take him, my darling. While you can. Love him. I can see that he worships the ground you walk on.'

Somewhere a loose shutter banged against the wall; the noise, or the interruption, broke the contact.

Eve whispered, 'I do love him so much. I want him to be *safe*!'

But the eyes in the mirror did not reply.

Then her mother said indifferently, 'Fetch my glasses, will you, dear? I left them in the study.' As Eve went to the door she heard her murmur, 'Or was it in –'

The study was much as it had always been since the great house was built, she thought. Shelves from floor to ceiling, now mostly filled with her father's ledgers and personal books. The rest lay empty, a reminder of the house's better days.

She heard the wireless from the outer hall, the night porter's prop for staying awake.

Her heart turned to ice. As it always did.

'The Secretary of the Admiralty regrets to announce the loss of HM Submarine *Skilful*, and of . . .'

And of . . . and of . . . and of . . .

'Next of kin have been informed.'

She clutched her hands across her breast and waited for her breathing to steady. It was always the same now. The real meaning of that flat announcement. The sense of gratitude, then of shame, sympathy for the men who had died somewhere, in what conditions she could only guess at.

She looked around the shadowed study. *Ian was coming back.* Then she remembered what her mother had sent her for. But there was no sign of her reading-glasses. Her mother had often come here to work on her various charities before suffering the shock of the bombing.

Eve smiled. She had probably left them in the desk drawer. It would not be the first time.

It was strange that she felt guilty at opening her father's desk. She wanted to laugh, to cry out that she had shared her love with her mother. She pulled out the drawer, careless of the sound. Her father was in the city.

Then she froze. At the back of the drawer was a big envelope, marked with the newspaper's crest and the bold sticker, PHOTOGRAPH – DO NOT FOLD. It was addressed to her. The posting date she did not even need to examine.

With great care she slit open the envelope and removed the stiff cardboard protection.

For several minutes she studied the photograph, to which was pinned the newspaper's compliment slip.

So clear. So vivid. Ian on his bridge, pointing at the sky, his beloved face so tense, so strong.

With the picture clutched to her breast she mounted the stairs and looked into her mother's bedroom. She was wearing her reading-glasses and studying an album of holiday postcards which she had once collected.

Had she forgotten that she had kept her reading-glasses near her? Or was it her way of reaching her daughter, to tell her that her father had intercepted the picture of the man she loved and had tried to keep it from her?

Eve ran to her room and threw herself down.

How could he?

Then after a time she left the bed and rested the photograph against her bedside clock, while she took out the white nightdress from her drawer.

19

Love and Remembrance

Spring seemed to have come late to the West Country this year. It was true that the skies were often blue and cloudless, and the hedgerows and cottage gardens bright with colour. But the Channel which remained unimpressed and restless along the Cornish coasts often crashed amongst the jagged rocks as if it were reluctant to leave winter behind.

Ransome walked up from the tiny ferry and paused to stare across at the boatyard. Like the rest of the Fowey Estuary it was almost hidden by landing-craft and small warships of every class and use, some of which had probably begun life under old Jack Weese's supervision. You could *feel* it along this coast, Ransome thought. Everywhere you went, in the narrow streets and in crowded harbours, it was more of a sensation than anything spoken. Like the murmur of far-off drums. Something which was stirring and yet filled with menace.

The war had moved closer again. Perhaps that was it. Along these shores they had seen enough of it, but never before had they been so involved in what was now inevitable.

Here in Polruan, directly opposite the place which even in memory had become his only home, Ransome could sense it. It was no longer the free-and-easy village it had been even during the darkest days of the war. There were troops and armoured vehicles all around, just as the vessels which would soon carry them into battle on the other side of the English Channel filled every creek and river, until invasion seemed to become a secret quite impossible to keep.

In other parts of the world the conflict raged on. In the Pacific and on the Russian front, where millions were said to have perished in that last bitter winter. In Burma, the forgotten Fourteenth Army was no longer in retreat, and even if the Allies in Italy were making only slow progress there were other benefits. The Italians, at least those lucky enough to be on the right side of the lines, had surrendered to the Allies, their fleet secured under the guns of Malta, a great achievement which had once seemed like a pipe-dream.

But the *here* and the *now* were more relevant. The sandbagged gun emplacements, the depressing barriers of barbed wire on tiny Cornish beaches where children had once explored and played. Many of them would now be in uniform, waiting for D-Day.

Ransome wondered what his parents really thought about the cottage in Polruan. Local people would know about it soon enough, but the events to come might put it into perspective.

He had mentioned this again to Eve when he had telephoned her to say that he was free at last to come to her.

She had replied, 'Just come. I'll be waiting. It has to be there, Ian. Don't you see? I want it to be clean, decent. To be able to face anyone and say, *This is how it was*. No matter what.'

Ransome turned and looked at the little pub, The Lugger, where he had taken her on that sunny day. Bare-legged, her eyes sometimes so grave, at other times laughing like another voice. Too young to go inside for a drink, but now he knew that she had loved him even then.

When he had called her from Falmouth to tell her he had secured the cottage she had gasped with disbelief.

'How did you manage it?'

He smiled now. Manage it? Old Isaac Proby who owned three of the little cottages had been more than eager to let him take it. People did not come here for their holidays any more. There were too many restricted areas, warnings of minefields, forbidden walks along the cliffs.

Old Proby had added, 'I'll air the place out. They gets a bit damp, y'know.'

Ransome walked up the little pavement. On one side it was a wall, to lean on and reflect, with a lower bank of cottages below, and then the water.

He paused to rest his elbows on the worn stones. It was really happening. So it must be as she wanted it. There might be pain enough later. He stared hard at the racing current, the way some moored landing-craft tugged at their cables and nearly dragged their buoys beneath surface.

It was going to be soon. They had been briefed and briefed until they could digest no more. Ships, commanders, landing instructions, army units, the whole strategy of invasion.

Many would fall that day, whenever it was. Some, like the disfigured airmen he had seen in the abbey, would wish they had.

He must give her no hint, no suggestion of what might smash down their happiness. It was a matter of odds, luck, and fate. He had now been over two years in command of *Rob Roy*, with thousands of miles steamed, and countless mines swept and rendered harmless. At the beginning he had imagined he would survive six months, and no longer. Today he was on borrowed time. The most dangerous of all.

He shook himself and walked more quickly up the sloping pavement.

There were plenty of khaki and blue uniforms about and he was glad to reach the tiny passageway which led to the cottage's entrance. Away from the salutes, the curious stares, an occasional twitch of curtains as he passed.

The rugged stones of the cottage were newly painted, and the tiny garden at the rear was a vivid confusion of rhododendrons and blue and purple lupins. The gardens of these cottages were allowed to grow much as they pleased, but Ransome knew that somebody had made an effort to tidy this one up.

The door flew open and she held out her arms to him.

He held her very tightly, his mouth brushing her long hair, neither of them speaking.

Beyond her he saw more flowers, and some fresh rhododendrons which she must have cut from the bushes and had arranged in a large copper pot.

There was a fire burning in the grate of the living-room and she twisted round in his arms as he took her through the door.

She said, 'I had to light it, May or not. It was so damp!' She was laughing, helping him with his cap and jacket, waiting for him to lose his nervousness. It was something she had not felt for a long while. Since the last time they had been together? Or when she had discovered the hidden photograph? It seemed like something destined. What she had wanted, always wanted. Now, with the door closed, and the sunlight reflecting on a framed print of Polperro, she wanted only for him to be happy, to feel at peace.

Ransome looked at the table, the knives and forks. 'But they're – '

She nodded, her eyes shining. 'Your father sent them across from your house, and some other things too.' A little of her courage faded and she added, 'I didn't bring much. It was a bit difficult.'

She waited for him to sit beside, if not in front of the fire, and watched as he filled his pipe. She looked around the room, remembering all those holidays, but picturing it as it might have been. A dog perhaps, or a cat like Jellicoe drowsing on the wall with one eye on the gulls.

She knelt by his legs and rested her head on his knees so that her hair hung down to the floor.

She said, 'I must ask. How long do we have?'

Ransome tried not to picture the ship, the other minesweepers waiting for the final decisions to be made. Sherwood had suggested that the whole thing might be postponed indefinitely despite all the weight of preparations. The Met reports were unfavourable. But so had they been before Sicily. And all the while the great armada waited. Ships and men. Flesh and steel.

'If I'm not recalled, two days.'

'There's no telephone here.' It was like a cry of protest.

He ruffled her hair. It was like warm silk. 'They always find a way.'

The coastguard knew where he would be. A message would reach him in minutes. After that –

Eve said, 'We *can* have some walks?' She looked up at him, searching his face. 'Please?'

'Of course. Lots.'

She lowered her chin to his knee. 'Your father sent a message too.' Her mouth trembled but she made another effort. 'He wrote that he would look after me when you left. That he would drive me – ' She broke off and wrapped her arms around him. 'Not yet, dearest Ian. Please, not yet.'

Ransome reached out to his jacket, which hung on a chair. He had intended to wait, but now she needed him: it was no longer just the other way around.

He took out a small package. 'I meant to get a proper box. Anyway you might not like it, it was just an impulse. I – '

She pulled off the wrapping and held the ring up to the sunlight. It seemed to glow, first red then white, the tiny rubies and diamonds flowing into each other.

In a small voice she asked, 'Where did you *get* it?'

Ransome took it gently from her and looked at it. *Rob Roy* had been in Alexandria and he had been ordered to Cairo, to meet some senior officers who had apparently been involved in supplying weapons to the partisans. Their beliefs and their politics did not matter. If they hated the Germans enough to pull a trigger they would be given arms to use for the job. God alone knew what would happen when the partisans and the vague resistance groups went back to being bandits again.

Without effort he could see the shop, the old jeweller watching intently while he had picked out this ring.

It was neither a wedding nor an engagement ring in the accepted sense. But it had seemed right for Eve.

When he had told her about the strange little shop she said, 'I think it's lovely.' She lifted herself higher and kissed him gently on the mouth. 'You're always full of surprises!' Then she looked at him, her eyes big and very steady. 'Put it on for me.'

She offered her left hand. 'Please.'

He held her wrist and said, 'It may not fit.' It was as if this very moment had also been a part of destiny.

He said, 'I do love you, Eve. One day – '

She raised her finger very slightly. 'Until that day – ' Then she withdrew her hand and held it to the sunlight again. 'We're engaged!'

They faced each other and laughed like conspirators. Like children. Then she got to her feet, and when he attempted to hold her she shook her head.

'I was going to be sensible. To make you eat something, or at least have a drink.'

She was backing away very slowly, as if she could not bear to lose sight of him.

'I can't *be* sensible, dearest Ian. I've wanted you for so long. Why be sensible now?'

He stood looking at her, watching the firelight playing in her eyes. So many emotions. Determination and a sweet unsureness, even fear.

She whispered, 'Give me five minutes.' Then she held up her ring and exclaimed, 'I'm so *happy*!'

She ran into the adjoining room and closed the door.

So his father knew all about it, but not, it seemed, her own. The consequences neither of them could guess; but there would be no regrets.

The war and the danger were alien, not even intruders in this place.

He hesitated, then pushed open the door.

He did not know what he had been expecting. That Eve might be in bed, her eyes on the door; nervous perhaps, shy now that the moment had arrived. Wondering if the reality would spoil the dream they had both cherished.

But she was standing by the window, one hand gripping the heavy black-out curtain while she peered towards the darkening estuary. She was wearing a white nightgown, with small delicate patterns of lace around the neckline and hem. Just two thin cords across her shoulders, her hair hanging free and shining faintly in the light from the solitary bedside lamp.

He saw her tense as he walked towards her.

She said, 'I – I wanted to be perfect for you.'

Ransome put his hands on her shoulders and was shocked to discover they were so cold despite the humid air and the fire they had left in the other room.

Very gently he turned her to face him, holding her at arm's length. Her hand released its grip on the curtain and fell to her side; she did not look up, as if she could feel his eyes on her.

He said in a whisper, 'You're so lovely, Eve.' He put one arm around her and pulled her against him. He could feel her supple body through the thin silk, the pressure of her breasts against him, and when she did at last look into his face he saw the warmth, the pleasure of his words shining in her eyes.

She threw her arms around his neck and shook some hair from her face.

'Wanton, and I don't care. I'm not going to spoil anything because I'm inexperienced. I want to be adult – ' It would not hold, and she nestled her face against his, her body trembling as she sensed his need of her.

'You may have grown up, Eve. But you're the same girl.' She did not protest as he led her to the bed and sat her down. 'You couldn't spoil anything, as you put it.' He sat beside her and kissed her gently at first, and then with a passion he had never known before. He felt his heart pounding like blood, and gripped her more firmly as her mouth responded to his, her lips parting while she drew him closer.

She lay back on the bed and spread her arms as if crucified. He touched her body, her breasts, caressing them through the silk. Then he leaned over her and kissed her, he did not know how many times. Through the nightdress, across her bare shoulders until she gasped, 'Oh, Ian, I never thought – '

She raised herself as he slipped the nightdress away, watching his eyes while she lay naked, her long hair across the pillows and over the side of the bed.

She whispered, 'Don't turn away.' She did not move as he undressed, and only the beat of her heart below one uplifted breast gave away her emotion, her longing for him, not just for this moment but for all the months, the dreams, the fears.

Then he knelt beside her and ran his fingers over her breast, down still further to the dark triangle he had seen through the nightdress when she had turned from the window.

She reached up and held his shoulders. 'I've never been with any other man. You know that, don't you?'

He nodded. 'I shall be gentle, my darling girl.'

'It's not that. I'm – quite small. You may hurt me.' Her fingers gripped him more tightly. 'But I don't want you to stop.' Her eyes were pleading. 'I can bear the pain . . . it will get better in time.'

She gasped when he touched her, as she felt his body dividing hers. Ransome slipped his arm beneath her shoulders and kissed her very slowly. He wanted to hold his breath, to prevent himself from crying out. He felt her back arch to receive him, then the first precious moment. She drew him down, her hands slipping down his back, pulling him until her nails must surely have broken the skin.

She gasped, 'Now, Ian, please, *now*!'

Ransome felt her body surrendering, then kissed her hard on the mouth as he entered her and was enclosed, received like part of herself.

They lay together for a long time, she on her side with one leg thrown across him, her foot playing with his.

She said, 'It was beautiful.' Her eyes were very near to his, filling her face. 'I knew it would be like that. I just knew. Now nothing can keep us apart.'

Ransome stroked the hair from her cheek. 'And I knew you would be as you are. When I saw you lying here it was all I could do not to take you then and there. You're so lovely, you've no idea.'

She moved closer. 'I want us to make love again as soon as we can.'

He smiled. 'Yes, you *are* wanton.'

They kissed, but this time the embrace did not break.

The next day they went for a long walk along the cliffs, and watched the sea. It looked angry and hostile, with serried rows of jagged breakers and blown spume.

Then far, far out to sea, almost hidden in horizon haze, they saw the ships. Ransome's heart sank: it was something he had hoped to avoid. Like the long arm reaching out, leaving nowhere to hide.

'What are they, Ian?' She clung to his arm, her hair barely contained by a scarf, her face so relaxed and happy he did not want to reply.

Suddenly a thin white waterspout made a flaw in the dull horizon, and seconds later a muffled boom thudded against the cliffs.

She said quietly, 'They're minesweepers, aren't they?'

He nodded. 'Trawlers out of Falmouth, most likely.'

She gripped his arm more tightly. 'They look so small. It's a wonder they hold together with great explosions like that.'

Ransome turned her towards a different path. No escape. The field where he and Tony had once hiked was commanded by a slit-eyed, concrete machine-gun bunker, the lush grass dotted with tall poles to prevent gliders or small planes from landing here.

She whispered, 'You will be careful. Promise!'

'Trust me.' He turned toward her and kissed her, tasted a tear on her cheek. 'I love you. We love each other. We were meant to share.'

They walked down the path, the sound of the sea fading behind them.

'Will you be going back to Codrington House?'

She shook her head. 'Not yet. Your father said I could stay with them for as long as I want. My mother knows. She likes you very much.'

'I'm glad.'

What was wrong? Was it seeing the minesweepers? She was going to stay with his parents. She would not feel so cut off there. His father's hand was in this too, he thought. He would know that the invasion was on the doorstep; he met more Admiralty officials and naval officers than anyone.

The thought touched his mind like a scalpel. They were his next of kin, and would be told first if anything went wrong.

He tightened his grip around her shoulders. She would be there, sharing it.

'It's been wonderful –' They turned into the street, and he saw the coast-guard's car parked as close as it could get to the cottages.

Oh God. He slowed his pace, trying to find the words. *I am afraid.*

He said, 'He's here to fetch me. It's a recall.'

She turned and stared at him. 'Not yet, Ian! We've only had one night together . . .' She tilted her chin and said in a controlled voice, 'I'm not being very much help, am I?'

They walked down to the car and the coastguard handed Ransome a sealed note.

He said, 'Came just now, zur, must be urgent. They'm sending a car for 'e.'

'I'll not be long.' They entered the cottage and stared around in silent desperation.

She said brokenly, 'I loved it here, darling!'

He watched her roll her nightgown and place it in her bag with great care.

'Just a moment.' He took it from the bag and held it to his face, the memories of their brief time together sweeping over him to torment him further.

'Such a lovely smell. I shall never forget.'

Their eyes met and held like a last embrace.

She said simply, 'It was the sachet. Roses and rosemary.' Then she came to him and whispered against his face. 'Love and remembrance.'

20

Day of Reckoning

HM Minesweeper *Rob Roy* completed another slow turn and settled on to the next leg of her prescribed sweep.

Standing in the forepart of the bridge Ransome watched the sweep-wire's float with its little green flag cutting above the waves, then trained his glasses on the other ships taking up station astern.

It was evening, very dull with a hint of drizzle, not at all like the end of a June day.

He heard Beckett's voice from the wheelhouse. 'Steady on two-zero-zero, sir.'

Ransome tugged his cap down over his hair and shifted restlessly. Like any other day and yet so completely different. He could feel it all around him: expectancy, relief, anxiety, and, most of all, the sailor's attitude of resignation. The waiting and the doubts were all behind them, although to the men working aft by the sweep, or at their guns and lookout positions, they could have had the Channel to themselves.

Ransome heard Morgan speaking to the coxswain again, and pictured his small company throughout the ship, on deck and in the engine-room. Commander Bliss had called a conference of all his captains as soon as Ransome had returned to Falmouth. The group was to be at first-degree readiness, no matter what the Met buffs had threatened about the weather. More delays and uncertainties, with some of the old hands already suggesting that the top brass had made another timely cock-up. Forty-eight hours of conflicting signals, more intelligence packs and recognition instructions.

Then Bliss had sent for Ransome and had announced without fuss, 'It's on. Tuesday morning we hit Normandy as planned.'

Now they were here in mid-Channel, heading towards the French coast. It was no longer a plan or a conception of one; it was not even next month. It was dawn tomorrow.

Ransome felt a shiver run through him. It was hard to imagine it. All those vessels, hundreds of them, converging from east and west to the great assembly point south of the Isle of Wight, already aptly nicknamed Piccadilly Circus. From Harwich, Chatham and the Nore. From Portsmouth and Weymouth Bay, from Plymouth and every inlet in the West Country; all those ships. Only a cruising gull would be able to get a complete picture. The forty-eight hour delay might cost them dearly. Too much. For even with air supremacy over the south coast, with the American and British squadrons keeping up unbroken patrols by day and night, the enemy must surely know by now what was coming.

When the minesweepers and other small support vessels of Bliss's group had sailed directly to their prescribed areas from Falmouth, they had only caught a glimpse of the massive build-up. Every type and size of landing-ship, tanks, men, and weapons, while other strange-looking craft followed close behind carrying steel bridges, portable jetties, and the vital supplies of fuel to keep it all moving.

They had been challenged several times by vigilant patrols and escorts, but Ransome had been fired on in the past by over-zealous commanders, and had ordered Mackay to be ready to flick the minesweeping lights on to reveal their intentions, rather than risk unnecessary injury or death.

He heard Fallows' sharp voice from 'A' Gun below the bridge and pondered again over Bliss's last-minute, private comments.

'That subbie of yours, Fallows. I've had a signal about him from the security chaps. A spot of bother about some forgery on a supply docket – pusser's paint going to the black market, would you believe!'

Fallows had certainly been behaving strangely, Ransome thought, but he had imagined it was over something else.

Bliss had added smoothly, 'It will probably mean a court martial – you know how it is, Ian. He'll certainly be required to face a full inquiry. It's your responsibility, of course, about when you tell him. You don't want any changes or upsets at this stage, with all hell about to break loose, eh?' He had smiled warmly. 'Entirely up to you.'

In other words, if anything misfired, Ransome and not Bliss would carry the can.

Ransome moved across the bridge past a look-out, and the young replacement signalman named Darley. It was all so fresh and new to him that he kept jumping up and down, fetching things for the yeoman, like a puppy with an old dog.

He peered astern, his glasses misting in the drifting drizzle and salt spray.

Ranger was on the quarter, dipping and lifting again in the steep swell; her outline was already blurred. It would be dark soon, but the sweep would have to be completed whatever happened.

He wondered briefly how Hargrave was managing with his first command, and what Gregory thought of his gaggle of motor minesweepers, which were somewhere astern with the Rescue M.Ls and *Bedworth*. Someone handed him a mug of cocoa, 'kye', and he felt it sticking to his throat like treacle. There was more than a hint of rum in it. Beckett's work, no doubt.

Ransome rested his elbow on his bridge chair and tried not to let his mind stray from his ship, the wires and voicepipes which connected him with the men who listened and waited; who had only him to rely on.

But he thought of that short stay in Polruan, the room which had been so small and yet barely able to contain their love. He recalled his surprise at seeing his own photograph in a frame by the bed lamp, as if it belonged there, had always been a part of the place. He had mentioned it, but she had said little about it. There was another story there somewhere, he thought.

He touched his coat pocket and felt the outline of his oilskin pouch. This time it held another picture, a small self-portrait she had shyly offered him just before they had set off for that last walk along the cliffs.

It showed her sitting at an easel, her knees drawn up and displaying those familiar paint stains. She had put *Barracuda* in the background – remarkably accurately, considering the boat had been under canvas for so long.

On the reverse of the painting she had written, 'To the dearest of men.'

It had not been the only message she had given him. The last one had been in a sealed envelope; she had handed it to him just before the naval car had driven him away, before he had had time to open it. She had called, 'Read it later on!' Then as the car had gathered speed she had shouted, '*I love you!*' And she had turned away. He had known it was because of her tears.

She must have selected the sonnet with great care. It had reminded him of his schooldays, but she had somehow brought it up to date, to their dangerous world, in her own handwriting. Like a calm pool in a forest.

Let me not to the marriage of true minds
Admit impediments. Love is not love

Which alters when it alteration finds,
Or bends with the remover to remove . . .

There was more, but in those first lines he could hear her speaking to him, reassuring him. As if she were here beside him.

Ransome recrossed the bridge, knowing that Morgan wanted to talk, but had been respecting these remaining moments of privacy.

He peered at the shaded compass repeater and felt his ship rolling heavily in the troughs. With an opposing current, and the heavy sweep trailing astern, *Rob Roy* was barely making seven knots.

He stamped his old leather seaboots on the deck and felt the restless strain thrusting into him again. Was it fear? Or was it fear of failure, of overlooking some small but vital point?

Directly below his feet Ordinary Seaman Boyes heard the thuds and glanced up at the wheelhouse deckhead. Beside him, the new midshipman, Piers, stared at him wide-eyed.

'What was that?'

Beckett lounged easily behind the wheel, his eyes on the gyro tape.

'No sweat. Just the skipper lettin' off steam.' He did not even bother to add *sir*. It didn't seem to matter, he thought, as he watched the ticking lubber's line.

There had been some cheeky comment when he had taken over the wheel. He would be on it until they'd done what they'd come for. Beckett was dressed in his best Number One jacket, with the shining gold-wire badges on each lapel.

He had rasped at the quartermaster, 'An' why not? This is the big 'un. It's got to be done right – look proper, see?'

Nobody argued with the coxswain.

He still felt the scar on his thigh where the red-hot splinter had torn into him; but what the hell. You lose something, and you fetch up gaining something. He had been awarded a bar to his Conspicuous Gallantry Medal, which he had got when the Old Man had got his gong from the King. Made 'em all sit up at home, although his dad had been enjoying His Majesty's pleasure in a different style.

The door opened and closed and the Buffer, carrying a heavy torch, glanced in as he made a final check on damage-control.

Beckett gave a lazy grin. 'I 'ope you've got a tin-'at for yer weddin' tackle, Buffer! Wouldn't like nuffin to get shot off!'

The Buffer snapped back, 'I thought *you'd* be wearin' yer brown trousers this time, Swain!'

Boyes watched the Buffer bustle away. He drew comfort from their casual banter, their warm hostility toward each other.

He tried to push Connie from his thoughts, but she kept returning. He saw her on the bed, then wrapped in his arms; felt his face flush as he recalled what they had done, and how she had guided him to that overwhelming climax.

He had tried to telephone her several times, a difficult and expensive exercise. The battery guardroom had been unable or unwilling to help him, but on the third occasion, with a queue of impatient and fuming sailors outside the only telephone box, her friend Sheila had been brought to speak to him.

'You're a nice bloke, Gerry, but in some ways just a kid. You're not like Connie

– you're like chalk and cheese. She's my best friend. I know more about her than most.'

'But I must speak to her!' A sailor had rapped with his coins on the glass.

She had said, 'Connie's fond of you, 'course she is. But it's not the real thing.' She had hesitated, balancing Boyes' despair against her own betrayal. 'She was in love once, with a bloke from this battery. He treated her badly, then he pushed off to North Africa, God rot him! Well, now he's back, and Connie's making a fool of herself all over again. So just forget it. Wouldn't work anyway. You'll be an officer soon. Then what?'

Boyes had left the box as if he was in a trance. He loved her. They would have managed.

On the messdeck it had been the tough A. B. Jardine who had asked, 'Wot the hell's up with you, Gerry? You got a face like a wet Sunday in Liverpool!'

The mess had been deserted at the time and Boyes had found himself spilling it out to Jardine, expecting him to mock him for his juvenile behaviour.

Jardine had regarded him thoughtfully. 'She sounds a right little raver.' Then he had relented. 'See 'ere, Wings, she's not for you. 'Er mate was right. She's not your sort, no more than I am. When you've got a bit o' gold on yer sleeve, you'll remember us, an' wot you've gained – least I 'ope you do.'

Boyes had stared at him. 'You knew?'

Jardine had laughed. '*Course!* The 'ole bloody ship knows. But it's different now, see? Maybe they was right to turn you down for your wavy stripe, but not no more they ain't. Even if you are going to be one o' *them*, you're all right, Wings. So just remember this lass as experience.' Then he had shaken his head. '*Love?* Gawd, Gerry-lad, she'd 'ave you fer breakfast!'

Boyes was still unconvinced.

The midshipman whispered, 'Do you think we'll be going into action?'

Boyes smiled. 'It's hard to tell.' He pointed at the vibrating plot-table. 'Now look at this – '

They all stared up as Sherwood's voice came across the bridge intercom.

'The float's no longer watching, sir!'

Midshipman Piers forgot his authority and seized Boyes' arm. 'What's he talking about?'

Boyes swallowed hard. 'It means that the Oropesa float has disappeared, gone below the surface. We must have snared something.' He looked for understanding, but there was none. He remembered Jardine's words. Maybe they had been right to turn him down for the chance of a commission: but not any longer. In the face of Piers's anxiety, he thought he knew what the tough seaman meant.

Beckett interrupted, 'Stand by, my beauties. Time to earn yer pay!'

Lieutenant Sherwood gripped a davit and watched the sea boiling up beneath the stern from the racing screws. They were making slow progress, but down aft, with the water rising almost level with the deck as *Rob Roy* pushed into the oncoming crests, they got an impression of speed.

He saw *Ranger*'s murky silhouette riding out on the quarter, the spray bursting above her stem as she held station on the leader. The remainder of the sweepers were already lost in early darkness. Sherwood buttoned the neck of his oilskin.

Inside the heavy coat he was sweating badly, but without it he knew he would soon be drenched to the skin and shivering. You couldn't win.

Stoker Petty Officer Nobby Clarke crouched on his little steel seat while he controlled the winch, spray dripping off the peak of his cap as he squinted into the criss-cross of foam from the ship's wake. Sherwood found he was able to accept all that was happening, what he could see around him, and that which he could only imagine from reading the intelligence packs.

They had all known it was coming. Now it was here, or soon would be. To have lived this long was the real bonus.

Had anyone else spoken such thoughts aloud, Sherwood would have torn him apart. *Once.* How could he have altered so much? He had believed it madness to consider a true friendship, let alone a marriage, in wartime. He could almost hear himself warning others against it. But that moment beside the parachute-mine had changed him.

He glanced around at the other shining figures in his party, the slender barrel of the after four-inch gun overhead.

Whatever happened to caution? To our disbelief in survival?

He smiled to himself as he recalled his unusual reserve when he had told Ransome, the day he had returned to the ship to take over Hargrave's work.

'I've asked her to marry me.' He had grinned, surprised at his own shyness, his new faith.

Ransome had shaken his hand warmly and then said, '*Snap!*'

So the skipper had a girl too, although nobody had ever guessed it. The news was another precious secret, like the one he had shared in Sicily.

Stoker Petty Officer Clarke snapped, 'The float, sir!'

The older hands could often sense such things. By the sound or the vibration of a sweep-wire.

Clarke exclaimed, 'There's somethin' there!' His eyes showed white in the gloom. 'Better tell the Old Man, sir.'

Sherwood snatched up the handset. 'The float's no longer "watching", sir.' He saw Guttridge peering down from the four-inch. The leading hand had come back from leave with a pair of black eyes. But he was a hard character, not a man to be laughed at.

'Captain here.' He pictured Ransome on the bridge, assessing it, making a plan, preparing another if it all went sour.

'Recover the sweep.' He hesitated. 'Take it easy, Philip.'

Sherwood nodded to Clarke. 'Bring it in.' He heard the Buffer panting along the side-deck. 'Clear the quarterdeck and take cover!'

He waited, half-expecting his limbs to defy him, to begin shaking.

'Nice and easy, Stokes. It's probably a bit of wreckage.'

Clarke said nothing, but reached out with a gloved hand to let the incoming wire slide over it. He remarked flatly, 'Clean as a whistle.'

Sherwood waited. Even in the poor light he could see the wire, bright and burnished, proof, if any was needed with old sweats like Clarke on the job, that the wire had been running along the bottom.

'Guttridge! Fall out the gun's crew.' Sherwood glanced around. He could barely see beyond the guardrail.

If it was a mine, it was coming in right now towards the counter.

'Pass the word to the bridge, Buffer.'

The Buffer stood his ground and called, 'Gipsy, tell the bridge. It's probably a mine.' To Sherwood he said affably, 'I'll stay with you, if you don't mind, sir.' He folded his arms and could have been grinning at him. 'I 'ear congratulations is in order, sir?'

Sherwood gave a short laugh. Maybe that was it. They were all going quietly round the bend without realising it.

'*Slower*, Stokes!'

Clarke gritted his teeth. He could feel it now, as if he and not the winch was taking the full strain, like a fisherman with a marlin on his line.

Sherwood got down on his knees and winced as a rivet dug into his leg.

'It's there. It must be.' He made up his mind. 'Tell the captain.' He reached up and added, 'Give me that flashlight, Buffer. I'm going to have a look, and to hell with the bloody black-out!'

He switched on the light and saw several things at once. The float trying to rise to the surface as it floundered towards the winch, the otter already shining brightly in the beam while it moved nearer. Directly below his outstretched arm was the mine.

Sherwood heard Clarke give a gasp, and as if from a mile away someone calling to the bridge on the intercom. The deck seemed to tilt right over, and he guessed that one screw had been thrown into full astern to pivot the ship round.

He saw the mine sway towards him, but found he could watch it without fear. Seconds only to live. He shouted into the spray, '*I love you!*'

Then the mine veered away, caught unawares by the violent change of course. It collided with the otter at the end of the sweep and the dark sea lit up to a vivid explosion.

Sherwood felt himself knocked flat by a solid waterfall which swept over the deck without making a sound. But as his hearing returned he caught snatches of cheering, and felt the Buffer thumping his back and yelling, 'We're goin' to need a new float, sir!'

A seaman called, 'All them dead fish! Pity we can't 'ang about to net 'em for the galley!'

Sherwood staggered to his feet. His cap had vanished, as had the Buffer's flashlight. *A bloody close thing.* There was nothing in the manuals about using a torch in enemy waters.

Down in the engine-room Campbell watched the revolution counters moving into unison again, and saw one of his stokers giving him a thumbs-up while the glistening machinery roared round within inches of his hand.

The whole place had boomed like an oil drum beaten by a giant hammer. Campbell looked for his E.R.A. and they exchanged quick grins.

Then he turned back to his dials, his lips moving to the tune of an old hymn.

> 'Sweeping, sweeping, sweeping,
> Always bloody well sweeping,
> Sweeping in the morning,
> And in the afternoon . . .'

Campbell wiped his streaming face. Alf Bone had been right to get out of it, he thought. Just for a split second back there . . .

He had felt his eyes fixed on the curved side, streaked with oil, each droplet quivering to the beat of the twin propellers as if it was alive.

Just for one agonising moment he had believed that which all of them dreaded had happened.

The telephone shrilled noisily beside his little metal shelf, where he kept his engine-room log.

'Chief here.' He had to press one grimy hand over his other ear.

'This is the captain. All right? Sorry about the noise – don't know what the neighbours will think.'

The Chief grinned and felt the tension draining away like sand from a glass. 'We're okay, sir. Let me know when you intend to do it again!'

On the bridge Ransome gave the handset to the boatswain's mate. To Morgan he said, 'Let's hope that'll be the last of them!'

Morgan removed his cap and allowed the spray to soak into his curly hair.

He had imagined that he actually saw the mine as Ransome had flung the ship hard over. Another moment, and – He felt his legs shaking. *No casualties, no damage.*

Then the boatswain's mate turned from a voicepipe and said unsteadily, 'Beg pardon, sir, but the gunnery officer is reportin' the starboard guardrail 'as carried away in the – er – bang!' It was all he could do to prevent himself from bursting into insane laughter.

Ransome climbed into his chair for the first time and nodded gravely.

'Tell Mr Fallows that I shall indent for a new one when we return to harbour!'

Mackay hid a broad grin, and touched his young assistant's arm.

'Like a bunch of kids!' But he did not hide his admiration, or his relief.

Long before dawn it was obvious to everyone that there was no last-minute change of plans. The full force of the attack was under way.

Throughout the night Ransome and the watchkeepers who shared the bridge with him had felt the air trembling to an unbroken procession of bombers flying toward the Normandy coast. There must have been hundreds of them, perhaps thousands.

And now, as dawn made a reluctant grey brushstroke on the clouds, the coastline was outlined by a backcloth of fire. Red and orange, with a wall of smoke rising like the gateway to Hell.

How must it look to the thousands of troops who would be in their landing-craft? Heading towards their next rendezvous, a cross on a map, an aerial photograph at some last briefing?

Very few of these many craft were yet visible from *Rob Roy*'s bridge, but Ransome knew they were stretched across the Channel, the rearguard still leaving the assembly area while the leaders were preparing for their baptism of fire.

Ransome levelled his glasses and watched the ripple of flashes which seemed to dart from the land itself. Seconds later the heavy shells began to fall amongst the invisible armada, while the air quaked to the echo of their explosions.

As at Sicily, the big ships were firing from below the horizon, the glow of each fall of shot giving shape to the land, like a terrible panorama of death.

Bedworth cruised through the support craft with an impressive bow wave, her signal light flashing briefly like a solitary blue eye.

'*Proceed as ordered*, sir.' Mackay lowered his father's big telescope.

'Slow ahead together.' Ransome rested his hands on the screen and watched the first low shapes of landing-craft butting into the choppy water abeam. No bagpipes this time. It seemed wrong somehow. They had survived this far. The greatest invasion of all time had begun.

He saw some fast motor launches leading the way as the larger landing-craft turned obediently to follow.

Part of the Canadian Third Division, heading for the beach codenamed Juno.

Ransome thought of the pipe-smoking major he had met on the beach in Sicily. Perhaps he was here too on this bleak, terrible morning.

It prompted him to call, 'Yeoman! Hoist battle ensigns! Let's show 'em!'

Mackay stared at him, then nodded. 'Aye, *aye*, sir!' He jabbed the young signalman. 'Here, Nipper, help me bend them on!' He laughed aloud. 'Something to remember, eh, kid?'

Morgan raised his glasses as the lenses glowed red from a fiery reflection across the water.

'Some poor devil's brewed up, sir.'

Ransome turned away as more waterspouts burst skyward amongst the lines of landing-craft.

He looked above and watched as the first great ensign floated from *Rob Roy*'s starboard yard, then a second one to port. This ship was too small for such a display; but it might give some of the watching soldiers heart while they waited, counting seconds, hoping the ramps would fall and their helplessness would end.

An upended landing-craft floated abeam, with two soldiers standing on the keel, casting off their boots and weapons as the hull began to sink beneath them. One of them waved, or it could have been a mock salute.

Great shells thundered overhead, and once when Ransome trained his glasses on a hardening ridge of land he saw a four-engined bomber fall like a leaf to vanish into the smoke. There was some sort of electrical storm making the clouds shine like silver, and a second plane fell without every sighting its objective.

Ransome watched, and found himself hoping. Praying. But no tell-tale parachutes drifted clear. Their war had ended, here.

'Port ten. Midships. *Steady*.'

Morgan turned and looked up at him. 'Steady on one-six-zero, sir.'

The minesweepers had achieved what they came to do. Even as the thought crossed his mind, Ransome saw some of the big warships which had doubtless been the last to leave the assembly point surging past, guns high-angled and already shooting far inland.

Sherwood climbed to the bridge. 'Sweep secured, sir.' He watched the tall waterspouts shredding down near the landing-craft, some of which appeared to be swamped, only to emerge as determined as ever.

Ransome said, 'Go and clear the after guns. Stand by scrambling-nets. We'll be needed in support soon.'

He heard cheering and saw some of his men pointing and gesturing astern.

Ranger and the rest of the flotilla had followed his example, and looked even smaller under their big White Ensigns.

Sub-Lieutenant Fallows stood with his hands on his hips and glared as Leading Seaman Guttridge strolled toward him on the forecastle.

'Buffer said you want some 'elp, sir?' It was as close to being insolent as he could get. Guttridge was still smarting over the hiding he had received when he had gone home to sort out his wife and her boyfriend. He had not expected the latter to be a six-foot tall commando, nor had he anticipated that her two brothers, both squaddies, would be there to fill him in.

She had screamed, 'You talk about bein' faithful, you slag! Wot about all the girls you've put in the club?' They had beaten the hell out of him. His body was still a mass of bruises. He was in no mood to put up with Bunny Fallows, bloody D-Day or not.

Fallows barked, 'This guardrail – ' He pointed at the trailing wires. The explosion had snapped a small shackle like a carrot. 'It's a *mess*!'

'Wot d'you expect me to do about it?' Guttridge saw the crew of 'A' Gun rising above the shield to listen to this unexpected diversion.

Someone shouted, "Ere come the Glory Boys!'

A tight arrowhead of motor gunboats roared diagonally towards the port bow, their cannon and machine-guns already tracking round towards the land. With their ensigns streaming from each gaff, and the oilskinned officers wearing their dashing white scarves, they looked every inch the schoolboy's dream of the country's heroes.

Some of the seamen waved as *Rob Roy* plodded on at a steady eight knots.

Fallows yelled, '*I'm speaking to you!* Don't be so bloody insolent or I'll have that hook off your arm!'

He had to grip the remaining guardrail as the combined wash of the three fast-moving gunboats thundered around the bows and lifted them effortlessly on a small tidal wave.

Guttridge watched the sub-lieutenant and hoped he would lose his balance and pitch over the side. There was not a single matelot who would offer him a line.

But Fallows was clinging to a stanchion, his eyes popping from his head as he stared down past the receding bow wave.

He wanted to cry out, to make himself heard and obeyed. But in those swift seconds he saw only the mine as it spiralled lazily from the depths, where it had probably been lying for years undisturbed.

Guttridge saw his terror and yelled, 'Hit the deck! *Get down!*'

Then the mine rasped against the hull, and the world fell apart.

Lieutenant Trevor Hargrave stared overhead as another great salvo of shells thundered towards the shore. It sounded like a dozen express trains passing at the same time, so loud that you almost expected to see something.

The seaman with the quarterdeck handset reported, 'Sweep secured, sir!'

Hargrave nodded. How long would it take, he wondered? To stop fitting *Rob Roy*'s faces to the men he now commanded?

He glanced around the bridge, at the crouching look-outs, the leading signalman who should have been Mackay as he took a couple of turns on a signal halliard and watched the big, clean ensign streaming out on the wet breeze.

Ranger was his command. *Mine*. He felt pride matched only by an unexpected sense of loss.

He saw *Bedworth* tearing through the groups of motor minesweepers, and smiled bitterly. In Falmouth he had bumped into an old classmate who was now a lieutenant-commander on the naval staff.

He had asked him about Bliss, and why he did not appear to get on with Vice-Admiral Hargrave.

His friend had grinned and punched his arm. 'By God, Trevor, they must be a close bunch in your family to smother such a juicy secret!'

When Hargrave had pressed him further he had explained, 'Your old man was once Bliss's commanding officer in a fleet destroyer. The *word* went round that he was chasing Bliss's young wife – and with some success to all accounts. No love lost since, it seems.'

Hargrave bit his lip. He found it easy to believe now, when once he would have defended his father's name from any quarter.

He felt the pain and the humiliation returning. The beautiful Ross Pierce had offered him her private telephone number.

'Next time we meet, Trevor, we *may* start a few fires together!'

And he had believed it.

He had phoned her at that number, a flat she owned with a Mayfair exchange, two nights before *Rob Roy* had received her final orders for Operation 'Neptune', the navy's equivalent of 'Overlord'. Obviously she liked him quite a lot, but had held him at arm's length, which only made him want her all the more.

His father had answered the call, and Hargrave put down the receiver without speaking. It still hurt him more than he would have thought possible.

Sub-Lieutenant John Dent, whose sister drove staff cars in the WRNS, exclaimed, 'From the W/T office, sir. The first troops are ashore!'

Hargrave looked at the bleak sky, the choppy sea with its mounting litter of upended or burned-out landing vessels.

They had done it.

He thought of his father and the Wren officer together and tried to accept what he must do. He would use them both, just as they were using one another.

He heard muffled cheers from the wheelhouse and leaned over the voicepipe.

'Stow the noise down there.' He glanced at the gyro repeater. 'The course is one-six-zero, not two degrees off!'

He knew he was being unfair, that he was taking out his resentment on those who could not retaliate.

He looked round again. New faces. Probably clinging to Gregory's memory, his methods and personality.

Spray dashed over the glass screen and soaked Hargrave's shirt. He saw the sub-lieutenant trying to suppress a smile and said ruefully, 'I was wrong. D-Day or not, collars and ties are *not* suitable.'

There was a livid flash, followed by an explosion that hit *Ranger*'s flanks like something solid. For an instant longer Hargrave thought they had struck a submerged wreck or an unmarked sandbar. Then he stared appalled at the tall column of water which appeared to be rising from the deck of *Rob Roy*, towering higher and higher as if it would never disperse. *Ranger*'s first lieutenant, a young New Zealander, clattered on to the bridge.

'Dead alongside, sir! She's hit a mine, God damn it!' He sounded personal, beyond belief.

Hargrave watched as the white column cascaded down, the way she seemed to rock right over, and stay there.

The leading signalman shouted, 'From *Bedworth*, sir. *Take command of flotilla. Rescue M.Ls will close on Rob Roy.*'

Hargrave stared at their sister ship until his eyes smarted. Pictures stood out like those in an album. Fallows, too drunk to answer his questions. Ransome in his little cabin, like the one he now occupied when *Ranger* was in harbour. Campbell, old Bone and the hostile Sherwood. Beckett and the Buffer, and the midshipman who had been killed.

He said harshly, 'Disregard! Make to *Firebrand. Assume control. We are assisting.*'

He pounded the screen with his fist as he had seen Ransome do. 'Full ahead together!' He was disobeying Bliss's direct order, but suddenly it no longer mattered. All the petty manoeuvring and the plans for his future counted for nothing.

Rob Roy was still his ship. She mattered. Men were dying unnoticed against the background of greater events.

He shouted aloud, '*Well, they bloody matter to me!*'

The first lieutenant and the subbie exchanged glances. There was more to their new captain after all.

Ransome leaned on the chart-table with Morgan crowded against him under the canvas screen.

Ransome said, 'We shall remain on the present course until we reach *this* point.' He tapped the pencilled cross with his dividers. 'Six miles offshore.'

Morgan rubbed his chin. It made a rasping sound, as he often had to shave twice a day.

He said, 'After that – '

The explosion seemed to be right beneath their feet. The noise was shattering, and the hull rebounded from it with terrible violence.

Ransome found himself on his knees, Morgan sprawled and coughing beside him. There was smoke everywhere, and when Ransome struggled to his feet he almost fell again, and knew that the deck's angle was increasing.

He reached out to help Morgan from the litter of broken glass and buckled voicepipes but a pain like hot iron lanced through his side.

Morgan clambered up beside him. 'What is it?'

Ransome clawed his way to the chair and held on to it, gritting his teeth against the agony. He gasped, 'Couple of ribs, I think!'

He stared round the tilting bridge, his mind shocked and dazed by the explosion.

Rob Roy, his ship, had hit a mine. It was probably fatal. He must think. Accept it. Carry out the drill he had always dreaded.

He shouted, '*Stop engines!*'

The reply came back from the wheelhouse. 'No communications, sir!' He heard Beckett coughing. Then he said, 'Bit of a potmess down 'ere, sir. Steering gone – compass – the lot – '

Ransome beckoned to Morgan. 'Take over. Clear the wheelhouse. I must speak with the Chief.' He stared, sickened, at one of the look-outs. He had been flung back from that side by the blast; his head was smashed against the grey steel like an eggshell. There was a smear of blood down to the gratings, and much more of it running in the scuppers. Mackay knelt on an upended flag-locker, mopping his cheek where a piece of glass from the broken screen had slashed his face to the bone. The boatswain's mate sat with hands folded in his lap as if resting. Only the broken handset and his bulging eyes showed that he had been killed instantly by the blast; he was otherwise unmarked.

If he had not been crouching over the chart-table . . . Ransome controlled his thoughts with a terrible effort and pulled himself toward the ladder. In his sea-cabin there was another telephone which was connected directly to the engine-room.

Even as he reached it, he realised that the engines' beat had ceased. The cabin looked as if it had been ransacked by madmen.

He pulled the handset from its bracket, and Campbell answered before he could speak.

He said tersely, 'Taking water fast, starboard side forrard. Losing fuel from the tanks there too.'

Ransome pressed his forehead against the cold steel and nodded, his eyes closed. He had already smelled the stench of fuel. He had been present often enough when other ships had died. Like their blood draining away.

'Get your men out of there, Chief.'

Campbell replied, 'The pumps are holding, sir. I'll stay with them.'

Ransome saw Sherwood watching from the door, noticed how his figure was set at a crooked angle; he knew it was the ship going over. Men were shouting, and he heard metal scraping across the deck, feet running, disorder when moments before –

Sherwood watched his anguish and said, 'All depth-charges are set to safe, sir. The Buffer's standing by with floats and rafts. The whaler's ready for lowering, but the motor boat's had it.'

He helped him to his feet, feeling his pain, and the worse agony for his ship. He did not mention that the motor boat which hung from its starboard davits had taken much of the blast when the mine had exploded.

Sub-Lieutenant Tritton had been smashed to the deck when the 'skimming-dish' had been hurled inboard, and was still pinned under the wreckage. Cusack was with him, and he had seen the frightened S.B.A. handing him his instruments. Sherwood felt sickened by the thought of his cutting away at flesh and then bone while the ship settled down more steeply in the water.

Shells roared from the sky, and a drifting L.S.T. took one below her bridge, where two abandoned tanks were already burning from the last straddle.

Sherwood considered it. They were just a few miles offshore, and those guns would soon shift their sights to *Rob Roy* once the L.S.T. had been put down.

Ransome asked, 'How many casualties?' He moved through the door, his arm around Sherwood's shoulders as they lurched toward the ladder.

'Bunny Fallows bought it, sir. Guttridge too. Some of 'A' Gun's crew are badly shaken up, but only Hoggan was seriously wounded.' He thought of the burly leading hand with the tattoo around his wrist. 'He's been blinded.'

The deck gave another lurch. Ransome pulled himself to the bridge and threw back his head to take several gulps of air. But for Campbell's quick thinking when he had stopped the engines, the next bulkhead would have collapsed under the strain, and *Rob Roy* would be lying on the bottom.

He heard footsteps and saw Cusack striding across the broken glass. Cusack sensed the question in Sherwood's eyes and shrugged. 'Had to take the leg off. No choice.' He helped Ransome into the chair and said, 'Let me take a look.'

Ransome said, 'Too much to do. Shove off and see to the yeoman.'

Mackay was peering over the rear of the bridge, then turned, his eyes red with shock and disbelief.

'*Just a kid!*' He stared around at their faces. 'That's all he was, for Christ's sake! What are we, that we can let this happen to boys like him?'

Sherwood climbed onto a locker, the same one that the young signalman named Darley had been using when he had reached up to free one of the ensigns which had become tangled in the halliards. The blast had flung him from the bridge like a bundle of rags. His slight figure lay on the deck below, his eyes still staring at the clouds as if he could not accept what had happened.

Ransome said, 'Get down there, Number One.'

Sherwood faced him. Was there any point in prolonging it? Then he saw Ransome's despair. 'I'll do what I can.'

Beckett climbed on to the bridge and touched his cap.

Like Boyes and the terrified midshipman who followed him he was speckled with chips of white paint from the deckhead, as if he had been in the snow.

'No casualties in the wheel'ouse, sir.' He stared at the L.S.T., which was now fiercely ablaze from bow to stern. 'A few bleedin' 'eadaches, that's about all.'

He saw Mackay and added roughly, 'Never mind. Yeo. Coulda bin anyone.'

Mackay picked up his father's telescope and wiped it on his sleeve. He did not even look up as another shell exploded in the sea less than a cable away.

Ransome tried again. *Abandon ship.* He had no choice, unless he put the ship before her people, his pride before their survival.

Morgan said hesitantly, 'Some R.M.Ls are heading our way, sir.'

Ransome levered himself to his feet. Thank God, Cusack had gone elsewhere where he was needed. He winced and clapped one hand to his side.

'Muster the wounded. Stand by to lower the Carley floats and rafts.'

He stared at the sloping deck, the corpses lying where they had fallen.

He was leaving her. After all they had done together. All those miles, and all those bloody mines she had swept so that others might be safe.

The hull gave another shudder, and the remains of the topmast, which had been felled by the blast, slithered over the bridge with the remnants of the shattered radar lantern.

If only they could move. He would get her home somehow, if he had to go astern on one screw all the way.

The Buffer appeared at the top of the ladder, his face like a mask.

''Ands mustered, sir. Eight wounded. Five killed.' He hesitated. 'Two missing.'

Ransome pushed his fingers through his hair. The latter must be Fallows and Guttridge. They would never be found. There would be nothing left.

The Buffer glanced anxiously at his friend. 'Okay, Swain?'

Beckett sighed. 'Not 'appy, Buffer.'

The Buffer looked around, like a man who has been robbed of something precious.

'Me neither.'

Some one said in a dull voice, 'There goes our bloody Senior Officer.'

So Bliss had seen what had happened. *Rob Roy* was already in the past, written off.

Ransome moved to the rear of the bridge and stared at the deck's stark angle. Both screws must be almost out of the water; the forecastle was well down, the anchors awash. If only –

Sherwood came back and reported, 'Bulkhead's holding, sir, though God knows how.' He thought of the gaping hole in the messdeck which had begun deep in the bilges before exploding upwards to the sky. Their private world invaded, soiled. Seaboot stockings hung to dry, floating in the gushing, foul oil. A letter from home, a man's cap with its best shoregoing tally, *HM Minesweeper*, still managing to shine through the filth. Like an epitaph.

Sherwood watched him, feeling it, as if she was his ship; sharing it.

'Shall I give the word, sir? If we stay here, the Jerries – '

'I know.' The two words were torn from his lips.

His hand touched the oilskin pouch in his pocket. Eve would know. Would be reaching out to him.

He nodded abruptly. 'I'll do it.'

He cupped his hands and saw them all staring up at the bridge, unable to accept it. Unwilling to leave.

Mackay stood up and stretched his cramped muscles. Then he trained his long telescope and said brokenly, 'If only you could see this, Nipper!'

Ransome thought he had finally cracked. Nobody could blame him.

Then Mackay said in a stronger voice, 'From *Ranger*, sir. *Intend to take you in tow.*'

Ransome stared at him. The flotilla had gone ahead as ordered; so how could Hargrave be here to offer assistance?

Sherwood looked at him.

'What do you think, sir?'

Ransome faced them. They had never been closer than at this moment.

'Make to *Ranger*. *We shall stick together.*' He heard the clatter of Mackay's lamp and said, 'We'll tow from aft, Number One.' He was surprised at the new strength in his voice. 'We might just do it.'

While Sherwood and the Buffer hurried aft to prepare the towing-hawser, *Ranger* was already turning steeply towards them, her deck angled over as far as *Rob Roy*'s as she came in on a diagonal course. Hargrave had assessed the danger from the coastal battery and was not wasting any time.

Ransome looked down at the great oil slick which was spreading out around his ship, flattening the waves like a greasy blanket. It might just help when the hawser took that first, critical strain.

There were more men on deck now, moving to the shouted commands, but there eyes were on the damage all around them. Most of the extra hands were stokers, sent on deck by the Chief, who with an E.R.A. had remained in the engine-room to nurse the pumps, as they fought to contain the great weight of water trapped between two bulkheads. If one more collapsed *Rob Roy* would sink in minutes.

Ransome heard Able Seaman Jardine exclaim, 'You should see the bloody hole in the side! You could drive a double-decker bus through it!' That was certainly how it felt.

He was relieved to see that the wounded were gathered near one of the big Carley floats, so that they would have a better chance if the worst happened. The dead had been covered with strips of canvas, and the little S.B.A. sat beside Sub-Lieutenant Tritton, oblivious to all that was happening, even when a shell whimpered overhead. He watched Tritton's face, which was the colour of chalk, holding his wrist and listening to his laboured breathing. It was to be hoped that Cusack had made sure he would feel nothing until –

He watched another float being manhandled toward the side. Could anything worse happen? Could he even begin to believe that the worst was behind them?

He thought of the one mine which had found them. After all the miles they had steamed, the risks they had shared, the mines they had destroyed.

It had probably lain there for years after being dropped, very likely by the British, to delay coastal shipping. Its sinker must have jammed when it had first been laid, and it had rested there undisturbed all that time until those jubilant motor gunboats had awakened it with their impressive wash.

He moved around the bridge, his boots slipping on the slanting plates, his eyes seeking and feeling her pain like his own. The blast had buckled the wheelhouse's protective steel like a piece of cheap tin, and swept down the starboard side, missing some, hurling others aside. Like the Oerlikon gunner who had died below the bridge. No wonder sailors hated wearing steel helmets, no matter how many times the order was enforced. The blast had ripped the helmet from his head so that he had been garrotted by the chinstay, as if by human hands.

He saw order emerging from confusion. Wires, ropes and strops filled one side-deck, and it all had to be moved by muscle-power. If they were attacked by an enemy aircraft there would be no point in trying to fight back. They needed every spare hand on the towing-hawser, and the power-operated guns were useless anyway.

He raised his glasses and saw Hargrave staring across at him while *Ranger* straightened up and backed stern first towards him, her screws beating up foam even through the great slick of oil.

A heaving-line snaked across and fell short. Then another, this time with a heavy piece of iron on the end, just to make sure. Hands reached out, and Ransome heard the Buffer give vent to some foul language as one of the seamen got under his feet.

But he studied Hargrave, saw him force a grin, and turn to call an order as his ship's screws stopped, then turned slowly ahead to avoid a collision at the last moment.

Morgan whispered, 'There she goes, see!'

The blazing L.S.T. was turning on her side, the tanks crashing down and through the thin plating while a few small figures ran away from the sea, which with an almost lazy contempt swept them from their final handhold, and swallowed them as the vessel took a last dive.

A shell crashed into the sea near one of the Rescue M.Ls. Then another, so that the launch gathered speed and scuttled into a bank of drifting smoke.

Morgan said nothing, but thought, *Now it's our turn.*

Ransome held his breath as the shining hawser began to nod its way across the gap. From the bridge, the line being hauled inboard by his men was invisible against the murky water, so that the hawser appeared to be moving unaided, like a great serpent.

There was a cheer as the eye of the wire was made fast and the slack taken in. Ransome looked at the faces of his men near the bridge. Cheering, some laughing, others weeping and holding on to each other, their best friends probably. For they had not all survived this time.

He turned away and saw Mackay watching him. The yeoman said quietly, 'She always was a good 'un, sir.'

Beckett had been observing *Ranger*'s agile movements, while she paid out the long hawser until its centre vanished into the drifting oil.

'I'ave to admit, 'e 'andles her fair enough. Still, *Ranger*'s got a good coxswain, o' course.'

Ransome gripped the oilskin pouch against his aching side.

He said, 'She trained him well. Like the rest of us.'

Ranger's siren gave a banshee screech and very slowly at first, then with more confidence, she took the full strain on the tow.

Ransome gripped the rail beneath the smashed screen and watched the other ship until she appeared to be obscured by mist.

Then he said softly, 'It's over. So let's take her home, shall we?'

KILLING
GROUND

For my Kim –

together we found love

Prologue

Dawn seemed slow to appear, reluctant, even, to lay bare the great ocean, which for once lacked its usual boisterous hostility. But there had been fog overnight which had finally dispersed, and the sea, which lifted and dipped in a powerful swell, was unbroken but for an occasional feather of spray. The sky was the colour of slate and only a feeble light betrayed the presence of another morning, touching the crests with a metallic sheen, but leaving the troughs in darkness like banks of molten black glass. Deserted, an empty treacherous place; but that was a lie. For, like jungle or desert, creatures moved here to seek cover from danger, to survive the ever-present hunters.

As the light tried to feel its way through the slow-moving clouds a few birds showed themselves, circling above the sea's face, or riding like broken garlands on the steep-sided troughs. To them the sea held no mystery, and they knew that the rugged coast of Ireland was barely a hundred miles away.

A deepwater fisherman, had there been one, or some wretched survivor on a raft or in a drifting lifeboat might have sensed it. The slight throbbing tremor beneath the waves – a sensation rather than a sound, which could make even a dying man start with terror. But there was no one, and forty metres beneath the surface the submarine moved slowly and warily as if to follow the line on the chart where her captain leaned on the table. His pale eyes were very still, his ears taking in every sound around him while he waited; the hunter again from the instant the alarm bells had ripped through the boat and brought him from a restless sleep to instant readiness.

He could feel his men watching him, as if he had actually turned to stare at them individually. Faces he had come to know under every possible condition, once so bright and eager but now blanched with the pallor of prison, their gestures the tired, jerky movements of old men. Like the boat, worn out with the weeks and months at sea. The stink of it: of diesel and cabbage water, or damp, dirty clothing which no longer defied the cold, of despair.

He glanced at the clock, resting his eyes in the dimmed orange glow. Two torpedoes only remained after that last attack on the convoy, which had almost ended in disaster. Some of his men would be thinking, *Why now? What does it matter? We are going home.* It was like hearing their combined voices pleading as one.

But it did matter. It had to. The hydrophone operator had reported a faint beat of engines. A large vessel, perhaps in difficulties. If it was anyone else he might have questioned it, disregarded it. But the seaman had been with him from the beginning in this command. He was never mistaken, and thousands of tons of shipping scattered the depths of the Western Ocean to vouch for his accuracy. The captain smiled but it remained hidden. The others were probably hating him for his skills now, when before they had blessed him for saving their lives. *The ears of the predator.*

He signalled to his engineer officer, who waited by his panel with its dials and tiny glowing lights, and without waiting for an acknowledgement made his way to the periscope well. Every step brought an ache to his bones. He felt stiff, dirty, above all exhausted. He thrust it from his thoughts as the air began to pound into the saddle tanks and the depth gauges came to life. What did he really feel? Perhaps nothing any more. The silent pictures in the periscope lens, explosions, burning ships and men – they no longer reached him.

To return to base was something different. There he might drink too much or forget too little.

He started as someone laughed. A young, careless sound. That was 'Moses', the nickname used in every U-Boat for the youngest member of the crew. The captain turned his eyes to the gauges as they steadied at fourteen metres. It was the boy's first voyage. Now his relief was pushing the nightmares into the darkness. He was lucky. For some reason the captain thought of his young brother, but saw him only as the round-faced student with his cap set at a jaunty angle, enjoying life, but sometimes being too serious, too outspoken about matters he did not understand. They had put him in the army despite his glasses and poor eyesight. Now he lay with two million others on the Eastern Front.

He tried not to grit his teeth. *I must not think about it.* For here, in the Atlantic, there was always danger; it waited like an assassin for the unwary, the one who forgot the need for vigilance just for a moment. He jerked his hand again and the forward periscope slid slowly from its well, while he crouched almost on his knees to follow it to the surface – his white cap, the symbol of a U-Boat commander, stained and greasy from a hundred encounters with deckhead pipes and unyielding metal, was pushed to the back of his head, although he never recalled doing it.

Slowly, so slowly now. The lens was nearing the surface, and he saw the first hint of grey. He tightened his grip on the twin handles as he had countless times, his mind quite steady, his heart beating normally. He could sense the unemployed men watching him still. But they were and must be like the boat itself – part of the weapon, an extension to his own eye and brain.

He licked his upper lip, feeling the stubble, and watched the sea's face begin to reveal itself. He switched the periscope to full power and turned it in a full circle before returning to the given bearing. *Empty.* No ships, no prowling flying-boats or bombers.

He blinked as the periscope misted over with spray, as if by doing so he would clear it. There was one patch of silver sunlight, which touched his eyes and made them the colour of the Atlantic.

And there it was. Drifting into the lens, then pausing in the crosswires as if snared in a web, while he followed the target and the details were fed into the machine behind him. The periscope dipped down again and he made himself stand upright, straddle-legged, his features impassive as he scraped his mind for any missing factor. A big merchantman, possibly a cargo-liner before the war; but why no escort? A ship that size – he glanced up as the lights blinked on to tell him that both torpedoes were ready to fire.

He almost laughed, but knew that if he did he might not be able to stop. A blind commander could not miss. What must they be thinking of?

The men closest to him saw his face and felt more at ease. *Get rid of those damned fish, then take us home.*

He gestured to the periscope operator and crouched down to take a final look. Nothing had moved. The range, bearing, even the feeble light were as before.

He gave his order and felt the periscope buck in his grip as first one, then the other remaining torpedo leaped from its tube.

Then he stared with chilled disbelief as a second ship appeared from beyond the barely moving target. The other vessel must have been lying hidden on the liner's opposite side, her engines momentarily stopped. Now with a bow-wave building up from her sharp stem like a huge moustache, she appeared to pivot around her consort's bows until she was pointing directly at the periscope. He had been too long in U-Boats not to recognise those rakish lines. She was a destroyer.

There was only one explosion. The torpedo struck the destroyer somewhere forward even as she completed her turn. The second one must have missed or run deep out of control. It was not the first time that had happened. A few of his men began to cheer as the explosion boomed against the hull, but the sound ended instantly as he swung towards them and ordered a crash dive.

He turned the periscope just briefly even as the water began to thunder into the tanks, then flung one arm to his face as if to protect it. Framed in the lens were a pair of racing propellers, as the bomber made her careful dive towards the shadow beneath the surface.

The U-Boat's captain was twenty-seven years old. On this bleak dawn he and his crew had just twelve seconds to live.

But this was the Western Ocean. The killing ground.

Part One

1942

1

No Reprieve

Any naval dockyard in the midst of a war was a confusing place for a stranger, and Rosyth, cringing to a blustery March wind, was no exception.

Every dock, basin and wharf seemed to be filled: ships being repaired, others so damaged by mine or bomb that they were only useful for their armament or fittings, all of which were in short supply.

Sub-Lieutenant Richard Ayres paused to stare down into one such basin at an elderly escort vessel, or what was left of it. She had once been a living ship, but now she was gutted down to and beyond the waterline. In the hard light Ayres could still see the blistered paintwork where men had once lived and hoped. From all the damage, it was a marvel anyone had still been alive to get her home.

Black shadows swayed and dipped over the battered hulk as gaunt cranes lifted pieces to be saved, and dropped the rest in rusty piles on the dockside. It was as if *they* were doing the destroying he thought, like untidy prehistoric monsters with an abandoned carcass.

He turned up the collar of his blue raincoat and shivered in the biting wind which came down from the north-west to change the face of the Forth into a miniature sea of white horses.

A dismal place to many perhaps, but to Sub-Lieutenant Ayres, who was nineteen years old and about to join his first ship, as an officer anyway, it was like the culmination of a dream he had once not dared to hope for.

His only time at sea had been spent in a tired, over-worked patrol-vessel named *Sanderling*, for the compulsory three months all officer candidates had to complete before being handed over to HMS *King Alfred*. There, youthful hopefuls were expected to be turned into officers in a further crammed three months, before being dropped right into it and packed off to war. Except that the poor little *Sanderling*, with her solitary four-inch gun and a few anti-aircraft weapons, had been worked so hard she had spent much of Ayres's allotted time either having a boiler-clean or lying at a buoy, while harassed dockyard men tried to find what had broken down this time.

Ayres shivered again. He had been two days getting here from the south of England. Trains that never arrived, another held up for hours in an air-raid – none of it helped.

He turned his back on the old ship and looked at the others looming from their moorings or peeping over the edge of a dock or wharf. Every kind, from powerful cruisers to the minesweeping trawlers which had once fished in these waters for herring and cod.

A coat of grey or dazzle-paint changed anything into a man-of-war; just as a building which had once been a swimming bath and pleasure centre in Hove had become a training depot where officers were manufactured overnight.

Boots grated on stone and he saw a tall chief petty officer in belt and gaiters pausing to stare at him as if unsure whether or not he should bother.

'Can I 'elp?' He cleared his throat and in those few seconds he took in all that there was to see. A brand-new cap and raincoat, the neat little suitcase; most of all, Ayres's pleasant open features. He added, 'Sir?'

Ayres produced his piece of paper. You never moved in the Navy without that. It had been almost the first lesson he had learned while he had been groping his way towards his goal.

'I'm joining the *Gladiator*, Chief.' He too was studying the other man. Old; probably retired when the war had erupted across Europe and their world had changed out of all recognition.

Gladiator. Just the name seemed to roll off his tongue like something familiar. Special.

The chief petty officer glanced at him again. 'You're Mr Ayres, then. They was expectin' you yesterday.' It sounded like an accusation.

Ayres flushed, something he still did far too easily. 'Yes, but – she was supposed to be at Leith, and when I got there – '

The other man nodded. 'Leith is full. They moved your ship here as soon as 'er overhaul was done.' He made up his mind. 'I'll call 'er up and get a boat sent over. She's out there with another of 'er class.' He looked away. ''Bout the only two of 'em left now, I shouldn't wonder.'

As he walked towards a little hut Ayres had not noticed before, he relented and stood facing the new officer, his white webbing gaiters squeaking on his boots. Why should it matter to this young subbie anyway? Nice as pie at the moment. But a little bit of gold on the sleeve, even a wavy stripe, could change a man; and not for the better. He said, 'My son served in one, the *Glowworm*, durin' the Norwegian foul-up. They're fine ships – never mind me.'

Ayres stared at him. It was like feeling a cold hand on the shoulder. Everyone had heard of the *Glowworm*. She had gone down with her guns blazing, and even then she had managed to ram the German heavy cruiser *Hipper*. It was like one of the stories he had read as a boy. Destroyers, greyhounds of the ocean, 'eyes of the fleet' as they had always been romantically described.

He heard himself ask, 'Did he – I mean, your son – '

The chief petty officer glared at the sparking river gun which spluttered from the nearby cruiser like a maniac signal. 'No. He's down there with 'er.' Then he was gone.

Ayres picked up his case and walked over to stand by his other belongings, thinking about his new ship. A destroyer. He had been more afraid of getting sent to a big ship, or of going to a clapped-out veteran like *Sanderling*. All her officers had been regulars, and like the chief petty officer had probably been on the beach until they were needed to fill the growing gaps in men and ships. When he thought of *Glowworm* and her fate he was surprised and relieved that he still felt the same excitement.

It was almost noon by the time the destroyer's motor boat coughed alongside the jetty and her coxswain, a massive Scot in a shining oilskin, dashed up the stone stairs and began to gather up Ayres's luggage with a few quick comments.

'Mr Ayres?' He did not wait for an answer. 'They were expecting you forenoon yesterday, sir.'

'I know. I was sent to the wrong place.'

The boat's coxswain did not hear. 'The Cap'n don't like to be kept waitin', sir.' He waited for him to clamber down into the cockpit and yelled, 'Shove off, Nobby! I'm ready for ma tot!'

The bowman grinned and vanished beyond the canopy with the bowline and in seconds they were scudding across the lively white crests. Ayres looked astern and saw the elderly chief petty officer in his belt and gaiters watching him from the door of his little hut. Over the widening gap of frothing water he suddenly touched his cap in salute, and for some reason which Ayres was too young to understand, he was deeply moved. Ayres returned the salute and realised that it was the first mark of respect the old CPO had offered him.

That was something else you had to get used to. The sailors who went out of their way to throw up a salute, especially if you had your hands or arms full of things, and the others who would enter a shop if necessary to avoid it.

The coxswain studied him warily. 'First time in destroyers, sir?'

Ayres shaded his eyes to stare at the impressive spread of the Forth Bridge which dwarfed all the ships which lay near it, or passed beneath the great span of angled iron which linked up with Queensferry in the south. If ever a single achievement proclaimed how man had tamed this part of Scotland, this bridge must be it.

The Germans had tried to destroy it, without success; in fact it was the first target on the British mainland to be bombed by the unstoppable Luftwaffe. There had been indignation and anger at the ease with which it had been done. Ayres doubted if anyone would even comment if it happened today. Too many battles lost, too many men and ships gone forever.

He started as he realised what the coxswain had asked. 'In *destroyers*, yes.'

The coxswain nodded, and when Ayres looked away he winked to his bowman. Green as grass. Just like all the others.

But for the bitter wind and the spray which leaped occasionally over the little boat's stem, it was a perfect day, a far cry from the time when Ayres had joined the little *Sanderling* as she lay in a filthy basin at Chatham Dockyard. Nowhere to sling his hammock, and not much of a welcome from the seamen who were to be his messmates for so short a time. He knew he had been tested to the full. The lower deck's usual brutal humour, reserved for any would-be officer; the foul language and jokes which made him blush; taunts because of his 'posh accent'; contempt for an amateur – he took it all, and more.

Until that air attack on a ten-knot convoy up the East Coast. The scream of bombs and towering columns of spray and smoke. The old merchant ships keeping formation no matter what, with the minefield on one side of them and shallow water on the other. No room for manoeuvre, and if a ship was badly hit she was ordered to beach herself and keep the main channel open. There were mastheads a-plenty along that coast to show how many had been sunk in the process.

Ayres had been passing shells from the ready-use ammunition locker as fast as he could to the old four-inch gun while *Sanderling* and the mixed bag of escorts kept up a rapid fire on the diving bombers until the sky was pockmarked with shellbursts, the filth of war.

A bomb had fallen too close to the ship's side and she had heeled over as the captain swung away from the explosion. Ayres had lost his footing and sprawled on the wet steel plates, his head striking a stanchion so hard that he almost lost consciousness.

A burly seaman, one of his worse tormentors on the messdeck, had leaped down to pull him from danger, and had shouted above the clatter of Oerlikons and the ceaseless beat of pom-poms, 'All right, Dick lad? One 'and fer th' King an' one fer yerself – just you remember that!' He had added awkwardly, 'See me at tot-time. That'll take your fuckin' 'eadache away!'

But that one act of kindness had changed everything for Ayres.

He caught his breath as he gripped the top of the canopy with both hands. There she was, lying at a buoy alongside her twin, her fresh dazzle-paint gleaming in the arctic sunshine so that she seemed to glow. She was exactly what Ayres had expected, had hoped for while he had studied the mysteries of gunnery and navigation, signals and square-bashing, all in a space of time which had gone by in a flash.

Gladiator, and he knew she was the nearest one by the pendant number *H–38* painted on below her forecastle, was every inch a destroyer, of the type built between the wars when the Royal Navy was paramount throughout the world, and the minds of planners still saw its role protecting the line-of-battle as in all other wars.

Dunkirk, Norway, Crete and the bloody campaigns in North Africa had changed all that.

'Our ship's over there, sir.'

'Yes.' It came out too sharply. 'Thank you.' But he did not want to share this meeting with anyone. He knew *Gladiator*'s statistics as well as his own. Three hundred and twenty-three feet long; built at Vickers-Armstrong at Barrow in 1936. Four four-point-seven guns; torpedo tubes; she even had radar in a sort of giant jam-pot above her business-like, open bridge. Two funnels gave her a rakish, dashing appearance – Ayres had got to know her silhouette at school, when *Gladiator* had been a part of the crack First Mediterranean Flotilla.

Ayres tried to look calm as the boat tore towards the accommodation ladder, where two sailors were already watching their rapid approach. Closer to it was possible to see the many dents and scars along her exposed side. What a story they could tell – coming alongside some stricken ship in convoy, possibly in pitch darkness, or taking shell splinters after an encounter with an enemy blockade-runner.

'Hook on, Nobby!' The boat churned to full astern and then idled to rest against the ladder despite the strong pull of the tide.

Men, appeared to pick up Ayres's bags. Weathered, tired faces, people whom he would know, really know, given half a chance.

The coxswain grimaced. 'Here comes Jimmy-th'-One, Nobby – watch out for flak!'

Ayres ran up the ladder and threw up a smart salute aft where a bright new ensign stood out stiffly from its staff between the ranks of depth-charges. A tall, unsmiling officer, his hands grasped behind his back, leaned over the guardrail and called, 'Wait for the mail-bag, Cox'n!'

The big man peered up at him from the pitching motor boat. 'Permission to draw ma tot, sir?'

'Later.' He turned to face Ayres like someone who had just dispensed with one pest and was about to deal with another.

'Ayres right?'

'Come aboard to join, sir.'

Ayres felt the man run his eyes over him from cap to shoes. An impassive, strong face, dominated by a large beaked nose.

'You're adrift.'

'Adrift, sir?'

'The Commanding Officer will want to see you. Right away.'

'The Commanding Officer, sir?' He had only spoken to the little *Sanderling*'s captain once and that had probably been an accident.

The big nose trained round towards him like a gun. 'Do you always repeat everything said to you?' He glared at some seamen who were dragging a new coil of mooring wire across the quarterdeck and shouted, 'Watch that paintwork, you careless idiots!' He said in a controlled voice, 'My name is Marrack. I'm the first lieutenant around here.' Surprisingly he held out his hand and Ayres was further taken back by the two wavy stripes on his sleeve. A 'temporary gentleman', like himself.

Ayres smiled. 'Thank you, sir.'

'And don't call me sir, except in the line of duty.' He watched the men with the mooring wire and added, 'Number One will suffice.' He did not smile and Ayres guessed that, like the use of words, the smiles were strictly rationed. A strange man – what had Marrack done before the Navy, he wondered? In his late twenties at a guess, but he acted with the authority and experience of one much older.

As an afterthought Marrack said, 'You will share a cabin with our other sub. At the moment anyway. I shall give you a list of duties, watchkeeping and the like, within the hour. But now go and see the Old Man.' His tone sharpened as Ayres made to hurry off. 'Not that way! His quarters are down aft, in harbour, that is.' He glanced up at the box-like bridge. 'At sea he's always *there*.'

Then, without another glance, Marrack turned and strode along the iron deck towards the forecastle, pausing merely to glance up at the smoking galley funnel as if to sniff out the ingredients of the meal being served.

'This way, Mr Ayres.' A wiry petty officer steward was watching him from the door of the quartermaster's lobby beneath X-Gun. 'We was expectin' you yesterday.'

Ayres gave a tired grin. 'So I hear.' He saw that his bags had been taken from the deck. He stepped over a high coaming and entered the white-painted lobby with its stand of Lee-Enfield rifles and a leading seaman, who was obviously the chief quartermaster, reading a magazine which was spread over the deck log. He did not even glance up as Ayres followed the petty officer steward down a steep ladder.

The new smells rose to greet him. Fresh paint, oil, people.

He removed his raincoat and the steward took it and folded it expertly over his arm while running his eye critically over his new charge.

He said, 'I'm Vallance, sir. I'm in charge down aft, an' the Old Man is at the top of the list so to speak.' He saw Ayres smile. 'Sir?'

But Ayres shook his head. 'Just a memory, um, Vallance.' He was still thinking of Vallance's description. *Down aft.* In *Sanderling* they had always referred to the officers as 'the pigs down aft'.

He paused and stared at the closed door with the small brass plate. *Captain.* Well, now he was one of the pigs!

Vallance watched his uncertainty. Ayres seemed like a nice young chap, as far as you could tell. He didn't even need a shave after two days on a bloody train. God, they'd be coming aboard in their prams if the war lasted much longer.

The bright new wavy stripe, the schoolboy haircut; Ayres's youth made Vallance suddenly depressed.

'A word, sir.' He watched, looking for any hint of arrogance. There was none. Encouraged by Ayres's obvious innocence, he added, 'Just be natural with the Old Man, sir. He don't like flannel, not from nobody, not even Captain (D).'

Ayres found himself nodding. Nothing was happening as they had told him it would. A chief petty officer who had at first not saluted him and then confided in him about his son lost at sea; a boat's coxswain who had asked him point-blank about his experience – even the First Lieutenant was not like those steely-eyed men in his magazine or in films about the war. And now Vallance was offering advice . . . or was he testing him to see if he was too weak to snap back at him?

But instinct made Ayres anxious, and he had to ask, 'What's he like?'

Vallance relaxed. A nice lad, not somebody to upset his wardroom.

'He's had a hard time, sir.' He looked above and around him. 'We've done some things between us – he's carried all of it. You can only handle so much . . . just be yerself, if you'll pardon the liberty.' He gave a slow grin. 'I'll have a nice bit of lunch for you.'

He watched Ayres's knuckles hesitate before rapping down on the door.

'Enter!'

Ayres turned to thank the steward but the passageway was quite empty. He swallowed hard and thrust open the door.

Unlike most wartime-built destroyers, *Gladiator*'s captain's quarters were almost spacious. They were situated right aft beneath the quarterdeck and divided into separate sleeping and day cabins. Even here there was a lingering tang of fresh paint, but the comfortable-looking armchairs and carpet still showed the wear and tear of too many Atlantic convoys when these same quarters had been used to accommodate survivors, wounded or otherwise, when the small sick-bay could no longer cope.

Beyond the bulkhead were the other officers' cabins, and of course, the wardroom. It was the one place they all met, to eat, to hold an occasional party, to wait to go on watch or for the hateful clang of alarm bells. Moving forward further still were the engine and boiler rooms, the ship's life-blood, which filled almost a third of the hull's capacity. Beyond them was the two-decked forecastle where the ship's company were crammed into their various messes, separated only by rate and department.

Seated at the desk in his day cabin, *Gladiator*'s commanding officer paused in writing a letter to look at the small old-fashioned coal fire which was kept burning in harbour. It made the place look lived in, or as the PO steward, Percy Vallance, would have it, 'more like 'ome'.

Lieutenant-Commander David Howard was twenty-seven years old, and, like his father and grandfather, had entered the Royal Navy as a young cadet. Nobody had ever discussed it; it had been the thing to do, taken for granted.

Apart from various training courses in larger warships, he had spent most of his service in destroyers and could visualise nothing else. At the outbreak of war he had hastily taken command of an old V & W class destroyer from the Kaiser's war, and within no time had been involved in the first shattering defeat in France, and the bitterness of Dunkirk.

Now it seemed a million years ago, the war as different from those early days as Agincourt. Immediately after Dunkirk he was ordered to take his elderly V & W, *Winsby*, into the Battle of the Atlantic. He had been in the same fight ever since, and in command of *Gladiator* for eighteen months. That, too, felt like years.

He stood up suddenly, light-footed as a cat, and walked to one of the few pictures which hung in the day cabin: the place he could only dream about when he was at sea. His sea cabin on the bridge was little more than a steel cupboard with a narrow bunk and a telephone. When you hit the damp blankets, fully dressed if you had any sense left, you did not sleep; you just died. The place of escape, beyond the anxious eyes on the bridge; away from the heaving grey sea, the pathetic lines of rusty freighters and tankers following like sheep. He smiled bitterly. To the slaughter.

He reached out and straightened the picture of his first command. Relics from the Great War about which his father rarely spoke, but the V & Ws were excellent seaboats, and had a sort of jaunty confidence which more than made up for their outdated machinery and overcrowded quarters. Without them, this war might have been lost before it had really begun in earnest. *Winsby* had been a happy ship, although it was becoming harder to remember all the faces, most of whom had been regulars like himself.

He turned his head to glance through one of the polished scuttles towards the land, and considered how this ship rated now. Every time she entered harbour, for whatever reason, he lost more and more of his skilled hands. Officers too, for promotion or advanced courses to try and keep pace with the war's mounting ferocity. It took time to train new ones; and when you did they were taken too.

All ships were like that now. Bakers and postmen, clerks and errand-boys. Only half of the whole ship's company of one hundred and forty-five souls were old enough to draw their tot. It made you sweat when you found time to think about it.

He half-listened to the muted beat of a generator deep in the engine room and pictured the engineer officer, Lieutenant (E) Evan Price, who had been in this ship since before the outbreak of war. What would happen if they took *him*? The ship might fall apart. He smiled and groped for his pipe but it was still in the jacket slung carelessly on the back of a chair.

His was a young face, which might turn any woman's head; his dark unruly hair needed cutting badly, something else which Captain (D) would most certainly mention when next they met.

He stared hard at the glass scuttle, which was streaked with salt like frost, but saw only his reflection. Brown eyes, lines at the corners of his mouth, the haunted look which had not left his face since that last convoy from Newfoundland, and which this brief overhaul, at Leith and here, had failed to disperse.

Some captains would have gone straight ashore after a convoy like that. To hide in some hotel, to get drunk, to seek the company of some bored tart; anything. But here, in this little-used cabin, was his escape. Hot baths whenever he chose; eating alone; listening to music; pacing the cabin to go over it all again as if to punish himself in some way.

Forty ships had sailed from St John's on that terrible convoy. They had been attacked by a complete U-Boat pack when they had barely covered a third of the passage. When they had passed the Liverpool Bar there had been only thirteen left. He had seen it all before, but somehow that convoy had affected him more than anything. A big tanker, its cargo of high octane fuel so precious to this embattled country, had burned for three days, and her company with it. Another ship, loaded to the seams with armoured cars and tanks, had gone done in thirty seconds, her back broken by two torpedoes. It went on and on, as if there was no mercy left.

He walked back to the desk and patted his jacket for his pipe.

Muffled by the bulkhead the tannoy squawked, 'D'you hear there! Hands to dinner!' The quartermaster would add beneath his breath, 'Officers to *lunch*!'

He sat down again and began to fill his pipe, his eyes on the photograph of his father which he had given him when their world had fallen apart. Dressed in naval uniform, a young face with the same twinkle in his eyes. He had not wanted his son to have a recent picture. This had been taken before the famous Zeebrugge raid in 1918, when unknown to him the war had only seven months left to run its bloody course. He had lost an arm and an eye, and had been rejected by the service he had loved more than life itself. He still managed to joke about it. 'What about Nelson? *He* managed!' In angrier moments he had said, 'Anyway, I couldn't do much worse than the blockheads who're running things now!'

Howard held a match to his pipe and saw the smoke drifting up into the vents. His hand was quite steady, almost stiff, as if he was consciously holding it so, like his muscles when the alarms sounded; how would it be the next time?

He sighed. He had promised to join Spike Colvin, his fellow captain in their sister-ship *Ganymede* alongside, for a few drinks before the next orders arrived. Howard looked at his watch. They would soon know. Convoy escort. But surely not the Atlantic again, not yet . . . He stood up violently, angry with himself for admitting the weakness to himself.

He heard himself call, 'Enter!' and saw the door open to reveal an unfamiliar sub-lieutenant standing beyond the coaming.

'Come in – it's Ayres, isn't it?' He held out his hand. 'Might have had to sail without you.'

Ayres shifted his new cap from one fist to the other. 'I went to Leith, you see – '

Howard pointed to a comfortable chair. 'Take a pew, Sub. Drink?'

Ayres sat down, completely baffled by this unusual welcome. Howard was not a bit what he had anticipated. He seemed very relaxed, and far more youthful than expected.

'Perhaps a gin, sir. I'm not much of – '

Howard opened the cupboard and poured two glasses of gin. The new subbie was no drinker then. The Atlantic would change that.

'I've put you down to share your watches with the navigator. He's RNR, a good officer, so I expect I shall be losing him too very soon. Number One will fix you up with your action and defence stations, etc – have you met him yet?'

Ayres recalled the big nose, the faint air of disapproval. The first lieutenant behaved more like a regular, straight-laced officer than the captain, who, Ayres observed, was wearing an old jumper over his shirt, and a pair of grey flannel trousers. Ayres looked at the jacket on the nearby chair, the tarnished gold two-and-a-half stripes. His mind fastened on the small blue and white ribbon on the jacket's breast. The DSC. In destroyers you didn't get that for nothing.

'You've joined the ship during a bit of upheaval, Sub.' Howard leaned back in his chair and allowed the pipesmoke to curl above him. He saw Ayres hold back a choking cough as he swallowed some of the gin, and tried to contain his disappointment. His other sub-lieutenant had joined the ship just before the refit, transferred from Light Coastal Forces after his motor gunboat had been shelled and sunk off the Hook of Holland. A withdrawn, tense young man who seemed to regard the transfer as some kind of stigma. Even the gunnery officer, an RNVR lieutenant, had only been in *Gladiator* for four months, and the new midshipman, a youth with a permanent round-eyed look of wonderment, had arrived when they had been in Leith. He continued, 'A third of the company are pretty new – a lot of them came on board just before the last convoy.' His voice seemed to linger over the word. Burning ships, men being swept past and swallowed by the racing screws, their cries lost in the thunder of depth charges. *Don't stop. Don't look back. Close the ranks.* The convoy commodore's signals never ceased. Howard wondered what that fine old man had been thinking when his own ship had been torpedoed and left astern to die.

Ayres felt the gin burning his empty stomach. What had happened on the convoy, he wondered? He glanced round the cabin, so still, apart from an occasional movement when another ship churned past. It seemed so wrong to put a beautiful destroyer like *Gladiator* on escort work. His gaze fastened on the ship's crest, which hung above the desk. An uplifted stabbing sword gripped by an armoured fist, the motto *Manu Forti* painted below it. Ayres had struggled through enough Latin at school to know it meant *With a Strong Hand.* Right for the destroyer, but not for the deadly boredom of convoy work.

Howard saw it clearly on the young officer's open features and said, 'In this ship we have no passengers, Sub. I'm telling you that right now so you can use every opportunity to learn from the more experienced members of the team. Pilot, with whom you'll be sharing watches, the First Lieutenant, and men like the cox'n, Bob Sweeney, and Mr Pym the Gunner (T) – they're all old destroyer hands who can teach you more in a dog-watch than six months in a classroom. If you have any problems, put them to Number One. He may seem a bit severe, but he was a barrister before he volunteered.' He forced a smile. He was getting nowhere. What did they teach them at the training depot? To die bravely? To be a bomb-happy survivor like the other subbie? 'He's a marvel with defaulters!' He put down his pipe and glanced at his empty glass. 'You'll feel new and awkward to begin with – everyone does. But remember this. You wear an officer's uniform now, and to all the other new hands you are just that. Someone to turn to, to hate if you like – but sometimes you have to come down on people like a ton of bricks. It's not enough to be popular.'

Ayres nodded. 'I wanted to be in destroyers, sir.'

Howard almost relented, but said, 'Keenness and courage go with the job – I have to take that for granted. But endurance and survival are what count in the end. Otherwise we are going to lose this war. Do you understand?'

Ayres swallowed hard. Nobody had ever said things like that to him. *Lose?* He felt confused, even betrayed, by the captain's blunt manner.

Howard watched his words hitting home. There might be no time later on. There never was.

He added, 'For the first time since the balloon went up, the enemy are sinking more ships than we can build.' He paused, counting seconds, trying not to remember Ayres's predecessor, his pathetic eagerness when he had stood on this same stained carpet. 'And the enemy are also building more submarines than we can sink, at present anyway. It is a brutal equation, but there it is.'

There was a shout from the deck above, the chugging vibration of a boat coming alongside. Marrack would deal with it. He could manage just about anything now.

Ayres said in a small voice, 'I'll not let you down, sir.'

'I hear you were in the *Sanderling*?'

'Yes, sir.'

Howard looked at him, his eyes in shadow from the hard sunlight. 'You'll find out anyway, later on when their lordships feel moved to announce it. She was sunk last night. A mine.'

Ayres was on his feet without realising it, the faces swimming back like pictures in his mind. The sailor who had helped him after the air attack. The elderly captain on his open bridge, an unlit pipe always in his mouth.

'Any survivors, sir?'

Howard shook his head. 'She was apparently in pretty poor shape. No match for a mine.' He stood up and added angrily, 'It's murder, nothing less.'

He held out his hand, 'Sorry, Sub. But this is the only place I'm allowed to let off steam.' He grasped Ayres's hand. 'If you get really rattled, talk to me if you like.'

There was a tap at the door and the first lieutenant peered into the cabin, his sharp eyes flitting between them.

'I thought you should know, sir. The guardboat has just delivered the pouch.' He stepped over the coaming, his neat, shining hair almost touching the deckhead. 'Otherwise I'd not have troubled you.' He laid the worn leather pouch on the deck and studied it thoughtfully. 'Our orders.'

The door closed and Howard realised that the sub-lieutenant had gone. He sat down heavily and said, 'You'd better assemble the wardroom at stand-easy this afternoon.'

Marrack waited, watching Howard opening the packet and breaking the seal. He added, 'Just us, sir. Our chums alongside haven't drawn a ticket this time.' He saw the captain's hands hesitate on the open packet. *He doesn't want to know. He's like the rest of us.*

To break the spell he asked casually, 'What do you think of Ayres, sir?'

Howard looked at his hands. Still steady enough. 'He'll shape up, with a bit of help.'

He drew the papers into the light and felt his mouth go suddenly dry.

Marrack remarked, 'I hope they give us a rest from the Atlantic.'

Howard did not answer directly but stood up again, moving to a scuttle. There was cloud about. It came suddenly here.

He answered slowly, 'No, not the Western Ocean, Number One.'

He turned away from the mocking glass and faced him. Afterwards Marrack remembered his dark eyes as being quite still, like a man already dead. 'It's North Russia, I'm afraid.'

Marrack said, 'I see, Dicey.'

Howard wanted to cry out or laugh. *Dicey.* The understatement for all time.

Marrack had his hand on the door clip. 'When, sir?'

'Last mail ashore tomorrow forenoon. We get under weigh at thirteen-hundred. I'll tell you the rest when I've read through this lot.'

As the tall lieutenant turned to leave Howard said, 'Thanks, Number One. If I ever murder the admiral, which I may well do, I'd certainly like to have you on my side.'

Marrack shrugged. 'It's a living.' He almost smiled. 'Like this one.' Then he was gone.

Howard opened the cupboard and rummaged about for something stronger than gin.

He could already sense the change around him. It was not merely leaving these quarters and returning to the bridge, the stage of battle. Not this time. Secret orders or not, the whole ship knew, or soon would. It was the Navy's way. Like a family.

He swallowed some neat brandy and thought of Ayres. What a way to begin.

Petty Officer Vallance entered the cabin and began to lay the table for his captain's lunch.

He only looked up once from his plates and cutlery.

He said, 'We'll need all our warm gear then, sir?'

The rest was over.

2

Open Boat

Lieutenant Gordon Treherne, Royal Naval Reserve, *Gladiator*'s navigating officer, wiped his binoculars with a piece of tissue and slung them inside his duffle coat. Beneath the well-used coat he wore a sheepskin-lined jacket and a heavy roll-necked sweater which had once been white. But even without the layers of clothing Treherne made an imposing figure, one that would not have been out of place facing the Armada, or the French at Trafalgar. Beneath his blue, folded balaclava his hair was as black as his beard, his eyes, with deep crowsfeet on either side, as blue as any ocean, He licked his lips and tasted the raw salt and tugged the towel tighter around his neck. He had taken over the forenoon watch only minutes earlier, and the towel was already sodden.

He glanced around the swaying upper bridge, open to the elements, a place so familiar at any time of the day or night that he would instantly notice if anything was wrong or different. Lookouts, equally muffled against the cold, their glasses moving to cover their allotted arcs; the yeoman of signals, always an early bird, crouched with two of his young assistants, stabbing the air with a gloved hand to emphasise this or that as the steel deck rolled drunkenly as if to hurl them all down. A glance over one bridge wing, and he saw the nearest Oerlikon gunner standing by his weapon, trying to stamp his booted feet quietly so as not to annoy anyone. Treherne's own new assistant, Sub-Lieutenant Ayres, was bending over the chart table, his legs straddled while he peered at their course and checked the pencilled figures beneath the shaded light.

Treherne smiled grimly. Eight-ten a.m., another forenoon watch, and the sea was only just beginning to show itself. Great sliding banks of grey glass patterned with salt and angry, breaking crests. It had been like that ever since *Gladiator* had left the shelter of the land to head north-west leaving the Orkneys abeam in the darkness and pressing on for the Shetlands. And on, and on, all three-and-a-half days of it in this savage, turbulent ocean. It might have been barely bearable but for their two small consorts, Flower Class corvettes, *Cynara* and *Physalis*, which, like their numberless sisters, had been flung together to fight in that separate conflict becoming known as the Battle of the Atlantic. Tiny single-screwed warships which were said to roll on a heavy dew. So *Gladiator* had had to reduce speed to the corvettes' most comfortable cruising rate of eleven knots. Destroyers were designed for the cut and dash of attacking with torpedoes, and retiring under a smoke-screen. But their role now seemed only to get convoys home and away again, and to kill the hated U-Boats whenever they had the chance. As for the convoys, the only rule concerned the speed. *It shall be that of the slowest ship in it.* So it was often the case that new, fast freighters had to crawl along with some ancient, dragging tramp-steamer which looked like something from the Great War, and probably was.

The two corvettes were placed out on either beam, smashing their way over the same impressive waves as *Gladiator*. With a quarter sea and a wind to make your gums ache, there would not be much to choose between them, Treherne thought.

Ayres approached him where he stood in his heavy leather sea-boots, one arm around the stanchion near a gyro-repeater. The sub-lieutenant seemed to rise up and then drop away as if in some weird dance, and when he eventually found a handhold he sounded breathless.

Treherne regarded him thoughtfully. Was he learning anything? He had asked him on their first watch together if he had had any maritime experience other than his seatime in *Sanderling*. Ayres had screwed up his face as if to conjure up something useful but had replied lamely, 'I was in the sea-scouts, sir.'

Treherne had made a joke of it, if only to take his mind off the ship which hit a mine in the North Sea.

But it was no joke really. At thirty-three Treherne was the oldest officer in the ship, apart from Evan Price, the chief, and Pym the Gunner (T), but there was nobody in the whole Navy as old as *him*. He wondered what the grumpy gunner thought of Ayres; they shared duties on the quarterdeck when entering or leaving harbour. The veteran and the innocent amateur. Treherne was a Cornishman, a professional seaman to his fingertips, who had spent his pre-war time in the merchant service, in one of the clean, fast banana ships which ran regularly from the sunny Windward Islands to Liverpool and Cardiff. *Gladiator* was often in Liverpool, the nerve centre of Western Approaches. It always reminded him of those faroff, impossible days: peaceful trips with only a handful of passengers to irritate you.

Ayres gasped, 'We shall be sighting Iceland today.' He hesitated and would have flushed but for the bitter spray. 'Er, Pilot.'

Treherne grinned and showed his strong teeth. 'Sure will, Sub. All lava-dust and people who hate our guts.'

'But I thought they were on our side.'

Treherne studied him sadly. So naïve. 'We occupied the place, otherwise the krauts would have got there first. It's not much of a prize, but it does have one of the biggest airstrips in the world – something which appealed to the Germans quite a lot. Anyone who holds Iceland commands the convoy routes to North Russia.'

He leaned over a voicepipe and snapped, 'Watch her head, quartermaster!'

'Sorry, sir.' The voice echoed tinnily from the wheelhouse beneath their feet. 'Steady on three-three-zero, sir.'

Treherne's eyes crinkled as they followed the ticking gyro-repeater. To himself he murmured, 'You too, mate!' Because he knew what the quartermaster was thinking.

Ayres wiped his wet face and blinked through the glass screen. The waves were enormous, but not too dangerous, or so Treherne had explained. When they broke across the maindeck he had known the bridge to be cut off completely from the wardroom; there was no way forward or aft along the iron deck except out in the open, and even lifelines couldn't save a man under those conditions. It had meant that the captain and the luckless officer-of-the-watch had been isolated, and forced to stand watch-and-watch until the sea moderated, and praying all the while that they would not be called to action stations.

'Is it pretty safe now, sir?'

Treherne looked at the captain who was sitting on his tall chair, which in turn was bolted to the deck. He was lying with his head on his arms below the screen, his body pitching with the violent movement, his duffle coat and hood black with spray and flying spindrift. 'Safe?' He considered it. 'With two corvettes in company and all our combined Asdic going, we should be. Mind you,' he looked astern, past the wildly shaking signal halliards and the funnel smoke which seemed to point directly abeam, level with the surging wavecrests, 'when we got close to the Rosegarden I did have a twinge or two.'

He saw the utter bewilderment. 'The Germans call that three hundred-mile stretch of the sea between Iceland and the Faeroes the Rosegarden. In the early part of the war every U-Boat, surface warships too, had to creep through that strip. We put down deep-level mines to make the U-Boats stay on the surface or at periscope depth so the RAF could have a go at 'em, but they still managed, in spite of that.' He added with unusual bitterness, 'Now the Germans don't have to bother going through the Rosegarden, unless *Tirpitz* comes out looking for trouble. When France chucked in the towel and our other allies went down like a pack of cards, they presented Mister Hitler with an unbroken coastline all the way from Norway's North Cape down to the Bay of Biscay.' He saw it in his mind's eye like a chart. 'That's about two-and-a-half thousand miles. Makes it nice and easy for them, eh?'

Someone groaned, 'Daylight, at long last!'

Ayres was thinking about his rare encounters with the destroyer's second sub-lieutenant, Lionel Bizley. He was only a few months older than Ayres but seemed like a veteran by comparison. They shared the same cabin because the new addition to the wardroom at Leith had been Surgeon-Lieutenant Jocelyn Lawford, a doctor so young that he must have only just completed his time in medical school. Prior to that, like many smaller warships, *Gladiator* had had to be content with a PO sickberth attendant. Had they any choice, most of the company would have preferred it to remain that way.

And yet Ayres had barely spoken a dozen words to his cabin-mate and they had met only when passing one another to go on or off watch, or to exercise action stations. His experience must have scarred him deeply, Ayres thought; and felt a certain respect.

The yeoman of signals snatched up his telescope, which he preferred to any binoculars, and stared across the grey water as a light blinked through the drifting spray like a bright diamond.

'From *Cynara*, sir. *Good morning.*'

Treherne smiled. Things were moving again. Somehow he had known Ayres had been preparing to ask him about the convoy, or worse, what the North Russian run was like. 'I'll call the captain.'

'No need, Pilot.' Howard levered himself from the tall chair and banged his boots on the wet, wooden gratings. 'God, I'm stiff. Any char about?'

A boatswain's mate spoke into a voicepipe and called, 'Told the galley, sir.'

Several of the tired-looking faces responded with grins. Tea from the galley would at least be hot when it got here. From the wardroom it would be full of salt-water by the time a steward had negotiated the deck and the unprotected ladders to the bridge.

Howard crossed to the chart table and rested his elbows on the stained paper.

About forty miles to go. He recalled their expressions in the wardroom when he had told them. A convoy to Russia. The new ones looking at the others for explanation or hope. Number One grim-faced; the chief, Price, probably thinking about the extra stress on his engines; Arthur Pym working his thin mouth in and out as he often did when he was troubled. Only Treherne had been his usual unperturbed self.

Howard straightened up even as a young seaman in a streaming oilskin tumbled into the bridge with a steaming fanny of tea. Dirty enamel mugs were produced as if by magic, and Ayres found time to notice that the char-wallah was the young sailor called Nobby, the motor boat's bowman.

Despite his misgivings, Ayres told himself he was finding his way. Faces had names, or some of them did; Pym the old Gunner (T) hated his guts; the first lieutenant no longer noticed him at all.

He heard the captain say, 'Call up *Physalis*, Yeoman. Tell her to take station on *Cynara* as ordered for entering harbour.' He swallowed the sickly, sweet tea and said, '*Good morning* indeed! All right for some!' More grins, as he knew there might be.

Howard stared abeam and thought he could see the other corvette as the lights blinked over the water.

He saw Treherne explaining something to Ayres. Like a rock. A corvette could be Treherne's for the asking. He had earned his own command. The true professional.

He loosened the clinging towel around his throat. A good, hot wash – no shave, just a wash in the reeling sea cabin abaft the bridge. Another dream.

He said, 'Warn all the lookouts. We may sight a local patrol or some fisherman selling his catch to a U-Boat.' That was not so flippant as it sounded. To Treherne he added, 'Begin the turn to the next leg in thirty minutes. I shall – '

'Radar . . . bridge!'

Petty Officer Tommy Tucker, the yeoman, pushed one of his young signalmen to one side and exclaimed, '*Shit!*'

Howard stooped over the voicepipe. 'Bridge. This is the Captain.'

The man hesitated, probably wondering if he were doing the right thing. 'I'm getting an echo. Very faint, dead ahead – about two miles.' When Howard said nothing he continued, 'May be a throwback from the shore. I – '

Howard was thinking rapidly, his eyes on the red button by his hand. 'McNiven, isn't it?' A face took shape in his mind. 'Keep watching. I'm looking at my radar-repeater now.' He winced as water ran off the canvas hood above the repeater and explored his neck like ice. 'I'm just getting a confused picture.' It was hardly surprising in this heavy sea, with the land mass of Iceland comparatively close.

McNiven said, 'Echo is stationary, sir. Very small.' He was a good operator, second only to his leading-hand.

Treherne asked, 'Shall I call up the corvettes, sir?'

Howard shook his head, still thinking. McNiven could see it, therefore it was not just a throwback. It was on the surface. Afloat but unmoving.

He bent over the voicepipe again. 'Any change?' McNiven came back instantly. 'None, sir.'

Howard said, 'Not a U-Boat. Too close to land to surface to charge batteries.' He saw them listening and realised he had spoken aloud. 'They've got seven hundred fathoms to play with around here.'

Another voice intruded from the wheelhouse. 'Cox'n on the helm, sir.'

'Very good.' Howard looked at Treherne and smiled. How did the old hands like Bob Sweeney the coxswain always know? Like the yeoman of signals, they never seemed to need the alarm bells.

Treherne asked, 'Fishing boat?'

'Not sure. But this is the time to be certain, eh?' Howard knew Treherne understood. How many ships had been sunk when lookouts had been thinking only of getting into a safe harbour, dry clothes, food which was not flung off the plate in a force nine gale? *Out of nowhere.*

He pressed the red button and heard the alarm shrill through the hull, the staccato reports on voicepipes and handsets as the men dashed to their action stations.

The first lieutenant joined Howard. 'Ship at action stations, sir. Trouble?'

'I'm not certain. Radar has reported a faint echo at three-three-zero. Unmoving, so not a conning-tower.'

Marrack squinted his eyes at the wet haze. 'Can't see a damned thing.'

'Radar – bridge!'

'Bridge.'

'I think it's a boat, sir. It just turned round. Drifting.' He sounded almost apologetic.

'You did well, McNiven.' He looked at the others. 'There's a northerly current just there, right, Pilot?'

'Yes, sir.' His bearded face was expressionless.

'Fall out action stations, resume defence stations.' Howard heard the feet thudding gratefully down ladders and along the deck. 'We'd better take a look. Maintain course and speed, Pilot. I don't want to shake the guts out of her in this sea.'

By the time Ayres had reached the bridge again from his action station which was by Y-gun right aft, the sea had brightened still further, and although the waves were too high to allow an horizon you could feel the depth and latent power. To starboard there was the hint of land, a purple shadow which looked like a fallen cloud.

'Object in the water, sir! Dead ahead!'

'Slow ahead together.' Howard climbed on to the forward gratings and levelled his glasses. He felt his stomach contract. 'Dead' was right. 'Warn the chief bosun's mate!'

'He's already there, sir.'

'He would be.' Knocker White, another one who was always ready.

He turned and saw Ayres standing by a signal locker, the hood fallen from his head as he stared at the boat drifting down the ship's side until it was snared by the chief boatswain's mate's grapnel. How far had they been journeying? What ship, and how long had it taken? Scarecrows. Torn, tattered faces, some eyeless, others fallen across the motionless oars. In the sternsheets a hunched figure with a cap down over his face, two faded stripes on the sodden jacket.

Howard called, 'Stop, together.' He saw the new doctor hurry to the guardrail, then pause as if he had been paralysed by what he saw.

Marrack snapped, 'There should be an officer down there, sir.'

Ayres tore his eyes from the horrific lifeboat, and knew Marrack meant him.

'I – I'll go, sir!'

Howard looked at him. 'Stay with the Buffer and his men. If you feel faint or sick, keep out of sight.' He added gently, 'But Number One is right. You've got to show them.'

Ayres almost fell as he lowered himself down the first ladders, past a grim-faced Oerlikon gunner and then to the maindeck itself. A few off-watch onlookers stood at the break of the fo'c'sle; others leaned out from their defence stations, sharing the moment.

Petty Officer Knocker White climbed from the boat and saw Ayres staring at him. Good lad, he thought, surprised that he should be there. He heard someone retching helplessly. It was the new doctor. God help us if we runs into the fucking *Tirpitz*, he thought savagely.

'I got the details, sir.' He pulled something leather from his oilskin; it was covered in mildew. He held it out for Ayres to see and said quietly, 'Poor bugger was 'anging on to the picture of 'is girl, sir. Probably the last thing 'e ever saw.' He waved up to the bridge and barked, 'Cast 'er off, Jim!'

The deck began to tremble again and white froth surged away from the great propellers. The boat seemed to hesitate against the side, as if reluctant to leave now that they had reached help.

Ayres asked huskily, 'What will become – '

The Buffer eyed him for a few moments while he watched the forlorn boat rocking as it passed over the destroyer's churning wake.

'The skipper'll signal for an RML, as it's so close inshore. They can deal with them things better than us.'

Ayres stared until his eyes were raw, oblivious to the biting air, everything but the lifeboat and its ragged occupants. It was as if he still expected to see the officer at the helm wake up and stare after them, to curse them, maybe, for leaving them.

He said aloud, 'I'll never forget.' He shook his head so that his schoolboy haircut ruffled in the wind. '*Never!*'

White, 'the buffer' as he was known in all ships, said, 'At the end o' the forenoon, sir, drop into our mess. 'Ave a tot with some of the *real* sailors.' He strode away to muster his men again, unable to watch Ayres's gratitude.

When he reached the bridge again to continue his watch Ayres saw the navigating officer studying him.

'All right, Sub?'

Howard turned in his chair. 'You did well, Sub. It gets easier in time. It has to, you see?'

Ayres moved to a corner of the bridge and tried to make himself small. He kept seeing them. Who had been the last one left alive? The girl in the photograph; did she know, did anybody at home realise just what it was like?

By the time the watch had run its course they were turning around the last headland with the bay opening up; beyond that lay a great fjord with snow and high ground beyond it.

'Hands to stations for entering harbour. Starboard watch fall in, first part forrard, second part aft!' The orders seemed endless. Lights winked and flashed from all directions and the yeoman was kept busy replying with his hand-lamp.

'Signal from ACIC, sir. *Anchor Off Videy Island.*'

Howard looked at Treherne and saw him grimace. That meant that the other anchorage was already filled. *The convoy.* 'Bring her round, Pilot.' He looked down at the forecastle and saw Marrack at the head of his men, the chief stoker groping around the starboard capstan, his breath like steam in the cold air. In England they would be hoping for a good spring in a matter of a few weeks, to give an illusion that the war was not too bad. Howard glanced aft and at the men around him. Spring would be a long time coming up here, with plenty of ice at the end of the journey. He saw Ayres's pale face, a youthful determination which had been lacking before. Thinking of that lifeboat still, probably the closest he had been to the war so far. He lowered his eye to the compass and took a quick fix on the brightly painted marker. 'Dead slow, together.'

'Coming on now, sir.' Treherne sounded calm, completely absorbed as usual.

'Stop engines! Slow astern together!'

Ayres trained some glasses on the nearest anchored warship. A big Tribal Class destroyer. He read her name on the plate by her quartermaster's lobby: *Beothuck*. Canadian, then. He felt himself shiver like that morning in Rosyth. *Just days ago.* It was not possible.

He turned, startled, as the anchor splashed down and the cable started to rumble out across the bottom.

Howard gave him a quick smile. 'You tell the wheelhouse, Sub. Ring off main engines.'

The vibrations ceased instantly and he heard the coxswain's surprised acknowledgement.

Treherne touched his arm as the watchkeepers began to relax and step down from their stations.

'Go and get that tot, Sub, the one that old rascal Knocker White offered you.' He saw the sudden embarrassment and added, 'You earned it back there. It's their way of telling you.'

Howard unslung his binoculars and wondered about a bath before he was summoned to some senior officer.

'I'll need the motor boat, Pilot. About an hour.'

The yeoman called, 'Signal, sir. *Captain to report to ACHQ when convenient.*'

'Acknowledge.' He ran his fingers through his hair. 'About an hour,' he repeated. Then he clattered down the ladder and made his way aft. Another landfall. Soon, another departure.

The tannoy came to life. 'D'you hear there! Men under punishment to muster!'

Howard paused at the entrance of the watertight door and looked along the destroyer's deck. *My ship.* In just the time it took to walk from the last bridge ladder to here, men had died and were still dying. But routine and duty ruled their lives nonetheless.

Other things stood out in his mind. Ayres had come through his first lesson, the new doctor had failed. The other sub-lieutenant, Bizley, was driving himself round the bend, or so Marrack had told him. That had to be dealt with promptly before it endangered some or all of them. Nobody else could handle it. Midshipman Esmonde had rushed on deck when the drifting lifeboat had bumped alongside, and had fainted. He might get over it. If there was only more time.

His day cabin door opened even as he raised his hand and he saw Petty Officer Vallance beaming at him. A fire was already flickering in the grate.

'Nice bath, sir, an' a clean shirt ready, special for the admiral, like!' Vallance saw and recognised the fatigue which the others rarely shared. The Old Man had got them here. He would go on doing it. Till it was all bloody well over.

Gladiator took the strain of her cable and swung to the swirling current. But Vallance knew it was their young captain who carried all of them.

The place chosen for the operational briefing was within the perimeter fence of Area Combined HQ where the Navy had joined with the Royal Air Force to control the destiny of every allied vessel. It was a grand name for a scattered collection of Nissen huts, all of which were dominated by a giant radio mast. Howard, with Treherne sitting beside him, looked around at the other naval officers who sat like pupils on rows of hard wooden chairs.

Howard guessed that this hut, larger than all the others, was normally used as a cinema for the many servicemen who were incarcerated on this inhospitable island. But the screen was folded up to the roof, and had been replaced by a long trestle table which faced the audience.

It had been four days since *Gladiator* had arrived at Reykjavik, and apart from moving alongside a fleet oiler to replenish the tanks, nothing much had happened. *Ganymede*, their sister-ship, had arrived to join them, delayed in Scotland only to collect and accompany two more corvettes. There were about twenty commanding officers and their navigators present, he thought, maybe more. It was to be that important.

Ganymede's captain, Lieutenant-Commander 'Spike' Colvin, nudged him with his elbow. 'Some of our chaps look as if they've just left school!'

Howard nodded, but through and beneath the unmoving fog of pipe and cigarette smoke he saw a few of the more experienced faces, the interwoven gold lace of the RNR, like Treherne, and several regulars like himself and Colvin. The majority were Wavy Navy, hostilities only; the new blood.

Howard wondered how they would all stand up to another run to Murmansk. Fifteen hundred miles as the crow flies, but far longer with all the detours thrown in. One of the worst sea areas in the world, even without the enemy.

The door opened and the little procession trooped to the table while the assembled officers got to their feet with much scraping of chairs. Rear-Admiral Henry Giffard took his place in the centre, ranked on either hand by his team of 'experts' and one naval commander whom Howard had already met. He was the captain of HMCS *Beothuck*, the big Tribal destroyer, who was to be the senior officer of the escort. A good choice it seemed, as he had done several of these trips before. He was a powerfully-built man with impassive features. One who would have no time for fools.

The rear-admiral was a complete contrast. Old for his rank, his chest brightened by a full rectangle of decorations most of which Howard did not recognise, he looked rather like a modern Pickwick. He was bald but for two white wings of hair, and he looked polished and scrubbed. When he put on a pair of small, gold-rimmed spectacles he *was* Pickwick.

He looked at them over the glasses and said dryly, 'Gentlemen, you may smoke.' He glanced pointedly at the drifting pall and added, 'If you must.'

Colvin grunted and immediately fished out a tin of duty-free cigarettes. Eventually everyone settled down and the navigating officers had their pads and pencils ready to hand.

The rear-admiral cleared his throat. 'Before I hand you over to the Met officers and my operations commander I should like to put you all in the picture. I shall of course be attending the convoy conference to address the ships' masters, but there are certain things they need not be told, yet, anyway.' Again that slow search of their faces. 'Our allies, the Russians, are having a very bad time of it. Too many retreats, terrible losses in men and materials, and more especially aircraft. The Luftwaffe dominates the whole front, and the Russians do not have the means to keep pace with the enemy.' He added with a certain irony, 'It has rather a familiar ring about it, don't you think?'

Howard thought of the way Britain's fortunes had suffered. Even in North Africa where there had been so many victories, the newsreels full of Italian soldiers surrendering to the Eighth Army, the situation was critical. One man ruled the Western Desert: Rommel, with his famous Afrika Korps. He was heading even now for Egypt, beyond which lay Suez, India, total victory. And nothing but the battered and demoralised Eighth Army could prevent it.

He recalled his own harsh summary, which he had offered Ayres. But he was no different from all the others who had not experienced the odds of battle. They wanted to close their ears or listen to Vera Lynn.

The admiral was saying, 'This will be a fast convoy. Almost all the ships are new – each will be loaded with essential weapons and aircraft, and tanks.'

Howard saw the Canadian escort commander look down at the table and sigh. He would know better than most what the admiral was hinting at. Their destination, Murmansk, as bleak as it was dangerous, had only one really functional crane, and that was capable of lifting just eleven tons at a time; far less than a tank. It meant more time lost and fretting over delays while they offloaded them on to any available slipway or jetty, using a solitary lifting vessel.

It was never made any easier by the thinly disguised hostility and suspicion with which the Russians behaved. Even the anchorage was far too deep for the tired escorts, and their allies persistently refused to allow any of them into the relative security of the Russian naval base at Polynaroe.

The men who manned the ships were more than bitter about this treatment, after all the risks they had taken to get there. Even then they still had to reach home again along the same dangerous highway. The convoys were beyond Allied air cover for the worst part of the passage, and the Germans used their Norwegian bases to full and deadly advantage.

Rear-Admiral Giffard dabbed his mouth with his handkerchief and Colvin whispered, 'Just had a bloody good lunch, I'll wager!'

Giffard removed his glasses and said, 'Unfortunately I have to tell you that intelligence reports suggest that the Germans may attempt a surface attack by cruisers which are said to be lying at Tromsø. There is a ring of steel around the place and even the Norwegian underground has stayed silent. There will be a covering force from the Home Fleet, a match for any such cruisers.'

Howard waited. Why was he hesitating, drawing it out?

Giffard replaced his glasses as if to afford protection. 'It is also rumoured that *Tirpitz* may make a sortie this time.'

If he had shouted some terrible obscenity the little admiral could not have had a greater effect.

Colvin said quietly, 'Jesus Christ, the battlewaggon could swallow this convoy and never notice it.'

Around the room officers were glancing at one another, seeking out familiar faces, starkly aware, not of their numbers, but of their complete vulnerability.

Howard felt Treherne stiffen beside him. Remembering *Tirpitz*'s giant sister-ship *Bismarck* which had escaped through these very same waters. Not before she had destroyed *Hood*, the darling of many a peacetime review and Britain's greatest warship, and sent a brand-new battleship, *Prince of Wales*, in full retreat from her great guns. The ill-fated *Prince of Wales* had shared *Hood*'s fate at the hands of the Japanese just seven months later.

They had sunk the German giant eventually, but it had taken most of the Home Fleet to find and destroy her.

While *Tirpitz* remained in her Norwegian lair the battleships and cruisers of the Home Fleet were tied down at Scapa Flow, just in case she came out.

Would the German Navy risk such an important battle-group on one convoy? Even as he asked himself the question Howard knew the answer. They would want to destroy *any* convoy that might help the Russians recover when the ice and snow released their ruthless grip on the Eastern Front. When the thaw came to those hundreds of miles of contested ground, Hitler would order his armies to attempt that which Napoleon had failed to do.

With Russia beaten into submission and slavery the enemy would double its efforts elsewhere. North Africa, and then – he thought of his father's little house in Hampshire, the pleasant garden from which you could see the old windmill on the top of Portsdown Hill on a clear summer's day. No amount of courage and sacrifice would stop them coming there, too.

He realised that the RAF Met officer was droning on about wind and snow flurries, about the fact that the ice-edge was still holding firm, later than usual, so that the convoy would have to sail closer to the German bases than had been hoped. Even around the approaches to the Kola Inlet and Murmansk there would be similar hazards although the port was selected in the first place because it was ice-free all the year round. It was also chosen because of the direct railway connection with Leningrad and the Baltic.

The Ops Officer was last, his hands in his reefer pockets, thumbs hooked over the sides.

He ended by saying, 'The convoy will not disperse, gentlemen.' He looked at their intent faces. 'It goes through. No matter what.'

To Howard as he turned up his coat collar and stepped over the dirty snow to find the jeep that had carried him here, those final words sounded like a covenant, a perfect epitaph.

3

From a View to a Kill

'Forenoon watch closed up at defence stations, sir!'

Lieutenant Neil Finlay nodded and trained his glasses on the nearest merchantman again. 'Very well.'

Finlay was a Scot and proud of the fact, and also of the knowledge that he was the first RNVR officer to be put in charge of gunnery in this hard-worked destroyer. Because his captain was a regular he was all the more determined to make no mistakes. If anyone else made any in the gunnery department, Finlay had left no doubts as to what he would do about it.

It had taken three days to marshal the convoy into their allotted positions and move out of Reykjavik, then north and into the Denmark Strait. Apart from a few minor collisions with drifting patches of ice they had managed without incident.

Now, with the sea rising and falling in a deep swell, they were in open water: the Arctic Ocean. There were thirty merchant ships in the convoy, arranged in five columns, with the commodore's vessel, a fine-looking cargo liner named *Lord Martineau*, leading the centre column. To protect them on the long haul to North Russia were six destroyers, eight corvettes, two Asdic trawlers and a tug. In the centre of the convoy was a converted Dutch ferry named *Tromp II*, described in the orders as an anti-aircraft ship. She was manned by naval ratings and her deck appeared to be crammed with short-range weapons, pom-poms and Oerlikons, while right aft by her stylish bridge she mounted two twelve-pounders. Lieutenant Finlay moved his glasses towards the other odd-looking vessel at the rear of the centre column, one he had heard Ayres asking about as soon as the convoy had got under way.

Another converted merchantman, her upperworks had been cut away but for her bridge and spindly funnel, while the upper deck was dominated by a long catapult. A Hurricane fighter stood all alone on the catapult, like some huge seabird which had landed there for a brief respite from its flight.

The first lieutenant's comment had been typically curt and scathing. 'Fighter catapult ship. If the convoy is sighted by a German recce plane they fire off the catapult and our gallant pilot shoots the German down before he can home the U-Boats onto our position.'

Marrack had met Ayres's unspoken questions with, 'After *that* he bales out, and we pick him up.'

Finlay smiled grimly. They were well north of the Arctic Circle. If the flier had to ditch he wouldn't last much longer than twelve seconds.

Tucker, the yeoman of signals, raised his telescope, his lips moving soundlessly. 'Signal from commodore, sir. *Mersey Belle is losing way. Investigate.*'

Howard stood up and gripped his chair while the signal lamp clattered an acknowledgement.

The ship in question was at the rear of the port column. She had already been told off by the escort commander for making too much smoke. Now what?

Howard shaded his eyes to study the great array of ships. Five columns of vital equipment, every hold packed with weapons, medical supplies and vehicles. Most of them carried deck cargo as well, crates and crates of aircraft destined to fill the critical gaps in Stalin's air force. The other five destroyers were out of sight, steaming in a widespread arrowhead formation ahead of the convoy. The corvettes were divided on either beam, their sturdy little silhouettes lifting and diving in the huge swell like lively whales.

Gladiator was two miles astern of the convoy, 'Tail-end Charlie', ready to do anything required by the commodore, or go for any U-Boat which might try to catch up with the ships on the surface. It was unlikely in daylight, for no submarine could outpace the convoy submerged.

'Half ahead together.'

In the wheelhouse Treherne was checking something with his yeoman, which was why Finlay had relieved him for a few moments. Finlay had lost no time in summoning their other sub-lieutenant and Esmonde the midshipman to the bridge to press home the main points of his fire-control system.

As the revolutions mounted Howard glanced at the trio of young officers below the compass platform. The two subbies, side-by-side but somehow totally apart, and Esmonde swaying jerkily with the uncompromising rolls and swoops, his features the colour of parchment.

'One-one-seven revs replied, sir!'

Howard raised his glasses again. The sky was very cloudy, with small patches of shark-blue here and there. No sign of snow as promised. No sign of anything for that matter. Even the far-off Admiralty had refrained from making signals. A covering force from the Home Fleet was somewhere to the north-west; there was supposed to be an escort carrier with it. Howard looked at the fighter catapult ship. At the moment that was all the air-cover they could expect once they had reached the limit of shore-based aircraft to the north-east of Jan Mayen Island, that lonely outpost at the very extremes of the ice-edge.

It was too calm. Bad weather was the best ally so close to enemy airfields and the deep fjords where the big surface ships were said to be hiding. Maybe the Met officer would still be proved right. If not . . .

'Slow ahead.' Howard walked to the side of the bridge and switched on the loud-hailer.

'*Mersey Belle*! Make more revs! *You're falling astern*!' He waited, tapping his leather sea-boot impatiently until two heads appeared on the freighter's high bridge. It was shining like glass, he thought. So, probably, was *Gladiator* as the freezing spray drifted over her. Marrack would have to get his people to work on the forecastle. A destroyer was not built to take a build-up of ice on the upper deck; too much top-hamper had been known to capsize an escort in heavy seas.

'Hello, *Gladiator*!' He had a Geordie accent you could cut with scissors. 'It's a spot o' shaft trouble. I'll have to slow down some more while my chief is working on it!'

Howard said, 'Signal the commodore, Guns.' He moved his glasses along the freighter's hull. The sea was lifting right up to her wash-ports one moment, then falling away to reveal her waterline. Deep-laden, like the rest. She had armoured cars on the upper deck; there were even crates of aircraft lashed across her hold covers. Not much chance if the cargo shifted, he thought. He often marvelled at how they stood it. They were, after all, civilians, but they bore the full fury of the enemy's attacks by sea and air. Howard had known merchant ships to pick up survivors only to be torpedoed themselves, then sometimes a second roar of destruction with the survivors crowding into other ships. And yet they always seemed to go back. This convoy's commodore, for instance, had been sunk twice already, and he was here again in the thick of it.

Finlay called, 'From commodore, sir. *The convoy will reduce speed to ten knots.*'

The yeoman lowered his lamp and said, 'Fast convoy, did someone say? A bloody snail could do better!'

Howard heard him. It was unusual for Tommy Tucker to show his feelings. *Edgy.* We're all getting like that.

He said over his shoulder, 'Take her round and resume position. Warn the messdecks first. She'll show her keel when we turn in this sea!'

A boatswain's mate switched on the speaker and touched his lower lip gingerly with his frozen silver call.

'D'you hear there! Stand by for a ninety degree turn to starboard!'

Ayres could picture it as he remembered the old *Sanderling*. Men seizing cups and food, others putting half-written letters away to prevent them from getting lost under-foot. It was strange, he thought. When he was in the little patrol vessel he had been desperate to leave her and go to the training establishment. Now, he could not get her out of his mind.

His silent companion, Bizley, gripped a safety rail and braced himself. He wanted to shut it all out. Be anywhere but surrounded by others he did not know, nor want to.

He was finding it harder instead of easier to sleep whenever he was off watch. It was always there, the vivid flashes of cannon-fire across the black water, sparks flying as the balls of red tracer had cracked over the hull. Men had fallen, some blinded by wood splinters from the deck, or hammered down by the E-Boat's rapid and deadly accuracy.

His commanding officer, a young lieutenant like Finlay, had fallen in the bridge, bleeding badly, one of his hands missing. In the dreams there was no fire, but he had known that the forward messdeck was ablaze when he had . . . He tried to accept it, to deal with it without lying to himself. There was nothing he could have done. The skipper would have died anyway. He chilled as he saw him again, reaching out with his remaining hand. Pleading with him without speaking. Two others had been trapped below when a machine-gun mounting had fallen across the hatch. They had been screaming still when Bizley had inflated his lifejacket and hurled himself outboard where two of the surviving seamen had been struggling with the Carley float. They had stared at him, their eyes white in the darkness, but they had shoved off without protest when he had yelled at them.

The motor gunboat had been carrying a full rack of depth-charges, and someone had failed to set them to safe when the hull had eventually raised its stern and dived from view. At fifty feet the charges had ignited and the sinking hull with dead and wounded still trapped inside had been blown into a thousand pieces.

That was last year. It seemed like yesterday. They had transferred him to general duties before sending him here, to *Gladiator*.

It was over. Finished with. Who could know now? The only other survivors barely remembered what had happened; they had been too busy trying to launch the float and escape.

'Stand by!'

Howard gripped the chair again. 'Starboard fifteen!'

'Fifteen of starboard wheel on, sir!'

Round and further still until they were dangling from any handhold they could find, skidding on steel and cursing, while the starboard Oerlikon gunner was heard to sing out, 'Any more for the Skylark?'

Gladiator asserted herself like the thoroughbred she was, lifting her sharp stem towards the clouds like the short sword on her crest. Water spurted from her hawsepipes as she plunged down again, surging around A-gun and bursting over the bridge in a miniature tidal wave.

They headed back to their allotted position before repeating the turn all over again.

Howard climbed on to his chair and watched the spread of ships as they appeared to slide back and forth across the salt-streaked screen.

Finlay said, 'You can cut along, Sub – you, too, Snotty.' He turned to Ayres.

'Bring her back on course, Sub.' He saw the genuine pleasure on Ayres's face. *That one couldn't hide anything if he tried.* He heard the others clattering down the bridge ladder. The midshipman was no better or worse than he had once been himself in his first ship. But Bizley – he was something else. He wondered if the Old Man had noticed. While Ayres was like a kid let loose in a toyshop, Bizley seemed to resent any sort of advice or instruction. As a sub-lieutenant he had probably been a big noise in his MGB, maybe even the Number One. Here, he was just another green subbie.

He was surprised that Marrack had not already come down on him like a ton of bricks. They shared the same watch after all. Perhaps he was sorry for him after losing his boat in the North Sea. Finlay smiled wryly. It was hard to imagine the first lieutenant being sorry for anyone.

Treherne appeared on the bridge and grinned. There was ice-rime on his beard.

'Thanks, Guns. I'll take over again.' He glanced across to the voicepipes as Ayres acknowledged the helmsman's report. 'Been a good boy, has he?'

Finlay nodded. 'He's got the makings, Pilot. Not too sure about – '

'*Aircraft, sir! Dead astern!* Angle of sight three-five! Moving right to left!'

Howard swung his glasses over the screen even as he slid from the chair. The signalman who had called out lowered his own glasses and exclaimed, 'It *was* there, sir!'

Howard continued with a slow sweep, rising and settling again with the ship. Only low cloud, with a sparse break where the aircraft had supposedly been. He looked at the signalman; just a boy, but he had already proved there was nothing wrong with his vision.

'Large or small?'

The youth, his cheeks and throat rubbed almost raw by his cold wet clothing, stared back at him, very aware that he was speaking to his captain.

'Large, sir. I'm certain it was.'

Treherne suggested, 'Could have been one of the big Yank planes from Iceland.' The signalman nodded, heartened that they actually believed him. 'Four engines. Flying just there through the clouds.'

The yeoman of signals said dourly, 'You'd better be right, my son!'

Howard walked to the chart table. 'Inform the commodore. *Aircraft sighted*, possible course and bearing.' A small voice seemed to ask, *theirs or ours?* It was the margin of life or death up here.

The yeoman reported, 'From commodore, sir. *Convoy will alter course in succession to zero-three-zero. Follow father.*'

Treherne chuckled. 'He sounds a lively old bugger!'

Howard saw fresh tea coming to the bridge and was glad of the interruption. The commodore was right about one thing. It was pointless to fly off their one and only Hurricane. It would never find the other aircraft in this cloud, and what if it turned out to be a Yank, or an RAF long-range anti-submarine patrol? It would mean a plane wasted with possibly a dead pilot as well. But the alteration of course was not good. It would add to the overall distance, and the destroyers, which used more fuel than any other ships in the convoy, would have to take on oil from the fleet tanker *Black Watch* earlier rather than later while the weather held.

Howard took the steaming mug and said, 'Warn all the lookouts. Double vigilance. It will do no harm anyway.'

He wiped the compass repeater with his sleeve and felt the ice cling to it. *The convoy will not disperse.* It was as if the man had spoken to him from Iceland. But if they had to fight, how long would it take the heavy ships of the Home Fleet to reach them?

He sipped the scalding tea and watched the ant-like figures through the glasses balanced easily in his right hand. They were working around the Hurricane. Making sure it would still fly if required.

He recalled the tough humour in the desperate days of the Battle of Britain. Join the Navy and see the world. Join the Air Force and see the next.

The watches changed, the bitter air was tinged with the smell of the galley. On the darkening sea the ships sailed on until in the deepening shadows the columns appeared to join like some gigantic Roman phalanx on the march.

A guessing game, so that Howard could picture the markers and flags on the operation boards in Iceland and the Admiralty, and presumably in Kiel, too.

When darkness had finally closed over the sea, Howard left the bridge and climbed stiffly down to his sea cabin. It had become a sort of ritual. A quick wash with warm soapy water, and a clean dry towel to wrap round his neck. PO Vallance thought of everything. He tried not to look at the untidy bunk. If he even just sat on it he would be finished. He looked at himself in a mirror and tried to comb the salt out of his unruly hair.

The telephone on the bulkhead scattered his thoughts.

'Captain?' He wondered if the petty officer telegraphist, 'Pots' Hyslop, could hear his heart beating down the line.

'From Admiralty, sir. *Immediate. There are said to be five U-Boats to the east of your position.*'

Howard nodded. 'I'm going up.'

The others were waiting for him and he was glad they could not see his face.

'Well, now we know, Number One. It was *not* one of ours!'

In the private, enclosed world of the chart table Howard and Treherne were leaning side-by-side while they stared at countless calculations, bearings and the pencilled line of their course. Behind them on the open bridge Howard could hear the other watchkeepers moving occasionally to restore circulation or to break the tension.

He picked up the brass dividers and moved them along the chart while he listened with half an ear to the ship, to the pattern of sound and movements. The dreary, repetitive ping of the Asdic, the squeak of B-gun as it was trained from bow to bow. Although every weapon was supposed to be safe from freezing, the special oil they used had been known to fail on rare occasions. Howard made a quick calculation on the pad and glanced at the misty, revolving picture in the radar-repeater. Like a faint beam of light as it passed across the invisible convoy, the unwavering shapes of the columns, the fainter blips of the corvettes' close escort on either beam.

It was unnerving, he thought. Another day with nothing untoward to report.

Maybe the U-Boat warning had been misunderstood by the coding staff at the Admiralty, or perhaps they were off after some other convoy.

The sea was calmer, with a long procession of low swells which lifted the ships with surprising ease before rolling on with nothing between them and the Norwegian coastline. Some of the destroyers had even managed to top up their bunkers from the fleet oiler, a nervous moment for any captain with his ship restricted by the hoses and lines.

He said, 'The motion is easier, Pilot.'

Treherne rubbed his eyes; they felt sore from the bitter air and from peering for the sight of the nearest ships in case there was a collision. On the previous night, one freighter had lost contact with the next ahead and had increased speed to such an extent that it had almost run the other vessel down. Somebody had sounded off his siren, either to warn the rest or from sheer fury at the culprit's carelessness, and had immediately been given a bottle by the commodore. As Marrack had remarked, 'The enemy don't need *his* bloody siren to find their way!'

Treherne replied, 'Ice, sir. There's ice about.'

'I think you're right.' He heard someone laugh; it sounded so out of place – like a lost soul, he thought. He was surprised anyone still could crack a joke with each dragging hour tearing at the nerves.

He could picture his men, huddled and crouched around the ship. Only half the company were closed up at their stations, but Howard had cleared the lower deck so that gun crews and damage control parties, stokers and fire sections could be close to hand if the balloon went up. Marrack was going round the ship for much of the time, keeping an eye on things, making certain that the men on watch were alert. Ready.

'We'll be up to Jan Mayen Island tomorrow, Pilot. The commodore will have to alter course if he wants to avoid the ice.'

Howard felt him start as something boomed against the hull. He said, 'If we remain on this course the pieces will get bigger than that one!'

Treherne grinned, his teeth very white in the faint glow. 'Lucky it wasn't a mine!'

In the privacy of the chart table, Howard seized the opportunity to say, 'Pilot, tell me about Ayres. Why did you swap him around with the other subbie?'

Marrack had already told him of the new arrangement but he wanted to hear it from the big, bearded navigator.

Treherne said, 'He's learned a lot in the past few days, sir. Bizley, on the other hand, has done some close-action, and I thought he would be better off with the after-guns and depth-charges. Ayres will do more good up here with me, I think, sir – anyway, that's what I told Number One.' He gave what might have been a shrug. 'So he changed the duties. I hope that was all right?'

Howard nodded. 'Good thinking.' He had always approved of his officers using their own initiative in such matters. It showed they understood, that they cared.

Bizley on the other hand had seen action in Light Coastal Forces, and according to his report he had behaved well when his boat had gone down. He had taken charge of the remaining survivors and had got them clear before the depth-charges went up. That sort of behaviour took plenty of nerve and guts. The report even hinted that Bizley might be recommended for a decoration.

They switched off the little light and backed out from under the protective canvas hood, shutting and opening their eyes to accustom them once more to the darkness.

Marrack had arrived on the bridge and said, 'Full readiness, sir. All watertight doors closed and checked.' The ship rolled steeply and an enamel mug jangled on the deck like Bow Bells. Ayres heard the yeoman of signals using some choice language to the man who had dropped it and recalled how he used to blush because of it. He saw Treherne speaking with the captain. He smiled to himself; 'The Old Man', as they called him, even though he was still in his twenties. He and the first lieutenant must be the same age, but Marrack looked much older. At that very second the two officers, who had been merely black shapes like the others around him, seemed to flare up like molten copper. Ayres exclaimed, '*Oh my God!*' He stared with disbelief at the expanding fireball which lit up the ships in the convoy like models on an uneven table. It took just the blink of an eye, and yet to Ayres it felt like an eternity before the shockwave of the explosion rolled across the heaving water and thundered against *Gladiator*'s steel flanks as if she, herself, had been hit.

Alarm bells jangled insanely and from every voicepipe the chatter of hoarse voices filled the bridge.

Howard could hear the men around him, their breathing strained and heavy, like people who had been running. In the flickering glare he saw their faces, grim, or shocked by the suddenness of disaster.

Treherne called from the radar-repeater, 'Two of the wing escorts are standing away, sir.'

Howard said nothing, picturing the corvettes, veterans of this kind of warfare, as clearly as if they were visible. Another explosion rebounded against the hull and for a moment he thought a second torpedo had found its mark. But it was aboard the stricken ship, and he could see the glow of fires beyond her bridge.

It was unlikely that the corvettes would make any contact, he thought. A U-Boat, probably sailing alone, had surfaced to chase after the convoy and had fired a torpedo, maybe more, at extreme range. The German captain was making off now, still on the surface, to call up his consorts to share the spoils.

Ayres pulled himself from a voicepipe and shouted, 'From W/T, sir, commodore has ordered *increase speed to fourteen knots.*'

The yeoman said harshly, 'No need to slow down any more. That was the poor old *Mersey Belle* that copped it!'

A blunt shadow passed between them and the spreading flames: *Bruiser*, the big salvage tug, known by most of the sailors as the Undertaker. She would assess the ship's damage, then either take her in tow or lift off the crew.

Ayres said, 'From commodore, sir. *Investigate but do not remain with Mersey Belle.*'

'Acknowledge.' Howard rubbed his chin, feeling the bristles. 'Too many damned signals.' He watched the flames intently. 'I've a feeling about this one, Pilot. Pass the word to damage control. Number One can rig scrambling nets as soon as he likes.' The flames were blazing higher than the freighter's derricks. Something really powerful must have been set alight by the explosion.

'Sea boat, sir?' Treherne's eyes were glowing like coals in the reflected inferno. He felt it badly. Most of the ex-merchant service officers were like that. Seeing a ship dying. Not a man-of-war, going down with guns blazing or trying to ram an enemy cruiser like the poor little *Glowworm*, but ships that worked for a living, in the Depression and in times of peace. Without them England would not, could not, survive. Howard felt the pain jar up his arm as he banged his fist on the unyielding steel. *And we are not protecting them. Not because we don't try, but because the enemy are better at it.*

He saw a shaded torch on the maindeck, men already moving to free the scrambling nets.

Treherne repeated dully, 'No sea boat then, sir?'

Howard raised his glasses and watched the other ship. Her shape had lengthened so she must have lost power on her engines and was drifting beam-on in the swell.

'Negative.' He realised how sharply it had come out. 'I'll not risk men more than necessary.'

'Escort commander reports no contacts, sir!'

Howard thought of the pencilled lines on the grubby chart where so many had leaned on it in the night watches.

'From Admiralty, sir. *Immediate. There are now six U-Boats in your vicinity.*'

The boatswain's mate muttered, 'Roll on death, let's 'ave a good rest!'

Howard watched narrowly as sparks burst up from the helpless freighter, and her funnel seemed to crumple like paper before pitching overboard in a great splash.

They were trying to lower a boat while the tug stood by, her screws beating up the water as she manoeuvred astern to keep station on the *Mersey Belle*. A ragged sheet of flame seemed to burst straight up through the deck where the tiny figures were trying to free the lifeboat's falls of ice. They were like dried leaves caught suddenly in a wind and tossed into the fire. Not men any more, who had loved and hated with the rest of them, but little burning flakes; nothing.

The yeoman said, 'From *Bruiser*, sir. *Mersey Belle has aircraft fuel on board.*'

Howard heard the brief click of his lamp and watched the tug's screws beat the sea into a mounting froth as she swung heavily away from the flames. So that was it. He felt his fingers gripping the binoculars so tightly that his fingers became numb even through his thick gloves. There had been no mention of that in the convoy report. A last minute decision perhaps, just to fill another space.

He felt his mouth go dry as a vivid red eye opened suddenly in the other ship's side to spread across the undulating water and set the sea itself ablaze.

'Port ten.' He did not recall moving to the voicepipes. He was just there. Where he belonged. *No matter what.* Those words again.

'Midships.' He heard the coxswain's thick voice, pictured the tense faces in the shuttered wheelhouse. The telegraphsmen, Treherne's yeoman with the plottable and its moving lights, Midshipman Esmonde who was in charge of it and the charts it might need. Faces like carved masks, picked out by reflected flames through the steel shutters.

'*Steady.*'

'Steady, sir. Course three-five-zero.' Howard lifted the glasses from his chest and said, 'Very easy, Cox'n. Like the last time, remember?'

He heard him sigh. 'Not likely to forget, sir.'

Howard strode to the side of the bridge and sought out Marrack's oilskinned figure by the guardrail.

'Number One!' He saw him peer up. 'This will have to be fast!'

Ayres wanted to throw the glasses aside but could not move. Half to himself he whispered, 'They're trying to swim clear!' It was as if he was there, right amongst them. The shining faces in the water, the bulky lifejackets dragging them back, the desperate terror of their thrashing arms as they made frantically for the slow-moving destroyer.

Treherne wiped his mouth with the back of his glove. *Gladiator* would stand out clearly in the flames; she was barely making headway through the water. At any second a torpedo might find her. He controlled his sudden anxiety with a physical effort. But he could hear one of the seamen repeating over and over again like a prayer, 'Let's get out of it, for Christ's sake. *Leave them!*'

Howard asked sharply, 'Where's the doctor?'

A signalman called, 'Sick bay, I think, sir!'

'I want him. Here and now.'

He lowered his head to the voicepipe, his lungs filled with the stench. They could not get any closer. At any second she might blow up, engulf *Gladiator* in her own pyre.

'Dead slow, Cox'n.' He heard Ayres give a quick sob as the fire overtook two of the swimmers. He imagined he could hear their terrible screams. More explosions ripped through the freighter from her keel to upper deck. All the crates were alight, and some of the armoured cars had torn free of their lashings and were hanging drunkenly through the bulwarks, or burning with everything else.

'You wanted me, sir?'

Howard did not turn his head from the dying ship. 'Yes, Doc.' It was amazing how calm he sounded. Perhaps it had got to him at last, and he really was going crazy. 'I want you to be there with your team when those sailors are pulled aboard. They will be frozen, shocked and close to dying.' He let his words sink in. 'There won't be too many of them this time.'

The doctor's face shone in the fires, his lips parted as he took in each part of the scene which seemed to be drawing closer by the minute. Howard heard him going down the ladder, his feet dragging. *Another second and I would have shaken the fear out of him*. He stiffened, craning forward.

'*All stop!*'

He hurried to the bridge wing again, and felt a lookout move aside for him. The first gasping figures had reached the scrambling nets while others reached out to catch the lines being thrown to them.

Some fell back retching and crying out as their hands, already black with their own ship's leaking oil, let the ropes slip through their grasp. Howard tightened his jaw as he saw some of Marrack's men clambering down the nets to help them, bowlines already made into heaving lines to pull them to safety. A few seemed to give up, and floated along the destroyer's side. Frozen to death even within yards of rescue.

Howard could feel the heat of the fires now on his face, saw steam rising from the lookout's duffel coat. *Oh God, just a few more minutes.*

One man was holding on to the nets but seemed reluctant to climb aboard. He was peering back towards his drifting ship but he was not looking at her. Above the roar of flames Howard heard him calling to someone who was still out there swimming, swimming. Then a terrible scream came from the sea of fire and the man on the nets completed his climb to the hands reaching out to help him. The scream had been his answer.

Marrack looked up at the bridge and waved his hands. *No more.* Or if there were, they were already doomed.

'Slow ahead together. Port fifteen.' He felt desperately tired. Like a sickness. A despair.

A dull explosion rolled towards them and more blazing fuel gushed from the ship's hull and crept up and down across the swell to the place where *Gladiator* had been.

'Half ahead together.'

The yeoman said, 'From commodore, sir. *Resume station.*'

Howard took off his worn, sea-going cap and shook his hair to the wind. The heat was fading already, the icy cold regaining its grip.

'Take her round, Pilot. Revs for twenty knots.'

He turned to watch as the *Mersey Belle* began to heel over, armoured vehicles splashing alongside, only so much rubbish now. There were two figures right up in the vessel's stern. *Don't let them suffer like that.*

He offered a silent prayer as some of the flames vanished and he heard the grating crash of metal as the ship began to break up, the stern half diving first in a great welter of steam and bubbles, the two lonely figures still there to the end. A last great explosion rocked the destroyer's sleek hull and then the sea was empty once more.

At first light they rejoined the convoy, and as the visibility improved Howard saw that the formation was as before. As if *Mersey Belle* had never been. He said, 'Fall out action stations. Get some hot food into the people. It may be the last for some time.'

Treherne asked quietly, 'And what about you, sir?'

Howard gave him a curious glance. 'Me? I'd like the biggest Horse's Neck in the whole bloody world, but I'll make do with some fresh kye if you can arrange it.'

Treherne glanced at Lieutenant Finlay who was climbing down from his fire control position, and gave a brief wink.

Just for an instant back there he had been worried. But Howard was OK. He thought of the men, dying in the water. *He had to be.*

4

Ice and Fire

Gladiator's small chart-room was situated abaft the wheelhouse and opposite Howard's sea cabin. The only light came from the chart table where everything was clearer to read and understand than the cramped ready-use hutch on the upper bridge.

Howard and his three lieutenants stood around it now, sharing the illusion of warmth after the biting cold of the open bridge.

Howard watched Treherne adjusting the course to another alteration from the commodore, oblivious to the condensation which fell like heavy drops of rain from the deckhead. Marrack and Finlay the gunnery officer waited in silence while they contemplated their own possible fate.

It was past noon, and the pace of the convoy had dropped to nine knots as more and more ice-floes cruised slowly down their ranks. The heavy tug *Bruiser* had steamed to the head of the convoy, ready to assist if one of the deep-laden ships got into difficulty, or to smash her way through with her tough, ocean-going hull.

The survivors from the *Mersey Belle* were aft in the wardroom. There had been only seven, but one had died an hour ago from his burns and other injuries.

Howard had accepted the news in silence. It was terrible what war could do to your judgement, he thought. *To me.* In those early days, learning the job, he would have been grateful, proud even, to have snatched just six men from the jaws of death. But experience made him ask questions now. Were a handful of survivors worth risking this ship? She had been stopped, outlined against the blazing fuel, an easy target for any U-Boat had there been one. They *had* to be worth it. *Otherwise we are as bad as the men who struck them down without mercy.* Every U-Boat commander knew that his weapon could be the vital one to win the war. Up here, in these bleak wastes, submarines and bombers alike were ordered to go for the main targets, merchantmen and aircraft carriers.

As one senior escort commander had told Howard, 'When the U-Boats start going for *us*, you'll know we're winning!'

He heard boots scraping on the deck overhead and wondered what Sub-Lieutenant Bizley thought about being on watch alone while Finlay was down here. He must have done it many times in his racy motor gunboat. But this was quite different. A powerful destroyer, a company of one hundred and forty-five to consider, and signals which might burst upon him from any direction: the commodore, the senior escort, or the distant Admiralty.

Howard still felt guilty at leaving the upper bridge even in the face of exhaustion. In the event of an attack, one more ladder to the centre of his 'stage' might make all the difference.

Treherne straightened his back, wincing. 'There it is, sir. We know that the ice-edge is still to the south-east of Jan Mayen Island. The convoy has to make a turn very soon or get scattered amongst the floes.'

Howard rubbed his chin, and tried to sip from his mug. It was empty, although he could not recall drinking the glutinous pusser's kye so beloved by sailors.

'At best we shall have to alter course to east-north-east, which will take us up to the final big change below Bear Island.'

Treherne grinned. 'Run like rabbits all the way for the Kola Inlet and our Russian "chums" – I don't think!'

There had been no more U-Boat reports, but they were out there somewhere. It was like fighting something unreal and unreachable, Howard thought. *Perhaps they know something we don't?*

He glanced at Marrack's impassive features. 'What d'you think, Number One?'

'*I think*,' he cupped his hands around the calculations on the chart, 'they're trying to herd the convoy as close to the ice as possible. In the summer we could have sailed further north, around Bear Island, but not now.'

Howard nodded, seeing the slow-moving columns going on and on like that drifting lifeboat and its tattered crew.

'I agree. The Germans probably know the Home Fleet has a shadowing force at sea big enough to cope with *Tirpitz*, if she is reported on the move. Then there will be our cruisers – *they* wouldn't risk an encounter with that big bastard, and in any case they would have been ordered not to proceed beyond longitude twenty-five east.' He smiled dryly. 'Just where we'll need them most, of course!'

Marrack grimaced. 'They seem more intent on keeping the battleships intact than using them for this job.' He spoke with all the intolerance and contempt shown by destroyer and small-ship men for the ponderous goliaths of the Navy.

The door opened slightly and Morgan, the navigator's yeoman, peered in at them. 'Fog warning, sir.' He glanced at his charts as if to check that nobody had put a dirty mug on them. 'Cox'n said it's quite usual so near to the ice.'

Treherne patted his arm. 'That ancient mariner would say anything!'

Howard snatched up the chart-room handset in one movement.

'Captain!'

'Bridge, sir.' Bizley sounded very calm. 'General signal from commodore. *Reduce distances to avoid losing contact.* To us, sir: *Remain on station and maintain contact by radar.*'

'Very good. I'll come up.' He looked at his lieutenants as he put down the handset. 'We've got the fuel, and even without air-cover after today, we may have one ally after all – fog. We could just shake 'em off our backs for a bit longer.'

He tightened the towel around his neck and fastened his coat once again.

Finlay bustled away to resume his watch, while Howard paused by the wheel-house door and glanced inside. It was almost hot in there, and he saw the men on watch stiffen, then relax again when they realised this was not an official visit.

The coxswain, Bob Sweeney, one of *Gladiator*'s only two chief petty officers, was standing near the plot table, red-faced and comfortable-looking as he chatted with one of the telegraphsmen. Sweeney should have been below, off watch. Maybe his instinct was warning him again.

Howard nodded. 'All right, Swain?'

Sweeney shrugged. 'Fog's goin' to be a proper pea-souper, sir.' He had a pronounced London accent and had been raised in Stepney in the East End before joining up at the age of fourteen. He had seen it all, and had been due for retirement exactly two days before the Germans had bombed Warsaw. The coxswain was the core of any small ship. He handled defaulters, attended to problems of leave and welfare when one of the lads' wives was having it off with the milkman while he was at sea. But in this ship there were not too many wives to worry about. For the vital task of entering and leaving harbour, going alongside another vessel, or at action stations, the coxswain was always there – at the wheel. It was good to know when all hell broke loose.

The man now on the wheel was the chief quartermaster, 'Bully' Bishop, a dark-featured leading seaman who was nicknamed for his savage temper when he was drunk ashore, which was often. How he had managed to retain the hook on his sleeve was a miracle, for he had lost all his good conduct badges along the way.

He said, 'I was in a fog once, sir.' His eyes never left the ticking gyro-repeater. 'Worse than this – '

The cox'n eyed him scornfully. 'That's right, Bully, you swing the lamp! The worst fog you bin in is when the shore patrols carry you on board!'

Howard heard them chuckling as he faced the cold again and climbed into the upper bridge.

He walked aft and peered towards the quarterdeck. But it was already lost in the slow-moving white mist, as if she had lost her stern completely. He made his way to his chair again and felt the cold air driving away the brief reprieve in the chartroom.

He said to the bridge at large, 'Good lookout all around.' He stared through the glass screen and watched the stem blunting itself in the bank of fog. 'Might hit some straggler up the arse otherwise.'

Their faces cracked into grins. They seemed to trust him, even the new hands. *I must never lose my trust in them.*

It was eerie, but far better than being up ahead with all those ships around you. Any collision at sea was bad enough. Up here it was a nightmare. Ice thudded and grated against the hull, and he found time to pity the little corvettes. They would take it badly, especially as they had just one screw to drive and wriggle them amongst the ice.

It would be dark soon. There was hardly any real daylight, and yet in the summer it would be reversed so that enemy aircraft could have a field-day.

Sub-Lieutenant Bizley trained his binoculars over the screen and watched his breath falling away to join the fog. He had been in Channel fogs often enough, but on this comparatively high bridge you felt as if the ship had lost contact with the sea, that only the thick mist was moving. He stiffened as Midshipman Esmonde moved across to join him. He was always understudying someone, he thought impatiently. More like a soft, stupid girl than a budding naval officer.

Esmonde asked timidly, 'Will this fog make much difference?'

Bizley recalled his disgust when the youth had fainted at the sight of the eyeless creatures in the lifeboat. Ayres had been close to that too. Now they seemed to think he was some kind of bloody hero.

'Why? Scared, are you?'

Esmonde seemed to cower. 'I'm not frightened. Not any more.'

The roar of an explosion seemed to come at the ship from several directions at once. The nearness of the ice and drifting banks of fog made a mockery of the frantic reports which echoed from every side.

Howard jabbed the button. '*Action stations!*'

He gripped the arms of his chair as the fog ahead of the bows seemed to change colour, to writhe as if some maniac painter had decided to change the substance of his canvas. Orange one second, deep scarlet the next.

Voices ebbed and flowed around him as his men ran to their stations, hearts pounding, throats suddenly like dust.

'Ship at action stations, sir.'

'Warn the Cox'n, Pilot. Be ready for an instant change of course and speed.' He held out his hand and touched Marrack's wet sleeve. 'Stay here for the present, Number One.' He heard Treherne speaking into the voicepipe, knowing that the coxswain would be ready for anything. But you had no room for chance.

Marrack polished his binoculars. 'Think that one may drift down on us, sir?'

'Not sure yet.' Howard tried to hear something else. There was more flickering light, but no further explosions. 'Strange. I thought it was a double bang.'

Marrack raised his glasses. 'I heard that. But too close together for topedoes, unless there's another sub out there.'

'Signal from commodore on R/T, sir. *Retain course and speed. Do not lose contact.*'

Treherne muttered, 'Some hopes!'

Howard shifted uneasily in his chair. Another long-range, unlucky shot. There was always the chance of a hit, especially if they were using the much talked-about homing torpedo.

God, those poor devils would stand little chance of being saved. He found himself wondering where the gap would be when the fog cleared and left them naked again.

'Radar – Bridge!'

'*Bridge!*'

Marrack held his ear to the voicepipe while his eyes flickered in the savage glow of fires.

He said quietly, 'Radar reports a strong echo at one-four-zero, three miles.'

Treherne exclaimed, 'Why the hell didn't he see it before?' But nobody answered.

Howard stood up as if he was afraid of disturbing something evil. Then he lowered his mouth to the voicepipe. 'Captain speaking. Who's that?'

'Whiting, sir.'

Howard spoke slowly to give himself time. Leading Seaman Whiting was the senior operator. A good man, who had been decorated for courage under fire at Dunkirk.

'What d'you think?'

The man took a deep breath. 'No doubt in my mind, submarine on the surface. Stopped for some reason.'

Howard turned to Marrack. 'Go and give them some support, Number One. It may be a false alarm, a wreck or a piece of one, but if so we should have detected it earlier when we altered course.'

He watched as Marrack hurried away. *It had to be.* Chasing the convoy while surfaced, then firing off a torpedo for fear of losing the chance in the fog. He said aloud, 'It's *got* to be!'

'Gunnery officer, sir!'

Howard found the voicepipe and spoke into it closely to exclude all the others. 'Yes?'

Finlay sounded as if he was right beside him instead of up there in his fire-control position.

'I had a thought, sir. There was a *double* explosion.' He sounded very crisp, as if he were lecturing trainees on the parade ground at Whale Island. It was always hard to see Finlay as a junior librarian, which was what he had once been.

'I heard it.'

'I think the Jerry fired two fish but one exploded prematurely. Maybe it was touched off by a drifting floe.'

Howard stared at the voicepipe, almost invisible now as the darkness closed over them again. The fire was still burning. Another dying ship; as if all the rest had been swallowed up.

He walked to his chair and said, 'Make by W/T to commodore. *There is a U-Boat on the surface three miles to the south-east of my position.*'

Treherne said in a fierce whisper, 'Suppose he orders us to stay put?'

Howard thought suddenly of his father, and it gave him a strange sense of comfort. 'Remember Nelson!'

The yeoman finished scribbling in his pad. 'Any more, sir?'

Howard looked up towards the sky and tried not to listen to the groan of metal as a ship began to break up.

'*Am engaging. Ends.*'

'Hard a-starboard! Full ahead together! Stand by all guns and depth-charges.' He heard the jingle of telegraphs and pictured the wheelhouse suddenly stirred into activity.

'Hard a-starboard, sir!'

'Steady! *Meet her!* Steer one-four-zero!'

He turned and looked over his shoulder as a shadow dashed up to the yard. Even in the early darkness the yeoman would not overlook that. The black pendant. *Am attacking!*

Sub-Lieutenant Lionel Bizley clung to a safety rail beneath X-gun's blast screen and stared astern at the mounting banks of *Gladiator*'s wake. As the revolutions mounted the ship appeared to bury her narrow stern deeper and deeper until the glistening deck was awash. It was a strange, sickening motion as the destroyer rose and plunged over each successive bank of swell, as if she were in her true element. The hull shook and trembled, the excitement of a wild animal going for the kill.

Leading Seaman Fernie, a great bear-like figure made even more bulky by the oilskin he wore over his other clothing, lurched across the deck to join him. He had been checking the depth-charges, making sure that the settings were correct. Fernie was also the captain of the quarterdeck, and knew every wire, shackle and rivet even in pitch darkness.

He shouted above the din, 'The bugger'll dive soon, sir!'

Bizley looked at him, thinking of his motor gunboat at times like these. *Gladiator* must be doing close on thirty knots despite the troughs and glittering patches of ice dashing past in the darkness. There was no other comparison but speed, and the wild excitement which churned at your insides like madness.

'The U-Boat might be waiting for *us* – have you thought of that?'

He did not hear Fernie's answer, nor did he care. In the little MGB there had just been him and the skipper and a dozen men. Here, he had to wait for the order, chase up anyone who was slow off the mark.

The crouching figure with the headset wedged beneath his hood yelled, 'Load with semi-armour-piercing! X- and Y-guns train to Green four-five!'

Bizley watched the two four-point-seven guns swinging round almost to their full extent even as the breeches opened and clicked shut like rifle bolts.

The communications rating called, 'Sub still on the surface, sir! We will alter course and engage to starboard!'

Bizley thought, Well, that's bloody obvious, surely? He snapped, 'Tell the gunlayers to check their sights while there's still time!'

Fernie watched him in the gloom, his eyes raw with salt. This young officer was a hard one to know. He grinned to himself. If you *wanted* to know him. He seemed to know what he was doing, but might prove to be a real bastard when he thought he had the weight. Not like poor Mr Ayres. A nice chap, but handling seasoned hands amidst a mass of mooring wires when entering or leaving harbour was not his cup of tea. Especially with the old Gunner (T) fucking and blinding all the while.

Bizley stared at the depth-charges right aft and recalled exactly when his MGB's pattern had exploded. If he hadn't ordered the float to be paddled away they would have gone up with them. It had become much clearer with each passing day and he could sense a sort of wary respect from some of the ship's company. What would have been the point of dying? The boat had been done for. The skipper would never have made it anyway.

Even *Gladiator's* captain, a straight-ringed regular who would have seen any flaw in his personal report, seemed impressed, especially at the idea that a decoration might be considered.

He thought of his father and mother, what they would say when he next saw them. His father was a local bank manager, at the same branch where Bizley himself would have ended up but for the war. Paying out cash to people who looked down on him, who were not fit to clean his shoes.

A telephone handset buzzed in its metal box like a trapped insect and Bizley tore it out and covered his other ear with one hand.

'Quarterdeck!'

It was the first lieutenant. A man with no emotion, Bizley thought. The one person who had made him uneasy by asking, 'Surely *somebody* ought to have set the depth-charges to safe when your boat bought it?' Not two officers sharing tea and a momentary break from watchkeeping. More like being in the dock, or how he imagined a court martial would be.

'The U-Boat is diving. Stand by to engage!'

Somewhere a thousand miles away a gong tinkled and instantly B-gun, which was immediately below the bridge, shot back on its springs, the jarring crash of the explosion making some of the new ratings squeak with alarm.

Fernie barked, 'Easy lads, that'll be a starshell, you'll see!' He glared at Bizley's back. *He* should have told them, not leave everything to others.

The bursting starshell made the seascape starkly beautiful, with patches of drifting fog breaking around the destroyer's headlong charge, while the hard glare transformed the swell into moving banks of searing whiteness. Bizley felt the deck tilting over, and saw the sea clawing over the side as the wheel and rudder went over.

He tried to hold his glasses steady while he clung to the safety rail with his spare hand. Just for a brief moment he held it in the powerful lens, before spray dashed over him and soaked him from head to foot.

He didn't know what he had expected. He had seen submarines alongside in Portsmouth, had even been over one when he was at school. Shining and purposeful within, and somehow placid-looking from the dockside, like basking whales.

What he had just witnessed had been something so incredibly evil he had been shocked by his sudden fear. He had even seen the tell-tale burst of spray as she had vented her tanks and begun to dive.

'Target bears Green four-oh! Range oh-one-two. Moving left to right!'

The slender guns moved in unison and then settled.

'Independent – commence!'

'*Fire!*'

Bizley gritted his teeth as both of the after-guns fired together, the shells tearing toward the starboard bow where he had briefly glimpsed the enemy. She would be submerged now, damaged or not.

Again the guns roared out while from the bridge and pom-pom mounting the arching balls of livid red tracer floated away towards the U-Boat's last position.

Bizley thought wildly that it would only take a few cannon shells to destroy the periscopes and she would come floundering to the surface. With something like a great sight of disappointment the revolutions began to fall away as the captain conned his ship at a more manageable speed in pursuit. Radar would give over to Asdic, the searching echo beneath the sea, like the stick of a blind man in a great empty room.

Bizley heard the breech-blocks snapping shut again.

'X- and Y-guns ready, sir!'

Surely at this range the German captain could not get away? He must have imagined that the convoy's escorts had closed in to protect the other ships. He stared at his crew of depth-charge handlers. '*You*, get ready to fire!' It was somehow characteristic of Bizley that he never bothered to learn the names of anybody but key ratings, or, of course, trouble makers.

He could picture the U-Boat – the *thing* – diving steeply, her commander using every skill to shake off his pursuer, the eerie ping of the Asdic against his hull.

Once the bridge have got a perfect position it will be left to me. Some new methods of firing depth-charges were coming off the blue prints, but for the most part these were the only ones in service.

A pattern over the stern, rolled off like great dustbins, while two other sets were fired abeam even as another pattern was rolled over the stern. In theory and the classroom, the explosions should make one great diamond-shaped design which ought to surround the target and sink it or force it to the surface.

A sudden explosion rolled across the water. Another ship torpedoed? Or the last one blowing up?

Bizley knew each charge took its time to reach the set depth. Even now . . . He swung round. '*What?*'

Fernie held out the handset and replied just as sharply, 'Gunnery Officer, sir.'

He snatched it. 'Bizley, sir.'

Over the line Finlay's Edinburgh accent was even stronger. 'Keep your team on the jump, Sub. If the U-Boat comes up, I need to know wherever it is, right?'

Bizley handed the big leading-hand the instrument and said, half to himself, 'I'm not a bloody child!'

Fernie patted one of his men on the arm. 'Could have fooled me, mate!' He gestured to the throwers. 'I give it about half a minute.'

The men peered at one another, their faces and scarves covered with frozen rime.

'Done, Hookey! Gulpers at tot-time!'

The communications rating shouted, '*Continuous echo, sir!*'

'*Fire!*'

Bizley ran to the guardrails and saw the port depth-charge flying lazily away, then it lost itself in a welter of spray. He knew without looking that a full pattern had rolled off the stern, and found he was trying to moisten the roof of his mouth, which felt like old leather. He stared as if mesmerised as a great column of spray shot from the sea astern, and the crack of explosions seemed to shake the ship from truck to keel, as if *Gladiator* and not the enemy was being torn apart.

Fernie called hoarsely, 'Come on, lads! Reload the throwers, *chop, chop!*'

Bizley shouted, 'Taken over, have you?'

The big leading-hand seized a stanchion for support as the deck tilted steeply once more. The ship had lost contact. The Old Man was going for another search.

He took time to confront Bizley's fury and thought of the pleasure it would give to poke him right in his stupid, arrogant puss.

But he was a good leading seaman, and was hoping for a chance to rate petty officer. They at least had space to stretch their legs.

He retorted, 'We're going in for another attack, *sir*. If we make a pass over the target with nothing to drop on 'em, it won't be *me* what gets a bottle from the Old Man!'

Bizley swung away. 'Don't be impertinent! I'll be watching you!'

The breechworker of Y-gun whispered sarcastically, 'Don't think 'e likes you, 'Ookey.'

The deck swayed upright again and men peered at one another, breathless with all the heaving at tackles and struggling with the unwieldy charges.

'Ready, sir!'

'In contact, sir!' The man in the headset crouched like an athlete and tried not to think of the target as a form of warship, which contained men, Germans, who wanted to kill all of them.

Minutes dragged by while the ship appeared to weave her own pattern through the sea, as if she and not her company was trying to sniff out her enemy.

'*Continuous echo, sir!*'

'*Fire!*'

Someone broke free from the huddled group of figures by Y-gun's open shield and ran to the guardrail.

'*We must have got it!*' His voice was almost breaking. 'She *can't* have got away!'

Fernie seized his arm as the great columns of water cascaded down and were soon swallowed up astern in *Gladiator*'s frothing wake.

'Hold your noise, Croft!' He shook him and felt the complete lack of resistance. Just a kid; he had only been aboard since Leith. What a way to begin. He glanced at Bizley's intent shape and hissed, 'Don't let *him* see you! Get back to your station!'

Bizley shouted, 'Next pattern!' He peered astern until his mind throbbed. But no slime-covered hull or bursting air-bubbles appeared. He glared angrily as one of his men fell sprawling while the deck lurched over in another violent turn.

Perhaps the submarine had been sunk after all. He had seen on the charts that there were places where the depth was as much as two thousand fathoms. Even now, the enemy could be falling like a leaf in that perpetual darkness until the hull was crushed like a tin can, and their lives with it.

'Lost contact, sir.'

Bizley heard someone say wearily, 'Gulpers, then?'

But all he could see was the shadow in the depths.

'Steady on zero-seven-zero, sir.'

Howard peered down at the faintly glowing compass repeater. Every bone in his body seemed to be protesting at once, and he felt that if he stared into the darkness and thinning mist much longer he would go blind. He heard the regular ping of the Asdic and thought it was louder than usual. Mocking him as he took his ship this way and that in a careful search. The area was becoming larger every time. The U-Boat could be miles away right now, or licking its wounds in readiness for another attack.

Howard realised that he had thought nothing about the convoy since he had seen the surfaced submarine, so black and stark in the drifting flare. He had heard the machine-gunners and pom-pom crews cursing and shouting as they poured tracer at the target even as she had begun to dive.

The wildness of battle after all the frustration of convoy duty, seeing their helpless charges marked down time and time again.

Howard lowered his head and felt his neck crack. 'Alter course ten degrees to starboard.'

Sweeney's muffled voice came back; a man of endless patience.

'Steady on zero-eight-zero, sir.'

He heard Treherne's clothing scrape over the chart table as he recorded this latest change of direction.

What does he think? That I'm obsessed, unable to concentrate on anything else? It was probably what they all thought.

A shadow moved from the bank of voicepipes and he heard Ayres say, 'The first lieutenant reports, *lost contact*, sir.'

'Tell him we're not giving up!'

Treherne straightened his back and hoped he had not forgotten to put some newly sharpened pencils in his coat. He had heard Ayres's careful message and Howard's abrasive retort.

He means he's not giving up. The thought troubled and impressed him.

Treherne started as Howard remarked, 'You know, Pilot, we've been fighting bloody U-Boats for two and a half years now.'

Treherne relaxed slightly. 'God, is that all it is?'

Howard shrugged his shoulders more deeply into his coat. 'And that was the first one I've ever laid eyes on.'

To himself he added bitterly, *And I lost it. Any moment now and we shall be recalled to the convoy. What was the point of* . . .

It was Marrack again, using the bridge speaker to save time.

'In contact, sir! Bearing one-five-oh, moving slowly right to left!'

Howard slid from his chair. 'The crafty bastard! He's crossing our stern, making a run for it!

'Hard a-starboard! Steady, steer one-five-oh!' He turned to Treherne even as the wheel went hard over. 'Warn Bizley!'

Again they tore through the uneasy water and dropped another full pattern of charges. *Gladiator* was doubling back on her tracks as the last towering columns fell back into the sea.

'Slow ahead together!'

A boatswain's mate called, 'Signal from commodore, sir. *Rejoin without delay.*'

There was a far-off explosion. Yet another victim? Or the unknown ship that had blown up in the fog?

Howard swung round. 'What the hell are those men doing?' They were cheering, the voices ragged and partly lost in the sounds of the sea and the great thrashing screws.

Treherne ran to the side and seized the screen with his gloved hands. 'Oil, sir!' He cocked his head and sniffed like a hunting-dog. '*You got him!*'

Howard stared at him blankly as his mind explored the pattern. 'Perhaps – we'll probably never know. Releasing oil is an old trick of theirs.'

'No contact, sir!'

The boatswain's mate coughed nervously. 'W/T office is waitin', sir!'

'Yes.' He thought about climbing into his chair but the effort was too much. 'Reply. *Am rejoining convoy. One U-Boat possibly sunk.*'

He heard Treherne rapping out the change of course and speed to the wheel-house and said, 'We can't claim a kill, but it will give the others some comfort.'

The U-Boat might still slip away, he thought. But it was already damaged, and would have a hard time of it to reach port in Norway.

Hitting back, instead of taking it all the time.

It was what it was all about. He found that he was in his tall unsheltered chair again.

Treherne said, 'I'll get some hot drinks laid on for the gun crews and watch-keepers.' He turned away, shaking his head. The captain was fast asleep.

5

Bright Face of Danger

'Afternoon watch closed up at defence stations, sir.'

Lieutenant Finlay nodded. 'Very good.'

The new watchkeepers moved restlessly, or glanced at one another as if to reassure themselves.

The yeoman pointed over the screen and said to his youngest signalman, 'Just you watch the commodore's ship, see?' He saw the instant anxiety on the youth's face and added·abruptly, 'I'm goin' to th' mess for some mungie – my guts are pleadin' for grub!' He touched his arm. 'Call if you need me.'

Howard was moving along the port gratings, lifting his binoculars every so often, watching the convoy, his ship, and the faces around him. They had found the convoy in the early dawn, with the promised snow-flurries outlining the bridge and gun mountings like pieces of a giant cake.

He raised the glasses and studied the distant columns of ships, partly lost in the irregular flurries of snow. He had noticed the change in the pattern on the radar as soon as they had caught up. Two more ships gone; one, hit by the torpedo, had burst into flames and after losing steerage way had somehow collided with the American tanker *John L. Morgan*. It must have been an agonising decision for the commodore, to steam on and leave the entangled vessels blazing together in a single pyre until that last explosion they had heard when hunting the submarine. What a hideous way to die. One corvette had boldly attempted a rescue and pulled seventeen survivors from the blazing sea. It was not many for two such large ships.

Someone handed him a mug of hot, sweet tea; so much sugar you could almost stand a spoon in it.

He leaned over the littered chart table and massaged his tired eyes until they focussed properly.

What had happened to the U-Boats? Was it possible, after all, that the one which had been damaged and then driven deep by *Gladiator*'s onslaught of depth-charges had been the only one close enough to shadow the convoy, and home others onto the precious targets?

He tried to think like the U-Boat's commander but found, not for the first time, that he could not. But he *might*, he just might have tossed caution aside when the fog had drifted protectively over the plodding columns of merchant-men, more afraid of missing the chance of a shot at them than of anything else.

It was like the scales of justice, he thought vaguely. You added the pros and measured the cons against them.

The commodore had decided to make his own judgement and altered course east-south-east sooner than expected. It would cut a day off their final passage, and if the U-Boats were elsewhere, there might still be a few odds in their favour.

He straightened his back and looked at the sky, knowing the young signalman was watching him despite the yeoman's advice.

A strange day. The sky was full of low cloud and the snow still swirled over the bridge, making the nearest ships difficult to recognise. That was good. Beyond the clouds he could see lighter, brighter patches, as if the sun might try to break through. He smiled grimly. That was bad.

What a barren place. It was impossible to see it set against all the other war fronts. Here, they were totally isolated and alone. Going on and on, with nothing gained by previous Russian convoys to offer even a hint of encouragement.

He wondered how his father was making out in the little house in Hampshire. Even if he owned a car, the petrol ration would have been denied him. There were local village shops, of course, but if he had swallowed his pride he could have visited one of the several naval establishments. There was one situated quite near, well outside the tempting target of Portsmouth, where he would surely have been offered some extra rations. No, he was not the type.

Howard's mother had died immediately after the Great War from the devastating 'flu epidemic which had followed the Armistice. He could remember little more than a shadow of her now. His brother, Robert, three years his senior, had often tried to describe her to him; instead she had become even more of a stranger.

Robert was an acting-commander now, on a course in Portland before being offered one of the new escorts, as second-in-command of a whole group. He would likely have found a billet nearby for his wife Lilian. That would mean the Guvnor, as they called their father, was all on his own. *Unless* . . . There had been another woman after their mother had died; maybe more than one. It was like entering the Navy in this family, he thought; you never really questioned it.

In his mind he could see him now. So different from here. Spring over Portsdown Hill and in the many villages lying off the Portsmouth Road which sailors had used for centuries.

The Guvnor had lost himself in his garden, digging for victory, so that he was almost self-supporting. What he did not need he shared with his old chum, Mister Mills. Howard could never recall his being called by any other name. An army veteran from that other terrible war, who nearly caused a riot in their quiet village by running the engines of his little van on Armistice Day while everyone else stood in respectful silence, heads bared, faces sad.

When someone had accused him of insulting the dead, Mister Mills, not a big man, had seized him by his lapels and had retorted hotly, 'What d'*you* know, eh? An' what do all those po-faced hypocrites know? You bloody well tell me that!'

He had served in Flanders, the Menin Gate, the lot. He knew well enough. They made a strange but companionable pair, Howard thought.

A voicepipe muttered tinnily and Sub-Lieutenant Bizley snapped, 'Forebridge?'

Howard paused with an unfilled pipe half drawn from his duffel coat pocket. It was amazing how the past few days had changed Bizley in some way. Tougher, more confident, and yet . . .

Bizley faced him, his face and eyebrows wet with dissolving snow.

'W/T, sir. From Admiralty, *Most Immediate. A large enemy surface unit has left Tromsø, heading West.*'

Howard returned to the chart and remarked, 'Not many other ways they could go, I'd have thought.' It gave him precious seconds to think, to escape their eyes as they listened to Bizley's clipped voice.

'When? Does it say?'

He pictured the other escort skippers like himself, the big Canadian in his Tribal Class *Beothuck*, Spike Colvin in their sister-ship *Ganymede*, all studying their charts, measuring the distances, weighing the chances.

Bizley returned from the voicepipe. 'Not known, sir.'

Howard stared at the jagged outline of Norway's north-west coast. The big warships had often used the Tromsø anchorage, *Scharnhorst* and *Hipper*, even the biggest of them all, *Bismarck*. It made good sense because of the heavily defended airfield there.

Perhaps this was the moment the Home Fleet had been anticipating, and their own heavy units were already smashing through the Arctic waters to seek out the enemy, cut them off from their base.

Over his shoulder he said, 'Call Pilot to the bridge, Sub.'

What men had braved capture and torture to provide this piece of intelligence? But where free people were oppressed, there would always be the brave few to outshine the collaborators and the black-marketeers.

'Sir?' Treherne's heavy boots thudded across the bridge while he brushed some biscuit crumbs from his beard. He listened to Howard's news and said, 'I think we've slipped past the U-Boats, sir. The one we put down – ' he grinned at Howard's frown, 'but can't "claim" must have been the only boat close enough to matter.' His grin vanished. 'As to this signal of joy from the Admiralty – well, we were sort of expecting it.'

Howard shrugged. Treherne was never afraid to speak his mind, to admit if he was wrong. Marrack was an excellent first lieutenant, but you could never imagine him admitting being wrong about anything.

'The Russians are supposed to be sending additional support for the last part of the trip.' He saw the scepticism in Treherne's eyes and added, 'But we have to be prepared to crack it on alone. We're in range of enemy aircraft all the rest of the way now, and tomorrow the Home Fleet will begin to withdraw.'

Treherne grimaced. 'Poor old Jack. Pull up the ladder, as usual!' He saw a shaft of hard sunlight lance off the gyrocompass and looked at the sky. 'All we have going for us is that we've lost them. So far.'

Howard stared ahead towards the elegant *Lord Martineau*, but the commodore's ship was still in visible.

Aloud he said slowly, 'The Boss knows a thing or two. But being blown up makes you careful.'

Treherne eyed him wryly. 'Also, sir, despite the RNR handle, he's still a merchant navy man at heart!'

The yeoman climbed onto the bridge and banged his gloved hands together. He studied the young signalman and said angrily, 'What did I *tell* you afore I went for some grub, Rosie?'

Howard turned aside to look at him and saw the youth staring over the screen, just as the starboard lookout reached the end of his own sector.

Ordinary Signalman Rosie Lee was almost incapable of speech, let alone the words of identification he had learned since he had completed his training. He pointed blindly and gasped, '*There!*' He swung round and looked at his captain and repeated, 'There, sir!'

Howard realised that it was the same signalman who had reported that other aircraft, the one that had directed the U-Boats. Even as he thought about it the starboard lookout swivelled his powerful glasses on their mounting and shouted, '*Aircraft*, sir! Bearing Green eight-oh, angle of sight three-oh, movin' right to left!'

Every man squinted into the patch of hard light where the reflected sky gave the sea its only pretence of warmth.

Howard found it as it flew, so very slowly; or so it appeared on a parallel track, like some huge disinterested bird.

He said, 'Signal the commodore.' Howard kept his words to a minimum so there would be no hint of despair. They had got this far, and had lost only three of their charges. *Until now.*

Disinterested this aircraft was not. He had watched them so many times circling a convoy in the Atlantic, close enough to see everything, but keeping out of range of the guns while homing the U-Boat pack onto their victim. It was a Focke-Wulf Condor, that great four-engined long-range reconnaissance bomber that had made history at sea between plane and submarine.

'From commodore, sir. *Increase to fourteen knots. Stand by for alteration of course.*'

They all turned as a sudden throaty roar thundered across the water like a marauding aircraft. It was the solitary Hurricane perched on its catapult, smoke darting around it while men cowered away, their reason and purpose lost in distance.

Howard said, 'The commodore's sending him in pursuit, for God's sake.' He looked away in case the others saw his sudden anger. This was not the Atlantic, and the Focke-Wulfe was within easy reach of its airfield and support.

Treherne observed mildly, 'He might catch the bastard, sir.'

Howard knew that Marrack and Ayres had come to the bridge but he was alone in his thoughts as he said, 'Tell W/T to make this request at once to the commodore. From *Gladiator. Request you withhold aircraft until –* '

He turned on his heels as the Hurricane roared along the catapult, dipped momentarily towards the eager water, and then climbed rapidly towards the clouds.

'Belay that!' Howard watched the fighter getting smaller and smaller until it was lost in another flurry of light snow.

The commodore wouldn't have listened anyway. A young man he had never met, and he had just seen him thrown away. 'For bloody nothing!' He realised that he had spoken the last thought aloud and added, 'Prepare the sea-boat, Number One. It'll be too dark to see anything soon.' He stared at the patch of bright sky, now so treacherous and empty.

Treherne asked quietly, 'Shall I sound off action stations, sir?'

'No, I shouldn't think so. They're in no hurry now. They've got all the time in the world.'

A boatswain's mate called, 'Sea-boat lowering party standing by, sir. The first lieutenant and th' Buffer are in charge.'

They all looked at the clouds and Howard heard the far-off trapping sound of machine guns. Like woodpeckers on a summer's afternoon.

Treherne watched him. 'He could stand a chance, sir?'

'Perhaps.' So Treherne was thinking of the pilot, and not his hopeless mission. He looked at the young signalman and tried to smile but his mouth felt rigid. 'Good work, Lee.' If only he would stop staring; his eyes seemed to fill his face.

There was no sound of a distant explosion or the great four-engined bomber dropping through the clouds. It was as if neither plane had ever been. Only the empty catapult made it a lie.

The Hurricane when it reappeared raised a cheer from some of the boat-handling party who waited by the whaler's falls while the crew in their oilskins and lifejackets prepared to be dropped into the water alongside. The cheer died instantly as the Hurricane dipped and then fought its way up again, the engine coughing and roaring out suddenly with fresh hope, as if the plane and not a man were dying.

The pilot managed to turn towards the slow-moving destroyer; it was usually Tail-end Charlie they were told to make for. Perhaps he could even see the men at the falls, the whaler already swung out above the sea, finding hope, praying.

There was a chorus of shouts as the plane staggered suddenly, then seemed to tilt right over on to one wingtip before hitting the water. It exploded in a livid fireball while fragments showered all around it. Then there was just the drifting smoke. Then nothing.

Howard said, 'Secure the sea-boat. Increase revolutions to resume station, Pilot.' He hung on to the rail beneath the screen and was as close to vomiting as he could remember.

He heard his orders being passed, the increased tremble of the bridge and fittings around and below him.

When he spoke his voice was calm again. Too calm. 'Make to commodore, *Aircraft lost. Pilot killed.*' He wanted to scream it out loud, as if the commodore and all those others might hear. Instead he climbed into his chair and held it all back. He could even offer a smile of sorts. Perhaps the cynical Mister Mills had been right after all.

'From commodore, sir. *Alter course in succession. Steer one-four-zero degrees.*'

By the compass platform Treherne filled an extra pipe with pusser's tobacco and watched the quiet preparations around him. *Gladiator* was at action stations and had been since the first hint of daylight. He saw Ayres at the voicepipe which connected him with Midshipman Esmonde and Morgan, his navigator's yeoman. They would be watching the plot-table, ready to change to a different scale of chart. To perform miracles up here if the whole bridge party was wiped out.

The captain was standing by his chair, his pipe well alight, the wind burning it away in minutes. He looked less tired now, Treherne thought. It was something he had never got used to with Howard. The prospect of action, set against the chance of surviving the day; his reactions were never what Treherne expected.

He often wondered if the captain had a girl somewhere. If so, he kept her safely stowed away. Treherne thought of his own wife, Carol, who had just walked out of his life after two years of marriage. He didn't understand that either; she was, after all, a sailor's daughter. He smiled to himself. Maybe that was the reason. Maybe she wanted something more in her life than hello and goodbye.

Treherne had been born and raised in the little port of Fowey. He had always wanted to go to sea, even as a nipper. It was in his blood; almost every family around that busy harbour had a sailor in its midst. It seemed natural, expected, perhaps that he should choose one of the local china-clay steamers for his first step. But he soon lost his heart to the deep-water ships, and the lure of the Caribbean had taken him all the way.

When his ship, packed to the deck seams with bananas, had crossed and recrossed the great Western Ocean, he had never thought that those same waters might one day be a terrible enemy, not only to him and his companions, but the one real, unbeatable menace to his country.

He felt the deck lift and slide as *Gladiator* came round on the new course and he heard Howard speaking with the coxswain in the wheelhouse. *The team.* Boots on a ladder and a welcome clatter of mugs as they waited for the promised hot tea in its dented fanny.

Here and there a light flickered in the convoy or there was a stammer of static from the W/T office voicepipe.

The commodore was getting jumpy. Rounding up his flock while one of the wing escorts entered the convoy and steamed fussily up the ranks of heavily laden ships. Demanding more speed and less smoke, telling one of the masters to watch his course, another to acknowledge signals and not just take it as read.

It was funny if you thought about it. Treherne was a highly-skilled navigating officer like so many RNR people who had once served in peaceful ships. He knew the dangers and the stupidity of some masters who preferred to go their own way, but he still resented the manner in which they were chased around by the Navy. They were, after all, civilians; they were also well aware that they were themselves the main targets. Bomb, torpedo, or the impartial mine – they faced it all, and still went back for more.

He realised that Howard had joined him, his pipesmoke thinning as he took another long puff. I must be getting shagged out, Treherne thought. I didn't even see him move.

Howard eyed him thoughtfully. 'Any views, Pilot?'

Treherne grinned and felt his skin crinkle where he had once got frost-bite in the North Atlantic. One of the reasons he had grown a full set.

'I think it'll be today, sir.'

Howard glanced at the men around him. Hands reached out for mugs to be filled, but the lookouts never took their eyes from their various sectors.

'I agree. No more signals about the German ship out of Tromsø. No bloody news of anything!' He seemed to make up his mind. 'You know what I think? They're going to come at us from the air.'

They both looked up at the fast-moving wisps of cloud. The sky would be properly blue when the day finally opened up. No cover.

The young signalman Rosie Lee stared up with them, as if to see something terrible there. But he heard Treherne chuckle and saw him hand his tobacco pouch to the captain. It was all right after all.

'God, look at the sun!'

Howard turned and saw the two funnels slowly light up like burnished copper as the first rays spilled from the horizon. It was as if the light were being poured across it, molten metal over a dam.

Faces became personalities again, the muzzles and barrels of the anti-aircraft guns shone as the sunlight played over the glistening ice and the huddled figures of their crews.

Treherne glanced at the White Ensign as it flapped out stiffly from the gaff. Their sea-going one, torn and shredded by a hundred gales. It could not last much longer. The yeoman of signals had a system. The best ensigns were used only in harbour, and for covering the dead awaiting burial. After that they took their chances aloft.

A boatswain's mate by the voicepipes called sharply, 'From commodore, sir! *Aircraft sighted at Red four-five. Four miles.*' He was squinting with concentration as he pressed his ear to the pipe. '*Believed to be Focke-Wulf Condor again.*'

Treherne thought of the exploding Hurricane. 'Cheeky bastard!'

But Howard's mind was exploring another route. The commodore was using his radio more than usual to save time. *Because he knows.* There was no hiding-place now.

He heard the crump-crump-crump of gunfire, far away beyond the head of the convoy. That would be the RCN's *Beothuck*; she mounted eight four-point-sevens in twin turrets. Most destroyers like *Gladiator* mounted only four. There was virtually no chance of hitting the German reconnaissance bomber, but the escort commander would let fly just to break the tension. The anger and frustration of seeing the big aircraft flying lazily around the convoy, just out of useful range, close enough to count the ships then radio back a full report. Loosing off a few shells was better than nothing.

He heard signalman Lee murmur, 'I'll bet it's the same one I saw!' He made it sound suddenly personal.

A voice yelled, 'There it goes, Green four-five, angle of sight two-five!' Right across the path of the convoy. But the sun was so harsh and bright that the aircraft only showed occasionally, like a sliver of glass or bright metal.

Howard lowered his binoculars, his eyes stinging. They would have a perfect view from up there, he thought. He tried to remember all the lectures he had endured on aircraft recognition. How many were there in a Condor's crew? It was eight. Probably sitting in the sunlight, sipping *erzatz* coffee while they speculated on their chances of getting back to base in time for lunch.

A party of men scampered down the starboard side, one with a big Red Cross satchel bouncing on his hip. Another part of the ship's intricate pattern, like the damage control party which would be waiting to douse fires, shore up bulkheads, patch holes while their messmates fought the guns. The six survivors would be doing their best, although one was so badly burned that he could scarcely move. Prosser, the sick berth attendant, had given him some bandages to unpack in case they were needed. It was very likely the same in the other ships which had managed to snatch up some survivors. To sit and do nothing, in pain or not, was worse than being occupied; work kept you from thinking the ship that had saved you might be the next one to catch it.

Sub-Lieutenant Ayres lowered his glasses and wiped his eyes with a glove. His breath poured through the blue and red scarf around his neck and mouth so that it looked like steam. Little gems of ice clung to the scarf as his breath froze on it.

He had seen the slow-moving aircraft, now a mere speck above the hard horizon. 'The bright face of danger.' He said it without emotion, his tone almost matter-of-fact.

Treherne looked at him searchingly. He guessed the scarf was part of the earlier Ayres. The schoolboy.

'What was that, Sub?'

Ayres gave a little shrug. 'Something I had to learn once.'

Howard moved to the forepart of the bridge. He knew what the big, bearded navigator was thinking. Ayres could easily give up right now. There was no fear any more. You only felt fear when you retained some hope of survival.

'From commodore, sir! *Aircraft approaching from Green one-five –* ' The rest was lost in the din of commands and the crisp Scottish voice of Finlay in his control position.

Howard looked at his bridge team. 'We shall close the convoy to offer anti-aircraft support. Revs for twenty-five knots, Pilot.'

He felt his ship begin to quiver as Lieutenant (E) Evan Price, the son of a Swansea collier, opened the throttles on his thirty-four thousand shaft horse-power like a man raising weir gates on a flooded river.

'Aircraft, sir! Bearing Green three-oh, angle of sight two-oh!'

Finlay's voice, calm and unhurried over the bridge speaker: 'Twenty-plus bandits! All guns stand by!'

Howard stood high on the forward gratings and watched A- and B-guns swinging onto their targets. The snick of metal, a man's quick, nervous cough like one in church before the sermon.

Finlay again. '*Barrage!*' He was speaking to one of his men but had left the speaker switch down. 'Ju 88's. Coming low. Feeling their way.'

Howard lifted his glasses. By excluding all the other ships it felt as if *Gladiator* was completely alone. He stared at the two arrowheads of aircraft. The sky was full of them, or appeared to be.

'From commodore, sir. *Open fire at will.*'

A seaman gave a tight laugh. 'Who's Will, then?'

'Barrage – *Commence!*'

Howard let the glasses fall to his chest and took a deep breath. *Here they come.* He heard the staccato crash of guns over the convoy, and as Finlay passed his order the bridge shook to the instant response from the main armament.

Howard saw the convoy spreading out on either bow, as if *Gladiator* would charge unchecked into its midst.

But he heard Treherne passing his orders, the bow-wave easing slightly. Below the bridge he heard the next shells clanging into the breeches. 'Gunlayer – target!' Then, 'Trainer – target!'

'*Shoot!*'

The sky was already pockmarked with drifting balls of smoke, as if it were indelibly stained and would never regain its colour.

Howard looked at the solid lines of merchantmen, their grey and dazzle-painted escorts weaving around them, automatics and close-range weapons blazing their challenge.

He said quietly, 'No, we are not alone.'

The leading aircraft thundered overhead, their wings reflecting the cones of tracer around them as they screamed towards the ships.

Then came the first bombs.

Chief Petty Officer Bob Sweeney, *Gladiator*'s coxswain, eased the wheel carefully as the wheelhouse shook and rattled to the crash of gunfire. Despite the steel shutters across the ports and windows the air was already filled with acrid smoke from the bridge Oerlikons as they kept up their harsh rattle, pausing only briefly for the loading number to slam on a fresh magazine.

On either side of Sweeney's thickset figure the telegraphs were manned by Bully Bishop, the chief quartermaster, and an able seaman named Melvin. A messenger crouched by the voicepipes while Midshipman Esmonde and the navigator's yeoman wedged themselves in a corner behind the vibrating plot-table.

Sweeney listened to the voices from the upper bridge, a shout from one of the lookouts followed instantly by more rapid fire from the main armament as well as other ships nearby.

He growled, 'Easy, lads. 'Ere they come!'

He concentrated on the ticking gyro-repeater and tried not to think of the bombers as they streaked towards the convoy. When *Gladiator* had been released from the Atlantic run to carry out a much-needed overhaul, Sweeney had gone home on leave. It was more of a formality than any sort of comfort. He no longer *had* a home, and his patient, long-suffering wife was buried in one of the East End's big communal graves.

It had been an eerie experience even for him, and he had seen just about everything from the Spanish Civil War to Dunkirk, from the Western Ocean to North Cape.

The worst part had been that he had not known where he was. The streets where he had grown to boyhood before joining the Andrew, where most of his relations had lived, worked, or been on the fiddle, had simply ceased to exist. A desert of flattened and burned bricks, the roads only marked by their broken kerb stones.

A sympathetic ARP warden had pointed out the place where his house had been. There was not even any wallpaper to show him its exact position.

'Hard a-starboard!'

'Hard a-starboard, sir!' The wheel seemed to spin in his meaty hands. 'Thirty of starboard wheel on!'

Boots skidded on the metal plates as the deck tilted hard over and Esmonde almost fell headlong, his face like a sheet.

'*Midships*!' Sweeney ground his teeth together as the bombs screamed overhead. The Old Man sounded cool enough. Just as bloody well. He added, 'Revolutions one-one-zero!'

The chain of dull explosions seemed to lift Sweeney off his feet, and he sensed that some of the bombs must have found their targets.

Bully Bishop exclaimed harshly, 'Why th' hell don't we go faster, 'Swain?'

Sweeney nodded warningly at the bell-mouthed voicepipe. 'Keep yer voice down! Wot's got into you then? 'Ad a bellyful already?'

Esmonde touched the navigator's yeoman's arm and felt him jump.
'Why don't we?'

Morgan eyed him wearily. 'Cause we've got to stick with the merchantmen!'

Sweeney heard the captain again. 'Steady on one-seven-zero.'

Someone whispered, 'Oh God, here they come again!'

Sweeney ignored him and listened to the muted beat of engines. Ju 88's, Guns had said. Twin-engined and heavily armed. They were no strangers to Sweeney. Again that insane scream of bombs, and over it all a mad cheer from one of the voicepipes. '*Got the bastard!*'

The explosion must have been almost alongside. Morgan jerked open a shutter in time to see a huge aircraft wing complete with black cross as it disappeared past the bridge.

Sweeney snapped, 'Shut that, Morgan! Don't want a splinter in me guts!'

How long it lasted he had no idea; he never once took his eyes from the compass to consult the wheelhouse clock. Smoke eddied around them until caught and dispersed by the fans, and their aching bodies were spotted with deckhead paint like snow.

'*Full ahead together!*'

Sweeney hid his relief as the telegraphs sent their message to the engineroom. Christ, he thought, the chief and his mob would be feeling it down there. You would never hear a bomb or see a torpedo until the side caved in and you were scalded to death.

The revolutions mounted and Sweeney tried to picture what was happening. A gong rattled sharply through the din of engines and gunfire, and for a moment he thought he had gone deaf.

'Cease firing!'

They stared at one another in disbelief. Morgan said thickly, 'Near thing.'

'Revolutions seven-zero.' Just as promptly the speed began to drop away. Howard must be standing right by the voicepipe, Sweeney thought.

'Sea-boat's crew, Pilot! Doctor to the bridge at the double!' Then he said, 'Cox'n up here, please.'

Sweeney automatically made to wipe the paint flakes from his cap and duffel coat. 'Take over, Bully.'

After the trapped confinement of the wheelhouse the sky seemed unnaturally bright through a great undulating pall of smoke.

Sweeney climbed the ladder, past the starboard Oerlikon where the crew were re-loading and checking over the firing mechanism, their eyes wild and glaring.

Sweeney had seen pictures of similar faces in his father's old books about the Western Front. Faces driven beyond hope, even despair, with only the madness left; the need to kill.

Sweeney stepped through the bridge gate and stared at the scene ahead of the ship with stunned dismay.

The convoy was scattered into uneven straggling lines, and the oil-covered swell was covered with the flotsam of battle. Broken lifeboats and packing-cases, bodies and men still, unbelievably, alive as they foundered towards the destroyer moving amongst them. Sweeney kept his face hard and expressionless as he saw the others: pieces of men, no longer human, just things.

He touched his cap. 'Sir?'

Howard swung towards him, seeing him for the first time. 'I'd like you to take over aft, 'Swain. Sort the wounded out in the wardroom.' He tried to smile but it did not reach his eyes. 'You know what to do.'

Sweeney shaded his face to study a dark shape in the far distance. The keel of an upturned freighter. There were men there too, some standing on the stricken hull. Sailors were often like that. Unwilling to quit their ship even at the end.

Howard said, 'You did well, 'Swain.' He lowered his eyes and stared at his sleeve. 'We lost seven merchantmen.'

Sweeney watched him gravely. A third of the convoy wiped out since they had left Iceland. God alone knew how many blokes had gone with them. He asked, 'Did we get any of *them*, sir?'

Howard stood motionless and stared at the drifting smoke. 'Two, and a probable.' He faced the coxswain. 'Pretty good deal for Jerry, I'd have thought?'

Marrack clattered onto the bridge, his nose probing around. 'Sea-boat ready for lowering, sir.'

His expression asked, *Is it wise?* But one look at Howard's despair gave him his answer.

Petty Officer Tucker levelled his telescope above the gently shivering screen. 'From commodore, sir!'

Treherne said heavily, 'I thought they'd done for him too.' He sounded dazed by it, sickened at the simplicity of slaughter.

Tucker continued relentlessly, '*Am abandoning ship.*'

Howard raised his glasses and found the elegant *Lord Martineau* drifting bows-on in a bank of smoke. There were flames too. She had been straddled several times by bombs, and with her massive cargo of tanks and armoured vehicles she would go suddenly when the time came.

'*Beothuck* is standing by to take off survivors.'

Howard saw the foremast and derricks topple over the side, the noise lost in the distance. *Eight then.* In what? An attack which had lasted only two hours.

He crossed to the other side and peered down at the deck where the whaler was already swinging above the sea, its crew grim-faced; hating it, not wanting to be left by their own ship.

'Lower away!' Marrack was standing on a washdeck locker, hands on hips, his nose trained towards the men at the boat's falls.

Howard said, 'Dead slow.'

'Vast lowering! Out pins!' Marrack watched as the oily swell rose evenly below the whaler's keel. '*Slip!*' The slender hull hit the water and with the helm lashed over was guided away from the destroyer's side by the long boatrope from the forecastle.

Howard forgot them and looked at the scattered convoy. Here and there a lamp stammered amongst the smoke, and the big tug was somehow managing to take a freighter in tow. The damaged vessel's bows were so deep in the water that her screw was lifted cleanly above the surface.

He watched the commodore's ship give another shudder, her stern sinking even as he watched. The strange hull of *Tromp II*, the makeshift anti-aircraft vessel, steamed slowly across his vision. But for her, the Germans could have wiped out the whole convoy. No bother at all. By the time she had passed, the commodore's ship was almost gone, obscene bubbles bursting around her as her heavy cargo began to break free and complete her destruction.

Treherne said, 'Escort commander has ordered the corvettes to carry out another sweep, sir, while the rescue goes on.'

'Good decision, Pilot, and a brave man to make it.' He said it with the bitterness which held him like a vice. All this way, and for nothing. It was a game where one player held all the aces. The Home Fleet support group had stayed well clear because of the U-Boat reports, and had retained their carrier for their own protection. The large enemy surface ship had failed to appear, and it was unlikely she would know that the Kola Inlet was so near. She was probably back in harbour. Another ruse, then?

'Stop engines!' He heard the Buffer's rough voice bellowing at his men at the scrambling nets and bowlines.

The gasping, anonymous faces in the sea alongside, soaked in oil, bloody and nearly done for.

I should be too used to it to care. But I do care. He found he was gripping the cold steel so hard that his fingers cracked.

Treherne said, 'Have another fill of mine, sir?' He was holding out his tobacco pouch, concerned. 'I'll join you in that first Horse's Neck when we get back, sir. If I may?'

Howard took the pouch but did not speak. Treherne knew he could not. Dare not.

Ayres moved silently to his side and whispered, 'I've never seen anything so terrible!'

Treherne made certain Howard was out of earshot and noticed that he had not managed to fill his pipe.

'Well, my lad, Winston Churchill has promised our wonderful allies, the Russians, that we shall push a convoy through to Murmansk every three weeks.' He turned his gaze from Howard's stooped shoulders. 'Can you imagine anything so bloody crazy, Sub? Like the Germans trying to send a convoy up the Thames Estuary!' He spat it out. '*The bloody bastards!*' But Ayres did not really understand who he meant.

The whaler was picking its way through the drifting wreckage, the carnage. They were still doing it when a Russian unit of six destroyers and a tug came to join them for the rest of the way.

'Tea, sir?'

Howard turned in his chair and took the chipped mug with great care.

The Russian senior officer and *Beothuck*'s captain were exchanging signals, while the convoy gathered its strength and tried to take up its positions again.

'Ready to proceed, sir!' Marrack was calm, as usual. 'We should be in port by dawn.'

But Howard was listening to the port Oerlikon gunner, who was squatting below his mounting and banging his gloved hands together in time with a quiet lament, which he recognised was sung to the tune of 'What a Friend We Have in Jesus.'

> When this bloody war is over
> Oh how happy I shall be,
> But we're here today and gone tomorrow,
> So let's get back to bloody sea . . .

6

When Do You Leave?

The great stretch of the natural harbour was the colour of dirty pewter, so that the craggy hills and fjords seemed without life or movement. Narvik, once a busy Norwegian port, was partly hidden in mist, and there was no horizon to separate land from sky.

The apparent lifelessness of the place was an illusion. Even as another snow-flurry blotted out some of the small houses above the harbour, a fighter roared out of the shadows, her engine shaking the hills and cutting a sharp passage across the sea's face.

The submarine moved slowly, her powerful diesels throbbing as if, like a wounded beast, she was returning to her lair to recover. There was barely any wash, and the men who stood on her casing, muffled to the eyes in their heavy clothing, watched the approach of land, some probably regarding it as some kind of miracle.

When the small minesweeper pushed abeam and tooted to them, nobody moved or returned the waves of welcome and admiration.

There were no such gestures from some nearby fishing-boats, for this was an occupied country where it was wiser not to display any feelings at all. A big launch detached itself from the powdery snow and surged to meet the incoming U-Boat, a lamp already stabbing through the gloom, so that the long, shark-like outline turned slightly to starboard as if on an invisible towrope.

At the rear of the conning-tower, on the 'bandstand', a flag had suddenly appeared, scarlet with black cross and swastika to match the ones on the launch and minesweeper.

By the periscope standard the submarine's commander turned his head to stare up at it, sharing the moment with the rest of his men. There would be other eyes watching from the land, he thought. Spies, terrorists, who would be quick to send word by their forbidden radios to London, to report their presence. Their survival.

With a kind of defiance the German threw off his weather-proof hood and jammed his white-topped cap on to his untidy hair. The white cap, the mark of a U-Boat commander.

They might even see the extent of the damage, he thought. He touched the side of the bridge, the buckled plating, the holes punched through it by cannon fire while they had gone into a steep dive. One man had been hit by splinters and had died a few moments after they had gone under. If the enemy's attacks had continued the sailor's corpse, with some more fuel, could have been sent to the surface. That might have convinced them.

Kapitänleutnant Manfred Kleiber had been in submarines for most of his naval service. He was now twenty-six years old, and until that last attack had never really considered the real possibility of being killed himself. It happened to others, for theirs was a dangerous trade.

But this time things had gone wrong; and he still searched his mind, trying to discover if he had failed in some way.

They had sailed from Kiel after a short refit to make their way north around the Faeroes, through the *Rosegarten* and then down to a new base on the French coast near Lorient. A change from these bitter seas, with only cold stares and hostility to greet a U-Boat's return. But he had received orders redirecting him to find and shadow the convoy. To keep pace with it, he had had to surface, and had been very aware of the dangers afforded by the ice and what it could do.

He had known the vents to freeze solid in Arctic waters, so that a U-Boat was unable to dive and would lie surfaced until an enemy flying-boat or bomber found her.

They had fired at extreme range, knowing it was the only chance to slow down the convoy, to fight for time to home other U-Boats to the area. Now he knew differently: that the other boats had been sent after the heavy British war ships to the north-west.

He had taken his boat into a dive, barely knowing if the damage from the torpedo which had exploded prematurely was fatal; realising only that he had done his best, and had managed to send one more precious supply ship to the bottom.

Even as he had reached up to pull the upper hatch behind him, and the tracer had shone so vividly in the dying seaman's blood, he had seen the destroyer ploughing over the sea towards him as if all else was excluded and it was a personal fight to the death.

When the hydroplanes had finally responded and the water had thundered into the saddle-tanks, Kleiber had retained that picture starkly in his mind. And later, while he had used every trick and skill which had managed to keep him and his men alive, he had recalled the destroyer's number as it shone in the bright tracers like the dead man's blood. H–38. He had looked it up in his soiled and well-used copy of *Weyers Kriegs-Flotten*: his bible. So now he had one up on the enemy which had so nearly sent them down into the crushing depths for the last time. HMS *Gladiator*.

But for the damage caused by the explosion Kleiber knew he would have had another attempt to find the convoy. And H–38.

Boots grated on the casing and he saw the seamen gathering up the mooring wires, kicking them free of ice.

Kleiber glanced around the narrowing anchorage. They could not stop here. It would be back to Kiel again to put matters right. By the time they eventually reached their French base it would be summer. They said there was fresh butter, wine and good food a-plenty in France. Women too probably, to get his men into more trouble.

He thought of his home in Hamburg. They would all ask, 'Home again? When do you leave?' Maybe it was like that in all navies.

He thought of the thunder and crack of depth-charges. He had grown to accept them, although he had heard that the enemy were acquiring better anti-submarine weapons.

But time was running out for the British. They did not have enough escorts, and could not provide air cover for the convoys where it was most needed. Whereas Germany was building more submarines, faster and bigger than ever before. It was a race which could only have one ending. The Americans could not offer much help; they were too enmeshed in the Pacific, fighting the Japanese and seeing the enemy drawing closer and closer to a homeland which had never known the destruction of war.

The Russians were falling back and the convoys to Murmansk must stop soon. Even the British, desperate, with their backs to the wall, would have to admit defeat there, just as their army was being defeated in the Western Desert. He paused in his private evaluation and passed a few brief orders down to the control room. The first heaving-line snaked through the thinning snow and soon had a wire eye bent on to it.

Kleiber saw the caps and greatcoats of senior officers waiting to come aboard. To hear his part of the game they played at HQ with their flags and coloured counters.

The diesels puffed out choking fumes and shuddered into silence.

Kleiber straightened his oil-stained cap and climbed down to the casing-deck.

'*Besatzung stillgestanden!*'

He saluted his men on the fore-casing, and only then did he turn to meet the visitors.

Respect had to be earned from these men. It did not come only with the white caps.

Lieutenant-Commander David Howard switched off the remaining light in his day cabin and felt his way to one of the scuttles. It took physical effort to unscrew the deadlight and then open the scuttle; weeks and weeks of being tightly secured had seen to that.

He held his face to the air and took several long, deep breaths. It was all so unreal, like the day cabin, or part of a nightmare, the strangle-grip which almost stopped his breathing when the alarm bells screamed out in the night, or when Howard had awakened in his bridge chair, the sky bright from some burning merchantman.

The only light here was a fine edge of deep gold around a solitary cloud, and soon that would be gone as night gave an even denser darkness to the Firth of Clyde.

After the bitter days and nights on the upper bridge the air here felt almost balmy. He strained his eyes as if to see the sprawling town of Greenock beyond the dockyard, but it was sealed-off as tightly as any cupboard. Here and there a boat chugged through the darkness, showing itself occasionally with a bow-wave, or some shaded light as it approached a mooring buoy. After so many weeks of endless duty, *Gladiator* had been sent back to Britain in this, the middle of June.

But not before she had completed another convoy to Murmansk and several hazardous anti-submarine sweeps to clear the way for a second, homeward bound.

He still thought of that convoy which had been the first for many of his company, when they had been attacked by aircraft. There had been one final victim before the ships were taken into the port for unloading. The freighter

Empire Viceroy which had been under tow with her stern high out of the water had gone down quite suddenly within sight of land. So the losses had risen to twelve, nearly half the total number when you considered that the fighter catapult vessel, and the converted anti-aircraft ship *Tromp II* had been counted amongst the thirty to be escorted from Iceland. It was ironic that none of the escorts had lost a man.

Reluctantly, Howard sealed the scuttle again and switched on all the lights. Even this place felt different, he thought. Damp, unlived-in; that was nothing new, but he could sense another change in the whole ship, as if there was surprise and not just relief at being here.

When he had opened the scuttle he had heard music blaring out from the messdecks and W/T office, the buzz of voices through the bulkhead where Marrack would soon assemble the officers and Howard would be invited to join them in what was theoretically their own, private mess.

He stared at the desk, the neat piles of papers and requests he had spent most of the day scrutinising and signing so that Ireland, the petty officer writer, could parcel them up to be collected by the guardboat.

Breakages, losses, reports on machinery and supplies, ammunition and fuel. He had to deal with it, stand in a queue with all the other commanding officers.

He glanced at the cupboard where he kept his personal stock of brandy but decided against it. Not yet anyway.

He crossed to the mirror inside his sleeping cabin and touched his face with his fingers. The first real shave he had had for weeks.

He thought suddenly of his ship's company, and smiled. They would care little for the neat piles of forms and documents. First priority was mail from home. Second, leave.

He watched his eyes as he smiled. Like a stranger. The lines around his mouth, the deep shadows beneath his eyes seemed to smooth out. He was twenty-seven. He had been feeling as old as time. Howard looked at the neat bed which Vallance or a messman would turn down for him. Another rare harbour ritual.

Would it work this time? He stared around with sudden anxiety. His quarters, usually so spacious, seemed to have shrunk so that he felt restrained. He knew it was because of the convoys, where his quarters had been the sea and the sky with only cat-naps in his hutch of a sea cabin to confine him.

He winced as he touched his face again – his freshly shaved skin felt raw and tender. Perhaps Treherne and some of the others had the right idea in growing beards. He thought of young Ayres. They said he did not shave at all yet.

A few familiar faces would be gone when *Gladiator* was committed to her next task. New ones to know and trust, or to have them trust him.

There was a tap at the door and Marrack stepped over the coaming, his cap beneath his elbow. He looked fresh and sleek; 'polished' might describe him best, Howard thought. He had come through it all very well, and had shown little concern for the hatred he had roused by his constant efforts to keep everyone on top line.

Marrack glanced past him at the cabin, like a detective looking for clues. 'All ready, sir.' He gave a brief smile. 'Bar's open.'

With a start Howard realised it was another rarity to see all his wardroom together at once. The place was welcoming and comfortable, with the foul-weather covers removed from the red leather chairs and club fender. All the usual wardroom clutter, pictures of the King and Queen on either side of the ship's crest, a rack of revolvers behind a locked glass door, an empty letter-rack, and beyond the barely swaying curtain which divided it from the dining section, the table, properly laid out, instead of the mugs and slopping dishes which had been common enough in the Arctic. Those officers who had been seated got to their feet, and Howard nodded to them. Another sea-change, he thought. Gilt buttons and ties, instead of filthy sweaters and scuffed boots.

A ship at rest.

Petty Officer Vallance held out a glass to him on a tray. It was filled almost to the top and he guessed it was a Horse's Neck.

Treherne spoke as he raised his own glass. 'The first one – remember, sir?'

Howard drank slowly, although he did not recall what Treherne meant.

'Relax gentlemen.' He perched on the club fender as Vallance and a messman refilled glasses and made notes at the little bar counter to make certain no officer conveniently forgot his mess account.

Howard said, 'I'll tell you what's happening – what *I* know, that is.'

That brought a few grins, except from old Arthur Pym the Gunner (T). In the deckhead lights his bald pate shone like a marker buoy, and his tight-lipped mouth was set in the usual sour disapproval. He looked ancient, and beside Ayres he could have been a grandfather.

Howard continued, 'The Asdic and radar boffins are coming aboard as soon as we move alongside tomorrow forenoon, then there's a boiler clean.' He glanced at the Chief, unrecognisable without his white boiler-suit and grease smudged cap. 'So be ready for the signal.'

It was a miracle how Evan Price and his engineroom crew had kept the shafts spinning in all seas under every kind of pressure. This morning, when they had made fast to a buoy, Price had come to the bridge to stare at the land, drinking it in.

When Howard tried to thank him for his efforts Price had shrugged and had offered his lop-sided grin, something originally caused by a loose wrench when he had first gone to sea, and said, 'I must be mad, sir. My dad was a miner, see? I worked to *better* myself, no down the pit for me, I said!'

Together they had watched the gulls swooping over the masts, sharing their momentary freedom. Then Price had said, 'Look at me now – I spend more time creeping about in the darkness than my Dad ever did!'

Howard saw Vallance taking his empty glass away to refill it. He had barely noticed drinking it. *The old wardroom devil.*

'We've got a list for the dockyard maties to lose themselves in for about . . .' He felt them tense and added, 'Three weeks. So there'll be leave for the port watch and the first part of starboard watch. Number One and the cox'n are already working on it.' He met their various gazes. 'We had the usual signals from Welfare, I'm afraid. Two homes bombed – one, Stoker Marshall, lost his whole family. Such cases get preference, of course.'

He looked at the crest; it enabled him to turn away from their eyes. What a bloody awful thing to happen. One of Evan Price's men. A stoker who had been aboard for over a year. To go through hell, half-expecting death to come bursting into the racing machinery, then to get back and be told about his family.

And for what? He remembered the smouldering anger of the Canadian escort commander who had come aboard in Murmansk. The commodore had died of wounds shortly after making his last signal and *Beothuck*'s captain had assumed overall charge. He had been ashore to discuss berthing and fuelling for the escorts, and the Russians had barely been interested. When he had told them something of the losses, the sacrifice in men and ships, one had merely commented, 'Then Captain, you should send more ships!'

The Russians had refused to allow them into their base at Polynaroe, but Howard had been expecting that. Worse, they had not permitted the landing of some of the badly wounded and disabled survivors.

And it was still going on, exactly as they had left it. One convoy, which had been reduced to three-and-a-half knots by a gale-force head-wind, had been attacked by aircraft and destroyers from Norway because some of the escorts had been running out of fuel and were detached to head for the Faeroes to top up their bunkers. A third of that convoy had been scattered and sunk.

You should send more ships.

He tore his mind from the shrieking bombs and the stricken freighters lurching out of line, sinking or on fire.

'This is confidential. After taking on new equipment and some replacements for our company, we shall join a newly-formed escort-group for a working-up period, yet to be decided. Questions?'

Finlay asked, 'Back to the Atlantic after that, sir?' So casually put, like a man asking about the cricket score.

Howard smiled. Finlay, perhaps more than anyone, had actually thrived on their discomfort in the Arctic. It was the first time his department had been able to fire on and actually hit a U-Boat, and the overall gunnery against aircraft had been faultless. He was losing his gunner's mate, who was going for warrant rank ashore, and one of his ordnance mechanics too.

He replied, 'I believe that may be so.' In minutes it would be all over the ship. A spot of leave, then back to the bloody Atlantic. Sugar and poison. He shook his head as Vallance made to refill his glass. Then he said quietly, 'I don't have to drum it into you,' his glance fell on the pink-faced midshipman, 'any of you, after what you have just seen and done. If anyone asks you what you're doing, tell them simply this: you are achieving impossibilities because each and every one of you has become a veteran, *just by being there!*'

Marrack said, 'Thank you, sir. I can speak for the wardroom as a whole, I think.'

Treherne grinned through his beard. 'You will anyway, Number One!'

Marrack frowned slightly. A witness had distracted his brief. 'We all appreciate what you have done, sir.' There was a murmur of approval, even from old Pym. 'We've lost a lot of good ships, but we saved quite a lot too. For myself, I'm proud to be a part of it.'

Nobody laughed at Marrack's remark, and for him it had been an outburst, Howard thought. The tall lieutenant meant every word of it.

Howard moved through them to the door where Petty Officer White, the Buffer, was waiting to do Rounds.

Howard hesitated, then turned away from his own quarters and ran lightly up the ladder to the lobby where Leading Seaman Bishop was leaning over the quartermaster's desk.

Howard could feel Bishop staring after him as he stepped out onto the deck, the breeze of the firth greeting him like an old friend. Had he been thinking that it was hopeless, wasted – marking time while awaiting the inevitable? The thought seemed to shake him bodily. All the parades and the training in peacetime, regattas and girls in low-cut dresses at wardroom parties in the Med. He had since been made to re-learn *everything*, no less completely than men like Marrack and Bizley. What he had been taught in those far-off days had proved utterly useless. Was that how his father's war had been, why Mister Mills had lost control of his feelings on that and probably other Armistice Days?

The shock seemed to steady him in some way. How could he have failed to see that the men who served *Gladiator*, and all those unknown ones who faced death and fear each time they put to sea, were too precious to waste, to be tossed away for nothing?

He remembered the Oerlikon gunner's little ditty. *Here today and gone tomorrow* . . . He gripped the guardrail and stared at the invisible town. '*Well, not if I can bloody well help it!*'

Vallance, who had padded quietly after him from the wardroom, paused and nodded to himself. The Old Man was letting off steam. Thank God for that. I've served a few, he thought, but I'll see the war out with this one.

Back in the wardroom again Vallance realised that Sub-Lieutenant Bizley was still slumped in his chair, some neat gin splashed over his trousers. The others were already sitting around the table, and there was a rare excitement at the prospect of the meal.

'Wake up, sir!' Vallance stepped back as Bizley stared at him, his eyes red-rimmed while he recovered his bearings.

'*What?*' He had been deep in thought when the gin had taken charge. Dreaming of the proposed decoration, what his parents and friends would say. He lurched to his feet, but not before Vallance had made sure he had scribbled his name on a bar-chit.

At the table old Pym was saying, "Course, in them days we didn't 'ave no big searchlights, y'see?'

Finlay peered doubtfully at the soup. 'I expect *you* had oil lamps, eh?'

Treherne reached for the bread, two helpings of it, brought aboard fresh that afternoon from Greenock. He held it to his nose and sighed. *Real bread.*

He saw Pym's watery eyes glaring at the gunnery officer and said easily, 'Go on, T, tell us about Jutland again, when you were in the old *Iron Duke* with Jellicoe.'

Pym regarded him suspiciously and then squinted at the deckhead. 'Well, as I may 'ave told you before, Lord Jellicoe was standin' right beside me when the Jerries opened fire . . .'

Vallance watched him and rubbed his hands while the messmen bustled around the table.

Normal again. Just one big happy family.

The naval van pulled up with a jerk after dodging a mobile crane and a whole squad of marching sailors. The driver called, 'Here she is, Sunshine, the *Gladiator.*'

After a momentary hesitation, the driver, a tough-looking leading seaman from the Railway Transport Office, climbed down to help his last passenger lift his gear from the back. Afterwards he wondered why he had done it; he could not recall helping anyone before.

The young seaman dragged his kitbag and hammock to the side of the jetty and stared slowly along the moored destroyer from bow to stern. She was a powerful-looking ship with fine, rakish lines, very like the ones he had studied in his magazine at school. She appeared to be littered with loose gear, while wires and pipes snaked in all directions and overalled figures groped over them, adding to the confusion with their tools and paint pots.

The driver stood beside him, arms folded, and said, 'She was on the Ruski convoy run 'til recently. In the thick of it.'

He glanced at the youth and wondered. Slightly built, with wide eyes and skin like a young girl. God, he thought, he only looks about thirteen. In fact, ordinary Seaman Andrew Milvain was eighteen, just, but certainly did not look it. In his best uniform, the jean collar still the dark colour it was issued, unlike the Jacks who scrubbed and dhobied them until they were as pale as the sky. Everything was brand new, straight off the production belt. He thought he knew what the driver was thinking, but he had become used to that.

A seaman in belt and gaiters, a heavy pistol hanging at his hip, walked to the guardrails and called, 'One for us, Hookey?'

The man nodded and said to Milvain, 'Off you go, your new home then.'

The youth picked up his bag and small attaché case and the gangway sentry came down the brow to carry his hammock.

The driver made to get into the van and looked back. There was something very compelling about the new seaman. So serious; dedicated, whatever that meant.

The sentry waited for the duty quartermaster to make an appearance and said, 'New hand come aboard to join, Bob.'

They both looked him up and down and the quartermaster asked, 'Where from?'

'Royal Naval Barracks, Chatham.' He had a quiet voice which was almost lost in the din of hammering and squealing tackles.

The quartermaster took his draft chit and studied it. 'Before that?'

'HMS *Ganges*, the training establishment where . . .'

The two seamen grinned. 'Oh, we know where *that* is, right enough.'

The sentry added, 'Where they make mothers' boys into old salts in three months, eh?'

The quartermaster glanced forward. 'I'll tell the Cox'n. You carry the load 'til I get back.'

The sentry grimaced. 'The chiefs and PO's are givin' the gunner's mate a sendoff. I'll bet there's enough booze there to float this ruddy ship!'

The other man nodded. 'I'm sort of bankin' on it!'

The sentry watched a Wren riding her bicycle along the jetty, her skirt blowing halfway up her thigh.

467

He called after them, 'Don't let Mister snotty-nose Bizley catch you!' Then he stared after the Wren. Rather be on her than on the middle watch, he thought.

Laird, the duty quartermaster, led the way through and around many obstacles. 'Half the lads are already on leave. I'm afraid you've come at a bad time.'

Milvain asked politely, 'That officer – Bizley, wasn't it?'

Laird heard the laughter and clinking glasses from the chief and petty officers' mess and licked his lips. He dragged his mind back to the question. 'Oh, don't worry about *him*. He's fairly new to the ship, a real little shit, but nothing we can't handle.' He turned to see the youth blush. 'Why?'

'My brother had an officer of that name. In Coastal Forces.'

A note of warning sounded in Laird's mind. 'Your brother – the skipper, was he?' He saw the sudden lift of the youth's chin, a brightness in his eyes. *Had*, he thought. He said casually, 'What do they call you, then?'

Milvain thought of his mother sobbing over him at the railway station, the other sailors watching curiously while they waited for their various transport.

He replied, 'Andy, usually.'

Laird said, 'Well, Andy, I'm sorry I put my foot in it. It happens. You'll see soon enough.'

The coxswain, massive and sweating, appeared in the doorway and beamed, 'What are all we, then?'

The quartermaster handed him the draft chit. God, he thought, the coxswain reeked of rum. The whole mess did. He said abruptly, 'His brother was Mister Bizley's skipper.'

The coxswain looked at the new arrival, Laird's remark slowly penetrating the fog of the sendoff for the gunner's mate.

'*Ganges* boy, eh?'

'Yes sir.'

'Not "sir" 'ere, my son. Cox'n will do very nicely.'

It was all coming back. Bizley's bravery when his motor gunboat had gone down, his efforts to rescue the survivors. Maybe even a medal . . .

'First ship?' He nodded slowly, picturing the various messes, the leading hands who ruled them like barons. 'I'll stick you in Nine Mess. Bruce Fernie is the boss there.' He stared down at him. Officer material most likely, he thought. *Ah well*. All eyes and innocence. Bet he had to watch out for his virginity at the bloody *Ganges*.

He belched. 'I'll make out a card for you. Just wait 'ere, my son.' He scowled at the quartermaster, '*You* can 'ave a wet, if that's what you're after!'

Milvain stood by the door and watched the petty officers laughing and drinking, as if they hadn't a care in the world. He looked around him, seeing the scars beneath the new paint. Russian convoys. He shivered and thought suddenly of his dead brother. He might have been proud of him.

A youngish-looking man in a raincoat, and without any sort of cap, ran up one ladder and paused to glance at him as he moved his attaché case out of the way. 'Just joined?'

Milvain nodded and remembered what the burly coxswain had told him. 'Yes, Petty Officer. From Chatham.'

'Welcome aboard.'

The coxswain reappeared with a card for the new rating, then froze as he saw the youth chatting away.

He said awkwardly, ''Ere's yer card.'

Silence fell in the mess as the newcomer went inside. Milvain heard him say, 'Just one then, I'm catching a train south as soon as I can.'

Milvain asked quietly, 'What does *he* do – er, Cox'n?'

Sweeney breathed out heavily. 'That was the captain, my son. Gawd, wot are things comin' to in this regiment!'

He watched Milvain climb down the ladder, looking around, trying to find himself in his new world. A grin spread slowly across his battered face. Wait till I tell the others about this. *What does he do?* But it was also a side to the commanding officer he had not seen before.

Back in the crowded mess he saw the Old Man chatting with the departing gunner's mate. Should he tell him about Milvain's brother? He decided against it. Wait and see, that was best.

Howard looked across at him. 'They're getting younger, 'Swain.'

From one corner of his eye Sweeney saw the duty quartermaster slip out of the other door in case the Old Man should see him here.

He nodded heavily, 'You're off 'ome then, sir?'

Howard studied him gravely, wondering how Sweeney would manage. There must be hundreds like him, thousands, like Stoker Marshall. Nothing left, and nothing to look forward to. He glanced at the mess clock. 'I'm off then.' He thought of Hampshire. The Guvnor's garden. It would be good to see him again. But the ship seemed to hold him. Howard shook himself and said, 'I've left a phone number in case . . .' He walked from the mess and went aft to retrieve his cap from the lobby. Time to go.

The quartermaster was just about to tell the sentry all about the party when Sub-Lieutenant Bizley strode aft, his cap at the rakish angle he seemed to favour.

'Somebody came aboard just now!' It was a statement. 'I should have been told. I'm OOD in case you'd forgotten!' He jabbed a finger at the sentry and snapped, 'Tighten your pistol belt, man! I'll not have you making this ship look sloppy, so don't you forget that, either!'

The QM hastily intervened for his friend's sake. 'It was another replacement, sir. Name of Milvain.' He watched him warily, like a cat weighing up a dangerous hound. He had not anticipated Bizley's reaction.

'What name?' He felt his mind reeling. It couldn't be. Even in the navy it was too much of a coincidence.

Sure of his ground now, the quartermaster said, 'Your last CO was his brother.'

They both stared after Bizley as he hurried away. He was almost running.

'Well, well, well, what tin of worms have *I* discovered, then?'

They grinned at one another like conspirators, while the gangway sentry gave up his attempt to tighten the offending belt.

The Buffer appeared by the after torpedo tubes and lurched towards them, his face flushed from the sendoff in his mess. 'Where's the officer of the day?'

The quartermaster replied innocently, 'Not sure, Buffer.'

'*Jesus!* The skipper's goin' over the side at any minute!'

At that moment Bizley made an appearance, but Knocker White was too full of rum to notice the corresponding smell of gin from the duty officer.

Howard came up, still wearing his plain, unmarked raincoat, and stood to look along the littered deck, wondering what Marrack would have to say about it.

He carried just a small grip; he would change into some old clothing when he reached home. The heaviest things in it were tins of duty-free cigarettes for the Guvnor. He could not manage a pipe with only one hand.

The three figures at the brow froze to attention, and the quartermaster moistened his silver call with his tongue, even as a taxi came to a halt on the jetty.

Aloud Howard said, 'Take good care of her.' Then with his fingers to his cap in salute he hurried down the brow, the twitter of the call still hanging in the dusty air.

Only once did he look back and upwards to the high, open bridge where he had stood for so many hours and days.

It was behind him now. But it would never leave him.

7

I Saw Him Go

The passenger seat of the small army fifteen hundred-weight lorry felt like iron but Howard barely noticed it as he stared out at the rich green countryside. Beside him a young lance-corporal, from Yorkshire by the sound of it, seemed eager to get as much speed as he could from the much-used vehicle.

Howard had not realised just how tired he was after the lengthy journey from Scotland. On the final leg of the trip from Waterloo he had fallen into a deep sleep and had been awakened by a porter tapping his knee to tell him that the train had reached the end of the line. It had been Portsmouth Harbour station which had been so much a part of his life even from childhood: the old wooden platform, through which you could see the water underfoot at high-tide, and the imposing masts and yards of Nelson's old flagship *Victory* rising above the dockyard wall outside the station. He could recall walking through the yard shortly after the start of 1941, when there had been a devastating air-raid on the city and anchorage. The continuous attack had lasted all night, and when a smoky dawn had laid bare the terrible destruction it had seemed a miracle that anything had survived. Over three thousand people were made homeless and famous buildings like the Guildhall and the George Inn were laid in ruins. Hundreds were killed and injured in that single raid, but the thing so engraved on Howard's mind was seeing the *Victory*'s fat black and buff hull unscathed amidst devastation, with shattered vessels all around her.

Today he had been standing frustrated by a deserted taxi rank when the lance-corporal had offered him a lift. He had barely stopped talking since they had joined the Portsmouth Road and headed inland towards the village where Howard's father lived.

It had been over a year since Howard had been here on leave and he was still trying to come to terms with the undertones of war which had changed almost everything. Hotels, once so popular with holidaymakers visiting Southsea and the Isle of Wight, were now billets and stores for the military. There were checkpoints everywhere, barbed-wire barriers and protective banks of sandbags around some of the buildings. More sinister, he thought, were the little newspaper stalls and tourist information huts with their faded posters and shuttered windows. He had supposed they were shut 'for the duration' until he had seen them close to, when his driver had been forced to slow down by a column of tanks crossing the road.

The huts were fake. Underneath their disguises they were solid concrete blockhouses from which machine-guns could cover the road with cross-fire. They were even here in the countryside, painted with camouflage or disguised as farm outbuildings. Like the tall poles poised in the fields to prevent aircraft or gliders from landing, they were a true reminder of the ever-present danger and threat of invasion, as was the fact that the nearest enemy airfield was less than ninety miles from this pleasant stretch of deserted road.

Howard thought of the grim newspaper headlines, the so-called strategic withdrawals in North Africa. What a familiar ring they had. *Would* the enemy ever come here?

He glanced at his companion, the crumpled khaki battledress, the youthful intentness on his face as he roared around a shallow bend and braked hard to avoid a marching squad of soldiers. A pleasant, homely youth, the sort you saw on the newsreels giving a hopeful thumbs-up before some disaster or other. What would he and his friends make of the battle-hardened Panzers and Wehrmacht, he wondered.

'Where are you from?'

He darted him a quick glance. 'Bradford, sir – can't you tell?' He grinned broadly. 'Th' Riviera of the North!'

'How long have you been in the Army?'

The grin remained. 'Ah, sir, I can't tell thee that! Careless talk you know!'

Howard smiled and thought of the one telephone call he had made to the ship. Marrack distant and self-assured, enjoying total power. 'Nothing to bother about, sir. Just chaos, that's all. If you don't bolt everything down it vanishes. Poor old Gunner (T) even lost his spare dentures!'

Howard leaned forward and said, 'Here it is, coming up on the left.' His mouth had gone quite dry, as if he was afraid of what he might find.

The lance-corporal looked doubtfully at the narrow lane which led off the main road. 'Tight squeeze, sir!'

'This will do fine.' He glanced at two figures in battledress similar to the driver's. Until they turned round. Each had a large coloured disc or diamond stitched to his clothing. 'Who are they, for God's sake?'

The driver watched him curiously. 'Eye-ties, sir. Prisoners of war left over from the desert, when we were chasing *them* for a change!' He took it for granted, and Howard was now the stranger here.

He explained, 'The trusted ones work on the land, y'see, sir. Big shortage of proper farmhands. They're even after our lasses if they get half a chance. One of our lads found his missus in bed with one when he popped home unexpected!'

Howard tried to come to grips with it. 'What happened?'

The huge grin reappeared like the Cheshire Cat's. 'The Eye-tie's in hospital, our bloke is in th' glasshouse! Worth it though, I'll bet!'

Howard groped for his bag and heard the tins rattle together. He pulled out one of them and handed it to the soldier. 'Duty-frees. Thanks for the lift.' He climbed down and walked into the lane, knowing that the unknown soldier was still staring after him. It seemed an age before the lorry's engine revved up again and left the lane in silence.

He stopped suddenly and stared at the house. Exactly as he had remembered it; cherished it. Seventeenth century – well, some of it anyway, but all of it very old. As a child he had frightened himself in his bed when the wind had moaned around its eaves, picturing the press-gangs marching through the night, or some felon hanging from the gibbet which had given its name to the hill outside the village.

The two POW's were inside the garden discussing things with his father. Of course, he spoke fluent Italian; or had once. Another picture formed in Howard's mind like an old photograph, he and his brother on holiday in Venice, his father in a white suit and panama hat. The locals had admired the Englishman with the one eye and single arm. *Capitano*, they had called him. Howard felt the bitterness again. But the Italians had been their allies in the war which had done that to his father.

At that moment the Guvnor looked up, his eye squinting in the bright sunshine. He hurried towards him, his arm outstretched. 'Good to see you, David!' He hugged him warmly. 'So *bloody* good!'

Howard looked across at the two Italians. 'What are they doing here?'

'Helping *me*, of course.' He sounded surprised. Like the lance-corporal. 'But never mind that, my boy, come inside and tell me all about it.' The bright gaze moved over him, missing nothing. The strain, the tightness around the mouth. The youth which had gone forever.

He seemed to notice a bicycle beside the front door for the first time. 'Almost forgot. Something quite extraordinary has happened today. Better come in and be introduced.'

It seemed fresh and cool after the lorry and the dust. The furniture was a bit more battered, the pictures on the walls not as straight as they might be. But the living room with its oak beams, and fresh flowers in the great fireplace where they had sat as children with their dreams, were as welcoming as ever.

Howard realised with a start that there was a young woman beside a window, her features lost in shadow behind the sun's probing rays.

She came to meet him and held out her hand. He thought about it afterwards. She had met him halfway. On equal terms. 'I'm very sorry to do this to you, Commander Howard. I didn't know it was your first day home.'

He released her hand and watched her as she turned towards his father. Younger than he had first thought; in her early twenties, with short brown hair, and eyes which might be green if he could see them properly. She was dressed in an old tweed hacking jacket and corduroy trousers. A green headscarf which she must have been wearing on the road lay across the sofa. He also noticed the RAF brooch, like a pilot's wings, on one lapel, and that she wore a wedding ring.

The Guvnor murmured, 'I'll lay on some tea, unless – ' He fixed Howard with his eye. 'Something stronger perhaps?'

Howard felt lost. 'Stronger for me.' He faced the girl again. What about you?'

She smiled, but only briefly. 'I shouldn't be here. No – I think I *will* have a drink.' She looked at his father. 'A sherry perhaps?'

What could she want? How could she possibly know when he was due here? He thought of the soldier's quip about careless talk. Somebody must be doing quite a bit of that.

He waited for her to sit on the sofa, then pulled out his pipe and pouch. Like those times on the bridge. Faced with the unanswerable question. Needing the time to fashion his observations. She looked up at him and in the cooler light he saw the tiredness in her eyes. Someone who had been and still was under pressure. She was very withdrawn, wanting only to accomplish her mission and leave.

She took the glass from his father and Howard saw that her hand shook slightly. It made her apparent composure a lie.

His father stared at him. 'I've got to tell the chaps what I want digging.' He did not wink, but he might easily have done so. 'I'll leave you to some privacy.' Then he was gone and they heard the excited chatter of Italian from the garden.

'A lovely man.' She sipped her sherry. 'You see, I thought my letter had gone astray, or that you might not wish to see me.'

He frowned. 'What letter?'

She took a deep breath. 'I'm Celia Kirke. My home is over in Chichester.'

'And you cycled all this way?'

'Hardly. I borrowed the bike from an oppo in Pompey.' She watched him as he crossed to the table where his father kept letters ready for forwarding to his two sons. No wonder he had kept this one. It was stamped with some official-looking numbers and dates, and had been signed for.

She said abruptly, 'I'll tell you, now that you're here.' She sounded less confident. Troubled. 'I was in the Wrens.' She stared at her glass. 'I was stationed at HMS *Daedalus*, the naval air station at Lee-on-Solent. Where I first met Jamie.'

Howard nodded. It explained her familiarity with things naval; her casual use of Pompey, slang for Portsmouth.

She was gripping the stem of her glass with both hands, and a lock of hair fell across her forehead unheeded.

She said in the same contained voice. 'He was a squadron-leader in the RAF. He was attached to the Fleet Air Arm as an instructor.' Her chin lifted as if with pride. 'He had been a fighter pilot in the Battle of Britain.'

Howard sat down opposite her and wished the sun was not so strong in his eyes. So her husband, Jamie, was dead. *Bought it*, as they said in all three services. Casually uttered to keep up the pretence and hold back the fear you might be the next one.

She looked at him with sudden despair. 'I'm not making any sense, am I?'

Howard stared at his unlit pipe. 'Where exactly do I come in, Mrs Kirke?'

'My husband was a fine pilot; everyone looked up to him, until – ' She hesitated. 'They told him he was grounded for good, that he would stay as an instructor, but not in the air.'

'He must have hated that.'

She did not hear him. 'Then there was this signal. Asking for volunteers. Pilots, anyone who could stay airborne and was mad enough to do it.'

'How old was your husband?'

She eyed him steadily. 'Thirty-one. Older than most. Flying was his *life*. Perhaps I didn't realise it before – ' She broke off and gave a small shrug. 'Catapult aircraft merchant ships, CAM for short.' She saw his instant response and added, 'Yes, Jamie was the Hurricane pilot aboard the CAM ship on your convoy to Russia.'

Howard stared at her. 'How did you discover all this?'

'Jamie's mechanic came to see me afterwards . . .'

The picture thrust into his mind. The Hurricane rising and dipping, pouring smoke as it headed towards them. *Tail-end Charlie.*

She said, 'He explained that it was your ship Jamie was making for – you know, how they're taught to do. I just wanted to see you, to find out.' She wiped her cheek with her knuckles as if angry that she might break down. 'You see, we'd had a row. The last time we were together.' She spoke faster now. 'I didn't want it to end like that.'

Howard moved across and sat beside her without looking at her. He could feel her tension, her sudden guard as if she expected him . . . 'Yes, I saw him go, Mrs Kirke. He was trying to reach us, although I think he must have been dead already when the plane hit the sea.' Then he did turn his head to look at her. 'I'm very sorry, but there's little more I can tell you. The Hurricane blew up. There was nothing.'

'Thank you. I had to speak to the man who might have saved him, had there been a chance.' She gazed at him for several seconds. 'Now I've met you, I know there *was* no chance for him.'

The Guvnor entered with a tray of plates but she stood up and shook her head. 'No, I must go now. But thank you.' She faced Howard again. 'Both of you.'

He followed her out of the house and waited while she put some clips around her corduroy trousers. Even the old and shabby clothing could not hide her attraction – perhaps it too was another sort of defence. He wondered what that last argument had been about.

She began to push the bicycle towards the gate. The two POW's were careful to avert their eyes but were probably watching all the same.

'What will you do now?'

She glanced at the clear sky. Looking, remembering, perhaps, when it had been filled with criss-crossing vapour trails, and schoolboys had shot each other down until luck deserted them. Like Jamie's.

'I shall go back in the Wrens.' There was no sort of doubt there, but Howard had seen her resistance almost break in the quiet, cool room. It was another side to the war. He had written to the parents of men who had been lost at sea, killed in action. He had even attended a couple of funerals because there had been nobody else. But this seemed more personal because he had shared it, and because of some unknown RAF mechanic he was a part of it.

'Perhaps we shall meet again some time?'

She looked at him. Her eyes *were* green, keeping him at a distance.

'Well, you know the Navy. Maybe we will.' She mounted the bicycle and tightened the headscarf under her chin.

She added, 'Take care of yourself, Commander Howard.'

He was taken aback by the old-fashioned way she said it. More like a mother speaking to her son than a young girl.

He called after her, 'If you ever need . . .' But she was already out of earshot.

The Guvnor had joined him in the sunlight and said quietly, 'Poor kid. She thinks she killed him, you see.'

Howard stared at him. 'He didn't stand a chance!'

'I've known men go like that. A letter, a rumour maybe, and you see death on his face. Mister Mills will tell you. It was the same in the trenches.' He put his arm round him and added, 'Try to forget it. I want to hear all about *Gladiator* and the bloody Russians!'

But that night as Howard lay in his old bed and listened to the vague drone of aircraft, 'theirs' or 'ours', he did not know, he found that he could not forget it, or the girl with the green eyes.

Gordon Treherne lay back sleepily on the disordered bed and tried to guess the time. He heard her humming in the other room and felt the returning need running through him like a fever in the Gulf. She had drawn the blackout screens across the windows. He ran his fingers through his hair and sighed deeply. So they had been *at it* for most of the day, and within an hour of his arrival at her flat.

Outside the room it was quiet, the town of Birkenhead bracing itself for another sneak air-raid. The shipyards were still, all work stopped until the new day. So many fine vessels had gone from here, he thought. He had served in a couple of them.

She came back into the bedroom, a tartan blanket wrapped around her nakedness. Her name was Joyce, and Treherne had met her shortly after the outbreak of war, over the water in Liverpool where she had been working in a pub to make a few extra bob. She was married, and her husband was now serving somewhere in the Royal Army Service Corps.

His eyes narrowed as he thought of the first time he had made love to her. Lust, need; there had been no thought of permanence then. Perhaps it had been the savage scar on her back after her husband had beaten her up, as he had apparently done quite a lot.

She stopped by the bed and put down a tray with some beer and sandwiches on it.

She smiled. 'Only spam, I'm afraid, Gordon. You must eat as well, you know!'

She gasped as he dragged her down and flung the blanket to the floor. 'You're lovely, Joyce!' He squeezed her breasts and pulled her closer, feeling the urge rising to match hers.

She had beautiful breasts and a body to match. She must have been quite lovely as a bride, he thought wistfully.

All at once he was above her, kissing her, while she moved her body against his.

When it was over they lay entwined, exhausted by their hunger for each other. He stroked her back and made her shiver when he touched the scar. 'If that bastard ever bothers you again . . .' He never used her husband's name, as if it was something foul. 'I'll take him apart.'

She nodded, like a child, then touched his beard. 'I'll never go back to him. I'll manage. I have before.'

'*We'll* manage, right, Joyce?' He did not know how, but somehow wanted it to be so.

She said, 'I've got a good job now, making duffel coats for the Navy!'

Treherne grinned at her. A real sailor's girl. God alone knew how it might end, but he knew that he wanted her for himself. She was not at all like his Carol, nor any of the brief affairs he had entertained in the Caribbean or various ports where they had dropped their cargoes of bananas. Joyce was different, and she was fun to be with.

They both jumped as the telephone jangled beside the bed. She made to pick it up but Treherne said, 'If it's that bastard, pass it to me! I'll tell him a few home-truths!' She watched his smouldering anger with quiet admiration. Gordon could make mincemeat of her old man. But she handed it to him anyway and whispered, 'It's for you.' It sounded like a question.

Treherne bit his lip. 'Had to leave a number, love.'

She retrieved her blanket and hurried towards the little kitchen. When she came back she found him sitting on the edge of the bed, his hands locked together, his face set in deep thought.

He looked at her, then held out his arms to her. 'I've got to go back, Joyce. That was the skipper.' He glanced at the telephone as if he could not believe it. 'Thought he was on leave.'

She clung to him and pressed her face against his chest. 'But it's not right, Gordon! You've only just got here!' She was crying now, her eyes red with tears. 'I wanted to have such a nice time with you . . .' She could not go on.

Treherne stroked her back and murmured into her hair, 'I'll make it up to you, love.' He was trying to remember exactly what Howard had said. It had been a bad line, too.

Then he said quietly, 'He wants me to take over as Number One, for the moment anyway.' She stared up at him, not understanding. He added gently, 'Second-in-command, that means.'

She wiped her face and eyes with one corner of the sheet. 'Second-in-command! Of a destroyer!' Her momentary pride vanished as she said in a small voice, 'You won't want me any more. Mixing with all those posh officers.'

Treherne grinned as he pictured the *Gladiator*'s wardroom, the old Gunner (T) minus his teeth, snoring in a corner after too many gins. 'Pusser' Finlay, and dear old Taffy Price, the chief.

He replied, 'You're my girl, Joyce. Next time I come I'll get you a ring.'

She stared at him with disbelief. 'But I'm still married!'

'I don't care. You belong to me, see? I want everyone to know it!' He let out a sigh. '*Posh* officers indeed!'

She looked at him searchingly. 'When do you have to go?'

'Tomorrow, love. I'll be back, probably sooner than you think.'

She looked at the blackout screen. 'Liverpool again?'

He nodded. 'Something like that.'

She moved against him and they lay down together. Too exhausted to make love, too sad to talk about the future.

When the first shipyard hooter sounded the start of another day, they had still barely slept.

Lieutenant Graham Marrack remained quite still, his face expressionless while he watched Howard standing by an open scuttle, the sunshine on his face.

Howard said, 'I don't see what all the fuss is about, Number One. Of course you must accept it. God, man, a command of your own – it's what any officer would give his right arm for!'

Marrack replied stubbornly, 'I'm very aware of the honour, sir. But there will be lots of people in the queue without my jumping the gun.'

Howard turned aside as a rivet-gun shattered the silence like an ack-ack fusillade. He did not know what angered him more. Losing the best first lieutenant he had ever known, regular *or* reservist, or Marrack's pigheaded attitude about accepting command.

'Look.' Howard faced him. 'This bloody war will last for years. If we win, there'll still be the Far East waiting, after that probably Russia, the way they're going on. But win or lose, the Navy must have good, experienced commanding officers. You've seen the green kids we're getting, willing to die, and that's what they usually do before they can learn anything!'

There was no movement in the little pantry and he could imagine Petty Officer Vallance with his ear pressed to the hatch, reaping a harvest of gossip for the chief and PO's mess.

'And anyway, if their lordships offer you this appointment it is not a *request*, Number One!'

Marrack frowned. '*Gladiator* will be going back to Western Approaches after this. Nobody has said so, but we both know it.'

Howard nodded and waited without comment.

Marrack finished his summing-up. 'You carried the lot of us last time. If I've learned anything, it's come from you, not out of books. You tell me that the Navy needs experienced commanding officers.' He eyed him calmly. 'And skippers need good subordinates.'

Howard smiled. 'Remember that when you take command, eh?'

As if to a signal they both shook hands as Marrack said, 'Of *course* I wanted it, sir. But not like this. I'd thought to stay in *Gladiator* for a while longer.'

Howard looked at the appointment lying on his desk. They must have worded it much the same in Nelson's day, he thought.

He said, '*Tacitus*. Flower Class corvette. She's in Western Approaches too.'

Marrack nodded slowly, watching him as if he wanted to forget nothing.

'We've seen her many times in the Atlantic.'

Marrack moved to the door. 'I've a few things to do, sir, before I leave.' He hesitated. 'Who will you get, I wonder?'

'Not another bloody lawyer, that's for sure!'

He saw the tall lieutenant give his private smile before he closed the door behind him.

Howard thought suddenly of his father, his obvious disappointment when he had cut short his visit after a call from Marrack. He could see him exactly as he had left him by the garden wall, his tousled white hair, the single, busy hand which could do almost anything. Like an extension of his eye and brain. *I shall give him a ring later on.* It seemed unfair that the Guvnor had grown so old.

That evening, when the ship was blacked-out alongside the jetty, Howard telephoned Treherne in Birkenhead.

He thought of it later. Treherne's surprise, which matched Marrack's stubbornness, so that they each had to be convinced in different ways.

He went on deck and looked at the tall cranes stark against the pale stars, and thought of the woman who had answered the telephone. Treherne was a dark horse. Full of surprises.

The gangway sentry stiffened in the darkness and Howard said, 'All quiet, Laker?'

'As a boneyard, sir!' The man grinned at him, pleased that the Old Man remembered his name.

Howard strolled along the iron deck beneath the whaler's davits, and thought about Treherne.

It was the first time that he could recall being so envious.

The red-faced coxswain stood massively to one side of the table and bawled, 'Quick march! 'Alt! Off cap!' He did not need to consult his clipboard. 'Leading Seaman Bishop, sir! Drunk an' disorderly!'

Lieutenant Finlay stared at the chief quartermaster across the little desk, his eyes hostile.

'Will you never learn, Bishop?'

The man met his gaze with equal animosity. 'Nuthin' to say, sir.'

The gunnery officer, who was OOD, glanced at the coxswain. '*Well?*'

Sweeney tilted his cap against the sunshine. 'Brought aboard by the shore patrol, sir. That was after bein' thrown out of the *Coach an' 'orses*, and then the wet canteen, sir.'

Finlay glanced at his watch. 'You're a fool, Bishop – your own worst enemy.' When there was no response he snapped, 'Stand over for first lieutenant's report!'

'On cap, right turn, double march!'

'Next!'

Sub-Lieutenant Bizley waited impatiently by the lobby door. He hated being made to understudy Finlay's duties, or anyone else's for that matter. In the motor gunboat he had been first lieutenant, gunnery officer and watchkeeper, and anything else that was thrown his way.

The tannoy squeaked into life. 'Stand easy!'

'That's the lot, sir.' Sweeney folded his list of defaulters. He did not sympathise with Bully Bishop, nevertheless he had seen some of the officers pissed enough in the wardroom. Probably not the gunnery officer, he thought. 'Pusser' Finlay was sharper than any regular he had known. He never bent the rules for anyone. Unlike Treherne. He gave a grin. Even Jimmy-the-One had been known to offer a second chance. Bishop would dip his hook for certain this time.

Finlay looked along the deck. There was less disorder and mess now, fewer power-leads, and only a handful of boiler-suited dockyard maties grouped around the new gun mounting amidships, a multiple-barrelled pom-pom. To hell with dockyard rules, he thought. *They* don't have to fire the bloody things.

'I'm going to look over this job, Sub. Take over for me, and let me know when the captain comes back. He's in the dock office, so watch out.'

Bizley looked sulkily at the coxswain. 'I'll see you at up spirits.' He was about to move away when he noticed the young ordinary seaman coming aft, bent almost double under a parcel of heaving-lines. He had seen Milvain several times, working ship with the part-of-watch still on board, and knew that the young seaman had been studying him too. He made up his mind. There would be too many people about when the hands turned-to again.

'Here, Milvain, put that lot down a moment. It's standeasy anyway.'

The youth looked at him shyly, and Bizley felt a chill run through him in spite of the sunshine.

'Sir?'

Bizley cleared his throat. God, he thought. I can *see* his brother in him. 'Just wanted to say how sorry I was about your brother.' If only he would stop staring. 'I was going to visit your family, but I was in a bad way myself.'

The youth nodded. 'They understood, sir. It must have been terribly dangerous, what you did. I read all about it in the newspaper.'

Bizley's eyes blinked. 'Newspaper? I didn't see that!'

Milvain plunged his hand inside his overalls and withdrew his paybook and wallet. He opened it carefully and took out the cutting, which had obviously been studied many times. 'Here, sir.'

Bizley stared at the article which had Milvain's brother's photograph, and one of himself he did not know existed. Probably obtained from the gunnery school when he had done a course there.

It was all there; words like 'courage' and 'unselfish behaviour, above the line of duty,' stood out like banners on a cinema.

Milvain offered, 'Keep it if you like, sir. I've another one at home.'

Bizley could barely think straight. In a way it was all true, so why should he feel guilty? He saw Milvain fumbling with his paybook and another photograph as he made to close it. To cover his excitement he asked, 'Who's that, may I ask? Bit young for a pretty girl like *her*, I'd have thought?'

The seaman held it out to him. 'It's my sister, sir. Sarah.'

Bizley held it to the sunlight. The same look as the youth who was staring at him with something like awe. '*Very* nice.'

'Wait until I tell her, sir. She was dying to meet you, to thank you for what you tried to do for Gregory.'

Bizley had had little or no success with girls. He knew that the Milvain family was very unlike his own, that the head of it was a major-general.

The tannoy again. 'Out pipes! Hands carry on with your work!'

Bizley nodded. 'Perhaps I *shall* be able to pay them a visit when I get some proper leave. It will be easier to tell them now there's been some time since . . .' He broke off as Finlay came striding aft to the bow.

The lieutenant exclaimed angrily, 'I *told* you to warn me, Sub!'

The captain was at the foot of the brow, a pipe in his mouth which he removed only to salute the quarterdeck as he came aboard.

Howard sensed the tension between them but decided to ignore it. It had been agreed that Treherne should take over as first lieutenant, for the moment anyway. There was no available replacement in any case, so he would have to go over the watch-bill with Treherne when he arrived.

'Ask Number One to join me in my cabin, will you, Guns?' He could tell from

Finlay's curiosity that Marrack had said nothing to anybody. He was playing it close to his chest. As usual.

He would tell the wardroom when Treherne was present; the others who were on leave would get the news later.

He looked at the bright sky. It was hard to believe that the ice and bitter weather had existed. That the convoys had ever been. He thought of the exploding Hurricane, and his father's simple explanation. 'She thinks she killed him.' Surely that was impossible?

He saw Marrack strolling towards him. 'It's on, Number One.'

Marrack smiled. 'Sun's over the yardarm, sir. Will you join me in a gin?'

Finlay glared after them and said, 'Don't do that again, Sub, *ever*! Or I'll have your guts for a necktie!'

If Bizley had retained any reservations about what he had done, Finlay's anger had dispelled them.

Just you wait, you Scottish bastard! You'll soon change your tune!

It was such a warm evening that the Guvnor could not bear to go indoors. He was on his knees, his hand digging into the soft earth like a grubby crab searching for food, while the garden around him was alive with bees and other insects, and a blackbird began a late bath in the dish he kept for them.

He would stay out as long as possible, watching the late sunshine; there was always a chance that someone would pause at the wall for a chat. Once inside the house the loneliness always tightened its grip.

Perhaps it would be another quiet night. The area had been lucky recently, as if the enemy was staying his hand while he concentrated on London and the northeast.

He thought of his two sons, especially David, who had gone back to his ship to face more problems. The refit was taking longer than expected. It would be the end of July by the time they went back to sea. He gave a satisfied grunt and pulled a fine bunch of radishes out into the sunshine.

'Not bad at all!' He slapped them on his patched gardening trousers, then laid them in a basket with some crisp-looking lettuces he had also cut that afternoon.

When Mister Mills dropped in for a glass of something they would share them and pass the time together.

He got painfully to his feet and felt a tiny insect fly into his eye. He blinked it away and dabbed his eye with his handkerchief. It was an ever-present fear. That the other eye would go bad on him.

He heard the muffled roar of engines from the road, voices raised in song. As regular as clockwork, he thought. The mobile anti-aircraft batteries taking up their positions for the night. He smiled grimly. Typical, Mister Mills would say. The old horse and stable-door policy.

The Guvnor opened his tin of duty-frees and lit one with great care. As he watched the smoke rising straight up by the greenhouse, he thought about his own war. That day at Zeebrugge.

He looked up as more wheels grated along the pot-holed lane. Some soldiers who had taken the wrong turning. It happened often enough. He walked slowly towards the gate and then stopped with surprise. A khaki Humber staff car was parked outside, almost filling the lane. A sailor sat behind the wheel and for a moment the Guvnor could not get his breath. He felt suddenly angry with himself. Getting senile. If anything was wrong they wouldn't send a bloody great staff car. It would be a telegram, like all the others which had been delivered around here over the months.

Anyway, sailors lost their way too.

He got a second surprise when a Wren officer stepped from the rear of the car and adjusted her tricorn hat over her eyes against the low sunlight. She wore two pale blue stripes on her sleeve – a second officer, then. She was slim and neat in her uniform, and it was only when she walked uncertainly towards him that he remembered. The shabby hacking jacket, the old corduroys; like another person entirely.

She paused by the gate and said, 'I'm sorry to do this to you again, Commander Howard.' She reached out impulsively and touched his arm.

He stared at her, sensing her nearness, her freshness and youth, so that he felt old and dirty by comparison.

'Please come in, my dear. I'm afraid it's in a bit of a mess!'

A voice called after her from the car. 'Don't be too long, Celia, we're late as it is!'

The Guvnor strained his eye but the car was in deep shadow so that he could not see the man, except that he too was in uniform.

'Ten minutes, Daddy!'

She walked with him up the path and took off her hat to shake out her short curls.

The Guvnor said, 'How can I help you? I'm afraid . . .' He smiled. 'There, now *I'm* apologising again too!'

She turned and faced him in the same direct manner she had used with David. 'I hope you like dogs.' She hurried on, 'Some friends of mine were bombed-out. The dog escaped. I would take her, but I'm back in the "regiment", as you can see.' She looked at him and added quietly, 'They were both killed. My friends, I mean.'

He saw her lip quiver and guessed they had been close.

He said awkwardly, 'Well, fetch her over, my dear. A dog would be nice company. I get fed up discussing Venice with my two POWs!'

She called, 'Let her go, please, Tom!'

The door opened and then the gate, as a plump Labrador padded curiously up the path.

She stooped down and ruffled her ears. 'She's called Lucy. She's not young, but she's such a dear. She'll eat you penniless if she gets the chance!' She hugged the animal and said, 'You can take care of each other. I'll come and see you one day!' When she stood up there were tears in her eyes.

He said gruffly, 'Be certain you do.' He walked with her to the gate and was astonished to see that the dog was already lying on the mat by the front door.

'See? She feels at home already!'

The girl replaced her hat, then leaned over and kissed him on the cheek. She said, 'Goodbye, again.' Then she was in the car without another glance at the yellow Labrador, who was snapping at flies by the mat. But not before the Guvnor had seen the gold lace on her father's sleeve. A rear-admiral, no less.

He watched as the big car reversed carefully, to the main road before turning across it towards Portsmouth.

Aloud he said, 'Don't keep punishing yourself, my girl. It's the bloody war, not you.'

He walked back to the gate and stared at his new companion. 'Well, now. That was a turn up for the book, eh?'

8

Convoy

David Howard returned the salutes of the dock sentries and presented his identity card to an armed policeman. Around him the place seemed to be teeming with sailors, naval and merchant alike, and although it had only just stopped raining there was an air of scruffy defiance which appeared to be Liverpool's stock in trade.

Howard slowed his pace as he approached Gladstone Dock, where *Gladiator* lay with many other Atlantic escorts. He had just left the imposing presence of the new Captain (D), a tall, powerful man with the battered features of someone who had been well-known on the rugby field in the impossible days of peace. Even the flotilla-leader had changed while *Gladiator* had been fighting to stay afloat on the North Russian 'run', as it was discreetly called in the press. Captain Ernle Vickers DSO, DSC, Royal Navy, had as his own command the *Kinsale*, one of the famous K's which had been almost the only new destroyers available when the war had begun. Like Mountbatten's *Kelly*, which with some of her consorts had been bombed and sunk near Crete in the spring of last year. Raked bows, with a single funnel instead of the usual pair, and an impressive armament, she would make any recruit's heart beat faster, Howard thought. Like her captain, whose record he knew very well; he was exactly what they needed when things looked so bad in the Western Ocean.

All the captains had been there to meet the great man, and Howard was relieved to discover that Spike Colvin's *Ganymede* and another of their old team, *Garnet*, were still with the flotilla. She was commanded by an impish two-and-a-half named Tom Woodhouse whom Howard had known for years. They had done the long gunnery course at Whale Island together as sub-lieutenants, and the instructors in that fearsome place had more than met their match with Woodhouse and all his practical jokes.

Most of the other ships had been less lucky and had been sunk in the first two years of conflict. Their names, the places where they had gone down, read like a brutal record of the country's lost campaigns. *Gipsy*, mined off Harwich just two months after the declaration of war. *Glowworm* dying bravely off Norway, *Grenade* and *Grafton* bombed and sunk at Dunkirk, and *Grenville* lost in the North Sea, all in 1940; the list seemed endless.

Captain Vickers had presented his own summing-up of events and the current measures, which it was hoped would cut down the appalling loss of tonnage in the Atlantic convoys. 'The enemy are already moving more submarines from the Norwegian and Baltic bases down to the Biscay coastline. Large surface units too, but at least the Air Force should be able to keep an eye on them after what happened in March.'

Howard recalled it well. While they had been riding out storms in the Arctic, dodging bombs and torpedoes while trying to protect their convoys, there had come one of those bright moments which flare up in all campaigns. A touch of hope, like the sun after a northerly gale. An ancient destroyer named *Campbeltown*, one of those transferred from the US Navy almost at the end of their useful life, had been expended like one giant, floating bomb when she had rammed the lock gates at St Nazaire and blown them to pieces. It had been the only dock on Hitler's impregnable West Wall which was large enough to hold and repair the battle-cruisers, or even the mighty *Tirpitz* if she ever left her Norwegian lair.

Destroyer men always felt different from anyone else. That one incident had convinced them.

Vickers had continued in his thick, resonant voice, 'We shall use new tactics too. To meet their wolf-packs of U-Boats we shall increase the use and deployment of small killer-groups. To this end the yards are now producing newer and faster frigates, solely designed to find and destroy U-Boats. If we can get these vessels to sea, and release other destroyers and corvettes from elsewhere, and *if* we can cling on until that time.' He had given an eloquent shrug. 'I will not dwell on the consequences of the *if nots*, gentlemen. You know them as well as anyone.'

Howard had found a quiet moment to explain to him about Treherne, and his new standing as first lieutenant.

Vickers had nodded, his mind already grappling with some other problem. 'I shall see what I can do. Good navigators are at a premium just now. But so are efficient escorts. I'll try and get you fixed up with an extra hand as soon as I can.' A pretty Wren had entered at that moment to present Vickers with a clip of new signals, and he had left.

Howard had pondered on the girl called Celia Kirke a good deal while his ship sorted herself out from the Greenock refit.

While his father had told him about his new companion, Lucy, he had thought about her even more. What had prompted her to do it after she had left so abruptly? There were so many things he wanted to know about her, even though he knew he was being ridiculous. An escape, then? Perhaps; but it stayed with him nonetheless.

The Guvnor had told him that the girl had been returning to Portsmouth, but when he had found occasion to speak with that naval base on the telephone and had asked casually about her, the Wren on the end of the line replied sharply, 'No second officers of *that* name here!'

Perhaps she had put it about that she wanted to speak with no one who might remind her of her husband's terrible death.

No wonder she had been so confident about returning to the WRNS; her father held flag-rank and could probably pull all the strings for her. But with the way the war was going it seemed unlikely she would have any difficulty in getting back to the world she understood.

Howard was pleased about the Labrador. His father had spoken of little else. Just what the doctor ordered.

The thought brought a frown to his face. He had hoped to get rid of Surgeon-Lieutenant Jocelyn Lawford, but doctors, like good Scotch, were apparently very thin on the ground. If Lawford was confronted with another convoy like the last one *Gladiator* had brought across the Atlantic, he would be utterly useless.

He paused and saw his ship waiting for him, her dazzle-paint shining faintly in the smoky sunshine.

If ever he was ordered into Portsmouth . . . He felt his lips move in a smile. *Pompey.* He would try and find her himself. It would probably mean the brush-off, he thought. Everyone would be after her once they knew what had happened.

He strode down the brow and touched his cap to the quarterdeck where the gangway staff and Sub-Lieutenant Ayres stood at attention.

'Hello, Sub, got you on duty already? Good leave?'

Ayres stared away, seeing nothing. 'My brother's missing, sir. In the desert.'

Howard watched his despair. 'I'm sorry.' How stupidly inadequate it sounded. Like all the other times. *I saw him go.* 'It's not definite, is it?'

Ayres shook his head wretchedly while the quartermaster and gangway sentry tried to melt away. 'Not yet, sir.'

He touched his arm impetuously. 'Keep your chin up. Come and talk if you feel like it.'

Treherne appeared in the lobby door and saluted. 'Orders have arrived, sir.' They fell in step and Treherne added quietly, 'I'm keeping the kid busy. Take his mind off it.'

They reached the door marked *Captain* and found Petty Officer Vallance hovering by his pantry.

Howard tossed his cap on to a chair and sat down at his desk where Ireland the PO writer had lined up his papers in order of importance.

He said, 'Drinks, if you please, Vallance.' His eyes skimmed the neatly worded signal and pictured one of the Wrens typing it, watched over perhaps by someone like the girl with green eyes.

'Day after tomorrow, Number One.' He glanced at him. 'It's confirmed, by the way. The Boss just told me he would do what he could to keep you with me, until – '

Treherne grinned. 'We can discuss *that* later on, sir. Thanks a lot!'

He was thinking of Joyce, her supple body taking him, holding him.

Howard turned over another sheet. 'Send for Sub-Lieutenant Bizley.' He waited for Treherne to speak on the bulkhead telephone and then said calmly, 'He's getting a gong after all.'

Treherne tried to look pleased, although he could not bring himself to like Bizley. He replied, 'There'll be no holding him now!'

There was a tap at the door and Bizley entered the day cabin, his features filled with curiosity, or was it something else? Like guilt?

'It's just been put in orders, Sub. You are being awarded the Distinguished Service Cross at their lordship's convenience. Suit you?'

But Bizley seemed unable to speak or take it in. His eyes moved instead to the solitary blue and white ribbon on Howard's reefer.

Howard smiled. ' "Like yours", were you going to say?'

Bizley stammered, 'T-thank you very much, sir! I never expected . . .'

Treherne looked at his empty glass. *Not much you didn't, you little twit!*

'More good news.' Howard ignored Treherne's expression. 'You are to be made acting-lieutenant on the first of the month. So you can put up your second stripe any time after that. You'll get all the bumf about it after we've done our next convoy.'

Bizley did not even hear him. He muttered something which made little sense and then found himself on the mat outside the cabin door.

He had done it. It was even better than he had dared to dream. He stared wildly at the single stripe on his sleeve. *Lieutenant Lionel Bizley.* It even sounded right, and he wondered dazedly if the King would make the award personally. He thought of Finlay and the others, and found himself laughing but making no sound. He was on his way.

The wardroom steward, PO Vallance, watched him around the curtain that hung across the pantry entrance. There would be no more peace down aft after this, he thought gloomily. Bizley was a proper little toe-rag, and would be a bloody sight worse now.

Two days later as *Gladiator's* narrow hull throbbed steadily to the deeper beat of her main engines, Howard sat at the same desk and thought of the sea cabin on the bridge where he would have to snatch his catnaps whenever possible. There was still a lot to do, and there should have been more time for the flotilla, or escort group as it was now termed, to work together. But Vickers had made his thoughts clear to each commanding officer. 'There *is* no more time. So let's get out there and beat the hell out of them!'

Treherne entered the cabin and waited for Howard to look up. 'Special sea dutymen closed up, sir. Postman's gone ashore with the last mail.' He hesitated. 'One man absent, sir.'

'Stoker Marshall? He saw him nod. The rating who had lost all of his family in an air raid. Where was he? What would he be doing?

Treherne spoke for him. 'He should be here, with *us*, sir. A lot of men have lost relatives.' He added harshly, 'My God, it seems as if the civvies get all the casualties in this war!'

Did he mean the people who crouched in their primitive air raid shelters, Howard wondered. Or was he still thinking about the merchant seamen?

He asked, 'What about young Ayres?'

'He's heard nothing more, sir.' He glanced up as a mooring wire was dragged noisily over the deck. 'Bit of a breeze across the dock. We may have to use the back spring to work her clear.'

More quivering from Evan Price's engine rooms. The beast stirring herself, getting ready to face her old enemy. At least they were in better weather this time.

Howard stood up and began the routine of patting his pockets for the things he would need. He wore a comfortable grey roll-necked sweater he had bought in Reykjavik, his oldest reefer and battered sea-going cap with a paint-stain on the peak. Binoculars, fresh towel. He glanced at himself in the mirror. Hardly what they might expect at Dartmouth or Greenwich.

'Fifteen minutes then, Number One.'

Treherne smiled through his beard. 'The old firm, sir.'

Howard nodded, remembering.

And so once more HMS *Gladiator* went back to war.

For many of *Gladiator*'s ship's company the days that followed their leaving Liverpool were more of a strain than if they had faced immediate action. Day in, day out, with a convoy of some forty vessels of every type and size, the escorts swept ahead and abeam of them seeking the telltale 'ping' of Asdic to betray a submarine, or, if half the rumours were true, a whole pack of them.

But apart from exercising action stations and testing guns, the hands worked watch-and-watch, four hours on, four off, a kind of stumbling sleepwalk in which they ate the greasy meals brought down to the messes, catching a few moments of rest where they could. Sometimes they slept on the steel decks where cursing watchkeepers stepped over them in the darkness, or faced a torrent of abuse from the ones who were forced to sleep by the vertical ladders which linked the messdecks to the world above.

Lashed hammocks stood like monks in their nettings in each crowded mess, not to be used in case they jammed a hatchway, or were needed as lifesaving floats if the ship bought it.

It was a dawdling convoy, the speed of which was that of the slowest vessel in it, in this case a Greek freighter that looked as if she had dropped out of a picture book from the Great War.

The old sweats were not surprised at this or much else either. Every kind of hull was needed, and those which should have been scrapped years ago were ploughing the Atlantic with all the rest. Long tankers in ballast which with luck would be almost awash on the return trip, every bunker filled to the brim with fuel, the life-blood of any war-machine.

Ships which had come from the Clyde and the Solway Firth, from Liverpool bay and Londonderry to join in this great array of salt-smeared and rusty silhouettes, around which the escorts plunged and harried like terriers. The merchantmen were more used to it, while for the lean destroyers the slow passage was hard to take, and for the new hands it was an introduction to the Atlantic roll and the seasickness which went with it. The slow lift of the bows, so that the ship seemed to hang motionless while the sea surged against one side, before giving that terrible corkscrew plunge down again, hurling water high over the bridge and sheltering gun crews.

Many a meal went flying, or untouched; personal possessions clattered about the messdecks in a mixture of spilled tea and vomit.

This, then, was the world Ordinary Seaman Andrew Milvain shared with the old hands – old to him anyway – and those like himself who had joined straight from the spit-and-polish of a naval training establishment.

Apart from the usual quips about his very youthful appearance and what the seamen called his 'posh' accent, he was accepted far more easily than he had expected. His quiet dedication and almost fanatical efforts to learn all he could, even when he was laid low with seasickness, won him both respect and curiosity.

As the forenoon watch was relieved on this particular day Milvain climbed down the ladder to join his new companions in the mess. Nine Mess was little more than a scrubbed wooden table, which was covered in oilcloth for the main meal of the day. There were benches to sit on, and the curved side of the mess was lined with cushion-covered lockers, above which the lucky ones stowed their cap-boxes and other personal items on shelves.

Leading Seaman Bruce Fernie, 'killick' of the mess, sat on one of the lockers reading an old newspaper while the meal was passed down from the deck above by the duty cooks. He glanced up and said wearily, 'All out of bloody tins again! I'll bet them buggers in the barracks do better!'

The plates were passed along the table where fiddles were fitted to restrain them when the ship rolled, which was often.

Fernie watched the boy tucking in busily, as if he had not eaten for a year. Tinned potatoes, tinned sausages, tinned carrots, with some kind of plum duff and watery custard to follow. 'Don't they feed you at 'ome?'

Milvain gave his shy smile. He was thinking of the letter he had written to his mother before the ship had sailed from Liverpool. *His first ship.* What she was like, and a piece about these very same men. Rough and tough for the most part, but always ready with grudging praise when he did something properly. He wrote of the captain, but left out the piece about mistaking him for a petty officer. He still blushed about it. But mostly he had told them about Sub-Lieutenant Bizley, the talk about the medal he was going to receive. They would like that. He often thought about his dead brother; he had been something like the captain in a way. A face full of experience, a match for any occasion from taking over the bridge to facing Bully Bishop across the defaulters' table, where he had indeed dipped his hood as Leading Seaman Fernie had prophesied.

He felt his stomach heave as the deck lifted again. If only the sea were visible. But the scuttles had the deadlights screwed tightly shut. That was hardly surprising as the mess was the closest one to the bows, directly below the main messdeck which ran the full length of the forecastle. They had pulled his leg about that too. He glanced at the deck between the messes. They had told him that some of the main fuel tanks were under there. Some joker had said, 'You won't feel a bloody thing, Wings. Straight up to the pearly gates!'

It was a Sunday, and as bridge-messenger Milvain had been kept busy with tea or kye for the watchkeepers, up and down the steep ladders, gauging the moment so as not to be drenched by an incoming sea, or flung bodily to an unyielding deck. He made up little sketches in his mind as he bustled about and tried to keep out of everybody's way.

The captain, hatless, his hair thick with spray as he chatted to the yeoman of signals, an unlit pipe between his teeth. The officer-of-the-watch, in this case Lieutenant Finlay, as he passed his helm and revolutions orders, or shouted over the loud-hailer at one of the merchantmen as they thrashed abeam.

On the bridge there was always a sense of purpose, whereas elsewhere the ship seemed to exist on rumour. The latest buzz had been about Bizley and his medal . . . Milvain could not fathom it out. Nobody seemed to like him. Even the bear-like leading seaman with his newspaper, usually a tolerant man, had remarked, 'That's all I need, a bloody 'ero! That sod will get your arse shot off and still expect a salute!'

Milvain was astonished and overwhelmed by the sea itself. It was like nothing he had seen, even in the cinema. This summer's morning when the watch had changed, and the weary lookouts and gun crews had scattered to their messes, the ocean had seemed all-powerful and fierce. Dark, dark waves and troughs broken only here and there by fans of spray, the whole lifting and falling, it seemed level with the bridge itself. When the sun found its way across the horizon he had felt no warmth, just salt hardening on his cheeks and lips. Then the sea would change, the colour a shark-blue which rolled along the columns of merchant ships with disdain, as if merely to display its latent power. He could not imagine it in a full gale as one of the boatswain's mates had described it.

Fernie had interrupted scornfully. 'That's right, Bill, swing the bloody lamp, will you?' To Milvain he added, 'Bill talks so soddin' much you'd think he was vaccinated with a gramophone needle!'

At first Milvain had flushed at some of the language he had heard, the embellished experiences some had had on runs ashore, but not now; not too much anyway. It was like the sea and the danger. It was there all the time. Something you had to accept.

One by one the men of Nine Mess found corners to lie or crouch into, their lifejackets worn loosely and uninflated. Just in case.

As it was Sunday, there was a make-and-mend for the afternoon. Then on watch again for the first dog at four o'clock. Order, routine, and, many said, boredom. But not Milvain.

He watched as the big leading hand opened his ditty box and produced some intricate ropework, turk's heads which he had fashioned into handsome handles for a chest he kept somewhere. Milvain was fascinated by it. Fernie's hands, like the man, were huge, scarred by his work as captain of the quarterdeck and in charge of the depth-charges there, and yet he could produce delicate mats of twine, and carving from old packing cases which would put a joiner to shame.

Fernie looked at him thoughtfully. 'You don't mind talking about it, do you, laddie?'

Milvain flinched. He knew now what *it* meant. 'No. Not really.'

Fernie peered down at his ropework. 'I lost one of my brothers at Dunkirk.' So casually said. 'I still miss him, strangely enough.' Again that steady stare. 'We never really got on, y'see, not close like we should 'ave bin. I think about that sometimes.'

Milvain stared at him. He had never imagined that this huge man could be moved by anything.

The fingers tugged at the rope. '*Sod it!* It's not right!' Then he said, 'I wouldn't 'ave too much to do with Mister Bizley, if I was you. I know 'is kind. In this ship I've seen 'em all.' He darted a glance at the opposite mess which was made up mostly of telegraphists, signalmen and supply assistants. A few snores from there, but nobody moved.

'But – but – the medal, Hookey? He's getting the same one as the captain's!'

Fernie grinned at his outraged voice. 'Bits of tin. This ship was awarded some gongs after one trip, and the lads 'ad to draw names from an 'at.' He stifled a laugh. 'A leadin' cook we 'ad then drew a medal, an' *he* was drunk and still ashore on the day of the action!' It amused him greatly. 'The Old Man, that's different. 'E earned it, 'e does every time 'e gets us back 'ome in one piece, in my book!' He changed tack and asked abruptly, 'Did anyone see Subbie Bizley when it 'appened!' He saw the sudden brightness in Milvain's eyes and said, 'Forget it, son. It's just that I don't see 'im as a ruddy 'ero!'

Milvain was still thinking about it when he went on deck and climbed to the bridge for the first dog watch. As he passed the chart-room which opened off the wheelhouse he heard the murmur of orders and acknowledgements as the watchkeepers handed over to their reliefs. It never failed to excite him. The shining brass telegraphs and wheel, and the gyro-repeater ticking this way and that, as the quartermaster, a very subdued Able Seaman Bishop, brought the ship on to a new course.

'Want a look?' It was Morgan, the navigator's yeoman. He led the way into the chart-room and explained the ship's track, speed and estimated time of arrival. There had been plenty of buzzes about that too, but now Milvain actually knew their destination. Halifax. *Canada*. His heart thudded. He had never been further than Bournemouth or Ramsgate until he had joined the Navy.

Morgan saw that he was impressed and added loftily, 'I'll try and get you transferred here if you like. With Jimmy-the-One doing two jobs at once it's more than enough for me. Besides,' he added accusingly, 'you're hoping to be an officer, right?'

'Well, yes. I thought that you . . .'

Morgan grinned. 'I failed.'

Milvain digested the information. 'When we reach Canada, I mean what . . .'

Morgan looked at the gently vibrating chart. 'Big convoy. Heard the Old Man discussing it with Jimmy.'

'What about this one?'

'Safe now.' He lowered his voice. 'W/T had a signal last night. A homebound convoy was clobbered to the south of us. Sounded like a butcher's shop.' He bit his lip as if the casual dismissal was no longer a protection. 'It's the full convoys the krauts are after, not the likes of this one.' He stared at him, but Milvain thought that he did not see him. 'The PO telegraphist was saying there were *thirty* U-Boats in the attack! Can you believe it? That's more than the bloody escorts!'

Sub-Lieutenant Ayres entered the chart-room and picked up some brass dividers.

Morgan guided Milvain to the door. 'You heard about his brother?'

Milvain shook his head although he guessed what was coming.

'He was in North Africa.' He drew one finger across his throat. 'Rest in peace!'

Milvain went down to the steaming galley to collect another fanny of tea. He was learning quite a lot.

Milvain was on the bridge for the morning watch when daylight uncovered the craggy shoreline in the far distance, and shortly afterwards they were joined by two Canadian destroyers and a dozen corvettes fussing around to divide and re-route the convoy, which had arrived without the loss of a man or a ship.

He was pouring the last of the tea for a boatswain's mate by the voicepipes, while lights clattered and winked in greeting from the Canadian warships. He heard the captain say, 'Local leave only tonight, Number One, whichever watch is due. But we go alongside the oiler first.'

Milvain heard Lieutenant Treherne say, 'God, look at that lot!'

He peered over the salt-splashed glass screen and saw a mass of deep-laden ships anchored in lines, and without asking, knew it was part of the next convoy. Their convoy.

Treherne raised his binoculars and added flatly, 'Lambs to the slaughter.'

Howard said, 'I'll take over the con, Number One. We'll go alongside, starboard side-to, if I can find the bloody thing!'

They both laughed and Milvain felt the cold fingers around his heart relax their grip. He tried to cheer himself up at the prospect of a run ashore in Halifax. A foreign country.

Across the bridge Howard was watching him. He said, 'Take it off your back, Milvain. This isn't *Boys' Own Paper*, this is the *real* Navy. You know what they say, don't you?'

Milvain nodded. 'If you can't take a joke, you shouldn't have joined, sir!'

Howard grinned. 'So be it. Off you go for another brew of sergeant-major's tea, eh?'

Treherne paused at the bridge gate, one leg hanging in space. 'You just made his day, sir.'

Howard stared past him at the moored merchantmen. So helpless. He replied quietly, 'You just murdered mine.'

9

'. . . And Don't Look Back'

At a steady, economical speed the U-Boat thrust her way through the dark water, white feathers of spray bursting occasionally from her raked stem to drift over the bridge like rain. It was cold, but not uncomfortably so, and after what they had been used to there had been few grumbles from the crew. The stores loaded at their new French base had been far more plentiful than usual, and baskets of apples had been wedged anywhere throughout the hull where there was still space.

The ocean had its usual impressive swell, but the tight knot of lookouts stationed around the bridge found it easy to keep their balance. In the forepart of the bridge the officer-of-the-watch levelled his glasses and hunted for the horizon. But it was an hour until dawn, and there was still nothing to betray it.

He could picture it in his mind, the endless expanse of ocean with no land beyond those sharp bows but the southern-most tip of Greenland, four hundred miles away. He was not new to this part of the Western Ocean, and often thought how aptly named that hostile wedge of land had become. Cape Farewell. It had certainly been the last sighting for many an unfortunate mariner.

The officer listened to the powerful throb of diesel engines vibrating through the narrow conning-tower while they sucked down the air from above to charge the batteries.

They would have to dive before too long, and rely solely on the electric motors to carry them as close as possible to the enemy.

He felt the usual tightening of his stomach muscles; one never really got used to it. Nobody who had been aboard during that last attack would forget. The sudden explosion of a faulty torpedo, the boat going into a crash dive as the destroyer had stripped them naked with a starshell. The depth-charges which had gone on and on. Afterwards they had stared at one another with dazed disbelief. They had survived – once again luck had stayed with them. He thought of the captain. Not even a blink. As cool as spring water.

He felt the sailor nearest to him stiffen slightly and knew the man who held all their destinies in his eye and brain was coming up.

Kleiber took several deep breaths to clear his throat and insides from the stench of diesel, boiled cabbage and sweat. It clung to his hair and body; it was like a scar, a mark of their profession.

He had been studying the chart, calculating and trying to guess exactly when it would happen.

A convoy was heading towards them from Halifax, or should be if the code-breakers at U-boat HQ were proved right. At least thirty ships, over half of them tankers: a twelve-knot convoy.

How did they know, *really* know, he wondered. Their own agents in Nova Scotia, perhaps? Or had this vital intelligence been transmitted by wireless? Information of such importance was usually sent direct by submarine cable laid on the seabed, which could not be tampered with. Maybe that had been too busy at the time, and some senior official had decided to risk a coded signal.

Kleiber looked at the sky and thought of the chart again. They were heading north-west, crossing the longitude of forty degrees west. Beyond that the convoy would have no air cover from land-based American or Canadian patrols. The gap, which reached as far east as longitude twenty, *was* the killing-ground. Only an aircraft carrier would suffice, and the allies reserved those to protect their capital ships, or their operations in the Pacific.

He thought suddenly of his mother during that last, unexpected leave. She had wanted to know about the war. A mild, gentle lady who had aged considerably; probably because of the scattered air raids and shortages, he thought. She loved and admired him, proud to a point of embarrassment, and always had a big photograph of him on display for the neighbours' benefit, the one of him shaking hands with the Führer after being awarded his second Iron Cross.

She had been proud too of his young brother, Willi, the first one in the family to enter university. She had asked Kleiber repeatedly during his leave how *it* could have happened. A cheeky youth with bad eyesight and student's cap, who had been doing so well with his work. His tutors had told her as much. Then, out of the blue he had been told, along with several other students, that he was required for duty in the Wehrmacht.

Kleiber thought he knew the reason but could not allow himself to believe it. Willi talked too much; but then so did a lot of students. They did not have the discipline and purpose of the armed services to restrain their high spirits. But Willi as a soldier? It was ludicrous.

He lifted his powerful Zeiss night-glasses from the cover of his oilskin and trained them abeam. But it was a fish, leaping from another predator. He readjusted the glasses and stared hard into the darkness. Seven hundred miles abeam lay the coast of Newfoundland, the home of some of the greatest fisher-men in the world. The convoy must have wended its way around that coast after leaving Halifax astern to the south-west. Getting the feel of one another,

zig-zagging and changing formation until the escort commanders were as satisfied as they could be. A few days later and the watchful anti-submarine aircraft
would dwindle in the distance. The convoy would stand alone.

He peered at his watch. Not long now. He remarked as much to the watch
officer who repeated his instructions down the voicepipe.

The lieutenant beside him smelt of cigars; probably some he had come by in
France. It made Kleiber think of his father, and he knew he had been avoiding
that too. His mind had to be empty of everything but the work in hand. His eyes
and brain had to be clearer than any prismatic gunsight. He moved away from
the others and listened to the thud of diesels dying away to be replaced instantly
by the electric motors.

His father had been little more than a motor-mechanic before, but his skills
had soon been recognised when the full demands of war were made evident. As
the pace had mounted, so his position had expanded and improved. His mother
had been pleased; there had never been much money to spare before the war.

Now he was in charge of a whole factory, not a large one, but one involved in
manufacturing small, intricate machine parts for tanks and half-tracks.

He had seemed much troubled this time and Kleiber had watched him lighting
a cheroot, one of a box he had given him as a present.

Eventually, after taking him to one side, he had explained that he had become
unhappy with the way he was expected to work. There were some kind of official
supervisors who came and went with lists and demands, longer working hours –
in fact a twenty-four-hour rota system was now in force. Kleiber had tried to pull
him out of his depression, and told him they never stopped for a minute in the
Atlantic. But it had been no use.

His father had stared at him anxiously and had spoken about the people who
were being brought to work as unskilled labour, under the supervision of the SS,
a unit of which was always at the factory.

Kleiber found himself recalling that conversation over and over now, when all
he wanted was to prepare himself for action.

His father had described them as prisoners, civilians for the most part, women
as well as men. Half-starved and frightened.

Kleiber bit his lip. The work to support the armed services must go on, no
matter what else was happening. Prisoners took no risks, and if they were criminals it was only right they should do something useful to help.

The lieutenant let out a quick breath and Kleiber moved swiftly to join him
again. The sky was lightening. There was an horizon of sorts, and he could even
see the U-Boat's bows, the saw-like net-cutter rising above it like a scythe.

The dawn strengthened, and although the light was approaching from the east,
the sky was so clear that he could see the stain above the horizon. The telltale
mark of drifting smoke. In such a vast span of open sea it could mean only one
thing. Ships, and many of them.

He called down the voicepipe and guessed he was the first of sixteen U-
Boats to make the sighting report. The others, as yet unseen and unheard, were
stretched out on either beam. They could muster nearly one hundred torpedoes
in the first salvoes.

He saw his men leaping for the oval hatch, leaving him alone on the narrow
bridge. It was always the most exhilarating moment. The thought of standing

here, doing nothing but wait for the sea to come roaring over the lip of the conning tower, riding the boat down like some armoured monster until he could feel no more. He snapped down the voicepipe and sealed it by turning the small cock. Then, without haste, he pressed the klaxon alarm before lowering himself through the upper hatch and dragging it down with a thud over his head. The boat was already going into a dive, the water surging into the saddle-tanks to force her under.

Checks completed, the boat glided up again to periscope depth. Kleiber signalled for it to be raised and knelt down to catch it even as it cut above the surface.

There they were, dark flaws against the pale horizon, moving diagonally; slow, tired, already doomed.

The exact moment of truth, the click of cranks which made the final settings to the torpedoes; the sudden chilling stillness.

The periscope hissed down.

'Feueraubis!'

'Fächer eins! . . . *Los!*'

'Fächer zwei! . . . *Los!*'

There was little more than a slight thud as each torpedo started up and flashed from its tube. Kleiber nodded to his engineer and felt the deck begin to tilt down again.

The attack had begun. It would not end until all the tubes were empty, or the boat was scattered across the bottom of this pitiless ocean.

'Signal from commodore, sir! *Alter course in succession, steer zero-five-zero!*'

Howard swung away as another explosion tore the morning apart, and was in time to see the tall white columns falling with deceptive slowness even as the ship began to veer out of formation, smoke and flames spurting through her side and upper deck.

Treherne called, 'Starboard ten! *Steady!* Steer zero-five-zero!'

Gladiator was at the rear of the starboard column and must turn earlier than the others to retain the protective shield on the convoy.

Howard had known it would be today; some of the others had had the same feeling, he thought. It had all started too well; the ships in the convoy were all veterans of the Atlantic and were quick to respond to the signals of the commodore and escort commander alike.

Thirty-two ships, over half of them deep-laden tankers, with four destroyers, six corvettes and an elderly sloop like Ayres's old patrol vessel to protect them. But no air cover, not even for such a vital list of cargoes. The first victim had been one of the tankers, a fairly new vessel which had protested to the commodore when the overall speed was further reduced to eight knots because of a freighter's engine-failure. She had been carrying high-octane aircraft fuel and had exploded in one tremendous fireball, fragments of metal and flaming debris scattering over and around the other ships, the heat so fierce that Howard imagined he could feel it against his face.

Three of the corvettes were working up to full speed as they charged to the attack, their progress marked across the grey sea by towering geysers of water as their depth-charges thundered down. Again and again, the sea's face was littered with stunned or gutted fish which floated through leaking oil, upturned lifeboats and meaningless human remains. Two more explosions on the far side of the convoy, and immediately two more, so that the roar blended together like thunder over the hills.

The yeoman of signals said harshly, 'There's another one, the poor buggers!'

The ship in question was already turning slowly onto her beam, steam shooting from her shattered engine room where her people must have died in the worst known manner.

Crated cargo, dismantled aircraft lined up like unfinished toys, were tumbling into the sea, and one of the lifeboats hurled its occupants down to join them as flames burned through the boat's falls before it could reach the water.

'*Redwing*'s calling up the commodore, sir! Requests permission to pick up survivors.'

Howard turned to watch some men floundering in the sea, staring up at *Gladiator* as she surged past, their cries and screams lost in the thunder of depth-charges and the roar of fans.

'Permission denied.'

The yeoman glanced at his young signalman. 'Don't gape at *me*, watch the bloody commodore!'

It was getting to him. Tommy Tucker, the hard yeoman who saw and heard everything that went on in his bridge but kept it to himself; a man who had seen sailors die horribly in the blaze of a convoy battle, or quietly and without dignity in the freezing water.

Howard heard the brittle edge to his voice. Just how much could a man take, and still be made to watch helpless sailors blown to pieces?

'Signal, sir. *Increase to thirteen knots.*'

The last ship to go had been the offending freighter with engine trouble. She would never delay another convoy.

One more oiler to explode before a lull fell over the heaving water. Once again the elderly sloop *Redwing* requested permission to search for survivors with the same response. It was the nightmare all over again. *Do not stop; close up the gaps.*

Howard massaged his eyes with his fingers. They should add: *and don't look back!*

He turned deliberately and trained his glasses astern. It was as if the convoy itself was bleeding to death as he watched. Two ships gone completely, four more either burning fiercely or with their decks already awash, their sacrifice marked by a bright sheen of oil as wide as the whole convoy. Boats, wreckage, and men who could only stare with stunned disbelief as the formation headed away.

Howard said, 'It's a pity they can't see this at home, Number One. The black marketeers, the people who brag about getting petrol for their cars despite the rationing.' He turned from the pitiful scene and added with bitterness, '*God damn them all!*'

Howard saw Ayres staring at him from the compass platform, the others around him, moulded together more than ever because of the horror they shared, the apparent helplessness which rendered them impotent while so many died. And tonight the U-Boats would rise like evil sharks to the surface to give chase with greater speed afforded by their diesels. The Admiralty had said there were ten U-Boats in the vicinity. How had they come here? Where did they get this information? Tomorrow would begin like this one. And the next, and the next.

There was a dull boom astern and he heard the Asdic report, 'Ship breaking up, sir!'

Treherne acknowledged it, his features like stone while he lifted his glasses to watch the remaining hulks falling further and further astern. The corvettes closed round their charges again, and Howard imagined their hands working feverishly to reload the depth-charge racks and prepare for the next encounter.

He said, 'See if you can drum up something hot for the lads to drink. The sandwiches are already done in the galley, though God knows the bread will be like asbestos after all this time!'

Treherne passed his instructions to the boatswain's mate and said, 'You knew, didn't you, sir?' It all added up. Howard's lack of surprise, his instructions about there being plenty of sandwiches well in advance.

Howard raised his glasses again as a diamond-bright light winked across the convoy. It was Captain Vickers's *Kinsale* at the head of the port column from where he controlled the escort and gauged the commodore's next move. He seemed to have that uncanny knack of guessing each manoeuvre, and had proved his skill as well as his worth from the moment they had left Halifax.

The yeoman said, '*Kinsale*'s got a contact, sir!' He almost yelled aloud, 'Black pendant's gone up! He signalled *Ganymede* to assist!'

Stiffly, like old men, the gun-crews and damage control parties crowded around their stations to watch as the big destroyer with the leader's black band on her squat funnel appeared to leap away from the convoy. The bow-wave mounted around her raked stem so that she seemed to dig her stern deeper into the sea to thrust her forward, while tiny figures ran to the quarterdeck to set the charges for the first pattern.

Angled towards her at ninety degrees, *Gladiator*'s sister-ship was swaying in a welter of yellow foam as Colvin brought her hard round, ready to surge across his leader's wake with his own set of charges.

'There she goes!'

There was a ragged cheer as the first charges exploded and hurled spray in the air like something solid. Then another pattern, and as the black pendant vanished at the destroyer's yard, *Ganymede* increased speed to pass across the area where the sea still boiled in torment.

The yeoman called, 'From *Kinsale*, sir. *Join the party!*'

'Starboard fifteen! Full ahead together!'

Howard lowered his eye to the compass. '*Steady!* Steer zero-eight-zero!' Over his shoulder he added, 'Warn Bizley, Number One. Full pattern!' It was like a touch on the shoulder, a chill breeze on the skin. He was almost surprised to hear himself say, 'Belay that, Number One. Tell Guns. Prepare to engage!'

He saw the boy Milvain swaying at the bridge gate, a huge fanny of steaming tea dragging at one arm.

Treherne passed his order and stared across at his captain by the compass. More charges roared down as *Kinsale* thrashed back along the same track.

Howard was aware of so many things at once. The new multiple pom-poms training soundlessly round to starboard, the main armament following suit as if they were about to engage the other destroyers. He also saw the old sloop

Redwing blowing out smoke as she increased speed to fill *Gladiator*'s gap in the defences.

More charges. He was even able to picture them, falling so slowly, down and down to detonate like savage eyes around the submarine's blurred outline.

He rarely thought of the men who served in them. The U-Boat was weapon and crew all in one. A mind of its own. The hunter.

'From *Kinsale* sir! *Remain on station. I have another contact at three-five-zero!*'

There was something like a groan of disappointment as *Ganymede* heeled over, showing her bilge as she turned steeply to follow the leader once more.

The yeoman exclaimed angrily, 'Lost the bastard!'

Howard said sharply, 'Look!' He raised his glasses and stared at the great surge of bubbles and oil which rose to the surface and rolled swiftly away into the troughs. Then, like an obscene monster, the U-Boat began to break surface, bows first until something brought her under control and she came down fully and untidily on the broken water.

Men appeared just as suddenly on the casing, flowing down the side of the conning-tower, their features lost in distance.

The boatswain's mate gasped. 'The buggers are goin' to surrender!' He was almost incoherent with wild excitement.

The yeoman rasped, 'Are they fuckin' hell!'

Howard shouted, '*Open fire!*' He stared at the surfaced U-Boat as it lay pitching in the disturbance of its own making. She had been damaged by the charges; there were jagged marks on the casing. But the U-Boat's long gun, larger than any of *Gladiator*'s, was already pivotting round until he was looking straight down its muzzle.

'*Hard a-port!*' That would give Finlay a chance to use all his armament, even though the move made *Gladiator* a larger target.

He saw the flash of the U-Boat's gun and heard the shell scream overhead before exploding far abeam. Then the air was ripped apart by the clattering pom-poms and the sharper crash of the four-point-sevens. Water-spouts fell near the submarine's hull and burst in the sea beyond it. Tracer clawed over the water and struck fire from the casing and conning-tower where some madman had managed to run up the German ensign.

The rapid fire of the lighter weapons cut down the U-Boat's gun crew like bloodied rag dolls, but even when the order to cease fire was repeated one Oerlikon gunner continued to rake the enemy's deck until his magazine was empty, and there were only jerking corpses to be seen.

Howard shouted, 'Continue firing! Tell Guns I want to be certain this time.'

Holes appeared in the U-Boat's saddle-tank, and he noticed for the first time that its hull was covered in slime and weed. It had probably been at sea for weeks, maybe refuelled in these same waters by one of their big supply boats, the 'milch-cows'.

He watched more shells burst alongside and found that he could do it without compassion. Even when some small figures appeared on the conning-tower only to be cut down by Finlay's withering fire, he felt nothing but the need to destroy this thing and all that it had come to mean to him.

Treherne said, 'Never thought I'd see the day!'

Howard did not reply but watched intently as the slime-covered hull began to lift into the air bows-first, smoke pumping from the shattered conning-tower. He steadied his glasses with great care and saw some small designs painted on the punctured steel plates below the periscope standards. Ships sunk. Men killed. A record of murder.

Two figures were in the sea, although it was not possible to know how they had survived.

'She's going!'

There was no cheering this time. Just the cold satisfaction of victory after so many, *too* many failures.

The U-Boat dived and Howard called, 'Take her alongside those men in the water, Number One.'

He saw Treherne's surprise and hurt. Because of all the men they had left to die back there. And now they were stopping for two of their attackers. Howard shook his head. 'They are not survivors. To me, they are nothing more than trophies. Evidence of a kill. It's not much, but – '

He ran to the side as a lookout shouted, 'Torpedo running to starboard, sir!' Just for a second or so he saw the steely line as it tore through the water and cut across the bows. If *Gladiator* had not reduced speed to wait for the two Germans, she would have taken the torpedo amidships. It must have been fired at extreme range, perhaps on the off chance of a hit after the first bloody and successful attack. They were lucky.

He felt the shock of the explosion and turned with sudden dismay as the little sloop *Redwing* began to settle down, the sea already surging through the great hole in her side. *Redwing* was on *Gladiator*'s proper station. Again he felt the chill breeze on his skin. *Either way it was meant for us.*

'Slow ahead together. Stand by to go alongside portside-to. Tell the Buffer to have all the hammocks brought up to cushion the two hulls as we come together. Yeoman, call up *Redwing* and tell them to hold on.' He thought suddenly of his ship's motto. *With a strong hand.* It was all he could offer now.

He watched the narrowing gap, saw the chaos where fittings had been flung to the deck, blood running on the steel plates as men had been crushed and broken. A ship dying.

'Stop engines.' He added to the voicepipe, 'Ease her in, Cox'n. We haven't got a lot of time.' Another quick glance. Perhaps even now a U-Boat's crosswires were holding *Gladiator* and her sinking consort like victims in a web. No, this torpedo had come a long way, otherwise *Kinsale* or *Ganymede* would have made contact.

'Slow astern starboard. *Stop.*'

Treherne stood high above the screen to watch the Buffer and his men reaching out to seize the first staggering figures from the other vessel. Sub-Lieutenant Bizley was taking charge, and he saw Lawford the doctor waiting by the guardrails with his SBA.

Treherne said urgently, 'She's going under, sir!' There was a curtain of steam hissing above the sloop's thin funnel and Howard wondered if any of the stokers had managed to get out.

The last one to be pulled roughly from the tilting deck was the *Redwing*'s captain, a bearded RNR officer, a bit like Treherne.

'Cast off! Slow astern starboard! Stand by with fenders!'

Howard watched the captain's despair. It was physical. Like an unhealable wound. *How would I feel if* Gladiator *went down, and I was left behind.*

'Pass the word to bring him to the bridge.' Howard lowered his eye to the compass again. 'Half ahead together.' When he looked again, *Redwing* was gone, leaving just the usual whirlpool, the rubbish and the oil. The commodore would likely give him a blast for stopping. 'What the hell – who cares anyway!' He saw some of the sailors grinning at him and realised he had spoken aloud. He felt a sudden warmth for these men, who trusted him, and who could still find a smile somewhere even when others had died. Not unknown merchant sailors this time but men like themselves. The same uniforms and badges, the same backgrounds and grumbles.

Treherne said, 'Steady on zero-five-zero, sir, revolutions one-one-zero.' He eyed Howard, the question still unasked.

Howard thought of the two Germans he had been about to take from the sea when the torpedo had suddenly appeared. He said quietly, 'What Germans?' He turned as the other commanding officer was helped up the bridge ladder.

The man stared uncertainly at the interlaced gold stripes on Treherne's jacket which matched his own, and then allowed Howard to guide him to the bridge chair by the screen, not so very different from the one he had just left.

Howard stood beside him and began to fill his pipe. There was nothing he could say to this man. The right words eluded him; the wrong ones would be an insult.

Redwing's captain touched his arm but stared ahead at the approaching convoy. 'Thanks.'

Perhaps there were no words.

Someone said, ''Ere comes the mungie! 'Bout time too!' as the sandwiches were brought through the bridge gate.

Gladiator seemed to shake herself. Once again routine was taking over.

On a grey blustery morning HMS *Gladiator* said goodbye to the convoy and with the other escorts headed for the docks.

Howard sat on the bridge chair and stared through the smeared glass screen while Treherne handed him a cup of steaming tea. Afterwards he knew he must have fallen asleep where he sat, and that Treherne had shaken his arm to wake him.

He shivered. It was cold on the open bridge, more like winter than autumn, but he knew it was not just the weather. He felt utterly drained, and was unable to share the relief of many of his men, the luxury of returning to Liverpool when others had died.

They had lost eleven ships from the convoy, five of them tankers, left astern like drifting pyres to mark their hopeless fight. But for a completely unexpected Force Nine westerly gale which had scattered the U-Boat pack, but had helped rather than hampered the remaining merchantmen, the losses would have been twice as many. From the eleven ships there were barely more than thirty survivors.

Howard swallowed the tea and watched the familiar silhouette of the Crosby

Light Vessel as *Gladiator* made another turn and followed the *Kinsale* up-river to the docks.

They had already been ordered to proceed directly to Gladstone Dock and refuel. They would be told eventually when the next convoy was ready for another long haul to Canadian waters. Howard tried to shut it from his mind. *Then back again.* The picture refused to budge. Men in the water calling for help. Ships sinking and on fire, the roar of torpedoes in the night. He even thought of the two survivors from the U-Boat they had sent to the bottom. With disgust sometimes, because he had been glad to leave them to die. To discover how it felt.

He slid from the chair and picked up his binoculars. 'I'll take over, Number One. You'd better get up forrard for entering dock.'

Treherne hesitated and glanced at the others. Ayres was bending over the ready-use chart-table, but was probably worrying about his brother, and if there was any more news. Finlay, who was the OOW, was looking at the shore, ready to remind the signalmen if there were any lights or flags which they should have seen. Tucker the yeoman was also watching, making certain that Finlay would not catch his team at a loss.

He said, 'Remember, sir, we got a U-Boat.' He forced a grin. 'After our chums blew it to the surface for us! That's a bonus surely?'

Howard bent over the voicepipe. 'Starboard ten. *Steady.* Steer for the mark, Cox'n.' He heard Sweeney's rumbled acknowledgement. How many orders had he passed down this voicepipe? Changes of speed and helm, emergency turns, and desperate zigzags to avoid drifting merchantmen or lifeboats. No wonder the wheelhouse always seemed such a haven of peace in harbour.

He replied, 'A drop in the bucket.' He tried to shake himself out of it. Like the hand on the shoulder again. 'But our people did well, especially when you consider most of them were at school a short while back.' He raised his glasses to look at the birds on top of the Liver Buildings. It was not really home, but at this moment it felt like it.

The yeoman called, 'From *Kinsale*, sir. *Captain repair on board when convenient.*'

Howard nodded. 'Acknowledge.' He saw the question in Treherne's eyes and said wearily, 'I'm about to get a bottle for going alongside *Redwing*, I expect!'

'Well, if that's all the thanks you get for . . .'

Howard waved to a small tug which was heading down-river, her crew lounging on deck like a bunch of old salts. He turned to answer but Treherne had gone. Seething, no doubt, in defence of his captain.

When convenient was a way of saying he should get shaved and changed before presenting himself in front of Captain Vickers. Maybe the commodore had made an official complaint about his act of mercy. Perhaps it was merely to decide who would take the credit for sinking the German submarine!

In fact it was neither.

As soon as *Gladiator* had secured alongside the oiler in Gladstone Dock, Howard walked across to board the big K-Class destroyer. He felt vaguely embarrassed in his best Number Fives, the gold lace very different from the tarnished, almost brown rings on his sea-going jacket.

Men were at work everywhere, washing down the decks and superstructure to wipe away the stains of battle. Others were dragging sacks of expended cannon shells, which would end up somewhere being made into fresh ammunition. A few would find their way to the stokers' messdeck to be fashioned into ashtrays and paperweights.

The *Kinsale*'s first lieutenant greeted him with a smart salute. 'Bad trip, sir.' He looked at the shore. 'Even this place looks good to me now!'

Howard eyed him gravely. First lieutenants as a breed knew everything, or should do. 'What's all this about, Number One?'

He shrugged. 'In God's name, sir, I really don't know. All I *do* know is that an admiral, no less, is with the captain right now.' He glanced at his watch. 'You're to go down as soon as you arrive.'

Howard could feel him staring after him, probably wondering if he was seeing the next candidate for a court martial.

A white-jacketed steward opened the door for him, but looked away when Howard was about to speak.

Captain Vickers greeted him with a firm handshake and smiled. 'Bloody good show, David!' But the smile did not touch his eyes.

Howard saw a tall rear-admiral standing by an open scuttle drinking coffee. He looked young for his rank, keen-eyed and alert like Vickers.

Vickers began, 'This is Rear-Admiral Lanyon, David. It's all very difficult – ' The admiral put down his cup and looked at Howard very directly.

'Lieutenant-Commander Howard is a good officer, so I'll come straight to the point. I was asked to come and see you myself, by my daughter actually. I understand that she came to visit you.'

Howard did not know what to say. He had never heard of Lanyon, and his daughter did not make any sense. Lanyon continued, 'You knew her as Kirke, her married name.'

Howard stared at him. That was why they had not known her at Portsmouth; she was using her maiden name.

'So when I heard your ETA at Liverpool I drove up.' He tried to smile, like Vickers, but it would not come. 'As ordered!'

'What is it, sir? Has something happened?' The hand on the shoulder. He should have known.

Lanyon said quietly, 'There was an air raid five days ago. I'm afraid your father was killed. A direct hit on the house.'

Howard walked to an open scuttle and stared out blindly. It was not happening. For an instant he had imagined something was wrong with the girl, then in the same split second he had thought of his brother. Even though he was on a course, things like that did happen. *But not the Guvnor* . . .

He heard himself ask, 'Was it – I mean did he . . .' He could not go on.

Lanyon said, 'My daughter could tell you. She went there afterwards, to find out. It was all over in an instant, I understand. He could have felt nothing. It's not much help, but it's better to know he didn't suffer.'

Captain Vickers asked, 'Drink, David?' He eyed him with concern. 'I'm damn sorry, I really am.'

Howard shook his head. Needing to be alone; not knowing what to do. 'No, I must get back aboard. We're alongside the oiler.'

Vickers said, 'Let your Number One take charge. Do him bloody good!'

The admiral looked at the clock. 'I'm to see the C-in-C very shortly.' He glanced at Howard. 'I'll run you down to Hampshire in my car when you're ready. Suit you?'

Howard nodded. *Suit you?* How he had put it to Bizley about his DSC.

'What about my ship, sir?'

'We'll manage.' The admiral held out his hand for his oak-leaved cap. 'There'll be things you'll want to do, I expect. Your brother's been a tower of strength.'

'I'll see you over the side, sir.' Vickers looked at Howard. 'You stay here, David. Long as you like, right?'

The cabin was suddenly empty and quiet, with only the murmur of a generator and muffled shipboard noises to remind him where he was.

All those miles and all those ships and men. And now this. The Guvnor. He buried his face in his hands to stifle his emotion. What a thing to come home to. Except like the coxswain and Stoker Marshall, he no longer had a home.

There was a discreet tap at the door and the captain's steward padded into the cabin, a glass, filled almost to the brim, balanced on his tray.

He said, 'My old chum, Percy Vallance, told me just how you like it, sir, so I fixed you a big 'un.' He watched him take the glass. 'Sorry about your spot of news, sir.'

'Do they know aboard my ship already?' He pictured them in his mind. Curiosity and sympathy. *See how the Old Man can handle this one.*

The steward shrugged. 'Well, you know the *Andrew*, sir, nothing secret for long in this regiment. It happened to me last year. It's something you don't forget.'

Howard stared at him. Just an ordinary man, who was serving as a steward probably because he could get nothing better. And yet one who had taken it on himself to go over to *Gladiator* and ask his chum how his skipper liked his Horse's Neck.

'Bombing, was it?'

The steward looked into the far distance. 'No, sir. My dad was a merchant seaman. Found dead with some of his mates in an open boat after they was tinfished in the Atlantic. I've thought of him a few times these last weeks, I can tell you.'

Howard thought of that other drifting boat and its silent crew; Ayres overcoming his fear and horror; the girl's photograph found with one of the ragged corpses.

'Thank you for telling me.' He put down the glass, surprised that it was empty. 'I needed that.'

The steward smiled, knowing that Howard was not referring to the drink. He followed him to the door and said in parting, 'Well, sir, as *I* see it, it's what it's all about.'

The *Kinsale*'s first lieutenant saw him to the brow and saluted again. 'Sorry about your news, sir.'

Howard returned his salute. *Nothing secret for long in this regiment.*

He found Treherne waiting for him but before he could speak said, 'I'm going south for a couple of days, Number One. Look after her for me, and make certain the lads get as much shore leave as you can manage.'

'I just heard, sir. If there's anything I can do . . . but then, you know that by now, I hope?'

Howard met his gaze and thought of how he had nearly broken down, but for an unknown man's simple kindness. 'I may have to hold you to that one day – and yes, I've always known that.'

He looked along the ship's deserted decks. The hands were below in the messes reading their letters, getting ready to go ashore.

Treherne watched him grimly, knowing what he was thinking.

Welcome home.

10

Every Time You Say Goodbye

The man Howard had known all his life simply as Mister Mills placed two mugs of tea on his scrubbed table and studied the young officer opposite him. 'I've laced it with some rum, David. Do you good. Besides, it's going to be a cold 'un tonight.'

Howard nodded and warmed his hands around the mug. Mister Mills was older, but did not seem to have changed all that much. The same shabby sports jacket, and the beret he always wore indoors and out, pulled tightly down over his ears like a lid. His house was as he remembered, filled with odds and ends, furniture too, which Mister Mills sold when he had the mind to. Some described him as a junk-man, but in these hard times of shortages and rationing, he had come into his own again. He bought bits and pieces from bombed buildings, found furniture for people intending to get married and to hell with the war; like his battered old van, he was a familiar sight around Hampshire.

Howard shivered and thought of the long, fast drive from Liverpool. It had been spent mostly in silence, with Rear-Admiral Lanyon apparently content to leave him to his thoughts while he went through endless clips of signals.

Of the war the rear-admiral had said very little except, 'Your fight in the Atlantic is the essential one. Things must turn the corner soon.' But he was unprepared to enlarge on that flash of optimism.

He had mentioned his daughter only briefly. How she had held up after her pilot husband had been killed in Howard's convoy to Murmansk. Even through the grip of his own worries Howard had sensed, strangely, that Lanyon had not really approved of Jamie Kirke. He had called him a hero, but it had sounded like a mark of distaste.

He tried not to think of the house he had just left. The stench of wet ash left by the AFS hoses which would cling until the place was rebuilt. Two walls, a solitary chimney-stack standing like a crude monument, all the rest a shambles of broken glass and brickwork, and a hole that covered half the site where the bomb had come screaming down.

Mister Mills had explained how it had happened. A sneak daytime raid intended for the dockyard again, but the enemy aircraft had been confronted by the whole weight of Portsmouth's defences, from the ships in harbour to land-mounted batteries. Their attack had been further snared by the new ranks of barrage-balloons, which had forced the bombers to swerve aside and be caught by the onslaught of combined anti-aircraft fire, 'Like a Brock's benefit', he had described it.

Mister Mills watched him now thoughtfully. 'I've salvaged some of his gear, of course. You'll be coming back here one day, eh?'

Howard heard himself reply without hesitation. 'It's still my home.' The rum-laced tea was helping and he said, 'Where's the grave?'

Mister Mills looked at the window, darker even earlier this evening. 'Other end of the village.' He looked at his companion again, perhaps seeing his dead friend as he had once been before Zeebrugge. 'It was a nice service. There were six killed that day, David.' He let out a long sigh. Remembering. 'A hell of a lot in a place this size. But the pub was saved – that was one blessing, I suppose.'

'Could you tell me again, please?' He watched him pour two more mugs and wondered why he had to know.

'There was an air-raid warning, nothing unusual, even in daylight. The gunfire got so loud I said, we're in for it this time, never guessing the bastards would jettison their bombs over here. So we went out to the little shelter at the back of the house, but the dog was frightened.'

Howard nodded and thought of the dog he had never seen. 'She would be. Her own home was bombed earlier.'

'Just as we reached the shelter, the poor old thing broke away and ran back to the house. Like a shot he was after her, telling me to get down.' He gave a sad smile. 'Well, you know what he was like.'

There was silence and Howard heard a car clattering along the lane. Mister Mills had heard the bomb coming; he was sure he had seen the blur of it a split-second before it struck.

He said, 'They were killed together. I was knocked out myself. When I came to, old Tom the gamekeeper and a special constable were bending over me, and everything seemed to be on fire. I was a bit concussed, *they* said.' He added with his old contempt, 'What the hell do they know?'

Killed together. He thought of the girl with green eyes. She would blame herself for that too.

Mister Mills went on, 'Your brother and his wife were here for the funeral – even the two Eye-tie gardeners came along.' He looked at Howard with sudden interest. 'That young Wren girl was here as well. Real upset, she was.'

The bombs had devastated one complete side of the little lane. The victims shared a grave together, as they had shared their lives in this quiet corner of England.

Mister Mills cocked his head as another car slowed to a halt outside. The rear-admiral had even organised that for him. Mister Mills offered, 'You can stay here if you like.' He tried to shrug it off. 'It's a bit quiet now.'

Howard shook his head. 'I've things to do, but thanks – for everything you did for the Guvnor. I'll not forget. Ever.'

Mister Mills shuffled after him to the garden with its sagging gate. He touched it and said half to himself, 'Must fix it. One day.'

Howard waved to the khaki staff car. 'I'll be in Portsmouth if you need me. And then . . .'

503

Mister Mills nodded. *And then.* How many times had he pondered over it in his own war? 'Back to the Atlantic, David?'

'Yes.'

They shook hands in silence. Two wars apart, but linked by what they had both lost.

As the big Humber swung on to the main road, Howard turned and gazed at the shabby little figure staring after him.

The driver remarked, 'God, that's a bad mess, sir.'

Howard said, 'It's my home.'

The car waved and the man said awkwardly, 'I'm sorry, sir, nobody told me.'

Howard stared at the blur of passing fields and hedges, the trees stark and bare of leaves. Another winter drawing near. More convoys. Then what?

Later, as Howard sat in a corner of the large barracks wardroom where he had been booked in by the rear-admiral's flag-lieutenant, he stared at the fire and tried to put together all he had seen and heard.

He toyed with the idea of phoning the girl and wondered if her father had already warned her off, or even if she needed to be dissuaded.

There was a great gust of singing and several of the more senior officers got up and departed with obvious irritation.

Howard glanced across to the activity at the long bar and saw some half-dozen sub-lieutenants, each with pilot's wings displayed above their wavy stripes, and guessed they must just have 'passed out' and were about to join their various squadrons. If they lived long enough, their role might be crucial in the months ahead.

He half-listened to their roar of voices as they kept time to the mess piano, the tune that of 'The Dying Lancer', and thought suddenly of the girl's dead husband.

> Take the cylinder out of my kidneys,
> The connecting rod out of my brain,
> The cam box from under my backbone,
> And assemble the engine again!

Howard stood up and strode to the door. He did not even see one of the bright new subbies nudge a companion. *Look at him. Another one who's bomb-happy!*

All three telephone boxes were occupied and he hesitated, wondering what she might say. If she would pretend she wasn't there and have someone else put him off. In the meantime the next verse had struck up, louder than ever.

> When the court of enquiry assembles,
> Please tell them the reason I died,
> Was because I forgot twice iota,
> Was the minimum angle of glide!

A plump paymaster-commander eased himself from one of the phone boxes and growled, 'They'll soon change their bloody tune when – '

Howard did not hear him finish, and the confined box seemed suddenly private and safe.

It took the best part of ten minutes while he checked the various numbers and extensions and endured the usual questioning and clicks from service telephone operators. And then, all of a sudden, he was through.

He asked carefully, 'Could I speak to Second Officer Lanyon, please.'

He waited for the rebuff, the curt disclaimer; all the while he could feel his heart pounding faster. *I must be really mad. Round the bend.*

'Putting you through, sir.'

She sounded cool and distant. 'Hello, who is that?'

He replied, 'David Howard, you remember when I – ' He stopped, already lost.

She asked, 'Where are you?' She had changed, her voice very low. 'Have you been to the house?'

He nodded, as if he expected her to see him. 'Yes. I'm at RNB. Just for a day or so.' The words were tumbling out as if he feared they would be cut off. 'Your father arranged it. I – I didn't know what had happened 'til he told me.'

She said quietly, 'I know. It was the least we could do. We heard about the convoy, what you went through.' The line clicked but there was no interruption. Maybe you did not break into a call, even one which mentioned naval operations, if the one concerned was a rear-admiral's daughter. She said quickly, 'There's a pub, this side of Gosport – *The Volunteer*.' When he said nothing she said, 'It's quiet, not used much by our people or HMS *Collingwood*.'

He said, 'I shall be there within an hour.' He could not believe what was happening. 'I'll find a friendly driver. I just want to tell you . . .'

A man's voice interrupted patiently, 'You've been disconnected, sir.'

'But I was just speaking to . . .'

'Sorry, sir.' Then what might have been a chuckle. 'It's the war, you know.'

Howard slammed down the telephone and hurried from the box. He almost knocked over a lieutenant who was about to leave the wardroom. They stared at one another and the lieutenant grinned.

'Sinclair, sir.' The grin widened. 'I was a CW candidate in your ship, the *Winsby* – you won't remember me.'

Howard's mind was still reeling, but suddenly a young, eager face formed in his memory. One of the many. He said, 'You wanted to go into submarines when you were commissioned, right?'

The lieutenant stared. '*Right*, sir! Matter of fact, I've a boat coming to collect me right now to take me back to the base at *Dolphin*. What about letting me show you off to my friends, sir?'

Howard's mind was suddenly clear again. 'HMS *Dolphin* – then you probably know a pub called *The Volunteer*?'

'Yes, I know it, sir. Bit too quiet for me though.' His eyes sharpened as he sensed the urgency of the question. 'I can get you there easy enough. I'm duty-boy at *Dolphin* at the moment, just came over with a message for the commodore here.'

Howard took his arm. 'Then lead on. I'll have that drink later, if I may!'

He turned to collect his cap from the table outside the wardroom and the young lieutenant who was serving in submarines, and who had once been a nervous CW candidate in Howard's first command, thought he heard him say just one word. *Fate.*

*

Howard pushed through the door and parted the heavy blackout curtains, which smelled of tobacco and dust. It was a cosy enough little pub, but after the darkness outside even the dim lighting seemed too bright. There was a fire in the grate where two farm labourers were sipping their pints, a large dog snoozing between them.

There were a few servicemen in the adjoining bar, but thankfully nobody he knew. He had never felt less like talking just for the sake of it. As the lieutenant named Sinclair had described it, *The Volunteer* was pretty quiet. It was hardly surprising, he thought. Sea-going sailors liked something a bit more lively after the strain of watch-keeping and staying alive, while shore-based ones preferred the plentiful if unimaginative food of the various barracks and establishments.

'Evenin', sir.' The landlord wiped an imaginary stain off the bar with his cloth while he watched the newcomer, his eyes moving professionally from Howard's two-and-a-half stripes to his DSC ribbon when he removed his raincoat.

'Horse's Neck, please.' He smiled to break the tension he felt. 'If you can still manage it?'

The man grinned. 'Ah, but if you'd asked for Scotch, that'd be different. I'd have called the police or the Home Guard in case you were a Nazi parachutist! Not had any Scotch for a year!'

Howard took his glass to a corner table while the landlord switched on the nine o'clock news.

Howard hardly listened. In any case he had heard the same sort of thing so many times it made little sense any more: 'During the night our bombers raided targets over the Ruhr and the U-Boat bases at Lorient. Seven of our aircraft failed to return.' He saw the landlord staring at the little wireless, his face grim. Maybe he had someone who flew the hazardous raids deep into enemy territory. The newsreader's well-modulated voice shifted its attention to the Russian front. *Stalemate*. The news was little better from the North American theatre, and he thought momentarily of Ayres and his missing brother.

A breeze fanned the curtain, and she was suddenly here. She glanced quickly around, as he had done, probably for the same reason. She sat down opposite him and removed her tricorn hat to shake out her hair. All the time she watched him, searching his face feature by feature.

'I hope you've not been waiting long?'

Howard signalled the landlord, who, like the two men by the fire, had been staring at the girl as if she had just stepped from the moon.

She said, 'A gin would be nice.'

Had she been going to ask for a sherry, but remembered the last time it had happened in the Guvnor's living room?

'Of course.' Howard moved to the bar and then stopped dead. The newsreader was just ending. Just a small item, which in any daily paper would qualify for no more than a couple of lines: 'The Secretary of the Admiralty regrets to announce the loss on active service of HMS *Redwing*. Next of kin have been informed.' He did not remember paying for the drink. Only that he was seated again, the glass gripped in his fingers.

She took it gently, her eyes studying him anxiously. 'What is it?'

'*Redwing*. I saw her go. That last convoy. We managed to lift off some of her people.'

He stared at the wall but saw only the ship settling deeper and deeper along-side. Dazed, bleeding men being dragged roughly to safety. *Redwing*'s captain on the bridge, his eyes blank with shock. He stared at her hand on his wrist but did not feel it.

'Tell me.'

'I must have been at it too long.' He looked at her hand and wanted to hold it, to let it all flood out. But he knew she would pull away, that he would not be able to stop this time. 'But I had this strange feeling – ' He looked directly into her eyes. The colour of the sea. 'It's impossible of course – '

He felt the slightest pressure on his wrist. 'Try me.'

Howard said, 'I think the torpedo was meant for us.'

She smiled and took her hand away as if she had just realised what she had done. 'Well, thank God it missed!' She raised her glass. 'I can't stay long.' She recognised his disappointment. 'My friend Jane is standing in for me. I simply wanted to see you. To make sure you were all right. It must have been hell for you when you got back.'

'I saw what was left of the place. Mister Mills has done his best.' He smiled with sudden affection. 'Bless him.'

'He's very fond of you, isn't he?'

Howard glanced round as the curtain swirled aside again and two soldiers thudded across the floor in their heavy boots, each looking quickly at the girl before discovering the dartboard on the far side of the bar.

She added, 'I met your brother and his wife.'

'What did you think of Robert?'

He saw her start with surprise that he should ask her. But her reply was in her characteristic, direct fashion. 'Well, I can see him as an admiral.' She smiled for the first time. 'He's not in the least like you.'

Howard grimaced. 'I suppose not.' It was strange, but he had never really thought about it. She was right. Robert was all one would expect of a regular officer. Very straight; but inclined to a stiffness their father had never needed.

When he looked again her smile had gone. She said, 'Will you keep the old house?' She saw him nod and added wistfully, 'I came to like it.' Then she seemed impatient, angry that she could not hide her emotion. 'Poor Lucy. But for me – '

Howard pulled the handkerchief from his breast pocket and put it in her fingers. 'Don't even think it. They were together. Each needed the other.'

He knew the landlord and the two men by the fire were watching intently, but did not care. They probably imagined they had met here in secret. Lovers, when neither was free. *Would that we were.* He said nothing while she dabbed her eyes, then studied herself in her compact mirror.

She said, 'I'm a mess!'

He reached between the glasses and took her hand very carefully. As a man will hold a frightened bird, trying to avoid injuring it. 'I'd like to see you again.'

She studied him curiously. 'I can tell you mean it, and not for the reasons I'm offered from time to time. But it wouldn't work.' She smiled, as if to ease the hurt. 'How would we manage? Have you asked yourself that?'

'Others do.' His voice was sharp. He was thinking of men who had tried to win her favours. *The young widow.* It happened often enough in wartime.

'Maybe.' She was still watching his face, looking for something, or someone. 'I know I couldn't. Not again.' She glanced at her watch. 'I must go. Really.'

He held her hand more tightly. 'Don't you understand? I've been thinking about you ever since that day when the Guvnor – ' He looked away. 'Sorry, I didn't mean to drag it all up again.'

Then they were both standing, and in the small bar he could hear the clock ticking.

'It's my fault.' She freed her hand very gently. 'Anyway, what should I do? Every time you say goodbye, it breaks your heart – didn't you know? That's why I'm soldiering on. I want to do something useful. Like you, and all the other people out there who are trying to win this damnable war!' She looked around at the intent faces with a kind of defiance which only made her appear more vulnerable. 'We shall probably bump into one another from time to time. My friend Jane and I are being transferred to Operations.' She hesitated, seeing the dying hope in his eyes. 'Western Approaches, in fact.'

He stared at her. 'Liverpool!'

She replaced her hat, then turned to face him. 'Well, it's not too big a place, is it?'

He would have followed her but she said, 'I've got my bike outside. You stay and have your drink. You've not touched it.' Then she said, 'I shall miss your father, and if you're interested, I think you're exactly like him.' With the same touch of defiance she held up her cheek, and for those few unreal seconds Howard tasted her skin and the gentle fragrance of her hair.

He heard the outside door slam, the far-off wail of an air-raid warning, and pictured her cycling through the darkness to the air station at Lee-on-Solent. He downed the drink in one swallow and picked up his cap.

The landlord nodded as he put the glass on the bar. They were in short supply too. Most of the pubs had the rule, 'no glass no drink', so that customers would refrain from gathering a little hoard of them at every visit.

'Nice lady, sir.' His eyes were full of questions. 'Not married, I see?'

Howard wanted to leave, to think alone. He replied brutally, 'She was. He was killed.'

Outside he paused to look at some searchlight beams wavering across the sky and to get his bearings. As he walked along the darkened road he was torn between despair and a lingering hope. Which, like the horizon and the night sky, had no clear division.

Howard returned to Liverpool after four days, during which time he visited the family solicitor, and spent a whole afternoon signing papers. Even in war there was apparently a lot to do when someone died.

He visited the communal grave, a sad little plot as yet without a proper stone to mark the remains of the six people who lay there. There were a few dead flowers and a fresh bunch of chrysanthemums in a stone pot. There was a card, too, with her name on it. She must have gone there without telling him before she left for a few days' transfer leave. Mister Mills had told him that she had made him promise to keep flowers there until the stone was properly installed; that was something else Howard had signed at the solicitors.

At Liverpool it was raining when he arrived, and by the time he had been aboard *Gladiator* for an hour it was almost as if he had never been away.

Lieutenant Treherne had told him that the group was expected to sail in three more days, or that was the latest buzz. He also told the story of Bizley, who with his second stripe and promised decoration was becoming unbearable. There was also a new navigating officer, Sub-Lieutenant Brian Rooke, one of those rare junior officers from the lower deck who sought and won promotion by way of a scholarship. Most of the other lower deck officers were much like old Arthur Pym: years and years of service from boy seaman, up and up via the Petty Officers' mess and eventually to wardroom with just a thin half-stripe to show for the long, hard slog.

Howard saw Rooke in his quarters, a tough, round-faced man of twenty-four, with a blue chin which apparently defied the sharpest razor. He had a brusque, business-like manner, and his personal report left Howard in no doubt that Treherne's replacement would prove an excellent navigator, if they could hang on to him.

But he had one failing, a chip on his shoulder a mile wide. As Treherne had said with gleeful relish, 'He thinks we're all turning up our noses at a poor ex-matelot!' Treherne had been thinking of Joyce at the time, and all her ideas of *posh officers*.

It was just November when the group left Liverpool to shadow a large westbound convoy which was to be met by Canadian escorts in the usual way. The convoy was attacked by long-range reconnaissance bombers, then U-Boats for much of the way; but using more aggressive tactics than before, Captain Vickers threw his group into the attack again and again and left the close-escort to the corvettes. They lost just two ships, but severely damaged a U-Boat on the surface one night in mid-Atlantic. It was a probable kill. The return run from Halifax with a fast convoy of modern tankers was mauled once again by a U-Boat pack south of Cape Farewell. Once more Vickers impressed it on his escort captains to follow his tactics whenever possible. Drive the U-Boats under, and keep them there so that they could not overhaul the heavy tankers.

It was a record. When they reached the Mersey they had lost only three tankers. Three out of twenty-seven.

Perhaps it had been sheer luck, or maybe the German HQ had misunderstood the convoy's intentions. They might even have withdrawn some of their powerful force of U-Boats for refitting and repair before winter really hit the Western Ocean.

As *Gladiator* headed slowly upriver towards Gladstone Dock, Howard stood on the gratings beside his chair and stared at the mass of dockyard personnel and servicemen who thronged the jetties and moored vessels to watch their return, and then to his amazement, to cheer as if they were the victors.

Leading the group, Vickers's rakish *Kinsale* was blaring 'D'you Ken John Peel?' on her speakers, adopted by the rugged captain as their own hunting song. Howard left the ship in Treherne's hands and watched the welcome, very moved by what he saw and heard. It had never happened before.

He heard Rooke say, 'Time to turn, sir.'

Treherne nodded. 'Very good.'

Howard did not even have to look. There had been times when he had barely been able to snatch a catnap at sea. Afraid that a youthful and barely-trained officer on watch would do something stupid, lose the next ship ahead in the dark or ram it up the stern by too many revolutions wrongly applied. Somehow, despite the changes, or because of them, they had become a team, and no matter what happened on the next convoy or the one following that, this delirious welcome was a tonic after what they had seen and done.

As the destroyers made their careful turn, one of the Wrens on the signal station's verandah called, 'They're coming, ma'am!'

Celia Lanyon removed her hat and took the proffered oilskin from a grizzled yeoman of signals; it came down to her ankles, but that did not matter. Out on the windswept verandah, the rain plastering her hair to her face, she felt the new excitement in the place, which she had never shared before. The flags soaring up and down, so bright against the grey sky and sombre town; the clatter of signal lamps; and then more cheers as the destroyer with *H–38* painted on her rust-streaked bow edged into view.

She found that she was waving and cheering too, without understanding it. They had called her a blue-stocking, stand-offish, before Jamie had come into her life. But she had never been like this.

Howard turned to watch the yeoman clattering off yet another acknowledge-ment, his hard features outwardly unmoved by something he probably thought was empty optimism.

Well, perhaps it was. Howard stiffened. But this time it was different. He raised his glasses and trained them through the diagonal rain towards the signal station.

Even in the bulky oilskin, hatless and with her hair clinging to her face, he saw her immediately. He hesitated, then removed his cap and held it high above his head before waving it slowly from side to side.

Treherne called, 'Stand by wire and fenders.' He glanced up at the captain, and gave a slow grin of understanding. Bloody good luck to him.

Ayres gave a nervous cough and Treherne leaned over the voicepipe.

'*Stop port! Slow astern port!*' Just in bloody time.

Gladiator was back again, and although there would be those who would grieve for the men who had died with the three tankers, others would see this as a small break in the cloud.

Howard watched until the signal station was hidden from view. There was hope after all. Perhaps for them, too.

In the same month of November two other events took place – unconnected, but they would prove more important than any of these men and women could appreciate.

There came to Liverpool a new commander-in-chief for Western Approaches, a tireless, dynamic and forceful admiral named Max Horton. He was neither a patient man, nor one who would accept defeat in any form while the convoys braved the Atlantic in all conditions.

The other event occurred in North Africa beside the Qattara Depression, near a place nobody had ever heard of. It was called El Alamein, where for the last time, at the very gates of Egypt, the battered Eighth Army turned and stood fast. Like the thin red line, some said. The retreat was over.

As Howard had thought. There was hope after all.

Part Two

- - - - - - -

1943

Part Two

1913

1

Victors and Victims

'Starboard watch closed up at defence stations, sir.' Lieutenant Finlay's voice was sharper than usual, a sure sign that he was on edge about something. Lieutenant-Commander David Howard licked his lips and savoured the last cup of coffee until morning. It was midnight, the middle watch standing to their various stations while the destroyer rolled easily from side to side at reduced speed.

Howard looked up at the heavy cloud layer, the rare glimpse of a star. It was mid-April, and already the Atlantic was reluctantly showing its mercy after the winter gales. Around and beneath the gently vibrating chair he could sense his ship's mood and that of her company. Just another year; a few months since his father had been killed in the hit-and-run raid, and yet everything was different. Even the ship was changed in some ways, but that was to be expected, he thought. He was lucky to have held on to Treherne as his Number One, and of course, the ship's core, Evan Price, the chief.

But he would soon be losing Finlay, although the gunnery officer had as yet not mentioned he was seeking a transfer to another ship. It was largely due to the bad feeling between him and Bizley, who after receiving his coveted DSC had used every opportunity to cross swords with Finlay, so that Treherne had been forced to stand between them on too many occasions. The wardroom was predominantly a young one still. Old Pym had gone at last to a shore job at HMS *Vernon*, the torpedo school, and was probably boring his recruits to death with his well-worn tales of Jutland. He had quit *Gladiator* as he had served her, a complaint on his tight mouth, a scowl for the growing intake of green and untried sailors. He was not missed. The new Gunner (T), only recently promoted from chief torpedo gunner's mate, was a different sort entirely. Bill Willis was round and jovial, and had a fund of yarns which had even forced Bizley to silence.

Midshipman Esmonde had left to be promoted to sub-lieutenant, although Howard found it hard to imagine him in any sort of real crisis where people would be looking to him for leadership. Treherne had described him as 'a squeaker'. A squeaker he would probably remain. His replacement was a midshipman of a very different kind. His name was Ross, a pale-faced youth who kept very much to himself in spite of their enforced mingling. Howard had spoken to Midshipman Ross when he had come aboard and had decided it would take more than a few months to make him relax. He rarely slept below when the ship was at sea, even in the worst weather, and at action stations he was usually the first at his station on the bridge. He had been serving in a big fleet destroyer called *Lithgow*, a powerful class of vessel much the same type as Captain Vicker's *Kinsale*. The ship had been in the Mediterranean, trying to force the convoys through to beleaguered Malta. A lucky ship, they had said. Until the day she had been attacked by a dozen aircraft all at once. When a rescue vessel had been sent to assist there had been just seven survivors on a Carley float, surrounded by oil and flotsam. Ross had been the only officer out of a company of over two hundred. But he was good at his work and eager to learn; together they probably served as his lifeline. How long, only time would tell.

Gladiator had also got rid of her doctor, much to most people's relief. The newly appointed surgeon-lieutenant, John Moffatt, a Dorset man born and bred, looked every inch a countryman, with rosy cheeks and what Treherne described as a turnip haircut. He was already very popular, and many swore he had once been a vet.

Howard stifled a yawn and thought of the two-month course they had been ordered to complete to their masters' satisfaction by the end of March, only days ago.

Howard had never believed they could have achieved so much or had so much to learn. It had been like going to school all over again. Tactical training ashore in class rooms, and periods at sea which had made the war almost preferable by comparison.

Admiral Max Horton, the new C-in-C Western Approaches, not only lived up to but surpassed all the stories previously told about him. In a few months the whole command was feeling his personal drive and demanding enthusiasm. He soon made it known that he believed in co-ordination, and the use of long-range aircraft with both the Navy and the RAF playing a full role. With extra fuel tanks they narrowed the Atlantic gap even more, and many U-Boats had been forced to run deep when they had discovered hostile aircraft where once the ocean had been theirs alone.

The active and aggressive use of hunter-killer groups was the basis of all new training, and *Gladiator*, with her consorts, had been in the thick of it. With a couple of elderly submarines playing at Germans they had evolved an entirely new method of attack. No longer used only as close escorts for the desperately needed convoys, they worked independently in small groups, sent to seek out the enemy in advance of any convoy due in any area, before a U-Boat pack could be mustered to attack and slaughter it as so many had been.

In some ways, at the beginning, it had been humiliating, and Howard had found himself resenting the bland instructions, the ruthless criticism after an exercise had gone wrong.

Slowly but surely, their instructors had won them round. The U-Boat, after all, had the whole ocean in which to hide. The old method of using depth-charges which took so long to sink and explode at the required depth was not enough. New ahead-throwing mortars with three barrels on each mounting, code-named Squid, were being developed and installed as fast as possible. The new pattern produced meant that the attacking warship could shadow a submerged submarine and still not lose contact if a salvo failed to encircle the enemy. Destroyers and frigates had previously lost vital minutes after they had dropped the old-style pattern over the stern, and had to turn as fast as possible to make another strike.

Until Max Horton's appearance at Western Approaches the theory on sinking submarines had changed little since peacetime, but the effect of the old-style depth-charges had been wrongly estimated. With the German hulls now being constructed of welded pressured steel, it was necessary to get a charge closer than sixty feet to do any lasting damage.

On *Gladiator*'s bridge one day after a fruitless attack, the tall, severe-looking commander who had been Howard's referee had remarked calmly, 'You see, old chap, Jerry's got six hundred feet to play with whenever he feels things are getting too hot.'

Howard had conned his ship slowly round for another attack, remembering all the other times – the lost echoes, the depth-charges killing nothing but fish. His tormentor had added, 'Remember, at four knots a U-Boat can *travel* six hundred feet while the charges are falling.' He had smiled at Howard's resentment. 'Now let's have another go, eh?'

Howard slid from his chair and crossed to the ready-use chart table. It seemed quiet enough. He smiled. *Spring in the air.* As he leaned over the chart and switched on the tiny shaded light he thought he heard Sub-Lieutenant Ayres humming to himself by the magnetic compass. He had been paired off with Finlay for watchkeeping duties, mainly so the first lieutenant could keep an eye on all of them. A sort of trouble-shooter, allowing his captain to keep his distance.

Ayres had certainly changed for the better. Like the news from North Africa, it was not just the continued advance of the Eighth Army against Rommel's invincible Afrika Korps. In their retreat the Germans had allowed one of their prison cages to be overrun. Ayres's brother had been found in it, wounded and still in a state of shock, but alive. The Red Cross had sent word to Ayres's home as soon as they knew.

Howard forgot him as he studied the worn chart, the one with a dark ring left by a cocoa mug like an ancient compass-rose in the corner.

One hundred miles south-south-west of Ireland's Bantry Bay and a convoy would be due to enter St George's Channel in two days' time. All being well. There had been many losses on the Atlantic run, but the deployment of new escort groups had managed to stop the score from rising like last year's brutal testimony.

He could picture the rest of the small group clearly in his mind, as if it was broad daylight. Three other destroyers, all veterans like *Gladiator*, steaming abeam in the new strategy to cover as much sea as possible with both radar and Asdic. One ship to the north of *Gladiator*, the other two equally spaced to the southward.

He was surprised that he could feel so relaxed. It was the first time he had been back in the field since their training had begun, and apart from exercising with the whole group they had covered just one small convoy until it had been met by other escorts from Gibraltar.

The training was over. He had to make certain that nobody forgot, even for a second.

They would patrol their beat, one giant rectangle, until the next convoy was safely passed through their area, unless they were required to offer support to another group or assist the air patrols. It was that flexible.

There was growing speculation about the new 'pocket' aircraft-carriers now being built. Tiny compared to a fleet carrier, they were converted merchantmen with wooden flight decks, from which pilots were expected to take off and land-on in any conditions. If it was true and it worked, the air gap would be closed for good. Convoys would sail with air cover from shore to shore, and no U-Boat would be safe to seek and attack them while on the surface. Like the sudden change of fortune in North Africa, it had once been a despairing dream. Now when the people at home listened eagerly to the news bulletins they could find hope instead of disappointment or fear.

All the way from Alex, household names which had changed hands so many times when the Eighth Army had been in retreat, would now be read out in the reverse order. Tobruk, Benghazi, Sirte and on to Tripoli, the ultimate goals being Tunis and Bone, Rommel's first toehold in Africa. A far cry from the crushing defeats and reverses of just a year ago. He sighed, and knew that Ayres had instantly stopped humming to listen.

What a pity the Guvnor had missed the change of luck. He switched off the light and stood up. *Luck?* Hardly that with all the ships sunk; all the men who had died at sea and on land, or had been hammered out of the sky. Hardly luck.

'Increase to half-speed, Guns. The others in the group will be checking the time and watching us on the radar. We don't want to hang about now and wake up some sleepy U-Boat before we can hit the bugger, do we?'

A shadowy figure moved across the bridge, a steaming fanny of kye swinging to the ship's motion.

Ordinary Seaman Andrew Milvain stopped dead as Howard said, 'We're losing you after this patrol, I believe?' He made it sound friendly and casual, as if he had not already written a good report for the young seaman, who was leaving to attend *King Alfred*, the officers' training establishment at Hove. There, all wartime RNVR officers cut their teeth and swotted to become midshipmen like Ross or subbies like Ayres.

'Yes, sir.' He stammered, 'I – I shall do my best, sir.' He glanced around him in the darkness, his shyness suddenly held at bay. 'But I'll miss the ship, and everyone. . . .' His voice tailed away.

I would feel the same. But he said, 'You've made a lot of friends. Just mind you remember them when you get your little bit of gold, eh?' He turned as the wheelhouse acknowledged the increased speed and the bridge began to vibrate more insistently, and the slow roll departed in *Gladiator*'s ruler-sharp wake.

'I'm going to my hutch, Guns.'

'Aye, aye, sir.'

Howard lowered himself to the next deck, past the stammer of morse and murmuring voices in the wheelhouse, on into his tiny sea cabin.

He sat down on the bunk and massaged his eyes. Just a few moments alone to think. He reached out and opened the thermos of tea he knew Vallance would leave for him and tried not to dwell on the girl who came and went with his thoughts like the sun and the moon.

He had seen her only once after the triumphant return to Liverpool. It had been unsatisfactory again, because of the brevity and also because she had had her friend, Jane, with her. *Holding him at arm's length.* When he had been enduring the frustration and demands of the training course with the group, she had also been away with some senior officer on some special assignment. Or so her friend had said when he had telephoned. The one called Jane had left him in little doubt that she was more than willing to stand in for Celia if he gave the word. He had not, and was strangely glad about his decision.

He swallowed the over-sweet tea and took the telephone from its hook.

Finlay responded at once. 'Forebridge, sir?'

'All quiet, Guns?' He had come to rely on most of them more than he could believe. He remembered his first command, the little V & W Class destroyer *Winsby*, a wardroom of recalled old salts or complete amateurs. It all seemed a long, long time ago.

He looked at his new perk, the small radar-repeater on the bulkhead, the light revolving steadily to pick out the little blips on either side. *A long time ago.* Now Howard as a young lieutenant-commander was the senior officer of the group, that was, until they rejoined the others, or whatever else Admiral Horton decided.

Finlay said, 'Passed three sweepers two miles abeam, sir. Making for base.'

Howard nodded. Minesweeping: the most demanding job of all. Day in, day out, every channel must be swept. Just to be sure, for this was one of the main fairways of Western Approaches, with convoys putting out to sea – or making the last miles into harbour, and safety. Until the next time. The men who worked the minesweepers complained it was boring rather than dangerous. But their casualty lists were unmatched.

'Buzz me in an hour, Guns, unless . . .'

He heard his dry chuckle. 'Aye, sir. Unless I need you.'

Howard laid back on the bunk and watched the revolving radar beam until it made him drowsy. He felt the ship lift and plunge beneath him and pictured his men trying to sleep in their messes or huddled at their stations, peering out at the black water.

Gladiator was feeling the change too. No longer a helpless escort, watching while others died. She was her proper self again. A destroyer.

His head lolled and he was instantly asleep.

The dream was rising to a frenzied climax, in which Howard was unable to speak or make himself understood. She was in his arms, watching his mouth, waiting for him to explain with just the hint of a smile on her lips. Despite her nearness, the touch of her body in his hands, Howard was aware only of danger, the need to protect her.

The background was so bright and empty he could barely look at it, and when she twisted round in his arms he saw another figure standing quite still, his back turned towards them, his arms hanging by his sides.

Even in the whirlpool of this thoughts he knew who it was, why he had come. He was dressed in a leather flying-jacket and fleecy boots. It was something Howard simply knew although he did not see them.

She laughed and ran from his outstretched arms towards the solitary figure, without another glance or any sign that she understood.

She held out her hands and the airman turned to look at her for the first time. But there was no face, just burned flesh and two angry red eyes. Her scream seemed to sear his brain like fire, but still he could not move.

Howard woke up, sweating and gasping even as the scream extended into the piercing call of the telephone.

He managed to speak. 'Captain?'

There was a pause. Like a question mark, he thought later. 'This is Treherne, sir.'

Thoughts burst through his mind and then slowly settled like spray after an exploding depth-charge.

The first lieutenant was on the bridge, but it was still the middle watch. He peered at the bulkhead clock. It was barely three-quarters of an hour since he had lain down. It had felt like an eternity, like torture. The ship was quiet apart from the engines' pulsing beat, and the occasional sluice of water alongside. No action stations, and yet . . .

'Are you all right, sir?'

Howard swallowed. 'Yes. What is it?'

Treherne seemed to turn away, to speak on another telephone perhaps, or to ponder on the captain's state of mind. 'Is your radar-repeater switched on, sir?'

'Yes.' Howard turned and peered at it, her scream still probing his mind. It was only a dream. He gritted his teeth. A bloody nightmare, more likely.

Treherne said evenly, 'Probably nothing, sir. But look at one-five-oh degrees, about ten thousand yards beyond *Hector*. Could that be an echo?'

Howard stared, watching the bright little blobs glow and then fade as the radar beam passed over them. Steering west, all on station, in line abeam. *Hector*, a pre-war destroyer which had seen plenty of action at Dunkirk and off Norway before coming to the Atlantic, was the wing ship. There it was. He felt his body tense on the edge of the bunk, the dream refusing to leave him. It was a very small echo, but it was still there when the radar beam passed over it again.

'Why haven't the other ships reported it?'

Treherne weighed his words with care. 'The conditions tonight might make a difference, sir. I've spoken with Lyons. He's known it before, where one ship can pick up on an echo at a greater range than others. Sometimes it's the set, but this time he thinks its the heavy cloud.'

Howard thought about it while he watched the repeater. Five miles was the kind of range for radar to pick up a surfaced U-Boat if that was what it was. *Hector* and her nearest consort *Belleisle* were nearer, but they had not so far reported anything.

'I'll come up.' He waited, knowing Treherne was still there. 'And thanks, Number One.'

It was cold on the upper bridge after his brief stay in the sea cabin. There were no stars at all now, the clouds almost as dark as the water.

'Call up *Hector*, Number One. Ask them if they've seen anything.' He studied the bridge repeater while Treherne called up the wing ship on the short wave intercom.

The little blip was still there. There were no patrols out here, or they would have been told. If it was a small Irish vessel she'd be showing lights. But then, if they had any sense they would be snug in port somewhere.

'Negative, sir. But *Hector* is keeping a good lookout.'

'What's the range now?'

'From us, sir?' That was Finlay.

'Of *course!*' He regretted the sharpness of his tone.

Finlay reported stiffly, 'Nineteen thousand yards, sir.'

Howard took the intercom telephone from Treherne and spoke to each captain separately. The result was the same. *Gladiator* was the only one in contact. Unless, of course, her set was faulty.

Howard spoke to the radar office. 'What's it doing now, Lyons?'

Lyons had no doubts. 'Its speed is much like ours, sir. I think it's stalking *us.*'

Howard considered it. 'Tell the other ships to reduce speed to nine knots.' He was thinking aloud. 'If that bastard thought we were four powerful destroyers we wouldn't see his arse for sauerkraut. I think,' he nodded firmly as if to convince himself, 'I *think* he believes we're part of a convoy. After all, they did change the sailing time of one a few days ago, right?' He saw them watching him in the darkness, as if he had suddenly become dangerous.

'We will continue at this reduced speed, course two-five-zero.' He heard Treherne repeating his instructions quietly over the intercom. When Howard had taken his first command to war there had been no such luxury as an intercom which could not be detected. No radar; few fully automatic anti-aircraft guns; and senior officers who for the most part had trained all their lives to believe in the Empire, on which the sun never set. Some of the new escorts coming off the stocks were even more effective and sophisticated.

Treherne called, '*Hector* has the contact, sir. Requests permission to attack.'

'Denied.' Howard looked over his shoulder. 'Sound action stations. Have the Gunner (T) check all watertight doors himself.' He could almost feel Treherne's surprise and added, 'Remember, Number One, he's new in this ship. I'm more concerned with staying in one piece than ruffling his feathers!' He added sharply, 'Or anyone else's for that matter!'

They were steaming almost parallel with the target, for that was what it had become. When the time was right, the four destroyers would pivot to port and in line abreast would charge down on the enemy at full speed.

He said to the bridge at large, 'Well, after this we might know if all that training and sweat did us any good!' It was a relief that somebody laughed. He tried to place the sound in the darkness. Of course, it was Richie, the new one-badge petty officer and yeoman of signals.

Poor Tommy Tucker the original yeoman had finally cracked. For him it could not have come at a worse time. His wife had gone off with a Yank airman when *Gladiator* was on her last convoy, and he must have been brooding about it during the group training. One of the admiral's instructors had tackled him on the bridge about some obscure signals procedure, but Tucker, who had seen every horror the war could throw his way, who had nursed his newly trained bunting-tossers until they could do almost anything, had taken enough.

'What the hell do you know, *sir*? The war looks pretty good to you, I expect, sitting on your fucking arse while others are getting theirs shot off!'

Howard had appealed on his behalf, but Tucker had been sent ashore under guard.

The authorities had two choices for Tucker. A mental ward at a naval hospital and perhaps a discharge, or a court martial and an eventual return to the Atlantic.

Tucker had rejected both options. With his usual hard efficiency he had found a tree and hanged himself.

Howard shivered. But he was still here, in his rightful place, on the bridge.

'Call up the group. We will attack when the target is due south of us.'

'Radar – bridge?'

Treherne was there. 'Bridge?'

'Target bears one-six-five, ten thousand yards!'

Howard stood up behind the forward screen. 'Tell the group. *Execute*, speed fifteen knots!' He sensed the sudden excitement crowding around him. 'Port twenty!' He heard Sweeney's hoarse acknowledgement. He wondered what the coxswain thought about Tucker. Changes in the small petty officers' mess were never welcome, especially for a reason like that.

'Midships! *Meet her*!' He swore to himself. He had allowed his mind to stray. 'Steer one-eight-zero!'

Hidden from one another in the darkness, controlled only by their radar and churning screws, the four destroyers had wheeled round to head at right-angles towards the target. The single ship, the *Blackwall*, on *Gladiator*'s starboard beam would be at the end of the sweep, like the edge of a door while the others swung round on an invisible hinge.

'From *Hector*, sir! *Lost contact!*'

Treherne said, 'Jerry got the message at long last, and dived.'

'From *Blackwall*, sir. *Have Asdic contact at one-seven-zero degrees, one thousand yards!*'

Howard said, 'Tell him, *Tally Ho!*'

'From *Blackwall*, sir. *Am attacking!*'

While the destroyer charged into the attack, the others took up their allotted stations for a five-mile box search. But it was not necessary. *Blackwall* was fitted with the squid mortars as well as her conventional depth-charges, and by the time *Gladiator* had completed her turn, the sea was already stinking of oil.

'Slow ahead together.'

With the ships spread out in the new formation it was unlikely that any other U-Boat could get close enough undetected to carry out an attack.

'Ship breaking up, sir.'

There was a ragged cheer from somewhere aft.

Howard leaned over the screen and peered at the heaving water. Another kill. It had gone like a clock. As all those brasshats had promised it would.

The port lookout called, 'Someone's got out, sir!'

Above the rumble of screws Howard could hear the coughing and retching. God alone knew how they escaped.

'Lost contact, sir. Target is now on the bottom.'

Howard looked at Treherne's shadowy outline against the grey paint. Imagination, or was it getting lighter already?

'Away sea-boat's crew, Number One, two extra hands to help with possible survivors.'

'Aye, *aye*, sir!'

Within minutes the whaler was hoisted out, lowered and then dropped into the sea to be carried clear by the boat-rope.

The Buffer appeared on the bridge, banging his gloved hands together as he always did when he was pleased about something. 'I've told 'em not to 'ang about, sir.' His teeth were white through the shadows. 'I'll bet that Jerry commander didn't know whether to 'ave a shit or an 'aircut, when 'e saw us comin' at 'im!'

They were all grinning at each other like schoolboys.

Howard thought of the past three years and sighed. *No wonder.*

Treherne said, 'I cleared the after-guns for the whaler, sir. Lieutenant Bizley volunteered to take charge.'

Howard ignored the sting of bitterness in his voice. 'Fall out action stations.' Howard trained his night glasses. 'Whaler's coming back. Have the falls manned. As the Buffer said, we don't want to hang about!' Almost before the boat had been hooked on and run up to the davit-heads, Howard knew something had gone wrong.

There were two Germans only, although neither might live after what they had gone through.

'Slow ahead together. Bring her round, Pilot.' Behind his chair he could hear Bizley panting, as if he had been running.

'It wasn't my fault, sir!'

'I shall decide that. Just tell me, right?'

'I had two hands in the bows, sir. But after we hauled the first German on board, the other started to drift away. He was calling out, choking on oil. One of the bowmen went over the side with a line and put it round the other German. Then – then . . .' He sounded dazed and lost, 'He just vanished under the boat. He never broke surface again.'

A massive figure in oilskin and lifejacket loomed through the bridge gate. It was Leading Seaman Fernie, who had been the whaler's coxswain.

He said harshly, 'It was the kid, sir. Young Andy Milvain from my mess.'

Bizley seemed to regain his composure. 'Go aft, Fernie, I'll deal with you later!'

Howard found that he had pulled out his empty pipe, remembering his brief words to the boy who had wanted to be an officer.

Fernie stood his ground. 'I don't care what *you* do, Mister Bizley! You ordered him over the side, an' I'll say as much if I'm asked!' He swung away as if he had lost his way.

'Steady on one-four-five, sir, one-one-oh revolutions.' A voice from the other world.

'Is that true, Bizley? *Did* you order him over the side?'

'Certainly not, sir. He was over-eager, always wanted to impress . . . you know, sir.'

'Yes. I think I do. Now get about your duties. I shall want a full report before we return to base.'

Treherne said in a hoarse whisper as Bizley's head and shoulders vanished down a bridge ladder, 'What a bloody awful thing to happen! What will his folks think? First one son, then the other. Who'll tell them, for God's sake?'

'I will, Number One.'

He turned as a muffled figure entered the bridge with a fresh fanny of tea. But Howard saw only the bright-eyed youth, Ordinary Seaman Andrew Milvain. His voice hardened. 'So take it off your back, Number One. It *happens*. All we can do is try and pick up the pieces!'

They both knew it was a lie, and when Howard looked again Finlay had resumed his watch, and the first lieutenant had disappeared.

Milvain's father was a major-general so was probably away somewhere. It would not be much of a home for his mother any more.

But in a few weeks or months when the boy's replacement had been settled in, he would soon be just another missing face, and his name would rarely be mentioned. Except by Leading Seaman Fernie perhaps. When one of his mess asked, 'D'you remember that posh kid, Hookey?' He would crush him.

Howard blinked his sore eyes as the morning watch clattered up ladders or slithered behind the gunshields to await the first light of another day.

Treherne came up to take over the morning watch and stood in silence beside his chair while the various voicepipes and telephones reported that they had relieved the others.

Then very soon *Blackwall* showed herself, throwing up spray and not a little smoke as she plunged over some short, steep rollers. When it was light enough Howard studied the other ship through his glasses. The victor. All grins on the upper bridge; a team job, but she had been the one to make it all work and leave the enemy in their tomb on the seabed. Howard had filled his pipe but did not remember doing do. He gripped it with his teeth and tried to strike a match below the shelter of the glass screen. He tried several times and then stared with shock as his hand began to shake uncontrollably.

'Light, sir?' Treherne did not raise his voice. Then he took Howard's wrist in his grasp and held a match to the bowl while their eyes met through the drifting smoke.

Howard exclaimed harshly, 'Christ, what's the *matter* with me?'

'Nothing.' Treherne tossed the match downwind. 'I asked for that last night. You'd just about had enough. I should have seen, understood.'

Howard removed his battered cap and shook his head in the wet breeze. 'I'll bet you wish you were back with your other ships, Number One?' He could feel the man's strength, the bond which linked them and perhaps always had. Like the thaw after frost; a first warmth.

Treherne bared his teeth through his beard. 'Well, bananas were a lot less trouble to deal with, sir, I'll not deny that!'

Howard watched the other ships taking shape against the endless pattern of whitecaps which had come with a freshening wind.

The hunt goes on. 'I'll make out a suitable signal for the C-in-C, Gordon. He'll be pleased. Another kill so soon – it must mean something.'

Behind his back he imagined he could hear Petty Officer Tucker's ironic laughter.

Sub-Lieutenant Brian Rooke stood by the chart table and watched Treherne as he checked over his calculations. It was stuffy and dark in the chart-room because the ship was preparing for her last night at sea. The remainder of the patrol had passed without incident, and hardly an hour had gone by, or so it seemed, without a signal of congratulations being received. Another escort group had sunk two U-Boats in as many days, so if any proof had been needed about the admiral's strategy they had got it loud and clear.

Treherne said, 'We shall have to stand off until first light, Pilot.' He still found it strange to hear someone else called that. 'I don't reckon on the Old Man dicing with all the local traffic *en route* for Gladstone Dock.' He thought of the strain Howard had shown, the way he always seemed to force himself out of it. 'Shan't be sorry to stretch my legs ashore.' He thought of Joyce waiting to welcome him. 'That was quite a patrol.'

Rooke regarded him warily, as if he suspected that Treherne was about to find fault with his chartwork. 'Is it always like that?'

The door of the W/T office slid open and Hyslop the PO telegraphist, a pencil behind one ear, looked across at them.

'First Lieutenant, sir? I've got something for the captain.'

'What is it?'

'Big raid on Liverpool, sir.' He glanced at his pad. 'Meant for the docks but the flak was too heavy apparently. They knocked down a few streets though. All incoming escorts are to land their medical officers to assist.'

Treherne kept his voice level. 'Birkenhead?'

The PO looked at his pad again in case he had missed something. 'No, sir.'

'I'll tell him.'

He found Howard in his usual place on the port side of the bridge, his glasses hanging loosely around his neck.

Howard did not move as Treherne read him the lengthy signal and the first lieutenant imagined he was thinking about his father, comparing the raids which had been caused by the heavy resistance of AA batteries which covered the real targets. Instead Howard asked, 'Were *our* people all right?'

Treherne looked at him curiously. 'I think so, sir. No reports of any damage to ships and docks.'

Howard stood up and moved about the bridge, his hands touching various pieces of gear and instruments as if he had not seen them before. He asked, 'What's our ETA?'

Treherne replied, 'Well, five o'clock in the morning, sir. But as I said to Pilot you'll not want to . . .'

Howard said, 'Make a signal to give our time of arrival *as calculated*, Number One. Is the raid still going on?'

'No, sir.' He looked at the sky as if he expected to see the glow of fires. He had seen The Pool like that often enough.

Howard nodded. 'Get on with it then. I shall speak to the other captains. It's my responsibility.'

Treherne hurried down the ladder again. Was he still thinking of his father, or was he brooding about the boy who had been drowned? *He takes everything on his shoulders*. He recalled how Marrack had wanted his own command more than anything. Well, he was welcome to it!

Howard replaced the intercom handset and tried to think clearly. There were raids every day; people died, but others managed to soldier on. He turned away. *What she had said*. It couldn't be. Not her. She might not even have been there.

'Permission to step aboard, sir?'

Howard turned. It was Moffatt the new doctor. Wrapped in a duffel coat, his cap jammed on his head like a pie-crust to keep it from blowing away, he looked more like a proper seadog than a medical man.

'Of course, Doc.' A thought flashed through his mind. 'Did Number One ask you to come, by the way?'

'No, sir. Although he did tell me about the air raid. I've got my gear all ready.'

'I'll be going ashore.' It came out too easily. 'You come with me.'

Moffatt asked quietly, 'Have you got someone there, sir?'

'Why does everyone *keep asking questions?*' He saw a lookout glance round and gripped the doctor's arm. 'Sorry, Doc. Not fair to pull rank. Yes, there is somebody I care about. Very much, although she doesn't know it.'

Moffatt regarded his profile thoughtfully. All bottled up. A man could take just so much. Howard's sudden confidence had touched him. He had always imagined a captain like Howard had no feelings other than for the job in hand. Not because he wanted it like that, but because it was his only way of staying outwardly sane.

Moffatt had got to know his fellow officers and many of the ship's company in his short time aboard. It was odd that nobody had let drop some hint about the captain's private life. After all, he had soon learned that there were no secrets in this *regiment*, as the sailors called it.

'Can't you take a nap, sir? Might help.'

'No. I shall more likely ask you for one of your pills to keep me on my feet.'

Bizley, who was OOW, said, 'Time to make the signal to the group, sir.'

'Do it then.'

Moffatt asked, 'What now?'

'We form line ahead before entering the final approach. There may be sweepers about, even a coastal convoy, although I don't know of any. But the raid may have delayed everything.'

He listened to Bizley's precise tones on the intercom. He was sullen rather than subdued, he thought. Perhaps it had been what he said; an accident. When he made his report, the chief-of-staff would very likely want to interview Bizley, as well as some of the whaler's crew.

He tried not to think of the young seaman. So eager, but he was dead, and a drunken lout like Bully Bishop was still alive.

As *Gladiator* and her consorts passed the Skerries and the northern coast of Anglesey the usual mood of apprehension closed over them for the men who had relatives and friends in the city. Treherne and the coxswain made all the arrangements for local leave for those concerned, and for once there was no idle chatter about the possibilities of 'a good run ashore'.

As the middle watch drew to a close and the ships headed due east towards the mouth of the Mersey the evidence of the raid hung on the air like something physical. There were few fires, but that did not mean much. Howard raised his glasses as the new yeoman of signals triggered off an acknowledgement to a guard boat's challenge. But of course, there would *not* be many fires, Howard thought. The raid had been intended for the ships and docks; the aircraft would be carrying high-explosive bombs, not incendiaries.

He thought of that other return, such a short while ago. The cheering, people thronging the waterfront to wave at them. The girl on the signal station verandah, waving with the rest, oblivious to the rain, her hair plastered across her face.

Shaded lights guided them through the entrance where the stench of charred wood reached everywhere. Torches glinted on the forecastle and he saw the first heaving line snake across, the eye of a wire hawser bobbing after it like some endless snake.

'*Stop port!*' Howard leaned out and saw some men standing by the guardrails staring into the first grey light of dawn. 'Slow astern port!' More wires, the sudden squeak of fenders as the hull came alongside the cats.

The engines quivered into silence and other sounds intruded. Ambulance and fire-engine gongs, the rumble of falling bricks as a bulldozer began to clear a road beyond the docks.

The officer-of-the-guard stepped aboard just as Howard climbed down from the bridge and saluted despite the early hour. Howard saw Moffatt hurrying after him and asked, 'Many casualties?'

The lieutenant was looking at the two German prisoners, one being carried on a stretcher. He replied, 'They're still coming in. Not really sure. Safe enough here though. I've never seen so much flak.'

Howard heard the coxswain bawling names selected for local leave and said, 'But none of *our* people?'

'Only up at the temporary planning room. Some Wrens were killed. Four, I believe.' He was still staring at the Germans, doubtless the first he had seen of the enemy, like most of them. He realised Howard was waiting and added, 'One was an officer. Poor girl had only recently transferred from down south.'

Moffatt was listening and said, 'I've told my SBA to wait with the Jerries. The first lieutenant has sent for the provost people.' He watched Howard's face. Like a man at the foot of the gallows. He snapped, 'Where did they take them – the Wrens, I mean?'

'Brought them down here, with the wounded ones. The sickbay is over . . .'

Moffatt retorted, 'I *know* where it is.' To Howard he added, 'I'll go.'

Howard walked past the quartermaster and sentry and down the brow, which had not even been properly secured yet. He did not see the curious faces, the orderly bustle of ambulances and helmeted police, their uniforms covered with dust.

'And where are *you* going, then?' It was a surgeon-lieutenant, a white coat slung over one arm.

'I'm *Gladiator*'s commanding officer.' He saw the man flinch as if he had sworn at him. 'I want to know about the Wren officer, so *don't waste my time!*'

The lieutenant glanced at Moffatt who gave him a quick nod, then said, 'One was killed, outright I should think; her friend was badly shocked, but she should be OK.'

Howard pushed past another white coat and opened the door. There were two girls lying on beds covered with blankets, their eyes closed, probably drugged.

The young second officer was sitting on a wooden bench, her head lowered, her coat and hair covered with flakes of plaster and paint.

When she looked up Howard almost cried out, as if she were also badly hurt. Her shirt was soaked in blood, her hands and wrists too.

She stared at him for a long moment, her green eyes very bright in the hard glare of sickbay lighting. Then she began to shake, her whole body quivering, yet she made no sound. Moffatt watched, holding the door with his shoulder as the captain raised her to her feet and then very carefully pulled her against him.

'Celia, it's me. Don't be afraid. Everything will be all right now.' Useless, mindless words.

Then she looked up at him again, and there were tears cutting through the grime on her cheeks.

She spoke in a small halting voice, like a child trying to explain something she did not understand. 'We were just sitting there. Jane had told me about the signal, about you and your group. The submarine.' She frowned, trying to remember. 'The teleprinters were making such a din. We knew about the raid, but there was going to be a flap on. The work was nearly done anyway.' She began to shake more violently. 'I – I think we both heard it coming. There was no sound afterwards. I suppose I was deaf or something. Then the emergency lighting came on and I tried to help poor Jane. She had no legs, and she was staring at me. I tried to help, but she was dead.'

'Over here, my dear.' Moffatt waited for Howard to guide her to another bed where she collapsed like a broken puppet.

Howard sat beside her, conscious of her bloodied fingers, which were entwined with his so tightly that he could barely feel them.

She looked at Moffatt for the first time, her eyes moving to the scarlet cloth between his two wavy stripes. 'Doctor.' One word.

'Yes, that's me.' Together they raised her and removed her jacket. The sight of it must have brought back the horror of her friend's death.

'*Hold her!*' Moffatt took her arm, seeing the blood, imagining what it must have been like, and thinking too of the German survivors who had been so grateful to him, and to some of the seamen who had brought them rum and cigarettes. The same men who had been trying to kill each other. It made no sense. 'She'll sleep now.'

Moffatt turned as two nurses came through the door. They both looked worn out but the older one managed to say, 'Thank God, the Navy's here!' To Moffatt she added, 'We'll take care of her. We can get her cleaned up in a moment.'

They all looked at Howard as he asked, 'Does her father know yet?'

The older nurse said sharply, 'We *have* been a bit busy here!'

Howard nodded. 'Can I use a telephone, please?'

Moffatt watched the other nurse as she took Howard to the door and pointed along the corridor. 'Just tell them I said it was okay!'

Moffatt said, 'I have been instructed to stay and give you a hand, Sister. I've brought my bag of tricks with me.'

'What was all *that* about, Doctor?'

Moffatt looked at the girl's upturned face. 'I'm not sure. But I think it was some kind of miracle.'

2

Moment of Peace

After a slow journey from Waterloo, stopping at every station, the train finally came to a halt at Hampton Court, the end of the line. Howard recalled very clearly the instructions he had received over the telephone when he had called to ask about Celia Lanyon. It had been her mother, and Howard was still uncertain whether the welcome had been genuine or if the admiral's lady had been unable to think of a way of putting him off. As he left the station and began to walk across the bridge over the Thames he was conscious of his uncertainty, which even the ageless view of Hampton Court Palace could not dispel.

He had travelled down from London after staying at the naval club, membership of which the Guvnor had insisted on for both his sons. *You never know when you might need a bed.* He had been right about that too. Most of the hotels seemed to be either full of Americans or prosperous-looking business men to whom the war had obviously been kind.

He paused in the dead centre of the bridge and stared along the river. It was easy to put the war aside when you took in this view, he thought. The pleasure boats were covered with awnings for the duration, and anything larger or more powerful than little punts and motor-cruisers had been commandeered long since by the Navy. But there were swans drifting by the banks, and only a few far-off barrage balloons marred the picture of tranquillity. He leaned on the warm stone balustrade and felt the sun on his neck.

He had written too many letters in the past to parents and wives when a loved one had been killed or lost at sea, but only when you came face to face with it did you understand the true shock of war.

He had visited Ordinary Seaman Milvain's family the previous day after telephoning Celia's home number. He knew that if he had done the visit first he would probably never have made the phone call to the house, which, if he remembered the directions correctly, he would be seeing for himself in about fifteen minutes.

Milvain's house had been very different from this riverside with its ancient trees and weathered buildings. It had been in a quiet, expensive street in the centre of Mayfair which had miraculously escaped any really serious bombing. One of the tall, elegant houses had been destroyed, but the site had been tidied up, leaving a neat gap in the street like missing teeth.

Howard had been unable to pay his visit before the news had arrived there in the usual fashion: *Missing and must be presumed dead.* God, it was common enough, but not easy to see for yourself.

In the high-ceilinged drawing room with the curtains half-closed Milvain's mother had listened in silence while he had tried to describe what had happened. She was a severe-looking woman, worn down by her latest loss, and not yet recovered from her other son's death. From a highly-polished table the two silver-framed photographs had regarded Howard as he told her of young Milvain's disappearance. His photograph had shown him as a very new recruit at HMS *Ganges*, a young open face, lacking the later intensity he was to gain at sea. The other was of a serious-eyed two-ringer, the one who had been Bizley's CO.

The only relief had been Milvain's sister, Sarah, a lively, bright-eyed girl who had confided that she hoped to be accepted for the Wrens. Howard noticed the hurt look her mother had given, the bitterness in her tone when she had finally spoken. 'It was to rescue some Germans, you say, Commander Howard?'

In that quiet room, London's traffic muffled by the curtains and the deserted street, Howard imagined he heard Bizley's voice, as if he had been there with him. '*It wasn't my fault, sir!*'

Howard had tried not to think of a memorial he had seen while attending a naval funeral. How long ago? It seemed like a hundred years.

When you stand there, think of us and say, for our tomorrow you gave your today. The Guvnor's war.

Milvain's father, a major-general, was up north; it was not explained what he was doing or how he had accepted the terrible news. Howard was ashamed, but he had been glad to leave the house in Mayfair, especially after Milvain's mother said in the same flat voice, 'He was just a *young boy*. Surely he should not have been given a man's job to do?'

He had recalled a signalman on *Winsby*'s bridge, cut down by machine-gun bullets from a Stuka dive-bomber. They had been going to the assistance of the crew of the East Dudgeon Light Vessel, which the aircraft had been attacking; still a mercifully rare occurrence despite the war's new height of savagery. The signalman had fallen at Howard's feet, his eyes losing focus even as he cried, '*Why me?*' His last words on earth.

Howard could share Milvain's mother's grief, and understand her sense of loss; nevertheless her words had seemed to follow him up the street like an accusation.

He paused now and looked along the tow-path, at Hampton Court Palace drowsing in the sunlight. He was out of breath already. Too many days and nights on an open bridge, too many vivid dreams when he finally got an opportunity to sleep.

Two sailors passed him and saluted smartly. Probably on leave, he thought as he returned the salute. Sailors would be rare around here unless they were free from the sea for awhile. He saw one of them glance quickly at his DSC ribbon; sensed the comradeship you usually felt when you saw the familiar uniform, so out of place inland.

He strode on, trying to recall what the girl's mother had said about their real house being used as recuperation hospital for officers somewhere. He wondered if she had told him to put him in his place, to imply, without describing it, that their home was rather grand.

For some reason he recalled the way Celia had described his brother. The future admiral. He smiled grimly. It was equally possible to see Lilian, his brother's wife, as *the admiral's lady*.

He saw a man in Home Guard battledress reading a newspaper's glaring headlines, his eyes very intent through some ancient steel-rimmed glasses.

Howard wondered if the news had been confirmed. Another setback at this stage would be disastrous.

The headline seemed to shout at him. *Rommel quits North Africa, Germans on the run.*

It was difficult to accept it, let alone take it as gospel truth. He had heard all about it at Liverpool while he had been fretting and waiting to see Celia before she was sent on sick leave.

Hitler had recalled the Desert Fox and left the final retreat of the Afrika Korps to General von Arnim. Nothing could stop the Eighth Army now. For once, the Germans were pinned in a corner of Tunisia, with only the sea at their backs. Without Rommel's inspiration, the general who had been admired by friend and foe alike, it seemed only a matter of days before the remaining troops surrendered, while others were forced to run the gauntlet of Allied submarines and aircraft.

While the U-Boat had gone to the bottom, and Milvain had been taken by the Atlantic as part payment, all this had been happening. Months, years of it, and it had suddenly burst out like a flower on a fast camera lens.

He stopped, breathing hard while he looked up at the imposing house which stood behind an equally old wall. It was hardly any sort of demotion, he decided.

Maybe he should go, now. Catch the next train up to Waterloo before he made a bigger fool of himself . . .

'You must be Commander Howard?'

He saw a tall, slender woman shading her eyes with a rough garden glove, while she held a basket of assorted tools in the other hand.

She put down the basket and tugged off a glove. 'I'm Margaret Lanyon. How do you do?' She shook his hand warmly. 'Come around the side gate and through the garden, will you? We don't use the front entrance much. The Americans camped in Bushy Park keep coming over to ask if the house is open to the public! If it wasn't for their lordships of Admiralty I could make quite a killing as a guide!'

Inside the pleasant, walled garden she paused and studied him, and he thought he could see her daughter somewhere in the scrutiny.

'I cannot thank you enough for what you did.' She smiled. 'May I call you David? I get quite enough spit and polish down at Pompey!'

'I wish I had been there sooner.'

She walked slowly amongst some roses and peered at the buds. 'Early this year.' Then she said, 'You saved her sanity, I really believe that. Her friend, poor Jane – well, it must have been terrible, for those other girls too. Jane was good for my daughter in her funny way. My husband thought she was a bit flighty, but I told him not to be so stuffy. They are young; there just happens to be a war on, but you can't expect people to toss their youth away because of it. They give enough as it is. Now she's dead. Celia insisted on going to the funeral. I went with her . . . it was quite awful, but I expect you know a lot about that aspect?'

Howard smiled and thought of Milvain's mother. 'A bit.' No, she was not like anyone he had expected.

'I just wanted to say something before you meet her. Be gentle with her. She's all we've got, you know.' She lightened it by adding, 'I think George wanted a son so much that Celia joined the Wrens just to please *him*!'

Howard faced her. 'I promise.' He thought he heard footsteps on flagstones and said quickly, 'May I ask you something?' He saw her nod and thought she already knew the question.

'Was she very much in love with her late husband?'

She did not answer directly. 'She told me what happened, that you saw him crash into the sea. I was shocked that she called on you, to ask you about it. And then your poor father – ' She seemed to shake herself mentally, before continuing, 'Jamie was in love. With himself. That is all I *can* say.' Then she said, 'Here she is! The one you really came to see.'

Howard turned and saw her looking at him, not in that direct fashion he had been expecting, but with an expression of shyness. She was dressed in a plain jumper and skirt, and afterwards Howard could not remember even the colour of them. It was as if everything was faded out, with only her face and eyes clear and distinct.

He took her hands in his and said, 'Celia, you look wonderful.'

She studied his face; remembering what, he wondered. That first sight of him in the sickbay, or did it spark off the horror when the emergency lighting had brutally laid bare her friend's injuries?

'How long have you got?'

He smiled. First things first. 'I was just telling your mother . . .' But when he glanced round they had the walled garden to themselves. 'We shook up our Asdic dome a bit. The ship has to be docked so the boffins can have a look at it.' He saw her eyes cloud as he added, 'I have to start back tonight, I'm afraid.'

She turned and slipped her hand through his arm as if it was the most natural thing in the world. 'All that way, just to see me. I had secretly hoped you might. Pity Daddy is at work. He was very touched when you phoned him about me.' He felt the pressure on his arm. 'So was I, afterwards. I must have made a terrible scene.'

He could feel her body trembling and knew that if he tried to comfort her it would get worse.

She said, 'Dear Jane. At the funeral they all looked at me. As if to ask, why Jane and not her?'

She was crying now; Howard felt her forcing out her words, controlling the sobs which were making her shake so violently. She said, 'I'm bad luck; you know that, don't you?'

'*No.*' He felt her turn and stare up at him but kept his eyes on the flowers, the blue sky above the old wall which must have been here when England had waited for Napoleon to invade, and long before that. 'I *don't* know.' He could feel her slipping away. He ought to have known it was hopeless. It had been her mother's way of warning him what to expect.

Then he felt her fingers reach up and touch one of his sideburns, heard her say in barely a whisper, 'It's a little bit grey, David.' She sounded suddenly angry, bitter. 'What are they *doing* to you?'

He thought of Treherne grasping his wrist to light his pipe when he had been incapable of it. How many times had he nearly split apart? And the next time – then what?

He replied, 'Never mind that.' He turned and held her at arms' length. 'Can't you see, girl? I'm in love with you.'

He waited, but she stood quite motionless in his grip, as if she had not heard him properly.

Then she asked quietly, 'Bad luck and everything? No reservations, just like that?'

Her mother appeared at the top of some stone steps that led from the rear of the house.

'I just heard the news, you two! The Germans have surrendered in North Africa!' She closed the door quietly and re-entered the house.

A tabby cat was dozing against the sun-warmed glass of a window and she paused to stroke it, to rouse a protective purr.

She murmured, 'They didn't hear a thing, Stripey. May God protect both of them.'

Captain Ernie Vickers stood, arms folded, while with several other officers he studied the new arrival at Liverpool.

'Well, gentlemen, she may not win any beauty contests, but in her and others to follow I think we will turn the battle of the Atlantic in our favour.'

Howard examined the escort-carrier moored on the opposite side of the dock. Her flight-deck was alive with activity, with figures crawling around and under the neat line of Swordfish torpedo bombers which had been flown-on at sea. The Swordfish, with its fixed undercarriage and open cockpits, looked like something from the Western Front, but it was an endurable and tough aircraft, and its relative slow speed and short take-off made it ideal for depth-charging submarines, and for reconnaissance far out in the Atlantic where no air-cover had been possible before.

Compared with the more majestic fleet carrier she was small – about half her bigger sister's size – but in the dock she seemed like a leviathan, squat and outwardly top-heavy.

Howard said, 'So we and the Americans are going to close the gap quite soon then, sir?'

Captain Vickers took out his pipe and rubbed it against the side of his broken nose, so that flesh seemed to move across his face unhindered. He looked at him searchingly, secretly surprised that Howard looked so fresh. He had been down south and back again within three days; that was something, with wartime train hold-ups. Word had reached him that Howard was badly shaken-up by almost continuous duty in the Atlantic. If it was true, he seemed to have overcome it.

'Next week, in fact.'

Vickers looked at the resting escorts, their hulls showing rust and scrapes from too many miles, too long at sea.

'The cargoes are going to get more valuable, David. More men for the next phase of the war. Troop convoys from Canada and the USA, from New Zealand and Australia. The South Africans have been in the desert all the time, so they at least should get there safely.'

'*Where*, sir?'

Vickers laughed loudly. 'Anyone's guess. But it's no secret that we'll get nowhere in stalemate. You always need the infantryman with his boots firmly planted on enemy soil before you can start thinking in terms of victory. That's where we come in, where most of you have been since the first weeks of war.'

They fell into step together. Howard was quite tall, but beside the broad-shouldered ex-rugger player he felt like a boy. *Kinsale* must have a larger bunk in her sea cabin than any he had seen.

Treherne was waiting with a tubby little man in overalls, who was wearing a bowler hat.

He saluted and said, 'Trouble, I'm afraid, sir.'

Vickers must have ears everywhere. 'The Asdic, Mr Robbins?'

The bowler hat nodded sadly. 'Big job, sir.'

Vickers regarded him coldly. 'I want *Gladiator* ready to sail with the group. You've got twenty-four hours. God, that should be enough!'

'Well, I expect the union will have a moan about it, sir.'

Vickers gave a fierce grin. 'Well, the *union* isn't putting to sea, is it?'

'I'll do what I can, Captain Vickers.' He added gloomily, 'It's asking a lot, you know.'

Vickers winked over his shoulder at Howard. 'Shouldn't have joined!'

He took Howard aside and added, 'That spot of bother over the seaman who was drowned last trip.' His eyes were very steady. 'Bad luck, David. But set against what your team achieved, and the sinking of another U-Boat – well, it's not worth stirring up the mud at some enquiry or other. The group has got a good name already; morale is higher than it ever was in the past, eh? Give the lieutenant a bottle and leave it at that. I'll keep out of it.'

Howard thought of Leading Seaman Fernie's anger and contempt for Bizley. 'I'll do what I can, sir.'

'You do that. I'll see you in *Blackwall* this evening. Ginpendant's going up. Celebrating the kill.' He strode away, touching his oak-leaved peak with his pipe-stem as he returned a seaman's salute.

Howard shook his head. If Vickers was ever troubled he never showed it. Like the admiral, he had once said, 'I want results, not excuses. And it starts right here with me!'

He walked along the side of the dock looking down at his ship, trying not to think of what might happen next.

She had walked with him to the station at Hampton Court. They had spoken very little and had paused in the centre of the bridge as he had done to look at the swans, the fiery sunset on the palace's historic windows. A moment of peace. Probably the first each of them had known for a long, long time.

She had said quietly, 'Take care of yourself when you cross London. There's bound to be a raid tonight.' She had shivered. 'A bomber's moon.'

They had stood side by side staring at the ticket barrier, the rear end of the train with many of its doors open as passengers climbed aboard. Mostly servicemen, Howard had noticed. Khaki and air-force blue. Cheerful grins, set against tears and clasped hands. Two redcaps stood beside the ticket inspector, running their eyes over the servicemen, always suspicious; looking for a deserter, a drunk, anything to break the monotony.

But the crowd was getting smaller, and the doors were slamming shut, while the guard unrolled his green flag and eyed the station clock.

So much to say. And there was no more time. Perhaps there never was.

She had said, 'You'd better go. You've got two minutes.' She had turned suddenly and looked up at him, her eyes pleading. 'What you asked, what you said . . .' She put her arms round him and somewhere a passenger gave a shrill wolf-whistle, finding safety in anonymity.

Howard answered, 'I told you. I'm in love with you. There's been nobody else. There couldn't be now.'

She had nodded. 'I shall see you very soon. I'm all right now.' She had smiled, and he was reminded instantly of the terrible dream. '*Really.*'

Then they had kissed. It was not an excuse, a last opportunity; it was simply something which seemed to happen, a natural response. The same way she had taken his arm in the walled garden.

'Come along, sir.' The ticket inspector had smiled. 'If it was *me*, I'd stay!'

Howard had hurried away and got into a compartment. When he leaned out of the window the train was already gathering speed; he waved until they passed the level-crossing and the station was out of sight.

Here, in the midst of a noisy dockyard it was still so hard to believe that it had really happened. When she returned to Liverpool might it all come back to haunt her?

He thought too of her dead husband, her mother's words. *Jamie was in love. With himself*. It was still no answer to his question, or what that last quarrel had been about.

Treherne watched him from the brow. He had also noticed the difference. The missing lines at each corner of his mouth, no quick impatient gestures when things went wrong. The new doctor had told him nothing, but he could put most of it together for himself. A woman then. One of the Wrens.

Treherne saw someone hovering by the lobby door. It was Vallance, a tray still in his hand, which was unusual to say the least. Treherne had often thought that the PO steward would make a perfect valet, a gentleman's gentleman.

'Something wrong, PO?' He kept his voice low in order that the captain should be at peace for awhile longer.

'Yessir.' He glanced over his shoulder. 'It's not my place, sir . . .'

Then it was trouble. Mess bills unpaid; wardroom silver, what there was left of it, stolen to be made into brooches by the engine room staff.

'Spit it out.'

Vallance took a deep breath and said in a quietly outraged voice, 'The gunnery officer, Mister Finlay, just piped up that he's got engaged, sir.' He screwed up his eyes to remember it as it had happened in *his* wardroom. 'Mister Bizley was, sort of out of it, y'see. Sir.'

Treherne nodded. 'Go on.'

Vallance said, 'So Mister Bizley calls out, who would want to marry *you*!'

'My God.'

'So with that the gunnery officer snaps back, "At least I don't go round getting our own people killed!" ' Vallance went on unhappily, 'They stood shoutin' at one another, and then Mister Bizley aimed a punch at him. Guns, I – I mean Mister Finlay threw a glass of Plymouth gin over him by return.'

Treherne tried to smile. 'I'm glad you noted the brand, Vallance.' But it was not a laughing matter. 'Who else was there?'

'Everyone, sir, 'cept the Gunner (T).'

Treherne felt the anger boiling up like thunder. In the merchant service it was very different. He had known boatswains and several bully-boy mates who would use their fists rather than make a big yawn out of it. This was not the merchant service however, and *Gladiator* needed her internal unity as much as her weaponry and engines if she was to beat the Atlantic.

Finlay was a fine gunnery officer, but nobody was worth that much. As for bloody Bizley, the *hero*, he knew what he would like to do with him.

The quartermaster, his eyes popping from what he had seen and heard, whispered, 'Cap'n's comin' aboard, sir.'

'Thanks, Laird.'

He met him at the top of the brow and saluted.

Howard glanced along the deck, deserted now but for a couple of electricians and a man with a teapot.

'Trouble, eh?'

Treherne stared at him. 'I was just going to deal with it.'

Howard gestured to the dockside. The wardroom scuttles were open. 'I'd have thought they could hear the row in Birkenhead!' Surprisingly he reached out and touched his sleeve. 'Not your fault, Number One. It's been coming, and like you, I had hoped it would sort itself out.' He nodded to Vallance. 'Bring me a drink aft, will you?'

'How was London, sir?' Vallance was so relieved to see him he could not restrain himself. 'Still showin' the flag, sir?'

Howard thought of the great open spaces outside Waterloo Station where there had once been many streets of little back-to-back houses; a market too, where even in wartime you could get almost anything from a tin of fruit to a puppy. All gone. Wiped out, not even the rubble left, only the kerb stones which marked where people had once played and lived, brought up kids, just so this would happen to them.

'Several flags, I should think.' He turned and looked at Treherne. 'I'll not throw away all that we've learned and endured because of childish behaviour from those who should know better. I'll see both of them. Informally, for the moment anyway, Guns first.'

It was not a happy few minutes which he gave to Finlay.

'I have seen you on my own so that I can speak my mind.' He did not ask the lieutenant to sit down. Very deliberately he took a swallow of Vallance's Horse's Neck, in his special glass. That had been another thing to fan his anger. Vallance had been embarrassed, ashamed even, when others in his position would have hidden their grins until later.

'You have become a very good gunnery officer in this ship. You can be proud of the way you have pulled your department together. Amateurs for the most part, and you have turned them into gunners. That is all I need from you, except your loyalty, see?'

Finlay exclaimed, 'It's not that, sir – he got under my skin . . .'

'And you forgot that you are one of my senior officers. Your childish behaviour comes back to *my* door, or don't you care any more?'

'Care, sir?'

'Well, you *are* applying for a transfer, I believe?'

Finlay's accent had become suddenly more pronounced. 'It's nothing definite, sir.'

Howard did not raise his voice; he did not have to. 'And you call that loyalty, do you? It's not what most people would term it. I know it's been hard for everyone, not just you – and it will get tougher, I shouldn't wonder. So if you're not prepared to show the responsibility you received with your commission, then by God I'll see you *are* replaced, and you can forget the transfer! I would make certain that you never trod the deck of any ship where you would abuse that responsibility! Now *get out!*'

Treherne entered and looked at him admiringly. 'I could see the steam under the door, sir!'

Howard ran his fingers through his hair. '*And* I forgot to congratulate him on his engagement.'

Treherne watched him, waiting to see the strain returning.

'I have to ask before you speak to Bizley – and I know it's a liberty – but what's she like?'

Howard eyed him severely and then smiled. 'I love her.' So simply said.

'Told her, sir?'

'Yes.' He looked at the empty glass and said, 'Tell Vallance.' He let out a great sigh. 'Then send in *Mister* Bizley. It's high time he was told a few home truths.'

Lieutenant Treherne clattered up a bridge ladder and paused to stare across the spray-dappled screen. Two days out from Liverpool, with the ocean reaching away like a shark-blue desert. No land in sight, no ships either. In spite of all Vickers's threats and persuasion the work-force had not completed the repairs on time, and there had been other delays while *Gladiator* had been refloated and prepared for sea.

Thirty-six hours behind schedule they had steamed down St George's Channel and then west into the Atlantic, the Irish coastline a mere purple blur lost in distance.

Treherne had been right round the ship, checking all the departments against the new watchbills and duty rotas he and the coxswain had prepared to make allowances for promotions and replacements.

Lieutenant Finlay was OOW, standing with his booted feet apart, his cap set at a perfect angle. Treherne smiled to himself. The parade ground. Sub-Lieutenant Rooke's buttocks were protruding from the chart table, and the yeoman was giving instruction to a pair of young signalmen. Like the captain, Treherne half-expected to see the taciturn Tucker in his place.

He crossed to the gyro-repeater as Finlay said, 'Steady on two-nine-zero, Number One.' He was still very hang-dog after the interview he had had with the captain.

Treherne nodded. Bizley would be relieving the watch. It was interesting to see the way he and Finlay managed to perform their duties correctly without seeming to notice one another.

Treherne polished his binoculars with a scrap of tissue. 'Are you getting spliced soon, or waiting until after the war, Guns?'

Finlay took it as a fish will snap at bait. 'It'll be soon, Number One, I hope. The war might last forever.'

Treherne grinned. 'Or you might go for a Burton beforehand!'

Finlay grimaced. 'That's a mite cheerless!' He darted a quick glance at the other watchkeepers. 'The Old Man . . .'

'What about him? Treherne knew exactly what was coming.

'Has he said any more about me leaving the ship?'

Treherne regarded him calmly. 'Not to me.'

'God, he gave me such a bollocking, Number One. After that party in *Black-wall* I *did* apologise. I don't know if it made any difference.'

Treherne said in a fierce whisper, 'What did you expect, you idiot, a fucking medal?'

'I don't see there's any cause to . . .'

'Oh, don't you. Well, even a thick-headed gunnery type should be able to remember what this ship was once like. Nobody could stand a watch without bleating either to the Old Man or Marrack. He carried the lot of us – you seem to have a very convenient memory! Most of the new gun crews couldn't hit a bloody cliff at forty paces! Well, that's over now. The skipper's got enough work on his plate, and the pace isn't getting any slower. You had it in for Bizley when he came aboard – now, with an extra bit of gold, he's trying to even the score. I'll be frank with you, Neil – I don't like him either, never have. But if all the people I've disliked since I went to sea as an apprentice were put in Trafalgar Square, there'd be no damn room for the pigeons!'

'Point taken, Number One. I suppose we've all been a bit on edge.'

The navigating officer ducked out of the screened chart table. 'We should rendezvous with the group the day after tomorrow, sir.'

His chin was as blue as ever, Treherne thought. He should cover it with a beard.

The day after tomorrow they would find Vickers, unless new orders had sent him off somewhere. Ready for another crack at any submarines that were making for some invisible point on this ocean, to meet and await the next convoy. The Jerries might get more than they bargained for this time. The new escort-carrier he had seen in Liverpool had already sailed even before the group, and there was said to be another one already on station. He thought of Joyce in her little flat in Birkenhead, the passion and pleasure they had shared until they could offer and receive no more. He had given her a ring as he had promised. She hadn't had an easy life, especially with her lout of a husband, but it had been the first time he had seen her really cry.

When he had tried to calm her she had sobbed, 'You care, Gordon! You *really do care!*' She had been stark naked on the bed at the time and he had gently smacked her buttocks and replied, 'Just want to make an honest woman of you!'

Now as he stared out at the dark-sided troughs of the Atlantic he was glad he had done it. Legally it meant nothing. But to her, and anyone else who tried to interfere, it meant everything in the world.

A boatswain's mate in a watch-coat turned aside from a voicepipe and looked at him. 'W/T office, sir.'

Treherne bent over the voicepipe. 'First Lieutenant?'

'Ship in distress, sir. Signal from Admiralty.'

Trehernen said, 'Send it up.' To Finlay he added, 'Ship in distress? That's not exactly rare around here, surely?'

Finlay grinned. Treherne's rough attitude to discipline and most things naval had driven some of his anxieties away. For the moment.

As he spoke on the telephone Treherne could picture the captain in his 'hutch', as he called it. Thinking of his girl, probably. Good luck to them both, whoever she was. He was pretty certain he knew her now. At the noisy party aboard *Blackwell* before the rest of the group had departed, he had seen a young third officer, one of her wrists in a bandage, who had been in the building next to where the other girls had been killed and injured.

He had seen Howard's face as he had turned to listen to something she had said about another Wren's dead husband, a RAF pilot who had gone down in a Russian convoy. It didn't need detective work to calculate the rest.

The third officer had probably had too much to drink. At one point she had elaborated to say, 'They were *madly* in love of course – '

Howard had said to him, 'I have to get back to the ship, Number One.' He had gone without another word.

It had been just after that when Finlay had tried to apologise to him for his own behaviour in the wardroom. Treherne shook his head. Poor old Guns. It must have been like playing hopscotch in a minefield.

'Captain?'

'Number One here, sir. Signal from Admiralty. A ship in distress somewhere.' He was relieved to hear a wry chuckle. The magic was still working.

'I'll come up. What's it like?'

'Nor' easterly, but not too bad.' He replaced the receiver and nodded with satisfaction. He could not remember him ever asking that before. He had always known, been down there listening, fretting. Not today, anyway. Howard appeared in a new, clean duffel coat. Probably one of Joyce's, Treherne thought.

The boatswain's mate pulled the little brass tube up the pipe from the W/T office and handed the enclosed signal to him.

Howard glanced at the blue-chinned navigator. 'Work this out on the chart, Pilot. It's only an approximate position, I expect, but in this weather it might not make it too difficult.' He took Treherne to one side. 'The ship was abandoned from the last eastbound convoy. After the other ships had left her astern a U-Boat surfaced and opened fire on the lifeboats.'

'Christ, what sort of people are they?'

Howard waited. He knew that Treherne was seeing himself out there, helpless in a lifeboat. A civilian at war. 'It seems that one of the boats played dead and waited for the sub to make off after the convoy. Then the poor fellows boarded their old ship and managed to get off this signal. There's been nothing further.'

Treherne clenched his fists. 'You should *never* leave your ship, not 'til there's no hope for her.'

Howard said quietly. 'I'm not so certain of that. This one is an ammunition ship, loaded to the gills with every sort of explosive you can think of. She may have gone down, in which case . . .' He walked to the chart and studied it for a full minute. 'Good work, Pilot, that was quick.'

Treherne saw a spark of pleasure in the navigator's eyes. A pretty rare sight, he thought. But the skipper always found time, no matter how steamed-up he might be.

'Look.' Howard probed the chart with some dividers. 'The next big convoy is expected to pass through that very area at night. No stars, remember?' He thought of that other time, her hand on his arm as she had whispered to him, 'A bomber's moon.'

Treherne rubbed his chin. 'There'll be bother enough for the convoy without having a giant bomb passing amongst them.'

'We shall get there first. Tell the Chief he can forget fuel economy for a bit. I want eighteen knots. That should do it. It will give the Gunner (T) something to do if we have to torpedo the wreck.'

Treherne strode to the other telephone, his mind clinging to those few men who had gone back to their ship despite the danger, rather than die like beasts under the U-Boat's machine guns.

'Asdic – Bridge?'

Howard lowered his mouth. 'Captain speaking. Is that Whitelaw?'

'Aye, sir.'

Howard pictured his face, younger than he looked because he had gone almost bald very early. Before 1940 he had been an ice-cream salesman at Worthing in the summers, and in the Odeon cinema for the winters. Now he was in charge of one of *Gladiator*'s most vital weapons.

'Well, have I got to guess?' If it was an echo it was both early and unexpected.

'The set's on the blink, sir.' He sounded despairing, angry. 'It's worse than it was before they fixed it in dock!'

Hoard covered the voicepipe with his hand. 'Go and see, Number One. We're losing the Asdic.'

Treherne and the others stared at him. Then Finlay said flatly, 'We'll have to make a signal, give our ETA for returning to Liverpool.'

Howard thought of the old Gunner (T), the unloved Arthur Pym, when he had once said so scathingly, *In my day we didn't 'ave no bloody Asdic nor radar neither.*

Marrack had answered with his usual cool brevity, 'Unfortunately, bows and arrows have now been banned by the Geneva Convention.'

Surprisingly, that one tiny incident among so many helped to steady him, when seconds earlier he had been stunned into disbelief.

The man in the bowler hat had said, 'The union will have a moan about it.' More than a moan apparently.

The new midshipman, Ross, had appeared on the bridge and was waiting to see if Rooke needed any new charts. He must have heard everything, and was staring out at the great, endless expanse of ocean as if he could see his own fate.

Howard watched him. In war, casualties came in all disguises.

He said, 'We're not going back. It should be obvious why.'

It seemed an eternity before Treherne returned to the upper bridge; in fact it was seven minutes.

He said, 'I've had a good look, and the Chief sent a couple of tiffies to give a hand.' He shook his head. 'It's gone completely now. Not even a white walking stick.' Nobody laughed, and the midshipman was gripping a stanchion as if the ship was already heeling over.

Howard heard her voice again. *I'm all right now. Really!* Was anyone?

'Very well.' He glanced at his watch. 'Eighteen knots, remember? Pilot, course to steer, *chop-chop*!' He looked at Treherne's grim features. 'Go round the ship again. Damage control especially. Take the Buffer and the Gunner (T) – he's a good seaman, I'm told.'

Treherne nodded. Boats, bulkheads, watertight doors, the lot. He knew the drill.

Howard glanced away. 'Have W/T code up a signal and pass them our estimated position every half-hour. So if the balloon goes up, we shall at least be able to tell the boss where we are.'

Treherne lowered his voice. 'If anything happens to me . . .' He shook his head stubbornly. 'No, let me finish, sir. There's somebody in Birkenhead. I've left a package for her at the base. But if you make it and I don't, I'd take it as a real favour . . .' He did not go on.

Howard thought of the woman's voice when he had telephoned about Marrack. He was moved. Was that still possible, after all they had seen and done?

He said, 'You can do the same for me, except she'll likely know before anybody.' He shook himself. 'We'll get through.'

Treherne hesitated. 'I think you're doing the right thing anyway, if that matters, sir.'

Howard stared after his broad departing form and said, partly to himself, 'You'll never know how much.'

Then he turned to look for the midshipman. 'Now let's have a look at the chart, shall we? I think we could manage a clean one. Help Pilot as much as you can, eh?'

He saw Rooke about to protest that he could manage on his own and added, 'It's good experience.'

Rooke nodded, understanding. 'Come on, Toby lad. Lesson one, sharpen all the pencils!'

A moment later, her bow-wave rising and tearing apart like a huge moustache, HM Destroyer *Gladiator* altered course and increased speed towards Rooke's little cross on the clean, new chart.

Howard could almost hear the music: 'D'you Ken John Peel?'

He saw a small figure, covered in an oilskin with a woolly hat pulled down over his ears, dragging a large fanny of tea through the bridge gate. He thought of the silent house in Mayfair. *He was just a young boy.* So were we all. Once. When he looked again the figure had gone. Perhaps it was a ghost after all.

When Treherne returned, the watch had changed and Bizley stood on the opposite side of the bridge to Howard's chair.

Howard said, 'We will stand-to at dusk. The hands will have to be fed at action stations. Speak to the PO chef about it.'

Treherne glanced at Bizley's profile. Still smouldering. At least Finlay had got over it. A bottle was a bottle. You took it and let it ride. Grudges were unwanted passengers in any warship.

He thought of what Howard had just said. It did not need spelling out. Howard wanted everyone possible on deck, with all watertight doors shut and secured in case the worst happened. They still had the radar but he thought of that last time, when a U-Boat had been stalking *them* instead of the other way round.

On his way to the galley Treherne met the chief boatswain's mate, Knocker White, who was supervising the laying-out of an extra scrambling-net near the midships pom-pom mounting.

'We're not goin' back in then, sir?'

'Did you think we would, Buffer?'

The little petty officer showed his uneven teeth. 'Nah, not really, sir.' He stared reflectively abeam. 'When I was an AB in the old *Revenge*, a right pusser ship *she* was, we 'ad a Jimmy-th'-One in 'er 'oo could make yer 'air curl with 'is language – but a real toff of course, in them days.'

Treherne smiled. 'Of *course*.'

'Old Jimmy-th'-One used to say, no matter 'ow bad things get, they can't put you in th' family way in this 'ere mob, so that was a bit of comfort!' He was still chuckling as Treherne walked away.

The momentary despair had released its hold. Treherne could even smile now. With men like the Buffer, how could they fail?

3

Something Worthwhile

The U-Boat was making good barely three knots as it pushed through the powerful undulating swell of mid-ocean. Steam rose from her casing-deck and conning-tower as the sun, which was directly overhead, gave an illusion of warmth.

All lookouts were in position, and the officer-of-the watch heard the search periscope move its standard; more eyes were busy from beneath his feet.

It was safe enough out here, but you never took unnecessary risks anywhere. Occasionally the lieutenant leaned over the side of the conning-tower to see how one of the seamen was getting on with his quick-dry paint and stencil as he adorned the grey steel with another kill, an American ship which must have been loaded with heavy metal. It had broken its back and gone down after just one torpedo amidships. An American escort had carried out several attacks, but the Yanks lacked the experience of the Tommies, and they had been able to run deep and slip away undamaged. Five other crewmen were lounging on the deck, their bodies naked to the sun, a luxury for their pallid skins and shadowed eyes. The captain allowed five at a time, to smoke, to stare at the sea instead of the curved interior of their boat when they waited to attack or endure a depth-charge bombardment.

One of the men below the conning-tower was playing a sentimental tune on his harmonica while the others listened in silence, or gazed at the vastness of the Atlantic, thinking of home, or that other impossible world.

The lieutenant sighed and straightened his back as the captain climbed swiftly to the bridge. The lieutenant admired and respected his captain; they all did. They depended on his skill and cunning for their very lives. But even in the confines of the boat it seemed impossible to know him, *really* know him. It was like having someone constantly present and yet separated by a thick plate of glass. And he was quite tireless. Each attack was fought as if it was the first one, nothing left to chance, no cutting corners because of all the other encounters, the strain and the anxiety.

Kleiber knew what the other officer was thinking but it did not bother him.

He was tired but would never show it, and his skin felt clammy with sweat beneath his sea-going clothing.

At least today, if things worked properly, some of their discomfort would be eased. One of the big supply submarines was due to rendezvous, part of the chain of *milchküh* boats as they were called, which met the U-Boats at special points, like one giant grid; if you missed one, there was another chance later on. The plan had trebled the sea-time of almost every ocean-going submarine. No longer did they have to abandon a patrol in order to return to base or lose time when making for their allotted area. It meant more strain on every crew, but it kept the boats at sea to attack and destroy as Donitz had planned.

This *milchküh* was new, and their boat was the first on its list. They might get a better choice from this huge travelling victualler's yard and machine shop rolled into one. Fuel, fresh water, food supplies, letters from home, newspapers; even the luxury of proper soap instead of the stuff which felt like slate after a few frugal washes.

Ammunition too, and perhaps they might replace the torpedo which had disgraced itself after one of their attacks on a small convoy. It had started to lose compressed air so that bubbles had surged from a bow-cap, a real gift to any keen-eyed observer in a reconnaissance bomber.

Kleiber would have to fill in a report when he eventually returned to their French lair. But nobody would dare to reprimand him now. There had been too many inexplicable losses amongst the U-Boat fleet of late. Good experienced commanders for the most part, not ones just out of tactical school.

There was also a leak in the forward periscope gland, which they might or might not be able to fix. But they could manage if it got no worse.

He ticked off the points in his mind like a written list.

Engines and motors, good. Results poor, but they had been homed on to a convoy which had been heavily defended for its small size, and they had managed to obtain just one hit.

He glanced at his watch. *Soon now.* He nodded to the lieutenant who spoke rapidly into the voicepipe. There was no risk of hostile aircraft out here, and the weather was fair for the Atlantic. They would have to open the big forehatch to take on stores, something which no commander wanted to do.

Kleiber had done it often enough to know the risks. He would wait until the actual rendezvous. The lieutenant had merely warned the deck party to be ready.

He tried not to let his mind dwell on the news from North Africa. It had to be faced. It was a reverse, but it would benefit the land-based forces in Europe and on the Russian front. Perhaps there would be a letter from his parents about Willi. The thaw would have come to Russia; the icy holes where the Army had fought and held the line would become slush and mud again. Poor Willi; his ideals had cost him dear. Kleiber glanced over the screen at the men on deck. Willi would be better off here, with him. He studied each man carefully. They looked undernourished, starved of fresh air and clean clothing. Worn, bearded faces, and yet there were few older than the mid-twenties down in the boat itself.

What would the Tommies and their allies do next? Attack through Greece, even after their disastrous lesson at Crete? France perhaps? He dismissed it instantly. He had seen some of the impregnable defences of the Führer's Western Wall for himself. Italy then?

His thoughts returned to Willi. Suppose the high command were already negotiating peace with the allies, to join together and smash into Russia, finish Ivan once and for all.

The lieutenant saw his mouth lift in a small smile and imagined Kleiber was thinking of home; a girl maybe.

Kleiber was picturing the high command on one side and Winston Churchill on the other. He could see no unity there.

A man shouted and he heard the offending periscope squeak in its standard. In the far distance there was a huge disturbance as slowly at first, and then more violently, the big supply-boat heaved itself to the surface, small figures spilling over the conning-tower like a team of athletes. One of Kleiber's men flashed off the recognition signal in response to the usual challenge. The supply-boat was already turning to make a lee for them to move closer alongside.

The supply-boat had surfaced too soon, and too far, he thought, and would waste valuable time with this manoeuvre. Which was why they had not detected its approach. A new milchküh; so maybe an inexperienced commander?

The man with the pot of paint grasped a safety rail and leaned back to study his work. There were over sixty such trophies painted there. Each one a blow for the Fatherland. He grinned at the solemnity of his thought and turned to shade his eyes to look at the other submarine. They might even have some special sausage, like that he had known as a boy in Minden.

He could not see the supply-boat because of the conning-tower. But he saw the captain's white cap, heard him speaking to the control room; one of the lookouts was waving, looking the wrong way.

The man turned and stared out to sea. The reflection was so hard it seemed to drain the sky of colour, but it deepened the grey-blue of the ocean. He blinked. It was impossible. He had been staring too long. Like pieces of glass against the horizon, a ship's bridge caught the sunlight. No; there was more than one, moving across the water faster than any ship. He heard himself cry out, the sudden scuffle on the bridge, and then the scream of a klaxon.

The seaman made to climb up the ladder but he had forgotten the lifeline, always insisted upon when working near the saddle-tanks. From the other side he heard men gasping as they ran frantically for the ladder, and then for the first time, the far-off drone of aircraft engines. *It was impossible.* He struggled, but the line had caught fast. There was a brief shadow and he looked up to see the captain watching him. A glance, nothing more, but the man knew what was happening. He heard the thud of the hatch, the sudden roar of vents as the sea thundered into the tanks to force the U-Boat down into a crash-dive. The man was still screaming as the first depth-charges exploded around the surfaced supply-boat, which with the forward hatch wide open was already doomed.

Then his scream was gone, and the little painted trophies were the last things he ever saw.

Kleiber waited for twenty minutes and then went up to periscope depth. He had heard the depth-charges, dropped from the low-flying biplanes which could only have come from a carrier. He swung the periscope in a complete circle and heard one last muffled explosion, which must have been caused when the supply-boat hit the bottom.

There was nothing, not even one of the strange-looking aircraft which he knew to be Swordfish. He could not even see any oil. It was as if nothing had happened.

He loosened his grasp on the handles; they felt wet, but it had nothing to do with a leaking gland this time.

Something scraped against the hull and he saw a petty officer staring at the curving steel as if he expected to see an intruder. The drowned seaman was still dragging there, his boots scraping against the saddle-tank in the undertow.

He felt he should explain. What was one life when set against so many? At night they would surface and cut the body free.

He leaned on the gently shaking chart table and stared at the wavering calculations.

He did not need to explain anything. He commanded, they did not.

He looked at the palm of his hand where there was sweat, when before there had been none.

The price of vigilance. *Survival.*

'Radar – Bridge. Ship now bears three-three-zero, range ten thousand yards.'

Howard stooped down and peered at the radar-repeater. Like something underwater, he thought, shimmering shapes before the revolving beam passed over the solitary blip.

He asked, 'Anything else, Whitelaw?'

'No, sir.' Whitelaw was probably surprised that he should ask. He would have told him had there been something.

'Revolutions for twelve knots, Number One.' He heard Treherne stir himself, the muffled response from the wheelhouse. 'Steer three-one-five.' It would be dawn soon; there was no point in displaying the ship's complete silhouette against a brightening horizon.

'Steady on three-one-five, sir.' Treherne sounded tense. With no Asdic, a submarine could be right underneath the keel and they would not know. It had been a long two days searching for this ship, and the next large convoy would be passing through this point to pick up additional escorts for the run home. It did not allow for any errors. A large convoy at night was bad anyway, especially as they had heard it had already been attacked and had lost three ships.

Bizley was OOW to help ease the work on the others, and because he was unable to control either his squid or ordinary depth-charges without the Asdic's eye to guide him.

He said the bridge at large, 'I thought the long-range recce bombers could reach this far out.' Nobody spoke and he added irritably, 'Just one bomb would have put paid to that hulk, surely?'

Howard spoke over his shoulder. 'There are men on that *hulk* – there were, anyway.'

Treherne exclaimed, 'They've suffered enough, I'd have thought?'

Bizley stooped over the gyro. It was to conceal his smile rather than to check the ship's head. It was always easy to bait the first lieutenant into an argument. What the hell did they really care? They had left enough men to die in the sea before; a handful more made little difference.

He saw Treherne and the captain with their heads together, while the navigating officer was hidden inside the canvas hood, busy with his chart with the new midshipman hovering nearby. Signalmen, lookouts, and just below the bridge the Oerlikon gunners moving their slender barrels from side to side, mistrusting every feather of spray, each sudden surge of water.

He thought of the girl he had telephoned before they had left Liverpool. Milvain's sister Sarah had sounded subdued to begin with, but had seemed to brighten up after a few moments, when she had realised who it was. She had told him about Howard's brief visit and had hinted at her mother's coolness towards him. It had been far better than Bizley had dared to hope. He could picture her as he had seen her in the photograph Milvain carried in his wallet. A good family too. It was strange that his CO, Milvain's brother, had not boasted about it. Father a general, their home a fine house in Mayfair. The things which rated very high in Bizley's suburban background. He had suggested they might meet when he was next on leave. To his surprise, she had sounded genuinely delighted. One hint of caution, however, when she had said that she would have to ask her mother.

Bizley had played his trump card. 'It's my decoration, you see. I feel it was really *because* of your brother – not what I did. I just wanted you to see it, share it.'

He glanced at the others around him. *I'll bloody well show you.*

Leading Seaman Fernie's anger was still a problem, but not as much as he had first thought. He had discovered that Fernie was sweating on getting made-up to petty officer. With promotion almost within his grasp he would be careful not to confront an officer with all the possible consequences of a court of enquiry. Bizley was still shaken by the captain's contemptuous reprimand – he had never had such a strip torn off him. It was so unfair; Milvain's drowning had been an accident, just as he had described in his report. He might have misunderstood when he had been ordered to assist the exhausted German on board. It was certainly not *his* fault. It was probably the youth's eagerness to please his lieutenant that had been the main cause of his accidental death. He smiled to himself. A kind of hero-worship. Milvain's sister would like to hear about that too, he thought.

'Range now five thousand yards. Vessel has turned end-on.'

Treherne muttered, 'Still adrift then.'

Howard thought of the ship beneath him. His men wondering what might happen. Each one of them would be fully aware that all the rafts and Carley floats had been loosened, ready to let go, and the davits turned out so that the whaler and motor boat were free to be lowered with minimum delay. And all the depth-charges were set to safe, so even if a U-Boat was careless enough to surface right beside them it would take too long to release the charges.

Finlay's gun crews were all standing by, ready-use ammunition set to be slammed into every breech, while full magazines were prepared for reloading the pom-poms and Oerlikons.

'Here we go!' That was the yeoman of signals. The horizon was making its first appearance, caught by a thin rippling line like beaten pewter, below which the sea was as black as ink.

Is the torpedo gunner's mate all clewed up, Number One?'

'Aye sir. The Gunner (T) has told him what's expected of him.'

Gladiator's twin quadruple mountings for the twenty-one inch torpedoes had never been used in the war except to put down damaged warships which were beyond recovery, and battered stragglers from convoys. Originally, the peacetime minds which had planned and designed a navy of the future had imagined only a faster war than the previous one. The same line of battle, with the destroyers, the fleet's greyhounds, waiting to dash against the enemy formations under smokescreens if need be and deliver a lethal blow with their torpedoes. The mentality of Jutland, Dogger Bank and the Falklands. Most senior officers had been selected originally from the gunnery branch; submariners and people who believed that the future fleet should be built around aircraft-carriers had often been seen as cranks.

The horrific losses at sea, both in merchant ship tonnage, and the proud names like *Hood* and *Repulse, Royal Oak, Barham* and rest had revealed the folly for what it was.

Howard was thinking about it, not for the first time, as he heard one of the torpedo tube mountings squeaking slightly as it was trained abeam.

In today's frantic shipbuilding programme, to equal if not beat the continued list of sinkings, torpedo tubes were considered more as useless top-hamper than truly dangerous weapons. For the anti-submarine war now being waged the deck space was better served by having more types of depth-charge mortars and dual-purpose light guns. Like his brother's newly formed escort group. All new frigates, some as large as *Gladiator*, and not a torpedo amongst them.

But even as he thought it, Howard knew that he had started as a destroyer man, and as an old hand he would so remain if he was given the chance.

'Smoke, sir!'

As the sky continued to brighten, to spill over the horizon and give the ocean its first hint of blue, they saw the great, low-lying pall drifting slowly in the light north-easterly wind.

Treherne said, 'Didn't realise she was burning, sir.'

Howard did not answer. It made the danger impossible to measure; the very real risk of a U-Boat stalking them was almost secondary.

There was probably enough explosive of one kind or another on board that ship to knock down a city the size of Liverpool.

'Doctor requests permission to come to the bridge, sir.'

That was Ayres, tense and brittle as the thing spread itself across the sky like one gigantic stain.

Howard said, 'Yes. All right.' He had barely heard the question. Surely if the fire was really dangerous the ship would have blown up days ago. He heard the doctor arrive in the bridge, but forgot him as he levelled his powerful glasses on the given bearing and saw the ammunition ship for the first time. A great wedge of a vessel, bows deep in the water, smoke coming from several places at once. No flames. Howard found he was biting his lower lip. But between decks it would only take a spark. Even at this range they would feel it.

He strode across the bridge to the opposite side, vague figures moving hastily out of his way.

He leaned over the side and saw the four torpedo tubes, the TGM's crew clustered behind them in their duffel coats, the distance making them look like attentive monks.

Finlay was covering the scene with his own team and said over the gunnery speaker, 'On this course, sir, you will be in position in seven minutes.'

'Thank you.' It was just an equation to Finlay, an exercise in which he would be an onlooker for once.

Howard glanced over at Treherne, his face regaining shape and personality out of the retreating shadows.

'Sir!' The yeoman was peering through his glasses. 'Signal!'

Howard let his glasses fall to his chest. He did not need to watch for more than a few seconds. It was *S-O-S*, slowly but distinctly spelled out by a powerful torch.

His mouth had gone quite dry. So there were survivors still on board.

Treherne said quietly, 'They've seen us.'

The doctor said, 'Maybe they've still got a boat, sir?'

He watched the captain, the way he was staring at the smoke as if he could neither think nor move. It brought back the stark picture of the girl in the sickbay, her shirt and hands soaked in blood, her shock and disbelief as Howard had taken her in his arms.

Howard stepped from the gratings and said, 'Call them up, Yeo. *Slowly*, so they can read you.' He rubbed his eyes, seeing the other vessel as she would appear in the torpedo sights. It would be so easy. Who would blame him? He continued, 'Ask them to abandon ship if they can. We will pick them up.'

The light clattered, the sound incredibly loud in the bridge's tense interior. Glasses were levelled on the eventual response, the blinking light their only, frail contact.

The yeoman was moving his lips as he read the careful signal. '*Unable – to – abandon.*'

Bizley swore. 'What the hell's the matter with them?'

A lookout murmured under his breath, 'Can't imagine!'

The yeoman lowered his glasses. 'They have seven wounded, two badly.'

Howard looked at their faces. Understanding, pity, anxiety. It was all there.

'Bring her round, Pilot, course to close with the ship. Tell W/T to prepare the signal. *Am in contact with ammunition ship. Will attempt to remove survivors from same.*'

Rooke called, 'Steady on three-five-five.'

Howard made himself climb into the tall chair. 'Increase to twenty knots.'

Treherne stood beside him, saying nothing, and he knew that some of the others must be stunned by his decision; hating him for it.

He said, 'What else can I do?' He turned and looked at Treherne. 'In God's name, what do they expect?'

'I've a suggestion, sir.' He watched him steadily, knowing that the wrong word could wreck everything. 'I'll take the whaler, and a crew of volunteers.'

'Just forget it, Number One. I know you mean well, but . . .' He swung round as more smoke belched over the other ship's shattered bridge.

Treherne shook his head. 'If you lay this ship alongside her in that state, we'll all be done for. I've seen plenty of fires at sea, and so have you. She'll be like a bloody furnace. Neither them nor us would stand a chance.'

Howard lowered his head. He could smell the fire now, like something alive.

Treherne said, 'Anyway, I'm more used to merchant ships than anyone else.'

Howard lifted his head and studied him intently. 'You really mean it, don't you? You're not just trying to save my neck.'

Treherne replied, 'If you work up to wind'rd, I'll get the boat ready.'

Moffatt the doctor had moved closer. 'I'd like to go with you, Number One.'

Treherne forced a grin. 'There – piece of cake!' He became serious again. 'At least we'll have had a damn good try, sir.'

Howard felt in his pocket but forgot his pipe as he said, 'She might go up at any minute, or she might burn for days, something we must not allow. There's also the real possibility that even now, while we discuss the value of human life, a U-Boat may be homing on to this smoke. Either way, if you're still aboard . . .' He reached over and gripped his arm. 'Well, I won't order you to go.'

Treherne nodded. 'I know. But it just happens to be part of the job I know something about.' He made an attempt at nonchalance. 'Remember what I said about the package.' Then, 'Come on, Doc, let's go and ask for some jolly jacks!'

At the bridge gate he stopped and looked back at Howard on his chair. He did not speak, but his eyes said all that was needed. Then he was gone.

Howard said, 'Slow ahead, together. Starboard fifteen.' He watched the great pall of smoke leaning over as if to engulf them in its stench of burned paint and seared metal.

He must show no doubt or apprehension. There were too many depending on him now.

'Midships.'

He watched the ticking gyro-repeater but saw only Treherne's face.

'Steady.'

'Steady, sir. Course zero-eight-zero, both engines slow ahead.'

'Hold her like that, Swain.' He made himself watch the drifting ship. Upwind of her, the damage was more clearly visible, the list more pronounced. The stern was in the best condition; he could even see her name, *Ohio Star*, but her port of registry had been seared off by the heat as Treherne had described.

He looked across at Ayres. 'Go down and take charge of the lowering party, Sub. Can you manage it?'

Ayres looked at him desperately, his face all eyes. 'Aye aye, sir.'

'I'll call down when to drop the whaler.'

The yeoman said, 'Boat's already manned, sir.' He looked at one of his signalmen. 'You know what they say about a volunteer in this regiment, my son – he's a bloke who's misunderstood the question!'

Howard looked away. It was all the same pretence. He seemed to hear her voice, her anger when she had exclaimed, 'What are they *doing* to you?'

Then he was off his chair and standing aft by the bridge searchlight and its painted canvas screen.

The whaler was lowered and he could see its shadow moving beneath the keel while the crew waited to man their oars.

'*Slip!*'

The boat veered away and Howard saw the doctor clinging on to his cap. He turned toward Bizley and said, 'Take her round again, but stay upwind. Same revolutions. No sense in charging about the ocean.'

The yeoman said, 'Whaler's lost in the smoke, sir.'

Howard jammed his unlit pipe between his teeth. 'Tell W/T to make the signal now.' *If that lot goes up we'll not get a chance to tell anyone.* But he kept the thought to himself.

Surgeon-Lieutenant Moffatt peered apprehensively at the huge overhang of the *Ohio Star*'s poop. *Gladiator* was not a large warship but the whaler's twenty-seven feet made him feel like a survivor himself.

Leading Seaman Fernie was the coxswain, the tiller-bar grasped in one gloved fist, and beside him, Treherne, already soaked from head to toe, gave the impression of unyielding determination. The volunteers for the boarding party were some of the *Gladiator*'s hard men. Like Bully Bishop the ex-chief quarter-master, and 'Wally' Patch, a pug-faced able seaman who was usually more in trouble than out of it. His friend, Tim Hardy, another AB, was no stranger to the naval glasshouse – a good hand at sea, but ashore he was known to drink and fight in equal proportion.

Moffatt enjoyed his middle-of-the-road status in the destroyer. Dressed like an officer except for the scarlet cloth between his stripes, he could nevertheless feel almost equally at home with the lower deck. In fact he knew some of them better than they realised, as Moffatt had been given the task of censoring their letters in the hunt for careless talk. He had discovered no secrets, but some of the more passionate letters had made even him blush.

But this was very different. The open boat rising and falling between the waves, the five oarsmen concentrating on the stroke and on Fernie's quick warn-ings and instructions. Moffatt had no idea how they were going to board the badly damaged ship. One false move and they would collide with her, or be capsized by some of the trailing wreckage alongside.

He heard Treherne exclaim, '*There*, Cox'n!' He sounded relieved as he ges-tured towards a dangling ladder. Moffatt wondered if Treherne had been as confident as his bearded countenance suggested.

There were two extra hands in the bows; Fernie was probably thinking of that other time when one of them had been the boy, Milvain.

'Hold water, port!' Fernie judged it with a skill Moffatt could only guess at. 'Ready, forrard!'

Treherne said, 'This must have been where they re-boarded the ship, Doc!' He had to shout, for the sea under the vessel's stern was like the tide in a cave. 'God knows what happened to their lifeboat. Either broke adrift, or was too badly holed by machine-gun fire!'

A voice called, 'This way, lads!'

Bully Bishop heaved back on his loom and snarled, 'Wot, no tea an' biscuits?'

Fernie snapped, 'Stow it!'

Treherne saw a man staring down from the rail. He was so filthy he could have been anyone.

'Three men will stay in the boat – keep her fended off, but make certain the bow-rope holds fast. I don't want the bloody thing stove in!'

One at a time, waiting for the whaler to lift against the ladder for a second or two, they scrabbled their way up towards the watching face, rung by painful rung.

Treherne was last. 'Up you go, Doc.' He gripped him as Moffatt's cap finally blew from his head and floated away along the side. 'I'll buy you another one if we pull this off!'

The man in the filthy dungarees stared at them, his eyes almost starting from his head. 'You came for us.'

Fernie said thickly, 'Looks that way, mate.'

The man said, 'If that murdering bastard comes back we'd be done for.' He rubbed his smoke-reddened eyes as *Gladiator*'s pale shape glided through the smoke and then vanished again. 'But your skipper'll be listening for those buggers, eh?'

Treherne glanced at the doctor. There was no point in telling him about the Asdic. There could be fifty U-Boats out there for all they knew.

'Lead the way. We'll have to get a move on.' They followed him to a great empty store which must have been the boatswain's place for stacking all the spare timber and cordage. That had been used for shoring up those bulkheads closest to the explosions. The second torpedo had flooded the first hold, and the weight of water had helped to steady the hull as well as covering the crates of explosives before the fires could reach them.

Treherne found the survivors huddled with their wounded, the only light below coming from holes in the deck overhead.

He made a quick count, fifteen in all, one of whom he realised was the ship's master. He lay propped against some rope fenders, breathing heavily while a youth held his hand and watched over him.

Moffatt said, 'Move along, Sonny. Let me have a look.'

The slight figure turned and stared at him. It was a Chinese girl, her fine features starkly beautiful in this terrible place.

The master said hoarsely, 'My wife, Anna.' He stared at the doctor's hands as he opened his bag and cut away the dirty bandage. 'A bullet, or piece of one.' He groaned as Moffatt probed around his bruised flesh. 'Just cruised past us and strafed the boats as he went, the bastard. He killed both the mates. Christ knows what happened to the rest. I thought he was going to stop and give us our position, a course for land or the shipping lanes. But he just stood there watching while his guns raked the lifeboats.' He had a Welsh lilt to his voice, very like the chief's.

Treherne asked quietly, 'Has that happened before?'

The ship's master peered at the faded lace on Treherne's sleeve. 'One of our mob, eh?' He frowned, trying to remember the question. 'I've been tin-fished twice before. The first submarine commander handed down smokes and some brandy before he shoved off.' He gasped with pain and added between his teeth, 'But that was in the early days. You know . . .'

'Yes, I know.'

Fernie called, 'This one's done for, sir.'

The master turned his head to listen. He said, 'Bulkhead's holding. We did get a pump going for a bit until it packed up. Now there's no power on anything. Just a matter of time.' He flopped back as Moffatt removed the needle from his arm.

'You can start moving him, Number One.' Moffatt, usually so gentle and curious about everything, was suddenly in charge. 'I'm afraid about this other chap.' He watched as Bully Bishop used his razor sharp pusser's dirk to slit open the man's bloodied trousers. He looked grimly at Treherne. 'It's got to come off. May be too late anyway.' He glanced around at the smoke-stains and the crouching, frightened figures. 'It's not exactly Harley Street, is it?'

The young Chinese woman was still beside him. 'It's all right, my dear, your husband will be well again when we can get him to the ship.'

She shook her head, her black hair shining in the smoky air. 'I stay with you. I help. I nurse in Hong Kong.'

Treherne looked at her. There was a story in her, he thought. Perhaps the captain, who must be well over twice her age, had got her away before the Japs had marched in.

Fernie held the badly injured man and caught his breath as the doctor pulled on his gloves and opened what the SBA called Moffatt's tool kit. He tried to imagine what Bizley would have done if he had been in charge. He realised the man was staring at him, his eyes flickering as the drug moved through him.

'Not me *leg*! For God's sake, *not that*!'

The girl dabbed his forehead, her eyes impassive as Moffatt made his first incision.

Treherne watched the big bearded leading hand. Like a gentle bear unless he was roused. Which was why Treherne knew Bizley had lied; just as he understood why the matter had been dropped.

He said, 'The first time I see you with crossed hooks on your sleeve, Fernie, I'll set up the pints until you're awash!'

Fernie saw the girl wrap the amputated leg in some canvas and carry it away. He murmured, 'A girl like that'd never let you down.'

He spoke so vehemently that Treherne guessed there had been someone special in Fernie's life too. *Had been.*

He thought of Joyce and knew he must see her again, even though he had been quite certain he was going to be killed.

Now he stared around, seeing the deck's steep angle, hearing the slosh of the sea between decks. A ship which refused to die, waiting perhaps to take others with her.

Wally Patch called, 'Just the wounded now, sir!'

Treherne touched Fernie's shoulder. 'Can you manage?'

The big man got to his feet, his eyes troubled. 'Yeah, I can manage, sir.' He spread his gloved hands. 'I'll be as quick as I can.'

'Don't worry. The Old Man will come closer when he sees the whaler.'

Fernie walked carefully up the tilting deck. 'Be seeing you.' He grinned. 'Sir.'

It was suddenly very quiet in the dismal place. Just the painful, regular coughing of one of the men who had swallowed too much fuel when he had dived to escape the machine-guns.

Moffatt looked at the girl, 'Go now. And thanks.'

She smiled briefly and went with Fernie.

Moffatt exclaimed, 'No use, can't stop the bleeding. His pulse is going.' Then he lowered his face and said brokenly, 'What a bloody awful way to die!'

One of the other injured men croaked, 'Never you mind, Doc, you done yer best. 'Is number was on it this time, that's all!' He fell back, exhausted.

Moffatt blew his nose. 'How do they stand it? Again and again?'

'I've often wondered.'

It seemed an age before the whaler returned and Fernie explained that the dangling ladder was almost out of reach. That meant that the ship had gone over still further, and might even capsize.

'It's going to be a rough ride.' Treherne watched Fernie and Patch tying bowlines around the helpless survivors. 'It's better than dying . . .' He broke off, startled, as a loud cracking sound seemed to come straight through the soles of his sea-boots.

Moffatt gasped, 'What was *that*?'

'Bulkhead.' He pushed him with the wounded towards the opening. 'Fast as you like, lads! The old girl's trying to take us with her!'

A man screamed in agony as he sprawled across the whaler's gunwale before being dragged to safety. More smoke exploded into the air, pressurised like steam from within so that Treherne was vaguely reminded of the geysers he had seen in Iceland.

He twisted his head and saw the destroyer swinging round, the sunlight flashing across the bridge screen where Howard would be watching, conning his ship to complete the impossible.

Treherne took a last glance behind him, the two corpses, the bloody parcel beside them. *So this is what it feels like.*

The deck gave a violent lurch and he heard the sudden roar of water, loud cracks as steel plates parted like plywood to the tremendous pressure.

When he climbed down the ladder he had to drop the last few feet into the sea. He clung to the whaler's gunwale as the oarsmen backed water away from the sinking ship. Treherne could see the hull rising over him and wondered if he had left it too late after all; overhead there was a glint of bronze from a motionless screw, which would never come alive again to the clang of the bridge telegraph.

Fernie waited for a seaman to put a bowline around the first lieutenant's shoulders and bellowed, 'Give way, starboard! Back water, port!' He glanced at the towering mass of burned metal as it started to dip deeper by the bows. There the inner fires had been so hot that the hull was black and shimmering from some isolated blaze.

Miracles did happen sometimes. Oil tankers which did not catch fire when torpedoed or bombed; or old veterans like the *Ohio Star* which had spared a few of her people, perhaps to tell the tale of her lonely fight with the Atlantic. An American name, a Welsh master and his lovely Chinese wife.

Treherne felt the bowman dragging at his arm but did not want to miss the moment, to leave without sharing it. 'There she goes!'

One of the less badly wounded clambered to the side and stared as the old ship suddenly lifted her stern and dived.

Treherne turned his head and saw that the unknown seaman was weeping, as if he had lost a friend. Perhaps he had.

The whaler rocked and plunged in the whirlpool that surged around the place where the ship had gone down – Treherne felt it pulling at his legs like something evil, trying to suck him away to follow the ship down and down, so many hundreds of fathoms where there was lasting peace.

He remembered very little after that except for the push and scramble of getting aboard *Gladiator*, with scrambling nets, by brute force, anything.

Faces, wild-eyed, stared at him, while others manned the falls and ran the whaler up to the davit-heads, the boat's usually neat interior slopping with water and bloody dressings.

The bells rang from the bridge, and *Gladiator*'s screws began to thrash the water into a mounting froth as she gathered speed. Men peered at one another, grinned or puffed out their cheeks with relief. The old girl was moving again. Hands reached out to touch Treherne's sodden jacket as he climbed heavily to the bridge.

He saw Howard standing away from the voicepipes as he finished putting his ship on course. He also saw Vallance with a mug in his hand. He had almost never seen the PO steward on the bridge before – Vallance was full of surprises these days.

Howard said quietly, 'It's rum, Number One. I know you don't usually go in for it, but it's the best I can manage at short notice.' He waited while Treherne took a great swallow. 'I'm damned glad to have you back!'

Treherne took another great swallow. 'The Doc did very well.'

'So did you.' He tried to make light of it. 'We even saved their lordships the price of a torpedo.'

Treherne said, 'In all this bloody war, I think that was one of the most worthwhile things we've done together.'

Then he fell silent again, thinking of the master who had now been sunk three times, and who would go back when there was a ship for him. And the girl who would be with him. That was the real difference.

He said, 'I'll go and freshen up, sir.'

Howard handed him his own duffel coat. 'Put this on. Please.' He had seen the sudden exhaustion, emotional and physical; it had been like that for him when Treherne had helped him when he had needed it most. 'It'll be okay.'

But Treherne hadn't moved. He was staring at the sea, and seemed to be grappling for something. Eventually he said, 'All these years, and this is the first time I've known what it's like to have a ship go down under you.' He looked at him, his eyes bleak. 'It's like death.'

4

■ ■ ■ ■ ■ ■ ■

Distinguished Service

The headquarters of Western Approaches was situated in a massive bomb- and gas-proof citadel beneath the rambling building called Derby House in the city of Liverpool. Concrete and armour plate had changed it from a big basement complex to the Navy's own command-post for the Atlantic battle, and had been its nerve-centre since completion in 1941.

No longer were the various sections scattered along the coast or in other ports; each part contained everything and was readily accessible to the boss, in this case Admiral Max Horton. Minesweeping, convoy plots, enemy activities and RAF Coastal Command; all could be contacted without delay by lifting a telephone, the secret information immediately sifted through a scrambler line. If not, the C-in-C would want to know why, and who was responsible. Its core was of course the operations room, one complete wall of which was covered by a giant chart of the battleground, in some places three times as high as the Wrens and operations team who controlled it. They climbed on sliding ladders to move the many coloured markers representing convoys, escort groups, known information about U-Boat packs and the tell-tale recordings of ship losses. There was another large map on an adjoining wall for the Irish Sea and local coastal convoys. It was fully staffed around the clock, so that what happened in the city above and around it ceased to have any meaning or reality. Only the great ocean and the ceaseless battle for supremacy between enemy and ally made any sense.

A youthful lieutenant regarded Captain Ernle Vickers with due deference. 'Captain Naish can see you now, sir.'

He held open a door labelled *Assistant to Chief of Staff*, and stood slightly to one side as if to hint that the interview would be a short one. But the tall captain who got up from his desk to shake Vickers's hand gave a broad grin. He and Vickers had been midshipmen together and were of about the same seniority.

'Good to see you, Ernle!' He glanced at the hovering lieutenant and added, 'No calls.' The lieutenant fled.

Naish seated his friend and produced a decanter and some glasses from a filing cabinet marked *Pending*, and poured two generous measures. He chuckled, 'I know you're not putting to sea, so you can enjoy some decent Scotch for a change. You can't see the boss – he's playing golf, can you believe? Like Drake and his bowls. This evening the Prime Minister is coming up specially to see him.'

Vickers tasted the Scotch, but refrained from asking his friend where he had obtained it. Naish would tell him in his own good time, if he wanted to. He watched Naish's hand moving a signal clip to examine some files underneath.

'I've just finished reading the report about *Gladiator*'s effort with the *Ohio Star*. Bloody good show, I think.'

'Howard's my best skipper.' Vickers waited. They were both too busy to waste time on a casual interview.

'Yes. He has a fine record. I see that his brother has just completed working-up his own escort group.' He got to the point. 'I've put forward the suggestion that Howard be recommended for the Distinguished Service Order, with a gong of some sort for his Number One. God, I think the whole ship's company should be decorated for the risk they took.'

Vickers had been there when the survivors had been landed; the Chinese girl had been wearing a petty officer's reefer jacket, and had brought cheers from the onlookers and ambulance men.

'That would be just fine. Howard deserves it.'

Naish gave a dry smile. 'I understand that you want him to be made up to acting-commander, so you'll have a proper brass-hat as your right-hand man. A bit young, but it would look good when he gets a new ship.'

Vickers grinned broadly. 'The day you prize Howard away from his precious *Gladiator* will be *the day!*'

He watched the man's hands tug at the other file, as if he was reluctant to spoil his news.

'Something rather awkward had turned up.' He opened the papers and Vickers saw the familiar stamp of Admiralty, and the words *Top Secret* in red.

Naish continued, 'An able seaman serving in Light Coastal Forces was killed in the North Sea a little time ago. His name was Hinton, not that it matters. After he was buried, an envelope was sent to C-in-C, the Nore – he was a Chatham rating, you see. Almost like a dying confession – he'd written it himself about a year ago.'

Vickers watched his friend's discomfort, a kind of distaste as he added, 'This chap made certain it would be handed to the proper authority in the event of his death.'

'That's a rum sort of thing to do, Geoffrey.'

Naish looked at him steadily. 'There's an officer in Howard's ship who was awarded the DCS for courage under fire when his MGB was sunk by enemy vessels. Not that far from where this poor chap was killed, curiously enough.'

'Lieutenant Bizley.' He could pick out the face quite easily. A competent enough officer, Howard had said. But a bit too clever for his own good.

'Yes, that's the name . . . It's probably all a waste of time – something that might bring a lot of unhappiness to others, a slur on the name of honour. This rating alleged that Bizley made no attempt to save the wounded, and the captain was still on the bridge, badly shot up when Bizley gave the order to bale-out. There were some others still trapped below, if that wasn't bad enough.' He leaned over with the decanter. 'I think we can do with another tot.'

'But if nobody knows for certain . . .'

Naish glanced at him angrily. 'Too many people know already. The admiral at Chatham, the Admiralty, and now the Special Branch chaps at Bath.'

'So the rubber-heel squad are already involved?'

'I'm afraid so. There was another survivor who got a Mention-in-Despatches. He is being traced. If he backs up this written testimony the whole rotten business will be out in the open.'

'Unlikely, I'd have thought. The other seaman would be in the muck up to his neck!'

'I read Howard's report on the drowning, that rating who was the brother of Bizley's late commanding officer. God knows what the family will have to say about that. Maybe it was only a coincidence. We'll just have to wait and see.'

'*I* knew about that, of course.' Vickers frowned. 'My ships and their morale are more important right now than anything.'

'I agree. But if Bizley lied to play the hero there is no way I can put the lid on it. The boss would have my guts for garters!'

'Shall I have a word with Howard?'

'No. This is between us for the moment. You might mention the possibility of a DSO. I think he's more than earned it.'

They both relaxed and sipped their drinks. The worst had been faced up to. The machine would take over from now on.

'Can we expect anything new in the near future?' It felt cleaner to get back to the war.

Naish pressed his fingertips together. 'A lot of troop convoys. The really precious cargoes. It will be all or nothing this year, I think, both here in the Atlantic and in the Med. The allies will have to make a stab at an invasion down there – to do that they need troops from everywhere. The Germans will know that too unfortunately – so it's business as usual, only more so!'

Just yards away in one corner of the large operations room, Second Officer Celia Lanyon was being shown over the layout by another Wren officer. Her name was Evelyn Major, a rather plain girl who had been a teacher at a fashionable girls' school in Sussex. She even referred to her Wren ratings as 'chaps' when she spoke to them, and Celia could well imagine her waving a lacrosse stick and calling 'Play up, you chaps!' But she certainly took her job at naval operations very seriously. Celia stared at the busy girls on the moving ladders, others sorting the great clips of signals that continually came and went to the hundreds of ships out on the Atlantic at any given time. Her glance lingered on an RAF squadron leader and the other girl said quietly, 'He's married. Anyway he's only a Met officer.' She flushed and exclaimed, 'What a twit I am – your husband was a flier, wasn't he?'

Celia walked to another table where the little pointers were marked with the various warship names, anything from a battle-cruiser to a lowly Asdic trawler. She touched the one now shown to be in port. *Gladiator.*

Evelyn did not miss it. 'You know her captain, don't you?' She smiled. 'Dishy.'

Celia stared at her. 'What do you mean by that?'

'Well, he's such a nice bloke, a lot of my chaps get hot pants when he calls in for something. We heard he came to see you when Jane bought it.'

Celia relaxed slightly. Maybe she was right. Maybe it was better so. Too much grief could tear you apart.

'Yes, he did.' She lifted her chin with something like her old defiance. 'As a matter of fact he telephoned me when the ship got in. To see if I was back from leave.' She hesitated, knowing what Evelyn might think. 'We're going out to dinner this evening.'

'You know you've been put into my quarters to share the place?' She saw her nod and wondered if she should continue. 'It's hard to be alone up here. I don't mind of course, can't see the point really. But should you want . . .' She looked embarrassed. 'Well, I can always clear off for the night.'

'It's not like that.'

'Look, I know what you've been through, but I think you're exactly what he needs. There was some talk . . .'

'Talk? What about?'

'You must have seen it with the Fleet Air Arm boys. Full of bluster and dash, but shit-scared underneath. Round-the-bend, because there's nobody who cares enough to listen.'

'Afternoon, ladies!' Captain Vickers strode past, towering over both of them and leaving a tang of Scotch in his wake.

It gave Celia time to recover herself. She asked, 'Commander Howard, you mean? Tell me – I must know.'

The girl called Evelyn touched her sleeve. 'He's nearly cracked up more than once. Just take a glance at the wall-chart. Every one of those crosses is a ship on the bottom. Can you imagine what it's like out there, month in month out? Holding on, existing while others are being slaughtered?'

Celia stared at the solitary name *Ohio Star*. He had been so casual about it on the telephone, and then she had seen the news report in the paper. Not just obscure names any more. Not this time. Names she knew, names he had mentioned. His most of all.

'Thank you for telling me. I've been too busy feeling sorry for myself. And yes, I do want to share your billet.'

'If you feel it coming on again, my girl, just spill it all to your Auntie Evelyn!' She glared at a small Wren who was staring at her uncertainly. 'What is it, old chap?'

'We thought you should know, ma'am. The C-in-C has just left Hoylake golf course and is on his way.'

'Thanks.' She grinned at Celia. 'You'd better escape while you can. See you here tomorrow. *Sharp*.' She watched Celia walk away, then pause momentarily to glance up at the huge wall-chart, her lips slightly parted as if she were seeing something evil.

Second Officer Major said briskly, 'Come on, chaps, no time for slacking, eh?'

But the mood eluded her, and all she could think about was those two lonely people. Together.

At such short notice the small restaurant, in what had once been one of the port's famous hotels, was not quite what Howard would have liked. One wing of the hotel had been burned out in an incendiary raid, and the empty, blackened windows greeted new arrivals like melancholy eyes. Once it thrived on the great ships which plied the Atlantic between England and the Americas, but now, like so many of the servicemen who stayed or visited there, neither the hotel nor life as it had been lived in those pre-war days, would ever be the same again.

But the food was good, the fish especially fresh and well-cooked, although it was hard not to think of the trawler-men who still plied the sea, with far worse now than the weather to worry about.

Howard watched the girl, who sat directly opposite him, and wished they were quite alone. But the place was almost full, mostly naval officers with their female companions. It was fairly easy to distinguish between the wives and the lovers, and he wondered if Treherne ever came here.

She said, 'I *am* enjoying myself.' She studied his face gravely. 'It was good of you to ask me.' Then she smiled and he felt his heart leap. 'Oh, come on, David – we're behaving like school children! I was so nervous when you rang I almost made some stupid excuse not to come.'

He laughed. 'I was feeling like a junior midshipman!'

She asked, 'What about now?'

He reached across the table and took her hand in his. He saw a few heads turn at nearby tables, but for once, did not care.

'I've thought about you a hell of a lot, Celia.' He saw her eyes widen at the easy use of her name. 'Kept me going when . . .' He shrugged. 'Well, when things got a bit grim.'

'It *was* bad, wasn't it?' She could hear her new friend's voice. *Because nobody cares enough to listen.* 'Tell me. I want to be part of it, try to help.'

His voice was almost distant. 'You need a break from it sometimes – but you can never have it. Every month you give to the Atlantic is more experience, more understanding of the enemy you hardly ever see . . . It gets to you, and sometimes you want to give up.' He raised his eyes and looked directly into hers. 'I expect you've seen the plot, the wall-charts, and all the other exhibits here. But they're ships you see being moved all over the place, ships with men, flesh and blood, who have to take everything the enemy can pitch at them. The skipper of the ammunition ship, for instance.'

She glanced down as his fingers tightened around hers and knew he was back there, reliving it.

He said, 'Tough as old boots. Just a handful of his men and his pretty Chinese wife floating on a mountain of explosives! But he'll be back at sea soon, you'll see.'

She said, 'If I had known, if I had only understood how bad it was. You might have all been killed.'

He smiled. 'As it turned out, the blessed ship went down all on her own. I doubt if the convoy knew anything about it when it passed safely through.'

An elderly waiter came to the table. 'Will you try the sweet, sir?' His tired eyes moved between them and he wondered if he should offer them the room with the double bed and the coal fire, for an hour or so.

She shook her head. 'No, thanks. But I should like some coffee.'

The waiter sniffed. 'It's not *proper* coffee, like the old days, miss.'

As he shuffled away she said, 'I wonder what they think *we* get?'

She realised that he was still holding her hand and when she looked at him she was startled to see the bright intensity in his eyes. 'What is it? Tell me.'

He replied quietly, 'We're friends, Celia, and I want it to be something much more than that.'

He expected her to pull away but she said steadily, 'I'm still here, David.'

'When you came to see me – that first time, remember? I knew you were so unhappy, and my father said that you blamed yourself for what had happened. I don't see you could be blamed for anything like that. I was there, I saw it. It's something you have to harden your soul to, otherwise I, for one, would be useless.'

The coffee came and they did not see it.

Then she said, 'There was a big scene on the last night when I was with him.'

Her lip quivered and Howard said, 'Don't talk about it if it troubles you so much. Nothing is worth that.'

She faced him in her direct way and said, 'Well, I think it is. You see, I have always been a bit – sheltered, isn't that what they say of girls who won't play games? I went to an expensive school where about the only men I ever saw were a clergyman and the gardeners.' She shook her head with something like disbelief. 'How I ever got the nerve to apply for the WRNS I'll never know. Dormitories packed with young girls all trying to outdo each other with their so-called adventures. A lot of them knew my father was a rear-admiral – well, he was a captain then – and they used to pull my leg about it. Was it just a game to me, they used to ask. I was never more serious about anything. I got my commission and went on attachment to the Fleet Air Arm . . . that was where I met Jamie. He seemed to be so full of life – nothing ever appeared to trouble him. I knew he had an eye for the girls – I think everyone knew. More than an eye in a few cases. Because I didn't "join in", and maybe because I was an admiral's daughter . . . I seemed to attract him. It was a kind of madness. *I* was envied for once, admired even for the way I handled it. I don't know if it would ever have worked out. He got very depressed when they told him he was to be grounded. Flying was his life, I should have realised that sooner. Flying, and all the adoration that went with it.'

The waiter's shadow was across the table. 'Would you like the bill, sir?' *She* would go to the ladies' to powder her nose as they always did. Then he would put it to the young lieutenant-commander about the empty bedroom.

Howard said, 'Two brandies.' He saw her start to protest and added, 'Large ones.' He faced her again and said, 'Sorry about that.' He waited, knowing that she was fighting it again.

She said, 'He was seeing some girl, one he'd known at his old airfield. We had a blazing row about it, and he told me about the job he had volunteered for. I asked him not to do it. He'd risked his life countless times. Luck can't last forever.'

She broke off and asked abruptly, 'Do you have a cigarette?'

He shook his head. 'Sorry, I'm a pipe man, but I'll get the old retainer to find some.'

She shook her head so that her hair fell across her forehead, and Howard could easily picture her as a schoolgirl. 'I don't smoke, David. I just thought this might be the time to begin.'

She watched the waiter place the glasses carefully on the table and said, 'This will do, though.'

Howard watched; she was unused to brandy too, he thought. It was best not to recall Vallance's Horse's Necks, which had grown larger and larger over the past months.

She faced him calmly. 'He stormed out of the house, telling me he'd do what he liked, and no stuck-up bitch would change him.' She swallowed some more brandy and looked at him, her eyes very green in the reflected lights. 'He came back that night so drunk he could barely walk. A different man, like somebody else – a stranger. Do you want me to continue?'

Howard said nothing. She was going to tell him anyway, no matter what it might do to her.

She said, 'He wanted me. He kept pulling at me, telling me I'd soon be rid of him. I tried to calm him, to find the man I had married – in the end I was fighting him off.' She gripped his wrist until her nails broke the skin. 'He hit me in the face and threw me on the bed.' Her eyes were quite level and unmoving. 'Then he raped me.'

'Dear God!' Howard pictured it as it must have been. Lust, anger, madness. And she had been made to submit to that and to the memory which had tormented her until now.

She said simply, 'The rest you know. He was killed shortly afterwards.'

Howard said quietly, 'If he hadn't been I think I would have done it for him.'

She released her hand very gently and said, 'The waiter is coming back. I'm told he makes "arrangements" for certain officers and their girlfriends.' She looked for her bag. 'So if I was ever in a position like that, I'm not sure I could . . .' She broke off as the waiter put down the bill on a dented tray.

'Everything all right, miss?'

Her voice was surprisingly calm. 'A very nice meal, thank you.'

To Howard she said, 'Take me home will you, please? I'll show you where I live.' As they walked to the door several heads turned to watch them, something which Howard resented more than he would have believed possible. She said, 'That will give the old goat something to ponder on!'

But Howard knew it was to cover what she had been trying to tell him. That she might never be able to make love again.

As they walked through the darkened streets and watched the first searchlights criss-crossing the sky she said, 'You see, David, I *do* care. Very much. I never thought I would again. Perhaps I didn't even know what I wanted.'

He turned her lightly in his arms. It was not happening. Another dream. 'I love you, Celia. I'll not change.' He held her, and they kissed gently, as if they were meeting for the first time. I'd never do or say anything to hurt you.'

Her hands were gripping his jacket as if she would not let him go, and at the same time knew that she must.

She said, 'I know that, David. That's why I want it to be *right*.'

They stood apart as two policemen walked past, their steel helmets shining in the faint searchlights.

All right for some, they would say.

Howard said, 'I'd like to see you again as soon as we get back.'

'Get back?'

'Well, you'll know soon enough when you go to your new job in ops. We're off again now that the maintenance commander has put a rocket under the Asdic people. Don't worry – we're getting pretty good at it now.'

'I'll be watching and thinking about you.' She lifted her head and looked at his outline in the darkness. 'I'm glad I told you about . . .'

He kissed her lightly on the mouth. 'Come on, I'll walk you the rest of the way.'

The smouldering ammunition ship, the inability to listen for U-Boats, even the next convoy; they were all far away.

This was now, and David Howard was young again.

'There's a sight for sore eyes, sir!' Treherne levelled his binoculars and studied the convoy, which was making a wide turn, hard sunlight flashing from tiers of scuttles and across the spacious bridge of the leading ship. Three ocean liners, well known on pre-war cruising posters, none of them a stranger to the Atlantic for those lucky enough in the Depression to be able to afford such luxury. Even their dull grey paint could not disguise their majestic lines, and even as the signal lamps began to blink between Vickers's group and the convoy's own close escort, it was possible to see that the leading ship's upper decks were packed with soldiers. They were mostly American, and had been handed over to their new escort in mid-Atlantic.

Howard loosened his coat; it was surprisingly hot in the open bridge, and he tried to estimate how many troops were crammed into each liner. All bound for Britain, and then after further training, to some point where an invasion must be launched.

'Port fifteen.' Howard glanced at the gyro-repeater. Like the other commanding officers in the group, he knew what to do. Half of them would sweep stern of the convoy's close escort; the rest would take station further to the south. The original escorts must have had their work cut out to keep pace with those powerful ships, he thought; it had made re-fuelling for the destroyers doubly difficult at sea because the liners stopped for nobody.

'Midships . . . Steady.'

'Steady, sir. Course zero-four-zero.' Howard smiled. The right direction anyway. They would be back in port in a couple of days if this weather held.

'Aircraft, sir. Bearing Green four-five. Angle of sight two-oh!'

'Disregard.' Treherne lowered his glasses. Even that was different now. The chill of despair when you sighted any aircraft was less evident. This one was a big Sunderland flying boat, crossing the convoy while the soldiers stared up at its great whale-shape and waved their caps.

Howard heard the clatter of feet on a ladder and knew Bizley had arrived to relieve Treherne for the afternoon watch. Was it noon already?

Bizley seemed to have recovered his old self-confidence, Howard thought. He was discussing course and speed and the air recognition signals as if he had been doing it all his life. At least he and Finlay were avoiding another clash, so Vallance's wardroom would be more peaceful.

Howard climbed onto his chair and thought of the girl he had walked home to her billet, the one she shared with the second officer they called 'Auntie'. It was still hard to believe it had happened, or how it had begun. She was shy; probably still very shocked by what she had told him. But it meant more than that to Howard. She had trusted him. He would never repay it with some clumsy attempt at love. But as he had held her outside the darkened doorway he had felt her pressed against him, and had known then how much he had wanted her.

Sub-Lieutenant Rooke called, 'From *Kinsale*, sir.' He held out the intercom handset, while Howard stared across the screen as if he still expected to see the leader. But she and the others were already out of sight, lost in a rippling mist created by the hard sunshine.

Vickers sounded as if he was on another planet, or was speaking through water.

'Received a signal from the Sunderland, David. Thinks they may have sighted a submarine, submerged and well astern of the convoy. They'll make sure she doesn't surface to try and catch up.' He gave a hollow chuckle. 'No chance of that, eh?'

Howard peered at his little radar-repeater. How huge the troopers' blips looked, the escorts – all destroyers for no corvette would ever keep pace with them – spread around them, a sure shield. *The most precious cargo of all.*

Vickers added, 'I've detached *Ganymede* to support. You remain on station, just in case.'

Howard relayed the information to Treherne, who was still on the bridge.

He said, 'They'll keep the bastard down. I don't expect the Jerry commander even realised the Sunderland had spotted him. Like a shadow in the water, I suppose.'

The yeoman of signals said, 'There goes *Ganymede*!'

Howard watched their sister-ship angling away towards the opposite horizon where another destroyer, Tail-end Charlie, was signalling to the flying boat as it cruised sedately overhead.

Howard thought of his friend Spike Colvin on *Ganymede*'s bridge, sporting one of the famous brightly-coloured scarves he had worn at sea as a subbie. He lowered his face to the radar-repeater again. He saw the blip made by the destroyer, a big modern one named *Mediator* over five miles astern. Then *Ganymede*, bustling through the revolving radar beam as if drawn on a wire.

It was a marvel Colvin had ever made command, he thought. He had committed every sort of prank imaginable. He had painted their class number on the grass with weed-killer when they were about to pass out from *Excellent*, the gunnery school. But it had rained unexpectedly and the enormous figures had appeared even as the captain had been about to conduct the passing-out parade. Colvin had confessed. He always had. Another time, at a Christmas party, he had loaded and fired a brass cannon outside the Devonport Barracks wardroom. It had, unfortunately, blown out most of the windows in the commodore's house.

The three troopships were completing another zig-zag, lights flashing to the close escort commander as they wheeled in perfect unison. No chances with this lot, Howard thought.

'Starboard ten. Midships. Steer zero-eight-zero.' He raised his glasses but it was difficult to see *Ganymede* now, and anyway one of the wing escorts blocked the lenses while she, too, made a rapid change of course.

Rooke still held the handset and shouted, 'From *Kinsale*, sir! Sunderland reports torpedoes . . .'

But Howard had already seen the flash, and then a second one. Against the eye-searing sunshine it was little more than a blink. By contrast, when it reached them, the double explosion was like a thunderclap; Howard felt the bridge quiver beneath his sea-boots as if they had run across a sandbar.

Treherne snapped. 'Where the *hell* was that?'

Howard was watching the blip which was furthest astern. It had to be the *Mediator*. There was nothing else that far out.

The Sunderland was already swooping down over the sea's glittering face, depth-charges ready to drop if it sighted anything. That was exactly what the second U-Boat had been depending on.

There was a double flash and even above the mist Howard saw the tall water-spouts shooting skyward, followed instantly by a great plume of black smoke.

'Captain Vickers – for you, sir.'

Howard did not need to be told. The second salvo from a different bearing had hit *Ganymede*.

'Sunderland's dropping floats, David. Take your section to assist.'

'Hard a-starboard. Full ahead together. Steer two-five-zero. Yeoman, take to *Blackwall* and *Belleisle*: Take station for search on me.'

Treherne watched him grimly. He knew exactly what Howard was thinking.

He had mentioned it several times; what a senior officer had once said to him. *When they start going for the escorts instead of the convoy, you'll know you're winning the battle.*

A powerful blast echoed across the sea, loud enough to muffle *Gladiator*'s racing screws as she worked up to maximum revolutions. A ship blowing up? It would not be depth-charges; the Sunderland would not dare with so many men fighting for their lives in the water. The enemy would know that too. In no time a second Sunderland joined in the patrol, but the U-Boats had gone deep and headed away from danger.

When *Gladiator* and her two consorts reached the scene *Mediator* had already vanished. She had been a big destroyer, newer and more powerful than Vickers's *Kinsale*. She carried about two hundred in her company. Of their sister-ship only the forward portion remained afloat. The torpedoes must have hit her amidships and blown her in half, the engine room exploding like a huge bomb.

Amidst the usual slick of oil and bobbing flotsam Howard could see a few struggling figures; not many.

'Action stations, sir?' Bizley sounded stiff and unreal, as if he did not believe what had happened.

'No. But clear the lower deck, and turn out the boats. Tell Ayres to stand by the Carley floats and scrambling nets.'

Treherne said, 'They're already dealing with it, sir.'

He trained his glasses on the *Ganymede*'s uplifted bows, and wondered how many might be trapped inside. He could see two tiny figures clinging to the port anchor, another trying to pull someone on to a waterlogged float.

'Slow ahead.' Howard heard the motor boat's engine cough into life as it was lowered down alongside. '*Stop engines!*' The moment of risk. He felt suddenly sick, as if nothing would stop him vomiting in front of them all.

'Boat's away, sir!'

Blackwall was already lowering her two boats near where the other warship had gone down, while *Belleisle* continued to circle round the scene, her Asdic listening for any tell-tale echo. But in his heart Howard knew there would be none. Two destroyers gone within thirty seconds. They had made their point.

When Howard eventually recalled the boats, and one solitary swimmer was hauled gasping and sobbing up a scrambling net, he had to report to Vickers that only fifty survivors had been rescued between them. Spike Colvin had not been found.

As the whaler was hoisted again, *Ganymede* released a great gout of filthy bubbles and vanished. The whaler's crew had managed to save the two men from her anchor. They had been lucky.

'Increase revolutions to resume patrol, Pilot.' Howard looked at Treherne, his eyes empty of expression. 'How does it feel to be winning, Number One?'

It took several hours to catch up with the convoy, and by then it was near dusk. Howard looked at the tall-sided liners and wondered if any of the troops realised what had happened, and would remember this day when their own time came to risk their lives.

He thought of their other sister-ship, *Garnet*, which was up there with Vickers's section. Her captain, Tom Woodhouse, had been at Dartmouth with him, another irrepressible joker – he and Colvin had been pretty close, too. Might he be thinking the same now? *Who's next?*

He pictured the girl in Liverpool, probably watching the plot right now as the two ships were reported lost. *Next of kin have been informed.* She must not go through all that again.

Later, as he sat in his chair and watched the first stars appear, he thought about it again. Perhaps like a ship's course on the ocean, their fate was already decided.

5

No Greater Love

Another full pattern of depth-charges exploded like distant thunder, but still close enough to shake the submarine from bow to stern. The men at their various stations stared unblinking at the curved hull, their eyes very white in the dimmed lighting.

It had been going on for an hour, even longer when you counted their failed attack on the small, fast convoy.

Standing by the periscope well, Kapitänleutnant Manfred Kleiber shifted his glance from the clock to the depth gauges. There was only one hunter up there now. That same single-screwed engine beat of a corvette, one of the convoy's escort. Perhaps they would give up eventually and hurry away to rejoin the others. He watched some of the men nearest to him, those at the hydroplane controls, the helmsman, the navigating officer. Their hair and shoulders were speckled with the cork-filled paint which had fallen like snowflakes from the deckhead during the last onslaught of depth-charges. Their faces were grey, pallid, even in the warm glow of the control room lighting. Dirty clothes; unshaven sunken faces. *The Grey Wolves*, as one patriotic newspaper had described them.

Those bastards should be here with us, he thought bitterly.

He could guess what most of his men were thinking, that they would soon have to break off the patrol and return to base. It had to be *his* decision. They had already passed the rendezvous time for the final meeting with a supply submarine. Surely they had not lost yet another one? Kleiber knew all about the new tactics, the hunter-killer groups which searched for U-Boats like professional assassins. Three of his own wolf-pack had failed to make contact, so they must have been destroyed. He thought of the base in France. It was high summer now – green fields, sunshine, good food. No wonder his men looked so desperate. He had addressed all of them when he had received the signal from HQ. The Tommies and their allies had made their first move since North Africa, and had succeeded in launching an invasion into Sicily. Not Greece after all, as his group commander had predicted, but they would be driven off or captured. Just like Crete.

His lip curled with contempt. What did he know? The allies were not only still there, but all resistance had ceased. Italy next – it had to be. The Italians had always been the weak link. Despite their outward belief in Fascism, they had proved to be jackals, an army that ran rather than fought to the death.

He saw the hydrophone operator's quick glance, and gave his orders: increase the depth by thirty metres, alter course ninety degrees yet again.

Kleiber was too experienced to need a headset. The thrum-thrum-thrum of the corvette's screw was like an express train. She had turned and was coming on another sweep.

Someone tip-toed through an emergency door, a rag covering his mouth and nose. Kleiber thought of the man who had died, after being hit by a piece of shell splinter on that other occasion when they had approached a convoy on the surface, working into a suitable position to attack. It had been a random shot from an escort, a ship they had not even seen. Just bad luck, for him. With the aid of a medical handbook Kleiber had amputated the man's arm himself when gangrene with its disgusting stench had pervaded the whole boat. He had died under drugs without knowing anything about it. His comrades had been sorry for him; he had been a popular crewman. Now, without exception, they had come to hate him, waiting only to rid themselves of the corpse and its constant reminder of death.

The hull shook wildly as another full pattern roared down. Several lights shattered, and a man cried out, his face cut by flying glass.

The corvette's engine faded again, but the hydrophone operator shook his head. The enemy commander was slowing down – a listening game, or perhaps pausing to await more support.

How much could the hull stand? Kleiber could feel them watching him. Looking for hope, despair, weakness.

He moved to the chart table and studied the pencilled parallelogram which showed the extent of the *milchküh* operational zone. It was no use. She must have gone down. With aircraft more and more in evidence across the once-safe area, they were prime targets, too big and too vulnerable to escape a sudden attack.

All at once, he was desperate to leave; to get back to base, to find out what was happening. Some of his fellow U-Boat commanders had been in the Mediterranean and had been employed against the supply train for the allied invasion. He thought bitterly of the last brief letter he had received from his brother in Russia. He was a fool to write as he did; if his letter had been opened he might have been punished for defeatist talk. But in it he had described the appalling food and shortages of medical supplies, ammunition and just about everything on the Russian front. Kleiber tried not think of what the enemy troops would be eating and drinking in Sicily. He had boarded British supply vessels before sinking them, in the rosier times, and knew well enough how well they lived. He made up his mind. He would tell his men, it would raise their spirits to head for base. A man could survive these conditions for just so long. The alternative could not even be entertained.

But first . . . He gave his orders without even raising his voice. He was not being callous; and if he was, it was the Atlantic's responsibility. There were two torpedoes left, and with only three hits and no definite kills throughout the whole patrol, Kleiber had felt disillusioned and frustrated by the latest setback of the supply-boat.

He heard the thud of watertight doors closing and could picture his men peering at one another as each door opened and shut on their private, sealed compartments. How would the dead man's relatives behave if they knew the last move he would make for the Fatherland?

The corvette was on the move again, her engine's thrashing beat fading as she prepared for a change of bearing, which at any time might bring her detection gear tapping at the submerged hull like a blind man's stick. A light flickered on the control panel. It was ready. The corpse was in an empty torpedo tube complete with any litter which the seamen had been able to gather. The engineer officer would supply some oil, but not much. Without the supply-boat it would be a long, painful haul back to France.

She was coming in to the attack; the loud cracks against the hull were the worst so far. She must have got a contact.

He snapped his order and saw the light flicker as the tube disgorged its contents into the sea. Kleiber could feel cold sweat beneath the rim of his soiled white cap. Like ice rime while he counted seconds and imagined the spread-eagled corpse, dressed in proper waterproof clothing, floating up to the sunshine, surrounded with odds and ends from the rubbish bins, and a quick discharge of oil. He felt his mouth tightening with the insane desire to laugh. It was to be hoped the Tommies didn't notice that their 'volunteer' had only one arm! Then he controlled his thoughts with cold determination; such hysteria was dangerous, destructive.

They were staring at the hull again, listening; straining every muscle for a sign.

Very slowly and carefully Kleiber brought his command round in a wide arc, the motors so reduced they were barely audible.

Round and further still, until the hydrophone operator reported that the corvette was stopping, and then that all hydrophone effects had ceased. Kleiber frowned, gauging where the sun would be when he went to periscope depth. He could see it all as if he were there. A boat being lowered to gather the evidence of a kill. If anything went wrong now the enemy commander would have no more doubts – he would *know* there was a submarine here. He might even have called for air support.

Kleiber nodded to his first officer and bent right down almost to his knees as the air was forced into the ballast tanks, the hydroplanes moving like fins to make the boat's movements slow and stealthy. At forty metres Kleiber ordered the attack periscope to be raised again, so slowly that he could hear the mechanic's rough breathing as he controlled it.

Faint green light, then purplish-blue as the lens cut above the surface. Kleiber saw the motionless corvette framed in the crosswires, her boat probably lowered on the opposite side to retrieve the grisly evidence of their 'kill'.

Kleiber did not linger long. Just enough to note the corvette's number: HMS *Malva*. Probably of all the warships in the Atlantic these stocky little vessels had been the U-Boat's greatest enemy.

The hull jerked twice and the periscope hissed down into its well as the boat gathered speed and swung away, the water roaring into her tanks again to carry her down deep.

A petty officer by the plot pressed his stop-watch and gasped as the exploding torpedoes threw the hull over, the sound sighing across and past them to be lost in the vastness of the ocean.

Moments later they heard the grinding echo of tearing steel, as the corvette began to break up on her way to the bottom.

Kleiber walked to the chart, shutting his ears to the crazed cheers and insane laughter which passed through the U-Boat like echoes from Bedlam. If the grand admiral ordered him to attack escorts as a priority, that he would do without question.

He must stop thinking of his brother and his starving comrades in Russia, and of the richly loaded food ships which he might lose because of this new instruction.

Above them, and failing further and further astern, the corvette's survivors floated in their lifejackets or struggled through the oil slick in search of a raft or some piece of wood to keep them afloat. There had been no time to make a distress signal; no time for anything; and most of all of these men would die before anyone came to search for them.

Among the gasping, struggling survivors, the dead German floated indifferently, unaware of what he had done, without even the satisfaction of revenge. In the Atlantic there was no such luxury.

The main operations room at Liverpool seemed even busier than usual. Second Officer Celia Lanyon shared a desk with her roommate, Evelyn Major, and together they were sorting through the latest signals which had been gathered by the SDO along another corridor in the citadel.

It was late afternoon, in the month of September, and all day the place had been buzzing with the news of the follow-up to the invasion of the Italian mainland. Wherever possible the Italians were throwing down their arms, offering their services to the allies, when earlier they had been sworn enemies. The complete collapse of Germany's strongest partner had been settled when the Italian flagship had led the main part of their fleet under the guns of Malta, that bombed and battered island which had once been one of Mussolini's hoped-for prizes.

Every day they had expected a reverse, another of the disappointments which had been their lot in the past years. But apart from the arrival of early rain in southern Italy, which had clogged down the movement of tanks and supplies, there was no sign of impending difficulty. There had been losses on the beaches when the Allied armies had first stormed ashore, while at sea the covering warships and bombardment squadron had been introduced to Germany's latest secret weapon: a glider-bomb which could be directed onto a floating target, and which had brought fresh problems to the fleet's gunnery officers. The flagship *Warspite* had been hit, and several major warships, including the US cruiser *Savannah*, had suffered heavy damage and casualties.

But down here in operations, despite the heartening news from the Mediterranean, defeat and victory remained strangely remote, like the city overhead. At this particular moment two major convoys were at sea, an eastbound and a westbound, which should be passing overnight some ninety miles apart.

The eastbound convoy was from Halifax, and included two large troopships as well as several freighters carrying vehicles and crated aircraft. As Celia checked the columns of names against the duty operations officer's list she thought of *Gladiator*, somewhere out there with the escort group under Captain Vickers's control. She had met Howard only three times since he had taken her back to the billet from the hotel – the group had been operating for much of the time from Iceland, to make certain that the flow of troopships reached port unscathed.

She remembered so clearly the moment when she had seen the two ships marked as lost on the plot. *Mediator*, and the one commanded by his friend, *Ganymede*. Just fifty survivors between them. It had torn at her heart like claws when he had told her. Even that he had been reluctant to do. As if he wanted to shield her from the true horror of the life they were sharing.

The enemy attacks on escort vessels were not coincidental; other ships had been mauled both by submarines and aircraft, with several new crosses on the plot to give grim evidence of this new phase of war.

The duty operations officer sauntered over to their table and nodded. 'Take a break. I have a feeling things will hot up shortly. The boss is here already, usually a bad omen.'

The tiny room where the officers could have tea or relax with a smoke was almost humid – the summer had been a long one.

Evelyn brought two cups of tea and one spoon. 'All there are left.' She sat down untidily and thrust out her legs like a man.

Celia thought of the way he had held her, how she had realised he had wanted her so desperately. She did not know, could not tell . . .

She looked up, startled, as the other Wren said, 'Auntie time, old chap. Isn't it about the right moment to spill the beans? If you don't, you'll drive yourself crazy. You've lost weight – something you never needed, not like *me!*' She became serious again. 'What does *he* think?'

Perhaps she was right. That it might help to talk. 'He loves me.' It sounded so empty that she said, '*Really* loves me. God knows, I'm bad luck – I told him that too.' She stood up suddenly and walked across the room. 'I'm afraid. I want him to love me.'

'And you think that you might not be able to give it in return? That he'll be hurt, get tired of waiting, something like that?'

She sat down again and gave a small smile. 'Very like that.'

'I think I know you pretty well, Celia. I know you're not the type to leap into bed with anyone you take a fancy to, and from what you've told me he certainly doesn't sound the type either. Otherwise you'd never have opened up to him about what happened with Jamie.'

Celia sighed. 'I do seem to tell you rather a lot, don't I?'

'Not much else to do up here.' She watched her warily. 'I have a cousin who's got a cottage up in the Lake District. I could easily fix it, next time you can both snatch some leave.'

Celia stared at her. 'What, a secret place, you mean? Just like that? A little black nightie and some perfume?'

Evelyn smiled. 'Has he ever suggested anything of the kind?'

Celia said nothing. Howard had told her about the girl he had once known, and, she suspected, had loved. He had just received his first command and had gone straight into the thick of it when, she guessed, he had won his DSC. The girl had not waited for him, and Celia wondered how it had affected him. She had been shocked when they had last met in that same shabby restaurant before he had sailed again for Iceland. He had seemed empty, utterly drained; even the news of his proposed DSC had had no effect.

'I would give myself to him tomorrow if I thought it would help. Give him something to – to hold on to.' She hesitated, remembering what he had said. *Can't you see, girl? I'm in love with you!* 'I wouldn't want to with anyone else.'

Evelyn said kindly, in her brisk, no-nonsense manner, 'Sounds suspiciously like love to me, Celia.'

She barely heard, remembering the flecks of grey in his hair, the lines at his mouth; the way he clung to her hand, like a lifeline.

'What shall I say? What must I do?'

They returned to the desk and she saw the chief of staff's assistant in deep conference with the other heads of department.

A Wren petty officer with a coder's badge on her sleeve bent down by their desk.

'The eastbound's in a spot of bother, ma'am. Their escort carrier has engine trouble and will return to Halifax. The westbound has another carrier, the *Seeker* – she will supply air cover from tomorrow.'

'Thanks.' Evelyn leafed expertly through her file and then handed the relevant flimsy to a messenger. Between her teeth she said, 'The carrier breakdown has delayed our eastbound.' She squinted at the plot. Almost too casually she added, 'The thirty-second escort group has been redirected. Two hundred miles. Should be all right according to the Met report.'

Celia watched the little counters appear for the first time: Captain Vickers's *Kinsale*, and then some twenty miles distant, the half-leader, H–38. There was a gap this time. Poor *Ganymede*.

And so it went on. Signals in and out, senior officers speaking to their various subordinates. The Wrens up and down the ladders, moving ships, marking some losses in a coastal convoy, with the RAF Coastal Command people listening to the latest Met reports, the availability of their new long-range aircraft from Northern Ireland, Iceland and Newfoundland.

The duty operations officer, an RNVR lieutenant-commander, said, 'One of the additional escorts has made a distress signal, sir.'

The assistant to the chief-of-staff folded his arms while the others around him poised themselves as they had done so many times.

Captain Naish stared hard at the plot. 'Make a signal to the thirty-second group – Captain Vickers will act on this. He must be the closest.' He waited for the telephone to click into action. 'How bad is it?'

'One torpedo, sir. Down by the bows. Requires assistance.'

'With this convoy coming through I can't spare any other escorts, Tim. The half-leader will be the most available – ask Vickers to detach *Gladiator*. She was the last to refuel.'

A door opened and without looking the girl knew it was the boss.

He asked, 'Which escort?'

'The corvette *Tacitus*, sir. Lieutenant-Commander Marrack.'

'Keep me informed.' The door closed again.

The two Wren officers looked at each other and Celia said quietly, 'Why can't they send someone else?'

Evelyn watched her unhappily, not understanding.

She said, 'He's often spoken of Marrack. *They* were friends too.' She pushed her knuckles into her mouth and then said in a small voice, 'Don't you see? After *Ganymede* and everything else . . .' She could not go on.

'I *do* see.' Evelyn stared at the plot but saw only the little marker, where a solitary escort lay at the mercy of the sea and the enemy. *Gladiator* would be on her way by now, and should reach the torpedoed vessel by dawn. Marrack's ship must have helped escort the carrier to safety and been trying to return to the convoy. She glanced at the two RAF officers. But there *should* be long-range air cover, even at that distance, when daylight found them.

Beside her Celia took the latest pad of signals from a messenger and waited for her vision to clear.

To herself she whispered, *Oh, David, I do love you so.*

The duty officer rapped out more figures and the ladders began to move again. 'To commodore. *There are now twenty-plus U-Boats in your vicinity.*'

Naish patted his pockets but had forgotten his cigarettes. He pictured his tall friend directing his killer-group to the eastbound convoy: *D'you Ken John Peel?* It was very apt. His glance fell on the latest female addition to the ops room. Rear-Admiral Lanyon's daughter. She would be a real catch for some lucky chap. But she looked strained and pale, and he suddenly remembered a rumour he had picked up at the club. As she stared at the small isolated counter, *H–38*, Captain Naish knew that it was no longer just a rumour.

Howard slid open the chart-room door and stared at Treherne and Rooke, who were busy with their calculations. It was all but dark beyond the ship, with thick cloud and the hint of rain. He should never have allowed himself to lie down in his sea cabin; it was always worse this way, the sudden shrill of the telephone, all his instincts forcing sleep and escape into the background.

'No further signals, Number One?'

'None, sir.' Treherne watched him, saw the battle Howard was already fighting.

Howard looked at Rooke. 'Well, *come on*, man, I'm not a bloody mind-reader!'

Rooke pointed with his dividers. 'Twenty-five degrees west, fifty-five north, sir.'

'I'm going up top.' Howard fastened his duffel coat, the one he had once offered to Treherne. 'By the time I get there I want the course-to-steer, and the ETA. I shall have a word with the Chief.'

He pulled the door behind him and for just a few moments stood with his back against the damp steel while he calmed his breathing.

On the other side of the door Treherne said quietly, 'Take it off your back, Pilot. He didn't mean to bite your head off. *Tacitus*'s skipper used to be Number One here. A pal of his.' He smiled sadly. 'One of the family, so to speak.'

Rooke sighed. 'In that case . . .'

Treherne made for the door. 'In that case, *get it right!*'

On the upper bridge Howard replaced the engine room telephone and listened to the regular beat of engines.

He heard Rooke and Treherne speaking by the ready-use chart-table, transferring the calculations which the navigator had just completed.

Rooke said, 'Course-to-steer is two-four-five, sir.'

Howard glanced at Treherne's shaggy silhouette. 'Bring her round. Revs for twenty knots. With the sea fairly calm, we shouldn't shake about too much, but better warn the watch below.'

'Aye, aye, sir.' They would be having their supper when *Gladiator* worked up to that sort of speed, big, sickening swoops across the unbroken swell. It was to be hoped the PO chief had not produced anything too greasy.

He heard Rooke say carefully, 'Estimated time of arrival will be six o'clock onward, sir. Daylight if the visibility's good.'

'Right.' Howard could sense Rooke's resentment, but it did not seem to matter. Once he would have apologised instantly for unfairly berating a subordinate. Those days had gone somewhere out here in the Atlantic. Tomorrow there might be air cover, or there might not. Two large convoys passing, vital supplies, and more troops to extend the victories in Italy, and elsewhere.

But at this moment there were only two ships he cared about, and Marrack would be desperate. His first command. What he had always wanted. Even the corvette's reported position was too vague for complete accuracy. There was never enough time when hell burst in on you.

He watched the sea creaming away from either bow, the spray starting to drift over the bridge or beat against the glass screen. Lucky they had been the last to take on fuel from a fleet tanker; otherwise someone else would be heading for that tiny pencilled cross down to south-west-by-south. The telephone in his sea cabin had torn him from another terrible dream. He had been helplessly watching her being raped by the man in the flying-suit; holding her down and laughing, laughing.

Treherne rejoined him. 'No more from W/T, sir. Keeping the air clear for the strategists.' He said it without bitterness, but Howard could feel the hurt he was sharing with him.

Treherne said unexpectedly, 'Had a bit of good news when we were in last, sir. My girl's husband got himself killed.' He chuckled in the darkness. 'He was pissed apparently, and got run over by an armoured car!'

They both laughed like schoolboys, and then Howard stared at him, knowing they were both going quite mad; there was no other explanation. 'Are you going to get married now?'

'Not sure, sir. My old lady walked out on me. I shall have to look into the legal thing when I get a chance.' He added sharply, 'If that bastard had laid a hand on her again, I would have done him in myself!'

Howard thought of what he had said to the girl in the restaurant. 'It must be catching.'

He leaned his head on his arms and felt the desire to sleep clouding his mind. But he knew that if he did, the terrible dream would be waiting to mock and torment him.

Instead he said, 'See if you can rustle up something hot to drink. It's going to be a long night.'

Howard buttoned up the collar of his oilskin as the rain slashed diagonally across the open bridge. It was heavy and surprisingly cold, a reminder, if anyone should need it, that autumn and winter came early to the Western Ocean. The lookouts were changed yet again to prevent them becoming dulled by the regular plunging motion, when they might miss something. The monotonous ping of the Asdic, the occasional shuffle of feet from the crew of B-gun below the bridge, all told of nervous readiness. If there was a battle going on in one or other of the big convoys, it was too far away to concern them. Everybody in *Gladiator*'s company would also be aware that they were drawing further and further from aid with each swing of the propellers.

Howard peered through the screen and saw the sea surging alongside. Beyond the curling bow-wave there was just the merest glimpse of the nearest troughs, riding past like heaving black oil.

Treherne was beside him again, trying to make sure he had forgotten nothing.

Howard said, 'We shall stay at defence stations, Number One, but I want both watches on deck, the hull sealed like a sardine tin. I've told Guns that he is excused watchkeeping – I want his control position manned and ready in case we need a starshell or something more lethal. He also knows that the short-range weapons will remain closed-up.' He mopped his face with a towel, but that was already sodden. 'This will play hell with visibility.'

'I've warned radar and Asdic, sir.' Treherne hesitated, unwilling to say it. 'We must expect the worst to have happened, sir.'

'Yes.' He sounded very quiet, his voice almost lost in the surge and spray of the old enemy. 'I realise that. But Marrack won't use his W/T any more. If there's still a U-Boat about, and we have to face that, it might pick up his signals.'

He heard the midshipman burst into a fit of nervous coughing. It often happened, and had got worse since the loss of *Ganymede* and *Mediator*. He had spoken to Moffatt about it, and the doctor had said angrily, 'I'll have a word if you like, sir. Some fool at the hospital must have been deaf and blind to send a kid like him back to sea so soon after losing his ship – he's a nervous wreck.'

Howard called across the bridge. 'Come here, Mid!'

Ross felt his way over the slippery decking and waited, mute in the darkness.

'I need all my most experienced officers up here. I've sent Mister Ayres down aft with the Buffer's party. You go and assist.' He looked away, thinking of the corvette. If the weather worsened they might not even find her unless they got help from a recce aircraft. 'And, Ross – I think you should have advice ashore. You've had a bad time.'

Treherne popped a piece of chocolate into his mouth and marvelled that Howard could adjust his mind to something so obscure.

The midshipman seemed to shake his head. 'I'd rather not, sir.' When Howard said nothing he added tightly, 'You know what they'll say, sir. They'll probably discharge me.'

Howard could feel his desperation. They probably would too, he thought. *It'll be my turn if I'm not careful.*

'All right. We'll see. Now you go and help Ayres.'

He listened to him groping down the ladder, his coughs beginning again. How old was he – eighteen? He was like one of the Great War people Howard had seen as a child. Still shell-shocked, reliving the hell which Mister Mills had sometimes described.

He wondered how the rebuilding of the house in Hampshire was progressing. It would give Mister Mills something to supervise; an occupation he badly needed now that the Guvnor had gone.

Howard's brother had wanted nothing to do with it. He already had a home of his own, although God alone knew how he was paying for such a grand place. But his wife Lilian had money, and knew exactly what she wanted for Robert and her own future.

Rain dashed over his oilskin and made his face feel raw. *Future* – how could anyone know?

'Time?'

Rooke called out, 'Five-thirty, sir.' He sounded unhappy, as if wondering whether he would be blamed if they failed to make contact.

Treherne picked his teeth free of chocolate. He usually saved his nutty ration for Joyce, but just this once he needed the energy they said it gave you. Joyce . . . She had been good about the telegram from the War Office. It had been followed by a letter from her husband's CO. He must have been drunk when he'd written it, he thought. It had made the man's death sound like a national disaster.

He said, 'Should get a bit brighter soon.'

'Convince me.'

Treherne tightened his collar but felt the rain running down his spine. 'Well, it says . . .'

'Radar – Bridge!'

'Forebridge?'

'Getting a faint effect at two-six-zero, about twelve thousand yards.' He fell silent as if, unheard, he were swearing to himself. 'Sorry, sir. Thought I'd lost it again.'

Treherne was peering at the radar-repeater. 'Nothing.'

Howard asked, 'What do you think, Lyons?' He was passing the buck, but he knew the man well. Someone who would appreciate the trust.

'Small vessel, sir. Appears to be stationary.'

Howard turned away, his blood suddenly tingling. 'Found him!' He walked to the compass. 'Starboard ten – Midships – Steady!'

'Steady, sir.' Sweeney was there without being called. 'On two-six-six.'

'Steer two-six-zero.' He groped for the engine room handset.

'Chief? This is the captain.' He stared at the darkness but saw Evan Price vividly in his mind's eye, down below the waterline with his racing machinery and steamy, tropical warmth. 'I think we've found her. But I want you to reduce to half-speed. Full revs or dead stop if I say so, right?'

He thought he heard Price chuckle. 'Isn't that what the bridge always wants, sir?'

Treherne watched him moving restlessly this way and that, and heard him say, 'Tell Guns what's happening.'

There was something unusual about him. An edginess which, if he felt it, he always managed to conceal. Except that once. Treherne wiped his binoculars; that memory always touched him. Like sharing something very private.

Bizley climbed into the bridge. 'Sir?'

Howard did not turn. 'Yes. I want you here, with me. Take over the con. Pilot will fill you in.'

Howard turned towards Treherne, and was surprised that he could suddenly see his bearded face and the battered cap he always wore on watch. A different badge now, but Howard knew it was one of his old company caps. A talisman maybe.

'Daylight, at last!'

It was little more than a grey blur, beyond which the sea and horizon were still one.

Howard said, 'I wonder if their radar is still working?'

Treherne said nothing. The blip on the radar might be something else. Or they might all be dead.

Sub-Lieutenant Rooke offered, 'I served in her class of corvettes, sir. The radar was always very reliable.'

'Thanks.' Howard laid out his busy thoughts. It could have been destroyed in the explosion. Anything might have happened.

Treherne tugged his beard as the radar operator reported no change, other than the range had fallen to ten thousand yards.

Howard said, 'Slow ahead together.' The motion seemed to become more violent immediately, loose equipment and metal mugs adding to the clatter of ship noises.

'Revolutions seven-zero, sir.'

Treherne remarked, 'We could fire a rocket, sir. We'd know for sure then.' Why were they slowing down? Prolonging the uncertainty, even the risk, if there was some survivors up there, five miles beyond the dark arrowhead of *Gladiator*'s bows . . .

Howard faced him and Treherne was stunned by the intensity of his stare. 'What is it, sir? Can I do something?'

Howard brushed against a stiff-backed lookout as he pulled Treherne to the port corner. 'You'll think me mad, Gordon.'

Treherne waited, holding his breath. He had noticed that Howard had often called him by his first name, even on the bridge in front of the others. It had pleased him, until now. Something was badly wrong.

'Tell me, sir.'

Howard lowered his voice, feeling his stomach contract to the savage motion. Or was it just that? 'I think there's a bloody U-Boat up there.'

Treherne felt the water on his spine change to ice. He was afraid to speak.

'It'll be submerged, otherwise Lyons would have picked it up by now.' His mind switched like lightning. 'Tell Asdic to cease tracking.'

He removed his cap and pushed his fingers through his hair. *What is the matter with me?*

Or was it some kind of instinct, living so long with this danger that he could sense the submarine, lying there like a shark, waiting for any rescuer who was coming to the corvette's assistance? To make the score two instead of one.

'Tell Ayres to prepare a full pattern, Number One.' His voice was clipped and formal again. 'Squid too.' He added with sudden vehemence, 'I'm going to get that bastard!'

A signalman whispered to his yeoman, '*What* bastard, Yeo?'

'Christ if I know, my son.'

The gunnery speaker squeaked into life. 'No target, sir.'

Radar next. 'Range now eight thousand yards, sir.'

'*Ship*, sir! Starboard bow!'

The light was spreading through the thick clouds to light up the sea's face in small glittering patches. Howard steadied his elbows on the wet steel and moved his glasses very slowly across the bearing.

Treherne said hoarsely, 'Corvette! It's her all right!'

Howard held his glasses with care as he examined the tiny picture, which grew and faded as the clouds bellied above it.

Her bows were very low in the water, and it was a wonder the bulkheads had not collapsed altogether. There was no smoke, just a barely perceptible roll as she drifted through the troughs.

Treherne asked quietly, 'What d'you reckon now, sir?'

'They must have sighted us.' He could see it in his mind. The despair giving way to hope. Alone no more. And a ship they would know well coming to the rescue. Howard shook his head as if he were arguing with someone visible only to himself.

'Call her up, Yeoman. Make our number.'

Bizley said sulkily, 'They must be blind!' He was suddenly remembering the sharpness of Marrack's tongue.

The light clattered noisily while everyone on the bridge peered at the little ship's dark outline, afraid they might miss something.

The yeoman of signals licked his lips and said, 'At last!' He watched the slow blink of *Tacitus*'s lamp then exclaimed, '*Contact at three-three-zero!*' He swallowed hard and stared at Howard. 'Then, *God bless you!*'

Howard flung himself forward. 'Full ahead together! Starboard fifteen! Steer three-one-zero!' He glanced at Treherne as the bells rang like mad things. 'Start the attack! Get on to Asdic and tell him – ' The roar of the explosion was deafening, and as Howard jumped on to a grating to clear his vision he saw the cascades of water still falling like an unwilling curtain, the sea's dark face pockmarked with a thousand falling fragments.

'Asdic reports, no contact, sir.'

'Tell them to *keep searching*!' He felt the sea roaring past the hull, but all he could see was the widening whirlpool of oil and other flotsam. Marrack had known the U-Boat was there, and had tried to warn him, even though he had known the price. *God bless you*. It was like hearing his voice.

Gladiator made two extensive sweeps but there was no contact. The U-Boat commander might have used a stern-tube for the final shot; either way there was nothing. When they returned to the place where Marrack's command had gone down they found only two survivors. Marrack would have had all his people on deck, gathered well away from the submerged bow section. It was not war. It was cold-blooded murder. A broken ship, like a tethered goat waiting for the tiger.

At noon a huge, four-engined Liberator found them and carried on with the search. There was no result.

Howard climbed into his chair as his ship began to reduce speed. It was one thing to die; another entirely to make the gesture which Marrack had known was taking away his company's last chance of survival. But for it, *Gladiator* would be down there with them.

He began to shake very badly and found he was helpless to prevent it.

Treherne moved beside him as the doctor appeared on the bridge. '*Well?*' He saw Moffatt glance at the captain but shook his head angrily. 'Leave it, Doc!'

Moffatt stared out at the brightening sea. 'One survivor was a signalman. Just a kid.'

Treherne glanced at their own signalmen, shocked and still looking at each other like strangers. 'Aren't they all?' he said savagely.

Howard seemed to rise from his own despair. 'A signalman? Did he say anything?' He would have been there on Marrack's bridge. The bunting-tossers, as they were nicknamed, saw everything.

Moffatt replied, 'They were trying to get back to the convoy after seeing the damaged escort-carrier into safety. Then after the explosion the U-Boat surfaced and opened fire with her deck gun. The corvette lost her W/T, and was barely able to stay afloat. The Germans must have realised or detected the SOS . . . they just stood off and waited. There were a lot of injured men after the first torpedo. Now they're all gone.'

Howard asked, 'What else did he say?' He knew there was more.

Moffatt sighed. 'When he saw your signal the captain called out, "My old ship. I knew it would be her!" ' He watched Howard as if uncertain whether or not to continue. 'Then he told the signalman to reply to you – the senior one was wounded. Then he said, "I've done for the lot of us." There might have been more, but the lad doesn't remember – he was in the sea being sucked down when he came to. Didn't even recall the explosion.'

Treherne remarked, 'It's often like that, Doc.' It was just something to say to break the tension.

Howard said, 'Course and speed to rejoin the group.' He twisted round in his chair and said, 'It's all right, Doc, I'm not ready for the men in white coats yet.' He strained his eyes, but there was nothing. Not even a wisp of smoke.

'Write this down, Yeoman, and pass it to W/T. *To Admiralty, repeated C-in-C Western Approaches. Tactitus sunk by second torpedo. No contact. Two survivors.* Get their names before you send it.'

Moffatt said dully, 'Just the one, Yeoman. The second man died.'

He heard Rooke speak into the voicepipe. 'Steer zero-nine-zero. Revolutions one-one-zero.'

Then Sweeney's thick voice. 'One-one-zero revs replied, sir.'

Howard watched the great curving wake as *Gladiator* came under command on her new course.

When he looked again Moffatt had gone. He said, 'Get the people fed, will you, Gordon. Go round the ship yourself. You know what to do.'

Treherne was about to leave but something made him return to the tall chair.

Howard stared at him, and there were real tears in his eyes as he said in a whisper, ' "*I've done for the lot of us.*" What a bloody way to be remembered, eh?'

Treherne touched his oilskin and said roughly, 'Well, you damned well saved all of *us* – and begging your pardon, sir, don't you ever bloody well forget it!'

Howard nodded very slowly. 'Thanks.' He studied him for several seconds, as if he were looking for something and, perhaps, finding it. Then he said, 'I'll speak to the lads over the tannoy presently.' He stared emptily at the ocean. 'But now I need to . . .'

'I know.' Treherne backed away. He had never spoken like that to any captain. He could not get over it. Like that other time – Howard had *known*. Most skippers would have gone charging to the rescue, eyes for nothing but the torpedoed ship. It might have been too late for all of them. To Bizley he said harshly, 'See that the Old Man's not disturbed, right?'

The lieutenant looked at him blandly. 'Something wrong, Number One?'

Treherne glanced at the oilskinned figure leaning against the side and dropped his voice. 'Just remember, *laddie*, but for him you'd have had your arse blown off just now.' He saw the sudden fear in Bizley's eyes. 'So shove that in your pipe and smoke it!'

Surgeon-Lieutenant Moffatt was seated comfortably in the wardroom that evening when Treherne entered, shaking water off his clothing like a great dog. 'I was thinking about our midshipman, Number One. He might beat this thing yet without being put ashore.' He looked up from an old magazine. 'What's wrong?'

'You can forget about Midshipman Ross, Doc.' He glared at the pantry hatch. 'Could I use a bloody drink just now? Trouble is, I don't think I'd stop, and it's still three days to the Liverpool Bar.' He sat down heavily. 'I've been all over the ship, Doc. He's not aboard.' He saw the shocked surprise on Moffatt's face. 'No point in going back to look for him. Anyway, we're ordered to rejoin the group at first light.'

'Have you told the Captain?'

'I'm about to.' He stared at the deckhead as if he could see the bridge from here. 'That's just about all he needs!'

'Why did he do it? Suicide?' Moffatt's mind was rushing through the medical books. 'Afraid of fighting it?'

The sea broke over the quarterdeck and sluiced away across the opposite side in a noisy torrent.

'Hear it, Doc? He lost the will to fight *that* anymore!' He slammed out of the wardroom and thought suddenly of Howard's words. What a bloody way to be remembered.

Next of kin have been informed.

6

▬ ▬ ▬ ▬ ▬ ▬

Nine Days

David Howard turned up the collar of his greatcoat and walked uncertainly out of the small railway station. The train had been unheated, and it seemed to have taken him all day to travel the sixty-odd miles north from Liverpool.

It was already dark and utterly alien, with a tangy edge to the air which he guessed came from the big lake.

He had no sense of place or direction, which was hardly suprising, and every muscle and bone was making a separate protest. Now that he was here he was not at all sure he was doing the right thing; maybe she had suggested it because she was sorry for him and nothing more.

He thought of the meeting he had had with Captain Vickers on the group's return from sea; the stern gravity in his tone which was new to Howard.

'You can't take everything on yourself, David. It has an effect on you, naturally, but I simply can't afford a weak link in my chain of command. You are the best commanding officer, your record second to none, and I'll make no secret of the fact I've suggested you soon get a lift up the ladder, a brass-hat, even if the war ends before you can confirm it. The fact is, David, it *happens*. It might be any one of us next time – you of all people should know that!'

Howard's mind had strayed to the song he had heard a seaman murmuring to himself. *We're here today and gone tomorrow.*

He had answered, 'I'm all right, sir. I won't let you down.'

'I'm depending on it.'

Had Vickers really understood, or would he insist on a transfer, or worse a shore job? Another bomb-happy veteran to flash his gongs at green recruits.

Vickers had continued relentlessly, 'I was going to suggest a bit of leave and put another commanding officer in your place.' He had held up a big hand to stifle his protest, '*Temporarily*. I knew you wouldn't care too much for that idea, eh?'

'She's my ship, sir.' He had even been surprised by the desperation in his own voice. 'I'd not leave her like that.'

Vickers had nodded and relit his huge briar pipe. 'I understand. I was like that myself. Once. Fact is, *Kinsale* is due for boiler-clean and radar check, I've already discussed it with the chief of staff.' His eyes had burned through the pipe-smoke. 'Would you trust your own Captain (D) in your place for say, ten days?'

Even as he had said it, Howard had known that the suggestion had no alternative which would leave him in command.

'Besides which, it might do your people good to be senior ship for the time being.' So it was settled.

He had telephoned Celia from the yard and had been astonished when she had mentioned the cottage owned by her friend's cousin. Her voice had been almost breathless, and it had been a bad line anyway. She had left him little time to discuss it, so intent was she on explaining about food rations, the destination, and how to get there.

She had ended by saying, 'I do so want to see you. I nearly made myself sick, thinking about you. And don't worry about anything – just come to the cottage. I'll be there, waiting.'

He had wanted to protest, to remind her what people would think and say. She must have known his very thoughts. 'Look, David, I don't care about anyone else. I just want us to be together, away from all the . . .' He had heard her catch her breath. 'From all the waste.'

But that had been then. Maybe she was not so certain now.

Two shaded headlights came on from the car park and an ancient Wolseley rolled forward into the forecourt. A gangling figure in a loose raincoat climbed out and shook his hand.

'My name's Major, Tom Major. My cousin told me to brighten the place up a bit for you.' He heaved Howard's case and respirator into the boot and added, 'It's a mite cold for October, but you'll be snug enough. I use the place, or did, for the summers up here.' He turned and looked at Howard in the dim glow of the headlamps. 'Welcome to Windermere.'

Howard wondered just how many other people knew. More nudges and winks. He settled in the seat and as an army car passed them he saw a sticker on the Wolseley's windscreen silhouetted in the headlights. *Doctor*. At best it explained where he got his petrol; at worst it sounded like some kind of plot, with Celia being used as the innocent instrument.

'Not far, bit off the beaten track. Where are you from – um, David?'

'Hampshire.'

The man grinned. 'Naval family. It would be.'

Howard watched the black trees skimming past. No place for the amateur driver.

'Been at sea lately?'

Howard tried to relax. His cousin had not told him much then.

He answered, 'Yes. Convoys mostly.' He didn't want to be drawn into conversation about it, but knew that the man was only trying to be friendly.

He said, 'So you're a doctor?'

'At the moment I'm *the* doctor! The others are either in the forces or helping out at the hospitals. This suits me. Doesn't give me too much time to think.' He pulled over and stopped suddenly, the engine thrumming quietly in the darkness. 'My brother was shot down over Germany, and now my young son can't wait to join up, as he puts it, *before the war's over.*' He turned and looked at him, but his face was hidden in shadow. 'Tell me something. Is it all worth it? *Are* we going to win?'

Howard tried to smile, but thought of the one survivor from Marrack's ship, the one Moffatt had described as just a kid. 'We have to.'

He wound down the window and felt the damp air on his face. Not the bitter touch of the North Atlantic with its tang of salt and fuel oil; a gentle, fresh breeze. No wonder the doctor loved the place. 'Otherwise all this is finished. It will never be the same again, but at least it will be *ours.*'

His companion jammed the car in gear and drove onto the lane again; it was even narrower than the one in Hampshire where the bombs had come screaming down.

Eventually he said, 'If you need me, my number's by the phone. I gather you've both been through it.' He shook his head. 'I'm not prying, but I'm here if you want me.'

'Thanks. I'm sorry I've been a bit screwed-up.' He thought of Treherne on the bridge after Marrack's ship had vanished. *Don't you ever bloody well forget it!* He found time to wonder how he and Vickers would hit it off.

'Here it is. Watch out for the puddles. The lake's over there. You can see it in the daylight.'

They stood side by side looking at the cottage's square silhouette. There would be a moon soon, and Howard thought he saw smoke from the squat chimney stack.

Then the doctor held out his hand. 'I can't lend you the car, but there are some old bikes in the shed.'

Howard watched him drive away, then turned and walked slowly towards the front door.

It opened wide even before he reached it and she was in his arms her hair pressed against his check while she hugged him. Then she took his hand and helped him in with his case.

She had a great log fire roaring in the hearth, and the place had been made to look lived-in, pleased with itself, as the shadows danced and flickered around the room.

Howard slipped out of his greatcoat and tossed his cap on to a chair.

'Let me look at you.' She was dressed in a white, roll-necked sweater and a pair of sailor's bell-bottoms. He held her again and then they kissed for the first time. 'I never thought it could happen. I shall probably find it's all a dream.'

She pinched his arm gently and said, 'See? I'm real!'

Her eyes were very bright, her cheeks flushed, and not merely from the fire. He noticed too that she was wearing her wedding ring. She saw his glance and removed it – like a guilty child, he thought. But there was nothing childish in her voice as she looked at him and said, 'I borrowed this one. It's not his. It's just that I've done a bit of shopping, and some of the people round here are – well, you know . . .' She held him again, but would not look at him. 'We are alone here. This is our place for . . .'

'Nine whole days.' He tried not to think of *Gladiator* leaving harbour without him. Vickers on his chair; the old destroyer hand. Probably he'd be loving every minute, he thought; Vickers made no secret of the fact he regarded the more modern destroyers as a collection of gimmicks.

She led him to the table; even that she had decorated with some sort of autumnal fern. 'Wine on ice – champagne, in fact . . .' She saw his disbelief. 'There is *some* use in being an admiral's daughter!'

They embraced again, uncertainly, as if they did not know what was happening.

She said softly, 'You can have a bath – it's all a bit Heath Robinson, but it works – then get out of uniform, and I'll give you a meal to remember.' She held him at arms' length, smiling at him; her heart was almost breaking at his expression. It was something like gratitude. Then she said, 'Stop worrying about me for once, and think of yourself. I said I was bad luck for you, that I'd never go through all that again . . . I'm still not sure if I'll be able – '

He touched her mouth. 'Don't, Celia. I love you. I *want* you, all for myself – no matter what.' She tried to release his grip but he said, 'Just be with me.'

'I must put a log on the fire.' As she stooped down, her hair falling over her forehead, she said quietly, 'You see, David, it came to me quite suddenly, that day when everything was so terrible for you and we were so far apart. I *want* you to love me. I don't think it's wicked or pointless because of the war – it's something I must have known since that day when I made you talk about Jamie, with never a thought for what you had just been through.'

He knelt behind her and put his arms around her waist while they both stared into the blaze.

'I don't know what I'd have done if you hadn't come.'

He caressed her and felt her muscles tense. 'I'd never hurt you.'

She stood up and watched him as he took off his jacket and tossed it on to another chair.

She said, 'You're not very tidy, *Commander*.'

Their eyes met, and each knew there was no going back, even if they had wanted to.

She left the door ajar and walked across the adjoining room, her bare feet noiseless on the scattered rugs. Through a window she could see the stark outlines of trees, the bright moonlight making the sky almost white by comparison.

She moved slowly past the table where they had eaten and talked, each trying to find the other. The champagne bottle stood upended in its bucket, the doctor's ice long turned to tepid water. They had left more than they had eaten; nervousness and the need of one another had seen to that. She stood quite still in front of the great fireplace and held out her arms to the fallen embers which had so recently been a roaring mass of flames.

She had been nursing him against her body, calming him, after he had cried out. She had felt the pang of jealousy, until she had remembered that the name he had uttered, Ross, had been that of the missing midshipman and not some other girl's.

Was that what had really become of Jamie? The war already become too much and he had wanted to end it, in the only way he knew. She was surprised that she could think of it now, without guilt any more, without anything more than curiosity.

Jamie had often spoken of his previous squadron commander, an ace, and all that went with it. He had been nicknamed Dicer because of the chances he took, and over the years of fighting he had shot down what must have amounted to a whole enemy squadron. Then, one day, flying alone in his beloved Spit, he had been attacked by a solitary Messerschmitt, and had crashed on a nearby beach. When the salvage team had arrived to clear the wreckage, they had discovered the firing button still at safe, the guns fully loaded. Was that how it happened? Too much flying, sated with all the individual killing. Like Dicer, perhaps Jamie had ended it in the way he had always expected to die, in close combat, but his death arranged by himself.

Without thought she took a shawl from the sofa and walked to the window and looked out at the arctic landscape. She could even see the same moonlight glittering on the lake through the trees.

She shivered as a vixen gave her shrill bark amongst the undergrowth, and pulled the shawl closer over her shoulders.

Then, trying to keep her mind clear, she thought of what had happened to her. Jamie had always been eager, even violent, needing to conquer rather than seduce her. She thought suddenly of her dead friend Jane, who had said more than once that the climax was the true delight of making love. The complete giving of one to the other. No wonder Daddy had thought of her as flighty.

Celia had never experienced it. Not even tonight when he had held her and touched her, and then entered her. David had been gentle and caring, as she had known he would be, but there had been some pain, and she had clenched her fists over his shoulders so that he should not know, or blame himself. It had been such a long while since . . .

She touched her breasts through her nightdress, as he had done, her thighs and the smooth skin where she had sensed him preparing her for that dreamed-of and feared moment when she would feel him come into her. He had fallen asleep almost immediately, and for hours she had held him, soothing his nightmares, praying that he would have no regrets when he remembered.

She found she was still shivering, and yet her limbs felt no chill. It was like hearing a voice, feeling hands gripping her arms.

She walked to the table and groped in the shadows for the brandy she had left untouched.

Like the time in the restaurant when she had secretly wished that the old waiter *had* offered the room; that they had taken it no matter what people had thought, or if her parents had got to know about it.

The brandy was like fire on her tongue. She tossed the shawl aside and the invisible hands propelled her forward again.

The room was full of moonlight, and on the opposite side of the bed she saw herself reflected in the old-fashioned wardrobe's mirror where their discarded uniforms hung together like interlopers.

She heard him stir, his breathing quicken, but she kept her eyes on her reflection as with slow deliberation she pulled up her nightdress, over her head, before throwing it towards a chair.

In the cold light her naked body, her fine uplifted breasts seemed to shine like sculptured marble. She said, 'You're my man, David.' She knelt on the heavy feather-bedded mattress and took his hand in hers. 'And I will be yours for as long as you want.' His face was in shadow but she could sense his desire for her as she pulled his hand to where he had touched her, roused her, entered her. Then she had been passive and frightened. Now she knew her passion for him had over-ridden everything.

They lay in each other's arms, her leg thrown across his body, prolonging it with their caresses and kisses. Quite suddenly she exclaimed, 'Take me, David. All you know, all you've wanted to do . . .' The rest was lost as he turned her carefully on to her back.

Outside, the vixen's cry went unheard.

A million miles away from that isolated cottage, Lieutenant Lionel Bizley pushed past two naval ratings and closed the telephone booth behind him.

Gladiator was getting under way in less than an hour, and if the formidable Captain (D) discovered what he was doing things would get nasty. But there had been talk of leave, two weeks at least, after this next operation, whatever it was. He had to let Sarah Milvain know about it. With luck he might be able to stay at their Mayfair house, provided her mother, who sounded a bit of a battleaxe, would allow it.

A house in Mayfair. In Bizley's suburban mind it was something between high society and Hollywood.

He had already revamped his own background, to make it suitable for Sarah's parents, especially the general if he happened to be there. He would describe his father as being in banking, maybe in the City. People were always impressed by finance. It was a joke when you thought about it. The dingy little high street bank in Horsham, where his father had been for most of his life. And his mother, who was undoubtedly proud of her son's becoming 'a real officer', as she had put it, more so since his DSC – she would be amazed when he told them where he had been and stayed, and about the girl he had met.

Through the glass he saw *Gladiator*'s chief quartermaster walking slowly back towards Gladstone Dock, an empty mail sack over one arm. It gave Bizley a sense of nervous urgency and he cursed impatiently as the telephone rattled and clicked in his grasp. 'Come on, *damn you!*'

Then he heard her voice. It was a relief to find it was not her mother, with so little time left to talk.

'It's me! Lionel!' He glanced at the queue outside the booth. 'Don't say anything, Sarah, we might get cut off.'

She sounded faraway, surprised. 'I hoped you would call.'

Bizley studied himself in the little mirror below the printed notice which said WHAT TO DO IN AN AIR RAID. Some wag had scrawled, *Try not to shit yourself!*

'Fact is, I may get some leave shortly. I was wondering . . .' She must have moved away to close a door somewhere. He flushed at the thought of their privacy.

'Sorry, Lionel, I'm back.' She cleared her throat. 'Leave, you say? That will be nice for you.'

It was not quite what he had expected. *Nice.* How his mother would have described it.

'Is something wrong? Are you all right?'

She said, 'I was listening for Mother. She's a bit upset.'

'I'm sorry. Give her my love. Tell her I'm still in one piece. I'm *longing* to meet her.'

'There was a man here to see her.' His lie seemed to have gone unnoticed.

'Man? What man?'

Somebody unseen rapped on the glass with some pennies but Bizley glared out, shaking his head.

He repeated the question and she replied, 'She won't say, but he was an official of some kind. I let him in. He was from the Admiralty. Mother got very upset. He apparently asked her a lot of questions about Greg – his death, things like that.' There was a sob in her voice. 'Why can't they leave things alone? He even mentioned poor Andy.'

Somewhere an air raid warning wailed dismally. It was strange to think it was all that way away, in London.

Bizley stared at the mirror at his own eyes, which were suddenly wide with shocked disbelief.

'Maybe he was just doing it for the records, you know.' But his mind seemed to scream at him. *They suspect something!* All this time, and somebody was probing what had happened.

He said, 'I'll ring again. Must go. Take care . . .'

'But it *is* all right, isn't it, Lionel? They're not keeping something secret from us – *you* would know, surely?' She was still speaking when he carefully replaced the telephone and pushed out into the shadows.

There was nothing to worry about. They had quite rightly accepted his report. And the two other survivors would know better than to interfere.

By the time he reached *Gladiator*'s brow he was sweating badly, as if he had been running all the way.

The duty quartermaster and gangway sentry were lounging by the lobby desk, and Bizley shouted, '*Stand up!* Smarten yourselves, or I'll have you in front of the first lieutenant!' But even that gave him no satisfaction.

The quartermaster adjusted his cap and muttered, 'I'd been 'opin' he might drop dead, Bill.'

The sentry grinned. 'Probably caught the boat up. I'm real sorry for the prostitute!' They both laughed.

In his small cabin Bizley knelt down and took a bottle of vodka from his locker. He had been given it on the North Russian run. He disliked it, but had been told it did not lie on your breath. He tossed some water out of his tooth-glass and poured until it was half-full.

It seemed to work.

Don't be such a bloody fool. Nobody knows. He touched the blue and white ribbon on his jacket and took another swallow. *Just keep your nerve.*

Over the tannoy the voice called, 'Special sea dutymen to your stations! All the port watch! First part forrard, second part aft, stand by for leaving harbour!'

Bizley stood up. That was more like it. Routine and duty. He would show them all!

David Howard lay on his back and stared at the ceiling. There was a smell of woodsmoke, mingled with another, of bacon. He had slept well, a night devoid of pressure and guilt, and he had awakened with her in his arms, wrapped around each other, and at peace. They made love with fierceness and sometimes in slow harmony, neither willing to think of the hours or the days. There was just four more left.

The door opened and she stood there looking at him. She was wearing his pyjama jacket and nothing more, not even slippers while she had been preparing breakfast, or perhaps it was lunch.

'We'll have another lovely walk today.' She moved to the bed and watched him with a tenderness she had never known. 'But first we eat. It's egg day today, a ration not to be missed!'

He rolled over and held her, then slipped his hand beneath the pyjama jacket and stroked her buttocks. 'You are quite shameless.' He pulled her down on to the bed. 'And I love you.'

She watched his eyes as he unbuttoned the jacket and touched her, his hand moving as if independent of its owner to explore and arouse her again. He had confided a lot about his war, and the more he had talked while they had sat by the fire each evening after their walks, their simple adventures, the calmer he had become. She had tried not to think of their eventual parting. In a matter of weeks it would be Christmas; the Atlantic at its worst. *This* would have to last.

She said, 'If you keep touching me there I shall forget about the eggs!'

He had not even blurted out his doubts again. The way he had blamed himself for not understanding what the midshipman might do, how he should perhaps have reacted differently to his friend Marrack's ordeal. Once in the night he had sat up staring at her, but she had known he was asleep. 'He just sat there waiting to die, and it was all because of me!' In the morning he had not remembered it, nor had he mentioned it since.

She felt his fingers move down across her stomach and gave up the battle. Afterwards they lay together and watched the cold sunlight lance across the room.

She said, 'I can still feel you, David. So deep. So much love.'

He raised himself on one elbow. 'We don't talk about it, Celia, but it's still there.' He touched her hair, and saw her watching him. 'I'd like to know – do you think you might change your mind?'

She stared at him, her eyes very green in the smoky sunshine. 'About us?'

He held her hand tightly in his. 'Would you marry me?'

'Hold me.' She buried her face on his shoulder. 'Is it wrong to want someone so much? To put *us* first, instead of the bloody war?'

He stroked her bare back. He had never heard her swear before. 'That's settled then.'

They both stiffened as the telephone shattered the peace and the stillness like an alarm bell.

She walked naked to the table and lifted the telephone to her ear, watching his face the whole time.

She said, 'I thought you might. Yes, I'll tell him. Bless you.'

She replaced the receiver and picked up the pyjama jacket.

'Who was that?' Just for an instant he had felt the same old dread.

'It was Mummy.' She regarded him gravely. 'We always tell each other where we are. You never know, these days.'

'You *told* her?' He reached out as she brushed against the bed. 'About us?'

She smiled down at him. 'I think she's always known.' She stepped back out of reach. 'Eggs first.' She wiped her eyes with the pyjama sleeve. 'No walk today. Let's keep this world to ourselves.'

7

Turning the Corner

Despite the powerful fans at either end of the huge U-Boat pens, the damp air was acrid with diesel as one of a pair of boats made ready to depart stern-first.

On the bridge of his own boat Kleiber watched with professional interest as more smoke puffed over the pier-like jetty which separated them, and forced several of the line-handling party into a fit of coughing. He knew the other boat's commanding officer, and they had been together for most of the war. It went no further than that. Korvettenkapitän Otto Schneider was the propaganda department's dream; either that, or he had some very good friends there. His rugged grin had appeared many times on newsreels and in the daily press. Usually seen with someone senior and important, either from the naval staff or a well-known party member. His conning-tower was covered with the record of his kills and the boat's insignia, a grinning shark in a horned helmet.

In Kleiber's view he was a boaster, a man who would snap at the most insignificant targets merely to add to his score. There was envy of course; Kleiber could accept that too. Schneider had bagged some important targets as well as the little fish, and probably the most decorated U-Boat captain who was still alive.

Before leaving this French base today, for instance, he had been bragging about a British corvette named *Tacitus* which he had put down some time ago; of how he had cruised around and waited for a second kill, the destroyer which had been despatched to search for her. He had known of Kleiber's interest in the British destroyer *Gladiator;* nearly all the veterans here did. Schneider had banged him on the back, laughing, as he had described the change of luck, when survivors on the stopped and torpedoed corvette had sent out a warning in time for the destroyer to start her attack. So the *Tacitus* had been sunk, and Kleiber could see the fresh little painting below all the rest to mark her destruction.

Schneider was waving to him now, as his submarine began to move slowly astern towards the harbour. Kleiber tossed a curt salute. Schneider was, after all, his superior.

How different it had been this time, he thought. Not even the staff officers had been able to reassure him that another supply-submarine would be on its proper station when he needed to restock and refuel. There had been some news from home, but the letters had shown a different address. The house had been evacuated after a tremendous air raid which had knocked down most of the streets he had known as a boy. His parents were all right, but his father's news was brief and uninformative where his work was concerned, as if he were now afraid that some official might open and read it.

There was no further contact with Willi, and the next winter had already come to the Russian front. How could he manage – survive?

A voicepipe chattered and was answered instantly by a petty officer.

Kleiber spoke to the control room and watched his men on the forecasing deck singling up the wires even as the great diesels coughed into life.

There had been another serious reverse last month, news of which had only recently been released to the public. The mighty battleship *Tirpitz*, the most powerful in the world, had been seriously crippled by a midget submarine attack in her Norwegian fjord. Nobody knew or would say how long it might take to repair this great ship, or how serious the damage was. But apart from the famous and successful battle-cruiser *Scharnhorst*, she was the last of their major warships still operational. It might mean that the enemy convoys to Russia would be able to increase without fear of attack by *Tirpitz*. Again, he thought of his young brother. Ivan would be strengthened by all this foreign aid and weapons; things might even deteriorate again on that terrible front, despite the sacrifices of the Wehrmacht.

The U-Boat service was the most dangerous in the whole Navy, but at least it was commanded by Admiral Donitz, who really knew and understood the men he directed and inspired. A successful submariner himself in the Great War, he was always ready to listen to his commanding officers on their return from patrols.

The battle over the Atlantic *had* to be won, and both sides were well aware of this. Survival, determination and courage rated as highly as new weapons and better equipment.

That had been another difference on his return to base. Some of the machine parts and replacements were from Kiel and other yards, spares taken from battered hulls too badly damaged to be repaired.

Kleiber stamped his fleece-line boots and considered what lay ahead. It was October, and outside this massively constructed bunker it was said to be snowing. They would have to be extra careful when cruising on the surface in Biscay. A radar-carrying aircraft could detect them even through snow, when they would be badly hampered by it.

He thought again of Schneider's jibe about the *Gladiator*, and wondered what sort of man commanded her. But she had probably had several; it was well known that the British had been so unprepared for war that commands had been handed out to anyone with even basic experience. It would be interesting to know, all the same. At the same time he was angry with himself for even considering it. War was not a game, not something for individual contests as Schneider seemed to think. It was for a perfectly co-ordinated machine, with one mind and one aim to control it.

There was something else which troubled him. This time he had not made the long journey to see his parents. Instead he had shared any such freedom with Ingrid. She was not German but Austrian, a nursing orderly in the navel hospital at nearby Lorient. He had first met her when visiting a wounded brother-officer there. She was dark, and when he had first seen her, her skin had been brown from the summer sunshine. Her hair was jet-black; she had told him her mother was Belgian. At first, whenever they had accidentally met, Kleiber had been attracted to her although he had told himself it was totally wrong, as well as irrational, to become involved. He had seen what it had done to others; a wife in Germany, a mistress in France or any one of the many countries where the swastika flew in conquest.

She, on the other hand, had seemed nervous of him, as if he had carried some scent of danger. But this time it had changed, and they had become intimate. It still unsettled him. He was out of his depth with her passion, her wanton abandon when they had intercourse. It was not love; so what might it be, and could it ever distract him from his demanding profession? If Schneider knew about that, the whole base would soon be made aware of it.

The conning-tower was vibrating less jerkily now as the engines settled down, and the reports of readiness in all sections were just being completed. If it were not snowing Ingrid might have been watching. You could see the Bay from the hospital. What did it matter? There would be another in her bed once he was gone. But it *did* matter, and it troubled him. Small hips and large inviting breasts, and a darting tongue which had at first embarrassed him and then goaded him to a madness he had not known before.

Bells clanged, and the last line was lifted from a bollard and hauled across to the casing to be stowed away until . . . When would that be? Very smoothly, the submarine began to thrust astern, the diesel fumes drifting over the bridge where the red ensign with its black cross and swastika hung limply against its staff. *When would that be?*

At the end of the last pier, his commanding officer stood gravely watching the dark, shining hull sliding out towards the thickening snow. Kleiber threw up another salute and guessed that the man was probably contemplating the empty berths, and wondering if they would ever be occupied again.

They followed a little launch with a shaded light until Kleiber was satisfied. A check with the control room; a last look around, although it was already quite dark, with the snow falling across the glistening hull like an impenetrable curtain.

Once out in open water it would be miserable for the watchkeepers under these conditions. But they would be changed regularly and could not complain. Kleiber felt something of his old confidence. For their captain would be here all the time until the first test-dive.

He and Schneider would remain in company in case of air attack while they were surfaced. Their combined firepower might be able to deal with the slower, heavier air patrols, although he preferred vigilance to a senseless duel which could soon be ended when reinforcements arrived.

The men stooping and crouching on the foredeck, struggling with the wires and fenders, glanced into the snow as the guide-boat gave a cheerful toot on its whistle.

They stared at its fading shadow with something like contempt. How much did a whistle cost, compared with what they were going to do over the next weeks?

Kleiber wiped his powerful Zeiss glasses and hung them carefully beneath his coat. Men moved past and vanished into the comparative warmth of the hull, and soon he felt the deck lift lazily to the first challenge of the Atlantic.

A petty officer hauled down the sodden ensign and folded it away, his eyes searching for the land. But there was only snow.

He had seen a choir of school children practising their carols for Christmas. They had fallen silent when they had seen him stop to listen.

He glanced at the captain's back. They would not return in time for Christmas; perhaps they would never return. He thought of one little French girl in that choir. About the same age as his own daughter, whom he had not seen for a year. She had looked straight into his eyes. He had never seen such hatred in anyone, in all his life.

Howard thrust his head and shoulders underneath the waterproof hood and switched on the light. He could feel the sleety rain hammering his oilskin and legs while he peered at the chart and compared Rooke's calculations with the latest information from the Admiralty.

He stood away from the table and felt the rain return to the attack. The snow had been bad enough, like driving blind through a fog. But at least he had been able to stay dry.

He pictured their companions, *Blackwall* to port and *Belleisle* to starboard, keeping in company as much by guesswork as by radar.

Treherne was waiting for him.

Howard gripped a stanchion as the bridge dipped over steeply and another big roller cruised against the hull.

He said, 'Convoy's all right apparently. No further attacks anyway. But one of the big tankers hit earlier is in trouble – even so, Captain Vickers and his section might be able to cope. He's with the air support group. *Seeker* will be able to provide air cover as soon as the weather improves.' He could see it all. The big convoy of thirty heavily loaded merchantmen, but, unlike the early days, with an impressive US and Canadian escort, now within five hundred miles of the Irish coast. They had lost two ships, and the tanker, one of the largest in the Atlantic, had somehow survived a torpedo without either blowing up or sinking. The convoy could not hang about for one ship, no matter how valuable. This was where the independent escort-attack groups could prove their worth. Vickers was out there somewhere, and the tough little escort-carrier might make all the difference. Howard added, 'They've sent the ocean salvage tug *Tiberius* from Plymouth. That great lump could bash through a hurricane if need be!'

He thought of Vickers's obvious pleasure when he had returned from his leave. 'You've done wonders with this ship, David! God, I'm almost sorry to be going back to *Kinsale!*'

They had sailed from Liverpool as a group almost immediately. Intelligence had warned of a buildup of U-Boats which were expected to go for the convoy like terriers. To lose only two ships from it was nothing less than a miracle. If they could still save the tanker it might give the enemy something to brood over.

There was another escort group to the north of the convoy, and a cruiser squadron on stand-by. The slackening of naval action in the Mediterranean had released more warships than anyone had believed possible.

'Take over, Number One. I'm going down for a dry towel.'

Treherne watched him leave. Was it the same man who had nearly broken down on this very bridge? It was as if he had been taken over by something even more powerful than fear and despair.

He heard Rooke passing his instructions to the wheelhouse, his body shining in the steady downpour. November already. Another year. He pictured their position, three destroyers, all veterans, some two hundred miles south-west of Land's End, and about the same westwards from Ushant. The enemy. Well within range of German aircraft, and yet it no longer felt so critical. The arrival of the little escort-carriers had changed everything. They were nicknamed Woolworths Carriers, or 'banana boats' by the lads – although here on the bridge they had refrained from the latter, he had noticed, for his benefit.

He thought of Joyce when he had told her about the solicitor's confidence that his first marriage could be proved null and void. Apparently desertion for whatever reason still counted for a lot.

She had been overwhelmed. '*Marriage*, you mean, Gordon?' Her eyes had shone with tears of happiness. So perhaps she had inwardly doubted his final intentions. 'I'll see you never regret it!' It had been a wild two days in her little flat.

He had been doubly glad to see Howard back in his chair. He had half-dreaded that he might be grounded for medical reasons; many commanding officers had gone under with less cause. The other reason for his relief had been the departure of Captain Vickers. It had been rather like having God on the bridge, and even for such a short time he had made his considerable presence felt. Treherne was not used to close contact with a senior, four-ringed captain, and had known that Finlay and some of the others had been amused at his efforts not to show it.

He peered at his watch. 'Midnight soon, Pilot. Have you sent a bosun's mate to rouse the starboard watch?'

Rooke said, 'Five minutes ago, Number One.' Even he seemed more at ease with Howard back in the saddle.

'Good.' He pictured Howard with his girl. What had they done? Where had they been, he wondered? He tried to think of them behaving like Joyce and himself, but was not so certain about that.

Rooke lurched across the bridge as the sea boomed against the side and flung a towering mass of water along the iron deck so that the superstructure seemed to shake from the weight of it.

'Think we'll be in for Christmas, Number One?'

'That would be nice.' He thought of Joyce, who would get all embarrassed when he suggested she came to the wardroom party. 'It would be my first in this bloody war, if so!'

A signalman groped towards them. 'From W/T, sir. *Two U-Boats destroyed by convoy's close escort.*'

The officers stared at each other in the drenching darkness. 'By God, Pilot, that evens the score a bit, eh?'

Howard had not mentioned Marrack again; nor would he. In most escort vessels and other small ships on active service it was the same. Gone but not forgotten. Anyone new and green who broke the rule would be met with chilling stares. He thought too of Midshipman Ross. How could he have done it? Just step off the ship into the darkness, to break surface in time to see *Gladiator*'s wake and nothing more. With luck he might have thrown himself over the side if he had to do it. The great screws would suck him into their embrace with only a split-second of agony.

Ross had not been replaced as yet. It was to be hoped that the next one had a better deal.

He heard Bizley's affected drawl on the ladder and steeled himself. He was definitely going round the bend, Treherne thought. Always asking questions about naval procedures, the various departments at the Admiralty, until the Chief had asked wryly, 'Are you thinking of asking for a shore job, then? Be an *admiral* next, see?'

The bridge messenger called above the noise of sea and rain, 'W/T, sir!'

Treherne moved to the voicepipe, his old sea-boots slithering the last few feet. 'First Lieutenant!'

It was the petty officer telegraphist himself, even at this hour. He had complained about stomach pains to Moffatt. Ulcers probably. Anyway they might lose him when they got back. It was a pity. He was the best.

Hyslop spoke distinctly up the voicepipe. 'From Admiralty, sir. *There are two U-Boats to the north of your position. Reported by RAF Coastal Command. Said to be heading north-west. Ends.*'

Treherne muttered, 'Thanks, it's enough as far as I'm concerned.' He looked at Rooke. 'Prepare the plot, old son. Two subs, hundred miles to the north. God knows where they are now. Too late for the convoy, I'd have thought.'

Reluctantly he picked up the solitary telephone by the bridge chair. 'Captain, sir?'

Howard stepped into the chart-room and watched Rooke busy with his dividers and parallel rulers.

He had been massaging his face and throat with a clean dry towel, thinking of the girl, *his* girl now, of their last embraces before they had parted, looking back at the doctor's holiday cottage as if they were leaving part of themselves behind. They had barely spoken when the doctor had called to drive them to the station. Wrapped in their individual thoughts, their hearts and bodies too aware of one another for words.

Howard had last seen her at the headquarters complex when he had attended a brief conference held for the various escort groups being deployed for the big eastbound convoy.

She had been standing by a noisy teleprinter which was churning out paper as if it would never stop. She had formed his name with her lips, and the three words, *I love you*, before they had been sent packing to their various commands.

If only he could have held her just once more. Felt her body against his, her hair brushing his mouth. In the same breath he knew it would have made their parting far worse.

'Two U-Boats, then.' He lit his pipe and marvelled it was such a luxury after the pitching, open bridge.

Rooke said warily, 'About here, sir.'

'I don't see why the RAF didn't give them a pasting, sir.' Treherne tried not to stare at Howard's relaxed grip on his pipe. Even his eyes seemed more interested than anxious as he studied the pencilled lines and bearings.

Howard said, 'Look at the time of origin, Number One. Not too much light when the Coastal Command people made the sighting. The Germans may or may not have seen the plane. It doesn't help us much.' He made up his mind. 'Give me those dividers, Pilot.' He felt them watching as he leaned over the table, gauging his own movements against the sickening lurch of the sealed chart-room.

'The Germans knew all about the convoy. It is an important one. A bit of face-saving will be called for.' He tossed down the dividers. 'Their high command is almost interchangeable with the Admiralty, you know.' He smiled briefly. 'Find that signal about the salvage tug, will you?'

Rooke hurried away and Treherne said, 'After the *Tiberius*?'

Howard looked at his disbelief. 'Why not? Without the tug, the tanker will be forced to remain at the mercy of the sea and the enemy. You can't expect either the convoy commander or the escort-carrier to hang about forever.'

Rooke returned and handed him the pad. Howard nodded, his eyes suddenly very bright.

'It must be that. These two beauties might well have a crack at the tanker themselves. A couple of days. Right up their street.' He picked up the dividers and waited for the deck to surge upright again. 'Lay off a course to intercept. To make good three-five-zero. I'll have a word with our two chums and put them in the picture.' He faced Treherne as Rooke hurried for the bridge ladder. 'It would be nice if we could stalk *them* for a change!'

Treherne swallowed hard. 'Very.' Could ten days really do that for anyone?

Howard heard somebody coughing in the wheelhouse but then it changed into a loud sneeze. For just a few seconds he had thought of Midshipman Ross. If only there had been more time to know him – to help him, perhaps. He listened to the boom of the sea and the great sluice of it alongside, and pictured him falling, his scream lost in the ocean's triumph. Out here, there was never enough time.

Howard said, 'I'll go up. Then, when I've spoken to *Blackwall* and *Belleisle*, I think I might have a catnap in the hutch. See that I'm called when the morning watch is closed up. It seems pretty quiet in this neck of the woods.' He hesitated before sliding the door open, remembering the time when he had turned on Rooke, and had been forced to crouch outside this same place while he fought his own destruction.

He said, 'So they bagged two more U-Boats, eh?' His eyes were almost boyish. Almost. 'Well, we'll make it three, Number One – at least!'

Treherne said, 'I did hear a buzz that you're getting a leg up, sir. If so, congratulations. There's nobody better. Will it mean leaving *Gladiator?*'

Howard sat on a locker and watched his sea-boots swinging to the savage motion.

'No secrets, eh? I thought it was just a suggestion!' He became serious at the sight of Treherne's anxiety. 'Leave this ship? Not now, not after all that we've done together. A brass-hat . . . Well, we shall have to see.' He touched the damp grey steel of the side. 'Leave you, old girl? To hell with that!'

The door closed and Treherne smiled to himself. Then he looked at the gyro-repeater as it ticked lazily back and forth and with a curse snatched up the bridge handset.

He heard Bizley's voice. 'Officer-of-the-Watch?'

'What the *bloody hell's* the matter with you, man?' He heard him snort. 'Check the helm – we're wandering about the ocean like a whore at a wedding! The Old Man's on his way up, so *jump about*, laddie!'

He waited for his anger to disperse and grinned.

He would have to watch Mister high-and-mighty Bizley. Something must have happened recently to make him so careless. Well, he could take a long walk on a short pier any time he liked; but when everybody else's arse was in danger it was no longer a joke.

Treherne looked at the chart. Two submarines – going for a kill, then on to another more valuable one. He heard the muffled clang of bells and the instant response from the engine room. By daylight *Gladiator* and her consorts would be close enough to the course taken by the big salvage tug.

He leaned on the chart and compressed the estimated positions between his large hands.

He thought of Howard's assessment, of his complete self-control. His beard parted in a smile. 'Here we go, then. Tally-bloody-ho!'

Howard swallowed the last of his scalding coffee and relished it as the heat roused his body. It was five-fifteen in the morning, but apart from an occasional greyness to starboard there was little hint of a new day. He handed the mug to a messenger and tried to settle himself more comfortably in his tall chair. He could feel the hard pressure of metal on his ribs through the layers of protective clothing, first one side, then the other as *Gladiator* plunged over serried lines of sharp rollers. It was raining, but impossible to distinguish it from spray flung back from the stem; it all tasted of salt.

The ship had been at action stations for half an hour after the latest signal from the Admiralty. Another aircraft of Coastal Command had reported seeing two tiny plumes of smoke when there had been a brief moment of good visibility. It was just luck; in such a vast area it might easily have gone unseen. It could only mean that the two U-Boats were still heading on the same course as before and were being forced to charge their batteries while still submerged. With growing air cover and the use of small escort-carriers, the enemy submarines were finding it less and less easy to surface and run on their diesels while charging batteries. Most of the submarines had been fitted with a breathing pipe which stood vertical with the periscopes when in use. The *schnorchel*, as it was called, had to be used with skill and great care. If the boat 'porpoised' with it raised, it would automatically close itself against an inrush of water. Unless the electric motors were brought into play instantly the interior of the hull would become a vacuum, the air sucked into the diesels to leave the crewmen gasping out their lives while the boat plunged to the bottom.

There had been reports of several of the big supply-submarines being caught on the surface with their hatches open while they prepared to service an operational U-Boat. Maybe these two U-Boats had been charging batteries while they still had a chance, in case their own rendezvous had been made useless.

As Treherne had remarked, 'It made a nice change!'

The Coastal Command aircraft had been at the end of its patrol, and had already dropped most of its depth-charges to help out a small westbound convoy. Aiming for the nearest little plume of smoke it had dived and released the last two charges. When the pilot had completed a turn around the area both U-Boats had dived, and there had been no sign of oil or wreckage. It must have given them a bloody headache all the same, Howard thought.

More air support had been promised when visibility improved, and the escort-carrier *Seeker* might be near enough to scramble her own Swordfish torpedo bombers.

The Admiralty had also advised that the ocean-going salvage tug was still on course. They had said little else in case the signal was intercepted and the code broken again.

Howard raised his glasses to peer abeam for *Blackwall*, but could see nothing but an occasional welter of heavy spray as her bows crashed down into the sea.

Treherne waited beside his chair, mopping his face and cursing the rain.

'They may split up when they realise we're on to them, sir.'

'Could be. *Belleisle* will remain on standby just in case that happens.'

Treherne fell silent again, seeing the ship as he had when the hands had gone to action stations. Main armament already angled out to cover both sides, the short-range weapons stripped and ready, spare magazines and trailing belts of heavy-calibre bullets prepared and unrestricted. Ayres was in charge of the depth-charges; Howard had decided it would give him more experience, while

Bizley was right here on the bridge, still sulking from the bottle he had rightly given him.

He thought of the engine room and boiler room staff, being tossed about in the din of roaring fans and thrashing screws. One false step and a stoker could end up as part of the machinery. And in the centre of his noisy, glistening world, Taff Price would be watching everything and everybody. Down there, *he* was captain and engineer all rolled into one.

'Call up the others, Number One. *Time to begin. Reduce to half-speed as arranged. Commence the sweep.* Pilot, warn Asdic and radar.' He held the luminous dial of his watch just an inch from his eyes before more spray dashed over them. 'Pass the word to the wheelhouse!'

He heard Bizley snapping his orders down the voicepipe and felt the heavy throb of engines drop slightly, although in the bruising motion it was hard to see much difference.

He watched his radar-repeater and saw the two blips of the other destroyers start to angle out slightly, so that the final formation became like the prongs of a giant trident.

If only the weather would clear, or the sullen clouds would allow some daylight to show the way.

Howard thought suddenly of the girl in that big operations room, watching, checking; a part of their team.

'Asdic – Bridge?'

Howard snatched up the handset. 'Captain!'

'Contact sir – echo bears zero-two-zero, moving right.'

Howard stared at Treherne. 'One of the bastards is doubling back. Maybe he's twigged us. Go and check the Asdic team. This has got to be just right!' Over his shoulder he called, 'Signal the contact to *Belleisle*. Repeat to *Blackwall*, but she needs to stay where she is in case the other bugger shows up!' He bent over the voicepipe. 'Starboard ten!' He watched the gyro-repeater begin to tick round as the wheel went over, boots slipping and men clutching for handholds everywhere in the ship. 'Midships – *Steady!*'

'Steady sir! Zero-one-zero.'

Howard smiled to himself. You could never disturb the coxswain.

'Very well. Steer zero-two-zero.' He saw the compass settle again and thought of the tense little group in the wheelhouse beneath his feet. Bob Sweeney, the quartermasters working the telegraphs and revolutions control on either side of him. The navigator's yeoman in his little allotted space with the plot-table, and a boatswain's mate at the voicepipes.

Howard added, 'We're after a sub, by the way.'

Sweeney gave a chuckle. 'Thought we might be, sir.'

'Asdic – Bridge.' It was Treherne's voice. 'Target still moving right, sir. Very slow, same bearing.'

Howard rubbed his chin. Suppose that aircraft *had* damaged one of them? This U-Boat would be off like a rabbit otherwise; they must have picked up the HE of at least one of the destroyers by now. Another trap then? He dismissed it instantly. The stakes were too high this time.

Treherne sounded as if he was concentrating every nerve. 'As before, sir. Moving right, but almost stopped.'

Bizley found that despite the streaming bridge he was still able to sweat. He stared through the gloom at Howard's motionless figure, perched on the edge of his chair where he could see and reach all that he needed.

'Aircraft, sir!'

Bizley gave a tense laugh. '*Where*, man?'

It roared directly overhead and moments later a recognition pattern of flares drifted through the rain.

Rooke said, 'It's getting brighter, sir!'

Howard nodded. A thread of silver had appeared beneath some of the clouds beyond the bows. A quick glance at the radar-repeater; both of the others were on station, *Blackwall* hanging back, ready to charge in to the attack if the manoeuvre they had trained and practised for so wearily began to go wrong.

He heard the murmur of commands over the intercom and guessed that Finlay was preparing his main armament. Just in case.

'Target seems to have stopped, sir.'

Howard looked at the radar again. Nothing. To the bridge at large he said, 'He's either shamming or damaged.' He took the intercom from Rooke and spoke briefly to the other captains. 'I'm going in. Widen your sweep for number two.' He put it down and blinked as a shaft of watery light clouded the caked salt on the glass screen. 'Captain Vickers would love this!'

He heard the snap of clips, as the yeoman bent the black flag on to the halliards.

'Come back to me, Number One.' He felt the deck shivering. Like a beast smelling something injured. 'Make to Admiralty, repeated C-in-C Western Approaches. *Am in firm contact with submarine in position whatever* . . . ' He saw Rooke scribbling on a signal pad. '*Am attacking.*'

A great shadow passed overhead, the engines' roar seeming to reach them long afterwards. If the second U-Boat was still hanging about it was unlikely it would risk coming to periscope depth. It was a great comfort. Treherne was back, his eyes on the compass as *Gladiator* followed Howard's instructions.

'Steady on zero-five-zero, sir.'

'Asdic – Bridge. Target stationary, sir. Same bearing.'

Howard snapped, 'He's going to fire blind.' He leaned forward. 'Full ahead together! Stand by depth-charges and mortars!'

Up, forward, and down deep, into each rearing trough, so that the ship shook violently from truck to keel as if she were ploughing over sandbars.

'Continuous echo, sir!'

Seconds later the sea erupted astern and on either beam, and torrents of water thundered down again even as *Gladiator* made a sweeping turn to loose off her squid mortars. More violent explosions which cracked against the bilges like shellfire. Howard bent over the compass again. '*Second attack!*'

Bizley said, 'Depth-charge party not yet reported, sir.'

Even amidst this uncertainty and danger Howard wondered why Bizley had bothered to mention it. They had not yet completed their turn, and Ayres had the best team anyone could ask for. It was probably to suggest that the young sub-lieutenant did not have the skill Bizley himself had displayed when he had been in charge down aft.

Howard put his eye to the ticking compass and gritted his teeth. *I must be getting like Number One where Bizley's concerned!*

'Steady on two-two-oh, sir!'

'Very well. Half ahead together.' He glanced through the screen in time to see *Belleisle*'s murky outline heading away, or so it appeared, as they lined up on the new course.

He saw Treherne glance at him. 'What is it, Number One?'

Treherne coughed. 'I thought I heard you say *softly, softly?*'

Howard smiled. 'Did I?' He tensed as the Asdic reported that the target was on the move again but still at reduced speed.

'Make to *Blackwall!* Attack!'

The other destroyer was thrusting over the waves, smoke trailing from her twin funnels as her revolutions mounted.

Her depth-charges seemed muffled, but Howards saw the sea churned up into tall pillars, as once again the surface seethed with the impact of the explosions.

'Stand by, Guns!'

'Asdic – Bridge. Bad interference – target's probably surfacing!'

'A- and B-guns, semi-armour piercing, load, load, load!'

Treherne was on tip-toe even though he was the tallest man in the bridge. 'Where *is* the bastard?'

The aircraft, a twin-engined Hudson bomber, roared throatily above the masthead, waggling its wings, glad to be making it a combined operation.

'*U-Boat surfacing! Starboard bow!*'

Howard flung up his glasses as the submarine's raked stem began to rise above the crests. 'Oh no, you bloody don't!' He reached for the handset. '*Open fire!*'

The two forward guns recoiled instantly, one shell exploding directly alongside the hull, the other throwing up a sheet of spray far abeam.

'Layer on! Trainer on! *Shoot!*'

The U-Boat had floundered to the surface and through his glasses Howard could see the deep scars on the conning-tower, some broken plates where a depth-charge had made its mark.

Treherne yelled, '*Got him!*'

Howard settled his glasses on the boat's conning-tower and felt a chill run through him. The grinning shark emblem in its horned helmet seemed to be staring directly at him. Almost to himself he said, 'That's Otto Schneider's boat, Gordon. My God we've done for one of their aces!'

Two more shells exploded against the slime-covered hull, and it gave a violent lurch and began to settle down by the bows, the cigar-shaped stern section rising from the sea to reveal the motionless screws. Nobody had appeared on the conning-tower, and when the sea reached the foot of the narrow structure which had been witness to so many sinkings, Howard saw the long columns of trophies, the one at the end being that of a corvette. Somehow he knew it was Marrack's.

He heard Treherne say thickly, 'That was the bastard who machine-gunned the lifeboats. I'd forgotten it. One of the survivors told me about the shark on the conning-tower. Sorry, sir, I just – forgot.'

'You were busy at the time.' Howard tested his own reactions but he felt neither elation nor pity. There was smoke now, probably from an electrical fire deep inside the hull. From a deadly weapon, something feared and hated, it had become a rigid coffin for Schneider and all his men.

Oily bubbles, obscene and horrific, surrounded the angled hull. The stern rose higher and higher, until it seemed to stand upright like some kind of marker, a memorial perhaps to all those this thing had killed and maimed.

Howard leaned over the voicepipe, '*Stop engines!*' He sensed the sudden confusion as the others dragged their eyes from the dying U-Boat to stare at him.

Treherne knew; or thought he did. 'Sir?'

The Hudson bomber was streaking back along its original course, a signal lamp blinking so rapidly even the yeoman could barely read it.

'*Torpedo approaching to starboard!*'

The U-Boat was about to make the final dive when the torpedo struck it and blasted the hull into great fragments, some of which were hurled high into the air by the force of the explosion.

Treherne watched the spreading arena of oil, the bubbles and the drifting pall of smoke. Far away he heard the old Hudson dropping her own charges where the other U-Boat must have been, while *Belleisle* increased speed to join in the search.

'You knew, didn't you, sir? Like that other time?'

Howard looked at him, suddenly drained when before he had felt nothing but the driving urge to find and kill the enemy.

'It was too far away. So it *had* to be an acoustic torpedo. I stopped our engines so it had nothing to home on to. Schneider's boat was the nearest thing.' He shrugged and even that made his shoulders ache. 'Someone up there likes us quite a lot, Number One.' He turned as the *Blackwall* split the morning apart with her shrill whistle. 'Slow ahead together. Signal the others to take station as before.'

Treherne gripped his hand. 'I'd never have believed it if anyone had told me!'

Howard watched Rooke laying off a new course, his fingers deftly working with ruler and pencil, but his mind still ringing to that last moment of triumph. He had probably not even thought of how near they had all been to joining Schneider's coffin on the bottom.

Schneider had been one of a few U-Boat commanders who had risen above their secret, faceless existence. Theirs was a dangerous war, and many more would pay with their lives for trying to reach just one target too many. But Schneider's reputation had been more than that of courage and success. It had created fear. He had even put down neutral ships, when there had been any neutrals left in this war, and was said to be dedicated, as if it was some private mission.

Howard walked to the rear of the bridge and stared down at the narrow shining deck, where Ayres and his men were all laughing and slapping each other on the back while they reloaded their racks. As well they might, he thought with sudden pride. Schoolboys and tradesmen against one of Hitler's crack commanders.

Treherne watched him light his pipe, saw the way his fingers were quite firm as he tamped down the tobacco and watched the smoke streaming over the bridge ladder.

'Fall out action stations, Number One. Our old Hudson will be sniffing around until it's relieved . . . I don't think even that bloody kraut will risk another attack.'

'You think it was the same one that almost got us before, don't you, sir?'

'Maybe.' He rubbed his eyes. 'See if you can rustle up some sandwiches, will you?'

He thought of Treherne's question and knew he had deliberately avoided it. Such things did not happen in wartime. He thought suddenly of Marrack and his little ship.

He said quietly, 'It was just for you, *Number One*.'

In spite of all the buzzes and informed sources, HM Destroyer *Gladiator* did not return to Liverpool in time for Christmas; nor did she remain in Gladstone Dock long enough to welcome the New Year. But not to celebrate their brief return and all they had achieved was out of the question, so a wardroom party was hastily arranged to fall somewhere in between.

Howard had no idea just how many people had been invited, nor did he expect *Gladiator*'s wardroom to be able to cope. A mass of figures, some from the other ships in the group, friends from Western approaches HQ, and many more who had worked on their behalf in the bitter months and years of the same endless battle.

The boss did not come himself though he had sent for Howard personally to congratulate him on his success as Vickers's second-in-command, and particularly his attack on Schneider's U-Boat and its destruction. Max Horton made no secret of the fact that it was a perfect example of his own strategy, the true co-operation between air and sea forces, something which had once been virtually unknown. Howard had learned that the salvage tug had finally reached her objective and, with air cover from the carrier *Seeker*, had got the big oil tanker safely into harbour.

Howard pushed his way through the throng, shaking hands, seeing faces he knew well, others he knew not at all. Captain Vickers towered above everybody, and was seen to place each empty glass on the overhead vent trunking. It was to be hoped that Vallance took them down before the ship left harbour again.

Then at long last he saw Celia by the door, Ayres pointing towards him to show her the way.

She gasped, 'Sorry I'm late. Last minute flap.' She removed her hat and shook out her curls. 'What a scrum! "Auntie" will be along later!' She took a glass from a messman's tray and looked at him, her eyes very green. For a few seconds the place was empty, but for them, the din around the wardroom no more of an intrusion than the normal sounds of the sea.

She said, 'You look wonderful. I'm selfish – I want you to myself.' She glanced at the nearest guests. 'They like you a lot, David. Auntie's chaps think you're the greatest!' She laughed and held his arm. 'When your signal arrived I just sat there and prayed. I'm so *proud* of you. Of everything about you.' She touched the two ribbons on his jacket. 'I love you so much it hurts!'

She saw Treherne pushing through the crowds with a pretty-looking girl in a brightly coloured dress.

Howard waved to them. 'That's Joyce. They're getting spliced quite soon.'

'Oh, David.' She dropped her eyes. 'I went down to Hampshire while you were away – it was official but I made a detour to see your – ' She hesitated, then faced him again. '*Our* house. Your friend Mister Mills is doing a fine job with the builders.' He felt her grip tighten on his arm as she whispered against his ear, 'We shall make love there!'

He led her across the wardroom until they had reached Vickers.

'Here she is, sir.'

Vickers swooped down and kissed her cheek. 'Lucky devil, David!'

He glanced at Howard's DSO ribbon and said, 'I gather that the official presentation is to be made in the New Year, by HM the K no less.'

The girl said, 'Will you take me, David?'

'Of course he will!' Vickers signalled to Vallance with a glass, mostly to avoid coming eye-to-eye with Lieutenant Bizley. What a bloody difference, he thought. He had been discussing Bizley earlier with his friend, the assistant to the chief of staff. It would be interesting to hear his views when he arrived for the party and saw the lieutenant for himself. Bizley was looking a bit the worse for wear, he thought. His face was red and shining, and Vickers guessed he had been drinking more than he should.

Captain Naish had told him the bones of the Special Branch report on the matter. They had run the other survivor from Bizley's motor gunboat to earth; he had been given a Mention-in-Despatches for his part in the affair. Just as Vickers had suggested when it had first been raised, the man had stuck to his guns, and had backed up Bizley's own account of the sinking, and the deaths of her small company. But he had made one thing very clear. He had been obeying Bizley's orders, and had been too busy lowering the float to see what had happened on the bridge. 'So there's an end to the bloody matter, Ernle. I'm only sorry it took so long!'

Naish had stared at him with amazement when he had retorted, 'Why not ask Bizley himself? I really don't see why we have to build a battleship to sink a ruddy dinghy!'

Vickers said abruptly, 'Maybe Captain Naish can't come, David. Would you like to say your piece before all your guests are awash? A bit of grub might do wonders then!'

Howard looked at the girl beside him. 'Ready, Celia? Can you stand it?'

She smiled and replied nervously, 'I am my father's daughter. We've shared everything since we came together.'

Howard caught Treherne's eye and the bearded lieutenant banged loudly on the pantry counter with a pewter tankard.

Eventually there was silence and Treherne said, 'I'm not one for speeches.' He looked across at them. 'But as Number One of this ship . . .'

Someone called, 'Couldn't they do any better, Gordon?'

Treherne ignored him. 'In a day or so we shall be at sea again, so in a fashion this is our way of welcoming 1944 and the hopes which will come with it. In the last twelve months we've lost a lot of good friends, and seen many a fine ship torn to ribbons out there on the Western Ocean.' He had their full attention now, and Howard saw a young Wren wiping her eyes with her handkerchief. *Part of the team.*

'I've been at sea all my life, and I'm a hell of a lot older than most of you here.

I've seen a lot of places, done a lot of things, some of which I'm not too proud of now.' He reached behind his back and took Joyce's hand in his. 'But I'd never been afraid, you see, not really *afraid* until I came to the Atlantic. With respect to senior officers present, never mind what *they* tell us, I think we've turned the corner, and next year the enemy will be on the run!'

He waited for some cheering to die down and added soberly, 'For my part, I own my sanity and survival to one man, and he's right here with us now.' He raised a big hand. 'I think our captain wishes to say something, for he's the one I referred to. Escort duty is the worst there is, and the Atlantic is a sewer where war is stealth, survival and murder.' He raised a glass steadily and stared at Howard across the others. 'You happen to be the bravest, most decent man I have ever met.' He turned away, unable to continue.

Celia gripped Howard's arm. 'Oh, David, I'm so glad to be here.'

There were claps and cheers as Howard stepped up on to the fireplace.

'Thank you, Number One. I could have made almost the same speech about you.' They raised their glasses to one another and he continued, 'We all know what we have done, what we might be required to do in 1944. Having a command is often, necessarily, a lonely job, so you learn to share your emotions when the pressure is temporarily removed.' He took her hand and helped her up beside him. 'So please share this particular miracle with us. What better place to announce our engagement, what better company to . . .' The rest was drowned by a wave of cheering and stamping feet. It was so loud, in fact, that not even Vallance saw Rooke, who was OOD, signalling frantically from the doorway.

Captain Vickers turned as the din of cheering faded away and saw his friend Captain Naish looking at him with quiet satisfaction.

He was ushered to the fireplace and after shaking hands with Howard and his girl he turned and faced the others; rather like a judge about to make a summing-up, Howard thought.

Naish said, 'Needless to say I add my congratulations to our young captain and his lovely Wren. I'm a bit late, but I didn't want to interrupt what I heard from the passageway.' His eyes settled on Treherne. 'I think you expressed it better than any politician,' he gave a dry cough, 'or *senior officer* for that matter!'

He looked around at their faces, young but old, tired but somehow elated by what they had seen and shared.

'I have to tell you, gentlemen, we have received a signal from Admiral Fraser's flagship *Duke of York*, which reports that yesterday he met with, and after a fierce engagement, destroyed the German battle-cruiser *Scharnhorst* off North Cape.' In the stunned silence he sought out Treherne again and said, 'We have indeed "turned the corner"!'

Vickers remarked, 'North Cape, in winter. The poor devils.'

Naish said coldly, 'Only three were picked up from the *Hood*, remember?'

Howard heard the exchange and wondered. Vickers, the fighting destroyer captain who had been in the thick of it for four years and yet could still find compassion for a brave and determined enemy. Naish, on the other hand, saw nothing but the impossible prize which this victory at sea might offer. Was it because it was harder to send others to fight than to face the immediate brutality of war? He knew he might never understand, and for a moment longer, would not care too much.

There was so much noise now as the stewards and messmen were struggling to lay out great trays of sausage rolls, sandwiches and other goodies. Howard doubted if anyone saw them leave; and together they walked along the deserted iron deck, with the noise of the wardroom party still ringing in their ears.

There was a moon of sorts, playing a will-o'-the-wisp game as it floated from one fast cloud to another. The ship's fittings stood out stark and black against the sky; the whaler's davits, and the rolled scrambling nets where men had clung to be rescued or had drowned within seconds of safety. The guns, covered to hide their smoke-stained muzzles, still reminders of Finlay's action against the last U-Boat.

There was more noise coming aft from the forecastle where they were trying to celebrate Christmas and the New Year all at once.

A gangway sentry straightened his back as he saw them.

Howard paused. 'They looking after you all right, Glossop?' He need not have asked; he could smell the rum at four paces.

The sentry bobbed his head. 'Er, congratulations, sir, an' miss. Just 'eard!'

She touched his arm. 'Thank you.'

They moved on and knew the sentry was staring after them.

They paused again by the guardrails, at the place where Treherne had suggested the midshipman had thrown himself over. Even that no longer seemed real, or relevant. That was his other world.

She was staring at him, her face very pale in the eerie light.

'It's hard to imagine what it's like when . . .' She looked at the motionless guns, the empty mountings. 'So still. At peace.' She faced him again and he could imagine her expression even though the moonlight had gone again.

'Up there.' She looked towards the square, uncompromising shape of the bridge. 'Where you are at sea.' Her voice faltered just once. 'Next time, I'd like to *know*. So that I can be there with you when you reach out for me.'

Together they climbed the icy rungs to the bridge, pausing to look into the gleaming, empty wheelhouse, where men had fought, hated and known fear. The only sound came from the W/T office where a solitary telegraphist was reading a magazine and eating a bun. He did not even see them.

She gripped his shoulders and said, 'All the way. Please?'

It was bitterly cold on the upper bridge, everything damp to the touch. They were lying outboard of two other destroyers, but they could have been deserted as they lay in the silent shadows.

He guided her to the high bridge chair and wiped it with a cloth before lifting her on to it.

She kissed him then, and they clung together for a long time.

Then she allowed him to help her down again and stood for a few more moments looking around at the distorted shapes and reflections, so that she would remember.

She said quietly, 'I shall be here. When you need me. Now that I know.'

They made their way down to the main deck again and she said, 'You'll never be alone again.'

A blacked-out tug surged past and *Gladiator* swayed very slightly against the other vessels.

She put her hand on the guardrail. It was as if the ship was stirring herself. Eager to leave and get back to the only life she knew.

Not yet. Not yet. I've only just found him.

Another year was just over the horizon; nobody could foretell what it might bring, what pain it could offer.

But for the two figures merged together by the guardrail, this was reward enough.

Epilogue

1944

Howard lay quite still and unmoving on the top of his small bunk as the telephone shattered his dream like an explosion.

It was Finlay, who was OOW. 'Sorry to bother you, sir, but Captain Vickers would like to talk on the intercom.'

'I'll come up.' How many hundreds of times had he said that? He swung his legs from the bunk and stared for a few seconds at the new cap with its bright oak leaves around the peak, which waited to remind him of what had happened. When he caught sight of himself in reflection or a mirror he barely recognised himself. A young face, with a commander's cap. Although he wore his old sea-going jacket the bright new stripes on that, too, seemed to accentuate a complete change. He stared around the tiny sea cabin. Even that thrust at his heart like a knife.

Vickers had been firm about it. 'Things have changed, David. New ships, fresh equipment and still not enough experienced officers to take command. The Navy's your career, and this accelerated promotion can do you nothing but good. You'll be an asset to your next assignment.'

He could still hear his own voice, protesting. 'What about *Gladiator*, sir?'

Just for a moment Vickers's tone had softened. 'With *Garnet*, she's to be cut down to a long-range escort. You know the idea; it's been very useful for some of the older destroyers, the V and W's for instance. *Gladiator* has a lot of good service to offer, but as a destroyer, with a commander on the bridge – well, I'm afraid that's over, or will be after the next convoy.'

Howard made his way to the upper bridge and looked across at *Kinsale*'s hazy outline. It was strange weather, cold up here, but the air was almost humid when you stood out of the Atlantic wind. It was nearly August, but the ocean was as grey as ever, the great unbroken troughs stretching away into the late afternoon sunlight like moving glass. Where had the last months gone? He thought of the wardroom party; Celia, with his ring on her hand; the moments of peace and happiness.

Then on to more troop convoys, from Canada and the United States, the final build-up which had exploded across the world's headlines on a bitter cold day in Juen, when the Allied armies had landed in Normandy, the shores of Hitler's West Wall, and were even now fanning across France towards the Low Countries, and south towards the Cherbourg Peninsula. The German High Command would have no choice but to evacuate their Biscay submarine bases, and return once more to their homeland. Otherwise the bases and pens would be cut off by the advancing armies and overwhelmed.

It would be a bitter pill for the U-Boat men to swallow. After all their successes, their near-victory in the Atlantic, they would have to withdraw to the old bases in Germany, with the dreaded Rosegarden to face once again.

Howard picked up the handset and heard Vickers say, 'Did I get you out of bed, David?'

Howard smiled. It was not Vickers's fault, It was nobody's. He glanced around the familiar bridge. So many hours; filthy nights, burning ships, dying sailors.

'What can I do, sir?'

'I've had a top-secret signal from the Admiralty. Two convoys are passing one another tonight, as you know; we shall be standing by to offer extra support. The fortieth escort group and a carrier are doing the same to the north.'

Howard waited. He knew all this. After tomorrow they would be heading back for Liverpool. He felt the catch in his throat. *Gladiator*'s final passage as a true destroyer, and his own last days in command.

Vickers continued, 'You read the reports about the *Burmese Princess* – well, something's gone wrong apparently. She's had a complete power-failure.'

Howard signalled quickly to Finlay for a pad and pulled a pencil from his pocket as Vickers gave him the ship's reported position. He saw that Treherne had arrived on the bridge as if he had sensed something unusual.

Vickers said, 'I hate to send you, but I'm needed here. It'll give them a bit of a boost if you're standing by. Air cover *will* be provided.'

'I'm on my way, sir.' He handed the intercom to Finlay as Treherne asked, 'Trouble, sir?' His eyes were on Howard's new cap as if he did not accept the change either.

'Put this position on the chart. About a hundred miles west of the Irish coast. We're going to offer support.'

Treherne's eyes sharpened as he studied the pad. '*Burmese Princess*. I remember her well. She used to be on the Far East run from Southampton. A cargo-liner – I never liked the mixture!'

'Well, she's not any more, Number One.' He watched him steadily. 'She's a hospital ship now.' She was packed with wounded soldiers, some from the Normandy landings in June, others, more badly injured, from the invasions of Sicily and Italy last year. Her power defect had slowed her passage considerably, and whereas hospital ships were usually left alone by U-Boats, unless escorted, this change of timing might lay her wide open to attack.

Treherne bent over the chart table. 'We should make contact around dawn, sir. No U-Boats reported in that area. All after the two convoys, I expect.'

'Very well, Number One. Course to intercept. Make to *Kinsale, Hate to leave you.*'

The reply winked back across the heaving, shining swell. '*Parting is such sweet sorrow. Good luck.*'

Treherne said, 'At least we might be back in the Pool before the others!'

Howard climbed into his chair and imagined her sitting on it. Holding her in his arms in this place which must have brought home to her his world; the daily acceptance of danger.

They had set the date for their marriage in October, when, Vickers had hinted, there would be some leave going. After that? He touched the rough grey steel. Not back to *Gladiator* again. Not ever.

He thought of the Normandy invasion. Did it mean that this would be the last summer at war? Was that just possible?

'I've been thinking, Number One.' He looked at him gravely. 'If I make a special request through Captain Vickers, would you be prepared to take command of her?'

Treherne saw the pain in his eyes. *He really loves this ship.* Treherne had known that almost from the beginning, but it was still a shock to see it in Howard's face, hear it in his question.

'Well, you know how I feel about a command, sir.'

'But *Gladiator*'s not just any ship.'

'I know it, sir.'

'Then at least think about it before we get in.'

Treherne watched as Bizley climbed into the bridge to relieve the OOW. He looked very strained, but his tone was haughty as ever as he took the con from Finlay.

Vickers had confided in Howard about the enquiries by the Special Branch. 'Would have told you before, but . . .'

That one word *but* counted for such a lot in this Navy, he thought. True or false, it mattered little. If Bizley's story was a lie, nothing could shift him from it now. He would be more insufferable than ever. Even that jolted Howard badly. Bizley would be someone else's responsibility after the next two days or so.

He tried to settle himself more comfortably as Finlay strode from the bridge, after giving Bizley a chilling glance. They would all be split up. Except the Chief, and the Gunner (T). Finlay was going on a long gunnery course, and Ayres to Portland for antisubmarine training. Bizley would probably be advanced to first lieutenant in some other escort, while Treherne . . . Perhaps he might change his mind. Howard looked at the scarred paint, the tarnished instruments nearby. She needed someone who understood.

The ship went to action stations to test guns and prepare for the night, then the starboard watch closed-up for defence stations as was usual. Gallons of tea and cocoa, greasy sausages and tinned potatoes. Men came and went about their duties, the ocean and the radar empty of surprises.

Howard dozed in his chair, awakening occasionally as W/T reported there was fog in their vicinity. But it was patchy, and when they drove through it they saw it clinging to the radar and rigging like ragged spectres.

It was sometime before dawn when the radar picked up the other ship, adrift, and as they were soon to discover, without lights or power. Usually the sides of hospital ships were brightly lit to display their white hulls and huge red crosses, a protection which, for the most part, had been successful. Hospital ships which had fallen to enemy action had been sunk by aircraft, dive-bombers, where there were only seconds to distinguish the difference.

Howard stood at the forepart of the bridge. 'Slow ahead together. Steer zero-six-zero.' Should be able to see her soon. To the yeoman he added, 'Be ready to call her up.'

Aircraft today, Vickers had said. Then what? A ship the size of the *Burmese Princess* probably carried several hundred wounded men. A tug might be needed.

He called to Treherne, 'Clear lower deck, Number One. Don't worry – I'm not sending you across this time!'

Treherne waited for the order to be piped, the watch below to come bustling on deck. Howard said, 'I could try to take her in tow. But it might be construed as an act of war by the enemy.'

'Ship, sir! Port bow!'

'All right, Yeoman!'

The Aldis lamp clattered noisily, the flash seemingly extra bright in the misty darkness.

A torch flashed back to them and the yeoman muttered, 'God, their power really *is* kaput!'

Howard watched the other ship looming out of the gloom; a cargo-liner as Treherne had described, and now that they were closer he could see the pale hull, ghostly against the moving water. He switched on the loud-hailer, his voice metallic as it boomed against the other ship and back again. *'Burmese Princess* ahoy! This is the destroyer *Gladiator!* What is the trouble?'

The other man sounded miles away, and was probably using a megaphone. 'Generator fault, Captain! It was good of you to come! These poor soldiers are being rolled about with no way on the ship!'

'How many?'

'Five hundred, Captain, bound for Halifax!' He seemed to brighten up and shouted, 'My chief has just reported that he's nearly ready to proceed!'

Rooke said, 'Generators – what a time to happen!'

Treherne retorted coldly, 'She's about twenty-give years old, Pilot! I reckon she's earned a bit of a rest!'

Bizley stood by the compass platform, thinking of his earlier fears. Nothing had happened. It had all been for nothing. When he got shot of this ship he would go and see Sarah. He was in the clear. What did they know about it anyway? He felt his confidence returning like the glow of vodka.

They were almost alongside now, the other ships rising above *Gladiator*'s deck like a cliff. There was a faint sound of machinery, and someone down aft gave a cheer. At any moment the sides would light up again; her errand of mercy would continue.

'Aircraft, sir!'

Three flares dropped from the clouds, and the yeoman triggered off an acknowledgement. A Coastal Command Hudson was circling around, widening its search area as it rumbled away into the distance, satisfied that help was on hand.

'Asdic – Bridge!'

Howard ducked down. 'Captain!'

'Strong contact at one-six-zero, sir. *Closing!*'

Treherne gasped, 'Christ, a sitting duck!'

Howard yelled, 'Full ahead together!' He stared through the screen as the other ship began to slide past. 'Tell W/T! Signal Admiralty, repeated C-in-C!'

'Both engines full ahead, sir. Steady on zero-six-zero!'

'Warn depth-charge party, Number One! Guns, stand by to engage!'

Gladiator was drawing well ahead of the hospital ship when the helm started to go over. Suction from the larger vessel, a mechanical defect – who could tell? Tilting right over, just as the photograph had portrayed her on her first trials, she charged across the *Burmese Princess*'s bows, so close that had the large ship been under way she would have sliced them in half.

Howard did not hear the torpedo as it hit the forecastle, but he was flung to the deck, buried by tons of water that stank of explosive. He tried to pull himself to his feet but cried out as pain took away his breath and left him too dazed to move. He was aware of lights in the sky, the rising scream of aero engines as the aircraft tore down to the attack. More explosions, bombs or depth-charges he did not know; it could even be beneath him in the hull itself.

Treherne was helping him up, and even as he propped him against the tall chair Howard knew the deck was already at an angle.

'Tell the Chief! Clear the engine room!' He dragged himself to the screen and looked over at the forecastle. There was nothing forward of B-gun. Just jagged metal where the blast had torn it away. Men were calling and running, and Howard remembered that he had cleared the lower deck. *Had he known that too?* Had the ship known, and shown her anger by turning to block the torpedo's path?

Someone shouted. 'They got that bloody U-Boat!' Then he broke off, sobbing, as he cried, 'It's *me*, Tom – speak to me, for Christ's sake!'

'Assess and report damage.'

Treherne stayed with him. 'I'll get the Doc.' Howard shook his head and fought against the pain. He must not faint now. He had trained all his life for this. The one thing that they all hoped would never happen. His mind would not accept it even though he knew *Gladiator* was finished.

'Just my ribs, Gordon . . . Christ, what a mess!'

There was a banshee screech of steam as the chief released the pressure on the boilers. Thank God he was safe. Another dread; it had happened to so many.

'Bulkheads are holding sir.' Rooke held the telephone to his ear but watched the instruments fall from his table as the list increased.

'Make sure the depth-charges are at safe – pitch the primers over board!'

Finlay had arrived. 'All done. I can't find Ayres though.' He stepped aside as the PO steward ran on to the bridge and helped to support Howard against the chair. 'I've got the photo of yer dad, sir. In the oilskin bag.' He was shivering, talking rapidly to conceal his terror. 'Will we be all right, sir?'

Treherne said, 'Shall I send the confidential books over the side, sir?'

He wanted to shout at Howard. *She's done for, can't you see? You've tried, but there's nothing more we can do except save ourselves.* Instead he said, calmly, 'Time to move.'

Howard peered at him. Celia would see it as she had seen all the others. Little black crosses. The secretary of the Admiralty regrets to announce the loss of HMS *Gladiator*. Next of kin have been informed.

Oh God, not for Celia! Not again!

He said between his teeth, 'Muster the hands.' He winced as the aircraft thundered overhead again; he realised that it was getting much brighter, with the hard, pitiless light adding to the shock and destruction.

And the chief was here now, hatless and with grease on his face, his eyes everywhere as if he felt unsafe up here on the bridge.

'Thanks, Chief. I'm glad you got your people out.' He groaned as the deck gave a lurch and something heavy came adrift between decks.

Price said, 'That bulkhead'll not hold, sir. I've had a look. It's weeping water like fury.'

'Very well. Clear the bridge, Number One. You take charge on deck.'

Treherne looked at him grimly. 'Guns can deal with that. I'm staying with you.'

Howard held on to his shoulder and nodded heavily. 'The old firm, eh?'

At the break in the forecastle some of the hands were already preparing to lower the whaler; the motor boat on the opposite side would not budge as the davits had buckled in the blast like cardboard.

The Buffer was striding about and turned as his friend the coxswain, with the wheelhouse party, joined him on the iron deck.

He grinned. 'Finished with engines, 'Swain?'

Sweeney looked at the dark lapping water and sighed. 'Too bloody old for this caper. It's a job in the barracks for me!'

Moffatt was kneeling on the sloping deck, his knees torn on the cracked plating as he knelt over Sub-Lieutenant Ayres.

'Get this officer to a raft, Buffer!'

Knocker White peered down at him. The bandages made it worse, he thought. Ayres had lost an arm and a leg in the explosion. It would be kinder to leave him with the ship. But he shouted, 'Dobson, Bully Bishop, over here at the double!'

Drugged though he was Ayres seemed to know what was happening. 'Help me. I can't feel anything!' He was still whimpering when they carried him away.

Bizley felt sick, from fear or from shock he did not know. They would be safe, those who had survived. The hospital ship was right here, a helpless spectator, but with boats and men in plenty. When they got back he would make the most of his survivor's leave and then – he clapped his hand to his pocket. *The medal.* His precious DSC was still in his cabin!

'Take charge, Cox'n!' He ran aft up the rising slope; the others did not even see him go.

It was frightening and eerie between decks. All the familiar places and memories. Shattered crockery and a puddle of coffee in the pantry, the wardroom curtains standing out from their rails at stiff, unreal angles. He slithered to a halt by his cabin and stared as Leading Seaman Fernie, carrying a large flashlight, came up the deck towards him.

'What are *you* doing here?'

Fernie faced him wearily. 'What does it look like?'

'When we get back, you'll bloody well regret this! My record is *clean*, do you hear?' He laughed and Fernie smelled the vodka.

He watched Bizley stagger into his cabin and drag at a drawer to find the little box he prized above all else.

Fernie heard the torpedo gunner's mate shout down the hatch. 'Come up from there, Fernie! We're baling out!' His head vanished.

Fernie felt the rage rushing through him, consuming him like blazing fuel on the sea.

With unexpected swiftness he swung the cabin door shut and threw on the emergency clips. He heard the frantic hammering, the faint shouts turn to screams, and then he walked away and up the ladder, sealing that hatch, too, behind him.

The ship shook again, and the men huddled together in the inflated life-jackets while the lowered whaler pitched alongside, oars and boathooks ready to fend off the torn metal.

On the bridge Finlay stood against the flag lockers, with their upended bunting strewn around as if there had been a wild party.

'Boat and rafts lowered, sir. I'm afraid we had to bring Dick Ayres back inboard.' He sounded suddenly at a loss. 'He just died. Three more killed, and Lieutenant Bizley is missing.'

Again the bridge seemed to shake itself and Howard said, 'Give us a hand, Gordon.'

Treherne looked at him in the strange light. 'If it's any use, sir . . . I *would* have accepted your offer – as it is – well, she doesn't need any of us any more.'

The three of them followed Vallance down to the side deck where it was almost impossible to stand. The after part must be right out of the water, the screws stopped as Schneider's U-Boat had been.

'*Easy*, sir!' Treherne watched despairingly as Howard tried to turn and look at his ship. At any second that bulkhead would go, but he stopped to listen as Howard said in a whisper, 'You were right, Number One. When you came back from that ammunition ship. It *is* like death.'

The whaler and floats paddled clear of the side while the boat tried to tow clusters of swimmers to safety from the inevitable undertow.

Howard sat propped in a big Carley float, Treherne holding his shoulders, Evan Price supporting him on the other side. The old firm, here to see her go. The last rites.

There was cheering too, waves and waves of it, and Treherne said quietly, 'It's the squaddies on the hospital ship. Look at them. Lining the rails, those who can stand, poor devils. They know she did it for them.'

Price said tersely. 'Oh God, there she goes!'

There was a devastating crack and *Gladiator* began to slide quickly into that churning whirlpool they had witnessed so often.

Then just as quickly, she was gone, with the sea still boiling as if she might yet burst up again with her old defiance.

As if to mark the end, all the hospital ship's lights came on, and after a further hesitation she began to lower her boats to assist.

Did ships really have souls? Was it because of pride that *Gladiator* had acted as she had, rather than face the ignominious saws and torches of some dockyard?

Howard let his head fall against Treherne's shoulder and stared at the clouds. He would tell Celia all about it. How they had lost the last battle; but had saved so many.

With a strong hand, even to the end.